Tania in China

Tania in China

BEN FOSTER

Matador
9 Priory Business Park,
Wistow Road, Kibworth Beauchamp,
Leicestershire. LE8 0RX
Tel: 0116 279 2299
Email: books@troubador.co.uk
Web: www.troubador.co.uk/matador
Twitter: @matadorbooks

ISBN 978 1800461 543

British Library Cataloguing in Publication Data.
A catalogue record for this book is available from the British Library.

Printed and bound by CPI Group (UK) Ltd, Croydon, CR0 4YY1
Typeset in 12pt Minion Pro by Troubador Publishing Ltd, Leicester, UK

Matador is an imprint of Troubador Publishing Ltd

About the Author

B EN FOSTER WAS BORN IN BEIJING, LATER A 10-YEAR EXILE TO Inner Mongolia. He holds a Ph.D. in history from Cornell University, and has been a university professor for three decades. The American Philosophical Society, Cambridge, Yale, Bloomsbury, Wiley-Blackwell and several professional journals published his books and articles; one of them was named "*Choice* Outstanding Academic Book" in 1994.

Acknowledgments

THE STORIES RELATED TO THE SIBERIAN DWARF CEDAR IN CHAPTER 28 were quoted from Varlam Shalamov, *Kolyma Tales*, trans. by John Glad (Penguin Books, 1994), pp. 25–30.

List of Characters

Family names come first in China. The Chinese characters and their approximate English meanings of the given names are provided in parentheses.

Bai Yu-Xian (白宇仙, "superman in the universe"), warlord in Southwest China
Bao Feng-Nian (包豐年, "abundant harvest"), Red Army officer

Chamberlain (張伯倫), the Communist International (Comintern)'s East Asia Bureau chief
Chen Dian (陳典, "role model"), Chen Han's older brother
Chen Han (陳漢, "real man"), nationalist general and president
Chen, Madam (maiden name Shang Yu-Xi, 商雨溪, "misty stream"), wife of Chen Han
Cheng Chu-Li (程楚力, "Hercules from Chu Kingdom"), communist agent in Shanghai

Dai Tian (戴甜, "sweetness"), reporter

Ding Qiao-Ran (丁巧然, "naturally talented"), bride of Gong Pei-Zhi

Dong Zi-Tian (董梓田, "catalpa tree in the field"), founding member of the Chinese Communist Party (CCP)

Duan Lin-Yu (段林峪, "tree-covered valley"), director of the nationalist Counterintelligence Office

Fan Jia (樊家, "family inclined"), warlord in Gansu and Qinghai Provinces

Fang Si-Liang (方思亮, "longing for light"), CCP undercover spy

Feng Zheng (馮正, "rectitude"), warlord in Northwest China

Fu Fang (傅芳, "pleasant fragrance"), Fu Lan's half-sister, Lu Shi-Yan's first wife

Fu Lan (傅藍, "blue"), Fu Fang's half-sister, Lu Shi-Yan's second wife

Gan Zu-Xun (甘祖訓, "ancestors' teachings"), founding member of the CCP

Gong Pei-Zhi (公培志, "cultivate steadfastness"), founding member of the CCP

Gregory (格利高里), Comintern's special envoy to China

Guo Jing (郭敬, "respect"), officer of the Sichuan troops

Hong Shi-Mei (洪詩美, "beautiful poetry"), wife of Si-Tu Wen-Liang

Hou Shi-Suo (侯石鎖, "stone lock"), high communist official, nicknamed "Broken Finger"

Jin-Xia (錦霞, "splendid clouds"), baby Si-Tu Wen-Liang's nurse

Robert Johnson (羅伯特•約翰遜), Russian specialist at Columbia University

Kang Yi-Jun (康益君, "to benefit the monarch"), elder brother of Kang Yi-Sheng

Kang Yi-Sheng (康益聖, "to benefit the sage"), Red Army telecommunication officer

Li Fan (李繁, "complexity"), originally named Lin Shuo (林朔, "the north"), internal security officer of the Red Army

Li Hong-Tang (李宏堂, "great hall"), warlord in Southwest China

Lin Shi-Xiong (林世雄, "hero of a generation"), CCP head of internal security

Liu Ming-Zhu (劉明珠, "bright pearl"), Lu Shi-Yan's fourth mistress

Liu Yi-Hao (劉一豪, "singularly majestic man"), warlord in Sichuan Province

Lu Di-Ping (魯笛平, "serene flute"), Red Army staffer

Lu Shi-Yan (陸士彥, "righteous and gifted man"), professor and founding member of the CCP

Martin (馬丁), Comintern's emissary to China

Meng Bo-Xian (孟伯賢, "manly and virtuous"), high communist official

Meng Xi (孟希, "rarity"), Meng Bo-Xian and Tania's adopted daughter

Mo Jia-Qi (莫家奇, "family genius"), high communist official

Pan Jin (潘勁, "strength"), nationalist army commander

Peng Xiao-Mei (彭小妹, "little sister"), Tang Shi-Hai's wife

Peter (彼得), son of Martin and Tania

Qi Shu (齊庶, "commoner"), union leader in WWI

Roy (羅伊), Comintern's special envoy to China

Shao Huai-De (邵懷德, "to embrace virtue"), communist commander of the 20th Army

Sheng Bao (盛寶, "treasure"), founding member of the CCP

Sheng Bing (盛兵, "soldier"), Sheng Bao's uncle

Sheng Wu (盛伍, "soldiering"), Sheng Bao's father

Sheng Ying (盛英, "gorgeous"), Sheng Bao's daughter

Si-Tu Hui-Xian (司徒慧賢, "kindness and virtue"), Si-Tu Wen-Liang's mother

Si-Tu Wen-Liang (司徒文良, "gentle and upright"), founding member of the CCP

Si-Tu Xiu (司徒秀, "nice-looking"), Si-Tu Wen-Liang's guardian

Song Pei (宋沛, "plentiful"), early member of the CCP

Su Ming (蘇明, "shining"), Sheng Bao's third wife

Tan Xue-Yu (譚雪瑜, "snowy jade"), Si-Tu Wen-Liang's foster mother

Tang Shu-Hai (唐沭海, "Shu River by the sea"), university librarian and founding member of the CCP

Tang Wan-Yi (唐婉儀, "delicate appearance and mannerism"), Tang Shi-Hai's daughter, Sheng Bao's first wife

Tania (塔妮雅), Comintern's emissary to China

Tania the Younger (小塔妮雅), Peter's daughter

Tao Yin-Hu (陶寅虎, "tiger born in the night"), Red Army commander-in-chief

Teng Wan-Chun (滕晚春, "late spring"), high school teacher

Tong Zi-Fu (童子福, "offspring and happiness"), member of the Grand Fellowship Society in Wuhan

Max van Aken (邁克斯•馮•艾肯), Peter's foster father

Wang Heng-Ji (王恆驥, "stamina and fine horse"), translator

Wang Xuan-Kui (王軒奎, "great carriage and strong man"), warlord in Guizhou Province

Wang Yu (王玉, "emerald"), Hou Shi-Suo's wife

Wei Hao-Qin (魏暭勤, "bright and diligent"), lieutenant commissar of the Second Front Army

Xia-Hou Dan (夏侯丹, "crimson"), party messenger from Moscow, Xia-Hou Ding's cousin

Xia-Hou Ding (夏侯鼎, "bronze vessel"), Red Army commander of the First Corps

Yan Shu (嚴術, "stratagem"), warlord in Shanxi Province

Yan Yan (閻妍, "blossom"), Lu Shi-Yan's third wife

Yao Xi-Wa (姚喜娃, "blessed baby"), Red Army officer

Yu Shao-Mei (虞少梅, "budding plum"), Sheng Bao's second wife

Zhang Wei (張威, "intimidating might"), warlord in Manchuria

Zhang Wu (張武, "militant"), Zhang Wei's son, warlord in Manchuria

Prologue

"I HATE HIM!" THE TEENAGE GIRL TANIA RETURNED HOME FROM school, shouted, and threw her bulky backpack onto the kitchen table.

"Whom?" mother Lynda asked. Motionless, she was glued to the latest article in the medical journal *Cell*. Life in this charming neighborhood of Kensington Hills had been pleasant and peaceable for many years since her marriage to Peter Fisherman, the Berkeley professor in the Political Science Department.

"My history teacher."

"Why?"

"He gave this impossible homework assignment! He is a nerd!" answered the girl adamantly, messing with her ruffled notes and battered textbooks.

"Well, when they're serious about teaching, some of them can be a little bit nerdy, just like me." The self-deprecating parent attempted to soothe her daughter.

"You are different. You are my mom. Besides, you are a professor, not a teacher."

"What's the difference? Both are teachers." The microbiologist Lynda realized this could become a long discourse and changed the topic. "What's the assignment anyway?"

"He said each of us must find an object owned by our grandparents and write a report about it."

"So?"

"So? Grandpa and Grandma are long dead. They never visited us. I knew nothing about them, duh!"

"That's not entirely true. You were named after your grandma." In walked her father, Peter. "We do have things from your grandpa and grandma."

"Really? Where are they? Show me! Why didn't you tell me before?" Tania could not wait.

Peter took the family to the hallway and stopped before an old trunk with elegantly carved full panels. A man in excellent health and shape, he opened the heavy lid and said, "Here they are. Pick anything you like."

"Woah! Treasure chest!" The puffed girl was full of excitement and anticipation. She rummaged through books, pictures, albums, papers, letters, and souvenirs, searching for the ideal object. Then a small wooden box caught her attention. "Tell me about it—I hope to know enough to fill out a report," said she.

"Oh, no!" The mother was incredulous.

"Why? What? What's the matter? Something bad?" Looking at the shabby box once more, Tania was surprised to see her mother's reaction.

"No, nothing. Just concerned that it may be too much too early for you, for now at least." Lynda tried to defuse the elevated anxiety.

"That's okay, I am sure she can handle that." Pleased with the daughter's choice, Peter seemed ready to begin a new conversation. "Your grandparents went through a lot in life, and this little box has been part of their extraordinary experiences. If you promise to be patient, I will tell you about their stories, and we can start tonight."

"I never had a chance to see Grandpa and Grandma, and I would love to hear every story about them! All of it!"

"That can last for quite some time," the mother warned.

"Daddy said I can handle it," the daughter responded.

"No rush. We can stop anytime and continue later, taking all the time we need," the father added.

The family moved to the cozy living room.

"So imagine yourself in a completely different world," Peter began. "That's where my mother and father, your grandparents, came from."

The spring of 1920—a few years after the fall of the Qing Dynasty. In Peking—the old capital city of China—peace was hanging in the balance as a weak central administration and several powerful provincial warlords competed for national dominance.

"I am leaving," Martin shouted, pacing in the room of a small hotel in the city. After more than two weeks in China, he saw his mission was going nowhere and had made up his mind. Tania, his wife, sat quietly in her chair and said, "Darling, be patient. We are making good progress and we can do it."

Still irritated, the husband slowed his pace. As his yelling receded into grumbles, Tania reached out for the tea set on the table. She knew him too well to allow his stormy temper to rage out of control. As he looked around for a chair, she noticed that he was pressing his right thumb on his left palm as he would usually do when upset. She filled up a cup and said pleasantly, "Have some tea, my dear?"

The husband had as good a reason to be frustrated as the wife had the good sense to be patient. They had been sent by the Communist International (Comintern) in Moscow to begin the monumental task of establishing a communist party and to instigate a working-class revolution in China, where more than four hundred million people lived, mostly rural poor, either illiterate peasant farmers or landless day laborers. Only a tiny fraction of the population worked for any modern industry. Few of the wage workers had a union; still fewer understood what a party was.

The prospect did not look good. Would they decide to push on? If so, did they know that their efforts were to turn China and their own lives completely upside down forever? Even if they did, a more difficult question remained—were all of those sacrifices worth it?

Chapter 1

Emissaries

1

G ROWING UP IN THE LOW COUNTRIES, MARTIN HAD NEVER minded the harsh elements. A strong and determined lad with an impetuous streak, his life next to the ocean had been invigorating despite the pungent, soggy, and salty smell from the treacherous North Sea.

Martin's father, a mechanic in Rotterdam, was a devout member of the Dutch Reformed Church, whose parents originally came from a poor rural hamlet forty miles away south of the low island of Tholen, in Zeeland Province, near the mouth of the Rhine River. A number of their neighbors and relatives had left the island decades ago. Lured by overseas ventures, many set sail to explore the Orient, while others headed west to the New World. Some became rich and famous, as their fashionable apartments and bustling commercial activity in the Old Port District would testify.

When Theodore Roosevelt was running for president in the United States, the toddler Martin heard neighbors whispering that TR's ancestors had also come from the tiny Dutch island Tholen. Surprised, he ran to ask Father, who calmly said, "Yes, similar to our Visser family, or Fisherman, the name Roosevelt came from the Dutch words 'het Rosen Velt,' meaning the Field of Roses—the small village where they had resided." It was only years later did Martin realize that Father did not tell him the whole story. Nicholas Roosevelt, the progenitor of the famed Roosevelts on the other side of the Atlantic, officially wrote down his name in full as Claes Martenszen van Rosenvelt, which meant the Little Fellow—Son of Martin of the Rose Field.

Martin's family had rich and powerful relatives for sure. But he never fully understood why Father remained tight-lipped about those relations. Perhaps Father was not happy about his own working-class status, and any direct or indirect association with the upper class would only embarrass him. Or perhaps he wanted his son to be self-reliant and not to expect any charity from anyone. In any case, the father's deliberate silence seemed to have worked. Martin grew up to become a diligent and skilled mechanic, with a profound sense of pride in his work that was instilled in him by his maternal parents.

They came from the Lys River region, one of the most productive flax-growing areas in the world. Martin could never forget that image from childhood—of both Mom and Grandma still working late into the night. With either a spindle or needle in hand, they were always spinning or knitting, knitting or spinning. In fact, it was their income from the delicate tablecloth, beautiful napkins, and bright laces they had made that enabled Martin to finish the Hogere Burgerschool while Father was sick.

He even remembered that, as a toddler, he was once playing with a big black rock, which had been a doorstop of sorts in the household for a very long time. Suddenly he heard Grandma yelling, "Martin, dear, please don't throw it away." When asked why, she, tears streaming down on the wrinkled face, said, "Look at the markings on the stone. It's the only thing I have left from your grandpa." Then she told him about the life of a flax grower who, among other things, would need many heavy stones to press flax down in a pit of water to ret. Retting, as it was called, as well as carting, crushing, rippling, braking, scutching, hackling, dressing, combing, and countless other toil year in and year out, had resulted in Grandpa's hands looking like the rugged surface of that broken stone. Grandma sobbed and so did little Martin.

Hard work never discouraged the boy, nor did it prevent him from pursuing his personal interests, of which his birthplace provided plenty. Conveniently located on the Rhine–Meuse–Scheldt river delta by the North Sea, Rotterdam ("a levee on the muddy stream" in Dutch) was like a revolving door—the first opening gate for outsiders to enter Europe and the last stop for Europeans leaving the continent, thus earning it the twin nicknames of "Gateway to Europe" and "Gateway to the World."

The city, with one of the largest ports in Europe, had been the renowned hub of ancient commercial ship lines and shipyards since the sixteenth century. It also witnessed extensive growth after the completion of the Nieuwe Waterweg in the nineteenth. Its industrial workers constructed the best railway systems and tram networks that could be found in a modern city, while its architects built the first skyscraper on the European continent. In the Old Port, majestic lime trees lined the promenade of the famed riverfront of the Boompjes, where the grand buildings of the East India House, the Rotterdam City Bank, and the Jewish Synagogue stood alongside the headquarters of the Dutch Steamboat Company and the Dutch Trading Company. Many celebrities claimed the city as their home, such as the humanist Erasmus, naval hero Piet Hein, philosopher Bernard Mandeville, theologian Pierre Bayle, composer Pieter Hellendaal, statesman Count Van Hogendorp, poet Hendrik Tollens, and painter George Hendrik Breitner. Hardly any resident would remain indifferent to the city's enterprising history and vibrant cultural activity.

What intrigued Martin, however, was a chance discovery. He was walking back home one day after school, and happened to take a left turn, instead of the usual right, at the corner of Hogendorp Square, where the big bronze statue of the count stood. As he passed a boutique, a bright object in the display window caught his eye. He stopped, gazed at it, and was inside the store before he realized it.

"How may I help you, my boy?" greeted the shop owner—an impeccably dressed gentleman in his mid-fifties.

"What is that… that… that thing?" Martin stammered, pointing to the object.

"Oh, my boy." The merchant's warm smile calmed his nervous visitor. "You see, young boy, you have good taste. This is a precious piece of the famed Chinese blue-and-white porcelain from the Ming Dynasty." As Martin received, held it in his hands, and slowly turned it around, he still could not figure out what on the earth the object was, as the words "precious," "porcelain," "China," "white," and "blue" buzzed in his head. "You see, my boy," the owner patiently explained, "this is a snuff bottle, the most exquisite ceramic made by the human hand." Now it all started to make sense as Martin continued his examination, with the owner whispering in his ears, "You see, young man, since the seventeenth century, the Chinese have turned this into an art form and their highly crafted snuff bottles have replaced the snuff boxes we commonly used in the West."

This little artifact was a cylinder shaped like a person's thumb, only two to three inches long and weighing no more than ten ounces. Against its spotless white background, a bouquet of three tulip flowers was beautifully painted in deep blue, brimming with life as if they had just been cut from a garden still soaked in morning dew. A silky lace tied the three corollas in the front, and the slender stems curved to the back, making a smoothly twisted pattern of a double Carrick bend knot. A band of floral meander enclosed the whole design and a translucent green jade shaped like a small ball and trimmed with golden inlays capped the bottle perfectly. Everything looked wonderful except… "If the snuff bottle is mainly for men, why is the picture so…" Martin was grappling for the right word. "So, so girlish?" He blushed.

"Well, my boy." For all his experience in the business, the merchant seemed stunned for such a question from a teenager. "You have a good question. You have a very good question, my boy. And… good taste, too." Unable to come up with any direct answer, his price tag of two guilders was cut in half. Martin was excited about his first collection, even though it had cost him several months' worth of savings from his allowance, which he dared not tell his parents.

This tiny little piece of porcelain would soon open a window to a whole new world for the boy, with questions flooding his brain every night: What was China like? What kind of people were the Chinese, who could craft such an exquisite artifact? Why did it have only two colors, not in red, white, and blue as in the Dutch national flag? Why did the snuff bottle made for men have an unmanly design of flowers, not of swords or pistols? Neither Martin's parents nor his teachers had the answers, so he decided to find out himself.

2

He remembered he had seen some museum paintings of porcelain objects, and he went back to revisit them as soon as he could. Thanks to the talents of those artists in the Dutch Golden Age, Martin quickly found out several stories. First, traditional earthenware used in ordinary households was as plain as those Cologne-ware bowls, jugs, tankards, and plates in his home. Mottled in the single earthly color of gray or brown, they were coarsely made potteries without any decoration. The jug and bowl in Johannes Vermeer's *Kitchen Maid* (1658) and the pile of dirty dishes in Nicolaes Maes's *Sleeping Kitchen Maid* (1655) and Adriaen van Ostade's *Peasants in an Interior* (1661) clearly represented this ordinary earthenware.

Any ceramic pieces that could be identified as what the boutique owner had called the Chinese blue-and-white porcelain showed only in the collections of aristocratic and royal families, such as those delicate ceramic plates and bowls that Floris van Dijck had meticulously depicted in his *Laid Table with Cheese and Fruit* (1615), Pieter Claeze in his *Still Life with Turkey Pie* (1627), Jan Jansz Treck in his *Still Life with Pewter Jug and Chinese Bowl* (1645) or his *Still Life with Beer Glass* (1647), and Abraham van Beyeren in his *Sumptuous Still Life* (1667). Apparently, the possession of a piece of imported Chinese porcelain had become a status symbol for those who had enough money to buy, use, and display it.

The third group of artifacts fascinated Martin still more. A young lady docent at Museum Boijmans showed him several huge cases of shining porcelain. In ubiquitous blue and white colors, they were decorative tiles, commemorative vases, bright dinning plates, and sophisticated coffee sets, all designed in the most regal style Martin had ever seen. "These are called Delft faience," she said. Martin was about to ask, "Why are they named after our neighboring city? Don't they have the same blue and white colors as the Chinese porcelain does?"

Fully anticipating such questions, since they had been asked by many visitors before, the young docent continued her elucidation in a voice as calm as in a prepared speech. "Delft faience, magnificent as it is, was an attempt to imitate the imported Chinese porcelain, which became highly desirable within the elite and court circles when the English and Dutch India Companies brought them back from the East. Indeed," she went on, "the response to this oriental treasure was so overwhelming that a new market started to emerge. These well-designed pieces of Delft faience"—she was pointing to the displays—"were commissioned by wealthy and royal families to show off their courtly taste—and, of course, the immense power and wealth behind it. When, in 1689, our Prince Willem III and his wife became William and Mary, King and Queen of England, they commissioned a large quantity of artifacts to redecorate Hampton Court Palace, including many charming pieces of Delft faience. Manufacturing and exporting faience was the most important business in Delft throughout the eighteenth century, and some of its most elegant products are still owned by the British royal family today."

When she finally paused to catch her breath, Martin quickly squeezed in a question. "Excuse me, Miss. Why are they called faience, not porcelain?"

Nothing could stop this young lady, whose slightly triumphant smile suggested that she knew this was coming. She politely responded, "Because the tin-glazed techniques were first developed by the craftsmen of Faenza in northern Italy. Today, they are commonly known as Delft blue, even though Delftware includes products of other colors. The young Queen Mary (she married at fifteen) was a passionate collector and promoter of Delftware. Her favorite supplier, the pottery of De Metalen Potrun by Lambert Cleffius, was the most famous Delft blue earthenware manufacturer. The Hoppesteyn pottery (named after the widow Wemmers Hoppesteyn and her son Rochus) came a close second. Daniel Marot and Frederick van Frytom were among the best designers of their times. Highly sought-after across Europe and increasingly around the globe, the Delft blue has become our Dutch national symbol. The Rotterdam resident John Francis Loudon owned the best private collection of Delftware. If you are interested, they can be seen in the Gallery of Honor at the Rijksmuseum in Amsterdam."

The docent's lengthy discourse, her monotonous voice notwithstanding, mesmerized Martin. Yet he was unsatisfied—the more challenging the topic, the more determined he was to delve deeper. From the copious listings provided by the docent, he clearly remembered that she had highlighted three distinctions between the Delft blue and the Chinese blue-and-white porcelain. One day, when the museum was quiet, Martin carefully took out his snuff bottle and compared it with a Delft blue on display. The lady was correct, Martin concluded. His piece, although small in size, was much thinner and whiter than the Delftware. Besides, the color of his blue was much brighter and shinier than any Delft blue in the showroom. The thinness and the brilliant dual colors certainly made his piece a superior product than the imitations. However, the little bottle's defining character was unquestionably the blue color, because its blazing luster was so strikingly magical, as if it were full of life under fire. The contrast between the intensity of his bottle's blue and the softness of its white was so amazing as to make all the Delft products in the room, for all their impressive sizes and stately designs, pale, dim, and lifeless.

Why could the ancient Chinese artisans achieve such a feat while the Dutch, Italian, and English could not? The docent had provided no answers. Martin knew he needed to learn more, which did not frustrate but excite him. An avid reader since childhood, he had a missionary zeal to tackle any topic, no matter how complex it might be. Insofar as his eternally squabbling parents could agree on one thing, it was that their son was unnecessarily too driven and too obsessed with solving problems for his age.

Indeed, once Martin was onto something, he would not stop until he got his answers. He soon learned that his native Rotterdam had a lot to do with the massive importation of Chinese treasures, which the nearby city of Delft had tried for years to replicate. Less than ten miles away, Delft was the favored seat of the stadholder William of Orange, also known as William the Silent, the great leader of the independence of the United Provinces. He, ancestor of all future monarchs of the kingdom, was assassinated during the Dutch revolt and buried in the New Church in the walled city. Delft was also the birthplace of the painter Johannes Vermeer, son of an innkeeper and art dealer, whose artistic reputation saw a significant resurgence two centuries after his death, even though the exact instruments (dubbed "Vermeer's camera" by some) and techniques he had used in some paintings of domestic scenes remained the subject of a heated academic debate. Father had told Martin that, for all its heritage, wealth, and fame, Delft, lying between Rotterdam and The Hague, had no port and was compelled to pay tolls to nearby port cities for its cargos. A settlement of wharfs and warehouses was therefore developed on the right bank of river Nieuwe Maas, where the Pilgrims had boarded the ship *Speedwell* to join the *Mayflower* in its voyage to the New World in 1620. Adjacent to the western vicinities of Rotterdam, the site was named Delfshaven or Port of Delft, which later became a borough of Rotterdam only a few years before Martin was born.

3

Legendary seafarers often returned home with grand pickings from the ancient past. Standing in the harbor, Martin believed that he could see the tricolor Dutch state flags and pennants flying under the expansive blue skies, along with exhausted sailors howling, anxious citizens shouting, strong waves gushing, fresh gales blowing, topsails folding, riggings and ropes whistling, blocks and gears shrieking. In a frantic race, dozens of local company yachts, official boats, and small vessels rushed to embrace the ships returning from their overseas voyages. No one wanted to be beaten by the other—all longed to be the first to take a peek at the precious cargos. The ships' overladen hulls were all ready to burst open any moment, threatening to rend asunder their dangerously bulging sterns—completely covered with gold-leaf carvings—into thousands of pieces and send them flying and kissing the fast-approaching natives.

Rotterdam was one of the six cities (along with Enkhuizen, Hoorn, Middleburg, Delft, and Amsterdam) where the Dutch East India Company (the VOC) had established a chamber. The company had sent no fewer than six thousand voyages to Asia, bringing back enormous wealth that heralded the Dutch Golden Age in the seventeenth century. Well over three million pieces of porcelain were delivered in the first fifty years, including dinner plates, fruit dishes, brandy decanters, salt cellars, mustard pots, and wide bowls, vinegar jugs, tea cups, and candle holders in various sizes.

The VOC paid the natives less than a penny for ten pounds of nutmeg on the Spice Islands of the East Indies, but could sell the same amount six thousand times higher at £25 in the European market. This kind of incredible gain made the arrival of the returning ships a highly anticipated event, which occasioned a spectacular public celebration every time, as marvelously depicted by the magnificent paintings by the artists Andries van Eertvelt and Jacob van Strij.

China was said to have continued to export large quantities of silk, tea, and chinaware to Europe, and until the early 1900s the Dutch vessels, along with those from Britain, America, Germany, Denmark, Japan, and Russia, still remained a large part of those trading activities.

Reading up on the Dutch East India Company's past not only helped Martin to understand the connection between his hometown and the China trade but also exposed him to the dark side of European history. The small maritime powers in Europe including Spain, Portugal, England, and the Netherlands, colonized large territories in Africa, America, and Asia for their own benefits. Dutch vessels benefited as much from the notorious slave trade in the Dutch Golden Coast of Africa as they profited from the spice trade in Southeast Asia.

The horrible stories and unscrupulous actions related to the Europeans' exploitation of the natives in their scramble for peppers, cinnamon, cloves, sago, nutmeg, and mace in the East Indies shocked Martin. In 1619, the Dutch forces defeated the Javanese, who had allied themselves with the English, and took full control of Jayakarta, the most strategic port on the northwest coast of Java. The port was renamed Batavia after the ancient German-speaking tribe in central Europe, whom the Dutch believed to be their forefathers. Thousands of Javanese were expelled, while hundreds of others were enslaved to serve their Dutch masters. An unknown number died in the conflict. Over a thousand Chinese were imported into Batavia to work. As their population grew, so did local resentment and hostility. Between five thousand and ten thousand Chinese laborers were murdered within the walls of Batavia in 1740, sending shock waves across the oceans.

4

"This is outrageous. Such injustice!" Martin thought. Gradually he gained a broad perspective that had eluded his coworkers. While many of them were union activists fighting for solidarity, his personal interest and knowledge quietly transformed him into an internationalist who was both deeply concerned with oriental affairs and strongly against European colonialism and imperialism.

A stint in Batavia as a reporter deepened his sense of social justice. He now understood how the powerful was controlling the powerless, how the oppressor was exploiting the oppressed, and how the wealthy foreigners were fleecing the poor Javanese. He realized how law and order was maintained by the imperial police force, whose chief task was to arrest the locals and have them beaten. Pampered by native manservants and maids, these European masters who belonged to exclusive clubs spent their time smoking and drinking aimlessly, all the while heaping scorn at the indigenous people for their supposed inferiority. The colonialists' high-handed attitude and insensitivity shocked Martin when he witnessed how one white policeman chased and beat a frail old Javanese woman senselessly.

In another incident, a white policeman was called upon to shoot an elephant that had trampled a person to death. Even though he did not want to shoot the animal, the officer felt he had to because a local crowd had gathered to watch the executioner demonstrate his brute authority. Martin would have found echoes of the incident in George Orwell's essay "Shooting the Elephant," where he wrote:

> When the white man turns tyrant it is his own freedom that he destroys… For it is the condition of his rule that he shall spend his life in trying to impress the "natives," and so in every crisis he has got to do what the "natives" expect of him. He wears a mask, and his face grows to fit it.

Martin's anger against colonial rule grew as his sympathy with the oppressed heightened. Or, as Orwell would say, "How can you make out that we are in this country for any purpose except to steal? It's so simple. The official holds the native down while the businessman goes through his pockets."

5

For the highly sensitive Martin, at twenty-seven, no event could have come at a more perfect time than the Russian Bolshevik Revolution in 1917, which shattered the traditional world of Western dominance.

Nothing could be more exhilarating for Martin than this epic upheaval, where tens of thousands of ordinary men and women rose to become masters of their own destiny. They were to build a new society, said Lenin and his Bolshevik disciples, where the divide between the rich and the poor, the powerful and the powerless, the rulers and the ruled, men and women, and between classes, races, and creeds, would forever disappear from the face of the Earth. This magnificent ideology and fantastic vision enthralled Martin, who rushed to Russia to embrace communism. His honesty, diligence, and knowledge soon earned him the appointment as the Comintern's first emissary to China. Nothing could compare to the thrill he felt over an impending worldwide revolution of the proletariat, and the alluring prospect that he was the chosen one to spearhead that glorious cause in China overwhelmed him.

Despite such heady feelings, Martin—who at six feet and three inches cut a fine figure with his blue eyes and chiseled features—couldn't help feeling anxious as he waited for an invitation to make his first-ever visit to the Kremlin in Moscow before his departure for China.

He finally received a call one afternoon to meet Mr. Chamberlain, the director of the Comintern's Asia Bureau, located in the Senate Building of the Kremlin. Moscow's heavily overcast gray skies did nothing to dampen the young emissary's spirit. He merrily waded through two feet of snow in the streets, which would not completely melt away until next May. The silhouette of the gigantic Savior Tower was still traceable despite the thick mist from falling sleet and layers of frost. No sooner had he shown his pass and entered the Kremlin than he was overcome by the solemnity of the surroundings. He slowed his pace as he strolled through the Cathedral Square in absolute silence. "This place is as big as Rotterdam within the old city walls," he said to himself. With the Assumption Cathedral and Annunciation Cathedral to the left, the Archangel's Cathedral and Ivan the Great Bell Tower to the right, the presence of Orthodoxy was as palpable as it was intimidating. Fascinated with the outlandish but magnificent architecture, Martin, who had grown up under the far simpler traditions of a reformed church, gazed at several huge crosses atop the brilliantly gilded domes in midair and almost forgot why he was there.

The chime of church bells reminded him of the time and he rushed toward the Senate Building. After passing the soaring rotunda of the Great Pantheon, he made a wrong turn and lost his way. The faster he tried to get out of the maze, the more it confused him. Running from one staircase to another, changing from one direction to the next, his heart was panting faster by the second. "This is terrible! Absolutely terrible!" he muttered in panic. Finally he bumped into someone who kindly pointed him to the right direction. Still Martin showed up fifteen minutes late for the meeting. The tall, stout, and thickly mustached Mr. Chamberlain was furious as he railed, "Comrade Martin, your tardiness has irrevocably delayed, ruined, and destroyed the great international revolution of the heroic proletarians, and you shall be charged as such at the Supreme Court of our Bolsheviks!"

Noticing that the poor man's profuse apologies could not quell the boss's anger, a third person in the room slowly turned around to inquire about the brouhaha. A nervous Martin could not predict the outcome of his fate, as the portly Mr. Chamberlain, head and shoulders down, started to converse in rapid Russian with the inquiring man, who was the shortest of them all. The conversation seemed to drag on for eternity until Martin saw the little guy turning toward him, glowing, "Really? The author of *The Future of Batavia*! Why didn't you tell me in the first place? Come, come to my office then."

Confused, Martin did not know what to do next. Scanning Mr. Chamberlain's stern face for any sign of permission, he reluctantly repeated, "Your... your office?"

"Yes, yes, my office." The person patted Martin's back, adding, "Vladimir Ilyich Ulyanov's office, or Lenin's for short." The pair were now arm in arm and hurriedly disappeared behind a side door, leaving the bewildered Mr. Chamberlain shaking his head over the curious turn of events.

The surprise meeting with Lenin lasted for several hours and, when Martin finally came out, it was almost midnight. Lenin, the champion of the total liberation of the working class, knew about his mission! Yes, yes, Lenin told the flattered emissary, he had not only known but also ordered the mission, which was of vital importance to the security of the nascent Bolshevik regime and to the ultimate success of the communist cause that Karl Marx had envisioned. As Martin left the room, his excitement was no different from that of a child receiving a Christmas present.

The overjoyed emissary, however, got lost again and could not find his way out of the colossal complex. "Damn it," he said as he started to panic again. As he reached a large landing from a flight of splendid marble stairs, he ran into the same person who had helped him earlier during the day. Only this time did Martin realize that this person was a very attractive lady in her early twenties. Evidently embarrassed not to have had the manners to thank her properly earlier, Martin said, "May I invite you for a cup of coffee please?" She smiled.

But an outing at that hour was not possible. Russia was engulfed in a terrible civil war and no shops or restaurants would remain open after dark during such tumultuous times. The two decided to go to her little flat nearby for a drink. When Martin had the first chance to take a good look at her while they were sitting down, he knew he was in love.

Women sometimes captivate men's attention for their outstanding beauty, at other times for enigmatic small things. It could be a polite greeting, a simple smile, or a casual laughter. It could be a flush of the face, a toss of the hair, a twinkle in the gaze, a turn of the neck, an innocent frown, a quiver of the lips, a teardrop, a soothing voice, a soft touch of the fingers, or a distinct aroma. It could also be a cheery expression, a witty story, a sharp question, a sarcastic comment, a humorous interjection, or an acute observation. Tania sat quietly in front of Martin for a while without saying a word. But her dignified deportment, along with her gracious style, was something that he had never seen in any woman before. He warmly recounted his meetings with Mr. Chamberlain and Lenin, but she did not seem to be as impressed as he had been—until he mentioned his mission to China. "China?! The people there saved my life." Her words burst out as quickly as her eyes brightened.

Her story began from the aristocratic Gorchakov clan. Tania told Martin that she was one of the descendants of Countess Maria, who had given up all her comforts and privileges in St. Petersburg to join her Decembrist husband, who had been banished to Siberia. After more than two decades of government abuse and personal sufferings, she passed away in the 1870s. Her dedication to her husband, support for his cause, enduring courage, and ultimate sacrifice earned her the title of Princess of Siberia. Maria's life inspired Tania's parents, who, rather than compromise their political principles in exchange for a pardon from the tsar, decided to continue their exile deep in the heart of Siberia at Nerchinsk, next to the borders with Northeastern China. Needless to say, the hard labor, brutal cold, and wretched living conditions over there ruined their health, and the mother was deadly pale and literally breathless after giving birth to Tania. The desperate husband implored local villagers for help. One of them went across the border and came back with a group of Chinese friends, who carried several sacks of flour, millets, potatoes, carrots, and cabbages, plus half a dozen chickens. One also brought a goat, saying its milk should be good for both mother and infant. The family was saved. Since then, the grateful parents had never failed to relay the story of their blessed baby and the stranger's nasty-looking goat for as long as Tania could remember.

The girl grew up with a rare blend of patrician grace and a profoundly tender heart for the underprivileged. For those who had met both Tania and her great-aunt Countess Maria, they insisted on the stunning resemblance between the two. Tania disagreed. She was proud of her clean, short, amber hair, which was distinctively different from the Countess's dark, long, curly hair. She also preferred her own down-to-earth hazel eyes over the Countess's sparkling green eyes, which she thought were too flashy. But Tania did share her great-aunt's lifelong passion for the classic treasures in Russian literature, music, and theater that the country had produced over the centuries. And, just like hundreds of Russian girls who idolized the country's literary giants, young Tania was secretly envious of the great-aunt who had been personally acquainted with the greatest Russian poet, Alexander Pushkin, who had written several exquisite poems for her.

According to the town's folk tale, in the spring of 1820, Pushkin accompanied Maria's family on a trip to the Caucasus. One morning the Sea of Azov came into view and the fifteen-year-old Maria and her younger sister ordered their carriage to stop. "Sophia and I jumped out and ran to the shore. The surface of the water," Maria recalled many years later in her memoirs, "was covered with waves, gentle, caressing waves, lapping at my feet, pursuing me back and forth as I ran." Unbeknown to the girls, Pushkin, whose carriage was behind theirs, had a chance to watch them from afar. The poet, widely famous at twenty-one, wrote in his journal that evening, "I longed, like the waves, to lap your feet with my lips." His amorous sentiments inspired by the lovely images of the beach were immortalized in *Eugene Onegin*, which the bard published as a collection of poems a few years later. Tania had always longed for the day when someone would compose romantic lines for her as beautifully as Pushkin had done for her great-aunt. Oh, those mesmerizing verses that she had recited thousands of times and would never forget:

How I envy the sea before a tempest,
The clapping waves never cease,
Dashing, flying for the shore,
Just to bow and kiss your lovely feet.

Tania's story deeply moved Martin, who, at that moment, believed that he had found his soulmate. "I will marry her and go to China with her," he decided.

Chapter 2

Peking

1

PEKING, THE CELESTIAL CAPITAL OF CHINA FOR SEVEN HUNDRED years, impressed visitors with its immense size. Nestled at the foothills of the rugged Yan Mountains to the northwest and commanding the North China Plain sweeping for miles upon miles from the east to the south, the city was the largest fortress of human habitation on earth. Like a giant black python, Peking's sixty-foot-high and fifty-foot-wide walls, made of special bricks weighing over thirty pounds each, extended for twenty miles in circumference and constricted the city tightly in a way no one could ever imagine. With the huge watchtowers rising seventy feet atop the walls and guarded by armed soldiers behind several hundred shooting holes, Peking's sixteen massive gates seemed intimidating to visitors.

But, once they stepped inside the city, its streets and roads were much easier to navigate than expected, thanks to the chessboard design by the original planners. This was especially true for the Inner City to the north, where most of the merchants, officials, and government employees lived. A first-time visitor would hardly have any difficulty finding his way back to his lodging as long as he remembered that the major avenues and wide paths in the city crisscrossed each other perpendicularly.

More problematic was the fact that no streets across town, large or small, were paved. They inevitably became a sea of mud after a rainstorm, stalling trucks, carts, rickshaws, cyclists, and pedestrians in hundreds of water-filled ditches and puddles everywhere. The narrow alleys, winding lanes, and tapered backstreets in the Outer City to the south, where most of the poor laboring families lived, simply exacerbated the problem, making travel after rain a big hassle like a fish struggling to swim in a pond of receding waters. When some scorching heat finally dried up everything, the overbaked road surface would turn into a sea of yellow powder that, as in the Sahara Desert, could cloud the skies whenever the wind blew. Whirling and mixing the Gobi sands with local dust, the strong seasonal winds from the northwest frequented the city between February and March, making the dirty cold spring air in Peking highly unpleasant.

Luckily for Martin and Tania, the weather was perfect when they stepped out of their small hotel one afternoon.

The pleasant sunshine blessed the entire city and warmed the hearts of those walking on the streets. The budding leaves of youthful green twigs on each tree painted a lively image against the backdrop of willowy stems in faint brown. A dozen house sparrows began their noisy games of chasing one another around the eaves. Even a middle-aged yellow dog felt cozy enough to lie down and expose his soft belly in the agreeable open air. All the signs indicated that the good spring days were finally here.

The couple felt particularly liberated after successive meetings with several groups of dubious visitors in the last few days. The first visitors were two strong men with exotic tattoos on their forearms, who barged into their room unannounced. "Want any job done in this neighborhood?" they demanded rather than asked. In an unabashed can-do spirit, they went on to enumerate their talents, such as blackmailing or spying on someone, robbing a bank, kidnaping a woman, triggering a riot, bombing a shop, purchasing illicit merchandise, locating rare antiques, maiming a foe, faking a suicide, or plotting a strike. In short, "If you can name it, we can do it." "And of course," they added, "we would let you know what the right price is." The two tough guys apparently believed that any foreigners who had taken the trouble to come to the city from a faraway land must be on some covert mission with loads of money to dispose of. As members of an underground society named "Fraternity of the East," they felt that they were entitled to be part of any transaction on their home turf.

Beyond the facade of ancient buildings, beyond the seasonal change of weather patterns, and beyond its share of clandestine activities, Peking had also entered a new phase of uncertainty after the fall of the Qing Dynasty in 1911, as Martin and Tania would soon discover. Although the followers of the Nationalist Party leader Dr. Sun Yat-Sen played a key role in toppling the Qing monarchy and gained extensive influence in Southern China, they did not have any control over the vast territories north of the Yangtze River. Taking advantage of the crumbling dynasty, several powerful warlords (former high-ranking military commanders under the Qing) turned parts of the country into their personal domains. Each became the exclusive possession of the regional military forces under their command, such as General Zhang in the Northeast, General Feng in the Northwest, General Yan in the West, General Li and General Bai in the Southwest, and General Wu in the East. Still, as the symbolic capital of the Chinese nation, Peking was the ultimate trophy in the domestic power struggle for these factions. But years of protracted conflicts failed to produce a definitive winner who was able to establish a central government strong enough to rule the entire country. The prevailing chaos, divisiveness, confusion, and instability had led to an unusual administrative vacuum, allowing for the first time in recent memory different political ideologies, diverse persuasions, competing platforms, and various associations to thrive.

The next person to appear before the couple was a Mr. Qi Shu, the self-appointed president of the Chinese Workers' Union. He recently changed its name to the Chinese Socialist Party, not out of principle but out of expediency. He started his organization shortly after World War I ended in 1918, when hundreds of laborers from China were stranded in Europe. These Chinese coolies were noncombatants, but hired by the Allied forces to transport ammunition, construct barracks, and dig trenches in the battle zones. The war's end left them with unpaid wages, health woes, and repatriation problems. Mr. Qi went to Russia to discuss these issues with officials from several European governments. To represent all the wartime laborers from China as one entity, he established the Chinese Workers' Union, which had nothing to do with any workers living in China. He happened to be in Moscow in 1919 when the first meeting of the Communist International was convened. He attended the opening ceremony and even gave a congratulatory speech on behalf of his union at one of the sessions. He quickly found out that all the other delegations—there were thirty-three voting delegates representing nineteen countries—had either socialist or communist as part of their party's name. He quickly followed suit and replaced "workers union" with "socialist party" in his organization's name just to be fashionable.

Upon entering the room, Mr. Qi quickly greeted Tania and Martin as if he were the host, they the guests. He shook their hands eagerly, declaring, "My dear comrades, long live Bolshevik Russia! Long live Lenin! I know him, my dear comrades. We met five times. (In fact, he only saw Lenin at the podium from afar during a rally.) We hugged. We shook hands. We embraced each other. We chatted. We discussed, and we…" As Mr. Qi went on and on about his union, his party, and his intimate friendship with Comrade Lenin, Martin and Tania began to understand that what Mr. Qi really cared about was nothing more than the workmen's "wages, benefits, and working conditions"—the exact concerns that Lenin had derided as "pure unionism," and the exact opposite of his ultimate vision of a global communist revolution.

A few days later, Tania and Martin received yet another visitor, whom they initially thought was Japanese. Mr. Wang proudly declared that he had translated so many treatises on Western political thought from the Japanese language into Chinese that all Chinese students of socialism and communism owed him a big debt. From Montesquieu's *Spirit of Laws* and Jean-Jacques Rousseau's *Social Contract* to Charles Darwin's *On the Origin of Species*, these translations had nurtured a whole new generation of Chinese intellectuals since the beginning of the twentieth century. Today, when many Western concepts had become part of the daily lexicon in China, few would realize that they had initially been retranslated from the Japanese language, such as politics (seiji 政治), philosophy (tetsugaku 哲学), society (shakai 社会), science (kagaku 科学), religion (shūkyō 宗教), freedom (jiyū 自由), culture (bunka 文化), and revolution (kakumei 革命).

As a longtime reporter for the Peking daily newspaper *Good Morning* stationed in Tokyo, Mr. Wang did more than anyone to introduce to the educated Chinese the latest Japanese scholarly works on social change. One was *A Theoretical System of Marxist Socialism*, written by Kawakami Hajime, Japan's most eminent Marxist scholar and a professor of economics at Kyoto University; the other was *A New Outline of Economics*, written by Fukuda

Tokuzō, a professor of economics at Tokyo Imperial University. Both works had been used extensively by several Chinese authors, whose adaptations of the two original versions had appeared in leading journals and magazines in China. As Martin and Tania wondered where this highly informative conversation was heading, what Mr. Wang said next totally surprised them. He wanted to have, through negotiations with the two emissaries, exclusive access to the German and Russian editions of Marx and Lenin's writings so that he could profit from the exclusive copyright of his future translations of those imported materials. Evidently, Mr. Wang was a gifted connoisseur, conscientious researcher, productive scholar, and an astute businessman rolled into one. But he was neither an ardent believer nor the trailblazing activist they were looking for.

"Do you know Sacco and Vanzetti? Are you here to collect donations? How are they holding up in jails? Tell them, we love them and we believe in their innocence. Just tell them to hang in there and they shall be freed in no time."

Before Tania and Martin knew it, they were bombarded by rapid-fire questions from the next group of five visitors. Each tried to speak louder than the rest, making it difficult to ascertain who was saying what, and absolutely impossible to engage in a conducive dialogue with any of them.

No sooner had they finished the first round of interrogations than two of them started to debate the validity of the evidence concerning the alleged gun used in the Bridgewater murder case in Massachusetts in early 1920. One said he was glad to hear Vanzetti's alibi. A swinging palm promptly landed on his face as a shrill voice pierced the air. "Are you saying Sacco was guilty, you idiot?" "Shame on the hypocritical capitalist legal apparatus! Down with the sham American court system!" someone shouted. "Free all the prisoners in the U.S., Germany, France, Spain, Italy, in all Europe, and in every country of the world," bawled another. "Bakunin is my hero," said one. "Nonsense! Proudhon is the true champion of the people," declared another. "No, no, no. Both of you were wrong. Kropotkin's ideas are the most viable and therefore truly revolutionary," retorted the third. To these proclamations, the rebuttals came fast and furious. "We anarchists believe in no authority, government, or hero worship of any kind!" "We are syndicalists," someone yapped, "not anarchists, you moron!"

By this time, the shouting match between the supporters of Vanzetti and those of Sacco, of Bakunin and of Proudhon, of Proudhon and of Kropotkin, of Kropotkin and of Bakunin, and between syndicalists and anarchists, had escalated to such an extent that a mad fistfight ensued. The hapless Martin and Tania had to shove all five out of the room before quickly shutting the door behind them.

Enough with these fruitless meetings, the couple thought. They looked at each other and decided it was time to take a break.

2

"Come on, dear, it has not been that bad." Tania held Martin's arm and tried to cheer him up as they took a walk outside.

"Tell me *one* good thing," he responded coldly, still upset.

"The weather is warm and nice today," she said, as she grabbed his arm and held it tenderly.

"That I can agree." He softened his voice, paused to take a deep breath, and reached out to squeeze her hand and hold it. "But that's as far as I can go," he declared.

"Well, let's see. The city is a heaven for photographers, wouldn't you agree?" Tania had an uncanny ability to look at things from an unusual angle.

Baffled at first, Martin turned around to look. As Tania saw the warm glow returning to his face, she knew she had won over her husband.

This oriental metropolis conducted much of its commercial activity in the open, and no district did it more so than the Outer City. Merchants set up stalls and sold goods of all sorts along the sidewalks, from small items such as cooking utensils, soap, hats, shoes, and clothing to large ones such as bedding, kettles, furniture, and livestock including chickens, ducks, and pigs. Offering a great variety of candies and toys in fancy wrappers, vendors paraded and advertised their merchandise by shouting at the top of their lungs. Housewives bought breakfast from food stalls on street corners, and bargained with farmers coming to their doorsteps over the prices of eggs, meat, fruit, and vegetables. Pedestrians read newspapers from neighborhood billboards, and then walked into a nearby teahouse to discuss current affairs. Looking for cheap rental accommodation, newly arrived migrants and poor students stopped to peruse announcements pasted on telephone posts. Yelling "Look out! Look out!

Vehicles passing," rickshaw men raced against each other through the crowds with astonishing speed and agility. After preparing some hot water on one high stool and sitting his customer on another, a barber began to sharpen a razor while telling some racy jokes for the benefit of both the customer and eager onlookers. Sweating martial arts experts performed amazing tricks, collected their hard-earned money at busy intersections, and entreated the crowd to come back for more shows next time. Waiting for their masters, several horses became restless and kicked their hooves in front of a tavern. A team of camels, with heavy loads on their backs, sneezed as loudly as they could to demand a rest, after trekking seven hundred miles all the way from Mongolia.

The whole place, the couple concluded, was buzzing and humming like one oversized county fair, where a photographer could find more real-life characters and more lively actions than anywhere else in China.

"Look at those faces! If only I could have the talents of Da Vinci, I would stay here for days to sketch them," Martin said enthusiastically, his spirit now fully restored.

Tania knew her husband's temperament well, and was glad to see how animated he had become simply by looking at the sea of human faces, from the beautiful and saintly to the pitiful and grotesque. Surely, his beloved Italian and Dutch masters would love these diverse faces. She said gently, "Yes. Rembrandt would be happy to be in this crowd too."

Oh, these faces of China—different yet real, old and young, male and female. Which of them had seen the pillage the city suffered during the Boxer Rebellion twenty years ago? Which ones were witness to the students' demonstrations during the May Fourth Movement just a year earlier? Hadn't that movement involved ordinary citizens and unleashed widespread anti-imperialist sentiments? The sea of human faces must have the answers, but they would not tell you voluntarily. This could be the charm of the city, which held many secrets that were waiting to be unlocked by those who cared enough to scratch beneath the surface.

"I think Peking is a wonderful place for architects," Martin said, offering yet another perspective.

They noticed that few Christian churches had been built here despite the laborious exertions by European missionaries to introduce Christianity to the celestial people for several centuries. Traditional Chinese temples, monasteries, and mosques dotted the city, their total number unmatched in any other Chinese city. The several dozens of huge royal gardens and big princely compounds were among the best examples of China's ancient architecture and craftsmanship. If any European were to visit a traditional house in any of the city's countless alleys, he or she would instantly be transported into a different world.

Guarded by a stone lion on each side, the heavily painted wooden front doors of the house exuded a calming sense of peace, harmony, and gravitas. Upon entering, the visitor would immediately notice a massive brick wall, which guarded the household's privacy from the prying eyes of outsiders. The centerpiece on the wall was a gorgeously carved stone relief, a symbol of blessing for the family. One needed to walk around the brick wall to its left side before the open courtyard would reveal itself, where the broad pathways lined with huge cypress suggested the family's history, wealth, and taste. Spacious and meticulously furnished, the main hall in the middle of the courtyard was where the most important family gatherings would be held, and where the host would receive guests. According to the dictates of tradition, the next best and large rooms facing the south belonged to the parents, while boys lived in the east wing of the compound and girls in the west. Side yards and rear gardens had seasonal flowers, fruit trees, fishponds, and grapevines, which provided ample shade and pleasure for the family to enjoy, free from the noise and chaos outside.

"If the city is a big castle," Martin remarked, "each household seems to live within a small castle of its own."

"Peace and tranquility has its price, doesn't it?" Tania commented.

"Which is…?"

"Exclusion, isolation, and self-centeredness," she replied.

"Are you talking about the family or the city?" he asked.

Tania paused, then said, "Both."

"Hum, that's an interesting point." Martin was intrigued by the reply. He considered himself well read in oriental studies and agreed with most European observers that the Chinese emphasis on family unity and harmony had been one of the greatest virtues they had inherited from Confucian times.

"If you think internal peace and harmony is not such a noble concept after all," he said, "why have the Chinese cherished it for long?"

"Tradition, I guess," said she. "Or the inertia of tradition." Tania's seemingly casual remarks really got Martin thinking. If what she said was true, it would mean that their attempt to introduce any Western thought would have to confront some enormous resistance in the form exclusion, isolation, and self-centeredness, which had been the Chinese way of life for several thousand years. How could anyone have the power to break that powerful tradition? He had no answer.

"My dear, do you think Peking is a romantic city?" Tania's new question interrupted Martin's train of thought.

"Yes, why? Ah, why did you ask?" Martin replied absent-mindedly, his mind preoccupied with his own set of questions.

"I mean we have been out for a while, but I don't think we have seen a boy dating a girl, or a girl holding her fiancé's hand. No one ever kisses another person, and no one ever hugs someone."

"Well, dear, the Chinese are known for their modesty and controlled expressions. Hugging, kissing, and public displays of intimacy are considered bad influences from the West."

"Look, what a pity if nobody would give someone a kiss right here and now," Tania insisted.

No sooner had Martin looked at the direction she was pointing than he felt a pull in his heart, as much as she did in hers. Both now stood next to the great moat, fifty yards wide, protecting the Forbidden City, where the deposed emperor and his family still resided. From the great distance between them and the royal palace, the walls of the Forbidden City seemed solid and impenetrable. No one was walking close to the moat, perhaps out of fear of the palace guards. No noise and no commercial activity in the nearby streets. The place was so quiet it was as if you had walked into a prohibited zone. But a fresh breeze did fill the air, which gently dispensed the tender but tantalizing fragrance of spring. Giant willow trees lined both sides of the moat, and thousands of green twigs began to dance as the sweet air breezed through to caress and play with each of them.

Against the warm afternoon sunshine, a unique watchtower of golden tiles and red panels rose as high as eighty feet into the skies at the corner of the palace walls, basking in splendid glory. Unlike the double-eave roof structures commonly found in many traditional Chinese buildings, this huge watchtower had three levels of roofs with the most intricate designs. Extending the exteriors of the first two lower levels, its builders constructed two protruding and decorative corners adding to each regular corner at both levels. The result was that, instead of four standard corners of any rectangular building, this palatial watchtower had twelve corners at each of the first two levels. A hip-roof covered every one of the twelve corners at the first level, and four hip-and-gable-roofs and eight hip-roofs covered the twelve corners at the second level. The last top level had four hip-and-gable-roofs of taller dimensions than those at the middle level, making the tower—covered with a total of twenty-eight marvelously curved and seamlessly joined and ornamented roofs—majestically balanced and absolutely enchanting.

"This is the most beautiful place I have ever been to. Look at this ancient tower and its exquisite designs," Tania said.

"And look at the environs," Martin agreed. "So quiet, so peaceful, and so elegant."

"I think this place is as romantic as the Eiffel Tower, if not more so. And I need a kiss," she demanded, raising her head proudly.

He complied.

3

When Tania and Martin returned to their hotel, the owner told them that several young visitors had stopped by and left a message in their room. "I hope they are not another group of anarchists or syndicalists," said Martin in trepidation as he opened the door.

"Oh look! Who said Peking is not romantic? We have been invited to see a show!" Waving the message to Martin, Tania could not be happier.

"Really? Let me see it." Martin remained skeptical.

Indeed, the nicely drawn flyer stated that there was a festival featuring several performances by local and visiting students, and that people in the surrounding neighborhoods were invited to attend it.

The following day, Tania and Martin set out for the event. Having been advised by the hotel owner, they asked their rickshaw man to avoid the Foreign Legations, where the embassies of nine nations and their troops were stationed. Nor did they tarry in the popular but crowded Prince Street, where many shops and commercial activities were concentrated. As they moved further north into a different neighborhood, the number of businesses dwindled and the level of traffic and noise lessened significantly. About five medium-sized elementary schools soon came into sight, followed by several middle schools across the street at a number of major intersections. Finally a free-standing library of modern sciences appeared, located between St. John's University on its right and a Methodist church on its left. A few blocks away, a lively construction project spanning several acres was underway. When they stopped to inquire, workers directed them to a big wooden marker, which had the names of a new private school and a sports complex, a novelty in China. According to anecdotes, the workers' supervisor shared, many businessmen, doctors, engineers, and professors in the area had sponsored the project and would enroll their children in the new school once it was completed.

"I would never expect to see so many schools so close to each other in one neighborhood," said an impressed Martin.

"This area should be named the Education District," Tania suggested.

A few minutes later, the couple found the sign they were looking for, and both nodded at each other as they proclaimed in near unison, "That must be the tricolored flag stated in the flyer."

Moving toward the direction of the distinct red–blue–yellow banner, the rickshaw man quickly took them to their destination—a fairly new brick building that was home to Peking University.

With the thick air of silence around the iron-fenced entrance and the modest surroundings, Tania and Martin could hardly believe that they had arrived at the place where several hundred students had gathered before taking to the streets, starting what would become known as the May Fourth Movement in China's history.

Next to the back walls of a mess hall stood a small and obscure athletic field, where the initial small protest had attracted its first crowd. Memorialized as Democracy Square years later, the big yard was now all but deserted.

Designed with symmetrical but unadorned facades, the redbrick building of four stories and a basement reminded Martin of the many similar structures in Rotterdam. Although devoid of any sophistication or huge expanse, the triangular pediment and the four Corinthian columns of the front entrance in particular indicated a heavy European influence. Only the small size of the front doors and the simple but ubiquitous trims of gray bricks over every window revealed the cost-conscious but functionally inclined nature of the planners. Once inside the hall, the structure appeared surprisingly spacious, comfortable, and airy. The crimson-hued wood floors throughout the building and the same colored wood molding and furniture in every room accentuated the importance of harmonious tranquility.

Yet it looked almost eerie since Martin and Tania did not see a single soul on the first floor. It was not until they walked to the end of the east wing that they finally met someone. He was collecting some magazines scattered on a desk in a double-sized classroom without a partition in the middle. All the books, journals, pamphlets, newspapers, shelves, and newspaper racks suggested to them that this could be the university's reading room or library.

The young man standing before them was tall and strong but seemed shy. His innocent round face flushed as he uttered, "How... ah, how can I help you?"

Several minutes later, following a dialogue in his broken English and their poor Chinese, they decided that another interlocutor was needed to rescue the conversation.

The young man left and soon returned with university librarian Tang Shu-Hai, a thin and handsome man in his mid-forties, who spoke fluent Russian and English.

Tang told the couple that the university was in a recess. He then went on to explain about the university's setup—God blessed his patience—which led Martin and Tania to realize that Peking University was spread out across three locations. The building with the library where they were in was called Campus One, which had the administration offices and classrooms for the humanities. Campus Three was a compound comprising both living quarters and classrooms for science students, which was located six or seven blocks down south from the administration building and very close to the construction site of the new private school. The scheduled festival was to take place at Campus Two, which was several blocks west in a residential neighborhood. Armed with such comprehensive information, Tania and Martin were ready to head out to the festival's venue.

"Please wait." Tang stopped them and turned to the young man. "Sheng Bao, can you get Dong Zi-Tian, who should be able to help this couple?"

Tania noticed that a slight frown flickered across the young man's face. He said, "I am not sure Dong Zi-Tian is here on campus."

"I am sure he is," Tang insisted. "He just told me that he would be in the seminar room in the west wing on the fourth floor."

The frown became more palpable. But, as the librarian's assistant, Sheng seemed to have little choice; he left.

Now that they were alone in the room, Martin began to confide in Tang about their actual mission in China. Tang told them that the best person to contact was a professor who, however, was no longer in town.

"Where is he and how can we find him?"

"He has left the university and now lives in Shanghai."

"What is his name?"

"He is Professor Lu Shi-Yan."

4

"Ah, here he is," announced Tang, and the couple stood up to greet the new arrival.

Although Dong Zi-Tian was also a young man, he instantly won the visitors over. As tall as Sheng but more heavily built, and having a more chiseled face and square jaw, Dong was an affable man who spoke excellent English. After exchanging greetings, they made their way to the western portion of the university.

The short walk was as pleasant as it was informative. Although it was a regular weekday, Dong told the visitors, the administration had granted a temporary recess to allow the students to disperse because the police were looking to arrest the activists among them. Still, preparations for a new round of action continued, with many students' organizations taking the opportunity to revise their strategies, and tonight's show was one of them.

While Dong's knowledge and inside information about the university reassured Tania and Martin that their visit would be fruitful, what they saw next was no less riveting. Originally the residence of a Qing princess, the royal entrance to this new site had a front door three times the size of a regular household, guarded by a giant stone lion on each side. A thirty-foot-tall and beautifully ornamented archway welcomed them to the first of the three huge courtyards of the compound. Well-laid-out cobblestoned pathways, five feet wide, led them into the campus's first courtyard, which was full of trimmed cypress hedges, manicured lawns, and well-tended flowerbeds.

As they walked along the path and enjoyed the picturesque scenery, Dong told them that the compound, about three hundred and fifty yards wide and five hundred and fifty yards long, was enclosed by a wall twelve feet high and four feet wide, made entirely by the same kind of high-quality bricks used to build the city walls. Although badly damaged during the Boxer Rebellion, the princely palace still had more than three hundred rooms and structures, including several grand halls, shrines, and temples. After passing a colorfully painted corridor and a ceramic-roof-topped side door, they entered the second courtyard, which was far bigger than the first. Standing before them were five mature and strong pagoda trees covered with thousands of small white flowers in full bloom, spreading a scent of mild sweetness. Under the leafy waterfall-like canopies, an open pond of lotus provided sanctuary to a shoal of large and small goldfish, which seemed to have a big appetite for the white flowers dropping around them.

Behind the pond was a grand hall, which was one hundred twenty feet long and seventy feet deep. Built on a raised two-tiered terrace made of bright magnesian limestone, it used to be the princess's main residence, Dong said. It now served as a lecture hall. The performances tonight would take place in this great building, which would soon host the British philosopher and mathematician Bertrand Russell, the American educator and philosopher John Dewey, and the Indian author and sage Rabindranath Tagore.

Inside the hall, at least several hundred people had already gathered. Most were students, professors, and teachers, with other professionals, middle-aged men and women, and even children, apparently friends and relatives of the university staff from the surrounding areas, making up the rest of the audience. Well publicized and carefully orchestrated, the event was truly a festival that attracted several delegations from nearby cities and provinces in Northern China. A big billboard announced that tonight's program would include a local opera presented by a students' troupe from Shanxi Province, a music rendition by Peking University's newly formed orchestra, and finally Henrik Ibsen's drama *A Doll's House,* performed by a students' company from the city of Tianjin.

When the evening started, a young female announcer came from behind the makeshift curtains and walked toward the front of the stage. In sharp contrast to the plain and one-piece robes found on most women and men, she wore a bright blue blouse and a long skirt of imported corduroy printed with flowers and appeared very beautiful under the spotlight of the grand theater. In a slightly nervous voice, she invited Dong to give an opening speech. Only then did Tania and Martin realize that he was the president of the students' union of Peking University, and had been one of the most active members of the students' movement since last year. Dong's brief but humorous remarks drew a big round of applause from an appreciative audience including the announcer herself, and the evening's program got underway.

The beat of gongs and drums marked the start of the Shanxi opera. Adapted from an episode of the classic novel *The Water Margin*, it recounted a popular legend of the hero Wu Song, who killed a tiger with his bare hands during a fight in the dead of the night, leading to his triumphant escape to join a rebellion. Often mixing gongs and drums with high-pitched strings, the music was much louder than what Martin and Tania—like most Europeans—were accustomed to. But they noticed that most of the audience were genuinely interested in the play despite their familiarity with the story.

The actors' painted faces were not that different from the ones seen in the more well-known Peking opera. Both used broad strokes of distinctive colors to represent different types of character, making it easy for illiterate audiences to identify them when the performances took place in the countryside. For example, a white face would often suggest a sly and immoral person who would resort to underhand tactics to achieve his goals. A red face would stand for a decent and honest person who would always remain loyal to his master, come rain or shine. A black face would be like the warrior Hercules, who had enormous strength, a good heart, but a terrible temper. The Shanxi students showed great passion throughout the play, and the intense fight between Wu and the tiger was particularly well done, thanks to the two performers' great acrobatic skills. At the end of the play, when the actors bowed amid applause from the audience, Tania and Martin noticed that the duo were sweating more profusely than anyone else on the stage.

The performance of the university's orchestra seemed to be the low point of the evening. Not entirely comfortable in his role, the student conductor did not seem to be in full command of his troupe. Nor did the team members coordinate well with each other. The group showed admirable courage by performing in public for the first time, even though they had been practicing together for only a very short period. In fact, most of them had not played any musical instrument before entering the university. Despite these obstacles, they played the traditional Chinese folk song *Autumn Moon Over Calm Lake*, the popular tunes *The Drizzle and The Nightingale*, and a song from Tchaikovsky's *Swan Lake*, which, for all their shortcomings, pleased Tania totally. To the delight of the audience, the orchestra also played the unofficial song of the alma mater, whose lyrics read in part, "the institute for the new century and the graduates for the new country." They ended their rendition with *America the Beautiful*.

The final and most anticipated part of the program was undoubtedly *A Doll's House*, which had for many years excited Chinese intellectuals more than any other literary work. It was hardly an exaggeration to say that the play by Norwegian playwright Henrik Ibsen started a cultural transformation, which introduced the new art form of modern drama to China as soon as Chinese translations of the play became available early in the century. Deeply impressed, many famous authors from Mr. Hu and Mr. Lu to Mr. Shen and Mr. Guo had showered praises on it. Mr. Hu Si edited a special issue for *The Youth* magazine to discuss the play. He also wrote his drama *When a Girl Marries*, which transplanted Ibsen's work into a Chinese setting. Few Chinese playwrights did not study Ibsen seriously and few Chinese actors or actresses could achieve fame without taking part in a stage play of *A Doll's House*.

Yet, Ibsen's message of individual liberty and particularly his powerful dramatization of a woman fighting for her freedom generated enormous controversy. His ideas and values, while inspiring hundreds of young Chinese, especially young women, to strive for independence and self-reliance, deeply troubled those who insisted on the traditional family structures, arranged marriages, parental authority over children, and the subjugation of women to men. Compounding these issues of social mores, the government banned actors and actresses from performing on the same stage, which was considered scandalous according to the prescribed moral codes of Chinese tradition.

Martin and Tania noticed that many women and men in the audience were chatting and eagerly waiting to see how this high drama would unfold.

It was gripping. The tight structure of the play, the well-executed acting, and Ibsen's impeccable dialogue moved everybody in the audience. They froze and almost became part of the scene as Nora made her final and most famous statement to her husband, Torvald—

We have been married now eight years. Does it not occur to you that this is the first time we two, you and I, husband and wife, have had a serious conversation? You have never loved me. You have only thought it pleasant to be in love with me… When I was at home with Papa, he told me his opinion about everything, and so I had the same opinions… He called me his doll-child, and he played with me just as I used to play with my dolls. And when I came to live with you… you arranged everything according to your own taste, and so I got the same tastes as you—or else I pretended to… When I look back on it, it seems to me as if I had been living here like a poor woman—just from hand to mouth. I have existed merely to perform tricks for you… You and Papa have committed a great sin against me. It is your fault that I have made nothing of my life… No, I have never been happy. I thought I was, but it has never really been so.

I must try and educate myself—you are not the man to help me in that. I must do that for myself. And this is why I am going to leave you now… I must stand quite alone, if I am to understand myself and everything about me. It is for that reason that I cannot remain with you any longer… I believe that before all else I am a reasonable human being, just as you are—or, at all events, that I must try and become one.

Judging by the audience's warm applause, the performance was very successful and the students' troupe from Tianjin seemed very pleased.

Dong later took Tania and Martin backstage. He introduced them to several key performers of the night—Mr. Tao Yin-Hu, who played Wu Song in the Shanxi opera, Mr. Gong Pei-Zhi, the orchestra's lead violinist, Mr. Gan Zu-Xun, who played Torvald in the drama, and Mr. Si-Tu Wen-Liang, who acted as Nora.

Still excited after they returned to the hotel, Tania said, "My dear, I can't believe Nora was played by a man. Mr. Si-Tu was really, really good."

Not long after, she asked, "Dear, do you think we should participate in the movement in China for love or for hate?"

Martin replied, "Perhaps for both. And you?"

"I will participate for love," said Tania.

"But love for whom and what? Like Nora, she had to choose to love Torvald or herself, didn't she?" Martin was perplexed.

"Love for humanity," Tania answered after some thought.

Chapter 3
Shanghai

1

"Y AN YAN, I RAN OUT OF INK," SAID PROFESSOR LU SHI-YAN LOUDLY while he was busy writing the last lines of a letter in his home office upstairs. A moment later, he asked again, "Yan, where is the fine paper I bought the other day?" Getting no answer, he stood up and walked to the open window. Yelling downstairs this time, he repeated, "Where are you, Yan? I have run out of ink and I need the fine paper I bought the other day."

"Need some help, Professor?" To his surprise, it was his student Dong Zi-Tian who responded from the yard.

"Where is Yan?" the professor asked.

"She went out to the market. Can I help you?" said Dong.

"Never mind. I'll ask her when she comes back. How are you this morning? Any new thoughts or suggestions? Why don't you come up for a talk?"

In his late forties, Professor Lu was the kind of person whom you would never forget after the first meeting. Dark and short but with broad shoulders, he was more strongly built than many Chinese intellectuals, who tended to be slender if not frail. Cutting a figure no less dramatic than a stage actor in a traditional Chinese opera, his jet-black hair shot up like a bundle of brushes perfectly trimmed on top, and his heavy mustache drooped sideways like a monstrous broom over his mouth. Daring, vigorous, and extremely obstinate, he was frequently at the center of a public controversy as often as he would be during a private conversation.

Born into a humble family in a small town in Anhui Province, Lu was a child prodigy. At the age of fifteen, he became the first person from his hometown to win the highest honor in the provincial examinations held every three years in China. Unlike hundreds of those young men before him who had built on such success to pursue a traditional career in civil service, he used his fame to propagate radical ideas for social change. When he was not yet eighteen, he started a local publication called *The Voice*, which was the first of the two dozen journals and magazines, big and small, that he would publish throughout his life. Spreading fresh ideas in public affairs and running biographies of international celebrities, *The Youth*, another magazine, launched in 1915, made him a well-known figure among the educated Chinese, especially among young school and college students. Mr. Cai Yuan-Pei, the highly regarded education reformer and president of Peking University, appointed Lu as professor and dean of the college of letters and humanities in 1918, completing his transformation from a provincial publicist to a national proponent of change. This new role would turn Lu into a pivotal figure in the May Fourth Movement.

It was around this time that Professor Lu, who was influenced by librarian Tang Shu-Hai, developed considerable interest in communism. He was enthralled by all that he had learned about the Russian Revolution and Lenin's Bolsheviks, who had successfully led the revolution. Lu was convinced that the key reason why the Chinese had tried but failed so many times to launch a revolution in the past was not because the enemies were too powerful and numerous but because the Chinese people didn't have a truly groundbreaking ideology around which to organize themselves. They were largely uneducated and ignorant, widely dispersed, and hopelessly divided. Yet, awaiting them were great tasks: achieving national salvation, restoring China's pride and integrity, and reclaiming her right to self-determination, free from foreign exploitation. To accomplish these tasks, however, an even greater challenge must first be overcome—how to awaken, educate, organize, and unite millions of people to participate in one common struggle. Neither Sun Yat-Sen's loosely structured Nationalist Party nor old-fashioned underground societies were up for the challenge. Only a completely new model, as demonstrated by the Russian experience, could offer China hope for the future.

A few days earlier, Professor Lu was glad to see Dong, who had come from Peking, carrying a letter from his good friend Tang. The letter mentioned several organizational matters he would like to discuss, while indicating that Dong could be entrusted as the go-between if the professor wished to communicate his ideas with his friends in Peking.

The professor had known Dong well; he was one of his prized students at Peking University. He immediately invited him to stay in his house, which had a spare room downstairs. This arrangement would no doubt facilitate their discussions over the issues Tang had raised in his letter, and Dong readily agreed.

Professor Lu's house was a typical "stone-gate-style" residence, which combined Western townhouse and Chinese courtyard structures, and had become very popular since its inception in Shanghai in the last century.

Originally a tiny fishing village close to the mouth of the Yangtze River, Shanghai was officially set up as a municipality in the thirteenth century. Rising to become the seat of regional administration in the mid-seventeenth century, it was selected, by the government after the First Opium War in 1842, as one of five port cities along the southeastern coast that were allowed to trade with foreign countries.

Located right in the middle of China's extensive eastern coastline and controlling the entry of the Yangtze, the country's largest river, no place was better suited than Shanghai for importers and exporters to come and trade. Yet the growing commercial and business activity quickly stretched the city to its limits. The existing city walls, only twenty-five feet high and hastily built in two months in the face of threats from Japanese pirates in the 1550s, had a circumference of less than four miles. This small domain was hardly enough for a local population of nearly half of a million, and it was far too small for the increasing number of domestic and foreign immigrants who were attracted to the city's rising potential throughout the second half of the nineteenth century. First the British, and then the American and French consulates, demanded permission to build their settlements outside the city walls, and negotiations finally led to the establishment of the so-called foreign concessions in Shanghai, where these foreign powers had their own police force and enjoyed extraterritorial privileges.

The development of international concessions fueled road and housing construction, as well as demand for public services, all of which helped to boost trade, business, and investment. Many of the projects, including broad avenues, fancy shops, trendy hotels, and dazzling theaters, would soon become major landmarks in Shanghai, famous not only in China and East Asia but also around the world.

A major artery crossing the entire French Concession from east to west, Avenue Joffre was named after the French marshal Joseph Joffre in World War I. Its western section—more than four miles away from the crowded and noisy old town—would eventually become an exclusive neighborhood for the wealthy. But its eastern section, close to where the northwestern portions of the old city walls (demolished by 1914) used to be, was popular with many middle-class Chinese residents, who were attracted to the new housing projects in the district and its convenient access to the newly developed public tram system. Only five blocks into Avenue Joffre from the east was the area where property developers had built many "stone-gate-style" houses, and Professor Lu's was one of them.

The so-called "stone-gate style" began as a figurative description, indicating that the thick and solid front gate of an alley was securely wrapped by a stylistic stone arch. Inside the alley, a row of the same style houses lined each side, making the entire alley an enclosed area once the huge and heavy front gate was shut. Such an arrangement was important to the initial construction projects in late 1800s because armed rebellions and violence frequently threatened the lower Yangtze regions in those days. As peace gradually returned, the practice of building an expansive stone-framed gate stopped but the name stuck; it could refer to either this type of old neighborhood in general or the distinctive housing style built since those days in particular.

A structure of gray bricks with red wooden panels as trims over doors and windows, every house inside the alley also had its own front entrance door and was a self-enclosed unit with high walls all around to ensure privacy. Like the row houses or townhouses in the West, all the units could have a uniform exterior, but they remained separate individual households, even though they could share common walls without any gap to save space and reduce cost. A typical "stone-gate" house opened into a yard, the size of which was usually a fraction of the one commonly found in Northern China. Facing the front door, a drawing room stood in the middle behind the small yard, flanked by one bedroom each on the left and right. A kitchen and a servant's quarters lay in the back behind the stairs, which were built against the back walls of the drawing room. The second floor had the main living room and bedroom for the head of the household and his wife, an office, a storage room, and a balcony. An extended version may also have a third floor or an attic.

2

When Dong went upstairs to meet his host, he laughed and said, "Nothing has changed, Professor."

"Like what?" Lu asked.

Dong pointed to a sign on the door of the professor's office. It read, "Fifteen minutes per visit."

"Oh, I see. It has changed, though. The old one in my office at Peking University only stated, 'Be Brief.' And as you know, to some people 'be brief' meant that they had the liberty of talking for a whole afternoon without any substance."

They both laughed and sat down.

A straightforward talker, Lu got down to business right away by stressing, "Studying Marxism is only part of the task. What is needed now is the immediate organization of a communist party."

Dong understood that the professor's opening statement was to counter the ambivalence shown by Tang in his letter, where he wavered between the need to strengthen the efforts to disseminate Marxism as an educational campaign and the need to establish a political apparatus as the first practical step in instigating a Bolshevik Revolution. In fact, Lu did not stress the importance of the latter at the expense of the former. He clearly understood that, given the level of literacy and education of the average Chinese, their understanding of Marxism or any new progressive thought was all but pathetic. The need for education of anything modern was paramount in a poor country like China. Yet, such a need, which could take forever to fulfill, should not stop them from taking concrete steps toward a revolution, or China would never see the end of her miseries.

His clear reasoning totally convinced Dong, whose youthful enthusiasm contributed to a robust discussion on several hot topics of the day. At the end of their lively tête-a-tête they came to these conclusions: First, nothing could save China from domestic corruption and foreign dominance except a grassroots revolution. Second, Sun Yat-Sen and his Three Principles of the People were not militant enough to trigger such a revolution, nor was his Nationalist Party effective enough to lead it. Third, the small size of China's working class made it all the more necessary to embrace the intellectual youths who had been exposed to Marxism and had the potential of becoming the vanguards of the movement. Finally, the future success of the Chinese revolution lay in the combined forces between the awakened industrial workers and a new generation of radicalized intellectuals and young students.

Based on these agreements, they further discussed the platform and political programs of the envisaged communist party. As for a plan of implementation, Lu suggested that he would start to organize those whom he knew to be potential Marxist believers in Shanghai. Next, he expressed hope that Dong would relay this strategy to Tang, and that they would organize a similar group of believers in Peking. Once that was completed, said Lu, the Shanghai nucleus would expand to the south and the Peking nucleus the north. After a network of several groups across major cities was established, they would then be ready to launch the national communist party.

By this time, Professor Lu was all glowing, his voice chirping, eyes shining, and mustache twitching, as though his entire body was filled with boundless hopes and great expectations. No less excited was Dong, who was about to reaffirm everything Lu had said when he heard a sound from downstairs.

"Mister, I am back. Look at what I have bought for you! And you would not believe what a bargain I had made."

Yan's incessant chatter continued as she made her way into his office upstairs. Dong rose from the chair, smiling, "Good morning, madam. Good to see you."

"Zi-Tian, good to see you too. And I am so glad you did not go out this morning."

"Ah, I have just finished a conversation with Professor Lu. Maybe it's better for me to go downstairs…"

"No, no, no. You stay, stay for lunch. See what I have bought from the market! I will cook sweet and sour fish, your professor's favorite dish."

"Yan, excuse me, Yan," Lu felt he had to interject or he would not have a chance to say anything at all. "I have run out of ink and I need the good paper I bought the other day."

"You wait for your turn, mister. I have not finished talking with Zi-Tian yet. Zi-Tian, guess what, I saw a beautiful girl in the market this morning. I think she is about your age, and it will be good if you can date her. So, what do you think? Should I go out and fetch her?"

Now, both men knew a whole new conversation was about to start, over which they had no control. Deflated, they fell back to their chairs, closed their mouths, and dropped their heads as Yan continued with her chatter.

3

At a street corner off Avenue Joffre, the front of the coffee shop "Oceana" did not impress the two emissaries, who were there to meet with Dong. Too many exotic colors on the exterior walls overemphasized its European flavor, while a sign with poor Chinese calligraphy failed to highlight its native roots. If Peking clearly showed what present-day China was and what her past had been, Shanghai struck them as a city where much of the old China had vanished, and a classic example of how quickly an Asian city could take on a Western facade. European-style buildings of big banks, department stores, hotels, churches, and government offices occupied the most prominent avenues and intersections in the city. Instead of worn-out ceramic tiles or weather-beaten wooden panels, pedestrians everywhere were greeted by ostentatious sights in the form of giant clocks, neon lights, soaring steeples, foreign flags, and alphabetic logos. Porters, drivers, rickshaw men, shoe shiners, and newspaper boys threw in an English word here and a French one there. Suits for men and skirts for women were as fashionable as the conventional long robes for both sexes. Cars, trucks, and trams began to replace horses and mules in the streets just as imported *Platanus* had displaced indigenous willows and poplars on the sidewalks.

Inside Oceana, soft lights and soothing music provided quiet relaxation for customers eager for some privacy. Although tiny, the shop offered an amazing array of choices—English tea, Turkish coffee, German beer, Japanese sake, Madeira wine, French pastries, and even Dutch sweets. Despite their disappointing first impression, Martin and Tania soon relaxed as they sat down. They were pleased to meet Dong, and laughed heartily when the latter recounted how he had tried to escape Mrs. Lu's attempt to matchmake him with a girl he had never met.

"She might have regarded you as her adopted son," Tania suggested diplomatically.

"No," responded Dong, "believe it or not, she is Professor Lu's foster mother."

"How come?" Both Tania and Martin were surprised. "Didn't you just tell us that he is the most fearsome warrior you have even known?" Tania asked.

"That's true," said Dong, "in so far as his political beliefs are concerned. As to his domestic life, he totally depends on Mrs. Lu. I mean totally."

Dong then started to share with them Professor Lu's life story. Yan was actually his third wife. His first wife, Fu Fang, was from an arranged marriage shortly after he became a local celebrity at fifteen. Her father, a powerful warlord in the province, sent a messenger to propose the marriage to Lu's mother, who had been a widow for many years. Believing that this might be the best thing for her only son, she agreed. The sixteen-year-old Lu Shi-Yan and the twenty-year-old Fu Fang met for the first time on their wedding day. Soon the difference between the erudite and restless Lu and the illiterate but contented Fu was too much to hide from anyone. Fu Lan, Fu Fang's half-sister, often came to visit the couple. She fell in love with Lu, who was also attracted to the sister's quick wit and feisty personality. Their love affair was highly scandalous, and both families banned them from ever seeing each other again. The young lovers refused to part, and ran away from the countryside to Shanghai, hoping to start a brand-new life.

Unfortunately, love at first sight was not the same thing as a mundane marriage. Fu Lan gradually became disillusioned with Lu, who, though extremely intelligent, rarely had any stable job or income; she left him after five years together. Never one to be deterred by temporary setbacks, Lu pushed on with his causes and often fell into debt. Running from one place to another, he took on various part-time teaching and editorial jobs to make ends meet. But he got very sick at one point, and was living in a dismal shed without food and fuel. Yan Yan, his student at an evening school for the city's young adults, happened to pass by the shed, and immediately took it upon herself to nurse her professor back to health. He recovered and would not let her leave his side. She, the strong-willed yet tender-hearted woman twenty years his junior, readily agreed. Since then, she had been her husband's most ardent supporter as well as his best friend and meticulous caretaker. She knew everything he needed before he knew it himself. He listened to her and obeyed her dictates at home without any objection, just like, according to his rationale, everyone else must listen to and obey him at work.

"I would never have expected Professor Lu to have such a fascinating background," said Martin.

"What a remarkable woman Yan is," said Tania.

"So, are you ready to meet them?" asked Dong.

"Sure, let's go." They agreed and the three left Oceana.

4

Professor Lu's drawing room was spotlessly clean, a reflection of his wife Yan's personality. A poised woman who was as proud as her husband, she was always looking immaculate. With her long, narrow head perched atop a slender but sturdy frame, she appeared to be taller than her husband. Grueling life and arduous work had taken a toll on her looks, but the bright eyes and the straight nose indicated she was anything but an ordinary woman.

A quick glance was all she needed to realize that the two guests Dong was bringing knew her history. Yan was not particularly upset about this since her past with her husband was an open secret. She would rather they heard the story from Dong since he was likely to cast her in the best light compared to others. Raised by a poor fisherman and a disabled mother on a boat, Yan had seen too much of this fashionable city's dark side to wallow in self-pity. She considered herself lucky to have entered Lu Shi-Yan's life, become his wife, and been able to take good care of him all these years.

As Dong helped her to serve tea to everyone around the table, Yan was all smiles, as if she did not know that her guests were familiar with her story by now. "Excellent jasmine tea, thank you," Martin said.

"You are most welcome," she responded. As she turned to Tania next, Yan could not help but notice this female guest's undeniable beauty and polished demeanor that would set many hearts aflutter. While handing Tania the teacup, Yan gave her a faint yet discernible smile, which intimated, "I have total control over my husband. What about you?" It was a smile that only another woman could understand.

After tea was served. Yan said in a sweet voice, "Please enjoy and let me know if you need anything else." She gave a curtsy, touched her perfect tresses, and withdrew to her room upstairs.

"Lenin's vanguard theory is exactly what we need now." Professor Lu nodded as Tania was explaining that Lenin developed the theory in *What Is to Be Done*, published in 1902. She and Martin felt encouraged that their meeting with the professor got off to a good start.

"When Marx and Engels were alive," Martin took his turn to expound, "they really didn't have a political party other than a loosely constructed workers' union. Lenin totally changed that. His Bolshevik party was not simply an extension of the working class but its brain, leader, and vanguard. Hard at work and with little opportunity for education, the industrial workers were too preoccupied with their day-to-day survival. They clung to trade unions, which were formed to protect their immediate interests. If left alone, the working class will become unionists at best, but can never develop its own class consciousness and fulfill its historical mission, which is, as Marx has pointed out, to bury capitalism and get rid of private property once for all."

"No wonder Lenin said class consciousness can be injected only from without," Lu said.

"Exactly," Martin agreed.

"That's why," Tania continued, "Lenin moved beyond Marx and Engel's *Communist Manifesto* and developed the vanguard theory, which has laid the ideological foundations and organizational principles for the modern-day Communist Party. As the vanguard of the proletariat, the party leads the working class, not the other way round. The party is also distinct from the massive body of the industrial workers. A tight organization (and a secret one before gaining power), the party comprises the most class-conscious members of the working class, as well as those from many other segments of society, including the intellectuals and the educated. The party in fact is a body of the most committed Marxist believers, whose understanding of the strategies of how to implement a proletarian revolution far supersedes that of most industrial workers themselves."

"Or, as Lenin puts it," Martin stressed, "the Communist Party is the organization of professional revolutionaries, whose sole mission in life is to promote and implement the communist revolution."

"So far so good. But"—Lu paused—"how can they be professional revolutionaries?"

"Good question," Tania responded. "The party members can become full-time revolutionaries because the organization collects membership dues and raises other funds. These can in turn support a small group of top organizers, who are the most dedicated, most knowledgeable, and most visionary leaders of the working class."

"How does the organization function as a party at the national level? How do the top leaders relate to local groups and their rank and file members?" he asked.

"The party operates on four basic principles," Martin explained. "That is, individual members must subject themselves to the organization, the minority to the majority, the subordinates to their superiors, and the whole party to its central leadership."

"Hmm, sounds quite one-sided. Did they ever work?" he asked again.

"They have worked perfectly," Tania said. "That is why the Bolsheviks won the revolution and took over Russia."

"For the establishment of a communist party in China," Martin declared, "Lenin has authorized the Comintern to provide one thousand dollars per month immediately to defray the cost of such efforts. Once the Chinese communist party is formally established, it will be accepted as a national branch member of the Communist International in Moscow, with the full support of Lenin's Bolshevik government, of course."

Just as Lu was about to say something, Martin, feeling the weight of his next statement, added in a soft but earnest voice, "Comrade Lenin would like no one else but you to be the first party chief of the new Bolshevik organization in China."

To Martin and Tania's surprise, Professor Lu did not seem to be pleased at all on hearing this. He stood up, took a few steps away from the table and then returned to the same spot. In his usual direct style, he said, "I will not be the appointed party chief as you had said. The Chinese communist party will not be a member of the Comintern, nor do we need the money from Russia."

"But you did agree with Lenin's vanguard theory, right?" Tania was confused.

"Yes, I did. I do think Lenin's theory of a vanguard party is highly valuable for us. I also believe that to establish such a party in China is of critical importance. But what Martin just said went beyond the internal structure of the new party. It touches upon a fundamental principle, which will guide the future relationship between the infant Chinese party, the Comintern, and Russia. To agree with what he suggested is to subject the new Chinese party to the directives of the Comintern and Russia."

Martin regretted that he had given Lu the wrong impression. He responded, "Professor Lu, I greatly respect your honest opinion. Perhaps I have made those suggestions a little too hastily. Please allow me to recalibrate them. Lenin and the Comintern have nothing but the highest hopes for the four hundred million Chinese people, who are engaged in an unprecedented struggle for their national salvation. Lenin and the Comintern see a rising China as their great ally in the East, and are willing to do all they can to help. It is with these most friendly considerations that they have made those offers and suggestions."

"Mr. Martin." Lu's response was as polite as it was firm. "I deeply appreciate the kind words Lenin and the Comintern said about my country. Please do convey to them my sincere thanks and gratitude. Yet an appreciation of sentiments is no substitute for principles, and I have no intention of changing my opinions."

Martin and Tania were at a loss. They thought the conversation had gone well, and they did not understand why it suddenly turned sour. What went wrong? What should they do next? How could they persuade this highly opinionated man to recognize that the conditions were ripe for establishing a communist party in an abjectly poor country despite the extremely hostile anticommunist environment around the world?

Martin stood up and said, "It's getting late. Why don't we talk about this some other time?"

"No, no need for that if the message is the same. Zi-Tian, please see them off," the professor ordered.

5

A few days later, Dong met the emissaries at Oceana again.

"What did he say?" they asked impatiently.

"Still the same things," he replied.

Dong did try to downplay the tension between his professor and the emissaries. He agreed with the latter that some financial sponsorship would be necessary for the future organization, that an affiliation with the Comintern could strengthen the new party, and that Lu would be the best choice as its first leader. He also agreed with Professor Lu that too much reliance on the Comintern and Russia would make the party look bad. It might also be problematic should any major disputes arise between the party and its foreign sponsors. Dong had attempted to speak to the professor again but their conversation did not last long. Lu again objected by saying that he would have nothing to do with the party if he had to accept directives from another country. "They are not the same things," Dong said as he tried to make a distinction between assuming the post of party chief and accepting orders from someone else. "Over my dead body" was the professor's response, which was something Dong didn't dare to relay to Martin and Tania.

Apparently, Lu Shi-Yan had made up his mind. He wanted no affiliation with the Comintern, nor would he accept its financial sponsorship. The new Chinese communist party must be a completely independent organization. At this point, nothing could change his mind.

Hence, when Tania and Martin asked for another meeting with the professor, Dong shook his head.

"As far as I know," he said, "in matters like this, the professor would never change his mind once it is made up."

"Really? How depressing," said Martin. The couple sighed. Even the music in Oceana did not sound as soothing as before.

After two more cups of coffee, Dong suddenly burst out, "How can I forget about him? He could be the one who may change the professor's mind."

"Who?" The emissaries asked.

"Librarian Tang Shu-Hai."

Tang was Professor Lu's best friend. According to Dong, the two men were poles apart: Tang was tall but feminine, Lu short and masculine. Tang was warm, diplomatic, flexible, gentle, and personable. Lu, on the other hand, was impassive, cold, dynamic, straightforward, obstinate, rugged, and distant. Or, as the Chinese saying went, "One is as pliable as silk and water, while the other as hard as rock and steel." For all their differences, Dong reassured the emissaries, both were decent men with their hearts in the right place. For all his apparent modesty, Tang was Lu's intellectual equal. He graduated from the Imperial University of Tokyo and could read and write in both Japanese and Russian. In fact, they not only complemented one another but also depended on each other. As the librarian of the most prominent national university in China, Tang liked Lu's *Youth* magazine and helped to promote its circulation. He also brought Lu to the president's attention, which led to Lu's appointment as a professor and dean at Peking University. Lu frequently asked Tang to write for his magazine, providing the latter with a great platform to spread his newfound faith in Bolshevik Russia and Marxism.

Tang came from a very traditional family in a rural village in Northern China, and had the same arranged marriage, like most young people of his generation. His bride had bound feet, and he had never met her until the wedding day, very much like Lu's experience. Yet, Tang treated his wife very well. He never yelled or quarreled with her, and remained faithful to her for more than twenty years. But, when he heard about Lu and Yan's plight, he went out of his way to help the couple, which eventually enabled them to move to Peking. Unlike many of his snobbish colleagues at the university, Tang also treated Lu and Yan with the same courtesy he had shown to others around him.

Lu's abrasive style did not sit well with some faculty members, who then launched an attempt to oust him. It was Tang who served as Lu's unfaltering supporter, by constantly highlighting the latter's valuable contributions to the university. Amid continuing pressure, the administration gave Lu a year's leave of absence, which was in fact a poorly disguised firing. Undeterred, Lu continued his militant activities from his residence in Peking. During a protest against corruption, he took to the streets to distribute flyers denouncing the government. He was promptly arrested and thrown behind bars. Again, it was

Tang who rallied the professor's friends and supporters to demand his release. He finally raised enough money, which included his own savings, to bail the professor out of jail. The last time they saw each other was when Tang helped Yan and Lu to board a train, heading south for Shanghai to escape persecution.

"Where is Tang Shu-Hai now?" Tania asked eagerly, as she and Martin felt a renewed sense of hope.

"He is still in Peking," Dong answered calmly.

"Then how could they get together?"

"For that, we need the help of another person."

"Who?"

"The professor's wife, Yan."

6

Two weeks later, when Professor Lu came downstairs for dinner, he was surprised to learn that Tang was hosting a family party for Yan, Dong, Martin, Tania, and himself. The small drawing room had rarely been used to entertain more than three people in the past. It suddenly looked crowded, as everybody now sat elbow to elbow around the small dining table. From the well-prepared dishes to his treasured bottle of Shaoxing rice wine, and several wine cups, Lu sensed that Yan had a hand in organizing the party. He could guess what was going to happen next.

Lu and Tang were such close friends that they could visit each other anytime unannounced, and neither one would be offended. Such an honor was accorded as a reflection their relationship—that they were not just friends but brothers. Although Tang's visit was unexpected, Lu was glad to see him. After all, Tang was one of the few friends he had who not only tolerated his eccentricities but also saved him from the police dragnet. He sat quietly next to Yan, waiting for Tang to begin.

Raising his glass, the tall Tang appeared more handsome than ever under the dim light from the ceiling, which almost touched his head. He said, "Today is my best friends Lu Shi-Yan and Yan Yan's wedding anniversary. Let's drink to their wonderful union and happiness forever!"

"Cheers, cheers!" Everyone but Lu joined in.

"Today is our anniversary?" He was perplexed.

"Mister, you correct every paper you read down to the punctuation in every line, but never remember my birthday or our anniversary," complained Yan.

"Yes, yes, my oversight, my mistake. Sorry, I am terribly sorry." Once his ego was deflated, the professor could sound apologetic, even humble.

"Professor and madam, congratulations on your tenth anniversary! What a big day in your lives and what a felicitous moment for all of us." Dong raised his glass.

Martin and Tania followed suit. "Congratulations on your tenth anniversary, Professor and madam! We are so honored to be here on this special occasion," Tania said on her husband's behalf.

"Eat, eat. Everybody, sit down and eat," Yan insisted. Although she knew the actual date of their anniversary, she was excited when Tang and Dong talked her into having the celebration tonight as part of their plan.

"Mister, your favorite sweet and sour fish. Let me know whether you think it tastes okay," Yan gently reminded her husband even as she was busy serving the other guests.

Lu got the hint. At any gathering where they had guests around, Yan expected him to compliment her and agree with whatever she said.

"Oh, the fish is terrific. Unbelievably tasty." Having recovered from his initial embarrassment, the professor now began to act like a host. "Come on, come on, please, don't be shy. You must all try it."

"As usual, I like your spicy Szechuan bean curd very much—it's a classic," said Tang.

"The green beans are so fresh and tender; how did you cook it?" Tania asked.

"Simple. They were dry braised," Yan responded casually, in the manner of a housewife who had total confidence in her culinary skills.

"Really? I hope to learn how to do it sometime." As a female guest, Tania was well aware of the need to massage the female host's ego.

"Sure, no problem. I will show you how when you have the time," Yan answered warmly, even though she regarded most dinner-table conversations to be pretentious and insincere.

"I love the chicken, especially the tomato sauce, very unusual," Martin said.

Such a remark from a male guest caught Yan's attention. She turned and asked, "Really? Why?"

"Tomato beef is very common in the West. I didn't know that tomato chicken is so common in China," Martin replied.

"See, mister, we have a food critic and real connoisseur tonight." Yan was honestly thrilled that Martin, the guest who tasted her cooking for the first time, had discovered her culinary adaptation.

"Cooking deboned chicken in freshly made tomato sauce is my new recipe to combine the east and west!" Her proud declaration, she feared, might not be convincing enough to hide her embarrassment that pricey beef was way beyond the family budget.

"Amazing, Yan. You are always the best." Tang now joined in the praises. "It's always good to have friends around, isn't it, Shi-Yan?" he turned and asked.

"Of course, of course. Thank you for coming all the way from Peking just for me and Yan," Lu heartily responded. It would be hard not to say nice things when one was surrounded by delicious entrées and savory wine.

"In China, we often say, 'a strong man needs three guys for help, and a beautiful flower needs green leaves for support.' Shi-Yan, if no friends had come, would you and Yan feel lonely tonight? Why can't we consider getting a helping hand from the Comintern and Russia?"

"Yes, I would feel terrible if nobody came tonight," agreed Yan.

Now, the truth was finally coming out. Lu paused a little and then said, "I did not refuse their help. I am just concerned that we might lose control over our own party."

"That was certainly not the intention of the Comintern or Lenin, right?" Tang asked Martin and Tania.

"No, no, no. Never. They only wanted to help," came the reply.

"Indeed, the Comintern and Russia want to help because, as we know," continued Tang, "the proletarian revolution is by nature an international movement, according to Marx's teachings. No single country can succeed unless the proletarians around the world would rise and bind together in true brotherhood. Thus, it is only natural that the Comintern and Russia would need as much help from us as we would from them."

"Yes, yes. The need for help is mutual; Lenin and the Comintern had made this very clear before we departed," Martin affirmed.

"I never said that we don't need any outside help," Lu stressed.

"But who else would help us other than Russia and the Comintern? The British? French? Germans or Americans? They are avowed enemies of communism, you know that, Shi-Yan," Tang pressed on.

"I understand that, if we were ever to get any help, it would probably be from Russia and Russia alone. No other country in the world is now willing to help us, and all the European powers are only interested in taking advantage of us. But I am afraid that we will be under the control of another foreign power if we tie ourselves to the Comintern as an organization," Lu explained.

"That would depend on how the Comintern handles its relationship with us. And I am sure it has no intention to control us, right?" Tang asked the emissaries.

"No, no, no. No control at all. It is all up for friendly discussion and negotiation." Martin gave a hasty assurance, even though he and Tania were not sure themselves how such a relationship between a national party and the Comintern would work.

"I also don't like the term 'party chief,' which sounds like a dictator. It reminds me of Sun Yat-Sen and his title in the Nationalist Party, which even requires every member to take a personal oath of loyalty to the chief. I hate that," Lu said.

"Well, that's just what it is—a term, a title, a name. It can change, I am sure." Martin responded.

"If I were to be the party leader, I wouldn't want to be appointed at all," Lu continued.

"Elections, elections, elections," Tania responded.

"So, can we basically agree with what the emissaries have suggested about the party affiliation with the Comintern and about the first party leader, not to be appointed but elected?" Tang asked.

"I am okay with that. But I am still not sure about taking money from them," the professor persisted. "As the Chinese saying goes, 'eating someone else's meals makes one meek, and taking someone else's money renders one submissive.'"

"This is certainly a legitimate concern. And we should never lose our independence because of organizational affiliations and financial ties to the Comintern. But let's be mindful of the current reality. Our party will be extremely small and vulnerable from start, like a newborn baby. Without the mother's milk, no infant can survive. It would take years before we have a membership big and strong enough to support any full-time vanguards. If we wait for that to happen, the party will die in infancy." Tang's analogy impressed Lu, who nevertheless did not want to concede.

"I know no politics, mister." To everyone's surprise, Yan interjected. "I am only a housewife. But I need money. Yes, I need every penny to survive every day. I need to pay the rent, pay for groceries, and I need to put food on the table. I need to pay the water and electricity bills. Yes, mister, I need money to buy your ink, pens, good paper, envelopes, newspapers, and books for your work. I am sure your party will need the same to survive too. It is not a shame to take someone's money when you do need help. It's a shame when you can't pay it back in kind and kindness." She sat down as the guests were about to stand up and applaud.

"Yan, what can I say?" The husband was fighting back his tears. "You are the best woman I know, and you always have a way of clarifying my thoughts." He then turned to his friends. "Comrades, thank you all for giving me and Yan the best anniversary tonight. Now, let's figure out the details of our agreement."

7

Summer in the Lower Yangtze River region could be unbearably long, hot, and humid, and 1920 was no exception. The largest and most fertile delta in China, this area had been the top producer of rice, grain, cotton, hemp, fish, tea, and silk for more than two thousand years. Emerging from a cluster of small towns and medium-sized cities all around, Shanghai rose to become, within a century, the largest urban center in the area for trade, textiles, manufacturing, shipbuilding, maritime transportation, advertising, banking, finance, publication and the printing industry, filmmaking, and entertainment.

Nowhere in Shanghai epitomized this drastic transformation more than the Bund. It used to be the swampy beach of the Huang Pu River, cutting through the eastern edge of the city to join the Yangtze less than fifteen miles to the north. Only a few decades ago, a large road was laid out, in the open field of the British Concession, along the left bank of the river next to the ancient trails used by generations of boat trackers in the past. If any person had a chance to visit this place, no one would fail to recognize the stark contrast between the old and the new, between East and West.

To the right side of the road and below the ancient trails, swarms of poor small wooden boats haphazardly lined along the Huang Pu. Dirty, worn, and weather-beaten, they belonged to the Chinese fishermen, petty merchants, and domestic marine transporters. Berthing at separate and designated docks, the much bigger and far more modern-looking iron ships and ocean vessels flew foreign flags—British, French, Dutch, German, American, and Japanese, and very few of them were owned by the locals.

On the left side of the road and overshadowing any oriental structures, a series of new buildings dominated the skyline—the Asia Building, the Shanghai Club, the Commercial Bank of China, the Great Northern Telegraph Company, the Sassoon House, the Yangtze Insurance Building, and Banque de l'Indochine.

"Look this way: I think I am back at the stylish river front of the Boompie in Rotterdam." Martin pointed to the gorgeous European-style mansions to his left.

"Look here: Yan could have spent much of her life on one of those badly discolored tiny watercrafts," Tania said, pointing to her right.

The afternoon breeze finally brought much-needed cool air during this long miserable summer, and the proximity to the beach offered them a panoramic view of the Huang Pu waters. They just learned that Professor Lu and his friends had formed the first branch of the Chinese Communist Party at his residence. Tang, they also learned, would soon set up another branch in Peking. Meanwhile, the professor used part of the funding the emissaries had provided to publish the party's first official monthly journal, *The Communist*, which would spread the news about their cause across China.

"Our mission is complete," Martin said with a big relief.

"I cannot believe that Professor Lu was convinced by Yan," said Tania, who still could not get over her surprise.

"As the Chinese would say, 'you think you are strong; there is someone tougher still.'"

"Or, as they say, 'water drops can drill through a rock.'"

"Can this apply to countries? Does China have similar dynamics as compared with the West?" Martin pondered.

"What do you mean?" Tania asked.

"I mean, China is feeble and weak on the surface, while the West is strong now. But this can all change."

"Yes, yes. This can certainly change," Tania was excited at the thought.

"And we are part of this momentous change," Martin said.

"Yes, we are," Tania said before adding, "You are also going to be a part of another momentous change."

"Of what?" he questioned.

"You are going to be *a father*," said Tania, beaming with the greatest pride and happiness she had ever felt.

Chapter 4

Epiphany

1

WHENEVER PEOPLE SAID THAT HE HAD BROUGHT TO LIFE A highly believable Nora in *A Doll's House*, Si-Tu Wen-Liang did not know whether he should take it as a compliment or an insult. The responses he got after each performance were more or less similar—even if their tone and choice of words varied—and they never failed to evoke mixed feelings in him. Born into a large and well-to-do family, he grew up under the close supervision of several capable women, who had shaped his life more than any male members of the clan. Their genuine love, compassion, and magnanimity warmed his sensitive soul and produced some of his fondest childhood memories.

Still, he was highly conscious of what had been missing from his formative years. Father was never at home. What was worse, he didn't have any boys of his age whom he could play with. But his doting matriarch had taught him long ago how to conceal his intense sadness deep inside, while presenting a perfect front—charming and playing to the gallery—when needed to please relatives and outsiders alike. His greatest skill lay in keeping his inner and outer selves totally separate. As he matured, his talent in managing both selves improved significantly, and his childhood frustration helped him to bring authenticity to the female characters' vulnerability and longings that he portrayed on stage. This conscious separation between performance and reality, or an unusual mixture of external beauty with internal pain, was the product not of deprivation but of his noble parentage and privileged upbringing.

Tai Lake, Si-Tu's hometown, was one of the most productive places in China's rural economy. Less than seventy-five miles west of Shanghai, the region formed part of the fertile Yangtze River delta, where the warm weather allowed farmers to plant and harvest crops two or three times a year. In the shape of a large pearl over eight hundred and fifty square miles, Tai was the third largest freshwater lake in China. All around its banks and between the lake and the nearby Yangtze, a huge web of small rivers, streams, ponds, and lakes connected every town and village, making water transportation the most convenient means of going anywhere. The same network of natural water also provided an ample source of irrigation for every piece of farmland in the region, a huge advantage that the rest of agrarian China could only dream of possessing, especially in the North and Northwest. Famous for its abundant harvest of rice, grain, cotton, silk, and fishery year after year, the Tai Lake region had been the coveted breadbasket of Southern China for more than two thousand years.

Literacy and education expanded as the bountiful output had kept living standards high. The Tai Lake region produced far more accomplished scholars than many surrounding areas, and provided a large reservoir of candidates for government posts throughout history. Since the time of Si-Tu's distant ancestors, the family had been known for its outstanding educational and literary attainments. His great-great-grandfather was the notable one who held high government offices, while every male household head from generations went on to serve in the government down to Si-Tu's father. The latter was first appointed as a county chief in Jiangxi Province, some five hundred miles away from home. Later he was transferred to another county in Fujian Province, seven hundred miles away. He served there for five years until he was transferred again to Hunan Province, which was nearly one thousand miles from home, where he eventually died. As a result, young Si-Tu rarely saw his father, and was left under his mother's total care.

The daughter of a neighborhood gentry, Si-Tu Hui-Xian or Mrs. Si-Tu—the double-character surname "Si-Tu" had been an honored official title since ancient times—was an excellent student of classical Chinese, history, philosophy, and poetry, who imparted all her knowledge to little Si-Tu Wen-Liang, her eldest son. Because the husband was constantly absent from home, she also took charge of the large household and its varied businesses. With the toddler at her side and two dozen house keys in hand, she checked out the compound grounds every morning, inspecting every room and giving orders to some fifty foremen, servants, maids, and laborers she met on the way. The image of his short and slim but determined mother directing every man around her left an indelible impression on the boy. Not a single day would pass without little Si-Tu seeing her acting as a shrewd planner, a stern disciplinarian, and an indefatigable supervisor. And given his mother's boundless energy and cheerful nature, she had always struck him as a superwoman—until one day when he saw her alone in her room, sobbing. He immediately went over to her and gave her a hug. Looking up to the beautiful face now covered with tears, he asked, "Mom, why are you crying?"

"How I wish your father could be here. I am so alone and I am so sad and exhausted," she sighed.

Behind that familiar austere facade, Si-Tu finally realized, was a fragile heart; behind that indomitable spirit, a vulnerability; behind that tireless body, inevitable fatigue; behind that beautiful face, an irrevocable pain. To a woman, a husband could not simply be in name, no matter how good and honest he was. He had to be at her side, and she must able to touch him, and feel his existence. Any forced separation for a married couple for whatever reason was the worst torment for a wife, who needed her husband more than anything else in the world.

From the excruciating pain and sorrow his mother experienced, Si-Tu too felt the dreadful absence of his father in his life as well. Yet nothing hurt him more than watching his mother suffer. Although still a boy, he knew he must be a man—the one person who was strong enough to help Mom, to be always at her side, would never let her cry again, and to make her happy and smile for as long as he could. The son suddenly realized that his mission in life was to take care of his mother, since there was no other man in the house to do it. Yes, he was willing to be her slave if that was the only way to make his beloved mother happy and smile again.

2

Apart from his mother, the boy was highly attached to his wet nurse and governess Jin-Xia, who, whenever Madam Si-Tu allowed, would take him to town. She grew up in extreme poverty and did not even know her family name. The name Jin-Xia, which meant "beautiful clouds," was given by her first employer, whom she started working for when she was barely big enough to wash clothes for his family.

She later married a local carpenter and gave birth to his six children before she was twenty-five. Still as strong as an ox, and as fast as a hare, she wore a huge black apron around her waist and carried little Si-Tu everywhere she went. Best of all, she could tell the boy endless stories and had an explanation for just about every question he asked.

"Nanny, why do people carry so many baskets in so many shapes and sizes?"

"Because they need to sell them to make money."

"How can they make money?"

"Because bamboo is cheap and baskets expensive."

"How would that work?"

"Well, a farmer needs to cut down bamboo and peel it into thin, smooth, long strips. They would then use the strips to weave those nice-looking baskets. It is a great skill that was handed down from their forefathers."

"Can you make one for me?"

"I sure can if you can find bamboo."

"Bamboo is everywhere here."

"It sure is. But it must be of the right age, and must be cut and peeled into proper sizes. You are far too young to do that."

Indeed, bamboo was another big source of income in the area. The sea of green bamboo covered every big hill and small slope, which made for a magnificent sight all year round. The acres upon acres of bamboo provided excellent yet inexpensive materials for the average farmer's family to make baskets, utensils, chairs, beds, tables, stools, drawers, and any other furniture for sale to townsfolk, which significantly increased their income. The region's silk and silk products were equally famous, providing ample employment opportunities for women and girls working at home, which was extremely rare for the rest of China.

Si-Tu loved it when Jin-Xia took him to the fish market, where he could watch and play for hours with crabs, shrimp, fish, clams, and mussels. Tai Lake and its numerous tributaries were a paradise for local fishermen, who earned as much as those who tilled the land. The fairground close to the southern town gate was his favorite place, where everything could be found—fresh produce, tea, fruit, trendy clothes, beautiful silk, handmade shoes, and a great variety of pottery, tools, and farm implements, fowl and other animals. He especially liked to see antique paintings, jade artifacts, traditional papers, brushes, ink, and inkstand made in the county of Jing from nearby Anhui Province. One day, while they were at the fairground, a small tea set caught his eye. As he was about to touch the teapot and cups, Jin-Xia warned him to be careful.

"Why?"

"Because they are very expensive."

"Why? They are so small."

"They are small. But they are the famed purple tea set made in Yixing—the best of its kind."

"Why? They are just teacups and teapot, aren't they?"

"Yes, but they were made of the special clay found only in Yixing, less than thirty miles from here."

"What's so special about the clay?"

"It's extremely refined and smooth, beautifully sculptured, and carefully blazed. This teapot can bring out the best flavor of the tea like no other. And these teacups and teapot can lock in the flavor much longer than any other set."

"Nanny, I have never seen you use these special teacups and teapot. How did you know so much?"

"Well, you are right. It's a privilege to use them, and not everyone has that privilege."

As they were getting ready to go home, Si-Tu begged her to tell him another story. The ever-patient and affectionate Jin-Xia allowed the boy to climb onto her back for a piggyback ride home. She then pointed to a couple of big colorful butterflies over a camellia tree and said, "I will tell you a story about two butterflies."

A long time ago, the gentleman Chen and his wife had a little daughter who grew into a beautiful young lady. Her long black hair was as shiny and soft as silk, and her delicate rosy face was as lovely as a flower. Although the father hoped to find a suitable partner for her, she insisted on going to school. "I already taught you the classics more than your mother has ever known," said the father. "I want to learn more," said the daughter. Father Chen gave in, but he knew that tradition forbade members of the opposite sex from sitting next to each other, and frowned on girls meeting boys before marriage. To indulge his daughter, he decided to find a private tutor to come to his house to teach Miss Chen, who would dress up as a boy for her lessons.

The first candidate was an old scholar, whose knowledge and reverence of Confucius were unmatched across the land. Yet his old-fashioned ways displeased the daughter, who was hiding behind a screen during the interview. The next applicant was a middle-aged man, who claimed to be the sincerest disciple of the renowned philosopher Zhu Xi. "Master Zhu Xi was no doubt a great Confucian, if not one of the greatest Confucian scholars after Confucius," Miss Chen said to her father. "But I also heard he was a hypocrite." The father had to agree; he was fully aware that Zhu Xi's devotion to Confucianism was as deep as his passion for prostitutes. The third candidate was student Zhang, who was preparing for the county examination for the first time. He came for the interview because he was hoping to earn some money for his journey. The young man's honesty and earnest attitude convinced both father and daughter that he was the right man for the job.

Days went by, the classes proceeded well, and Miss Chen and her family were pleased with the tutor, who was indeed a highly promising young scholar. But, one day, Tutor Zhang failed to show up for his class. And then the second day, and the third. Miss Chen was concerned. Dressed up as man, she and her maid went to the local inn, only to find her tutor lying in his room, terribly sick. Miss Chen took him back to her residence and urged her parents to allow him to stay there. She argued that he should be allowed to regain his health so he could fulfill his responsibilities as her teacher. Knowing how headstrong their daughter was, her parents had no choice except to accede to her request.

Indeed, Miss Chen had fallen in love with Tutor Zhang. But the teacher did not realize that the student who adored him was actually a girl—despite the hints she had given him, such as dropping her brush on the floor for him to pick up, or asking him to correct her handwriting style more frequently than necessary. All Tutor Zhang knew was that he was very fond of this lively, smart, and handsome student. He thought they had become very good male friends, more than just a tutor and his pupil. He was grateful to receive a hand-painted fan, not realizing that it was Miss Chen's sign of her love for him. On the day of his departure, he even promised to come back to see his student as soon as he finished the county examination, not realizing that it would be the last time they would see each other in this world.

Soon after Zhang left, Father Chen arranged a marriage for his daughter. Miss Chen was miserable and refused to obey her father. She waited and waited for her beloved tutor to return and rescue her. But he did not show up and Miss Chen was forced to marry a man she did not love. Upon hearing the news of the wedding, Zhang was heartbroken. He finally understood all the signs that she had tried to give him. He also realized how much he loved Miss Chen. The irreversible loss and the insufferable pain he suffered led to his premature death three months later. Miss Chen, true to her promise to be with her lover forever, jumped to her death from a cliff.

Although the two young lovers never became husband and wife, their death moved Heaven, which turned them into a couple of butterflies, one black, the other yellow. Some people believed that the black butterfly was Zhang, the yellow one Chen. Others insisted it was the opposite. But they all agreed that the two beautiful butterflies always flew as a pair and were never separated.

3

Jin-Xia tried not to make any noise when they returned home. To her surprise, a maid was already waiting at the front door and instructed her to take the boy to see madam immediately. "Bad omen. Maybe she suspected I had told Wen-Liang another love story on the way home." Jin-Xia now regretted telling the boy the butterfly tale. She did remember that Mrs. Si-Tu had chided her several times for telling the young boy love stories. "It would not be good for him. It can undermine his moral values and distract him from his studies," the madam had said. While Jin-Xia dared not to disagree with madam, she privately wondered how any child could grow up without listening to love stories. In fact, she asked herself, how could anyone live without love?

"Good evening, madam." Jin-Xia was all smiles as she entered the hall. "How are you this evening," she dutifully inquired.

"I am fine. How is Wen-Liang?" madam asked.

"I am fine, mother." Si-Tu was fully awake by now.

Dinnertime was the most pleasant part of the day. After hours of stress and hassle, the family could at last sit down together around the table to have a good meal with plenty of fresh vegetables, sautéed meat, steamed fish in a pool of ginger slices, delightful side-dishes of fruit and nuts, and freshly brewed hot tea—nothing was more enjoyable than the family eating together in the quiet compound before sunset.

"Jin-Xia." Mrs. Si-Tu finally broke her silence toward the end of the meal. "You need to pack and leave tomorrow morning…"

"Madam, I was wrong. I will never repeat my mistake again. Please, please forgive me." A distressed Jin-Xia started begging for mercy. She loved the boy, his mother, and his family. She had served them faithfully for years, and she would never want to lose her job.

"What do you mean you were wrong?" Mrs. Si-Tu was perplexed. "I only wanted to ask you to send Wen-Liang to his uncle's house tomorrow morning."

"Oh, really? Of course, of course, as you wish, madam," Jin-Xia was so relieved that she almost fainted. She later learned that one of the boy's childless uncles had gotten very sick and relatives suggested that adopting a son might cure him of his illness, a common superstitious practice in rural China in those days. The request was extended to Mrs. Si-Tu, who, after consulting her distant husband, reluctantly agreed. Thus, Jin-Xia was given the unpleasant assignment to take little Wen-Liang away from his mother and send him to a stranger's house the next day.

Tears—all the three of them were drenched in tears when the moment to say goodbye came. None of them knew when they would ever meet again. Only Jin-Xia's endless stories soothed the boy's intense agony on the way to the uncle's house. But the costly separation failed to stop the uncle's health from deteriorating further. He died a few months later, and little Si-Tu was left to live with the widow as the only male in his new home.

Widow Tan Xue-Yu, a beautiful name meaning "precious jade as white as winter snow," was a classy lady, who came from a distinguished and wealthy landlord family. She received an excellent education as a child, and her knowledge about the classics surpassed that of Mrs. Si-Tu's. After her husband's death, Si-Tu's foster mother devoted all her energy and attention to the boy, hoping to turn him into the best student of traditional values and classical learning. She woke him up early in the morning, sat with him to watch him study all day, and would not allow him to go to bed until he had finished all the recitations and homework she had assigned him. Extremely uncomfortable with these restrictive rules and feeling totally isolated from everything else except old books and his new mother, Si-Tu could only mourn his unlucky fate and imprisonment. Not a single day passed without him missing Mrs. Si-Tu's warm touch, cheerful voice, and vibrant personality, or Jin-Xia's uncontrolled laughter, quick steps, and the tranquilizing warmth he felt while lying on her back, listening to her fantastic stories.

Gradually the boy accepted the reality, and once again found himself subjugated by a domineering lady who, he also realized, loved him deeply in her own way. His boyish obedience and excellent progress in his studies helped Si-Tu to form a new bond with Tan, who would later discover that she had become equally dependent on her foster son.

For all her intelligence and education, Tan had no experience in the real world. Her total lack of knowledge in business and finance, coupled with the wicked side of human nature, made the widow an easy target of unscrupulous schemes and dirty tricks concocted by her friends, relatives, and neighbors. They claimed that her late husband was heavily in debt. They waved real and forged documents in her face and threatened to sue her. They demanded the land, the oxen, the barn, the garden, the tools, and the household furniture as payment. At her wit's end, the dispirited widow turned to the only person she could trust, Si-Tu.

Young or old, a man's natural instincts would immediately kick in as soon as a woman asked for his help. Little Wen-Liang went into action right away and proved himself to be the worthy foster son of Mrs. Si-Tu in no time. After examining his uncle's records, documents, profits, and expenses for several days, he eventually made a complete list of transactions, which included dates, places, and the names of all the parties involved. He then called a family meeting, requesting all the concerned parties to attend. Standing in the middle of the hall, little Wen-Liang held the papers high in the air, declared some debts justifiable, and dismissed all the rest as false claims. He warned those present that they should not even think of taking advantage of his foster mother as long as he was alive. Everyone should be honest with each other, and should treat each other with the same kind of respect and decency that Confucius had taught the Chinese people many centuries ago. It was a great shame and disgrace that they had to be reminded of these fundamental values, which they had learned since childhood. And he, continued the boy, would never call those present aunts and uncles again if they refused to mend their ways.

Shocked, embarrassed, and truly impressed, the visitors left the meeting feeling like those parishioners who had just received a good scolding from a furious minister in church.

Many were amazed by his oratory skills. "This boy could really command such a big crowd."

"He could really articulate his thoughts well."

"He did his homework and had all the facts."

"He held the moral high ground."

Amid the chorus of praises, someone summed up their feelings for the boy: "I wish I had a son like him."

As for Tan, being overjoyed was an understatement to describe her feelings after the meeting. From then on, Si-Tu was no longer just a foster son, but her friend and confidant. His devotion to her, absolute loyalty, and remarkable ability to handle crises made him the only person in this world whom she could depend on.

4

Just as Si-Tu was starting to feel happy and comfortable living with his foster family, tragedy struck. And "tragedy often comes in pairs," as the Chinese idiom went. Both Widow Tan and Mrs. Si-Tu contracted tuberculosis and passed away within a few months of each other. Worse than his father's absence and more traumatic than his adoption, the twin losses left him motherless for the first time. The Si-Tus were a large and influential clan, and the young boy had at least two dozen uncles and aunts in nearby communities. Each of them was wealthy enough to take the boy in. None did. Poor Si-Tu understood that he was of no value to his relatives, who considered him a potential burden at best or an immediate embarrassment to the family name at worst. There were rumors that his original infant name, which meant a "big legendary bird" in

Chinese, was a curse to his two young mothers, who died in their mid-thirties. Others maintained that, by taking the moral high ground in defending Widow Tan, the boy had alienated the clan elders, who, once humiliated in public, would never be willing to help him under any circumstances.

So much for the belief that "blood is always thicker than water." So much for the traditional family values, filial affection, and noble tenets of virtue, good-heartedness, and social harmony known to all adults who claimed to be devoted students of Confucius. If you were poor and without any inheritance, Si-Tu realized, no one—not even your closest relatives—would care about you. The unfortunate boy was left all alone and could have died had he not been rescued by the loyal Jin-Xia, who took care of him for as long as she could. Much later, Aunt Si-Tu Xiu, a distant relative who worked for a railroad company in Tianjin in Northern China, heard of his plight. She became Si-Tu's legal guardian and took him to live with her.

For most people born and raised in Southern China, the North was an awful place to live in—the weather was dry, cold, and miserable, its people primitive, rude, and vulgar. Thus, the relocation of a southerner to live in the North was tantamount to a death sentence, having to trade the comfort and abundance of the warm South for the unbearable miseries of the icy North. But Si-Tu was glad to embrace this unexpected transplantation, which finally freed him from his despicable relatives. He felt the excitement of seeing snow for the first time. He liked the exotic dialect and the down-to-earth conversations of his new neighbors. He even envied the native men, many of whom had long beards and muscular physique. A typical southerner, Si-Tu was slim-built and quite short by northern standards. Worse, his classmates initially took him to be a girl owing to his fair skin and soft-spoken nature. He decided to change. He would grow a beard and mustache. He would exercise hard to build up a strong body. For the first time in his life, he felt he must grow up fast to look, sound, and act like a real man.

Aunt Xiu had been widowed many years ago and had no child of her own. Smart and always neatly dressed, she, with a delicate round face and an agile body, was still very attractive in her late forties. An honest and kind guardian, she cared about the boy and wanted to provide him with a good home. But she had neither Mrs. Si-Tu's business acumen nor Widow Tan's passion for intellectual pursuits. Well schooled when young, Aunt Xiu could speak some English and

Japanese, and was therefore much valued at her company, which had many international businesses and foreign customers to deal with. Although only a secretary, she had a stable income that was enough for the household expenses. After work, she would spend many hours at bars, restaurants, ballrooms, poker games, and majiang tables. Gregarious, sparkling, and savvy, she had a quick wit and perceptive skills to deal with all kinds of men—she relished their attention but fended off their advances. Si-Tu was often amused to watch her playing those games, in which she was always hunted but never caught. He admired her seamless tactics and masterful interpersonal skills, which allowed her to conduct the games any way she wanted. He also appreciated her ever-present courage and diplomacy, which enabled her to sail through any situation— good, bad, or even hopeless. But her total lack of any ambition dismayed Si-Tu, who did not want to be trapped in a life of mediocrity. At the same time, he did not want to offend his benefactor by leaving her. An ideal chance came his way one day when he saw an admission advertisement for Nankai School, a highly reputable educational institution in Tianjin.

A newly established private boarding school at the beginning of the century, the founders of Nankai emphasized physical education as much as book learning, which had remained unchanged across China for generations. The sound early education Si-Tu received made it easy for him to be accepted by the school. A few days after the new term started, Si-Tu was surprised to discover that Miss Teng Wan-Chun, the instructor of classical Chinese language, was also in charge of track and field for his class. To his mortification, Miss Teng soon noticed his scrawny body and lack of stamina. He came last in the running race, and jumped only slightly higher than the girls, who could beat him in the throwing event. "So much for the 'big bird,'" he heard someone mocking, and was so ashamed to face the class that he would have cried if not for his teacher's gentle encouragement.

Miss Teng took the students back to the classroom and said, "Some of you mentioned a 'big bird,' which reminds me of a story about a legendary bird—a phoenix. Let me tell you about it."

In the twelfth century, two cousins, a boy and a girl, grew up together, played, studied, and read poetry together. They became so fond of each other that the boy gave the girl a jade hairpin in the shape of a magnificent phoenix as a symbol of his love for her. They got married when the boy was twenty and the girl sixteen, and continued to study and make poems together. Their life was so full of joy every day that they considered themselves the happiest couple on earth.

The boy's mother was not pleased with the daughter-in-law, who, she believed, was a distraction to her son's career. He should focus on his preparations for the official examinations, she thought, not on composing meaningless poems with his young bride. She then forced the son to divorce his wife; he resisted at first but eventually succumbed to his mother's pressure. The marriage ended, breaking the couple's hearts. Ten years passed. Although both remarried, they could not forget each other.

The son was Mister Lu, one of the greatest poets during the Song Dynasty. One day, he happened to visit a local garden, where he ran into Lady Tang, his first and true love. Out of respect, she presented some homemade wine to him and left the garden. All the bittersweet memories came flooding back as he began to taste the wine. He then wrote a poem titled "Phoenix Hairpin" on the garden wall, which read,

Pink hands so fine,
Gold-branded wine,
Spring paints green willows palace wall cannot confine.
East wind unfair,
Happy times rare.
In my heart sad thoughts throng:
We've severed for years long.
Wrong, wrong, wrong!

Spring is as green,
In vain she's lean,
Her silk scarf soak'd with tears and red with stains unclean.
Peach blossoms fall
Near desert'd hall.
Our oath is still there, lo!
No word to her can go.
No, no, no!

A year later, Lady Tang returned to the garden and found the poem on the wall. Grief-stricken, she composed a rejoinder, using the same title, "Phoenix Hairpin":

The world unfair,
True manhood rare.
Dusk melts away in rain and blooming trees turn bare.
Morning wind high,
Tear traces dry.
I'll write to you what's in my heart,
Leaning on rails, speaking apart,
Hard, hard, hard!

Each goes his way,
Gone are our days.
Like ropes of a swing my soul groans always.
The horn blows cold,
Night has grown old.
Afraid my grief may be descried,
I try to hide my tears undried.
Hide, hide, hide!

Lady Tang never recovered from her broken heart; she died a few months later when she was twenty-seven. Mister Lu lived until eighty-five, but he never stopped thinking of his first love until his last breath. He visited the garden often, and each time he would write a commemorative poem full of pain, sorrow, and regret. But none of these poems would become as well known as the very first one that Mister Lu had written on the garden wall.

"Class," Miss Teng concluded, "the story suggested that the phoenix was only a symbol of love, which could come in various shapes and forms. But the greatest testament to love could be expressed in only one way—in the form of a man who could remain faithful to his woman, stand up for her, and protect her when she was most vulnerable. If he failed to do that, and chose to compromise his principles in order to conform to orthodoxy, his soul would never be at peace. The moral of the story: never ill-treat the weak and do not worship the powerful."

5

When the class was over, Miss Teng took Si-Tu to her office and discreetly asked about his background. Extremely embarrassed, he reluctantly talked about his past to a stranger for the first time.

A recent graduate of Teachers College, Columbia University, Miss Teng was almost six foot tall and had the perfect athletic body. She knew how hard it must be for the young man to recount his unusual childhood and to confess his pains and his deeply hidden weaknesses. She remained calm and impassive as he spoke, lest he feel even more wretched. After he had finished talking uninterrupted, Miss Teng had only one thing to say: "You need more exercise."

Si-Tu was immensely relieved. There was nothing wrong with him after all, and all he needed was more workout and sports practice, which was not a problem for him. He was glad that he had had the chance to talk about his past to this towering yet hardly intimidating lady. Thank goodness, not all tall and strong northerners were as frightening as southerners had envisaged. Si-Tu believed that he had now found the path to salvation, with Miss Teng as his guardian angel.

And exercise he did. Adopting Miss Teng's advice as his holy creed, the boy went to the sports field every morning earlier than anyone else, and in the evenings he would continue practicing until dark. His arduous labor paid off and his sports performance improved. Nothing flattered him more than seeing Miss Teng smiling, who must be happy and satisfied with his progress.

Si-Tu finally understood that she was the ultimate feminine figure he had always longed in his sixteen years of existence. He simply adored everything about Miss Teng. In the sports arena, she ran as fast as a deer, competed as ferociously as a tiger, screamed as loudly as a wolf, and laughed as freely as a dolphin. But, once she walked to the podium in the classroom, she changed into a serene and confident scholar. She could engage her students in intense discussions about literature, and then getting them to reenact history on stage afterward. Her sensitiveness and unique perspective shed new light on many poems Si-Tu had already learned, while her melodramatic rendition uplifted poetry to a completely new level for him. Looking at her standing tall in front of the class daily, he thought her voice was tender and sweet, her smile lovely and warm, her face bright and reassuring, and her blue dress simple but perfectly fit.

One morning, she rushed into the classroom after the school bell had rung and apologized for her tardiness, which was uncharacteristic of her. Little droplets of perspiration began to ooze out from her freckled nose, as her beautiful bosom rose and fell as she gasped for air, while her stretched blue gown revealed part of her long ivory legs underneath.

For a brief moment, she stood frozen in that pose like a statue, as if to allow someone to take another good look. Si-Tu panted and could not hear, see, or think about anything else; he was simply bewitched by that enchanting profile of hers. He then realized that he had fallen in love with his favorite teacher.

Chapter 5

Predicament

1

"Si-Tu Wen-Liang, please come to the railway station and fast!" Dong Zi-Tian was yelling over the telephone. "Come, you must come quickly! Tania is very sick and we need your help."

For the last two days on the train back from Shanghai to Peking, Tania had first felt very weak, then started to vomit, and finally her nausea and insomnia became so bad that Martin and Dong were really worried. They decided not to continue the journey to Peking but to get off at Tianjin right away, hoping that Si-Tu's knowledge of the city would help them find a good doctor for her.

They made the right decision. Some ninety miles southeast of Peking, Tianjin was located at the junction of two canals and three rivers dividing the city into many sections, which made it extremely difficult for any stranger to find his way. After Si-Tu arrived at the station, Dong briefly explained the situation. Si-Tu then hailed two rickshaws. As soon as he had helped Tania and Martin to get on to the first one, he said to the rickshaw man, "The Water Tower Medical School, be quick!" He and Dong followed them in the second rickshaw.

"The Water Tower Medical School—an interesting name," Dong remarked casually after he could finally breathe a little easier. He knew that his friend Si-Tu could be trusted to make the best choice under the circumstances.

"It's the first medical school to train female doctors in China, I think," Si-Tu replied. "It also has the first and best nursing school in China."

"Oh, I see." Dong appreciated Si-Tu's tactfulness in dealing with Tania's health emergency, even though they did not know what was wrong with her. Still curious about the school's name, he asked again, "But why 'water tower,' which doesn't sound feminine at all?"

"Because the school is located at Water Tower Street," replied Si-Tu.

"You see," he continued, "when Tianjin was first established as an outpost to protect the capital, Peking, the small garrison town had no running water. To fetch fresh water in the morning, every household had to send someone out to the banks near the Bai River, where a station or tower was later constructed for the convenience of the locals and vehicles plying the area. This section of the street was hence named Water Tower Street, and the Female Medical School decided to establish itself here. Longtime residents, however, preferred to call it 'Water Tower Medical School,' and it became so popular that few natives could remember its official name today."

"Interesting," said Dong. Place names, he knew as much Si-Tu did, usually had some charming tales behind them if anyone ever bothered to ask.

Tianjin had three train stations. The one they just left was the West Station, which, constructed in 1910, was an imposing two-story building of red bricks in the neoclassical style. The last major stop before Peking, it was not the closest station to the medical school, but it did allow them to see more of the old Tianjin than other routes. First going east though the streets between Ziya River and the South Canal, the rickshaws turned right at Grand North Boulevard, which was a broad thoroughfare running straight toward the heart of Tianjin. Crossing the South Canal over the Silver Bridge, they entered the old town through its northerly gate and continued onto the North Avenue until they arrived at the town's Drum Tower. It was actually a bell tower built at the exact center of the old rectangular-shaped township of less than two square miles. They then made an immediate left turn onto the East Avenue, which would lead them out of the old town's East Gate and directly to where the Water Tower Medical School was, right at Bai River's edge.

Founded in 1902, the school several years later hired the visionary Dr. Jin, who was a graduate of the Bellevue Hospital Medical College in New York, as its president. She was the first female Chinese who went overseas to study in the 1800s, the first Chinese with a medical degree from a Western university, and the first female president of a Chinese medical school. Under her leadership, the Water Tower Medical School and its affiliated nursing school she helped found were among the best medical institutions in China at the time.

The school had a modest stone-arched front entrance, but a huge compound inside. Everything was in perfect order, and everywhere looked clean and meticulously maintained. Tania was taken to the clinic, which was in a building to the left side of the compound. The three men waited in the reception area. Except for a few nurses walking in the hall in their standard white caps and gowns, the place was as quiet as any hospital. The doctor finally came out and told Martin that Tania was fine. As a precaution, she had taken some blood samples for tests, but the results would be out only the next day. Still, the doctor thought that Tania's symptoms were largely due to her bodily reactions to her pregnancy. While the reactions did look a little severe, they remained within the normal range of a female's physiological reaction to pregnancy, unless her test results showed something else, the doctor added. She did suspect that Tania's childhood malnutrition, the different diet in China, and her recent long-distance travels could have contributed to the severity of her symptoms. Tania, the doctor concluded, needed rest, better nutrition, and a suitable diet more to her liking, which should help her to regain her health. She also warned them that any infection affecting the mother could be harmful to the fetus.

All were quite relieved. Dong and Si-Tu warmly congratulated the couple on Tania's pregnancy, which they were hearing for the first time. Si-Tu suggested that, since Tania would need some good rest, she and Martin could stay at Aunt Xiu's house for the time being.

"Would that be intruding?" Tania politely asked.

"Not at all," Si-Tu assured them. "Aunt Xiu is a very nice person, a perfect hostess. She would love to have you stay. And your health is the most important thing right now."

"What about you two, then? Where would you stay?" Martin asked.

"I think Zi-Tian would like to share my dorm room on campus, wouldn't you?" Si-Tu turned to his friend, who nodded his head in agreement.

2

Si-Tu and Dong were about the same age and they had known each other since the May Fourth Movement two years ago, when one was a prominent student leader in Peking and the other in Tianjin. They became acquainted after working closely together to coordinate students' activities and public demonstrations in the two nearby cities. But they never had had a chance to get to know each other on a personal basis until now.

After settling in the two emissaries at his aunt's house, Si-Tu took Dong to his university, a few miles outside the city.

As soon as they arrived, Dong noticed a full-length dressing mirror securely framed next to the campus entrance. "What's that for?" he asked.

"Personal appearance is very important at Nankai, which has a strict dress code," responded Si-Tu, who took several seconds to check his image in the mirror, making sure his attire conformed to the school's regulations from top to bottom.

"No wonder people say nice things about Nankai students, who always look sharp and smart in their uniforms," commented Dong while reading the campus dress code inscribed on the wall, "Face must be clean, hair must be cut, uniform must be neat and buttoned up."

As the two friends walked into the well-laid-out campus, where a broad tree-lined pathway led them to several new classroom buildings, Dong said, "I never realized that Nankai is so much bigger than Beida (the nickname for Peking University)."

"Yes," Si-Tu agreed. "Beida started life with some existing but separate structures in an old urban neighborhood, whereas Nankai has a completely new campus in the suburbs."

"Mr. Zhang, the president of our university, is truly a visionary," Si-Tu continued. "To the native inhabitants of Tianjin, the phrase 'nan-kai' literarily means 'south' and 'open,' describing the open field outside the city's South Gate. It used to be a no man's land, wild, desolate, and swampy. But Mr. Zhang saw its potential. He raised enough money to purchase over a hundred acres of the land some years ago to build this modern university, which now comprises three colleges, a state-of-the-art science building, a fine library, and a research institute."

"True, Nankai is really one of the top universities in the nation," Dong said. "I also heard that Nankai has a unique system compared to all other educational institutions."

"Yes, it does," Si-Tu nodded. "Unlike how most universities are structured, Nankai is not just a single institution of higher education but a group of interrelated schools and institutions including an elementary school, a middle schools for boys and another for girls, a coed high school, the university, and the research institute for economic development. Or, simply put, Nankai covers the entire educational spectrum from grade school to postdoctoral research."

"This is truly an all-inclusive system and a highly ambitious scheme." Dong was impressed.

"Yes, only an educator as daring as Mr. Zhang could ever attempt it," Si-Tu said.

"One benefit of the system, I heard," Dong said, "is that the best students from any of the Nankai schools could be recommended to move to the next level of studies directly without any interruption."

"True," Si-Tu replied. "I was recommended by my high school teacher Miss Teng Wan-Chun to join Nankai University without taking the general entrance examinations that most high school graduates have to take."

"Aha, Miss Teng Wan-Chun, haven't I heard about her too?" Dong's tone suddenly changed, his eyes twinkling.

"It's not what you think." Si-Tu sounded defensive.

"Then why are you blushing?" Dong pressed on.

"Well, there was nothing between us," Si-Tu insisted.

"Ho, ho, ho, 'you two' already," Dong teased his friend.

"Okay, okay, let me tell you the truth." Si-Tu realized it was futile to hide anything from Dong and decided to come clean about his relationship with Miss Teng.

According to Si-Tu, his interest in his teacher did not escape other people's attention. He did want Miss Teng to know his feelings, and he was not embarrassed at all to show that he admired and adored her. As to what the rest of the world might think about it, he could not care less. His behavior certainly raised eyebrows among some students and teachers. At a time when the prevailing social norms viewed any close contact between an unmarried man and woman as unacceptable, many of them considered the intimate relationship between a female teacher and a male student to go against the very grain of tradition. Yet they also recognized Si-Tu to be a brilliant student and Miss Teng an excellent teacher with impeccable records, and both had never shown any signs of improper behavior. Wavering between doubt and discomfort, and curiosity and fascination, the staff and students largely held their peace and did not say anything openly in front of Si-Tu and Miss Teng.

One day, Miss Teng asked Si-Tu to come to her office. In her usual calm manner, she asked if the rumors she heard about his feelings toward her were true. Si-Tu nodded his head. Then she said, "Wen-Liang, I know you are a very promising student. You should concentrate on your studies because you have a great future ahead of you. You should not think too much about romance at this stage in your life."

"Miss Teng, do you remember the story about the phoenix hairpin you told us? Didn't you tell us that one should remain faithful to his true love, lest he regret for the rest of his life?"

"Yes, I do remember that. But... but... we are different..."

"How so? We are only different in age. But I don't care. I love you, and I will always do."

"It's not about you, Wen-Liang. It's about me."

"Why, what about you? Don't you like me?"

"No, no, Wen-Liang. You know that, and everybody knows that I like you a lot."

"So, why? Why can't we love each other?"

"Because we are teacher and student."

"Who said teacher and student can't love each other?"

"No, no one said that. The reason is that I have made a vow, many years ago, to remain single for life."

"Why?"

"Because I have committed my body and soul to the salvation of our country. Before our motherland is completely free from oppression and abuse, I can't even think about love, marriage, or family."

"I will commit to the same cause, and we can fight together as a couple."

"A romantic relationship is hardly compatible with a great social movement; they will get in each other's way. One has to choose either country or self-interest."

"Then, I can wait, or we can wait, wait until we succeed in the cause and then marry."

"I may not be able to wait that long."

"Why?"

"Because… because… please, please don't tell anyone else, Wen-Liang. I have a terminal disease called leukemia."

"I can't believe it. You are so healthy, so strong."

"I am healthy and strong only on the surface."

"I can't believe it. I will take you to a hospital, the best hospital, the… the Water Tower Medical School. Yes, yes, the Water Tower Medical School!"

"Wen-Liang, it was the doctors at the Water Tower Medical School who did the tests and diagnosed my illness."

"No, no, I don't believe it. They must have made a mistake. There must have been some mistake somewhere." Si-Tu was so devastated that he started to cry.

"Wen-Liang, don't waste your time on me. I really appreciate your warm feelings toward me, and, believe me, I will forever treasure them as long as I live."

"No, no, Miss Teng, please don't say that. I love you, and I will love you always, no matter what. And I can wait. Yes, I will wait no matter how long it will take for you to recover, and I will never leave you alone."

Hearing that, Miss Teng hugged Si-Tu and, looking straight into his innocent eyes, gave him a most tender kiss on his forehead.

3

"So, that's where we are today," concluded Si-Tu.

"Oh, what a story you have, Wen-Liang!" Seriously touched, Dong wanted to know even more. "Was that it? Just a kiss? Nothing more?"

"Yes, just a kiss," answered Si-Tu. "But it was the sweetest kiss I have ever had, and that's the kiss I will never forget."

"Did you ever go on a date with her?" Dong probed further.

"Well, yes and no. We did go to the Nine Dragon Lake one Sunday. A very beautiful late afternoon in the fall, as I remember: half of the sky was covered with brilliant clouds like a giant piece of the most magnificent brocade. The kaleidoscopic colors beamed down on hundreds of lotus on the lake, forming a vast blazing carpet. She told me that she had been betrothed to a childhood boyfriend, who was also her amiable classmate, most loyal confidant, and a true soulmate. Both came from wealthy families in the same northern province of Shanxi, and everyone was looking forward to celebrating their forthcoming nuptials. But five years ago, on a similar weekend afternoon, she received the shocking news that her fiancé had died in an accident. Heartbroken, she was so traumatized by the loss that she decided she would never love again. It was simply too painful one day to lose someone whom you had loved so much and for so long, she said. She paused for a moment and added, 'That was the state of my mind until you came into my life.' In that glorious afternoon and against the backdrop of hundreds of alluring lotus, I could see that her serene, pale face outshone them all."

"Wow, what can I say? Wen-Liang, you and Miss Teng are such a perfect couple. It's real sad that you can't marry her. Is she getting any better now?" Dong asked.

"No, not really. I accompanied her to a number of hospitals several times. But even the most optimistic doctors said the same thing—that she has between a few months and a year or two left."

Not wanting to talk about Miss Teng anymore, Si-Tu decided to change the subject. "What about you? Who is your girlfriend? You must now tell me everything."

"I don't have any girlfriend, you know that," Dong protested.

"That was a year ago. Anything can change since then." Si-Tu was not about to go easy on his friend.

"Really, what I am telling you *is* the truth. I really don't have *any* girlfriend," Dong said in all seriousness.

"You must be kidding. I don't believe you," Si-Tu retorted. "Let me guess…"

"Well, you can guess as much as you want to. I am telling you, I don't have a girlfriend." Dong remained unruffled.

"Hmm… you may pretend not to have a girlfriend now"—Si-Tu was starting to enjoy their conversation at last—"but I can see from your face that there is indeed someone in your heart."

"So, you are a fortune teller now? Who then? Can you name anyone?" Dong challenged him.

"Let me see, she must be someone beautiful, tall, lively, and attractive."

"Go on, what's her name then?" Dong did not blink.

"It must be Tang Wan-Yi, the female announcer the other night. I know her, and I saw the way she looked at you that night, full of passion and admiration."

"Tang Wan-Yi? You mean librarian Tang Shu-Hai's daughter? No, no way. You are crazy."

"Am I crazy? Are you sure? So, you are sure. Okay, let's guess again."

"Please do." Dong now felt confident that Si-Tu would lose this wild guessing game.

"Now I know it, I know it. I know her name," Si-Tu said teasingly, while watching Dong's facial expression closely, like a highly experienced detective.

"Say it, just say it. I am sure you will be wrong again," Dong said, eager to call his friend's bluff.

"Her name is…" Si-Tu held his breath as he looked for clues in Dong's eyes. Finding none, he uttered one word that finally jolted Dong. "Tania."

4

Dong dropped his nonchalant act immediately at the mention of her name. He did not understand how Si-Tu could have discovered his secret. "Was he so smart that he could read my mind, or was I so stupid that I had unwittingly revealed my feelings through my body language?" he wondered. Although Dong might be a few months older than Si-Tu, his friend seemed to be the more perceptive one—an astute observer of human nature.

Now that the cat was out of the bag—even though Dong still had no idea how Si-Tu got it right—it was Dong's turn to tell his life story.

The son of a dirt-poor peasant farmer, Dong grew up in a remote hamlet that was so isolated from the world that he saw no more than fifteen people in his neighborhood until he was ten. Jiangxi Province, where he was from, was one of the most impoverished areas in China. Although lying south of the Yangtze River, the region had more inaccessible mountains and rocky hills than productive plains, more wild forests, trees, jungles, and bamboo than cultivated farmlands. Devoid of basic communication and transportation facilities, large parts of the province came under the control of local bandits and outlaws. For the average family, the cycle of life revolved around poverty, hunger, and lawlessness, with robberies and murders a daily occurrence. Few could break free from this vicious cycle or the eternal abyss of chaos, fear, and despair.

Dong Zi-Tian was the name the father gave to his son, which meant catalpa tree and land, a reflection of his lifelong dream to own a piece of property lined with trees. When Dong was barely four years old, his father was killed in a shootout between the neighbors and a group of robbers. To survive, his mother remarried another poor peasant farmer from a village twenty miles away. Because she was widowed with a child, the bridegroom did not have to pay any dowry, a huge financial burden for the majority of the rural poor. For the price of a meal, two chickens, and a bottle of cheap liquor—paid to the go-between—the farmer managed to lure the widow into marriage. No sooner had mother and son entered their new home than he changed into a tyrant. A walking skeleton with a pumpkin-sized head, he shocked everyone in the village with his brutal penchant for beating his wife and stepson half-dead every other day. Mother cried every night, and Dong hated him, always thinking either of killing him or escaping from him at the earliest chance.

One day, a provincial inspector, accompanied by an entourage, happened to pass by the village. He saw a boy practicing his handwriting on the ground. Intrigued, he asked the boy for his name, and queried him about his skills. The boy was Dong, who claimed to be able to write with both hands. What he didn't say was that he was too poor to buy any paper, and that his wicked stepfather would never allow him to practice reading or writing at home. The inspector insisted on a demonstration, which Dong duly provided under the watchful eyes of curious neighbors. With his left hand, Dong wrote "Too Great the Hero," and with the right hand, "Too Small the World." Because he had practiced on the stiff ground for so long, Dong's handwriting on paper exhibited a rare but mature manly style despite his age, which captivated those present. Childlike yet animated, his style was so distinct that few calligraphers could imitate, no matter how diligently they practiced in their comfortable study chambers. Extremely pleased, the inspector instantly awarded Dong a hundred silver dollars, saying that he hoped the boy would become an accomplished scholar someday.

That evening, mother and son shed tears of joy as they counted the silver dollars, thinking that this could be the life-changing event that they had been praying for all these years. They could use the money for the boy's education, and mother might finally be able to buy some decent clothes for herself. Suddenly, there was light and hope in their wretched existence.

The next morning, the money was gone. The stepfather had stolen it and was having a fabulous time at gambling houses and opium dens. Furious, Dong and his mother complained to the village elders about the man's act. But the elders were hardly sympathetic to their plight, with one saying the stepfather had every right to anything in his house. Another elder called it a trivial domestic dispute and said such an issue could not be fairly adjudicated by outsiders. Quoting Confucius, a third senior villager noted that, since the man was the head of the family, his wife and son were obliged to obey him even if they did not like his decisions.

Heartbroken and devastated, Dong ran away from home and wandered aimlessly for several days in the wilderness. One day, he came across a large river and jumped into it, believing that he would never find any justice in this world. When he next opened his eyes, the boy found himself lying on the floor of a small shed. An old fisherman had saved him.

Having been given a second lease of life, Dong decided not to dwell on his miserable past. He took on all kinds of odd jobs to support himself in the day, while studying hard in the evening in the fisherman's shed. His hopes of eventually bringing his mother to live with him were dashed when she died a few years later. His savior, the old fisherman, also passed away not long after. Dong then found a job at a small printing company in Nanchang, the provincial seat of Jiangxi. The company provided him with room and board, but he had to work as an apprentice without pay. His menial job enabled Dong to survive and to continue his self-education, which he had never stopped pursuing.

Through his sheer hard work and determination, Dong finally gained admission into Peking University, making him the happiest person on earth. A young man with extraordinary energy and a burning desire for learning, he quickly attracted the attention of several professors and librarian Tang Shu-Hai, who had once locked the reading room without realizing that Dong was still there studying long after the library's closing bell.

When the tall and handsome Dong first realized that Tang Wan-Yi might have some interest in him, he was terribly excited. The only daughter of librarian Tang, she, an innocent yet vivacious student with a beautiful round face and rosy cheeks, was one of the most attractive young girls on campus. Whenever she stopped by with an excuse to talk to him, Dong could see that many people would look at them in a weird way, their faces showing various emotions, from disbelief and discomfort to envy and even anger. Many students at the university came from well-to-do families, and most did not like to see a humble fellow from a rural province having a relationship with an urban and upper-class girl. Although he was not one to be easily intimidated, Dong knew that he should not allow their relationship to develop further. He did like Tang a lot. But he also realized that the difference in their family backgrounds was too big to ignore. He had nothing to offer this girl who deserved so much better.

Then, when one day Tang dropped by to talk to him, Dong asked her out and told her what he thought about their relationship. Tang was very sad, for Dong was the first young man whom she had any serious interest in. The romance had not even started when it ended. Luckily, neither one had invested too much into the relationship, so the separation was not too painful. To their surprise, they even ended up as the best of friends since they fully understood and trusted each other.

The episode taught Dong a big lesson. He realized more than ever that emotions were serious matters and that, as a man, he should handle them with great care or he could easily send the wrong message and hurt an innocent person. He refocused all his attention on his studies and believed that he would not be interested in another girl for a very long time. Yet, the moment he met Tania in the library for the first time, his self-restraint melted away. To be fair, few people would not be attracted to Tania, given her undeniable beauty and grace. But what attracted Dong was something far more than her good looks and demeanor.

A girl could dress up very nicely, a young lady could be stunningly beautiful, and a mature woman could be sophisticated and fashionable. But, behind such exteriors, inner qualities such as profundity of the soul and superb understanding of the mind could never be imparted or replicated. Such qualities came from years of education and would only grow with experience. They represented what the most sensitive souls would learn and absorb. They were shaped by the fortitude, forbearance, and pious devotion that existed only in the most decent of human beings. They embraced the prime of femininity as much as they represented the pinnacle of humanity.

Tania was one of those who embodied these qualities. Her magnanimity needed no makeup nor was it a make-believe, and it could be seen in everything she said and did.

Dong sometimes asked himself why he was even interested in a married woman. The answer was that he could not help it. Love could be at first sight; love was also irresistible when it came. Pure love, love for the sake of love, was particularly so. It was the kind of love that came with no ifs and buts, or any form of reservations. Dong knew that he was truly in love this time; his feelings toward Tania were so strong that he often could not keep them under wraps, especially when she was near him.

Perhaps because he had such a deprived childhood, Dong was also looking for something beyond a simple companionship. He did not want just a girlfriend. She must also have the kind of feminine maturity, warmth, and wisdom that he had been yearning for all these years. Dong's miserable past had also led him to see the world in black and white. His entire life had revolved around his uncompromising stand against injustice and his relentless fight for fairness. Consciously or unconsciously, he transported these assumptions and experiences into his expectations of his future partner, who should be not only pleasant and beautiful but also moral and righteous. He saw all these qualities in Tania, who was the very personification of virtue that he had dreamed of for years.

Dong was an extremely sensitive person and could be easily offended whenever anyone tried to patronize him. Although Martin had become a good friend, Dong thought that he had a condescending attitude that was common among Europeans in China. But Tania was different. She was always very gentle and considerate in her dealings with everyone.

When Tania fell ill on the train, Dong became angry with Martin when he seemed to be unconcerned about her condition and continued talking to some fellow passengers. When Tania was about to vomit, Martin remained seated and did not seem inclined to help. It was Dong who had to accompany Tania to the toilet at the other end of the train. He also asked a conductor to help bring some hot water, which Tania greatly appreciated. Knowing Tania was too sick to eat, Martin went to the dining cabin alone to have his meal. Dong, however, was thoughtful enough to ask a waiter to bring some fruit to her seat. It was little acts such as these that left Tania with a good impression of Dong.

5

"So, what do you plan to do next?" a sympathetic Si-Tu asked.

"I don't know," Dong confessed. "I don't even know whether I would ever be able to tell Tania about my feelings for her."

"It is a difficult situation," Si-Tu agreed.

"Let's take a walk," they said to each other, almost at the same time.

A few hundred yards away outside the campus, they came to a small town called Eight-Mile Heights, where several houses, a post office, and a bus stop could be found. "I know you may be interested in the name," Si-Tu said. "The distance from the Drum Tower or the center of Tianjin through its South Gate to here is exactly eight miles. Many years ago, the wasteland in between was filled with big ditches, small creeks, and various ponds and swamps of different sizes until this little raised hilltop. Thus the name Eight-Mile Heights."

"The place may not look that impressive at all today," continued Si-Tu, "but it used to be a very important military post, which controlled the highways coming in and out of South Tianjin. Because it was the last defense of Tianjin's South Gate, a fierce battle was fought here during the Boxer Rebellion."

"Oh, I think I have heard of that too," said Dong.

"Yes, that was only about twenty years ago, right here on this ground we are standing," Si-Tu recalled. "General Nie set up his defense with five thousand men against the allied forces of six thousand, while another five hundred Japanese soldiers attacked him from behind. Hours later, after four of his horses got killed, he was severely wounded, and both his legs were broken, but he still refused to surrender until one bullet hit his chest and another smashed his skull. The loss of the heights finally opened the way for those foreign troops, who went on to blow up the South Gate. Tianjin fell."

"What a bloody battle, what a heroic story!" Pointing to a stone obelisk before a bridge not far from them, Dong asked, "What's that?"

"That's the monument to commemorate the battle. And the Eight-Mile Bridge, the first front line of that battle, was renamed General Nie Bridge."

As they strolled along the road, Dong and Si-Tu felt that they were entering a hallowed ground, where they could still smell the heavy gunpowder, feel bullets whizzing by, see the flames of flying explosives, and hear the neighs of the general's horses.

Not far from the old battlefield, delightful farmland extended for miles before their eyes. Dong was surprised to see that these were rice fields, not the wheat and corn fields commonly found in Northern China. "This is the famed garrison rice," Si-Tu said. "First cultivated by the Ming government troops stationed in the Tianjin area more than two hundred years ago, the garrison rice is of higher quality than the common rice we grow in the South."

"Really? How could that be?" asked Dong, "Northerners prefer wheat over rice, don't they?"

"Yes, most northern farmers plant far more wheat than rice, which needs warm temperatures and a lot of water to grow. The southern suburbs of Tianjin are one of the few exceptions, however. After years of trial and error, a special kind of rice has been developed to suit this area, where plenty of sunshine and highly nutrient water from nearby rivers are available. In the South, farmers typically grow rice two seasons a year. Their rice output is high, while the quality is not as good as this garrison rice, which can be harvested only once a year."

"That makes sense—quality over quantity," Dong began to agree with Si-Tu, who seemed to have studied these regional specialties and varieties.

"You need to see its grain to believe it," Si-Tu said. "As crystal as little jade and as bright as snow, the round garrison rice is shorter in size but richer in content than the southern rice, which tends to look pale, translucent, elongated, and reddish. It has such a tender, crisp, and slightly sweet flavor that one has to see and taste it to know the difference."

"Oh, I am so tempted. You must treat me to this Tianjin delicacy the moment we get to the city." As a southerner whose daily staple had been rice all his life, Dong would have never thought that he would be asking for northern rice, suggested by Si-Tu, who was also a typical southerner.

Tianjin had expanded beyond recognition for the last several decades, largely due to the rapid growth of foreign concessions. Whereas Shanghai had only three settlements, by the French, English, and Americans (the last two later merged into one common settlement), Tianjin had as many as nine concessions extending along both sides of the Ha River, making the new city more than ten times larger than the old town. The British, French, Japanese, and Germans had their concessions in the 1800s. After the Boxer Rebellion was crushed by the joint forces of the Eight-Nation Alliance in 1900, several of the allied powers demanded their concessions, including the Russian, Italian, Austro-Hungarian, American, and Belgian governments. Each of them had the authority to run the concession as its own territory, which led the locals to call them "The League of Nations." Few visitors would not be struck by the presence of so many foreign flags, foreign troops, foreign police forces, foreign personnel, and numerous buildings of different foreign styles in one place.

For Chinese patriots, these foreign intrusions on Chinese soil collectively served as the most painful reminders of the humiliating defeats that China had suffered for years, as well as how corrupted their own government had become.

"When would we be able to take them back?" Si-Tu and Dong asked themselves as they passed the districts in those foreign concessions. "Our new party will for sure liberate China and restore its past greatness and glory," they both agreed.

The two walked and talked all night long. They talked about the new communist organization they had been involved with in Peking and Tianjin. Both were looking forward to the first national convention that would be held in Shanghai, where the two of them would be representing their local organizations. They would soon see each other again, working together to ensure the success of the first major gathering of the nascent Communist Party in China.

When they returned to Si-Tu's dorm, it was almost daybreak. The excitement that had built up from their heart-to-heart talks had yet to subside. Thinking that the two good friends would soon officially become comrades-in-arms, Si-Tu suggested, "Why don't we write down some words for each other?"

"A good idea," Dong agreed.

Both were good calligraphers. Si-Tu was an expert in the tradition of Master Yan, who had been highly influential since the Song Dynasty, while Dong was closer to the style of Master Cai from the Han Dynasty. So, in the twilight of Tianjin and in the small campus dorm room of Nankai, after the necessary brushes, ink, and papers were carefully prepared, the words Si-Tu wrote for Dong were "Ever Loyal to My Dear Friend," and those by Dong for Si-Tu "Ever Faithful to Your True Love."

6

That afternoon, Si-Tu took Dong to Aunt Xiu's house to visit Tania. She, sitting in a sofa, had recovered considerably. "Thank you, my dear friends," Tania said warmly as she saw the two coming into the room. "Thank you for helping me. And especially Si-Tu: thank you for finding me such a nice doctor at very short notice."

"Please don't mention it. That's what friends are for, right?" Si-Tu responded. "So, did you get the lab test results? What did they say?"

"Yes," Tania said. "The results are back and they are fine."

"Except..." Martin paused, unsure if he should continue.

"No big deal," Tania said. "Except that my white blood cells count is low, the doctor said."

"Not just low, *very* low, *extremely* low," Martin stressed.

"Oh, what does that mean then? Is it serious?" Dong asked, as Si-Tu looked concerned.

"No, not serious, at least for now," Tania said.

Martin continued, "The doctor told us that the low count for her white blood cells suggested some deficiency in her immune system. It may not matter for now, but it does make her body vulnerable to infections, which can be bad for her health and the fetus."

"Let's talk about the things we need to talk about," Tania suggested, trying to change the subject.

The four then discussed for a while about the arrangements for the upcoming national convention. Before Si-Tu and Dong left, they inquired about the couple's plan.

Martin looked at Tania for a few seconds and said, "Considering her pregnancy and current condition, I have decided to send her back to Russia as soon as possible."

Si-Tu looked at Dong and said, "That might be the best answer to her situation."

Chapter 6

Frustration

1

T O THOSE NOSY NEIGHBORS IN THE SMALL VILLAGE OF BOXWOOD, Sheng Wu, the head of the Sheng family must have been unbelievably lucky lately. First, he survived several horrible wars in nearby provinces during his five-year conscription and returned home miraculously in one piece, without even a scratch. Second, he used his savings from his monthly pension in the army to marry a decently good-looking girl from another village, who managed to bring into his household a small but nice dowry. Third, he expanded his small plot of land into a three-acre estate by acquiring the adjacent land belonging to two other families. Fourth, he doubled the output of his rice production by increasing the water flow of his irrigation line, after hosting a lavish dinner party for the village elders who controlled the allocation of the spring streams coming down from the mountains to the village. Fifth, he tore down the old thatched shelter and used his increased wealth to build a new five-room house made of tiles, complete with a kitchen, yard, barn, stable, and rice mill. Last but not least, his young wife had just given birth to a healthy and handsome boy, the first of four children that the couple would have in the next few years. To most of Boxwood's residents, who firmly believed in providential bliss, the Sheng family seemed to have everything that a farmer would ever need in this world, and they must be the happiest people on earth.

The years went by fast, and the parents were eager to marry off their eldest son so that they could have grandchildren as soon as possible—the typical parental yearning in China since time immemorial. However deeply rooted this tradition may have been, the arranged marriage with a twenty-year-old girl displeased the fifteen-year-old son, who then ran away from home. He returned home a few years later, only to stun his parents with the news that he had married a city girl.

This engrossing Boxwood tale quickly became a legend across the county of Jute, which most urban residents elsewhere would have never heard of. Located in Central China, Jute was only eighty miles away from Wuhan, one of the major cities in China and the largest one on the Central Yangtze. Yet, the stark contrast between city and county could not have been more pronounced here. As the critical north–south artery crossing the middle of the nation, the railway from Peking to Wuhan ran right through the southern edge of the Township of Jute, while the rest of the county saw nothing but miles and miles of treacherous mountains sadly named Big Farewell. Few outsiders had ever come to visit the tiny hamlet of Boxwood, hiding deep in those forbidden mountains, nor would any local villagers ever leave their residence. The runaway groom-to-be Sheng Bao was one of the few exceptions, who not only thought about leaving but also did leave in the end.

2

Like father, like son. Both Sheng Bao and his father were practical and hardworking. Both were frugal and intelligent. Both were extremely driven and ambitious. Headstrong and as stubborn as a mule, both were passionate believers in their own righteousness. Father Sheng Wu was an indefatigable workaholic and a fantastic accountant with an elephant's memory. He could compute with two abacuses at the same time by using both his hands. He had an eye for details and would never miss any deadlines listed in his schedule. Never one to allow his loan or credit to go bad, he always remembered who owed him what, where, when, how, and why. As one who was ahead of his time, he realized the importance of diversification, and gradually moved away from just farming into the business of buying and selling rice. He operated the rice mill for many local families, which turned him into a key rice dealer in the community. He used the constant supply of bran from the mill to raise pigs, which he would then sell at the market. He made out small loans to neighbors and collected interest. He used the profits to reinvest in land or to rent out parcels of land to tenants. After cultivating ties with several dry goods wholesalers and retailers, he participated in their businesses by issuing credit notes stamped with his name. These merchants, in turn, would accept his notes as payment from customers, ranging from farmers, laborers, and hunters to landowners, traders, friends, relatives, and residents in the region.

The more the father's businesses expanded, the more labor he hoped to extract from his eldest son, who started to help out in the fields when he was just six. He sent Sheng to school during the day, and required him to work on the accounts books in the evening. An impatient man, Sheng Wu was never pleased whenever he discovered that the son was reading something else instead of working on the balance sheets. He ordered Sheng to clean the farm tools, repair the grain pounder, prepare the paddy fields for cultivation by planting seeds, pulling out weeds, and irrigating the fields, cut the corn, thrash the rice, hull the grains, shear the animals, feed the pigs, fetch the fuel, deliver goods, collect rents, and run errands. With never-ending tasks to be completed in the fields and around the house all the time, the eldest son was always the first to be called on to finish them.

Tall, hardy, diligent, handsome, and extremely smart, Sheng had a big frame and a prominent forehead, while his full lips and bright eyes, as attractive as those of his mother's, softened and accentuated his round, manly face. His passion for reading and learning grew as fast as his mind and body, which, he believed, should not be devoted exclusively to the father's business enterprise.

As time passed, Sheng's strong desire to pursue his own interests put him on a collision course with his father, whose own ambitions were ever expanding. Any boy born into a peasant farmer's family, the most common type of rural household in late nineteenth-century China, was bound to start working in the fields as soon as he could walk, and Sheng was no different. Amid the searing sun and endless sweat, along with his father's yelling and generous use of his fists, his little body was forced to work overtime daily. Like most fathers of the time, Sheng Wu was temperamental, greedy, and driven, with dreams of joining the middle class by working their young to the bone. Sheng Wu himself had been in the same situation in the past, as had his father, his father's father, grandfather, and every forefather before them. Pushing and ordering his son around, Sheng Wu did not think for one moment that he was doing anything different from any other peasant farmer. His eldest son was, by default, the parents' first unpaid laborer. "Say nothing and do whatever the elders told you to" was the dictum generations of children had followed, and the father expected no less from Sheng, whose hard work would bolster the family's fortune and whose silent obedience would boost his paternal authority and pride.

3

While Sheng worked hard at all the tasks assigned to him, the little boy was not one who was easily intimidated, not even by his terrifying father. His sweet and devoted mother was his first line of defense, who would save him time and again from his father's explosive temper and violent fists. As he grew older, he discovered a new tactic to deal with the old man. When he was about twelve or thirteen, his father invited some important friends and customers to the house one day. He asked Sheng to serve tea, and then in front of the guests, called him lazy and useless for his apparent tardiness. Incensed, the boy dropped the tray on the table and retaliated by quoting the classics that an elder must be kind and affectionate. Besides, said he, old people should do more work than the young. "Since you are more than three times older than me," Sheng protested, "*you* should serve *your* guests *on your own* and not to pass this damn simple job to me!" Shocked, the father immediately looked for a broomstick to give his son a good beating, while all his guests, equally shocked, watched the boy dash out of the house as fast as a rabbit, disappearing into the nearby rice paddies.

As the family drama continued to unfold, half of the village started to follow it with great interest, albeit from a discreet distance. They watched, listened, and evaluated the curses, attacks, and counterattacks flying back and forth as the furious father chased after his headstrong son.

When the boy reached the edge of a small river, he threatened to jump if the father came any nearer. Silence reigned briefly before a new round of demands and counterdemands were exchanged. The father insisted that his son should apologize and "ke tou" (to kneel down and strike one's head to the ground) as a sign of submission. Sheng said he would perform the "ke tou" on one knee only if his father promised not to beat him. The father–son standoff finally ended when the mother appeared to take both of them home. Years later, Sheng would proudly recalled that "when I defended my rights by open rebellion my father relented, but when I remained meek and submissive he would curse and beat me even more."

The situation was now clear to the belligerents. Whereas the father believed that he had every right to dominate the son, the latter was determined not to be dominated. Whereas the father thought that, as the king of his castle, he could rule the boy any way he wanted, the latter became even more defiant and determined to disobey the older man's orders. Sheng Wu concluded that he had to find a way to tame his son. He consulted a fortune teller, who told him that the boy needed an anchor in life. Sheng was destined to have the fate of water, he explained. Soft and gentle, water was the origin of life and the source of happiness, he said. Water could be silent, discreet, peaceful, calm, harmless, and even charming at times. But it was also powerful and dangerous, he pointed out. Water could be restless, boundless, swift, aggressive, and turbulent when it gathered momentum. It could even be highly destructive when it unleashed its fury all at once, as in torrential tides and raging floods. Sheng Wu agreed completely with the fortune teller's diagnosis. But he wasn't sure what the anchor should be for the son or where to find it. He and his wife pondered over their son's future for quite some time until, one night, both suddenly woke up at the same time, turned to each other, and said: "Find him a wife!"

4

Whenever Sheng got upset, he buried himself in books. The boy was a voracious reader who could devour a dozen books in a few days. He particularly enjoyed the Chinese classics and admired their legendary heroes immensely. He memorized everything related to their lives and could recite many literary episodes of their careers verbatim. But, when the boy was really depressed, he would go and talk to Uncle Sheng Bing.

The Shengs were the largest clan in Boxwood, where most residents were all closely related. A distant relative, Uncle Bing became a hired hand for Sheng's father after losing his land many years ago. The boy called him "uncle," not so much for their blood ties but because of the intimate bond they had formed over the years. In his late forties, Uncle Bing was like another father to Sheng, only much nicer and gentler. His broad knowledge about farming and his unfailing willingness to help the boy saved Sheng from many sticky situations. Most of all, Uncle Bing had so many amazing personal experiences that the boy always wanted to listen to his stories.

"Uncle, were you ever married?" Sheng asked one day.

"Yes. But why?" The uncle had heard about the family's plan to marry off the boy, and anticipated his next question.

"How was your marriage?" the boy inquired.

"It was good at first. But it went bad, very bad, soon afterward."

"How come?"

"I was drafted to be a soldier, and she was gone when I came back a few years later."

"Were you sad?"

"Of course."

"Why didn't you marry again?"

"Well, my boy, marriage is a very serious business. If you are not ready, you shouldn't get involved."

"What do you mean 'you are not ready'?"

"Marriage means that a man and a woman are going to live together for a very long time and build a family together. If the man doesn't know what will happen in his own life, he should not have a wife."

"Then how can one know what will happen in his life?"

"He must know what he wants to do with his life first, and then he would have some idea."

Sheng paused for a long while and said at last, "Uncle, I think you are right. I must know what I want to do with my own life first before I can consider marriage."

Uncle Bing agreed with his usual smile, which was most reassuring to the boy.

"We must take a trip together!" the boy suddenly shouted.

"Why? Did your father allow it?"

"He ordered the trip," Sheng replied.

5

Like the boy's father, Uncle Bing was lean and short. His chiseled face and suntanned body were so bony that there seemed to be no flesh or blood under his skin. Like the boy's father, he was an incredibly tough guy who was never sick or ever tired of working. He, also like the father, was one of tens of thousands of farmhands who had been conscripted into the army to fight wars or battle rebels and bandits in the last few decades. Never able to refuse the boy's demand for stories, Uncle Bing shared his experiences in the conflicts with Sheng as they climbed down the big mountain toward Jute, where they were supposed to deliver several loads of dry goods including local tea, herbs, and animal fur that Sheng's father had collected at Boxwood.

Sheng knew that his uncle had been wounded more than once, having seen the scars on his back and forearm. "Were you ever afraid during those battles?" he asked on several occasions. "Not really," his uncle said. "And you will get used to it if you have seen so many corpses and killings every day," he explained.

They started the journey quite early before dawn so as to avoid traveling under the sun for too long during the day. The mysteriously invigorating morning air, the intoxicating smell of grass, the melodic sounds of birds, and the refreshing bath of the mountain mist added a spring to their steps.

"Why do people fight?" Sheng asked. "Why are there so many wars?"

"Because many were poor and desperate," his uncle said.

"You mean those rebels and bandits?"

"Yes, they were poor and desperate people."

"Weren't they devils and monsters as the governmental officials said?"

"No, the government never told us the truth."

Uncle Bing then told the boy a story. A tenant farmer named Young had a nice family and rented two acres of land to till. Unfortunately, a severe drought destroyed his crops and the family was struggling to survive. Unable to pay his rent, he begged the landlord for an extension, which was granted. He managed to plant his crops the next year, but a big flood destroyed everything, bringing in its wake diseases and infestations. The desperate tenant repeatedly pleaded for mercy from the landlord, but to no avail. Instead, the latter ordered the tenant to be arrested. Government soldiers immediately came and threw him into jail, where he was badly beaten and mutilated. When his incarceration finally ended several months later, he found out that the landlord had raped his wife, sold his house, terminated his tenancy, and disposed of the land. The landless, homeless, and penniless man left his hometown to join a group of bandits in the mountains, and never returned.

"To hide his past, he changed his name to Sheng, who was my great-grandfather," the uncle concluded his tale.

"Unbelievable." Sheng was totally fascinated. "Your great-grandfather was so brave to take up arms and fight back. He was a hero!"

"Not really," Uncle Bing said. "Bandits rarely survived for more than a few years."

"Why?"

"Because they had no good leaders."

"Were Liu Bang and Xiang Yu heroes?" asked the boy about the two best-known rebels in Chinese history.

"They were okay. But they were really not leaders of the poor," his uncle responded.

"How about Song Jiang and the one hundred and eight warriors?" the boy said, referring to the famous characters from the novel *Water Margin* by Shi Nai-An.

"Those rebels did everything they could while they got the chance. They eventually failed, however."

His uncle's accounts got Sheng thinking, and the notions of the poor and leadership lingered in his mind for a long time afterward.

"If you said the rebels and bandits were good people and if you were so sympathetic toward them," asked the boy, "why did you join the government troops to suppress them?"

"I had no choice. You see, son," Uncle Bing continued, "a man as downtrodden as I am now, I could either work myself to the grave, starve to death, be killed as a bandit, be beheaded as a rebel, or be conscripted to fight till my last breath. This means that I would surely die in misery and go to hell one way or another. Being poor, I have no hope, no choice, and no future in this wretched life." As he spoke, a few tears rolled down from his sunken and dry eyes that were filled with sadness, bitterness, frustration, and despair.

6

The mist was finally lifted by midday, which meant that the two had walked for six hours nonstop. At the end of a winding hilly road, they saw a beautiful temple, where a young monk guarded the entrance. Uncle Bing talked to the juvenile, who seemed to be indifferent toward the two visitors. But, when his uncle started to use some sign language, the monk allowed them to enter the compound. A master monk soon came out and talked to the uncle for a while. Before long, a good meal was served and they had some decent rest under a circle of big cypress trees.

"What did you say to the little monk?" Sheng asked.

"Nothing," he said.

"I don't believe you," the boy said as he lay himself on his uncle's lap, staring into his eyes. "I saw you talking to him using some secret signs."

"Nonsense; there were no secret signs," Uncle Bing insisted.

"Okay, okay, you don't trust me. I knew it. You never trusted me at all." The boy sounded upset.

Uncle Bing could never bear to see the little boy upset, even if he was just pretending. "Okay, if I tell you, you must promise never divulge this to another soul, including anyone in your family."

"I promise," the boy said.

"I belong to this underground organization called Grand Fellowship," his uncle said, and began sharing with Sheng the secret signs, codes, and rules of his organization. And then he said, "We must leave now or we will not be able to reach Jute today."

The last three-mile track took them more than four hours, and they finally arrived at Jute around bedtime. They found the streets unusually quiet, but did not think much about it. They settled at a small inn next to the shop where they were to deliver the goods. After a quick meal, they went to bed, thinking that their job would be done early next morning.

But a great disappointment awaited them. Employees at the store told them that a group of bandits had raided several businesses in the town several days ago. The store owner had fled, and they had no money to pay for the goods. "Where did he go?" Uncle Bing asked.

"He went to Wuhan," said one employee, "and you may be able to find him there."

7

Wuhan turned out to be an even greater disappointment, because the two outsiders found themselves walking into the worst food riots in the city's history.

Located at the intersection of the Han River and Yangtze River, Wuhan was the collective name of three townships—Hankou (north of the Yangtze and east of the Han), Hanyang (north of the Yangtze and west of the Han), and Wuchang (south of the Yangtze). Because of the topographical shape of the land and the large volumes of the two rivers, the region was very rich in water resources and produced plenty of farm goods. Known as "The City on the River" or "The City on Lakes," Wuhan was known for its nearly two hundred lakes, streams, and ponds around the city and its suburbs. Yet, seasonal trade winds, common in most parts of China, dominated the region, which was highly susceptible to big swings in weather patterns, from extreme drought to incessant rainstorms.

In recent years, the Wuhan region had been battered by a spate of very bad weather. First, farmlands were entirely flooded, only to be baked later by the scorching sun, turning this once fertile ground into wasteland overnight. Hundreds of peasants and farmhands lost their homes, and hundreds more ended up begging for food to survive. Grain supplies and prices became the most critical issue for the city dwellers, especially the underclass. One poor man, Huang, made his living by fetching fresh water from a nearby river and selling it to the community. A bout of illness that left him unable to work for weeks depleted all his savings. One day, the ailing Huang gave his last dollar to his wife to buy a pound of rice so that the family could have a meal that night. He then mustered all his strength to return to work. When the wife went to a local store, the owner insisted on charging her a dollar and a dime, making the purchase impossible. She was so humiliated and distraught that she threw herself into the river and drowned. When Huang and his two small children learned what had happened that evening, they went to the river and committed suicide at the very spot where the wife had killed herself.

Such a family tragedy enraged the whole city. Several hundred people protested in front of the municipal government, demanding justice. Several other groups took matters into their own hands, and began to attack those businesses that had profited from the widespread calamity by hoarding basic foodstuffs. Several rice merchants were beaten, their shops smashed, and residences burned. The city was thrown into chaos, and police and troops were called out to quell the unrest. The situation did not calm down for several months, causing nearly a hundred people to be killed on the streets, several dozen houses and government buildings burned, and thousands of dollars' worth of property destroyed.

During one of the violent street clashes, Sheng got separated from his uncle. Unable to find him anywhere, the boy decided to stay in Wuhan for a while, hoping that the two might soon be reunited.

The city could be charming once it had picked up the pieces after the riots. The market center for tea, salt, cotton, grain, timber, farm animals, medical herbs, and imported goods, Wuhan had established itself as the hub of commercial activities in Central China for centuries. The reputed pathway connecting nine neighboring provinces, the city also saw in recent years the rapid expansion of railway construction and numerous new industries from textiles, metallurgy, and shipbuilding to weapons production. With rapid growth of commercial boats and shipping lines, its ports connected inland China with Liverpool, Vladivostok, and Rio Janeiro in ways that no other interior cities could. Some foreign visitors went as far as to compare the fast-changing Wuhan with such industrial powerhouses as Chicago, Pittsburg, and even New York.

Few words could describe how amazed Sheng, the country boy, felt while walking through a giant gate to enter the city. Eyes wide open and heart pounding, he could not believe how thick the walls and how magnificent the watchtowers were. Everything here, from the heavy beams to the brilliant gilding, must have cost a farmer's fortune to build, he thought. To this newcomer, everything the local residents took for granted was a novelty to him. They wore shoes instead of sandals. Men covered their heads with hats, and women opened umbrellas to shield their faces and arms from the pleasant sunshine. Early in the morning, old or young came out to the streets to buy breakfast, instead of making it at home. They had something called electric lamps, which were a thousand times brighter than the kerosene light he always used at home. Hardly any pebbled streets were not lined with stores, shops, and businesses, where venders were howling, wagons passing, customers bargaining, obscenely enticing smells escaping from restaurants' open windows, little boys and girls running, giggling, and chasing one another. These urban activities, so common here every day, were more dazzling than the best New Year's parade Sheng had ever watched back home in Boxwood village.

Emerging from the edges of the ancient Lake in the Clouds, the earliest settlement of Wuhan could be traced back to two thousand years ago. Wuchang, the newest of the three townships, was built in AD 223, when the king of the Wu dynasty constructed a small but strategic garrison on the south bank of the Yangtze. To command the massive waterway, he also ordered the building of a watchtower on the northeast side of a hill named Yellow Swan. The locals called it Snake Hill, opposite the Tortoise Hill across the river. Over the years, the name of the fortress had been changed half a dozen times, its size greatly expanded, and the original tower redesigned and rebuilt into a grand structure—the Tower of Yellow Crane.

One of the most famous structures in Southern China, no tour of the city would be complete until one had visited the tower. Constructed on an immense base on top of Snake Hill, the three-story tower was almost one hundred feet tall. Its unobstructed view allowed visitors to see city's panorama, the mighty waters of the Yangtze, and miles and miles way beyond. On a clear day, Sheng believed that he could see as far as Jute and the Big Farewell mountains in the distance. Like all visitors before him, few would not be impressed by what they saw as soon as they climbed to the top floor of the tower. Some left commemorative poems on the wall, which had become much treasured in the annals of Chinese literary tradition, and one of them was composed by Master Cui in the eighth century—

The yellow crane has carried my friend away,
All that remained is the tower of this crane.

Where did they go and when would they return?
All the traces have gone with the clouds for a millennium.

Bright Yangtze waters are chasing the green Hanyang trees,
On the Island of Parrots stand lush sweet grasses.

Would sunset show me the way back home ever,
Why do I feel as blue as how the smoky haze has obscured the river?

Standing on the tower, Sheng felt that he was experiencing something more exhilarating than the sentiments expressed in Master Cui's poem, which he really liked. When he looked around from the gigantic tower, he felt the openness, the grandeur, the freedom, the limitless future, and the sudden awareness of his own great potential that he had never realized before. Instead of melancholy, he felt the weight of his responsibility and a grave sense of mission. Yes, he believed that he had an answer to Uncle Bing's question of what to do in the future—he had been called upon to fulfill some grand purpose in life. Coming from the tiny and desolate village of Boxwood, he was able to climb to the top of the world. He had witnessed it all, and now his responsibility was to change the world. He remembered that, the last time he visited the tower, he had run into a tall and gaunt man who was looking through the same window as he was. Unaware of his presence, the stranger sighed, "What a view! And what a pity that not everybody would fully appreciate it."

"What a time! Only true heroes can seize it and change the world," Sheng joined in, speaking almost to himself.

The man turned around and saw Sheng. He showed immediate interest in the teenager, whose bold thoughts apparently impressed him. He introduced himself as Tang Shu-Hai and talked with Sheng for some time. At the end of the long conversation, he said, "When you have a chance to visit Peking, you must stop by the Peking University to see me." He then waved to a girl standing nearby. "Come here, Wan-Yi, let me introduce you to this young man, Sheng Bao."

8

The next time Sheng met Tang Shu-Hai again, he was no longer a boy but in his mid-twenties. At six feet and five inches, he was unusually tall for a Chinese man, and, coupled with his handsome features that included large piercing eyes, it was easy for the young man to stand out in a roomful of people.

Years of farm work since childhood had made the well-built Sheng tough and strong. He rarely got sick and loved nature. Unlike most city folk, he could walk for miles at a stretch without feeling tired, but refreshed and energized instead. He enjoyed camping and outdoor life as much as he enjoyed reading books. Yet his initial encounter with the people at Peking University turned out to be a humbling experience.

As a society that never embraced the concept of equality, traditional China prided itself on social harmony at the expense of a strong penchant for divisiveness. Some were related to age, blood relations, ethnicity, or gender, while other prejudices arose from the vast disparity between the rural and urban, the educated and ignorant, between the haves and have-nots, the north and south, the coastal areas and inlands, and between the metropolis and provinces. These prevailing geographic-cultural divisions and socioeconomic subdivisions also produced a potent byproduct—the Chinese obsession with separating insiders from outsiders.

The first thing the snobs at Peking University noticed was Sheng's accent. Whereas most people here spoke Mandarin, his distinct southern twang attracted nothing but laughter. He did try to correct himself, but his attempts at imitating the way they spoke worsened, not improved, his pronunciations. He once made the innocent mistake of confusing "everybody" with "human body." Thereafter, he was stuck with the humiliating nickname of "human body" every time he attended a public gathering. Meanwhile, Sheng prided himself as a skillful writer who graduated first class in Chinese literature after three years of study at the normal school in Wuhan, which also happened to be a prominent educational institution in the province of Hubei. Yet, many students and professors at Peking University considered his style crude, loose, and dated, while some others thought it to be wild, incoherent, or journalistic at best. Such dismissive comments deeply hurt Sheng, whose self-confidence largely arose from the belief that his masterful command of Chinese literature, history, and politics had been one of his greatest intellectual achievements.

He quickly found out that, whereas his speech and debating skills had been greatly admired by his fellow classmates back in Wuhan, he was never at the center of attention in Peking. For those university students and professors who had come from wealthy families and worthy backgrounds, they talked about Locke, Montesquieu, and Rousseau in politics, Aristotle, Hume, Kant, and Russell in philosophy, and Voltaire, Dickens, and Tolstoy in literature. Sheng's extensive knowledge of the Chinese classics only qualified him as a quiet bystander in those conversations. One of the main reasons for the gap, he thought, was his inability to read and speak any foreign language. He tried to learn some Japanese at first, then Russian, and finally English and French, but had problems grasping a new language. He eventually gave up, just as he had stopped changing his accent. Foreign languages were not his cup of tea, just as Mandarin was of no great interest to him. He switched to reading a series of translations, which consumed much of his time and energy at the Peking University Library, where librarian Tang had hired him as an assistant.

Reading was a panacea for his woes, so it seemed. Satisfied with his self-education pursuits, Sheng was confident that his knowledge of the world was not inferior to anyone else's. Biographies of political leaders in world history, such as Peter the Great, Catherine the Great, Napoleon, Washington, Lincoln, Wellington, and Gladstone intrigued him as much as such powerful rulers in ancient Chinese history, such as Yao, Sun, Yu, Qinshi Huangdi, and Han Wu Di. Sheng's ambition was to become a great man, and only the lives of a small number of great heroes would truly impress him. He loved a big world map he had found, and studied it with great interest, fully anticipating the era of global geopolitics that he was entering. He also skimmed through Adam Smith's *Wealth of Nations*, Charles Darwin's *Origin of Species*, Herbert Spencer's *Logic*, John Stuart Mill's *Ethics*, Jean-Jacques Rousseau's *Social Contract*, and Montesquieu's *Spirit of the Laws*, while Greek mythology, European literature, and natural sciences were at the bottom of his reading list. Other than traditional Chinese novels and politics, only biographies of great politicians and some global geography would command his serious attention.

Sheng never intended to become an armchair scholar. Extensive social theories put him off, no matter how sophisticated they might seem or how famous their authors were. He needed some practical advice and applicable principles that he could quickly adopt. Far better than those vain university professors and graduates, he knew China's real story inside out, and was keenly aware of the grave disparity between rural and urban China from the bottom up. Foreign abuses and domestic inequalities tormented him. Yet none of those idolized Western theorists offered him much insights into his concerns, not even some of the best-known texts of radicalism at the time, such as *The Class Struggle* by Karl Kautsky, *Socialism in Thought and Action* by Harry W. Laidler, and *History of Socialism* by Thomas Kirkup. Their detailed chronology of the labor movement in Europe and North America did suggest the encouraging prospect that a worldwide revolution of the proletariat was on the horizon. But their page-after-page elaborations never matched the few powerful words in the small pamphlet by Karl Marx and Frederick Engels—*The Communist Manifesto* (1848)—which had plainly stated that the "history of all hitherto existing society is the history of class struggle." "The theory of the communists can be summarized in the single sentence—abolition of private property," continued *The Manifesto*, "and they openly declare that their ends can be attained only by the forcible overthrow of all existing social conditions." Sheng, like many ardent patriots of his generation, never forgot these unassuming yet captivating words once he had read them. They had such an electrifying effect on him that he was determined to uphold these straightforward principles till the end of his life.

9

Power, authority, tradition, establishment, prestige, orthodoxy, hostility, antagonism, prejudice, or condescension never bothered Sheng, who had grown up a rebel against all forms of oppression, with his own father as his first opponent. When things got tough, he got tougher. He thrived under pressure and was excellent at managing crises. Although he had a penchant for challenging the status quo, he knew when to pick his battles and when to avoid meaningless and costly skirmishes. He had long learned how to hold his tongue, swallow his pride, and wait for the right moment to be bold and aggressive. He was also learning how to become a good strategist and a good tactician at the same time, essential qualities for a man preparing for a political career.

For a stranger to survive in a new environment, a southerner in the North, a farmer's son among intellectuals, a high school graduate in a famous national university, and a provincial novice in this splendid capital city, he needed friends and lots of them. A series of attempts convinced Sheng that he was not about to have many in Peking. He had no sterling academic credentials, just a local diploma, nor could he boast of any kind of overseas experience. He was not an officially registered student at the university but a lowly temporary employee serving the institution's smug students and egotistic faculty. His base, it seemed clear, should be back in Wuhan, where he had goods friends, supportive teachers, and adoring classmates. He knew the people there, their accent, the land, rivers, country roads, and mountains. In familiar Jute and beloved Boxwood his deep roots lay.

One of the bright spots, though, was his admiration for this ancient city of Peking and its eternal beauty. A history buff, Sheng had traveled far and wide and frequently on foot. Whenever possible, he would stop by those renowned historic sites, such as the hometown of Confucius, the battlefields of Red Cliff, the real water margin in Shandong Province, the city of Xuzhou in Jiangsu Province, and Baoding in Hebei. Each time he visited a new location, his sense of mission was reaffirmed, and no place had completely taken his breath away until he saw the Forbidden City for the first time. The absolute beauty, unmatched grandeur, and astounding glory of this imperial palace, more than all other secondary sites combined, demonstrated to him in unmistakable terms what supreme power and ultimate prestige really meant.

Another tender spot was his lingering feelings for Tang Wan-Yi. Unlike many library users, who treated the assistant as a servant, she was one of the few people who had been nice to him. Whenever she needed some help in the reading room, she would first say "Mr. Sheng, please" and then "Thank you." Those few simple words led Sheng to suspect that she might still remember their brief first meeting at the Tower of Yellow Crane several years ago. But he was not certain and dared not ask her, lest such a question embarrass her. Growing up in the countryside taught him enough about animal needs, but very little about courting a city girl. He could tell that many students had an eye on her; she was nevertheless closer to Dong Zi-Tian than anybody else.

Both Sheng and Dong were from the South, both started as country boys, both were of similar built, and were about the same age. For the life of him, Sheng could not understand why Tang was more attracted to Dong than him.

An unexpected chance came one afternoon when Sheng attended an event in a park in the southern part of Peking. The Pavilion Park used to be owned by the royal court, with extensive grounds, several ponds, and one giant lake, which had been turned into public gardens after the fall of the Qing Empire. Far away from the city center and poorly maintained, the Pavilion Park looked more like a piece of abandoned land than a good place for recreation. Sheng liked it precisely for its wildness, which brought him closer to nature in this crowded city.

He was lost in his thoughts when he suddenly heard a yell for help near the lake. Sheng rushed to the spot, only to see Tang's bicycle in the water, while a group of her university friends were milling around, totally clueless about what to do. Sheng jumped in and got the bike back onto dry land in less than five minutes. The onlookers now realized that the water was not as deep as they had thought. They quietly left, embarrassed at not having the courage to help the young woman in the first place.

The grateful Tang started helping Sheng to dry his robe and to clean the mud and weed from the bike. They soon realized that the bike's front wheel was bent and Tang could not ride it anymore. Sheng suggested that he would take the bike back, while Tang could take a rickshaw home. She refused, saying that it would be unfair and she was willing to walk with Sheng back to the university.

What a pleasant five-mile walk it was for Sheng! Tang asked him so many questions on the way that he wished the walk could have been an extra five miles longer.

"Were you afraid of water?" Tang asked.

"No, never. I began swimming in my family pond as soon as I started to walk on land."

"So, you are from…"

"Yes, I am from the South and from the countryside."

"Oh, I see. There must be a lot of water there, unlike our North."

"That's true. The mighty Yangtze runs through our entire province from west to east, and I have swum across it several times."

"Really? Amazing! So, you live by the Yangtze?"

"Yes and no. I was born in Jute County, but I attended school in Wuhan."

"Wuhan? I know the place. Father took me to climb the famous Tower of Yellow Crane once."

"Yes, I know that too because I was there on the same day."

"Amazing! Absolutely unbelievable! So we have met before?"

"Indeed, we have."

Sheng could see Tang's eyes shining with joy at the memory. He believed that he would have many more stories to tell her on the way home, and in the days ahead.

Chapter 7

Faith

1

AFTER A YEAR'S WORK, MARTIN REPORTED TO THE COMINTERN IN a dispatch to his boss.

Dear Comrade Chamberlain:

You may recall from my last communication that the Chinese Communist Party was first launched in Shanghai in August 1920. The former Peking University Professor Lu Shi-Yan led the effort, which involved several of his close friends. They published the party's official journal "The Communists" in Shanghai.

I am now pleased to report that in July this year, thirteen delegates from six cities attended the first National Congress of the Chinese Communist Party in Shanghai, representing a total of sixty-three members from six branch organizations in Shanghai, Peking, Tianjin, Wuhan, Changsha, and Canton.

After lengthy discussions, presided by Dong Zi-Tian, the Congress adopted the party's program and constitution. It also elected a leadership committee of three—Professor Lu in Shanghai as the general secretary,

Dong Zi-Tian in Peking as secretary of organization, and Si-Tu Wen-Liang in Tianjin as secretary of propaganda.

This is a significant Bolshevik victory in China.

Long Live the Communist International!

Working Men of All Countries Unite!

Martin wanted to add more highlights from the conference in his message, but he finally decided not to expand his official report beyond the major events. Instead, he began to write a personal letter to Tania, now in Moscow, to express his concerns. He knew her to be an astute observer, whose valuable feedback would help shape his opinions. Besides, his frenetic pace of work in a foreign land had deprived him of a chance to slow down and clarify his own thoughts, which had become rather disorganized lately.

As Martin had told Tania in their private discussions earlier, China was very different from any other societies they were familiar with, and especially different from the industrialized European nations like Germany, England, and the Netherlands. Modern industries were few and far between here. Both the number of factory employees and their literacy rate remained pathetically low; few of them had ever heard of Karl Marx, much less read his works.

What made Marx attractive to the small group of educated individuals, such as Lu, Dong, Si-Tu, and Tang Shu-Hai, was not because they were desperate proletarians but because they were highly sensitized Chinese nationalists. They, first and foremost, were distressed by the decline of this once great country, which was now riddled with corruption, filled with miseries, and abused by both domestic and foreign enemies. Eager to save China and restore her past glory, they had been searching for an effective solution for years, but were sorely disappointed to see the repeated failures of the old reformist movements led by Mr. Kang and Mr. Liang and the more recent one launched by Sun Yat-Sen's Nationalist Party (Kuomintang). The Russian Bolsheviks' rise to power seemed to have provided them with an alternative model at this critical juncture in China's history.

With the bourgeoisie's failure, their courageous Chinese friends concluded, the true patriots or the communists should take over. Only they and their collective actions would ultimately save China from her tragic dismemberment. Instead of a full-fledged proletarian revolt against capitalism, they sincerely believed that the first step of this revolution was to reestablish China's national integrity, sovereignty, and independence, followed by the implementation of Marx's plans for socialism and communism. In this sense, they were more nationalists than Marxists, just like the mass movement they were about to initiate was more patriotic in nature than proletarian.

But Professor Lu and his associates probably chose this path due to the serious dilemma they were facing. To launch their monumental crusade for China's salvation, they needed the participation of tens of thousands of ordinary citizens, who by and large were uneducated, greatly divided, highly unorganized, and greatly apathetic to any issues beyond their immediate interests. Oppressed, poor, illiterate, docile, and fatalistic, the average Chinese had always played the role of obedient subjects under the established system and never had the tradition of active participation in public affairs. Other than involvement in some secret societies, few of them had had any experience in political organization. The general population, however, could be prodded to unleash their incredible energy by exploiting their fears and sense of desperation, by spreading a message that was simple, direct yet incendiary.

If history was any guide, the Boxer Rebellion showed how fast extreme antiforeign violence could spread. Sun had also exploited the Hans' ethnic hatred against the Manchus, which contributed significantly to the fall of the Qing Dynasty in 1911. The new Communist Party could tap into the deep reservoir of xenophobic feelings to advance its cause. In other words, the Chinese communists could use Marx and Marxism as a means to achieve not the real proletarian goals but their nationalistic agenda.

When Tania received Martin's letter, she agreed with her husband's concerns and reservations. But she thought that Martin might have been too critical and too pessimistic about their Chinese friends. Yes, she reminded him, most Chinese including university students and professors did not read the original German, English, French, or Russian treatises on communism, and she had no means of judging the quality of the Chinese translations of those imported foreign works. Their knowledge of Marx, Marxism, Lenin, and Leninism was thus quite limited, to say the least. But she never doubted the sincerity of Lu, Tang, Dong, Si-Tu, and others, who had professed their commitment to Marxism.

China did have its special conditions, she continued. In this poor and nonindustrial country, it might not be a bad thing to adjust the standard doctrines to suit indigenous realities. The efforts of their patriotic friends to incorporate nationalism into the new communist organization might be not only useful but also necessary in China, where the rhetoric of nationalism was an effective rallying call for most Chinese. The key was, Tania pointed out, that the leadership of the Communist Party must be absolutely clear about these distinctions—that nationalism could never substitute for communism, and that they should never sacrifice the party's Marxist ideology for immediate practical needs.

In the end, both felt good that they had taken the time to share their views, which helped them to better understand China and their Chinese friends. Insofar as the next task was concerned, they did not reach a complete consensus. Tania, who always looked up to Lenin and Trotsky as her idols, thought that identifying the charismatic leader within the organization should be the top priority. Still troubled by the thought that a communist party could have so little knowledge about Marxism, Martin insisted on implementing some immediate measures to change the status quo, such as having a new training program for the new party.

2

Beyond what Martin and Tania had observed, the launch of the Chinese communist organization also gave birth to some embryonic elements not immediately visible to foreigners. They were latent but potent ingredients that, after years of fermentation, would gradually change society. Downright radical in outlook and extremely small in size, the new party was among the several hundred political groupings that had emerged in China since the 1890s. Nobody could imagine that in less than three decades this tiny and obscure group of enthusiastic patriots would expand rapidly and become powerful enough to defeat all its rivals and take control of the whole country.

Much of its stupendous strength came from the new party's remarkable cohesiveness, which was based on its faith in Marx as the infallible godfather and on embracing Marxism as its unassailable creed—Martin's reservations about the new organization's limited understanding of communist theories notwithstanding. As much as how early Christianity had steadily routed the pagans, and how early monotheist Islam had swiftly defeated the polytheists, this institution of modern theology spread with an astonishing speed in the miserable and godless oriental county, where the converts exhibited the kind of zeal, piety, sacrifice, and hard work that only saintly missionaries and the most fervent religious believers could match.

The leap of faith was solidified by Lenin's skilled adaptation of orthodox Marxism, which established both a centralized leadership atop the party structure, and a total submission of the rank and file to their leaders. Few political organizations in the industrialized countries had similar structures; still fewer would subscribe to Lenin's highly authoritarian doctrines, which ran against the ever-widening demand for democratic processes in Western Europe and North America at the time.

China was in a completely different situation. An agrarian society for several thousand years, this monarchical nation's autocratic practice had always been the convention not only in politics, but also in the Chinese social life, cultural activity, and educational systems. Thus, whereas the German political activists Eduard Bernstein and Rosa Luxemburg had voiced strong opposition to Lenin's dogmas, their Chinese counterparts embraced them with little hesitation. In fact, insisting on the ideas that "individual members must subject themselves to the organization, the minority to the majority, the subordinates to their superiors, and the whole party to its central leadership," Lenin's four-layered organizational principles were not all that dissimilar to the long-held Confucian dictum that "a king must always be the king, just as the ministers shall always be ministers, fathers always fathers, sons always sons, husbands always husbands, and wives always wives."

No transplantations were ever seamless and without cost, and few inheritances without mutation. The blend of Lenin's imperious doctrines with deeply rooted native traditions was one of the few inventions the Chinese Communist Party had created. This adaptation or communism with Chinese characteristics did allow the party to gain strength in its early years. As time went on, the combination of the repressive elements from two orthodoxies would only get worse than when each was acting separately.

The international scope of the communist movement opened not only old wounds but also produced new ones. As Martin and Tania had correctly recognized, nationalism had a strong and pervasive influence in and out of the Chinese Communist Party. For most Chinese people and many members of this new party, Russia was no different from other foreign powers, having had eyes on Chinese border territories from the northwest of Xinjiang to the northeast of Manchuria for the longest time. For the Chinese, Russian imperialism was no better than that of the British, French, Japanese, Americans, or Germans. A close connection with the Russians would thus arouse as much suspicion as that with any other foreign state. Many Chinese patriots vividly remembered that, from the Treaty of Nerchinsk in the seventeenth century to the Treaty of Peking in the nineteenth, the Russian Empire annexed the vast region from Lake Baikal to the Amur basins, which had been part of the Manchus' historical territory. All told, Russia gained over half a million square miles of land from China—more than all the concessions obtained by other foreign powers combined. Only a decade ago, the Russians and Japanese fought a war on Chinese soil for dominance in Manchuria. Most recently, the Bolshevik regime's encouragement led to the declaration of an independent Outer Mongolia—which was not recognized by the Chinese government until the end of World War II.

What compounded the twisted issues of imperialist clashes of the past were the current unequal relationships between Moscow and the diverse communist parties in Europe and Asia, and between the Comintern and the leadership of the respective affiliated national parties. Although they were not exactly the same entity, both the Bolshevik government in Moscow and the Executive Committee of the Comintern considered themselves the undisputed leaders of the global movement of the proletariat. Therefore, their decisions should be taken as direct orders that each national party must obey. Insofar as the top personnel appointments within each member party were concerned, no office holders would be deemed as legitimate unless they were sanctioned by the Comintern and Moscow.

These controlling policies and practices were unsurprisingly met with resentment from the national parties, and Professor Lu was not the only one who had explicitly expressed his dislike for such arrangements. Yet, since the Soviet Union and the Comintern were often the only sources of outside support for the national communist parties, they swallowed their pride and followed the directives of the Comintern and Moscow, sometimes against their very own judgment when it came to dealing with their internal affairs and domestic situations.

Furthermore, the Comintern ultimately listened to Moscow, never the other way round. Motivated by national interests, the Soviet Union's foreign policies could be as expansionist and imperialistic as they were protectionist and self-serving, which were not consistent with those internationalist principles the Comintern was supposed to uphold. In such cases, the Comintern had to adjust its decisions to follow Moscow's directives, which were at odds with many of Marx's glorious principles related to the common cause and common interests of the proletarians all over the world. Worse, the Russian communists and their leaders had violent internal conflicts as frequently as in any political party. The rise and fall of the different factions could, through their spokesmen at the Comintern, have drastic impacts on the national parties outside Russia.

As a subordinate member of the Comintern, the Chinese Communist Party frequently had to bear the brunt of those brutal internal struggles taking place in a foreign land thousands of miles away, and to pay the heavy price of accepting the sham doctrine of internationalism in the communist lexicon.

3

Different delegates left the party's first national congress with different impressions. In a small but nicely decorated hotel room, Peking delegate Gong Pei-Zhi woke up the morning after the convention feeling totally elated. As one of its two secretaries, he and Sheng Bao had been terribly busy for the last two weeks, recording and transcribing the proceedings. The heavy workload, which left him with little free time, came at the most important juncture in his life. He had just got married a month earlier but could not stay with his pampered bride, Ding Qiao-Ran, who became very upset. Now the meetings were finally over, and they could spend all the time together any way they wanted. Best of all, they were about to leave in a few days for New York City for their long-delayed honeymoon. As Ding was still sound asleep, Gong sat up and leaned against the headboard, savoring a quiet moment to enjoy his marriage at long last.

A nineteen-year-old man from one of the richest families in China, Gong joined the Communist Party for fun. His family and ancestors had been preeminent merchants in Shanxi Province in Northern China for several hundred years. Growing up in a highly protected and privileged environment, he never knew what poverty meant for the millions, nor did he ever work for a single day to understand labor. If anyone wanted to know what wealth could buy, he would only need to go and see this family's living compound, which was a massive fortress of thirty-five continuous acres. Covering the entire face of the northerly slope of a hill, it consisted of one hundred and twenty-five courtyards and over one thousand, two hundred rooms, where the living space was not measured by yards, but by acres. No local or county administration would adopt any policy without consulting the Gong family beforehand, and no government officials at any level would pass this area without paying a tribute to its family elders first. Whenever Gong fancied something in town, he could simply take it and the family chamberlain would pick up the tab. If he wanted something that was not available locally, the family's business networks across China and in several foreign countries would order it for him. When he was five, he demanded an Arabian horse, which a house guest had casually mentioned during his brief visit. The family arranged to acquire ten of them in a year and to build a special stable for the imported beasts, only to have the boy losing all interest in them by then.

His proud parents of course hired the best private tutors for Gong, who was later sent to the top schools in the province and then to the nation's capital to attend Peking University. He was an excellent student in classical Chinese, and learned to speak French, German, and English. Western music enchanted him, and Gong also began to learn how to play the violin, not because he aspired to become a violinist but because he noticed that girls seemed to like boys playing a musical instrument. Highly intelligent, versatile, and gregarious, he was a tall, handsome, and elegant young man, who had a girlish obsession with his own appearance. Always in great shape and immaculately dressed, he methodically groomed his thick jet-black hair and polished his clean-shaven face every morning so as to present his best side once he stepped into the public view.

As one who was easily enthralled with anything fresh and exotic, Gong developed sufficient interest in Western philosophy, political theories, and Marxism, which seemed to be in vogue among some university professors and students. So he quickly devoured several books, declared himself a Marxist, and bragged about it to impress everyone on campus. When he came to Shanghai to attend the national congress, he refused to stay with other delegates housed in the dorms of a local school. Horrified by the idea of sharing a cramped room with another person, he insisted on staying at a nearby hotel with his bride, using their newlywed status as an excuse. Two weeks of wearisome debates and endless discussions overwhelmed Gong, who was totally uninterested in such detailed and tedious pursuits. If this experience suggested what party activity might look like in the future, he wanted no part of it.

Ding was still fast asleep. An unexplainable ire rattled Gong's mind. "What a pathetic place," he said to himself as he looked around. "Look at the cheap furniture. Look at the distasteful colors. How can they even call this miserable place a hotel? They don't have champagne and roses for the guests. They don't serve milk, coffee, and toast. They don't have bacon, butter, cheese, and eggs in the morning, but only serve traditional Chinese breakfast like the plain and tasteless porridge, pickles, and steamed buns. Oh, how I miss the Astor House Hotel and the delicious Greek souvlaki they provided at the dining hall. Yes, I need to wake Qiao-Ran right now so that we can go out to catch a show and then dance all night at the Astor."

By the time the newlyweds arrived at the Astor, they discovered that the hotel's entrance had been blocked by police. Perplexed, they talked to several bystanders and learned that a crime had been committed in the hotel last night. Some said it was a burglary, others said a murder, and still others claimed it was a burglary and murder. In any event, nobody was allowed in or out of the building while the police were investigating. As the couple was discussing what to do next, a person approached them.

"Gong Pei-Zhi, good to see you here," the person said, extending his hand.

"Gan Zu-Xun, good to see you too," Gong said. "So, why are you here? Shouldn't you be on your way back to Canton by now?"

Gan, another convention delegate, was from Canton in the deep southern province of Guangdong. He was probably the only one among the thirteen delegates whom Gong had befriended. Although about Gong's age, Gan's receding hairline and full-grown mustache made him look thrice his age.

"Yes, yes, I am supposed to return to Canton soon. But first, you must let me know who this beautiful young lady is."

"Yes, Gan Zu-Xun, my wife Ding Qiao-Ran," Gong began the introductions. "Qiao-Ran, this is my friend Mr. Gan, who is also a delegate to the convention."

"No wonder you could never focus on the meetings. You have such a lovely bride. Where did you hide her? Congratulations! And I am so envious," Gan started to tease them.

"Let's go inside for some coffee," Gong suggested as he saw the policemen taking down the barricades as a prelude to their withdrawal.

"Just coffee? You must be kidding! I already missed the wedding party..." Gan protested.

"Okay, okay, dinner, my treat," Gong gave up and before Gan opened his mouth again, adding, "and anything on the menu, of course."

The three walked gaily into the grand lobby of the Astor, the best hotel in the city and the whole country.

4

The son of a small landlord in Guangdong Province in Southern China, Gan received a Western-style education earlier than most of his contemporaries in the country. While the majority of the population had yet to encounter any foreigner in the heartlands of China, many local residents in Guangdong had long engaged in trading with their European counterparts, and missionaries preaching Christian gospels were a common sight in the province.

The early exposure to outside influences also bewildered Gan's generation, whose interests ranged from monarchism and anarchism to liberalism, from constitutionalism and federalism to parliamentarianism, from radicalism and progressivism to pragmatism, from syndicalism and unionism to socialism, from the Young Turks, Fourierians, Fabians, and Bolsheviks to Marxists, and from Kropotkin, Kautsky, Sen Katayama, Debs, and Lenin to Sun Yat-Sen.

Brave insurrectionists against the Qing Empire were Gan's early heroes. But the ones who had the greatest impact on him were Mr. Zhao, Mr. Jing, Mr. Huang, and Mr. Hua. All of them were Guangdong's natives, all attended Peking University, and all were staunch believers in various brands of anarchism. They formed a society called Essence and circulated numerous publications in Peking, Shanghai, Canton, and other major cities in China.

Essence was the most active and influential organization at Peking University, and had a fast-growing membership. Eager for change, its members ardently opposed authorities, government, and any social constraints against the individual, and strongly supported free love and free marriage. They translated numerous works by Kropotkin, Goldman, Proudhon, and Bakunin into Chinese, which gained a huge following among the young readers, so much so that the Professor Lu and Mr. Hu invited them to compile a special issue for the *New Youth* magazine on Henrik Ibsen, his life, and his famous play *A Doll's House*. This literary publication of both English translations and Chinese commentaries set a milestone in Chinese drama history, social thought, and culture change.

However faithfully Gan had followed his idols to Peking University and however much he had perused those incendiary publications, he seemed indecisive in taking a stand. Growing up in China, where tradition had been everything and everywhere, a typical Chinese youngster had too much baggage to shed before he could make any drastic and radical decisions that would turn him into a social outcast. Gan weighed the pros and cons of every theory he came across, and in the end remained incredulous, unconvinced by any of them. He liked the tone and rhetoric of many militant nonconformists, but felt more comfortable with keeping them at arm's length, in touch with their ideas but steering clear of their radical practices.

Naturally timid in character, Gan never considered himself an activist. He loved observing activity and social events, but he was not one to challenge the established social order. After considering his own weaknesses and strengths, he decided to become a journalist. A highly intelligent writer and knowledgeable person, he enjoyed the profession, which allowed him to use his talent to report on important social events while keeping him out of trouble by not becoming part of the event itself. His good and diligent reporting provided him with a decent living and gained him a reputation not only in several local newspapers in Canton but also in those syndicated ones in Peking, Tianjin, and Shanghai.

Gan had originally planned to leave Shanghai right after the congress ended. But rumors about a crime at the Astor Hotel triggered his professional instincts, and he rushed to the scene as quickly as the police. By the time Ding and Gong arrived, he had already talked to several persons and was ready to write the first report for his newspaper, *The Canton Herald*.

When the sumptuous dinner was over and after Ding had left with a girlfriend for the powder room, Gong asked, "What happened here last night?"

"Do you really want to know? This can spoil your honeymoon," Gan hesitated.

"No, never mind. Qiao-Ran is not here and I am curious," Gong persisted.

"Okay, I don't think anyone has the complete story yet. But here are the bits and pieces I learned," Gan lit up his cigarette. "There seemed to have been a robbery in a luxurious suite here last night. But the strange thing is that the guest of the suite was nowhere to be found."

"Who's the guest? If they couldn't find the guest, how could they know there was a robbery?" Gong got curiouser and curiouser.

"Good questions. Many are asking the same, but the hotel is not releasing any information about the case or the guest." Gan deliberately paused. "You really want to know?"

"Yes, yes, of course," Gong loved this kind of stuff as much as anyone else.

"I heard," Gan stressed, "the guest is none other than the girl who had just won the title of Camellia at the last citywide beauty pageant."

"Hmm, that's interesting. Where is she now? Is she okay?" Gong asked.

"That's the question everybody wants to know, especially the police."

"I hope the answer will not suggest a bigger crime or scandal than what you have uncovered."

"Me too. But who knows? There have been so many unresolved cases now, especially in the city."

"Yes, those mysteries, especially when they involve girls."

"Well, talking about girls, you seem to have a pretty good taste." Gan changed the subject.

"You mean Qiao-Ran? Well, she is okay. How about you? When are you getting married?" it was Gong's turn to pry.

"I don't know. I don't know much about girls."

"You liar! I saw you with a pros—" Gong stopped in mid-sentence.

Men were not known for their discreet actions. Regardless of their creed or politics, most Chinese males saw nothing wrong in pursuing girls or seeking out prostitutes. "I have no choice. Unlike you, I don't have that kind of money and appeal to marry a rich girl," Gan said defensively.

"Nonsense. Qiao-Ran is not a rich girl and I found her from a magazine cover," Gong retorted, half-bragging.

"Okay, I really wish you and Ding Qiao-Ran a long and happy marriage."

"You know me, Zu-Xun. Nothing stays with me for long. Remember what I said to you about the violin I had?"

The reply did not surprise Gan. When both of them were at Peking University, Gong did mention that he would never purchase the most expensive violin, because he knew that a new and better one would always emerge. No matter how much Gong liked a girl, a new and prettier one would come his way sooner or later. Was there ever eternal love, as most romantic men and women would like to believe? Gan wondered.

At this point, Ding returned and proclaimed, "Darling, let's go dancing!"

Gan stood up and said, "Please, you two lovebirds go ahead first. I will catch up with you later. Please excuse me."

"Are you sure you don't want to go? You may meet someone you like," Gong suggested.

"I am sure. I need time to finish writing my report so it can be printed in tomorrow's newspaper back home," Gan replied.

5

The Wuhan delegate Sheng Bao did not feel any more relieved after the convention ended than before it began. Because he had been courting Tang Wan-Yi, he came to the convention feeling slightly apprehensive that her father Tang Shu-Hai might pay extra attention to how he would perform at the meetings. If girls always feared their future mothers-in-law, boys dreaded facing their future fathers-in-law just as much. Strange as it seemed, more than half of Chinese parents tended to think that either their future daughter-in-law was not good enough for their son or their future son-in-law not good enough for their daughter. Sheng was afraid that he might be in the latter category.

Tang Wan-Yi never invited him to see her parents while he was in Peking. Tang Shu-Hai did not talk to him in private throughout the convention, nor did he mention his daughter before he returned to Peking after the convention. Sheng was really not sure about what Tang Shu-Hai was thinking about his relationship with Tang Wan-Yi. This prolonged uncertainty troubled him, as he had no clue on how to interpret Tang Shu-Hai's silence. He quickly reviewed his activities during the meetings and found nothing amiss. He was punctual at every scheduled event, and diligent at work as a recording secretary. Except for his thick dialect and imperfect handwriting, he couldn't recall making any serious blunder at the convention.

Or was it Tang Wan-Yi who had changed her mind? It could not be, for he had received a letter from her recently, saying that she missed him. The bottom line, Sheng suspected, could be that her parents did not like his family background, since the urban–rural divide had been the greatest social barrier in China for generations. Tang Shu-Hai studied in Japan, and was on the distinguished faculty (librarian and professor of political science and history) of Peking University—the premier institution of higher education in China. By contrast, he was a nobody from the most remote village of Boxwood in the most obscure county of Jute. But Sheng, who never gave up on anything once he had made his mind, was not about to give up his pursuit this time either. He reexamined the steps he had taken once more, believing that what he had done was good enough to win Tang Wan-Yi's heart.

Frankly speaking, apart from flashing brute masculinity, young men knew few tactics on chasing girls in China's vast countryside, where some tribes continued to resort to kidnapping the bride. The prevailing practice of arranged marriages had totally eliminated the need for courtship, which deprived young people of the natural ability to search for their mates. Even as new cases of spontaneous love emerged, it was still considered a taboo for an unmarried young man to meet an unmarried young woman in private. Few people knew how to proceed and still fewer understood the art of dating. The difficulties Sheng faced went beyond those conventional ones. He, a country boy, was chasing a city girl at the nation's most prestigious university. Luckily, Sheng's extensive readings of Chinese history provided him with ample stories about traditional love affairs and old-fashioned courtship tactics. He carefully screened the stories he knew, and told Tang Wan-Yi the ones he believed would have the desired effect. The first story he told her involved his native province and was about a love affair between a northerner and a southerner, which Sheng thought would be a particularly fitting analogy of their relationship.

Many years ago, Sheng began, the young man Mu Rong came on a boat with his merchant father, Mr. Mu, sailing from the north to the south. After a long journey of three hundred miles, they docked at Wuhan. Mr. Mu started to teach the son how to conduct the business of buying and selling, which he thought was more important than reading and writing, which most boys were learning. The son followed the father's instructions in business every day, but continued to practice his literary skills every evening, thinking he would become a good scholar in the end.

One night, the father went out for a gathering at a friend's house. While the son was reading some poems on the boat, he saw some shadows flashing against the window. He stepped out from the cabin, only to see a young girl about fifteen years old on the deck. She was very pretty but quickly walked away into the darkness.

Father and son completed their business over the next several days. They pulled the anchor, and sailed back to the North. They stopped by a lake one day for a rest. That night, father went on shore to visit a friend and the son stayed behind to guard the cargos. An old lady came aboard and said to the young man that he was responsible for her daughter's illness. Stunned, Mu asked for an explanation. The old lady said that her only daughter Miss White had become extremely sick since the night she heard him reading poems. She would not eat or drink, only thinking about Mu. Therefore, he must marry her or she would certainly die, said the woman.

Mu was delighted to hear this for he did like the girl he had seen. But he said that his father might be against the proposal. Upset, the old lady insisted but to no avail. She felt deeply humiliated at his rejection. Before departing, she angrily said to Mu, "If you don't want to marry my daughter, your boat would not leave here, nor would you return to the North anytime soon." When the father came back, Mu told him about the old woman's visit and her marriage proposal. Mr. Mu laughed and said he did not know her and she must be joking. Father and son then went to bed.

The two woke up the next morning only to find out that part of their boat was now stuck in a pile of rocks under the water. Since floods often washed debris, sand, and rocks into the lake every year, the father said, a boat could get stuck sometimes. "No worry," said he, "you shall stay with the boat and I shall take the road back home to get money. I shall return next spring when the rising currents will allow the boat to float again. We then could sell our goods and make a profit a hundred times higher than usual, because our boat would be the first to reach the North." The father then left for his land journey.

When dusk fell, the old lady took her sick daughter to the boat, where the son was alone. "See what you have done to her? Now you must take care of her." No sooner had she uttered these words than she dropped the girl in his cabin and left. Mu slowly stepped over to the bed and, feeling sorry for the girl, asked how she was feeling. Miss White said, "I will languish if I don't see you, but feel so bashful when I do." Her sweet expressions and pleasant voice delighted Mu, who was willing to do everything to help her recover. She said, "If you would please recite the poem in the special tone of 'Royal Palace' by Master Wang three times, I would be cured." Mu was more than glad to oblige and he began:

As leaf after leaf the exquisite silk robes fold and flow,
To the opposite side the golden phoenix and silver geese go.
Dancing to the left and dancing to the right unveil the symbol,
That ten thousand years of peace appear in the middle.

When he recited the poem the second time, she was able to sit up to join him. As they read the poem together for the third time, she was completely healed.

Mu and the girl started to live on the boat as a happy couple until one day, when Miss White seemed sad. When Mu asked why, she said that his father was about to return, and he would not approve of their marriage. "What shall we do then?"

"I'd better leave the boat for now to wait until you can convince your father."

"But where can I find you?"

"Please don't worry. I will find you." Then Miss White disappeared.

Mr. Mu returned and was not pleased to hear the son's plea, thinking that he must have been fooled by some prostitute. He was nonetheless satisfied after checking out that all the merchandise on board was intact. A few days later, it started to rain, and the rising waters finally made the boat afloat again.

Father and son returned home, unloaded the boat, disposed the cargo, and made a great deal of profit. The son became very sick, however, due to the separation from his beloved Miss White. No matter how many doctors were consulted, none could find a cure. Mr. Mu was really concerned. After he learned the real reason for his son's illness, he decided to take the son in their boat to go south again, looking for the girl. After they arrived at Wuhan, they searched all the nearby regions along the Yangtze, asking every mariner and fisherman they met. Nobody could tell them anything about the old woman and Miss White.

"Where were they? Did they know that the Mus were looking for them? Were they hiding from them?" This time it was an impatient Tang Wan-Yi who interrupted.

"They were the rare white dolphins living in the Yangtze River, one of the few surviving mammals in the freshwater rivers of China," Sheng Bao responded.

"What a beautiful tale. What happened to them in the end?" she asked.

"Well, according to legend, the mutual affection that Mu Rong and Miss White had for each other moved the heavens, which approved their union. Thus they were finally declared husband and wife, had several kids, and lived happily thereafter."

6

"Nonsense!" Tang Shu-Hai was offended when his daughter recounted Sheng Bao's story, and how he was planning to marry her. "The cheap fable from *Strange Tales from Liaozhai* by Pu Songling. Don't you see, Sheng Bao was using the Miss White tale to seduce you?"

"Daddy, that's not nice. I am only asking for your opinion. He was not seducing me, and I can't be seduced."

"Living together before marriage, isn't that enough? What else did he say to you?" a suspicious Tang Shu-Hai persisted.

"He told me another tale," the daughter said calmly.

"Another tale!" the father's eyebrows were raised.

"Yes. He said that a young man saved a wounded deer in the forest. The little deer was in fact a fairy. When she grew up and met the young man again, she asked him to marry her."

"See, that's what I mean. Seduction, total seduction! No nice guy should tell a girl such racy stories, especially when she is not married."

"Daddy, I don't understand why you are so upset. I said I would like to know what you think on this matter. I thought you had a good impression of Sheng Bao."

"Yes, I did. But look at this and read it." Tang Shu-Hai pointed to a newspaper on the table.

She picked it up and saw the headline in bold letters: "Beauty Queen Camellia Killed by Her Suitor at the Astor in Shanghai."

"So?" Tang Wan-Yi was perplexed.

"So, it's a dangerous world out there. You are a young girl and you have to learn how to protect yourself." Her father tried to control his emotions.

"So you are saying that Sheng Bao could be a murderer?" she said.

"I'm not suggesting that at all. You know that, don't you? Your mom and I have only one child and that's you. You are our dearest and you are our life. We can't even bear the thought that you would get hurt because of some careless silly mistake."

"I know, Daddy. I love you too. I love you and Mom." Tang Wan-Yi's voice softened.

"Besides, marriage is a very serious matter. If you make the wrong choice, it can ruin your whole life," Tang Shu-Hai began to explain patiently, as he had done many times before.

"I know that too, Daddy. I know you love me and therefore you care about my marriage and future." Tang Wan-Yi was, after all, a very innocent girl who enjoyed the warm protection of her parents.

"Okay, I am glad to hear that. Then, shall we hold off our decision for the moment? And please allow your old-fashioned parents to have more time to think it over, about your date and the relationship between you two," Tang Shu-Hai suggested calmly, having regained his composure.

"Of course, Daddy. I am not that desperate to get married," said Tang Wan-Yi candidly. She bade good night to her parents and went back to her room.

"Why were you so rough on our daughter?" Tang Shu-Hai's wife, Peng Xiao-Mei, finally opened her mouth, after maintaining her silence throughout the whole conversation.

Born in a small village in Northern China, Peng was a short, frail, and very traditional Chinese woman with bound feet. She had had an arranged marriage with Tang Shu-Hai, who was also a country boy. As time went on, he became a learned scholar while the illiterate Peng remained a housewife, whose fragile health was steadily declining. She never said anything disagreeable to her husband whenever there was a third person in the room, including in front of their daughter. She strictly observed the traditional harsh rule that the wife should never contradict her husband, no matter what. Once in private, however, she would speak up her mind because she knew that Tang Shu-Hai was a very good husband and father. He was loyal and loving, both as husband and father, and she trusted him to always act in their best interests.

"You don't like Sheng Bao because he is from the countryside?" Peng tried to find out.

"Not at all," Tang Shu-Hai responded. "You and I are both from the countryside too. Why should I bother?"

"Then why were you so upset about those stories? You know, as much as I do, country folk always tell racy stories and dirty jokes," the wife reminded him. "That's what young people—well, even old people—do when they are courting."

"Of course, I know," said Tang Shu-Hai, who understood perfectly that telling indecent stories was a universal pastime for all ages and both genders in most places across the country. But he wished that his future son-in-law could be a person of a different caliber and with a more refined taste.

Besides, he did have a really serious reason not to be thrilled about Tang Wan-Yi's relationship with Sheng, but he could not decide whether he should tell any of them about it.

Long after the couple went to bed, Peng could feel that Tang was still awake. Something was bothering him, and she wanted to know what it was. "You can tell me what's going on and why you are still upset," she whispered.

Tang held his breath for a while and finally said to Peng, "I have received a death threat in the mail and you must promise not to tell Wan-Yi."

Peng put her arms around her husband as if to prevent him from slipping away. She now understood why her husband did not like the idea of Tang Wan-Yi getting too close to Sheng. One death threat in the family was enough. There was no need to endanger the well-being of their only child, who might have gotten a little too deep in her relationship with another revolutionary. It was a dangerous world out there, as her husband had said. Tang Shu-Hai finally fell asleep, while Peng started to worry about her husband and daughter, and their family's future.

Chapter 8

Action

1

"THE MORE YOU FEAR IT, THE FASTER IT COMES." WHEN THE PARTY gave Sheng Bao his first task, he knew that he had to work with the person he had been avoiding—Tang Wan-Yi's father, Tang Shu-Hai. The party instructed them to organize the railroad workers and to instigate strikes at the most important transportation artery in China—the Peking–Hankou Railroad. Clearly, the party's plan was to duplicate what the Russians had done in their revolution, which started with workers' uprisings in urban centers. Nobody knew whether the same strategy would work in China, but it was worth trying when no apparent alternative was available. Thank goodness, while the party told them to work as a team, it also instructed Tang Shu-Hai, who lived in Peking, to focus his efforts on the northern section of the railroad, and Sheng to concentrate on the southern terminal of the railroad—Hukou, which was next to where he lived in Wuhan just across the Yangtze River. While the two should collaborate, they did not have to face each other every day.

Modern railroad in China was not much older than young Sheng, and the earliest ones had ceased to exist by the time he was born. Shortly after the construction of some experimental railroad tracks, they were promptly

126

dismantled because of the psychological fear their monstrous presence had created among ordinary citizens and mandarins alike. Sheng was a teenager by the time the Peking–Hankou Railroad was completed, and it proved to be an extremely profitable enterprise. The success of the railroad led to a fierce competition for its control, involving local businessmen, big merchants, regional warlords, governmental officials, and foreign investors. Everybody wanted a big share of the pie, which was never large enough for their appetites. The growing railroad business brought employment opportunities to local communities, and several big and small towns along the line—especially Changxindian (near Peking), Baoding (Hebei Province), Zhengzhou (Henan Province), and Hankou (Hubei Province)—provided many jobs for engineers, operators, mechanics, firemen, conductors, porters, repairmen, servants, and common laborers. These skilled and unskilled workers constituted a significant portion of the emerging working class in the three provinces. But changing them into militant proletarians was not as easy as Marx and Lenin had prescribed.

When Sheng set foot for the first time in a shantytown of railroad workers, he was shocked to see the same kind of suspicion that he had encountered at the Peking University campus. From the way those workers looked at him from head to toe, he instantly understood that he was regarded as an outsider, who would be treated accordingly. As soon as he opened his mouth, they laughed at his rustic tongue, his affected urban tone, his supposed intellectualism, and his inability to understand their slangs and cryptic euphemisms. When he asked them about the oppressed status of laboring men, they retorted, "We earn a buck a day here—ten times more than we used to. How much do you earn, pal?" Sheng was too embarrassed to answer because he didn't have a regular job. As a full-time professional revolutionary, he survived on the one hundred yuan he received from the party every month to cover his living costs and organizational activities.

Dodging the question, he then proposed to help them organize. "Thank you. No, thank you," said they, "We have had our own organizations for a VERY long time." What they meant was that they had numerous fraternities, associations, and clubs primarily based on their birthplace and hometown connections, such as the Henan faction, Hubei faction, Hunan faction, and Fujian faction. What they did not mention was the various clandestine organizations they belonged to, such as the Hungs, Tongs, Triads, Brothers, Fellows, Masons, Purples, Blues, Crimsons, Knives, Daggers, Lotus, Chrysanthemums, and Secluded. Nor would they reveal the existence of dozens of small cliques and infamous gangs secretly controlled by local thugs in their neighborhood.

The next day Sheng went to visit one of their clubs, where no fewer than fifty workers gathered. Some of them were playing cards, some playing majiang, some drinking, and the rest smoking, watching the games, or eating sunflower seeds. As he was about to inquire how one could join the club, two big men— one with a small head and the other with massive tattoos—came over and said, "That's easy, mister. It depends on how much you want to bet on the games." They then dragged Sheng to the majiang table. "Sorry, sir. I don't play majiang," he said, struggling to get out of the predicament. The two men laughed wryly and pushed him out of the door, yelling, "If you can't play the games, don't ever come here!" Sheng persisted in visiting the club several times but failed to make any progress. Disheartened, he thought to himself, "No matter how hard you try to liberate the workers, they simply don't want to be liberated." Were they really content with the life they had now? He wondered. Did they know that they were being exploited by the devilish capitalists? When would they ever understand their destined mission in history? When would they begin to show their class consciousness or to wage a proletarian revolution? The answers to these questions seemed elusive in the face of the cold reality before him.

Wuhan, notoriously known as a burning furnace for its excruciating heat and intolerable humidity, was a terrible place to live in summer time. Flies, mosquitoes, bedbugs, insects, centipedes, and sometimes even snakes invaded Sheng's bedroom, making him sleepless day and night. In desperation, he would sometimes run away to Snake Hill to escape from the insects and get some cool breeze. When that offered no relief, he would jump into the Yangtze River to have a good swim, which would finally cool him down by midnight.

Appointed as the party's plenipotentiary, Dong Zi-Tian came to Wuhan to assess the situation there. He listened to Sheng's complaints and suggested that helping workers to improve their literacy might be a way to break the impasse. Because most railroad employees, including some of the highly skilled workers, were largely illiterate, Tang Shu-Hai and several members of the Peking branch, Dong informed Sheng, had set up an evening school at Changxindian. Although elementary and primitive, the evening school taught workers how to read and write some simple Chinese characters, something totally unthinkable for the laboring classes in the past. The educational program allowed Tang and fellow party members to gain considerable trust from the railroad workers, who gradually agreed to organize several associations under the party's control. The progress Tang and others had made was hugely significant, Dong told Sheng. Changxindian, previously an ancient township composed of two villages, Chang village to the South and Xin village to the North, was a critical pathway southwest of Peking. It now had a large industrial population, which was quite rare in China. From a traditional traveler's rest area outside Peking, it had become a major stop along the Peking–Hankou Railroad that, in addition to a passenger terminal, was home to several cargo stations, mechanical plants, maintenance facilities, and repair shops, all employing several thousand workers.

Dong's suggestion seemed feasible and Sheng indicated that he would definitely try the same strategy in Hankou. He would improve his efforts, Sheng promised, and would not fail in the task the party had given him. After Dong left, he could not help feeling that he was once again overshadowed by Tang and Dong, who always seemed to have better luck with their assignments than him.

Sheng was a quick learner who had matured a lot in recent years. A highly intelligent country boy from Boxwood, he was intimately familiar with the critical importance of personal relationships in one's life. Boxwood had taught him how to navigate the intricate networks of friends and foes among family members, clansmen and neighbors. The experiences he had from Wuhan and Peking to Shanghai taught him a great deal about perverse human nature at marketplaces, school classrooms, university campuses, party meetings, and the shantytowns of the laboring population. Everywhere he went, he was viewed and treated as an outsider. The natives, the educated, the elites, the wealthy, and even the poor workmen had their own circles of friends, who invariably pitied, looked down upon, laughed at, and excluded him. No matter how smart he was, a country boy from the bottom of society could never survive on his own alone, which Sheng Bao now understood perfectly. He must have a circle of his own friends who would always be loyal and supportive of him. This circle of people would be his lifeline, and the success or failure of his career would totally depend on it.

The sad reality was that Sheng had no acquaintance, no friend. He was not a native of Wuhan, where, after years of residence, he still had no strong ties with the locals. He did not even know the name of any common laborer on the railroad. He had no means to break that invisible yet impenetrable wall between him and those railroad workers he was supposed to organize.

Although Dong had remained calm and considerate throughout their conversation, Sheng could tell something was amiss. Both men were southerners, both were from the countryside, and both understood the extremely creative ways in which many rural folk conveyed messages of pride and superiority to each other, such as by a simple glance or a subtle demeanor. They had met at Peking University where Dong was a prized student in the eyes of the professors, and a highly visible student leader among his peers. Many girls loved him, including Tang Shu-Hai's daughter. Sheng, however, was no more than a humble employee, who served many but attracted the attention of none. This time round, Dong was Sheng's direct boss and had bluntly told him to learn from the Peking branch, of which Dong was also the official head. Sheng dutifully showed his obedience not his jealousy, lest any indiscreet gesture upset the plenipotentiary.

That night, swarms of mosquitoes and a deep sense of frustration, envy, and anxiety troubled Sheng for hours. Not until dawn did he finally make peace with himself, thinking, "I can't give up. I can't quit. I can't blame others. I can't allow them to laugh at me. I must show them that I can do the job. And I must try out some new strategy at the slums as soon as I can get there."

Sometimes miracles did happen. Just as Sheng was feeling desperate, he got the breakthrough he had been craving for. After missing the regular ferry he usually took every morning across the Yangtze to the Waterfront District on the other side of the river, he boarded another one, which stopped at a neighborhood in Hankou that he had never had a chance to visit. He asked several people for directions and finally found his way to his destination— the Riverbank Station, one of the biggest terminals of the Peking–Hankou Railroad. As he walked past the Temple of Prosperity (called the "Liu Family Shrine" by the locals), he unexpectedly ran into Uncle Sheng Bing. The uncle was as surprised and excited as Sheng was. The two quickly found a small tavern nearby and sat down to talk.

After they were separated from each other, Uncle Bing wandered for days looking for Sheng. He later drifted from place to place, but eventually settled in Hankou, where he found a job on the railroad. Now he was a small boss leading a gang of fifty manual laborers employed by the railroad company. Most intriguing but not entirely a surprise to Sheng, the uncle also reestablished contact with his organization—the Grand Fellowship. This meant that Uncle Bing could certainly introduce him not only to the labor force but also to the closed society he belonged to. Sheng would be an "outsider" no more. His face glowing with excitement, the young man was now confident that he would finally be able to penetrate into the totally unfamiliar territory of the urban working class. Overjoyed by this miraculous rendezvous with his beloved uncle, Sheng stood up and said loudly, "Waiter, your best liquor and dishes for my table!"

2

Sheng had good reasons to be envious of Dong, who had the best job among them all. No one would dispute that Lu Shi-Yan and Tang Shu-Hai were the most senior and best-known members of the party. Yet both had full-time jobs (Tang was on the faculty of Peking University and Lu had accepted the appointment as Secretary of Education in Guangdong Province), and could not pay close attention to the organization's day-to-day affairs. Dong was therefore assigned to preside over the first national congress on their behalf, and was elected as one of the three members of the party's national leadership committee. He was also the party head of the Peking branch, working closely with Tang on major undertakings in the North. As the party's representative, Dong was appointed the plenipotentiary of the Pan-Chinese Labor Associations, which was under the auspices of the Chinese Communist Party. He was authorized to travel around the country to inspect and direct the nascent labor movement in major cities, such as Shanghai, Peking, Zhengzhou, and Wuhan. Moreover, he was the director of the Russian Study Program and had the power to select those party members who would be sent to Moscow for training. Except for Sheng (who knew he had no talent in acquiring a foreign tongue) and Gong Pei-Zhi (who had decided early on to study in the United States), everybody in the party saw this program as a great opportunity and earnestly wished to be part of it.

Looking at the list of some thirty applicants in front of him, Dong knew he had an unpleasant task ahead. The party was so small and not everyone could go, or there would be no one else left. Nor everyone was suited to go, unless he could speak some Russian. Dong must cut down the list significantly, which could hurt their enthusiastic comrades. Since Professor Lu was far away, Tang asked Dong to conduct a preliminary review to eliminate the most unqualified candidates. He then asked Martin to help Dong make the final selection.

"Well, let's see who is first on the shortlist," Martin told Dong who had eliminated more than two-thirds of the applicants.

"Hou Shi-Suo," Dong responded. "Family background: urban poor. Education: none. Occupation: textile operative."

"Hmm, interesting. Good family background. Good working-class identity. But no education at all?"

"None. As you know, illiteracy is widespread in China and particularly among the laboring classes. However, as a textile worker in Shanghai, Hou is the only member of our party who comes from a working-class background."

"What a pity. Then, let's see how well he may do in the Russian Study Program. Next," said Martin.

"Tao Yin-Hu. Family background: farmer. Education: elementary school. Occupation: unemployed."

"The name sounds familiar."

"That's right. A year ago you saw him performing as Wu Song at Peking University."

"Yes, yes. He was quite a martial artist. Can he speak Russian?"

"I don't think so. Hopefully, he could perform just as well in the Russian Program." Dong paused and then suggested, "Learning Russian may not be his strength. Instead of sending him to Moscow, could the party send him to some military school in China, which may make better use of his talent?"

"That's a good suggestion. According to the Bolshevik experience, an armed struggle is unavoidable. The question is not whether it will happen but when. It's better to be prepared than be sorry. We will talk about this with Lu Shi-Yan, Tang Shu-Hai, and Si-Tu Wen-Liang."

"The next candidate is Lin Shi-Xiong from Hubei Province. Family background: landlord. Education: high school. Occupation: small merchant."

"Good education, but dubious family background and occupation. Do you know him?"

"No, I don't."

"Then, put his name aside for the moment."

"The next applicant is Mo Jia-Qi from Canton. Family background: landlord and merchant. Education: BA in history, *summa cum laude*."

"Well, that's impressive. Can he speak Russian?"

"Here he says he can read and speak Russian."

"Excellent. He definitely qualifies." Martin got excited. He had strongly pushed for this leadership training program because he was convinced that the Chinese could never accomplish anything unless they seriously improved their knowledge of Marxism and Leninism. Once he saw a university graduate, his usual concerns about family background and occupation surprisingly dissipated.

"Agreed. Mo is the youngest member of the party and is the most promising," Dong said in confirmation.

"Also from Canton is Gan Zu-Xun, a journalist. He was from a landlord family with a middle school education. No knowledge in Russian."

"Hmm, not good," Martin somehow frowned upon the words "landlord family" this time and said, "Next."

"The last two candidates are Song Pei and Meng Bo-Xian. Both are from Hunan Province, and both are from rural families. Both are high school grads, and both know some basic Russian."

"Intriguing. Are they related?"

"No, they are not related. But they do share very similar backgrounds, which is not uncommon in China," Dong explained. He could tell that something was bothering Martin, who seemed to be in a contemplative mode.

Martin was calculating: seven candidates, one illiterate, one elementary school, one middle school, three high school graduates, one college bachelor. One from the working class, a small merchant, a journalist, and one unemployed. The majority were from landlord or rural family backgrounds. Was this the reality that he had to deal with? Where were the proletarians of this country? How could it be called a communist party when none of its primary members was an industrial worker, save for one? Yes, the Communist Party in the Netherlands had many members from the bourgeois class. But it was also a party led by educated scholars, schoolmasters, and lawyers, such as Herman Gorter (poet), David Wijnkoop (son of a distinguished rabbi), Willy Kruyt (minister), Henri van Kol (engineer), Gerret Mannoury (mathematician), Willem van Ravesteyn (historian), Jan Schaper (artist), and Pieter Jelles Troelstra (lawyer). Where were the educated people of China?

Suddenly, Martin realized that Dong was looking at him, waiting for his decision. He tossed his head back to refocus his mind and said, "Okay, let's do this. You need to find a safe place to set up a classroom for the language training as soon as possible. For now, and except for Tao Yin-Hu, we can ask Hou Shi-Suo, Lin Shi-Xiong, Mo Jia-Qi, Gan Zu-Xun, Song Pei, and Meng Bo-Xian to come for the Russian classes. The final list shall be decided after the preliminary training is over."

3

Finding a place for the program was no problem at all. New schools appeared in Peking every day in this new era of novel ideas and rapid change. Rental business was booming, and the local newspapers were filled with commercials on a great variety of classes and education, from bus driving, policy academy, journalism, wellness, martial arts, foreign languages, massage, acupuncture, quilting, knitting, and embroidery to palm reading and soap making. It was the students who proved to be the bigger problem. When Dong saw them in person, he finally understood why no one should ever trust a résumé.

Hou Shi-Suo, the only member of the working class in the party, faked his credentials. Growing up in the Northern District across the Suzhou River, he lived in a narrow street close to several textile factories in the working-class community of Shanghai. But he was never a textile worker himself, nor did he ever have any steady employment. A neighborhood rogue, he made his living by harassing people and bullying others. Many women considered him highly attractive, since his elongated face was endowed with an exotic aquiline nose between two benign yet vigilant eyes. Medium-built, agile, dexterous, and extremely smart, he had learned to play numerous small tricks to become a street magician, which earned him a loyal following of scoundrels, rascals, beggars, orphans, cripples, pickpockets, streetwalkers, drifters, homeless people, and the like.

He commanded them the way a general would with his army, whose word was law, the definitive order, the absolute command, the last lifeline, and the final judgment. He could gamble like hell, fight like a devil, and get drunk like crazy. Admirers and detractors alike called him "Broken Finger," in reference to the half index finger on his left hand that he had lost in a street fight with a rival gang. A natural businessman, he made a small fortune by selling leftover fruit at street corners. In summer at dusk, his followers would bring him the discarded apples and pears from local stores they had collected at no cost. Using a tiny sharp knife of two and a half inches like a magic wand, he would peel every fruit in a few seconds, get rid of the defects, and slit the rest into small pieces to be sold at retail in the evening.

There was nothing he would not do if there were profit to be made, from buying and selling drugs to kidnapping women and smuggling children. He became a legendary sales agent in the cigarette business by sending out his numerous followers as venders to all corners of his territory. He gave them strict sales quotas without pay, and only told them to hit the targets by whatever means they saw fit. The disciples understood the message from their supreme boss, whom they regarded as their fabulous role model, his scandalous career notwithstanding. They went on to harass, bully, and push any passersby to purchase cigarettes, lest they were showered by the boss's angry spit and torrent of verbal abuse. Hou awarded those who had managed to meet the quotas with no cash but cigarettes, and his order for the next day would be to sell more cigarettes. For the brisk business and amazing sales volumes, Broken Finger received huge sums of commissions from the cigarette companies and kept all the money to himself.

Using his most loyal worshipers, Hou had built a wide but secret spy network comprised of busybodies, informants, bodyguards, taxi drivers, servants, cooks, maids, nurses, nannies, waiters, and waitresses at every shop floor, ship dock, police station, opium den, brothel, restaurant, marketplace, tea shop, movie theater, hotel, and dancing hall. He knew all the important businesspeople in his territory, including every bit of dirty secrets from their directors' meeting halls to their bedrooms and majiang tables. Although he had never worked as a regular employee for a single day in his life, he controlled the labor force in the neighborhood, where factory foremen had to consult him before hiring anyone. While in Peking, Hou was more interested in making contact with local gangs and learning new tricks from them, than attending the boring Russian classes.

When Lin Shi-Xiong came up to Dong one day and asked whether he could show him how to write with both hands, the latter was pleasantly surprised. He did not know where Lin got to know about his skill, but was pleased to oblige. "The key," said Dong as he was demonstrating how to use his left hand to write, "is to focus your eyes on the direction your hand should be moving, not the hand itself. You may feel strange at first, but will get used to it as you keep practicing. And you will soon find that it's not hard at all to write with both hands."

"So, what you are saying is that writing with either hand is simply a matter of habit?"

"Exactly. Everyone can do it if only you are willing to practice."

"Call me Shi-Xiong," Lin said and went on to discuss calligraphy and recent cultural events with Dong. Both were passionate admirers of several famous painters, calligraphers, and poets from the past. They recalled the tragic losses during the Boxer Rebellion when the allied troops from eight foreign countries pillaged the capital. The foreigners plundered royal palaces and princely estates, destroyed buildings and monuments, and looted hundreds of thousands of pieces of treasures like ancient paintings, manuscripts, porcelain, and bronze. "It's such a shame that today one has to go to the museums in London, Paris, Tokyo, and New York to see those rare and brilliant Chinese masterpieces," Dong sighed.

"I heard many eunuchs continued to steal treasures from the Forbidden City after the last Qing emperor was dethroned," Lin said.

"Yes, I have heard a lot of similar stories," Dong replied.

"Do you think it's true? Where could I find antique stores in the city?" Lin inquired.

"The Glaze Market in the Southern District has numerous antique shops," Dong said and then joked, "So, you are hunting for some treasure?"

"Not at all. I am as poor as a church mouse. But I would like to go and see. Peking is such an ancient city full of dynastic history and valuable artifacts. I will not miss the chance to see them while I am here." With that, Lin said goodbye and took off for the marketplace.

Dong could not tell whether their conversation marked the start of a mutually beneficial relationship. Lin somehow impressed him as a scholarly type who knew a great deal about Chinese history and culture. He followed closely the latest archeological developments, and knew the stories of the oracle bones and the Dunhuang caves like the back of his hand. But Lin also seemed to be a calculative person, who was never entirely honest about his true intentions. He came across as one who would study your background thoroughly and then designed a plan to approach you while keeping all the cards to himself. He would use you, get what he wanted, and dump you right afterward.

What kind of student was he? Dong wondered: an antique collector or a student of the Russian language?

4

The next morning, a loud pounding at the door woke Dong up. "Dong, you are the director of the training program, correct?" Song Pei burst in, shouting.

"Yes, yes, I am the director." Dong tried to calm him down, offering him a chair.

"I have to say this—you must expel Gan Zu-Xun from the program!" Agitated and emotional, Song was panting, his cheeks flushing, and his voice shaking.

"Please slow down. Tell me what happened," Dong said.

"He was fooling around with my wife!" Song said angrily, his broad mouth and thick lips quivering.

"Are you sure?" Dong had heard rumors about Gan's conduct, but he still wanted to know what Song had to say.

The two discussed the incident for half an hour. Song then left, still feeling upset. Dong pitied him. What a poor husband, he thought. He also pitied himself. "What am I? A family court judge?"

A young school graduate in his twenties, Song was the most serious student in the program. Tall and heavy in frame, yet mild in manners and meek in mentality, he got up early every morning as any dutiful beginner would and studied the Russian language all day—not an easy task for one who was married at sixteen and now the father of two boys.

Demanding a highly sensitive hearing ability and subtle use of the tongue, the Russian pronunciation troubled Song, who could never figure out how to speak the soft consonant correctly, let alone the inconceivable "L" sound at the end of the letter "P." The Chinese language stressed the importance of the different tones of the vowels, not the wide varieties of the consonants—thus making the Russian consonants sound inaudible and meaningless to him. Grammatical rules and mandatory variations based on gender, on singular or plural, and on the frequent shifting context of aspect, mood, and action of the verb further bewildered him.

Drastically different from any alphabetical language, the most commonly used Chinese characters comprised several thousand ideographs, which could be difficult to learn at first. But once they were chosen, their shape, form, and pronunciation in a sentence would not change any more. On the contrary, declension in the Russian language or the endless alterations in spelling and pronunciation, according to a series of rules, standards, and matrixes riddled with hundreds of exceptions and irregularities, confused Song, whose best years to learn an alien tongue had passed. An excellent student of Chinese classics, literature, and history notwithstanding, the adult Song was nevertheless deeply entrenched in the familiar mode of all the past formalities and finalities of his native language. This prior strength now turned into a big learning block against him.

Adding insult to injury, someone else was having fun with his wife behind his back while he was struggling to study. Dong now could certainly understand Song's frustration, which was not entirely without basis. Just a few days earlier, Dong also heard rumors that Gan had tried to seduce Hou's wife, who was, by everyone's estimation, a remarkably cheerful young beauty. It seemed, Dong thought, Gan had to be warmed to change his behavior or the program would be in jeopardy. He must talk to Tang about what needed to be done.

5

"Absolutely unbelievable!" Tang burst out as he listened to Dong's report. "We allowed them to bring their spouses to Peking so that they could concentrate on their studies. Look at what has happened. What a shame!" He agreed that the conduct of several party members was simply unacceptable, and asked, "What about Mo Jia-Qi and Meng Bo-Xian? How are they doing?"

"Mo, claiming he knew Russian all along, rarely showed up. He is said to be visiting his friends across town," Dong replied.

"Meng Bo-Xian?"

"Meng is at the program every day, but seems to be not in good spirits."

"Why? What happened to him?"

"He has just broken up with his girlfriend, I heard, and therefore has been quite down lately."

"See, Zi-Tian, we must have discipline and fortitude. We can't allow such bourgeois behavior and sentimentality to erode our party. We must do something to stop this dangerous trend."

"Of course. I will find a chance to talk to the program participants."

"No, no, no. Don't wait for a chance, but talk to them immediately right after you return."

"No problem. I will do as you say," Dong agreed, feeling that, as the program's director, he was partly responsible for the present disarray.

Moments later, Tang regained his usual composure and said to Dong, "On second thoughts, I will go and talk to them. The success or failure of the program lies in their attitude and behavior, for which they must promise to rectify."

"Shu-Hai, I can talk to them. I am the director and I am responsible for the situation," insisted Dong, who was very grateful for Tang's strong support. Seniority was a big deal in Chinese society. Although Dong was the program's official administrator, many thought he was too young for the post. Tang's presence would certainly demonstrate that the most respected senior member of the party was fully behind this young director.

"Don't worry, Zi-Tian, I will go," Tang continued. "You have another job, which needs you to go to Tianjin tomorrow."

Realizing he had a new mission, Dong relaxed and asked, "Sure. Please tell me about it."

Tang took out a small packet and a letter from a drawer and handed them to Dong, "Wen-Liang asked me to give these to you. All the instructions are in the letter."

"Wen-Liang! How is he? Haven't seen him for a long time." Dong was excited to hear about his friend.

"He is fine. He is on an important mission," Tang replied but did not elaborate.

Dong understood the party rules for these matters and did not push for more information. He simply said, "Good to know that. I will leave for Tianjin tomorrow."

6

Si-Tu Wen-Liang's message had two parts. Dong went to meet the branch members in Tianjin and delivered Si-Tu's first message. The second message was contained in that small packet, which Si-Tu wanted Dong to give to Teng Wan-Chun.

It had been more than a year since the long overnight talk between the two, which cemented their friendship. As Dong walked toward Nankai, all the warm memories of that meeting came back, as if it happened yesterday. Tianjin had grown significantly. New streets were extending to the suburbs, where silence was giving away to noisy traffic and bustling commercial activity. Once a desolate path hiding in the wilderness, the old road from the South Gate to the university was now crowded with pedestrians, buses, and wagons. The willow and poplar trees were much bigger and taller now than the last time he saw them. He felt that he could see the Dragon Lake lying far away where healthy, strong, and tall lotus plants were visible. It was there that Si-Tu reaffirmed his love for Teng. What a perfect couple, Dong said to himself. Genuinely happy for his friends, Dong had also secretly wished that he might one day have a romantic experience that was as beautiful and memorable as theirs.

Nankai University had also expanded in size by adding more classrooms and new buildings. Far more students and professors were walking on the campus now than a year ago. At the heart of the university, the carefully planted trees nicely lined around a big rectangular pond, reconstructed from a swamp, and their vigorous foliage and lush canopy had begun to show the great charm that the designer had originally envisioned. The only thing that had not changed, it seemed to Dong, was that students still stopped in front of the mirror and double-checked their uniforms and appearance before entering the university compound.

Finding Teng was not as easy as Dong had thought, even though he had met her before. Nankai had so many departments, divisions, and branches at different locations that he finally had to enlist the help of one of her colleagues. She took him to Teng's dorm, which was a tiny single room in the housing quarters for the staff. The place was eerily quiet and she lay motionless in a small bed, which was about half the size of the room. Under the dim light, Dong could see how sick Teng was. A lively and lovable person just a year ago, she had now been reduced to a colorless skeleton. Not until she heard her colleague whisper "Si-Tu's friend is here" did Teng manage to open her eyes. Patently in extraordinary pain, she wanted to sit up but any small exertion cost her a great amount of energy, of which little was left in that frail and shrinking body.

"Please remain as you are. No need to sit up, please." Dong wanted to stop her. But she succeeded after several attempts.

Realizing that the longer he stayed, the more pain Teng would suffer, Dong cut to the chase. "Wen-Liang is on a mission, and has asked me to come and give you this packet."

Dong then helped Teng to open it. Inside there was a letter and something else in a paper wrapping.

She began to read the letter, and tears immediately rolled down her face. She sobbed uncontrollably. Neither her colleague nor Dong said anything, nor did they attempt to console her, knowing some emotional release might be good for her. Finally she turned to the wrapping and tried to open it, fingers shaking. Her friend helped her and an exquisite small lacquer box was revealed. She opened the lid, finding a pair of heart-shaped beans attached to a soft light blue silk pad. Bathed in brilliant crimson, the beans were almost a quarter-inch in diameter, which she had never seen before. She turned to the part of the letter where Si-Tu explained,

I stopped by an ancient town in remote Southern China and found the beans at a marketplace. They are the famous "love beans" often mentioned in folklore and legends. Locals said that they would grow only on giant love trees, which could develop long branches and deep roots to reach and hug each other. Once ripe, they would never perish or discolor. I have nothing valuable for you, but this pair of love beans may be the most fitting gift I can give to you—my dear and dearest.

He ended his description by citing a popular rhyme:

Pretty little love beans,
Would you keep it a secret?
Please bring her this message,
How ye I miss.

Tears were once again running down Teng's cheeks as she recited the other half of the same rhyme:

Pretty little love beans,
Would you keep it a secret?
Please bring him this message,
How ye I miss.

The friend helped her to lie down, fearing that she had become too emotional and exhausted for the day. Yet Teng insisted that Dong tell her everything about Si-Tu. She was not tired, she insisted, and wanted to know everything about her Wen-Liang.

Dong began to relate the details of Si-Tu's recent life and activities, some from his personal knowledge, some from stories he had heard from others, and some he simply made up to fill the gaps. He wanted to let Teng know what a wonderful man Si-Tu was, how much he was admired and respected by his colleagues, how he always had Teng on his mind, and how much he loved her.

Teng smiled. She understood that not every word she was hearing was true, but she was still very happy—it was as if she was making tangible contact with her Wen-Liang through those words. She promised to pen a reply and requested Dong to come back the next day to collect her letter.

Dong left with a heavy heart. He had met Teng a few times before, and, as Si-Tu had described, she embodied action, promise, hope, and life. But he could not believe what he had seen today: a beautiful girl who had completely succumbed to a terrible disease.

When Dong showed up the next morning, Teng had already passed away, but not before using her final moments and the last ounce of her energy to finish her letter to Si-Tu. It ended with these words:

I will go with you to see the beautiful lotus on Dragon Lake anytime you want to, and my soul will always be with you like the gentle breeze every spring would bring…

Dong cried. He cried for Teng Wan-Chun, for Si-Tu Wen-Liang, and for their unconditional devotion to each other. He didn't know how to bring this tragic news to his friend, and he was deeply worried that Si-Tu would be devastated when he knew that his beloved Teng was no more.

Chapter 9

Fusion

1

The party sent Si-Tu Wen-Liang to search for a safe place in Shanghai, which would serve as an underground national headquarters for the organization. A few days after his arrival in the city, he received the news of Teng Wan-Chun's death, but had no time to mourn the most painful loss in his life. He continued to work hard on the highly sensitive mission, and found out that all the leads provided by Hou Shi-Suo were useless. They were the names of local thugs, drifters, and jobless whose dubious behavior and heinous reputation made them totally unfit for involvement in the party's mission. Yet Si-Tu did not agree with his aide Cheng Chu-Li, who suggested severing all contacts with them. "You never know," he said, "they may turn out to be useful at some point in the future."

Si-Tu viewed people and life from a pragmatic yet constantly evolving angle. Everybody came to this world for a purpose, he believed. All had a particular role to play, no matter how inconsequential the person might seem at some point. Things could change, and sometimes even the most powerful elites might just need the help from the most humble. When he was a toddler, he closely observed how his young mother managed the large household. She ran a tight ship with sharp eyes and an open mind, but never with an iron hand. She understood perfectly everybody's ability and responsibility, from the maids and manservants to cooks and street sweepers. Some might be more important than others, but all could be useful at a certain juncture. He, as the general manager of this top-secret mission, must use all the skills he had and all the resources available, no matter how irrelevant they might seem for the moment, to establish a safe haven for the party.

Weeks went by and Si-Tu reported two things that had hindered his efforts. First, landlords were generally reluctant to accept a single man who wanted to rent a large house. Second, they were also quite suspicious of a renter who did not have any bank account but could afford to pay the high rent in cash for an extended term. To be absolutely safe, he suggested, these doubts must be eliminated from the start. The party agreed but its solution came as a shock: Si-Tu must get married right away.

For the first time in his life, Si-Tu felt so depressed that he asked Cheng to join him for a drink. He told him about the situation and asked Cheng for advice. "I think the party meant a fake marriage, which would not prevent you from having a real marriage later," Cheng said. "But how could I face Teng Wan-Chun, who just passed away recently?" Head down and shoulders shaking, Si-Tu sounded really sad and poor Cheng was thinking how he could share his superior's pain and predicament.

Losing the one you had desperately loved was heart-wrenching. Being forced to marry someone you didn't even know was akin to having your heart broken for a second time. Yet, as a member of the party, he had pledged his whole life and total loyalty to the cause, which required him to obey its orders and decisions unconditionally. How to help his friend resolve such conflicting emotions, Cheng had no idea. A much younger man than Si-Tu, he did not even have a girlfriend. He felt so sorry for his boss, whom he greatly respected. He also felt deeply embarrassed that he could not do or say anything to help Si-Tu at all. The only thing Cheng could do was to drink one cup after another with his boss until he passed out before Si-Tu did.

Miraculously, by the time the bride with the bank account arrived, Si-Tu had completely recovered from his agony. Neither the bride nor anyone else would suspect that anything out of the ordinary had ever happened. While Si-Tu was a sensitive man who could even be highly emotional at times, he was also the most disciplined and sensible member of the organization. As far as Cheng could tell, his boss had never lost his cool under any circumstances and possessed the most amazing ability of self-control. Deeply impressed when he saw for the first time how much his boss could handle alcohol, Cheng would never see Si-Tu get drunk again after that night.

When Si-Tu and Cheng met with Hong Shi-Mei, the boss's assigned wife, both men were impressed. She was such an attractive lady that Cheng believed the two would make a perfect couple. Under the permed pitch-black hair, Hong's lovely eyes shined as two bright gems. Her cute little nose on the oval face was endowed with a dimple on each cheek, making her smile acutely sweet, warm, and tender. While her small and pointed chin showed her innocence, her long, smooth, erect, and yet delicate neck spoke of her elegance, pride, and sophistication. Not quite twenty years old, Hong came from a big, rich family. Her mother was the fifth wife of the father, who did not like the daughter but nonetheless provided her with a good education. Not yet a party member, she belonged to the youth organization affiliated with the party. Her special upbringing, maturity, and sincerity about the cause landed her with this highly unusual assignment. To Si-Tu's delight, Hong liked drama as much as he did and had performed in some of the same plays as he had. They seemed to have much in common in terms of their family background and experience, which would stand them in good stead as they prepared to play their respective roles in the bogus marriage.

The strategy worked and every landlord they met seemed to have realized instantly the potential steady income from the newlyweds—the happy merchant and his young, beautiful wife. Every landlord tried every trick in the book to convince this wonderful couple to choose his place as their new residence. Here were the amenities, one pointed out, and there were the discounts he was willing to give. They preferred peace and quiet? No problem. He would never show up here again unless they asked him to. Their credit history? Oh, please, no need to mention that at all. The check issued by the British Jardine Matheson Co. said it all, which was more than enough to cover their initial payment and security deposit. When would the place be available? Of course, any time they pleased. Well, in fact, the landlord corrected himself by saying that his place would always be ready for them whenever they were ready to move in.

A few trips around the city allowed Si-Tu, Cheng, and Hong to compare the different locations they had visited. For good communication and transportation, Si-Tu avoided the areas beyond Suzhou River, even though many plants, factories, and working-class residences could be found there. For better cover and legal protection, Si-Tu finally chose a place in the English Settlement, where the rule of law was much better than the districts controlled by Chinese authorities. Situated at the end of a small lane north of New Gate Street in a middle-class residential community, the family house was an enclosed three-story building, providing them with enough space and a quiet environment for their covert activities. The house had several entrances, which would be useful during an emergency. It was also adjacent to a burgeoning industrial neighborhood only several blocks away, where the maze of working-class houses could provide them with additional places to hide or conduct clandestine actions.

Si-Tu then realized they needed one more thing to complete the setup: a housekeeper. Hong was a dedicated comrade who promised to take care of all household matters. But her role was that of a fair lady of the house. For safety reasons, Si-Tu could not allow her to do all the household chores like a real housewife. A merchant family should hire someone to do the manual work, lest it arouse the suspicions of the landlord and their neighbors. His request, precautionary in nature and yet entirely reasonable, was granted without delay.

Soon after they moved into the new rental place, the housekeeper arrived. She was Lu Shi-Yan's wife, Yan Yan.

2

After two years of persistent agitation and encouragement, workers of the Peking–Hankou Railroad finally went on strike as the party had hoped. Yet the long-anticipated action started not from Peking or Hankou but in Zhengzhou—the provincial seat of Henan, which lay south of Peking and north of Hankou.

Considered by many the birthplace of Chinese civilization, Henan had some of the earliest archeological sites, where countless prehistorical treasures had been uncovered, including tombs and burial grounds, grain production and storage, community structure and housing, royal palaces, city walls, oracle bones, weapons, earthenware, utensils, tools, metal work, bronze, and much more. Zhengzhou, along with Changxindian and Hankou, was established as one of the three primary depots of the Peking–Hankou Line, which ran from the north to the south. In recent years, the newly constructed Long-Hai Railroad (going east/west) also selected Zhengzhou as its hub, which connected the east coast to the remote western inland provinces of Shaanxi and Gansu. Thus, the two transportation systems crisscrossed at Zhengzhou, making it the most convenient railroad stop that could go in all four directions at the very heart of Central China. Anyone with political power understood the vital importance of Zhengzhou depot, just like the organizers of the railroad workers, who selected the city to launch the largest industrial union in history. The strike was triggered by the warlord government's decision to thwart a plan in Zhengzhou to shepherd all the workers and employees of the Peking–Hankou Railroad into one big union, which would pose a huge threat to various warlords in the region and their foreign backers, who had invested heavily in these railroads. If the plan succeeded, this single union of more than thirty thousand employees could control seven hundred miles of railroad operations, and had the potential of shutting down major industrial, commercial, and military activities north of the Yangtze River.

Authorities in Northern China were seriously alarmed. General Wu, the head of the warlords who held the reins in government, originally positioned himself as a friend of labor. He acted as a patron for the railroad workers by offering them some small benefits every now and then, and even allowed them to set up clubs and evening schools. But he also saw himself as the patriarch of the workers, who must show nothing less than total obedience to him. A powerful new union would certainly undermine his absolute authority over the railroad lines, which were vital to his finances and military mobility. He sent in several thousand soldiers to Zhengzhou to quell any attempts to set up such a union. Clashes between soldiers and workers ensued at meeting halls, local streets, hotels, and restaurants. Many workers and their delegates were roughed up and injured. Realizing the serious danger they were facing, union organizers decided to cancel the inaugural meetings in Zhengzhou, and moved them to Hankou to continue with their efforts to form the new union.

Hankou turned out to be no more favorable than Zhengzhou, as the city was controlled by warlord Xiao. As ordered by General Wu, Xiao ordered his troops to block the Riverside Station, prohibiting any union activity in the area. Yet the success of two recent brief strikes—one taken by the railroad employees of the Long-Hai Line, which lasted a week and the other by the rickshaw men in Hankou, which lasted for two days—gave union activists false hope that the authorities were bluffing, and they could be defeated in no time by the powerful alliance of railroad workers. A general strike was then called, which brought to a stop to several thousand railroad cars, civilian and military, passenger or cargo, making the entire Peking–Hankou Line look like a giant ghost town. The infuriated warlords poured in more troops to force workers at every facility to return to work.

While trying to escape the onslaught by armed soldiers, several workers in Hankou were shot dead. Sheng Bao quickly assessed the situation and told the workers to withdraw. It was pointless to let the unarmed workers face hundreds of soldiers fully equipped with rifles, bayonets, hand grenades, and machine guns. As he and many workers were leaving, Uncle Sheng Bing saw the soldiers marching toward them. He ran as fast as he could to warn Sheng, but was shot in the back. Uncle Bing fell immediately to the ground and died in a pool of blood.

Several workers who witnessed the shooting dragged Sheng away and ran like hell until they reached a safe place a good half-hour later. Only then did the workers get a chance to tell Sheng that his uncle was dead. Sheng froze as he tried come to grips with Uncle Bing's sudden demise. As a professional revolutionary, he knew this was the reality he must face every day. He must be prepared to be harassed, abused, arrested, tortured, or killed at any moment by the government, police, soldiers, and their supporters. This was the price that any revolutionary must be willing to pay for the sake of the cause. No pain, no gain. Sheng just could not believe that he would have to pay such a price so soon, one that involved someone so dear to him.

Yet Sheng was surprised that he did not feel like crying, for reasons he could not explain. Life was transient in nature, while death could happen to anyone, anytime, anywhere, and for any reason, good or bad. Unfortunately, human life meant little throughout most of Chinese history, especially for the lower classes. Like everyone else who was quite familiar with this bitter truth, Sheng was not totally numb, nor was he utterly shocked at his uncle's death. Or, perhaps, he possessed some unique ability to rationalize such an ultimate sacrifice. No matter how brutal the reality could be, he could deal with the tragedy by an enormous inner strength, which could uplift him from a sorrowful stage to a normal calmness in no time, as if he was immune from any woeful feelings that most people would have at a time like this. Sheng calmed down quickly and went on to discuss the next step with his workers.

The general strike ended in failure after three days. All told, at least forty-five dead, several hundred wounded, fifty-seven of them seriously, and over two hundred arrested and imprisoned at fifteen stations along the Peking–Hanou Line, making the strike the bloodiest event in modern-day Chinese labor movement. No railroad strike ever occurred again, and only a handful of industrial strikes would take place in the next several decades.

Less than two weeks later, another piece of bad news came. The workers' strike and unrest at Changxindian near Peking were also brutally suppressed by General Wu and his troops. Worse, Tang Shu-Hai got arrested. Charged as a Russian spy by Wu's secret police, he was sentenced to death by a hastily assembled martial court, and quickly executed. The party lost one of its most respected leaders, whose death set off a huge public protest in Peking. He was buried after a long funeral procession consisting of his students, friends, colleagues, and several hundred ordinary citizens in the city. Tang Shu-Hai's wife, Peng Xiao-Mei, could not bear the blow and passed away a month later. In this tumultuous times of fast-moving events, Tang Wan-Yi suddenly lost both parents. Devastated and overwhelmed, she could no long stay in the same city where they had died; she came down to Wuhan to look for Sheng.

What a reversal of fortune. Only a little more than a year ago, Sheng had been afraid to see Tang Wan-Yi and meet her family. He knew that his humble rural background and unsophisticated family could not meet the expectations that Tang Shu-Hai had for his future son-in-law. Now, Sheng had suddenly become the only person Tang Wan-Yi could count on in this world. "Maybe this is a good sign," Sheng reasoned, "that I am pretty lucky to have the good fortune to escape the dangers while receiving blessings at the same time." Maybe it was all predestined and he was protected for something—something bigger and larger than any individual could hope for in this world. Yes, he could be special and he could be destined to become not only a person of good fortune but also a truly important man.

Without much discussion, Sheng took Tang Wan-Yi to his residence and the two began to live together as husband and wife.

3

The Russian Study Program's decision to send Meng Bo-Xian to Moscow did not make him any happier than before. All his colleagues saw him as a pathetic fellow who was always feeling sad due to one reason or another. The family fortune had greatly declined because of its poor management by his father, Meng would relate to his friends. Growing debts and the family's falling reputation weighed heavily on the mother, who became seriously depressed and committed suicide when he had only been seven years old. The father abandoned all the children, who were sent to live with several relatives in different places. The family was completely shattered and Meng became a foster child, moving back and forth among the families of four kinsmen in three different cities in a decade. They fed him but made him understand in no uncertain terms that he was not to stay with them forever, or to compete with their own children in matters of inheritance and favors. His female cousin, the only member of the clan who showed some genuine feelings for Meng, confessed that she could not marry him even though she loved him. Family pressure forced her into a betrothal with a man twenty years her senior, who was believed to be a propitious choice for her even though she had never met him. Love was such a pitiful matter, such a pretense, such a delusion, such an abused word, such an empty notion, and such a luxury for a person like him. In fact there was no real love in this world, Meng concluded.

Apart from Meng, the other three who were selected to go to Moscow were Mo Jia-Qi, Lin Shi-Xiong, and Song Pei. Hou Shi-Suo, a restless street hustler who could never sit still for more than half an hour to focus on his studies, was sent back to work on local assignments in the party's southern bureau in Shanghai. So was Gan Zu-Xun, whose misconduct with several women led to his dismissal from the program. Both men believed Dong Zi-Tian was the one who blocked their advancement and thus hated him immensely, even though they had no choice but to obey the party's orders.

The original plan was for Martin to lead the small team to Moscow and help them settle there for a year-long study program under the Comintern's auspices. But a new order came suddenly, which required him to go to Canton immediately for an important meeting with Lu Shi-Yan. Dong was then reassigned to lead the group on the long journey to Moscow.

Just as Dong fretted over how to cope with Meng's perpetually gloomy mood on the cross-continental journey, he was delighted to discover that, except for the serious but reticent Song, the other two members were fantastic storytellers. An astute student of Chinese dynastic history, Lin could rattle off an amazing amount of details about court struggles and royal infightings from dawn to dusk. And looks could be deceiving. Mo's youthful face and crew cut betrayed little about how smart he actually was. Never missing a chance to shine in a crowd, big or small, he was not about to be overshadowed this time either. Sentence by sentence, his tales rivaled those of Lin's as Mo recounted the intimate lives of the most famous and powerful ranging from Alexander the Great, Caesar, Peter the Great, Napoleon, Washington, and Bismarck to Elizabeth, Maria Theresa, and Catherine the Great.

Partly tired and also to stop the escalating tensions between the two rivals, Dong asked, "Why haven't our Han Chinese produced some great people like these lately?"

"Because we have been beaten too many times," said Meng, "first by the Manchus and then by the devilish Europeans."

"Yes, we do need our own strong men and powerful leaders," Lin proclaimed.

"That's true," Mo concurred. "Most Han Chinese followed the teachings of Confucius. We have too many armchair scholars than brave warriors on horsebacks."

After the train left the last stop Shanhaiguan by the Great Wall and continued further into Manchuria, everybody felt that Northeastern China was like a colony under foreign occupation. The Japanese ran the Southern Manchurian Railroad and the Russians the northern one. In their respective territories, no Chinese money was accepted, while Japanese stores, merchandise, and police were as numerous in Shenyang as Russian refuges, merchants, and newspapers in Haerbin. Everywhere inflation remained high and goods expensive, streets dirty, houses run-down, local residents ignorant, sallow, and emaciated. No one could believe that this was the place where the legendary Manchurian cavalry had risen to conquer Central China and establish the once formidable Qing Empire three hundred years ago.

As the train finally left China and was about to enter Russia, Dong knew that they were passing Tania's birthplace near Nerchinsk. A most tender feeling warmed his body and he looked eagerly through the windows, hoping to find any outstanding traces that might help him remember this foreign and yet sweet place where Tania had lived. He could not image what she might look like after almost three years, but he was certainly more anxious than anyone in the team to reach Moscow as soon as possible. That was where she was now, and that was where he could meet her again, something he had long yearned for.

Like a sick old man, the train made loud cranky noises, smelled terrible, and moved at a snail's pace. After three weeks on the road, the huge forests and rolling ridges still seemed endless, while the final destination remained hidden hundreds of miles away, invisible and unreachable. The journey was moving toward its last leg as much as it was searching for the world's end. Sliced by pristine rivers and lakes, the immense Russian landmass was matched only by the infinite blue sky, which never failed to display her eternal splendor. Few people would not be impressed or, as the Scottish philosopher Francis Hutcheson once said, "The ability to perceive beauty is a superior sense of man."

4

More than six thousand miles away in the opposite direction and deep down in Southern China, Martin rushed to Canton to meet Lu Shi-Yan. The Comintern had a major new policy toward China and the emissary's task was to convince the leadership of the Chinese Communist Party to form an alliance with Sun Yat-Sen's Nationalist Party or Kuomintang. A little apprehensive when he received the instructions, Martin knew the meeting would not be easy because Lu had rejected similar suggestions in the past. Besides, he also knew how stubborn Lu could be, and few people would be able to change his mind once it was made up.

A rather warm and exotic place near the South China Sea, Canton was the first port city to open trade with European countries in modern times and its streets were filled with more commercial activities than anywhere else Martin had seen in the rest of China. As he took a rickshaw and passed the Old Town to look for Concord Street, the bright colors of tropical fruit stands, the fresh smells of seafood stalls, the big crowds at neighborhood teahouses, and the unfamiliar, omnipresent, and soft voices in nasal Cantonese amazed him. The great varieties of dry goods, bamboo products, toys, tools, and imported merchandise lined hundreds more shops along the sidewalks. Everywhere, striking announcements in bold characters, giant posters, colorful emblems, company logos, business billboards, commercial signs, discount flyers, and sales banners attracted throngs of people, making the city a shopping paradise for country folk and city dwellers alike who could hardly resist the ubiquitous temptation of buying and selling.

Originally located close to a range of big hills and small mountains to the north, Canton expanded several times in history toward the south. Lu lived on the top floor of a three-story building in the New Town section adjacent to the Pearl River, which would have been a very nice piece of property just like one of those in the waterfront district in Rotterdam. Despite a big development project that entailed removing large sections of the old city walls for the construction of new roads in the last few years, Concord Street looked narrow, crowded, but super convenient. The building where Lu lived seemed to have been recently constructed, for the new paint on the wood frames and the stuccoed facade did not look as garish as often found on some older houses. The big difference was that, unlike the straight vertical designs of Rotterdam apartments, many of the newer buildings in Canton were constructed in the veranda style, which was very popular in the business and commercial districts in Southern China, as it was across Southeast Asia. To shield the stores from the scorching sun and to protect customers from sudden rainfall, the ground floor had porch-covered pathways that allowed shoppers to continue shopping rain or shine. The storeowner's family usually occupied the second and third floors, and, if there were any rooms to spare, they could be rented out to augment the household income.

As Martin entered the room, he was greeted not by Yan Yan but a woman whom Lu introduced as Liu Ming-Zhu. Martin never saw her before and suspected that she could be Lu's fourth wife. To avoid any indelicate intrusion into Lu's private affairs, Martin did not say anything, lest it further complicate his already thorny task. The windows were wide open, and both men could overhear customers bargaining with shop owners downstairs. Horns were blowing long and short, telling them that several ships were passing through the river. From time to time, a warm but pleasant breeze sneaked out from the riverbanks and wafted through the open windows, bringing the damp salty air from the nearby delta.

After Martin explained his mission, he saw Lu's thick eyebrows and bushy whiskers twisting—not a good sign. The professor's answer was indeed an absolute "no." "The two parties," Lu said, "have very different platforms, and comprised different kinds of peoples, fighting for different social and political goals. Such an alliance would not only be impossible but also self-destructive. The alliance would defeat our own purpose of forming a communist party in the first place, and would have a seriously disturbing effect on our organization. How are we going to explain it to our members about this muddling action? How are we going to maintain our own identity? How are we going to explain to them the need for our own very existence?" Lu did not mince his words.

"The alliance is a strategic move to gain strength and expansion, which will not alter the party's purpose and long-term goals," Martin explained. "At present China is not yet ready for a proletarian revolution and may not be for a very long time. Our current goal is not to liberate the working class in an immediate socialist revolution but to engage the much broader social movement aiming at China's national independence and territorial integrity in the face of foreign interventions and abuses," he said. "For these matters, the Nationalist Party and the Communist Party have a lot in common and the two parties certainly can collaborate as political allies. This new united front can consolidate the various forces of the revolutionary camp, expand our influence, and achieve success much faster than a single party is able to accomplish on its own," Martin stressed.

"But if the alliance and united front require our party members to join the Nationalist Party, many may leave our party for good," Lu insisted. "The party of Sun Yat-Sen is a much older and bigger countrywide institution. For those who want to join the Nationalist Party, they would see no need to maintain our own party as a distinct organization. For those who don't like the Kuomintang in the first place—and there are many of them in our party—they will be greatly disappointed and their morale will be so badly affected that many may never return to work for our party again." Lu continued to press his case.

In the end, neither one could persuade the other after several hours of discussion. Martin left Concord Street feeling dejected. He recalled how Tang Shu-Hai had helped to change Lu's opinion when they met for the first time several years ago. But now Tang was dead, Tania was not here, Dong was in Russia, and even Yan did not show up. Where was she, the zesty and feisty woman who could manage her husband Lu like no one else could?

5

Several interrelated individuals and offices controlled the direction of the Chinese Communist Party, and the erratic Lu was but one of them. He considered himself the godfather of the party and wielded his power like a patriarch. Few party members dared to challenge his authority due to the enormous prestige he had gained before the party was formed.

Yet, many also understood that the Comintern was his superior that could impose its orders on him. His position as the party's general secretary notwithstanding, Lu was only a regional official who had to obey the directives of the Comintern, which commanded the compliance and obedience of all national communist parties around the world. As the Comintern's emissary, Martin had as much authority as Lu in directing and supervising the Chinese Communist Party, even though this foreigner's formal position was that of a liaison officer, acting as an intermediary between the two sides. Ultimately, Martin was authorized to ensure the implementation of any orders from the Comintern, while the Chinese Communist Party, including its general secretary Lu Shi-Yan, had the obligation to comply with them.

Towering above them all was the Russian Bolshevik government, whose control of the purse strings provided it with the most effective leverage over a nascent organization overseas like Lu's party. Strong adherence to the same ideology did not guarantee perfect harmony. The national interests and foreign policies of the Bolshevik government might not exactly be in tune with what Lu had in mind for his party and country.

As a newly established regime under constant threats from several European countries in the West, the Bolshevik government also needed to secure the country's extensive borders in the Far East. A China under a unified government and sympathetic to the Russians would greatly benefit that goal, and the Bolsheviks had every reason to make sure the revolutionary forces in China unite and succeed. If that could materialize soon, it would help protect Russia's backyard and she would be free from the dangers of facing two or more enemies from both east and west. Such a grand scheme of geopolitics required a credible and yet friendly national government in China, which Lu's incipient Communist Party was unable to achieve anytime soon.

In fact, Lenin's Bolshevik government was pleased with the encouraging developments in Sun's Nationalist Party, and even promised significant financial and military support to the delegation Sun had sent to Russia, headed by his right-hand man, Chen Han.

Meanwhile, the Comintern duly adopted a new policy urging the Chinese Communist Party to join forces with the bourgeois Nationalist Party and to assist it in achieving power as soon as possible. Clearly, what was imperative for the Russians were their national interests, not the plans and aspirations that the Chinese communists had for the liberation of the working class in China.

This significant shift in outlook and policy threw Lu off guard, and he had to adjust his lofty ideological convictions to fit the pragmatic needs of the Bolsheviks. When idealism clashed with reality, the former could rarely win even in the camp of zealous communists, Russian or otherwise. By the same token, when internationalism was confronted with national interests, the latter would always prevail despite the grand rhetoric and tantalizing promises repeatedly made by the demagogue Lenin, the radical Bolsheviks, and their professed noble government of the proletariats.

Mr. Chamberlain, who was a typical Moscow snob, had wired Martin several times, urging quick action to ensure total compliance by the Chinese. Martin was caught between a rock and a hard place. Party rules required him to overcome any objection as soon as possible, while his intuition told him that the more he pushed, the harder the implacable Lu would resist. "Those damned bureaucrats and overlords in Moscow," Martin said to himself, "who always give you orders but never understand the myriad complications in this old and mystifying oriental country."

Unlike Chamberlain and the other ignorant but arrogant bureaucrats at the Comintern headquarters, Martin was well aware of the delicate balancing act that he had to play—to push for China's support without alienating the Chinese. Moscow did hope that the Chinese communists would obey her orders to help Sun's party to succeed, but it certainly did not want to lose their support and loyalty completely. After all, this obscure and insignificant organ might someday grow into something big in the future. And the smart Russians were willing to keep all their options open, to continue to bet on the Chinese communists, and not to abandon them right away.

So, how could Martin carry out his orders while avoiding total chaos, given the conflicting political policies and national priorities, and clashing personal egos? This conundrum tormented Martin for several days, until he woke up one morning with an idea. "Let me play the numbers game," he decided.

A few weeks later when Lu met with Martin again, he was surprised to see that Si-Tu Wen-Liang from Shanghai, Sheng Bao from Wuhan, and Tao Yin-Hu from Peking were also present. Lu instantly realized that the emissary had planned to outvote him. He quickly suggested that Gan Zu-Xun should join the meeting since every local branch except for Canton was represented. No one objected and the meeting began.

Martin opened with a detailed statement of the Comintern's instructions. Lu tried to hold on to his objections and everyone in the room understood the grave task before them—their deliberations would decide the party's fate one way or another for years to come.

Gan spoke first. As Lu's protégé, Gan agreed with everything that Lu had said. His deferential and monotonous performance surprised no one, for his lack of independence was well known within the party. Some believed him to be an opportunist, while others considered him a spineless character too meek to make any stand. Still some even went as far as to suggest that Gan learned how to flirt with women from Lu himself.

The masculine Tao then rose to speak, who was not a very articulate person. After a brief mentioning of the lately failed strikes in the North, he went on to confess that he was impressed by the training he had received from the military academy in Paoding, run by the nationalists. "I agree with the alliance," said he, "because I think a good military training can be useful for us in the future."

"I am not sure what is the connection between military training and the alliance," Gan interjected.

Nervously, Tao added, "I mean, our party really doesn't have the resources to provide any military training for now, and maybe for a very long time to come. Why not ally ourselves with the Nationalist Party, which could give us access to the necessary training provided by their existing military staff and facilities?"

"What you did not mention," Lu suggested, "is perhaps the potential of receiving commissions from the Nationalist Party?"

"Yah, yes," a flustered Tao hastily defended his proposition. "Receiving officers' commissions would allow us to control more troops. I don't see why this is wrong."

"Okay, this can be discussed later after we settle the alliance issue," Martin said. Hoping to move the discussion forward, he asked, "Who will speak next?"

"I would like to say a few words." Sheng stood up. Having never made any formal speech at a meeting like this, he was as nervous as Tao. "I agree with Tao Yin-Hu that a continued reliance on waging strikes by unarmed workers alone would not seem practical, as the recent tragedies on the Peking–Hankou Railroad have shown. We need strength, we must expand, and we have to become strong fast enough to prevent such tragic losses. There are two ways of expansion—one is through our own efforts and the other is through an alliance, which, I must say, are not mutually exclusive. You all know the stories of 'horizontal alliance' and 'vertical alliance' during the warring periods of our history, I am sure. The former is one of several weak kingdoms uniting against a mighty state, and the latter is one between a big kingdom and a small one uniting against their common enemies. No matter which model we choose to follow, forming an alliance can be a very important and useful strategy for our party at the current stage of development."

Sheng sat down, pleased that his speech went much more smoothly than he had anticipated; especially as his confidence grew toward the end, after realizing that everyone was listening carefully.

Now the meeting looked set to end in a two-to-two split, and because the proceedings excluded the emissary from voting, people turned to Si-Tu, whose stand would tip the balance of the debate. Si-Tu clearly understood the critical role he was about to play. In his usual calm manner, he began, "I am very conscious of the seriousness of the issues under discussion. I greatly respect the views expressed by Professor Lu Shi-Yan and Comrade Gan Zu-Xun. I also greatly respect the views and opinions expressed by Comrade Tao Yin-Hu and Comrade Sheng Bao. I would like to add that I trust that, in matters as grave as the ones we are now facing, the Comintern's new policy Comrade Martin has relayed to us represents the best interest of proletarians worldwide. We may need temporary adjustment and we may have to alter our present practices. We may even need to make some sacrifices by putting our long-term goals on hold. But all this is necessary for the greater good of the communist cause and for the ultimate success of the international working-class movement. For these reasons, I would agree that we adopt the policy of alliance."

6

Study, meeting, more studies, and more meetings, almost another year had elapsed before Dong Zi-Tian finally got a chance to visit Tania in Moscow one Saturday afternoon. He was pleasantly surprised when Tania gave him a warm and affectionate hug, which he had never received from anyone else before. He understood that, unlike most Chinese who shunned physical contact, it was customary for Westerners to hug each other as a form of polite greeting. Yet the wonderful feelings of close body contact and the inexplicable intimacy and warmth that came with it still amazed Dong, who, jolted by the fresh experience, began to appreciate the hugging habit. Sometimes, it seemed to this young man who had never received much affection other than from his mother in his childhood, body language was much more powerful, direct, and effective than any words in conveying people's feelings and emotions. The passionate hug from Tania nearly electrified him from head to toe, while her soft hair strands were kissing his face and the slight scent of her perfume caressing his senses.

The two looked at each other for a while. Both smiled and could see happiness in each other's eyes. Tania noticed Dong's ardent and adoring gaze. She understood what it could mean and said, "It's so good to see you."

"You too," said he and then froze, feeling silly.

Tania smiled again. "Do you have any plans for the weekend?"

"No, not much," Dong responded mechanically. "Our study program has kept us so busy all this while that I have no need to plan anything for myself."

"Would you mind if I take you to see a place?" Tania asked, sweetness radiating from her beautiful face.

"No, of course not," Dong said, instantly rejuvenated.

"Okay, let's go and visit Leo Tolstoy's homestead, which is not far from here."

Dong thought she meant the Tolstoy Museum in the heart of the city. Yet Tania's "not far" turned out to be one hundred and fifty miles away in the southwestern vicinity of Tula, a small town. He jokingly said that it must be a uniquely Russian concept of distance—anywhere within five hundred miles was "not too far." Tania laughed heartily with Dong, pleased that he had finally relaxed.

A train took them to Tula in what turned out to be a slow but peaceful journey. The two talked all night, as any long-separated young couple would do when they were finally reunited. Tania told Dong that she had a baby boy named Peter. Unfortunately, she would have to send him to a foster home because she had received orders to return to China soon and continue her mission with Martin. Dong told her all about the events in China after she had left, and diplomatically inquired about her health.

"I am fine," Tania said gently. "I am really fine. How about you?"

"I am fine too," Dong said. Then, summoning all his courage, he added, "I just miss you."

"I miss you too, my good friend," responded Tania, recalling all the attention and care he had given when she was terribly sick on the train from Shanghai to Tianjin.

"I… I… I mean I love you," Dong said.

"Oh, Zi-Tian, that's so sweet. I love you too." Tania paused before adding, "as a true and dear friend."

They then each took a deep breath as if they were both relieved of some burden, while at the same time delighted about the frankness of their conversation. Their love for each other was platonic, and the candid expressions of how they felt about one another were liberating for both. The gracious Tania had noticed a long time ago that Dong adored her. There was nothing unusual about a young man falling in love with a woman even if she were married. A wonderful woman could attract a man's attention at any stage of her life, and his heartfelt admiration would always be the best compliment for her.

Dong was glad that he finally had the chance and courage to tell Tania about his feelings toward her. He never intended to disturb Tania's marriage, and her well-being was all that he cared about. He only knew that, as a man, he should not be afraid to tell a woman he loved about his true feelings.

They continued looking at each other for a long time, in silence. Their mutual gaze generated the warmest, the most affectionate, and the most magical feelings that only a loving woman and an honest man could share with one another.

A brief morning shower gave the homestead a good wash and presented it in the best color and shape possible. Straight, tall, and thickly dressed birches lined the country road, called Prospect by the family, leading to the heart of the four-thousand-acre estate where Tolstoy had lived for more than half a century. The main mansion was a two-story white building of more than thirty rooms. The most important was of course the one with a black leather couch lying in a corner, on which Tolstoy and all his thirteen children had been born. In the study a writing desk of Persian walnut occupied one big chunk of the space close to the wall, where Tolstoy wrote the world-famous *War and Peace* and *Anna Karenina*. His pen, pencil, ink, and inkstand were still lying on the desk, a pencil-knife in a drawer, and a book half opened to the side, all of which seemed to say that the writer had been here a few moments ago, leaving the room only temporarily.

It was said, Tania told Dong, Tolstoy could speak fifteen languages, and at the age of fifty he began to learn Ancient Hebrew and Greek in order to read the original texts of the Bible. This was only confirmed when they learned that twenty-two thousand books in thirty-nine languages had been kept in Tolstoy's library, which, to Dong's delight, contained a copy of *Tao De Jing* by the Chinese sage Laozi.

They came out from the mansion and proceeded to the next major stop. Tolstoy's grave was remarkably simple: a low and lonesome earth mound, covered with green twigs and some fresh flowers, in a small piece of clearing amongst the overgrown woods not far from the edge of a long ravine. Dong was particularly impressed by the absence of any tombstone, inscription, or sign—a common sight at any traditional Chinese gravesite. Visitors could choose to stand and pay a quiet tribute to the man who was still widely regarded as "the genius of Russia" and "the guardian of Russia's soul."

"A great man does not need much to be remembered," Dong remarked, a few feet away from the plainest memorial he had ever seen.

"Except for the three hundred and fifty-plus servants, peasants, and laborers who had kept him alive," she retorted, smiling wryly this time.

Dong laughed too. This was why he adored Tania, whose wit and sharp mind never ceased to delight him. Coming from a humble family, he saw simplicity as a laudable virtue in a life of plenty. Yet, Tania, a rebellious descendant of the nobility, could easily detect any irony and be merciless against any sign of duplicity.

"Okay," Tania told Dong, "let's go and see how this poor aristocrat has survived on this puny estate of gardens, lakes, orchids, meadows, and forests." They burst into another round of laughter, and off they went to take a less trodden path to explore the property.

Chapter 10

Confusion

1

"Yan Yan, please…"

"Go away!"

"Yan, please listen to me."

"Go away, you bastard!"

"Yan, I am sorry."

"Who cares! Get out from my house! I don't ever want to see you again!"

"Yan, listen, please let me explain…"

"Shut up and go! You shameless cheater!"

"Yan, please, I beg you. I was wrong and I am truly, truly sorry."

"GET OUT of my sight! You ungrateful degenerate!"

"Please, please, Yan, please give me one more chance…"

"Tell that to your wicked mistress!" Bang! The door was shut, and Professor Lu Shi-Yan had never felt this dejected before in his life.

Few things seemed to go his way these days, which perhaps all started when he began to have an affair with Liu Ming-Zhu, a singer at a Canton nightclub. Always sanguine and self-assured, Lu had an ego as big as his ambition. He believed in his virility and considered his ability to charm women as one of his key strengths. He lived in a time when the men from the elite class in China often took mistresses into the household as their second, third, fourth, and fifth wives—the number was only limited by what the men's wealth could afford—in addition to their official first wives. Viewed not as a bane but as a long-accepted social reality, this practice had had a lasting impact on the population as a whole. Many Chinese men, from the educated to the ignorant, regarded chasing girls, women, or prostitutes as a fun game. And many young girls saw nothing wrong in becoming the concubine of a powerful but older man as long as they could have an easy life.

Lu was never part of the ruling class; he was instead one of its most outspoken mortal enemies in public life. But as a well-known scholar—like many old-fashioned, learned, and yet licentious scholars before him—he enjoyed the attention of women in his private life, seeking comfort in their company and having romantic flings with them. A professed liberal, he strongly supported free love and was adamantly against arranged marriages. While Yan saw true love as total commitment between a man and a woman for life, Lu justified his behavior by distinguishing love from marriage. He thought he was entitled to pursue other women as long as he kept his marriage with Yan intact. Thus, whereas Yan believed that her husband's extramarital affair had betrayed their love and violated their marriage vows, Lu insisted that his relationship with his mistress did no harm to the marriage and was totally acceptable based on the existing mores in society.

Despite these different standards and conflicting views about love and marriage, such liaisons had remained the greatest temptation for both sexes through the ages—the source of endless arguments between wives and husbands, and the perpetual conundrum for millions of men and women whose blissful experiences coupled with everlasting quarrels, miseries, and tragedies could never be fully explained.

Compounding the mess in his personal life was his defeat at the last party meeting, which upset him greatly. Lu understood the party rules and had to accept the majority's decision to form an alliance with the Nationalist Party. But he was deeply disturbed by how the majority was achieved. He was literally outmaneuvered by Martin, who had for the first time played politics with him. Worse, Lu was outvoted by his loyal disciples. In a country where unassailable seniority should always prevail, Lu was confident that his established status in the party would be good enough to force the junior members to toe the line, just like an old and popular Chinese maxim had stated, "Even if he has studied but one day with the master, the student should always treat the master as his father for the rest of his life."

A champion of democracy in print and a vocal opponent of the old regime, Lu, like all his friends and colleagues, had no experience on how to apply democratic principles in real life. Lu viewed the party as his personal possession and since he was the founding father and its headman, he ran the organization like a family business. His will and opinions were synonymous with party directives. Rarely tolerant of different ideas and oblivious to the concept of shared governance, he was accustomed to others obeying his orders, not the other way round. The democratic process of give-and-take was entirely alien to Lu, whose immersion in Confucian classics since childhood had ill-prepared him for his current party position. Deeply hurt by the recent defeat and seriously concerned about his own reputation, Lu was also afraid that the incident was a signal that the party's junior members would no longer follow his lead. Not willing to reconsider how to improve his own leadership style, he glumly concluded that the defeat indicated his declining power in the organization. "Is this not the beginning of the alienation process Marx had alluded to?" Haunted by this dreadful prospect, Lu fell into a prolonged state of self-pity.

Personal authority and institutional strength could be strange things and, as in the lives of any couple, the balance between the two was exceedingly difficult to achieve. When the party was small, like a newborn baby, it needed the protection of the parents, whose painstaking care was his blessing. Yet, when the infant grew into a man, he naturally wanted independence and would resent the parents' heavy-handedness sooner or later. If the party officials continued to dictate, the dogmatic leadership would quickly become a roadblock to the healthy growth of the institution.

Lu, for all his intelligence, was not able to see that. His knowledge and expertise encompassed mostly Chinese literature and history, which provided little insight into how to manage this modern political apparatus. Nor was he able to learn much from the Russian Bolsheviks, whose leadership style was as deplorable as that of any medieval ruler and feudal chieftain. Lenin's assertion on the proletarian dictatorship reaffirmed the least democratic practice in history, and had left a devastating impact on communist organizations around the world. Sadly, the totalitarian form of government and the authoritarian form of organization exemplified by the Russian Bolshevik Revolution not only supported each other completely but also fitted into the darkest side of Chinese tradition perfectly.

At the practical level, the party had developed several regional branches since its founding. Each of them began to rally around its local leaders, who had also become powerful players in the party. The central leadership could not ignore these new developments, and had to rely on these regional offices and local leaders to expand the organization and to carry out its policies. The increasing expansion of regional/local branches and the growing number of party affiliations greatly strengthened the organization as a whole. Meanwhile, the emerging leadership at the regional and local levels were becoming bolder and would even challenge the party's top leaders sometimes. As the general secretary, the egocentric Lu was not prepared to face the new situation. Uncomfortable with it, he refused to refresh his leadership skills to keep up with the times. He had somehow wished that however much things might have changed, the party would still remain his pet (and he, its rightful and sole owner)—an outlandish dream that was totally shattered by the recent episode.

If Lu was surprised to realize that the party had outgrown its leader, never would he imagine that he, its founder, would one day become the sacrificial lamb in the party's first internal strife.

2

The strategy of grafting had worked, and the policy of alliance turned out to be a huge success. Once the pact was signed and once the Nationalist Party allowed the Chinese Communist Party to develop within the alliance, Lu's tiny organization expanded faster than anyone had anticipated. From a small group of a few hundred people, the communist membership ballooned to over fifty thousand nationwide in less than three years. The communists outpaced the nationalists in growth and organizational expansion, competed with them for official posts at every level, and even won a number of national appointments that were disproportionately larger to the size of the organization itself.

While many were excited about the party's progress and rapid development, Si-Tu Wen-Liang was deeply concerned that additional financial support was yet to come. He received word that the Comintern had again dispatched special envoy Tania to Shanghai. She carried all the necessary instructions and documents on how to set up an undercover but legitimately registered trading company, whose income would provide the party with all the money it needed. "Where is she?" Si-Tu was fretting the whole morning when Tania failed to show up at the scheduled time.

"Maybe she was delayed," Cheng Chu-Li responded, hoping to lessen his boss's anxiety, "Maybe she missed the train. Or maybe our security escort has missed her."

"That's impossible. The first principle in our line of work is to be on time, no matter what," Si-Tu said firmly.

"Then what could be wrong?" Cheng asked.

"Anything can go wrong," mumbled Si-Tu.

Suddenly, they heard a shout. "Si-Tu Wen-Liang, where is Wen-Liang? I must see him right away!"

In came Yan Yan, who was panting heavily. "Wen-Liang, Wen-Liang, you must go and rescue Tania immediately!"

"Slow down, slow down." Si-Tu tried to calm her. "Tell me what happened."

Yan said that she was at the market this morning when she saw a rickshaw passing by. She was surprised to see Tania in it. Although their eyes met just for a few seconds, Yan immediately knew Tania was in trouble. A woman's sixth sense was often well developed and Yan's was exceptionally so.

"Are you sure about what you saw? Are you sure it was Tania?" Si-Tu wanted confirmation even as he was starting to plot his next move.

After Yan detailed the location, time, and possible directions that the rickshaw was heading, Si-Tu ordered Cheng to use any means necessary to find the vehicle immediately and locate Tania's whereabouts.

Three days later, Si-Tu and Cheng successfully executed a plan to save Tania, whose story would stun everyone.

When she and Dong Zi-Tian returned to China, they said farewell to each other in Tianjin. Dong proceeded to Peking, and Tania changed to another train on the Tianjin–Nanjin Line to go south toward Shanghai. A man on the train began flirting with her, making her very uncomfortable. She tried unsuccessfully to shake him off. "Another hopeless womanizer," thought Tania, who desperately wanted to reach Shanghai as soon as possible. But the moment she stepped out from the

Shanghai station, two big men grabbed her and forced her into a rickshaw, which sped away. Only then did she realize that she had been kidnapped.

"Luckily, Yan saw you in the rickshaw and came back immediately to tell us about it," Si-Tu told Tania.

She turned and hugged Yan warmly. "Thank you. You saved my life."

"No big deal. No need to mention it," Yan said calmly, although her decorous response indicated that she was pleased with her splendid performance and the praise given.

Rivalry between two women was a delicate art. It should be subtle, but not to the degree that nobody would notice it. It should be keen, but not to the degree that everyone would consider it rude. Yan was a master of that art. Perhaps growing up in a poor family, she always felt inadequate before those well-educated intelligent women whose dignity and grace naturally attracted many people's attention. What she had was her razor-sharp wit, her street smarts, her acute reading of human nature, her fast reflexes, and, most of all, her innate good-heartedness.

Tania's equanimity came from her self-assured noble background, which she did not have to improve in any way. She was born a member of the upper class, whose superior social status and upbringing were undisputed. She could afford to stay above the fray during those trivial quarrels and to always remain dignified.

Since the incident, however, Tania and Yan had become fast friends; their recognition of each other's strengths and weaknesses had put the relationship on a new footing. The kidnapping clearly showed Tania's vulnerability, while Yan's sharp instincts and timely intervention made the emissary's rescue possible. Neither side would need to prove anything to the other anymore. The princess had been humbled, while the action of the humble was undoubtedly noble. Both now could finally stop vying for who was the better woman, but deal with each other as equals.

3

Yet the incident continued to trouble Si-Tu, who wanted to find out more about the man Tania had encountered. Who was he? A spy? An undercover detective? Or simply a rogue or an admirer? If he was just a womanizer, then it could be Tania's plain bad luck. But, if he were a spy who had been following her, it could mean something much more sinister. The safety of the party's entire underground network in Shanghai could be in danger.

So Si-Tu asked for more details about the man on the train—his face, height, features, behavior, attire, and just about everything else. As he and Cheng analyzed the descriptions provided, one name came to their minds: Gan Zu-Xun.

When Si-Tu confronted Gan several days later, he admitted to everything. Yes, he had chased a foreign-looking lady on the train. Yes, he passed the information to a human trafficker and pocketed a hundred silver dollars. For the price of a thousand silver dollars, the trafficker was about to sell Tania as a concubine to a rich man (a sad but common practice at the time) when Cheng caught up with him. Only one aspect of this terrible incident spared Si-Tu from his worst nightmare—Gan did not know Tania's true identity.

Following Si-Tu's investigation, the party decided to expel Gan, who was neither surprised nor angry. "Who doesn't love girls? Who doesn't like money?" he said to himself. "Show me a boy who has never chased a girl, or a girl, after a boy? If they exist, there must be something wrong with them," he reasoned.

Gan was essentially a confused product of his time, one who was full of conflicting ideas and faced with tantalizing choices, but had few clear directions. He started as a naturalist and animalist, and firmly believed human biology and Freudian psychology to be the foundations of man's behavior. Sexual drives and sexual pursuits should never be shunned but experienced, even if not fully comprehended.

Part of him was also Taoist and Sophist, combined with an Epicurean bent. He could be exceedingly detached from those worldly concerns that frequently bothered some other people, such as the prices of groceries in the morning or the color of his tie in the evening. Yet, whenever needed, Gan was able to come up with all kinds of weird theories and bizarre defenses to justify his self-interest and self-centered actions. And, when he did that, he could go on for hours without any sign of embarrassment or shame. Pretty soon, most people around him would realize that the only thing meaningful to Gan was his own pleasures, plus all the means, standard or otherwise, to obtain them.

Intellectually speaking, Gan was a probing agnostic and restless skeptic who happened to be attracted to the ideas of communism but was not altogether convinced or committed to them. He was, by nature and temperament, a loner not suited to any organization. He loved adventures and excitement, and was forever looking for ways to circumvent any rules that might constrain his liberty and freedom. He was gregarious only to the extent that any relationships formed would not infringe upon his free will and individuality.

The expulsion freed him from the organization, which had increasingly become more of a source of irritation than of comfort, and he was delighted about it. "Lu Shi-Yan has fooled around with women as much as anyone else. Why not expel him? For these hypocrites, whoever wants their company must be an idiot." With this thought and self-comforting justification, Gan went on to open the help-wanted section in a newspaper and started to look for his next move in life.

A man with his talent and ambition, Gan would never be happy with any humdrum job, such as an advertising agent, a salesperson, an office worker, a bank accountant, or a merchant clerk.

As a well-traveled newspaperman and well-informed writer, he knew the country was undergoing some profound changes. Anywhere south of the Yangtze River were battle-scarred war zones. Propelled by the new nationalist army's successes, the Northern Expedition advanced rapidly across several provinces and was fast approaching Shanghai, the heart of the Chinese bourgeois classes and the stronghold of their extensive wealth in the South.

Although sectarian fights over power and territory had never stopped, the North was looking relatively quiet for the moment and Gan did not believe the nationalist forces would proceed to march beyond the Yangtze River anytime soon. He was thinking therefore of looking for some position over there that might provide him with a comfortable life while sparing him from all the moralistic shenanigans he had experienced with the communists.

Three powerful men controlled much of the public affairs in the North—General Zhang in the Northeast, General Yan in the West, and General Feng in the Northwest. Even though he commanded the largest army among the three, General Zhang's chief goal in life was survival. The long-running conflict between the Japanese and the Russians over Manchuria had been a constant headache for the Zhang family for years. The increasing presence of the

Japanese military forces and the unyielding attitude of the Russians to protect their interests had only made General Zhang's life even more miserable. Gan thought that he would be better off if he stayed clear of that troubled area.

Ostensibly having the second largest military force in the North, General Feng did not control any territory central to the urban political establishment in the North and the only places he did control seemed to be too poor, too desolate, and too remote for Gan, who could find no joy living in an area whose only neighbor was Mongolia.

The bright spot seemed to be Shanxi Province in the West, where its leader, General Yan, was purported to be an enlightened commander-ruler. General Yan's father was a struggling small money lender in rural Shanxi. After the collapse of the family business and the father's suicide, the young boy became an orphan who begged from village to village to survive. He tried everything to earn some income, from being a stable boy to a street hawker selling homemade biscuits. His childhood hardship made him realize the importance of good financial management, and he devoted much of his administration's energy to improving the economic conditions of the province.

For all his limited and old-fashioned education, General Yan was a surprisingly open-minded governor. He was open to Sun Yat-Sen's Three Principles of the People as much as to Marx's communism and Russian Bolshevism. Most of all, to improve education, General Yan donated his own money to schools and strongly encouraged college graduates to come to Shanxi to teach, which seemed to be a very good reason for Gan to go there. He had also heard that General Yan had nine wives and so would probably care little about Gan's colorful personal life.

Thus decided, Gan sat down and wrote a polite letter to introduce himself to the general, explaining why he would be an excellent choice as the general's personal aide, one who could handle all of his paperwork dealing with matters from family business to international affairs. He dropped the letter at a post office, went to a club, and danced all night there.

Three weeks later, the general's reply came and invited Gan to come. Shanxi, the general said, was about to undertake a grand scheme of comprehensive reconstruction, political, economic, financial, and educational. It would be his great honor to welcome any educated persons, especially one such as Gan, to come and play an important role in the grand scheme. The general ended his letter by saying that a person as well qualified and highly experienced as Gan would no doubt make a significant contribution to the reconstruction of his humble province.

"What do you know?" said a delighted Gan to himself after reading the letter. "The dismissal from the party has helped me to land the best job of my life. Farewell, Shanghai, and goodbye, miserable South. I will enjoy a much better life and greater freedom somewhere else."

4

Not until he had to find out Tania's whereabouts did Cheng understand why Si-Tu had said that "everyone has some use in society." Hou Shi-Suo's network of beggars, busybodies, and informants turned out to be amazingly useful— nothing in the city, from the fanciest hotels to the dirtiest street corners, could escape their eyes. In less than two days they discovered the exact location where Tania was being held, the human trafficker's name, his bodyguards, and coconspirators. A rescue plan was then drawn up and swiftly executed, and Tania was freed the next day.

Both Cheng and Si-Tu were impressed with Hou and his team, who were handsomely rewarded for their critical contribution to the success of the rescue mission. Hou was entrusted with further responsibilities to organize the poor in the working-class neighborhoods, preparing for Shanghai's liberation once the Northern Expedition Army came to the city. One morning, a rumor started to spread that a stealth force of two thousand soldiers, dressed in plainclothes, had sneaked into the city, indicating the final assault on the city was imminent. At numerous street intersections some large posters were found, declaring,

> Citizens of Shanghai:
> For the last several months, the brave Northern Expedition Army has defeated the troops of the corrupt warlords seven times. They have given up three southern provinces and can no longer provide any meaningful defense of the city of Shanghai, which will fall into the hands of our Northern Expedition Army in no time.

We now call upon you to remain calm when the final attack begins. The North Expedition Army will do all we can to protect the lives and properties in the city.

Fellow Citizens, Brothers and Sisters,
Stand Up and Join the Fight against the Evil Foreign Invaders!
Down with the Corrupt Warlords!
Long Live the Northern Expedition Army!
Love Live the Great National Republic Revolution!

Banners, posters, and flags suddenly appeared everywhere, spreading exciting radical messages across the city: "Welcome the Northern Expedition Revolutionary Arm," "Down with the Foreign Imperialists," "Down with Devilish Warlords," "Down with Their Running Dogs," "Long Live the Working Classes," "Long Live the Republic of China," "Proletarians All Over the World, Unite!"

The revolutionary fever reached its peak when thousands of demonstrators stormed the Bund, shouting, "Freedom, Equality, and Democracy," "Long Live the Laboring Classes," "Long Live the Citizens of Shanghai," "Long Live Liberty and Revolution," "Down with the Foreign Imperialists," "Long Live the Republic of China!"

China was awakening, and so were its people. The long-awaited Chinese national movement for liberation seemed to be around the corner, the working class was going to champion this unprecedented event in history, and the city of Shanghai was soon to become the beacon of hope for China that St. Petersburg had been for Russia in October 1917.

When the Northern Expedition Army finally arrived after overcoming the final resistance, the whole city was jubilant. Flowers and slogans once again filled the streets, and the soldiers held the best victory parade that residents had ever seen in their lives—a grand parade of a Chinese army led by a Chinese commander, instead of foreign troops.

Marching ahead of his men, General Chen Han, the commander-in-chief of the Northern Expedition Army, was mounted on a big white horse and no doubt the most heroic figure of the day. Newspapers lavished praised on him and young girls with fresh makeup were crazy about the general. Slim, young, clean-shaven, and extremely determined, he led the Northern Expedition to a successful conclusion that even Sun Yat-Sen could only dream of when he was alive.

As a token of his appreciation for the overwhelming local support, General Chen ordered two big ornamental plaques made and delivered to Hou and his teams of followers and workers. One of them was inscribed "Labor Is Sacred" and the other "Long Live the Laboring Classes!"

No one could be prouder than Hou at that moment and a general holiday was declared for the entire city. Bars, saloons, restaurants, coffee shops, nightclubs, theaters, hotels, and dancing halls were open day and night. With soldiers and friends, customers and guests coming in droves, the hospitality and entertainment businesses were having their best days in decades.

At the time, neither Hou and his followers nor Si-Tu, Cheng, or any of their colleagues knew what was happening behind closed doors. General Chen had secretly met several of his domestic donors and foreign sponsors, who insisted that the communist menace must be stopped before they would provide any further financial support to the general and his troops. The general assured his powerful backers that he would take decisive action in return for a loan of thirty million Chinese yuan.

With the general's approval and in collaboration with his soldiers, Chen's allies from the underground world carried out the bloodiest purge ever in Shanghai. A high-ranking union leader was murdered on the night of April 11, 1927. The next morning, several thousand armed men in blue denim overalls with white armbands brutally attacked workers' clubs, unions, and their headquarters in the working-class districts of the city, where no fewer than four hundred people were shot and three hundred others arrested. The raids and rampage lasted for several days. Anyone suspected of radical activities could be arrested immediately, including some innocent passersby who had happened to pick up a few flyers on the ground. Many were summarily executed without any trial. Bloodshed, gunshots, arrests, imprisonment, and executions replaced the colorful banners and flags from just a week ago. The city of revolutionary pride turned into hell overnight, with the reds being hunted down and persecuted. The purge later spread to seven cities in Southern China and the final death toll was estimated to be as high as thirty-four thousand, with an additional forty thousand wounded and twenty-five thousand arrested.

5

The worst moment in the Communist Party's brief existence, those appalling events in China also humiliated the Comintern and Moscow, which had promised the marvelous future of a united front. Both decided to do something to reverse the trend. Lenin's death a few years earlier had led to a series of internal power struggles. Stalin eventually rose to the top when he managed to defeat several key competitors: Leon Trotsky (the preeminent Marxist theorist and founder of the Red Army), Lev Kamenev (the head of Soviet Russia and acting premier), Gregory Zinoviev (the head of the Comintern), and Nikolai Bukharin (a full member of the Politburo). Stalin and Trotsky particularly clashed over what should be the correct policies for China, when the Chinese nationalists launched the Northern Expedition from Canton in 1926, hoping to defeat the various regional warlords and unify the nation.

Presenting himself as the legitimate successor to Lenin and the faithful defender of orthodox Leninism, the pragmatic Stalin had urged the political factions in China to maintain Lenin's alliance policy. He instructed the Chinese Communist Party to continue to ally itself with the nationalists, support the expedition, and not to implement a communist revolution. In the true fashion of an exalted Marxist, Trotsky beseeched the party to oppose the Kuomintang and push forward with a full-scale proletarian revolution. The Chinese communists, he pointed out, should never entrust the bourgeois, especially its right-wing elements, to lead the nationalist revolution. But Stalin, in a fervent speech before three thousand sympathetic party activists, countered, "Why drive away the Right, when we have the majority and when the Right listens to us?" Never as polished a theoretician as Trotsky, his homily then went on to elucidate,

The peasant needs an old worn-out jade as long as she is necessary. He does not drive her away. So it is with us. When the Right is of no more use to us, we will drive it away. At present, we need the Right. It has capable people, who still direct the army and lead it against the imperialists… Also, they have connections with the rich merchants and can raise money from them. So they have to be utilized to the end, squeezed out like a lemon and then thrown away.

Stalin's calculated schemes prevailed and the Soviet government funded the Kuomintang during the expedition.

But General Chen's bloody massacre was a real slap in Stalin's face, whose "squeeze it like a lemon" speech was never published and remained the butt of jokes within communist circles for decades. Outraged and not to be outmaneuvered, Stalin ordered the Comintern to send in a new team to take charge of the Communist Party in China. Meng Bo-Xian, the top graduate of the Russian Study Program, was selected to lead the team. They arrived in China in the summer and immediately planned and directed the first armed struggle in the party's history.

The Northern Expedition displaced no fewer than five major warlords in Southern China. And the policy of alliance resulted in great success as well as great confusion. It split the communists into two camps as it did the nationalists—between those who supported the united front and those who were against it. Many of the Nationalist Party's left wing in Wuhan condemned Chen's actions and even attempted to strip him of his powers as the commander of the expedition army and to expel him from the party. Under the orders of Meng and his team, a small group of communists and left-wing nationalists decided to orchestrate a military mutiny to resist the onslaught by Chen and his right-wing followers.

They found an opportunity in Nanchang, the capital city of Jiangxi Province, where several battalions controlled by Tao Yin-Hu and some other communists were stationed. In late July, Dong Zi-Tian and Si-Tu Wen-Liang rushed to Nanchang to meet with Tao and to launch the armed insurrection. After four hours of fighting, they took control of the city on the morning of August 1. That afternoon, a newly formed committee of the Nationalist Party of the Left, including a dozen communists who had been active within the Kuomintang, issued a declaration against General Chen and his right-wing supporters. They also formed a new government separate from the official one headed by the nationalists. The armed rebellion and the creation of a rival government effectively ended the united front between the two parties under the auspices of Moscow and the Comintern, and the ensuing open hostilities between the nationalists and the communists would continue into the next decade.

Unfortunately, thousands of enemy troops quickly closed in on the rebel soldiers, who were now publicly declared traitorous mutineers and lawless bandits subject to capital punishment if caught by government soldiers, police, or anyone else. Confronted with the overwhelming number of government troops, Dong, Si-Tu, and Tao decided to give up the city and retreat to the countryside in the neighboring southern provinces of Fujian and Guangdong. However, they made the fatal mistake of dividing their forces into two midway, and each was soundly defeated soon afterward. Within less than three months, defeat and exhaustion cost the lives of one-half of the insurrectionists, while diseases, starvation, and deserters further decimated the ranks. Only a few hundred soldiers and officers managed to survive the catastrophe.

One debacle after another triggered an emergency party meeting, which must quickly come out with a viable solution for the communists at this pivotal moment. Two dozen delegates came to Wuhan, the industrial center in Central China and a relatively safe place at the time. To Professor Lu Shi-Yan's great surprise, he became the target of the meeting. Delegates blamed the latest setbacks on his willingness to form the alliance with the Nationalist Party. His ineffective leadership, they insisted, gave the nationalists the opportunity to slaughter their communist comrades, who were totally unprotected and unprepared.

Lu pointed out that he had been the one who was against the alliance policy. The party adopted the policy only because several of them vetoed him at their last decision-making meeting. As the person who was against the policy in the first place, why should he be blamed for the "ineffective" leadership now?

As Lu looked around, he could not find Si-Tu and Tao in the room, and was told that they were with the Nanchang insurrection troops. "What have they done," asked he, "such as Comrades Tao Yin-Hu, Si-Tu Wen-Liang, and Sheng Bao, who have strongly supported the alliance and who have subsequently held high positions in the nationalist government? What have they done to prepare us from the sudden attacks by the right-wing nationalists?"

Sheng was the only one present who had voted for the united front at the last party meeting. He stood up and said, "Making alliance is different from taking the lead in the alliance. I hope Comrade Lu Shi-Yan would not make excuses for his responsibilities as the general secretary of the party."

"I admit I have made terrible mistakes, which have contributed to the tragic losses we are suffering. My awful underestimation of the brutality of the nationalist right wing pains me every day, which is a lesson I shall never forget,"

Lu confessed. "But I can't accept the insinuation that my personal failing was the only thing to blame. No one in the party had the foresight, including all of us who were either doubtful or passionate about the alliance."

"If no one did anything wrong, why have things gone so badly?" Sheng retorted.

"Maybe, we could improve on some structural weaknesses and communication inconsistencies in the future," Lu proceeded cautiously, knowing his next statement would be explosive. "For example, two days before the Shanghai massacre, I received clear instructions from the Comintern not to alienate the right-wing nationalists, whose influence and power we may still need."

Sheng and every other delegate in the room were stunned. Lu was obviously pointing his finger at Martin, the Comintern, and even Moscow. As the national party chief, he did something no communist was supposed to do—questioning the correctness of the venerated Comintern, its emissary, and the infallible Moscow, and by doing so he was essentially challenging their authority as well.

"How dare you say that? What do you want?" Sheng yelled at Lu. "Do you want to blame the Comintern and our beloved Stalin for your failures?"

Lu could not remember what exactly happened next. He only saw everyone in the room standing up and pointing their fingers at him, shouting that he was the only culprit behind the recent calamity, and that he should be fully responsible for it.

Truth and reality did not seem to matter to the delegates. The party needed someone to blame. They could not blame the Comintern, which was their overlord. They could not blame the Russians, whose support, be it political, financial, or military, was still needed. Nor did the delegates want to blame themselves. Most of them should assume some form of responsibility for the crisis, especially Si-Tu, Tao, and Sheng, who had not only enthusiastically supported the alliance policy but also assumed important official posts in the nationalist government. Instead, they pointed their fingers at Lu, the old and vulnerable man whose stupendous arrogance had long alienated most of his younger colleagues. He became the scapegoat for the worst disaster the party had ever suffered since its founding.

Professor Lu never recovered from the way he was abandoned by the party. He protested against his dismissal from his party's post but to no avail, and eventually decided to form a rival faction within the party. Moscow and the Comintern labeled it reactionary, which deterred most of his former colleagues from supporting him. Ironically, Lu Shi-Yan—who more than anyone else in China was responsible for the Communist Party's birth—was the first lemon to have been squeezed out of its juice by his own organization and then conveniently thrown away.

Chapter 11

Reset

1

If there were only two people who best understood early twentieth-century Chinese politics, General Chen Han must be one of them. Although not one of the Nationalist Party's senior members, he was the first and the youngest of them to realize the vital importance of the military in government and society.

Smart and energetic, the general was the sturdy son of a salt trader in Southern China. Like most boys from those well-to-do families, his life had been mapped out for him long before he was born, which was about everything else but the military. He was to study Confucian classics, pass official examinations, and become one of those mandarins who would receive government pensions for the rest of their lives. Behind this mundane scenario lay a serious lesson obtained from years of painful experiences in the past.

Wealth was doubtless essential in life, but it would be meaningless without the blessings of political authorities in China. Power and money were hardly ever separable in this country, and even the wealthiest households would need the government's protection at all levels, because even the lowest bureaucrats were allowed to harass them at will any time. Despised and mistrusted by the general population, the merchant class in particular had historically been regarded as the lowest of the low in society since the time of Confucius, when the state controlled all economic and trading activities. Private entrepreneurs and merchants relied on government approval and contracts to engage in any lucrative business, and fears of uncertainty and vulnerability always haunted them since any slight alteration in tax policies, market regulations, and administrative practices could easily affect their entire business operations. They therefore would love to have family members serving in the government, hoping that this insider's connection to officialdom would enable them to gain privileges and contracts while hedging themselves against any precipitous change unbeknown to outsiders. Establishing such a connection might take several generations to achieve, but all wealthy families considered it absolutely necessary and well-worth the investment.

Thus designed, Chen's youthful life was unfolding without a hitch until one day the family received the shocking news that his older brother Chen Dian had been arrested for his involvement in a murder case. Considered the most talented and the most handsome of the Chen boys, Chen Dian was a restless child. Never content with the old-fashioned career the parents had arranged for him, he found his destiny in the great cause of rescuing China from the multitude of grave problems she was suffering. Like many rebels of the time, he believed corruption in the Qing Dynasty to be the root of all evils, and conspired with his friends to overthrow it at all costs. They plotted to assassinate a prince, who was a top official of the central government in Peking. But the plot was exposed after their homemade bomb failed to explode. Chen Dian and several others at the scene were immediately arrested. Only his family connections, exceptional gift of the gab, and, according to many, extremely good looks (he was believed to be one of the four most attractive men in China at the time) saved him—with the judges being impressed enough to commute the capital punishment to life imprisonment.

When Chen visited his brother in jail, their conversation changed his life forever. Chen Dian told him that China desperately needed a new kind of hero. All her enemies had been armed to the teeth, including the Qing court, foreigners, warlords, and even the local hooligans and bandits. But the Chinese patriots were too weak, too disorganized, and too naïve. They had a great deal of passion, but no political power or weapons. They had to buy daggers, make hand grenades, steal rifles, and smuggle explosives, which made them pathetic opponents of any well-trained professional troops. They would never become a real force to be reckoned with in society until they had their own army in the tens of thousands, just like their foes. Otherwise, the patriots could be crushed easily like Chen Dian, who was now a wretched captive left to rot in jail. Although stunned by his brother's revelation, Chen was convinced Chen Dian was right, and resolved to heed the latter's advice to embark on a new path in life. Chen dropped out of the conventional civil service course and enrolled in a military school in Northern China. After his graduation, he went to Japan to pursue further military training. Determined to save his country in the way Chen Dian had suggested, Chen believed that he would become the real hero China needed.

Chen's talent and experience drew the attention of the top leaders of the Nationalist Party, including Sun Yat-Sen, who appointed him president of the Huangpu Academy—the new military school established by the revolutionary government in Canton. Excited about the nationalist movement, many talented and enthusiastic young men joined the academy, and Chen made sure he interviewed every one of them himself. While questioning their knowledge, background, and interests, Chen would also examine their personal traits, to see who among them could become potential candidates for a long-term relationship. Those cadets who frequently received the president's attention realized its significance and reciprocated by demonstrating their loyalty to him. Within a few years, the Huangpu Academy had successfully trained hundreds of officers ready to serve in the Northern Expedition Army. As the academy's president and commander-in-chief of the Expedition Army, General Chen also succeeded in creating his own inner circle comprising a selected group of followers who were extremely loyal to him.

As the patron saint of his followers, General Chen was blatant in using his power of patronage. He would promote his favorite officers faster than others, and reward the troops devoted to him with better pay, better uniforms, better weapons, better supplies, and better equipment than those given to other army divisions. These officers and their troops became the core force under General Chen's personal command, and were answerable to no one else in the nationalist camp except him. Thus supported by a section of the military that was firmly under his control, General Chen's status and influence in the party quickly soared and the success of the Northern Expedition eventually propelled him to the top leadership position in the new national government in Nanjing. However, neither the officer corps of the Huangpu Academy nor the national government of Nanjing was as solidly behind him as General Chen would wish them to be. The majority of the Huangpu graduates were certainly nationalists and, among them, officers Hu, Gao, Tang, Pan, and Lin were on the list of his top favorites. Yet, under the alliance policy, a number of Communist Party members also had enrolled at Huangpu and several of them later became the backbone of the communist military unit, such as the unpolished but upright Tao Yin-Hu. In fact, he was Chen's classmate some years earlier at the military school in Northern China. Tao served as a drillmaster at Huangpu, and enjoyed the kind of genuine respect and wide popularity that even Chen would envy at times.

For the older nationalists who had served Sun long before General Chen appeared on the scene, not a few of these elderly statesmen considered themselves to be his legitimate successor, and Chen's rapid rise in the party kindled jealousy and hatred in them. Surprisingly, Chen Dian, recently released from jail, soon became a national superstar who commanded a broader public appeal than his brother. Many senior advisors within the party considered Chen Dian a much better leader and wanted him, rather than Chen, to lead the nation. In typical Confucian modesty, Chen Dian refused, insisting that China had suffered enough from the myriad infighting and divisions of the past. He did not want to add to the new national government's enormous burdens by engaging in a power struggle.

Indeed, even though the government in Nanjing claimed to be the new sovereign authority nationwide, no more than one-fifth of China obeyed its orders. The actual areas it firmly controlled included only the southeastern portion of China close to the cities from Nanjing and Shanghai to Hangzhou along the eastern coast. It had some nominal control over several nearby southern provinces, but had to yield the southwestern part of China to the powerful regional chieftains, especially General Li and General Bai. Moreover, it had no authority at all in the vast territories north of the Yangtze River, where General Yan dominated the West, General Feng the Northwest, and General Zhang the Northeast. Each of these powerful men had hundreds of thousands of troops under his own command.

How to subdue these regional rulers and exert real control over the whole nation became a top priority for General Chen, whose ability to govern would be seriously tested. If history were any guide, this would seem to be a monumental task for anyone. However, General Chen showed great ingenuity and adopted varied tactics to accomplish his goals in less than two years. What underpinned his successful strategy was the familiar Machiavellian belief that there were "no permanent enemies or friends, only perpetual interests."

He first neutralized General Li and General Bai by driving a wedge between the two longtime allies. He then defeated General Li's troops on the ground, forcing them to retreat to the southwest. Knowing many of General Bai's soldiers were captives from the army of warlord General Tang, he brought the latter to the front line to urge his soldiers to abandon Bai, which they did. The regional resistance finally collapsed in the face of a new round of swift attacks by the national army. Li and Bai were left with no choice but to enter into a peace agreement with General Chen. They promised their allegiance to the new national government in return for financial support from Chen.

At first glance, the military situation seemed absolutely hopeless in the north, where four hundred thousand of General Feng and General Yan's combined forces started attacking the army of two hundred thousand soldiers under the central government. Feng's ferocious cavalry and Yan's heavy artillery devastated the government troops, and General Chen was at one point only five miles away from Feng's fast-moving soldiers on horseback. Yet again, the wily Chen found a vulnerable spot among the allied powers, which allowed him to beat them separately. He observed that Yan, true to his duplicitous nature, was the more cautious of the two, always moving one step behind his ally. So he decided to deal with Feng first. As one who was familiar with all the corrosive habits and lethal weaknesses of the warlord soldiers, General Chen sent undercover agents to bribe General Feng's subordinates, including offering them huge sums of cash, tons of opium, and several thousand prostitutes drafted from nearby cities. The plot worked: General Feng's fierce attacks subsided and his alliance with General Yan evaporated.

In the end, everybody adhered to the same creed of "no permanent enemies or friends, only perpetual interests." General Yan's opposition came to an end when he found out that his backyard was threatened by General Zhang's troops from the northeast. A forty-million-yuan loan had purchased Zhang's loyalty to General Chen's central government and Zhang, according to the secret deal with Chen, quickly sent in his massive Northeastern Army to attack General Yan's troops. To preserve his dignity, he sought peace with Chen, who allowed Yan to govern the province of Shanxi as his exclusive domain in exchange for his allegiance to the central government.

One last act of a theatrical feast had to take place before General Chen would finally be declared the president of a unified China. Before the inauguration, he had a cordial meeting with the now defeated General Feng, exchanged their dates of birth, and the two went through a series of elaborate rituals to become sworn brothers. Since Feng turned out to be five years his senior, Chen had to bow and call him "elder brother." Strict tradition also dictated that Chen, though now the commander-in-chief of the whole Chinese army, must show his deference to Feng by allowing him to walk ahead of Chen, and by allowing Feng to sit on his left, instead of right. A man as egotistic as anyone, General Chen swallowed his pride to follow these quaint protocols to massage General Feng's ego of equal size. Chen understood perfectly that even a vanquished warlord could be of some use in the future, since he still controlled a large number of soldiers, and Feng's extensive military experience and renowned leadership skills might also be needed someday.

2

All told, nearly three hundred thousand soldiers died in those brutal military campaigns, which involved more than one million, three hundred thousand troops. It was one of the bloodiest armed conflicts in history, which exhausted both the regional warlords and Chen's central government. Meanwhile, a small contingent of eight hundred men led by the revolutionary Sheng Bao was trying to survive in the remote mountains five hundred miles away. Despite his total lack of military experience or even training, Sheng was ordered by the new communist leadership to start an uprising in rural Hunan, which was supposed to be one of the several thousand nationwide. A few days later the poorly orchestrated revolt failed miserably, and most of his hastily assembled followers fled. Sheng then took those who remained to Big Leopard Mountain on the Hunan–Jiangxi border to hide. It was clear to him that a successful communist uprising in China was not going to happen anytime soon as the

RESET

party's new leaders had hoped. Stuck in a desolated area, he now had plenty of time to contemplate his next move.

Sheng gradually came to the same painful realization as Chen, which was the utmost importance of the military in Chinese affairs. Repeated tragedies, failures, and bloodshed had shown him in unambiguous terms that, no matter how big or small it was, no organization could accomplish anything in China without a substantial military force. The principle applied to the previous Qing Dynasty, the regional warlords, the great patriot Sun Yat-Sen, his restructured Nationalist Party, the triumphant Northern Expedition, the hardliner General Chen, and to the recently consolidated national government. The glaring exception was Sheng's own Communist Party, which had no army of its own. It was precisely because of this great disparity that the Communist Party suffered the most, with its fearsome opponents treating it like a sacrificial lamb that could be slaughtered at will.

The need for an army was one thing; building one was quite another. While the Russian Bolsheviks had had success with an armed urban insurrection, it had been difficult for the Chinese communists to duplicate the strategy, as the failure of several working-class strikes had indicated. China's proletarians were small in number and had little or no education, completely different from the scenarios that Marx had envisaged for the industrialized European countries. Most were disorganized, low-skilled, and despondent laborers who were not suited to leading any modern revolution. Apart from being under the watchful eyes of armed police and government troops in those sizable population centers, these industrial workers were also largely controlled by employers' unions and secret societies, whose strong anticommunist stand was extremely difficult to change. Thus, finding those who would be willing to join the communist cause in significant numbers was the first challenge that needed to overcome before a military force entirely controlled by the Communist Party could be built.

Sheng suddenly recalled that his dear uncle had been a soldier for years. In fact, his father and many of his relatives, clansmen, and family friends had also been soldiers. The excited Sheng realized that the rank and file of any Chinese military force, past and present, were filled mostly with the sons of small farmers and lowly peasants. The rural population was after all the main source of an endless supply of manpower for all Chinese armed forces throughout history, for purposes both good and bad. Yet, would the same rural population

187

support a communist cause? If so, how? And, even if this was feasible, how could he, the firm Marxist believer, reconcile with the ironic conclusion that the proletarian revolution in China would be championed by the peasantry?

Nearly all the initial members of the Chinese Communist Party had rural roots and connections. Some were the direct offspring of farm families, such as Sheng himself and Dong Zi-Tian. Some were either born in small towns or grew up in an environment close to the countryside, such as Lu Shi-Yan, Tang Shi-Hai, and Si-Tu Wen-Liang. But the education they had received based on Confucian tradition since childhood was all about how to escape the toil in the field as fast as possible, and how to leave the farmland behind for the city as quickly as they could. Nor did their recently adopted new idols Marx and Lenin require them to pay much attention to farmers and peasants. These petty bourgeoisie, according to Marx and Lenin's theories, were conservatives at best and reactionaries at worst in any proletarian revolution. In agrarian China, where ninety percent of the population lived in the countryside, no one could deny their existence, but few people, including the most dedicated students of Marxism and Leninism, seriously cared about their fate. In a brief directive, the party did, as early as in 1923, declare the need to organize the rural population. But few local branches acted upon it except in several places, such as counties in the provinces of Gangdong and Fujian. Sheng was among the few party members who not only participated in the rural uprisings but also studied the rural population carefully.

Several extensive investigations in a number of counties in the south convinced him that the rural population, especially the poor, could become a significant force for the party. Typically in a county of seven thousand households, his surveys indicated, five percent of them were rich landlords, ten percent were substantial farmers, and fifteen percent were landless day laborers and itinerant craftsmen, such as carpenters, masons, roofers, brickmakers, tanners, weavers, tinkerers, and repairmen. The vast majority, seventy percent, of them were small tenant farmers and poor peasants, who were struggling to make ends meet.

Such a frustrating situation could certainly be used to the party's advantage. His experience told Sheng that during the heyday of the Northern Expedition, when it generated enormous response in the countryside, the small tenant farmers, poor peasants, along with the rural craftsmen and laborers, had provided ninety percent of the recruits for the expedition army. In addition, no fewer than two hundred counties across rural China had set up peasants associations, which involved as many as ten million ordinary country folk. They enthusiastically supported the Northern Expedition by taking some unprecedented actions, from subscribing to public bonds, establishing elected local governments, forming small cooperatives, and setting up evening schools, repairing roads, bridges, and dams to even allowing women to divorce. This profound transformation clearly showed, Sheng reasoned, that the lowest strata of Chinese rural communities were eager for change, which could be extremely useful for the party. If only the Communist Party could adopt a correct policy and provide some incentives, a huge portion of the rural poor could be turned into a major fighting force for the communist cause, just like what they had done for the nationalists. The key was, obviously, correct leadership and correct policies.

3

As Meng Bo-Xian read the reports from Sheng, he was elated. A totally transformed person, Meng changed from a sullen pessimist to a fiery optimist after he had finished his studies and returned from the Soviet Union. Sheng's reports confirmed what Meng had learned in Moscow, that the fundamental issue in the Chinese revolution was about the peasantry.

But China and Russia were thousands of miles apart, and the two countries had arrived at the same conclusion only after a great deal of blood had been shed. Although Lenin proposed the policy of alliance, he died soon afterward. Stalin and Trotsky were competing for the top party position, and the China question became a pawn in their competition. Insisting not on the proletarian but on the nationalist nature of the Chinese revolution, Stalin bet on the bourgeois leadership represented by the Nationalist Party, or Kuomintang. Through his control over the Comintern, he repeatedly exhorted the Chinese Communist Party to ally itself with the Kuomintang and not to alienate the powerful General Chen, who was spearheading the highly anticipated Northern Expedition.

A clever player in the game, Chen knew the importance of military and financial support from the Russians. He flattered Moscow by getting his party to apply for Comintern membership, and sent Si-Tu Wen-Liang, now a joint member of both parties and a high officer at the military academy, to represent him. Si-Tu testified before the Comintern's executive committee that Comrade Chen was devoted to the Chinese revolution. He assured them that "the Chinese revolution will correctly solve the peasant question" and that "the Kuomintang will fulfill its historic task."

No sooner had the Comintern accepted the Kuomintang as a sympathetic member of the organization—a fact long concealed to cover Stalin's huge blunder—than General Chen took off his mask and orchestrated the infamous purge in Shanghai, which led to the death of hundreds of communists and their supporters. Still not ready to give up on the Chinese bourgeoisie, Stalin then threw his support for the Kuomintang's moderate wing, led by Chen Dian. He praised Chen Dian for "leading a decisive struggle against militarism and imperialism." The moderate and left-leaning faction of the nationalists, Stalin went on to say, "will in reality be transformed into an organ of the revolutionary-democratic dictatorship of the proletariat and peasantry."

It was clear that, even after the bloodbath in Shanghai, Stalin continued to consider the nationalists, not the communists, to be the leading force in the Chinese revolution. The only thing that changed was that he had switched bets from Chen to Chen Dian. For all Stalin's enthusiasm, the honeymoon did not last long. Just a few months later, Chen Dian's nationalist faction purged and killed hundreds of communists elsewhere in China as brutally as his brother had done earlier in Shanghai.

The Trotskyites agreed with the Stalinists that China had four principal political and social classes—(1) the warlords, their domestic supporters, and the foreign imperialists behind them, (2) the bourgeoisie, (3) the proletariat, and (4) the peasantry. They differed from the Stalinists by insisting on the permanent proletarian nature of the Chinese revolution, which should be led by no one but the proletarians and communists. They were highly suspicious of the alliance policy, and strongly disagreed with Stalin's repeated pampering of the Kuomintang's leaders, from General Chen to Chen Dian.

When Meng compared these conflicting views with the reality in China, he believed that both the Trotskyites and the Stalinists were right on some points but could be wrong on others.

The Trotskyites were correct in their short-term tactics but their general assessment of China's political situation was wrong. The Stalinists and the Comintern were almost exactly the opposite—they were correct in their long-term strategic assessment of China but were wrong in their immediate implementation of tactics and policies. Although the Trotskyites were right to emphasize the importance of the communists' leadership in the current stage of the Chinese revolution, they overstated the proletarian component in it. The Stalinists erred the other way. They correctly realized the bourgeois and nationalistic character of the Chinese revolution but, as a result, they deliberately subjected the Communist Party to the total control of the nationalists, which soon turned out to be a huge disaster.

The Chinese communists paid a huge price not only for those erroneous directives they had received from Moscow but also for the confusion arising from the intraparty struggle there. As the heated debates between Trotsky and Stalin intensified, they split the Russian Communist Party and the Comintern into different factions. These partisan disputes spilled over to China and divided the Chinese communists, who were confused about whose orders they should follow. Micromanaging a revolution from thousands of miles away was never a good idea; it was a recipe for disaster.

Hardly visible at the start, the first communist-style partisan split established a pattern, and the subsequent ones would be even more messy and costly. Marx's noble ideas gave birth to modern communism, Lenin's organizational principles cast the party in a strictly autocratic frame, and Stalin's thirst for power taught every communist how to play dirty in working-class party politics.

4

Roy, the Comintern's new special envoy, knew how to be "special." Handpicked by Stalin, he believed he was the overlord of everyone he was about to meet. First, he summoned Martin and Tania, and blasted them for four hours. "Wimps, cowards, idiots," shouted he. "How stupid and absurd you have been! You have ruined a perfect revolution in China because of your failure to carry out the Comintern's orders. No, no, no! Don't even attempt to argue with me," he continued. "The Comintern is always correct, and so are Stalin's directives. You are hereby dismissed as the Comintern's emissaries, and your new assignments will depend on how seriously you confess to your terrible mistakes and how badly you want to reform yourselves."

Livid yet helpless, Martin was speechless as he came out from the meeting. "The worst pig I have ever seen" was the only thing he managed to say at long last. Tania was equally upset at first, but she soon realized the futility of trying to reason with an unreasonable man. "And a dirty one as well," she added, recalling the lascivious gleam from behind the oversized thick glasses on Roy's oversized nose.

"What is this?" Roy threw a pile of papers in front of Meng. "Garbage! Absolute trash! Complete nonsense! Total hogwash! Worthless junk! Utter rubbish!" He took a breather while looking for the next expression from his rich lexicon to vent his dissatisfaction over Meng's carefully prepared plan of the party activities for the coming year—the perfunctory act any boss had to perform in front of his subordinate.

The two had met each other a long time ago in Moscow, when Roy was an aspiring Comintern employee. Meng knew about his aristocratic background, which Roy never failed to mention whenever he had a chance. Nor would he ever let his listeners go without the casual revelation that he was of Aryan stock. According to Roy, he was the grandson of a prince whose grandfather was the great-grandson of another prince in India, where several thousand kingdoms had produced tens of thousands of those princelings over the past several thousand years. This stupendous heritage blessed him with Peharnism—the most ancient philosophical tradition in the world. As such, he naturally possessed a remarkable ability of talking wildly, passionately, and endlessly without the least hesitation on any topic—the most outstanding manifestation of his intellectual attainment, social importance, and metaphysical profundity. Once Roy opened his mouth, none of his speeches would end until he had exhausted all the pronouns in the vocabulary, and a brilliant one often ended with a meaningless "but."

Adding to his aura was the authentic Oxford accent he firmly believed he had acquired when he was a visiting fellow at St. John's College. By smoking a pipe, wearing a beret, and walking with a second-hand walnut cane when he was not even twenty-five years old, Roy thought he had totally transformed himself from an eminent Indian prince to a *bona fide* English gentleman. A gentleman without any gentleness, as far as Meng could tell. Knowing his background and habitual traits might lessen the pain of those who were meeting Roy for the first time. But Meng had another secret tool to deal with his new boss, which was to throw just a few Russian words in his face. The self-appointed doorkeeper of oriental philosophy and the personification of occidental gentility notwithstanding, Roy was an awkward Russian speaker who would somehow be frightened out of his wits and tremble uncontrollably when hearing the words Товарищ Рой (Comrade Roy), as if the formidable Stalin were standing right behind him.

Meng, the top student in Moscow, quietly waited for his turn to speak. Then he simply asked, "Товарищ Рой, what shall we do next?" Startled, Roy looked up to meet Meng's steady gaze for a few seconds until he stopped shaking. He hastily moved to another subject to hide his embarrassment.

Running the Comintern was not that different from running a corporation, the astute Roy observed, namely, performance was everything. A person who aspired to replace Chamberlain as soon as he could, Roy needed something new and big to happen quickly to boost his résumé. Here he was in China and he was not about to lose this opportunity to shine while he was there.

"The plan was totally inadequate, insufficient, inconsequential, and inappropriate," he began. "We need new ideas, new strategies! Bold ideas, and bold strategies! We can't wait. China can't wait. Russia can't wait. Comrade Stalin can't wait. We need action. Big, bold, quick, and decisive action! The victory of the Chinese revolution is right around the corner! The proletarians in Asia, in the Soviet Union, and around the world are waiting for us to give the capitalist system the final blow! We must stand up, assume responsibility, and join the greatest struggle of the proletariat worldwide when that day comes!"

"Comrade Roy, I did plan a thousand uprisings across China for the next year," explained Meng.

"Please, special envoy, not comrade. Special envoy, I repeat," insisted Roy, feeling pity for his Chinese associate, who never understood the seriousness of his title and office. "How often should I repeat this again?"

"Okay, Товарищ Рой," Meng smiled, wryly.

Shaking his head, Roy continued, "We need a completely new thinking. The proletarian revolution is facing the most critical moment in history.

Comrade Stalin has already drawn a big blueprint, which was unconditionally accepted by the Comintern. The Chinese Communist Party therefore must act accordingly to play its part in this international revolution. Now, I ask you to call a meeting of the party's top leaders immediately. I need to talk to them in person and convey the Comintern's orders right away."

5

A meeting soon took place and the participants, included Martin, Tania, Dong Zi-Tian, Si-Tu Wen-Liang, Tao Yin-Hu, Hou Shi-Suo, and Lin Shi-Xiong. Most of them had not met the special envoy and hence were eagerly waiting to see and hear from him. Accompanied by Meng, who gave the brief introduction, Roy rose to the podium amid warm applause and began his eight-hour speech, of which the heavily condensed excerpts were as follows:

"History has shown that great events need great ideologies and great leaders. Peharne (pronounced "pǝ-Hä-ni"), the illustrious sage often portrayed as a dejected and wandering mendicant, laid the foundation for the all-encompassing philosophical amalgamation of Peharnism. All great philosophies and great religions have legendary figures, powerful deities, and popular incarnations, such as Shiva and Bhairava, Vishnu and his avatars Krishna and Rama were as an integral part of Hinduism, as Gautama was to Buddhism, Master Kong to Confucianism, and Muhammad to Islam.

"In the modern struggle for communism, the proletarians cannot achieve any progress without the comprehensive guidance of Karl Marx and his closest friend, Friedrich Engels, whose scientific investigations have produced the most effective weapons to fight against capitalism. Their grand theories of the surplus value, historical materialism, class struggle, and scientific dialectics have proven to be the only universal truths that will lead the proletariat to liberation.

"The October Revolution in Russia could not have succeeded without the leadership of Lenin, whose ideas, theories, and principles, based on the latest Russian experience, have further expanded Marxism. His Bolshevik party was the forerunner of today's Russian Communist Party, which has remained uncorrupted amid the rising tide of diverse reformist persuasions and revisionist attacks. Bolshevism or Leninism continues to lead the worldwide communist movement after his death.

"Today, the great leader Stalin has carried on that glorious Marxist and Leninist tradition. Under his marvelous leadership, Lenin's vision of 'socialism in one country' has become an undisputed reality that even the international enemies have to recognize. Comrade Stalin is the greatest hope the working classes have for their ultimate liberation around the globe.

"Comrade Stalin has led the Soviet Union into an unprecedented phase of new development. He launched a political revolution in the party from the top down, and defeated both the Left Opposition and the Right Opposition, both the New Opposition and the United Opposition. Comrade Stalin exposed a series of devilish enemies of the working class, from Leon Trotsky, Lev Kamenev, and Gregory Zinoviev to Nikolai Bukharin, who were summarily expelled from the party.

"Those who continue to oppose Comrade Stalin will not be tolerated and will be resolutely purged from the party to ensure the one hundred percent absolute purity of the vanguard of the working class.

"Most exciting is Comrade Stalin's first five-year plan to develop the command economy, which is fast transforming the Soviet Union into the most advanced industrial nation in the world in a way that no other economic system can. Thousands of farmers are joining the collectives and productivity, agrarian and industrial, has soared in the fields and in the factories of the cities.

"Meanwhile, capitalism is facing its worst and terminal crisis, as Marx had long predicted. The Great Depression, starting from the crash of the New York Stock Exchange in 1929, is quickly spreading across major European countries including Great Britain, Germany, Italy, and France.

"Capitalism everywhere is declining fast and the socialist Soviet Union led by Comrade Stalin is rising to a new conclusive victory. The final countdown is at hand and the Comintern therefore has ordered the Chinese Communist Party to speed up its action and to join this pivotal international struggle of unprecedented historical significance without delay.

"Any hesitation, any inactivity, any reservation, and any slow response will be absolutely unacceptable, and those responsible will be severely disciplined according to the rules of the Comintern. If any leading individual of the party refuses to carry out the Comintern's orders, he will be stripped of his office immediately. If he continues to refuse to reform, he will be expelled from the party and replaced with the one willing to follow the Comintern's lead. If the whole party continues with its inaction, the organization will be kicked out of the Comintern.

"The Comintern has decided the following: the Chinese Communist Party must immediately organize no fewer than ten million peasants and prepare them to attack major cities in these provinces—Henan, Hebei, Shanxi, Shaanxi, Hunan, Hubei, Kuangdong, and Fujian.

"The Chinese Communist Party must immediately organize no fewer than one million workers and prepare them for uprisings in these cities—Shanghai, Wuhan, Peking, Canton, Qingdao, Xuzhou, and Nanchang.

"The Chinese Communist Party must immediately raise no fewer than five hundred thousand soldiers to form a brand-new Red Army to be ready for the final assault on capitalism and for the final takeover of the country.

"But..."

Roy's protracted silence perplexed Si-Tu, Dong, Tao, and Lin, who looked at each other, waiting for the envoy to finish his sentence. Meng quickly came forward and said, "Anyone has any questions?"

Realizing this might be the end of Roy's speech, those present paused for another few seconds. Finally, Tao stood up and said, "We had an armed uprising in Nanchang only a couple of years ago. We then had twenty thousand soldiers and failed to repel the enemy's counterattacks. I believe we will have less opportunity to infiltrate the nationalist troops today compared to the time when we had the alliance with the Nationalist Party. I am not sure that we will succeed in armed revolts in big cities anytime soon."

"Tao personifies the typical pessimism I had just warned about in my speech," said Roy, who was not happy that the first question challenged his basic assessment of the situation in China. "As I have stated, and I believed that I have stated it clearly, that the revolutionary conditions have totally changed within the last few years. Capitalism is declining, is on the path of defeat, while the Soviet Union is winning in every category—political, economic, and diplomatic. The Chinese Communist Party must seize this opportunity and take strong and swift action, so as not to lose this priceless opportunity in history."

Roy looked around and saw that most of the delegates were not as enthusiastic as he had expected. He then realized that someone was absent and asked Meng, "Where is Sheng Bao, the one who has had some military experience?"

"He is in Fujian, regrouping his troops. It is too far away for him to come for this meeting," Meng replied.

"Hmm, the so-called guerrilla expert, I hear. Is he hiding from action too?" Roy persisted.

"Not exactly. He has informed the Central Committee that his reorganization of the troops may take a month or two to complete."

"See, that's exactly what I was talking about. Total anarchy, total disarray, total confusion, total indifference, total loss of control, and total breakdown of authority. Where is the party solidarity? What a shame! What a despicable situation! What you have now is complete chaos, complete disorder, and complete disregard of party commands and discipline. Contact Sheng Bao now and tell him that this special envoy must see him right away. He must leave everything and come to see me immediately!"

Chapter 12

Pains

1

"**D**O YOU HAVE TO GO?" ASKED TANG WAN-YI, WHO DID NOT KNOW why she raised the same question every time her husband was about to leave, even though she already knew the answer.

"Yes, I have to," replied Sheng Bao without betraying any emotion as he packed his things.

"Do you know for how long?" she asked again, but immediately regretted it.

"No, I don't," said he, giving his standard response to her same question.

"Would you come back to see us?" her feeble voice shook so much that she could barely hear it herself.

"I really don't know." He started to frown and she stopped asking.

Tang and Sheng were part of a generation where the men and women, revolutionaries or otherwise, became obsessed when they were in love but then paid little attention to their spouses after marriage. Passionate romances, triumphant or fatal or aborted, grabbed headlines, topped the list of bestselling books, became fodder for dramatization, and had inspired poetry for ages. Once that stage of searching for love had passed, few understood how to transform that wonderful passion into a viable marriage. Spontaneous and fervent love stories frequently became classics in literature, while the inevitably mundane marriage life usually ended forgotten, never to be immortalized in any ode.

Although Tang adored Sheng, the energetic and dedicated revolutionary, she had yet to figure out how to live with her highly driven husband on a daily basis. Confucian teachings and social conventions stressed feminine virtues such as loyalty and obedience to men, and her beloved parents' relationship epitomized such old-fashioned behavior.

Tang was also little prepared for marriage life, having tied the knot with Sheng hastily after losing both her parents within a short period. A young city girl and a northerner, she tried everything she could to adapt to her husband's southern and rural habits. Sheng, for one, was totally convinced about the inseparable connection between red-hot peppers and a red-hot rebellious spirit. Thus, Tang would cook many pepper dishes whenever he was home, even though she did not like hot and spicy food at all. She would eat rice with him every day even though she preferred pasta—the staple food in the North. She tolerated his habit of not washing his feet before going to bed, a common practice by peasants. She endured his loud snoring and never complained about it, lest that offend him.

She had borne Sheng three children in the past five years, even though she did not want to be like those peasants' wives who were expected to produce like a sow. But what Tang feared the most was that her husband seemed to take everything for granted, and all that he was concerned about was how she should behave as a dutiful wife, not about his own role in their marriage. The romance and tender feelings toward each other during their courtship just a few years ago had vanished into a distant memory.

Granted, Sheng was a patriot, an important organizer, and a professional revolutionary engaging in an extraordinarily worthy cause. But was it against the rule that he should sometimes show his tender loving care toward her? To be sensitive and considerate of her feelings? To ask and accommodate her wants? To share her endless household chores? To pay some attention to the children's education and welfare? Was it too much to ask of a man to be mindful of these matters? Or was it too much to demand them from a professional revolutionary? Was dedication to the revolution totally incompatible with the role and responsibilities of a caring husband?

Tang had no answers and Sheng never paid attention to these questions. He believed that there were only two kinds of matters in the world—the big ones (such as a cause, a revolution, and the country's future) and the small ones (such as family, marriage, or any personal issues and sentiments). While both categories demanded his attention, the second type of issues would never be as important as the first. As a professional revolutionary who had devoted his entire life to the grand schemes of the first category, he was entitled not to be bogged down by personal things. If there was a conflict between the two, the second should always yield to the first and so should his wife and children to him, each of whom was responsible for a completely different kind of activity. This might not sound egalitarian but, Sheng reasoned, for the sake of the big cause, for the future of the country and its people, and for their ultimate long-term interests, anything personal, temporal, and inconsequential—or everything in the second category—could and should be sacrificed.

A great cause and a great revolution needed great leaders who must be willing to endure great pains and face great sacrifices. In the name of the revolution and for a better tomorrow, Sheng believed that he was destined to become such a leader and he was never to waver in the face of any difficulties. Since Tang had chosen him to be her husband, she should do the same without any complaints.

Tang never regretted her choice. She loved Sheng, the tall, handsome, and resilient man who had impressed her with his determination to save the country when they first met at the Tower of Yellow Cranes. Just like Sheng, she understood what a noble cause he was involved in and was aware of the dangers he had to face and the sacrifices he had to make every day. As his wife, she would never stand in the way of the cause, nor would she want to distract his attention purely for her and the children's sake. A strong patriot herself, she would never do anything that might compromise his principles or tarnish his name as a communist. She knew that, as one of the party's top leaders, he should be a role model for others. He must be tough and selfless, and must focus all his energies on revolutionary activities, instead of family affairs. When the moment came, everything, including his wife and children, that could be sacrificed would be sacrificed for the sake of the cause and in the name of the revolution.

What Tang wanted was a reassurance that he cared about her as his wife, and that he would sometimes show that she still mattered in his life as much as he did in hers. A word, a gesture, or any sign of tenderness was all that Tang needed, which would make her happy, thinking he still loved her as wholeheartedly as when they first dated. She needed to feel his manly reassurance, to embrace it; she needed to see it, and to receive it unequivocally. Any small but warm gestures or tiniest expressions of love and care from the husband would be the ultimate vindication of her existence as his wife.

The day prior to his departure, Sheng returned home, shouting, "Come out, Wan-Yi! You wouldn't believe who is here!"

Tang, who was in the kitchen, rushed into the yard in front of their house—a thatched structure of bamboo, straw, mud, and adobe. Her right hand held the dampened apron at her waist—she had been washing all morning in the kitchen—and she raised her left hand to block the bright sunshine so she could see the visitor.

There stood a lovely young woman, whom Sheng introduced as Dai Tian.

"How are you?" Tang greeted her as she tried to recall who the woman was.

"The talented Dai, the famous newspaper reporter, remember?" Sheng said enthusiastically and then requested, "Prepare some good dishes for lunch, okay?"

Back in the kitchen Tang began searching for ingredients, but, except for some dry peppers and a few cups of rice, she had nothing. "How can I make the guest happy?" she wondered nervously, "If I can't, he will be upset." Finally she decided to sacrifice an egg-laying hen to please her husband and his guest, even though it was one of the last two hens she had raised for the children.

An hour later, Tang brought the dishes to the dining table. Sheng was elated and said, "Dai, please eat all you can. The best dishes my wife had ever cooked—chicken soup, fried chicken with hot peppers, and the homemade pickles mixed with fermented black soybeans—your favorite."

Tang excused herself and went back to clean the kitchen. She could hear Sheng and Dai talking cheerfully about how they had met two years ago and what had happened since, and began to feel sorry for herself. She believed that she and Dai were about the same age. But from her looks alone—the short-haired guest was wearing a smart uniform complete with a pair of short military boots—Dai appeared at least five years younger. She must still be single, Tang thought, judging from the way Sheng talked to and looked at Dai. "Unlike me, the mother of three, with the weather-beaten face and wrinkled hands; I must have long passed the stage of being attractive to my own husband or any man," Tang sadly concluded.

She did not mind that Sheng had good friends, even female ones. Away from home all the time, he needed company, which was quite understandable. His political activities and organizational responsibilities also requested him to be in touch with a wide range of people from various professions. She totally understood that Sheng enjoyed meeting with people of knowledge and talent, particularly those who shared the same interests as he in classical literature and history. If Dai happened to be one of them, why not?

After lunch, Sheng and his guest continued to talk for several hours, and the conversation covered a wide spectrum of domestic and foreign topics. The highly intelligent Dai seemed to have traveled far and wide. London, Paris, Berlin, New York, Los Angeles, and San Francisco—she had been to all these amazing places and written numerous newspaper articles about her overseas experiences. An avid reader of such foreign authors as Fyodor Dostoyevsky, John Milton, Charlotte Brontë, Jane Austen, Charles Fourier, and Theodore Dreiser, she was one of the few Chinese female writers who had published several novels and whose literary talent was well recognized in literary circles.

A personal friend of Mrs. Sun Yat-Sen, Dai was also under the private tutelage of Mr. Lu—one of most famous writers since the May Fourth Movement. Dai's close ties with both Mrs. Sun and Mr. Lu helped open doors to the families of many upper-class elites and the intelligentsia living in the urban areas across China. She used her distinguished and varied social connections to serve as an undercover courier, traveling frequently between Sheng's Red Army's base in rural China and the communist headquarters in cities like Shanghai or Wuhan. She was one of the most indispensable figures in the organization and Sheng, often isolated in some locale without access to information, always spent hours talking with her whenever they got a chance to meet.

Although slightly jealous of their closeness, Tang had actually learned a lot just by listening quietly to their long conversation. She could not believe that Dai, a single woman, had so many accomplishments under her belt at such a young age. How Tang wished that she could have the same opportunity to be as well informed, well traveled, well published, well acquainted with famous personalities, and well versed in both Chinese classics and foreign literature as Dai. But, above all, Tang wished that she could be as talented as Dai in writing articles and stories, which was something she knew Sheng appreciated most. Tang noticed a long time ago that her husband, an enthusiastic student of Chinese classics, literature, and history, always let his guard down in front of talented female writers and would enjoy talking with them for hours. If only she could polish her writing skills, Tang imagined, she might have the same effect on her husband.

By the time Dai finally finished debriefing Sheng, the kids were already back home, yelling that they were starving. Tang handed a sweet potato to each of them, promising that dinner would be ready in a few minutes. Picking up some dry branches and straw as fuel, she went into the kitchen and started to build a fire in the low earth stove on the dirt floor. Flickering flames soon reflected on her weary face as she started to ponder seriously about the meal she needed to prepare right away, instead of how to improve her writing skills tonight.

2

The demotion hurt Martin deeply. He could not believe that the Comintern would send such an idiot like Roy to replace him, who had more experience and knowledge about China than anyone else in the organization. He also believed that the current directives from the Comintern, as related by Roy, were impractical at best and wrongheaded at worst. Having just experienced the brutal cleansing by General Chen Han and other hostile nationalists, China was not yet ready for a nationwide uprising, which would only expose the small and weak Communist Party to extreme danger. Stripped of his office and feeling powerless, Martin did not know what to say in his report of self-examination and rectification, which would be reviewed by his foolish new boss, Roy.

Nor did Tania know exactly what to do this time. Both of them felt trapped by the Comintern's bureaucracy and its inflexible structure, manipulative rules, and stifling regulations. Tania suggested a delaying tactic, by not voicing their true opinions or submitting their reports at this point, even though this would only further infuriate Roy. Instead, they should claim that they needed some time to reexamine all the new information and their past experiences in order to present a thorough account later. Meanwhile, they should indicate their plan to focus on another important task they had been ordered to accomplish—to establish a trading company in Shanghai to help finance the communist movement in China.

The proposal was reluctantly accepted by Roy, who knew what they were up to but also understood the limits of his power. However much authority he believed he had, he had no means to force Martin and Tania to confess their sins.

However, Tania soon discovered that the diversion strategy did little to heal Martin's wounds. Making money had never interested him, and collecting furs in Russia and selling them in China further dismayed him. He became restless, more irritable than ever, and finally started to drink heavily. Tania was deeply concerned for she had seen too many men ruined by the bottle. Then she received disappointing news about their son Peter, who complained about the foster home he was staying in. An idea came to Tania and she told Martin, "Why don't we find a place for Peter in America, where you may have some relatives who would be willing to take him in?"

Martin heartily agreed and started to make the necessary arrangements. Through his family's good network, the couple finally chose the family of Max van Aken in Amsterdam in upstate New York as the new home for Peter. Martin took leave from Roy and was soon on his way to fetch Peter and accompany him to the United States.

Born a princess from a noble family, Tania had never thought business to be her cup of tea. Yet trading in Siberian furs and buying Chinese tea, salt, silk, and porcelain for the Russian market intrigued her, and she quickly became known as the smart shop owner on Avenue Joffre in Shanghai. For a decade after the October Revolution, about twenty-five thousand to fifty thousand Russians had fled the country and arrived in this metropolis and international free port, where foreigners were not required to have any passport or visa. Many of them settled along the rather empty street, making it their home in this foreign land. Affectionately called "Little Moscow" by the locals, this section of Avenue Joffre in the French Concession was lined with stores, restaurants, coffee houses, bars, tailor shops, bakeries, barbershops, pharmacies, fashion salons, and dance halls. Almost a thousand businesses mushroomed in less than five years, transforming the rustic Avenue Joffre into one of the most delightful shopping districts in Shanghai. Customers could try out European fashion in the afternoon, go to a Turkish or Middle Eastern restaurant for supper, enjoy a jazz band while gaming at a bar or watching a cabaret, and spend the whole night at the ornate ballroom until dawn.

Tania was glad that her store could blend in so well with this bustling European business community full of Russian flavors, which turned out to be a perfect cover for her secret mission. She made many friends and acquaintances among these Russian exiles, who provided valuable information to her about everything from local gossip and commercial activities to municipal politics and international diplomacy.

To her great delight, Yan Yan lived not far from her and the two often went for afternoon tea together. The ever practical and observant Yan told Tania that, behind the fuss and buzz on Avenue Joffre, poor Russian men worked as bodyguards, doormen, janitors, waiters, laborers, dockworkers, watchmen, and chauffeurs. Many of them often ended up in beggary, just as it was common for those poor Russian women to become prostitutes. According to rumors, as many as eight thousand Russian prostitutes were working in the city. Many were rape victims, while others were the poor captives of human traffickers. Tania realized just how lucky she had been to escape this tragic but not uncommon fate for thousands of Russian women in China.

The most sensitive topic, though, was about their husbands. Tania did not want to mention it initially but the question came out in the end. "I heard you have left Lu Shi-Yan?" She looked at Yan nervously.

"Yes, that was some time ago," Yan did not seem to mind at all. "It's all over now," she added.

"Don't you miss him?" Tania asked.

"Me? No, never," said Yan resolutely.

"I heard he has been very sick lately. Don't you want to go and see him?"

"I... I don't know..." Yan paused.

Detecting a chance, Tania said gently, "I think Lu is still a good person. Besides, you have loved him so much and you had always been with him when he was sick."

Tears began running down Yan's face even though she did not say anything. So much pain, so many memories, so much humiliation, so much pride, so much tenderness, so much hate, so much resentment, and yet so much love—Yan's conflicting emotions raged in her heart, and she could no longer maintain her composure. "Yes, I was always there when he was sick because I loved him so much, I loved him so much." Yan buried her face in her hands as her uncontrollable sobs shook her whole body.

"Yan, my dear," Tania patted her friend's arm and said softly, "take it easy. We all make mistakes and we all need forgiveness. If you want to go and see him, I can go with you."

"Really?" Yan raised her head, her beautiful big bright black eyes still brimming with tears.

"Of course," said Tania. "I will go anytime whenever you are ready."

"Tania, you are my best friend." If not for the constraints of traditional etiquette, Yan would have hugged and kissed Tania, whose sensitive soul had seen through another woman's predicament.

A moment later Yan asked, "How come you are so... so..." Searching for her words, she tried to sound as appreciative as she could. "So nice? And so kind?" But, as one who hardly ever lost any verbal contest or emotional high ground, she quickly changed tack. "What if this happened to Martin? What if he had betrayed you? What would you do then?"

Yan's sharp and direct question surprised Tania. She paused. "I don't know. I honestly don't know what I would do if that's the case."

"Bad question. My fault. Never mind, my mistake. What a silly thing to say." Yan quickly apologized, realizing that she had put her friend in an awkward position.

3

The next day the two women went to see Si-To Wen-Liang. After hearing Yan's request to visit Lu, Si-Tu did not respond immediately. Under normal circumstances, the sympathetic Si-Tu would have granted Yan Yan's request without question. But the problem was that Lu had become a highly controversial figure in the Communist Party, and allowing Yan to visit him might cause problems for the party.

"Yan, I don't know how to put this more delicately," Si-Tu, a man instinctively bashful and diffident before a matron, said quietly, like a boy confessing to a mistake before his parent. "Lu is no longer the secretary-general of our party.

But he is still your legal husband, and I have no personal objection to your wish to meet with him. But Moscow and the Comintern are very upset with his several public announcements declaring support for Trotsky and opposition to Comrade Stalin. The party therefore has cut all ties with him. And, if you were to visit him at this time, our party will have a difficult time in explaining this to Moscow and the Comintern."

"I don't care about what Moscow and the Comintern think about my husband. All I know is that Shi-Yan is sick. I am his wife, and I need to see and take care of him. I really don't understand why anyone would care about a wife visiting her sick husband." Yan clearly had a different perspective from Si-Tu.

"Okay, Yan, how about this?" Si-Tu attempted to calm her down. "I will ask Cheng Chu-Li to find out about his situation, and then I will let you know."

"Why do you need permission to breathe? I am here right now. Why don't you just ask Cheng to take me there right away? Why the delay? What if Shi-Yan dies tonight? Then I will never have a chance to see my husband for the last time in this world!" Yan started to cry as if Lu was indeed dying.

Tania tried earnestly not to laugh at Yan's performance. Si-Tu understood her tactic too but he was more concerned that, if this conversation did not end soon, he might not be able to do anything for the rest of the day, or even for the next several days.

"Okay, okay. Chu-Li, why don't you take Yan and Tania to see Lu at this address?" Si-Tu whispered the secret location to Cheng's ear, even as he detected a triumphant smile on Yan's face. "And please note, Chu-Li, nobody should know about this, absolutely nobody," he firmly told his faithful assistant.

As the three walked out of Si-Tu's office, his wife, Hong Shi-Mei, walked in.

"Who are these women?" she asked.

"You have met them, Shi-Mei. Yan Yan, the housekeeper at our headquarters. And Tania, the wife of Emissary Martin from the Comintern," Si-Tu reminded her.

"Why were they here?" she persisted.

"Oh, Yan wanted to see her husband, Lu," Si-Tu found her inquiry odd but kept his calm.

"Why did they stay for so long?" Hong seemed to have more questions.

"Not very long, my dear, just a few minutes," he explained.

"Just a few minutes? I saw you talking and chatting with them for over an hour," the wife protested.

"Not at all, Shi-Mei. Maybe half an hour at the most," clarified the husband.

"Nonsense. I saw you flirting with them, I saw they enjoyed flirting with you, and I knew why they looked at you the way they did!" Hong then burst into a half-hour enumeration of the minute details, real and imagined, of how the two women turned their female charms on her husband, how he had reciprocated using his virile charisma, and, most of all, how all these deviant behaviors would never escape her eagle eyes.

"Shi-Mei, please, not again. I swear they came here with a request, which was discussed and settled. Nothing more, nothing less." Not the first time he was interrogated, Si-Tu tried to defuse the tense situation even though he was very upset over this unnecessary interruption and her unwarranted suspicions.

"What request?" Hong was not about to give up easily.

"You must have heard it, Yan wanted to meet her husband, Lu."

"Then why was Tania here?" Hong finally revealed the real target of their conversation.

"Tania and Yan are friends. She wanted to support Yan," he explained.

"What an excuse! If Yan wanted to see her husband, what has that got to do with Tania? I knew it. She simply wanted to come here and flirt with you, Si-Tu Wen-Liang!" Hong's voice started to quiver, as if she was about to cry.

"Shi-Mei, you are such a wonderful lady. Why get so upset over something that does not exist?" Si-Tu tried to appease her and patiently said, "Let me get you a cup of water."

He stood up, poured a cup of hot water, handed it to his wife, and helped her to sit down. The warm water did soothe Hong and she seemed to have calmed down considerably after emptying the cup. Si-Tu took her to the bedroom and talked with her for a little while more until she finally felt exhausted and dozed off.

4

By anyone's estimation, Si-Tu was one of the party's key members from the start. Most of them, especially the women, would also consider him to be one of the most handsome men they had ever seen. While his thick beard, dashing eyes, erect nose, chiseled face, and thick, jet-black hair looked mesmerizing to some, his good taste, broad smile, and gentlemanly manners captivated others. Hence, Hong always felt insecure whenever she found out that Si-Tu had been talking with some women. She became particularly jealous when he was meeting with a beautiful woman, such as Tania, even though he had repeatedly professed that he had no interest in other women. Arranged either by parents or institutions, marriage could be an excruciating trap and a terrible prison for a highly individualistic person. What amazed most people was not only how Si-Tu had gotten into such a marriage in the first place but also how he could have endured it for as long as he had.

If Si-Tu displayed striking fortitude in keeping his unusual marriage intact, his ability to survive the intensely convoluted factional strife and partisan conflict could only be described as incredible. Despite being one of the most highly intelligent, highly skillful, and highly polished veterans of the party, Si-Tu was never at the apex of the party leadership, even though he had consistently held various critical offices next to that highest position. This might be due partly by design, and partly by choice.

Like all great achievers, Si-Tu was not an unambitious person, but he knew his limitations. He believed early on that his bourgeois family background had disqualified him from leading a working-class organization. Instead of aiming for ultimate control over the organization, his mission in life was to undergo a complete transformation from petty bourgeoisie to true proletarian. Besides, he clearly understood his personal strengths and inherent weaknesses, which would only make him a good manager, not a superb national spokesman for his cause and organization. He could be a good hands-on supervisor, but not a visionary strategist. He was more comfortable with implementing a policy than making it. He enjoyed the day-to-day operations of his organization more than making grand strategies for it. Modest, thoughtful, and effective, he was a model operative but never a remarkable pioneer, an imaginative creator, or a bold architect. He was more willing to follow someone else's lead instead of leading others. He was more comfortable to work behind the scenes than to be at the forefront.

Thus, even though Si-Tu was never at the very top of the party, he was always at the front and center of its every major operation. More than any other senior party members, he knew every minuscule detail of this organization, both confidential and public. He knew all the party's top secrets, its clandestine spy rings, its communication lines, its diverse divisions, its vital statistics, its complicated personnel management, its inner sanctums and hidden offices, its foreign contacts and international connections, its past glories, its ongoing campaigns, its internal scandals, its worst failures, its historic dirty deals, and its never-ending propaganda schemes. Nothing escaped his watchful eyes and nothing would be too small for him to handle. With his boundless energy, Si-Tu slept little at night, and working twelve, sixteen, and even twenty hours a day was not uncommon for him. He was a demanding boss who terrified those incompetent staff. He could gain people's trust quickly but never tolerated those who betrayed him. His fingerprints were all over the areas the party had expanded to, and his control over the organization went much deeper and wider than any of those top officeholders could imagine. In fact, not a single party leader could effectively lead this organization without his support and collaboration. No matter who held the party's top national offices, Si-Tu was the *sine qua non* of the party.

When Cheng returned, he immediately reported to Si-Tu about everything that had happened during the two women's meeting with Lu. The former secretary-general was terribly sick, suffering from pneumonia, Cheng said. Bedridden and coughing blood, he was nonetheless as stubborn as ever, claiming that he wanted to write a strong rebuttal against Stalin, whose wrong policies toward China would lead the Chinese Communist Party to ruins. When Yan suggested he should care more about his health than politics, he retorted that imprisonment and the sickbed had always been the best time and place for him to clear his mind and focus on perfecting his ideas.

"What was Yan's reaction?" the boss asked.

"She was very sad, and she was unusually patient and attentive toward Lu. She said she would never leave him again, and was thinking of moving in with him to take care of him."

"What did you say?" Si-Tu calmly inquired, testing Cheng's loyalty and intelligence.

"I said this would need official permission and the party might not allow it," Cheng replied, hoping he had passed the test.

"Good," the confirmation ended the assistant's anxiety. The boss asked again, "What did Yan say?"

"She said she didn't care," Cheng replied. "She will come to see you again to ask for permission, and to beg if necessary."

"What about Tania?" Si-Tu shifted his subject to maintain control of the conversation.

"Tania was very emotional too," Cheng reported. "She helped Yan to clean the room and comforted the distraught Yan."

"Anything else?" Si-Tu never missed a chance to know the smallest details.

"Oh, Tania said it's a shame that the party would treat Lu Shi-Yan, the founder, so poorly and so disrespectfully. And she suggested that the party should find a doctor to attend to him immediately, and to provide all means possible to improve his living conditions and medical treatment."

Cheng paused but he could not tell Si-Tu's true feelings from his boss's face, which showed a series of solemn yet placid, caring but detached expressions. Finally, he said, "Okay, Chu-Li, you go to the Presbyterian Church Hospital tomorrow and look for Dr. Fred Connelly. Tell him that I would appreciate it if he could visit and check on Lu Shi-Yan. Also, let Yan know that she can visit Lu no more than three times a week. She can't stay there overnight. As for Tania, tell her not to visit Lu anymore."

"Yes, I understand," Cheng answered.

"Once again, no one should know about these visits," Si-Tu reiterated. "If Moscow finds out, we will have a hard time explaining."

"Understood." Cheng responded confidently as usual. The unquestionable ability to maintain total secrecy and confidentiality was a prerequisite to working for Si-Tu, and that was exactly why he had kept Cheng as an aide for so long.

"Also, your group should be on alert," Si-Tu continued. "Hou Shi-Suo will be coming back from Wuhan any day now. He will bring back important new instructions from the Politburo and the special envoy. Your group needs to be fully prepared when he arrives."

"Yes, of course." Cheng answered like a soldier, as he sensed the serious nature of his task from Si-Tu's voice.

5

Hou Shi-Suo and his wife Wang Yu had a great time in Wuhan. It was not their maiden visit to the city but the first time on the party's expense. As the head of a special unit directly responsible to the party's central leadership, Hou was in charge of a secret division of bodyguards and henchmen to protect the safety of top party officials. He could spend a huge amount of money whenever he desired, which only made his meager comrades envious. When he met Roy for several extended discussions about current affairs, the special envoy was deeply impressed with Hou's working-class background, his assessment of the organization, and his utmost dedication to the communist cause. Roy hinted that, when the time was right, Hou, the real representative of the laboring masses, could lead this proletarian organization. Greatly flattered and energized, Hou, although required to report to Si-Tu as soon as possible, decided not to leave for Shanghai immediately but to extend his stay for a day of fun.

The morning air felt so delicious following the usual long and warm day before, with vendors yelling in the distance urging residents to sample the traditional products they had been selling for years. Always an early bird, wife Wang went out of the tavern to buy breakfast. She regarded her husband as the world's greatest hero, who had rescued her from a brothel and then married her despite her past. She was willing to do anything to serve and please him. When Hou finally got up about an hour later, he saw not a breakfast but a full banquet on the table.

The energetic and proud Wang, an astute connoisseur of local food wherever they traveled, was cheerfully explaining everything she had bought from the market. "These dry golden noodles are refreshingly warm and only mildly spicy," said she. These pickled duck necks—chewy but tasty and good for both meals and snacks. Crunchy rice donuts—well baked, crisp, and yummy but best consumed with some sweet potato chips. Twisted dough sticks— deep fried, wrapped in glutinous rice dipping in sugar powder, and irresistibly delicious. Steamed dumplings—fresh, juicy, and slightly pungent due to a touch of black pepper inside. Fresh fish soup stewed with chopped dough sticks—a warm and soothing dish for the hungry stomach, highly fulfilling every time. Exquisite shrimp from nearby lakes sprinkled with wild red peppers—hot on the palate but amazingly delightful to the senses. Fried potato cakes—served on top of sliced green-bean tofu rolls with sensuous fillings inside, succulent, and heavenly. And, last but not least, pickled fish fillet salad dressed in specially mixed colorful local sauces.

"You are going to feed an army." Hou was delighted, as most men would be in front of such tempting dishes. He picked up a steamed dumpling, tasted it, and remarked, "Umm, it's good. It's really good. Very fresh and juicy. Perhaps even better than the ones we often had in Shanghai due to the special kick of the black peppers—a unique ingredient not used in other steamed dumplings I have tasted. But a successful combination, I would concede." Steamed dumplings were the venerated Shanghai specialty popular not only among native residents, but also in many restaurants around China. Giving credit to a different version of the dumplings in a different city was not easy for Hou, who prided himself as a firm defender and loyal advocate of Shanghai cuisine.

Wang blushed—nothing would make her happier than pleasing her husband. "Good, good. Then try some of this, this, and this..." She lined up the dishes, earnestly waiting for him to try them and give his verdict.

When Hou finished the meal, completely relaxed, and was ready for tea, the wife asked timidly, "So, what is your favorite dish?"

"Well, let's see..." He hesitated. "That must be, if I have to say, the pickled fish fillet. A unique dish."

In China, the most common way to serve any fish was to cook it. A cold fish fillet salad did not seem to be a typical Chinese dish. Wang was elated again for she had deliberated for a long time at the market before finally deciding to buy the fish fillet and give it a try. "Oh, I am so happy that you liked it." She wanted to reveal to him that the fillet was really made of fish skin, but decided against it. Given Hou's temperamental nature, she was afraid that the revelation might cause him to explode with rage and ruin a perfectly good morning.

So Wang related how she was struggling with the choice and how she finally made the decision. The story earned her the lavish praise that she had yearned for—"You are such a doll, a clever baby, and a devilish bitch"—followed by Hou's wildly passionate kisses all over her lips, eyes, cheeks, and ears.

"Let's go out," Hou told his wife after the smooching and fondling ended. "We have some business to attend to," he said as a friend, Mr. Tong Zi-Fu, from Wuhan's Grand Fellowship Society, arrived.

Their first stop was a horse racing track. A local history buff, Mr. Tong told the couple that Wuhan had three tracks for horse racing, while Shanghai had only one. The one they were going to was not far from where they stayed. "Are we heading away from the Bund?" Wang asked.

"Yes, Mrs. Hou," Mr. Tong replied. "The racecourse to the east, just over the Japanese Concession at the Bund, is for foreigners alone. The one we are heading to is in the western section of Hankou above the railroad, which is for the Chinese."

"Why two separate racecourses?" Wang asked.

Well, several years ago, Mr. Tong began, a wealthy merchant Mr. Zhang went to the east racecourse, which was the only one in town at the time. He was stopped by the guard, who said no Chinese were allowed to enter. Humiliated and outraged, he called for a meeting that very night with a number of fellow Chinese merchants and businessmen, who decided to build a new one for themselves. A wealthy real estate developer, Mr. Liu, provided the land. "So here it is. The Chinese racecourse is one of most successful businesses in Wuhan today," concluded Mr. Tong.

"Where is the third racecourse?" Hou was curious.

"The third one is called the International Racecourse, my brother. It is north of us, in between the Chinese Racecourse and the Foreign Racecourse," answered Mr. Tong.

"Indeed, three racecourses in one city—that is marvelous," Wang exclaimed.

"Yes, I think that's quite rare in any city in the world," Mr. Tong agreed.

"That's why Hankou is called China's Chicago, I hear," Hou said.

"Likely so," said Mr. Tong. "Look at the riverfront. There are literally miles of ships lining up along our ports and docks on the Yangtze River and the Han River day and night. Regardless of distance, domestic commerce, international trade, railroad transportation, and cargo ships all come down here. Going overseas, any passengers can leave Wuhan aboard a ship sailing to Japan, America, Italy, England, France, Germany, Egypt, Brazil, and more."

"Well, that's impressive," Hou said. He did take Wang to see the Bund the other evening, and both thought the Bund here in Hankou was bigger and more spacious than the one in Shanghai. The mighty Yangtze was the undisputed number one river in China and its massive water surface here at midstream in Wuhan was much wider and more majestic than that of the Hanpu River in Shanghai.

The first horse race was about to start. Hou found the racecourse to be as big as the one in Shanghai, perhaps even bigger. The relatively new facilities and fresh paint made the stadium attractive and hundreds of enthusiastic race fans were anxiously waiting for the competition to begin.

Bang! There was the shot. Hou, Wang, and Mr. Tong were totally engrossed in the race, waving, shouting, and cheering all the way like everyone else.

The first race ended in less than three minutes. Hou won two hundred yuan for his bet. "I love this race!" shouted Wang, "I love Wuhan!"

6

After an exhilarating afternoon of five races, Hou pocketed a total of eight hundred yuan and the overjoyed Wang kissed him and repeatedly called him "genius." Mr. Tong took the happy couple to a nearby teahouse and ordered some desserts for them. Just as the bubbly Wang was about to ask what was next, Hou said, "Mr. Tong will take us to the opera."

"How wonderful!" Wang started to kiss Hou again.

"Madam, the opera we are going to watch is distinctive to Central China." The ever-patient and polite Mr. Tong explained, "This region used to be the Kingdom of Chu in ancient times. The style of the show therefore is called Chu Opera, just as Peking opera was named after the northern tradition and style it has inherited."

The introduction somehow failed to impress Wang, who loved to attend performances of all kinds, musical, comical, or melodramatic. Style was never an issue. What really mattered to her was the type of stories in the shows. Even though she was illiterate, she was a sensitive soul who especially enjoyed watching those familiar romantic scenes in any traditional plays, and who often cried with those actors and actresses over their characters' tragic fates.

No sooner had Mr. Tong informed them that tonight's opera was based on of the romantic classic *The West Chamber* than Wang stood up and screamed, "What are we waiting for?"

Mr. Tong laughed and courteously obliged. He took the couple to a grand theater and settled them in a luxurious box overlooking the stage, one of the best seats in the theater. Wang could not help but said loudly to Hou, "Did you arrange all this?" The husband nodded and Wang threw her arms around his neck. "Thank you! Thank you! Thank you! I can't believe it. This is the most beautiful theater I have ever been to! And the best seat I have ever had!"

Hou took his seat but did not say anything. He looked to his friend, and both smiled.

As the play was about to begin, Wang noticed Hou whispering into Mr. Tong's ear for a few seconds before quietly disappearing from the box. She pretended she had seen nothing and continued to focus all her attention on the stage. Based on her past experience, she knew what Hou was up to, but decided to maintain her silence, and simply enjoy her evening at the opera.

Wang's instincts were correct. Everything that had happened throughout the day was a charade. Hou had carefully planned it all with Mr. Tong to entertain and distract her so that Hou would have a chance to sneak out to meet his mistress for the evening. He had used the same ploy countless times in the past to visit his mistresses or prostitutes. Wang knew it but she had no power, courage, or will to confront him, and Hou knew that as well. He was confident that Wang's embarrassing past and hopeless situation made her extremely vulnerable, which was exactly why he had married her. Wang would never disobey him because he had purchased her from the brothel. He owned her just like a piece of furniture. Plus, she used to be a prostitute and thus was forever stigmatized by society. Shunned and despised by everyone who knew her, she would never have the guts to stand up and defend her dignity as a woman, much less her rights as a spouse in this unequal union.

"This is man," Wang thought, bleeding in her heart. "This is Hou Shi-Suo. So cruel, so calculative, so devious, so mean, so unscrupulous, so heartless. And yet so pretentious, so hypocritical, so crooked, and so evil." She then tried to forget the brutal reality by focusing on the opera and crying profusely over the heart-wrenching stories of women, both on and off the stage.

Along with opium and gambling, prostitution was one of the three most widespread banes in modern China; Wuhan was no exception. Prostitution was legal in the city. Each year, the contributions from no fewer than three to five thousand registered prostitutes were the second largest to the tax coffers in the city, where no man who wanted a prostitute would ever fail to find one.

Hou, with his large network of friends and informants, would have no problem finding one anywhere anytime. In fact, he even had to pick and choose from those local prostitutes, who had been divided into several classes according to their looks and backgrounds. He quickly rejected those from Shanghai, having seen their ilk too many times already. He also eliminated the ones from the North immediately, believing northerners to be too strong and too rough for his taste. A woman from the southeastern province of Fujian, he surmised, could be exotic since he had never met one before. But he eventually settled on a southern girl from the next province, Hunan, thinking a southern female would have the kind of delicacy and tenderness he desired.

A fellow under Mr. Tong's command took Hou to the alley where the girl lived. He entered the yard according to prearranged signals. The girl was waiting and Hou was delighted. Without much ado, he took her straight to the bedroom.

When Hou finally returned to the tavern, he found Wang was already fast asleep. Mr. Tong had sent her back after the show, as the two men had planned. Hou undressed himself and went to lie down next to Wang. Feeling neither guilty nor regretful, he fell asleep within seconds.

7

Ever disdainful of any theory, Hou held a simple notion of life, which agreed completely with the social Darwinist idea of natural selection and survival of the fittest. The world was a jungle and a bogus morality, he believed. Everyone was selfish and you had to do what you had to do to survive. Willpower and deception were the only means to fight those who were stronger than you. Strength and duplicity were also the means to exploit those who were weaker than you. Only in this way could you protect and advance your own interests. And, if you didn't, someone else would do that onto you. Sympathy, mercy, and charity had never worked in this world. They were the creations of intellectuals and scholars, good for no one but those pitiful women and frail men who could never stand on their own but forever relied on superior forces for their protection and livelihood.

The next morning, Hou woke up fully refreshed. The dutiful Wang again bought the goodies for his breakfast; neither of them mentioned anything about last night.

Hou had booked their tickets for a ship scheduled to leave for Shanghai in the morning. They quickly packed up and left for the port. The dock was already very crowded, and many passengers and travelers hastily passed each other to look for their vessels. As the couple passed through the third dock and finally located the ship heading for Shanghai, Hou suddenly stopped. An amateur magician with messy hair in his mid-forties was playing a card trick on a small platform, surrounded by two dozen onlookers. They cheered when the magician mysteriously produced four aces from a random selection of the deck of cards.

Hou was intrigued. He joined crowd despite Wang's exhortations that they had only a few more minutes left to board the ship.

Hou went up to the magician and said, "Would you mind if I shared a trick with you?"

"Of course not." The fellow was in a good mood, having already collected a few coins for his morning show.

Hou smiled. He then moved forward and showed both his hands to the crowd. "You see anything?" he asked.

"No, nothing," those watching him replied.

"Good. But look again." As he uttered these words, Hou quickly turned around, his hands now reaching toward the magician.

Before anyone could say anything, Hou retrieved a bowl of golden noodles from under the magician's flying hair strands, which stunned him and the crowd.

"I believe this most famous local delicacy is yours," Hou gently handed the bowl of steamy noodles to the dumbfounded magician and pushed through the crowd to join his wife.

8

Hou was not the last passenger to board the ship as it prepared to depart. But Wang still blamed him for his tardiness and childish obsession with magic games. "That's quite all right. We both had a good time, didn't we?" he responded cheerfully, still relishing the big surprise he was able to pull off a moment ago.

Unbeknown to him, several undercover detectives walked up and stealthily surrounded him from behind. Before he could do anything, four pistols were pointing at his head and one voice shouted,

"Hou Shi-Suo, you damn communist, you are under arrest!"

"I think you got the wrong person." He tried to remain calm even as he started to stagger.

"The wrong person?" The chief detective waved to the magician who had suddenly showed up. "You, tell him!"

Also an undercover detective, the magician took off his wig, wiped the makeup from his face, and told Hou, "We have been following you for a long time. Show me the index finger of your left hand and we can then confirm your identity."

"Broken Finger" Hou collapsed while Wang fell to the floor, weeping hysterically.

Chapter 13

Telegrams

1

Away from the noisy downtown and on a quiet street in the northwestern corner of the city of Nanjing, Director Duan Lin-Yu was about to leave the office for the weekend. He told his assistant that he might return a little later than usual on Monday morning because he planned to visit his ailing father in the countryside. Assistant Fang Si-Liang, his trusted right-hand man, promised that he would work through the weekend until the boss returned. He escorted Duan to his car and told the chauffeur where to go. After the car left the compound, Fang went back into the two-story building to continue his work for the rest of the evening. A perfect weekend would again be spent in the boring office, he complained to a coworker, who said "good luck" even as he was rushing to get out from the building as fast as he could for the much-awaited weekly break.

A firm believer in the idea that only modern industries and enterprising businesses could save China, Duan was among those who had gone overseas to pursue science and business studies in Western countries in the early 1900s. He studied science at the Carnegie Institute of Technology in Pittsburg and obtained a master's degree in electrical engineering. Much valued by General

Chen Han, Duan was invited to build the first high-powered radio stations in Shanghai, Nanjing, and other cities for the general's new national government. Because the two men were born in the same county, a highly valued personal connection in the ubiquitous network of social relations in China, General Chen took a personal interest in Duan. He was lavished with several important government contracts and frequently traveled between the largest commercial center Shanghai and nearby Nanjing, the nation's capital. Duan's solid scientific expertise, astute business acumen, and close personal ties to the president helped him to rise in the government. He was appointed the first director of the newly formed intelligence bureau, and his primary responsibility shifted from handling construction projects to the eradication of the clandestine communist movement.

The easygoing but indefatigable Fang was also from the same county. A country boy who had worked hard to make it in the city, he graduated at the top of Duan's training class for telegraphic communications and was chosen as one of the bureau's earliest employees. One day, the director asked Fang to visit his aging and ailing father, who lived in the countryside, on his behalf. When Fang discovered that the lonely old man was living in a deplorable condition, he helped clean the house and cook a nice meal for him. He also bought some herbal medicine and showed the old man how to take it. Before Fang left, he even helped him to take a bath, which moved the old man to tears. It was only several months later that Duan learned about what had happened from a third party, and he appointed Fang as his personal secretary.

The two men soon developed a kinship and everyone in the building realized that Fang was the director's favorite. But few were aware that it was a domestic crisis that had taken their friendship to a whole new level. For all his worthy education, exceptional intelligence, and remarkable social status, Duan could not control his sexual urge. And, like many men, he kept several mistresses and frequently visited prostitutes. One day, his wife stormed into the office building, demanding the director to come out and explain why he had not returned home for the past few days. Fang quickly hid the boss in the office and came out to console the hysterical woman. He swore that Duan was away on a covert mission, which had been assigned directly by the president. The director was in a real dilemma, Fang explained, because he had to be away from home but could not tell her where he was going.

"Please understand his difficulties, madam," said Fang, "Your husband is one of the most dedicated and most trusted officials in General Chen's government. He is very proud of you for your unwavering support and understanding all these years. I hope you will understand him this time as well."

Although still doubtful, she stopped crying and yelling. After another hour of cajoling, Fang was finally able to send the exhausted wife home.

His domestic crisis might have ended quickly but Duan knew that General Chen hated scandals. If his wife were to make a scene again, Duan would not only be humiliated in front of his entire staff but also faced possible demotion or even dismissal from office. But, since Duan could never stop seeing his mistresses, the spymaster, in close collaboration with his aide, devised a strategy that would allow him to continue cheating on his wife. Whenever Duan decided to see another woman, he would inform Fang first and let him invent an excuse to explain the director's absence from home. The cover story could be either "the boss had to go and see his ailing father" or "the boss was assigned to conduct a serious investigation" or "the boss was out of town for an inspection." Confident that his smart and competent aide would be able to keep his indiscretions under wraps, Duan left it to Fang to make all the necessary arrangements so that he could have fun. Fang was able to carry out his assignment so well that the boss's wife no longer complained as much as before, and Duan's life became a lot more pleasant.

Duan had crafted the perfect strategy except for one thing—Fang Si-Liang was a communist spy planted inside the heart of the government.

The evening after Duan left for his long weekend passed quietly for Fang until it was almost midnight, when an urgent telegram came in, which was sealed and labeled "Top Secret for the Director Only." Fang was sitting in the leather sofa and sipping coffee in the director's office. He had seen such messages before and knew that most of them was just garbage. Less than half an hour later, a second telegram came in with the same label, and five minutes later a third one arrived. Now Fang was alarmed. He stood up and quickly walked to the safe box on the wall where the top-secret codebook was kept.

Security had several levels in the intelligence bureau, and Director Duan used to keep the only copy of the codebook in his pocket all the time. Only he and no one else, including Fang, could decipher any telegram addressed to him, even if the person could open it. Fortunately for Fang, and unfortunately for Duan, another minor incident led to a critical change.

One day, while the director was having too good a time with his mistress, the codebook dropped to the floor. Duan did not realize it until the next morning when Fang came to the house to pick him up. The aide suggested that, for security reasons, the director should not carry the codebook while seeing a mistress. The boss thought about it and agreed.

With the help of the codebook, Fang was able to decode the three messages within minutes, which shook him to the core—Hou Shi-Suo had been captured in Wuhan; he had confessed and would be delivered to Nanjing in a gunboat the following day.

2

One of the highest-ranking officials in the Chinese Communist Party, Hou was deeply involved in ensuring the party's security, and he knew the organization's entire structure and operations inside out. And, as the head of the special unit, Hou held all those vital secrets that Duan's intelligence bureau had tried for years to obtain, such as the address of the party headquarters, the residences of senior party officials, the locations of undercover party offices, the makeshift places for party gatherings, and the communication codes and methods between the party's headquarters and other branch offices in different provinces. Once Hou decided to betray his comrades and reveal these secrets, the party's top leadership and the entire organization faced the unprecedented danger of total annihilation.

Fang was panting as a number of ominous scenarios went through his head. Even though he could not ascertain the exact nature of Hou's confession, his long underground experience told him that he must assume the worst. But, because his position was so secret in the party, Fang had no one nearby to turn for help, nor was he allowed to call anyone by phone for fear of interception. What could he do? And, no matter what he decided, he must act quickly before the gunboat arrived. Within a few minutes the fearless and cool-headed Fang managed to calm down, after realizing that he still had a chance. Sailing from Wuhan to Nanjing along the Yangtze River would take at least twenty hours to cover the three-hundred-mile distance, while Shanghai was no more than two hundred miles on land from Nanjing. If he could catch a train, he would be able to beat the gunboat by several hours, which would give him enough time to forewarn his comrades at the party headquarters in Shanghai.

The earliest train took Fang to Shanghai at dawn, and he immediately went to see Cheng Chu-Li. They then rushed to Si-Tu Wen-Liang's house, and he was equally stunned by the news. But the three men knew they had no time to be distraught. They quickly decided to split in three directions, to inform as many top party officials as they could, and to assist them in evacuating from Shanghai right away. After three hours of frantic work, they accomplished the most amazing escape from the city before the arrival of swarms of government detectives and armed police officers seeking their arrest.

Hou was furious. He had warned the Wuhan authorities not to wire Nanjing, for he knew there was a communist spy in the intelligence bureau. He had also urged them to send him to Nanjing as quickly as they could, but not by boat. While refusing to give out any information to the Wuhan local police, he was prepared to reveal all the secrets he knew about the Communist Party to General Chen in person. A vain man as he was, Hou assumed that, since the general's most important goal was to destroy the Communist Party, he would then become the biggest hero by helping Chen to achieve it. And he expected General Chen would therefore bestow on him the biggest possible prize, which could be a large sum of money, a high government post, or anything else he would ask for.

Now the value of his intelligence was much diminished. Top communists fled right before their eyes, because the stupid telegrams had been intercepted. The Wuhan authorities insisted that they had feared hijacking on land, and thought that a gunboat would be the safest choice. Hou insisted that they simply wanted to claim some credit for the success by sending those premature telegrams, which ruined the whole plan. Now the blame seemed to be squarely on the quivering Duan, whose personal shortcomings and negligence had let to the big blunder. To everyone's surprise, General Chen was not as upset or as outraged as his subordinates had expected him to be. He praised all those involved for their efforts, encouraged all of them to collaborate better next time, and confidently told the roomful of his men, "The fleeing communists will not survive much longer anyway, for my troops have completely besieged them in the countryside where no one could escape, not even a fly."

3

Compared with the noisy urban life, the countryside in the southeastern part of Jiangxi Province was an idyllic paradise. The slowly rising mountains to the east separated the region from Fujian Province, which was next to the Pacific Ocean. The swirling hills to the west made room for a broad basin that had nurtured hundreds of local farming families for generations.

As one of the fortunate evacuees from Shanghai, Tania particularly enjoyed the new rustic environment. The moist, soft, and fresh air gently woke her up in the morning and completely liberated her from the dreaded nightmares of Siberian storms, the suffocating spring dust in Peking, and the piercing siren of police cars in Shanghai. As she stood up and looked through the window, she was captivated by the scenery before her, and realized she had not felt this relaxed for a very long time.

Black and fat water buffaloes chewing, whining, and slowly shaking their restless tails as they were driven to work in the fields. A family of sparrows chasing one another as they performed incredible acrobatics while dashing and flying inches away through tall grass. Upset over the silly sound and disturbance, a big long-necked gander with a crimson comb jumped and spread its enormous wings to protect its goose. From the nest under a bushy camellia, a mother duck was leading her twelve fuzzy ducklings for a big swimming lesson, carefully crossing the river right at the foot of the village.

"Is this the heavenly *Peach Grove Utopia* described by the great poet Tao some fifteen hundred years ago?" pondered Tania. All around her the front doors were opening, men talking, girls giggling, pigs howling, babies crying, bellows puffing, utensils clashing, white smoke rising—everybody knew a freshly prepared breakfast would be coming soon from the warm kitchen in every household at any minute.

The colors here were mesmerizing, Tania thought while looking beyond a small fenced yard. While the massive curtain of floating mist hid small trees and broken walls on the ground, the morning dew washed away the dirt on every grimy leaf and on every rejuvenated old brick. Not until the full sun came out in midday would the giant white firewalls show their splendid glory, the dark brown wooden framework of the house reveal its ancient authenticity, the worn-out bluestones disclose the ages of the plat streets, and a sea of gray roof tiles over the village tops demonstrate their sprawling immensity.

Few colors could compare with the brilliance of the rapeseeds in full blossom—tens of millions of little golden flowers forming a single piece of rolling blanket glittering for miles.

The innocent greens of young rice paddies in the distance seemed tender and delightful as much as the nearby colossal Chinese banyan, with its half an acre of evergreen canapé at the center of the commons, was nothing short of stunning and magnificent.

The sap green tea plants nursed the best emerald buds in the sweet bosoms of their lively hedges.

Slope after slope of blue-green bamboo protected their lime-green sprouts underneath, shooting up an inch every few minutes and turning yellow to green by the day.

Against the gorgeous blue skies, mountains of tall horsetail pine, old cypress, and strong camphor trees provided the solid greens in the backdrop, only to be accentuated by some huge black boulders nestled in the hills, the deep red surface of the winding dirt roads, and the bright crystal-clear streams disappearing into the valleys.

The overwhelming sense of peace and quietness brought with it trepidation. Martin had been moody since his return from his overseas trips and the evacuation episode did little to lift his spirits. Even though he brought back some lovely photos of Peter, which thrilled Tania, Martin seemed to have lost the fire in his belly.

"Come on, dear, you must tell me what's on your mind," said Tania, knowing the reticence of a man was not always a good sign.

"I don't know what I am thinking. I just have some questions," mumbled Martin.

"Okay, good. Let's hear them," Tania encouraged him.

"Well, I wonder if Lu Shi-Yan was correct after all." Martin's opening statement surprised Tania.

"Remember when we first met him," Martin continued in a low voice, "he strongly objected to the idea that the Chinese Communist Party should subject itself to the rules of the Comintern. I admit, the Comintern's initial support was crucial to the establishment of this new party. Now, I think we both have realized how complicated the domestic situation in China can be. But the party's major actions and policies are still dictated by someone like Roy, who has lived in Moscow for years and knows little about the realities in China. Isn't this a mistake? Isn't this the key reason for some of the most serious failures of late?"

Martin's poignant reflection got Tania thinking. She knew such thoughts and doubts could get the two of them into serious trouble. Even though they were no longer emissaries, the couple remained employees of the Comintern, which could expel them anytime if anyone were to leak their conversation to the boss in Moscow. But Tania could see the reasoning behind Martin's train of thoughts, and she was eager to hear more.

"As I traveled to the United States," Martin recalled, "I saw the extent of the economic devastation, now better known as the Great Depression, in many countries. Yet I doubt this crisis can easily translate into a brand-new revolution on a global scale as the Comintern hopes. Its overly enthusiastic attitude and overly optimist assessment of the international situation have led to an overly aggressive policy in China, aiming at a nationwide proletarian success within a year or two. Worse, it has appointed the snobbish Roy as the special envoy to execute the policy. And now we have to face the devastating consequences."

Martin paused and Tania understood that he meant those big failures of hastily organized urban insurrections in recent months and the series of wild attempts by the poorly trained and poorly equipped rural guerrillas to attack several heavily guarded large cities, resulting in the loss of hundreds of thousands of innocent lives.

"So, what do we do then?" asked Tania, who now seemed to share his views.

"That's a tough question. That's what has been troubling me so far," Martin replied without giving an answer.

Silence. The couple knew they were caught in a dilemma that had been building for some time. The communist movement had never been known for its tolerance of dissenting voices, which originated from Marx's uncompromising views of social classes and class struggle. While insisting on the bitter conflict between the bourgeois and the proletariat in modern society, orthodox Marxism sought the complete overturn of the capitalist system and held an unshakable belief in the absolute goodness of the collective ownership controlled by the state, leaving little room for self-reflection, mediation, compromise, reform, or evolution. The organizational structure and disciplinary rules Lenin had invented for his Bolshevik party exacerbated the ideological radicalism he had inherited from Marx. Stalin's brutal dictatorial style and blatant personality cult pushed that trend to the extreme, and all those with opinions that were at variance with his views or were not in line with the Comintern's orders would be labeled as anti-Stalin, anti-Comintern, anti-Leninism, anti-Marxism, anti-Bolshevism, anti-Soviet, antiparty, anticommunism, or counterrevolutionary. These dissenters, considered bourgeois agents and enemies of the people hidden within the party, would be promptly and ruthlessly purged for the sake of ensuring the purity of the revolutionary ideology and maintaining the solidarity of the proletarians.

The buzzword within the organization was to "hold the party line"—to follow orders from the top without making any fuss. The couple had two choices: To protect themselves from harm, they need not do anything, just to close their eyes, seal their lips, and simply obey instructions, even if this was against their conscience. Or they could voice their concerns to the Comintern and satisfy their conscience—and risked being purged.

Tania and Martin debated for a long time, and finally decided that they would write a private letter to the Comintern to express their views. But the letter would be composed in such a way that it would come across as one person's opinion; only one of them would sign it. Thus, they hoped, the Comintern would treat the letter not as an official correspondence but as a single individual's private viewpoint, which might help to mitigate the shock and reduce the possibility of being seen as openly critical of the authorities in Moscow.

4

The Red Army commissar Sheng Bao did not understand why he had been facing so much opposition lately. Since his rise to the head of a major army division under the communists' control, he had been called "warlord-like," "undemocratic," "arbitrary," "heavy-handed," "patriarchal," "ambitious tyrant," "opportunist," "escapist," and "rightist." He did the best he could to save the Red Army, defeat the enemy troops, and protect the regional base for the newly established Soviet government in southeastern Jiangxi. His flexible guerrilla warfare tactics had worked, leading a forty-thousand Red Army to resist the government's extermination campaigns three times in eleven months, even though they were faced with enemy troops that were three, five, and even ten times bigger in those attempts. Still, his detractors were not appreciative of his efforts and tried to oust him time and again. Sheng started to believe that he was a victim of a much more sinister plot.

Acting on suspicion that members of the secretive Anti-Bolshevik Corps had penetrated the Red Army, four thousand, four hundred soldiers and staff members were charged and arrested. Many were brutally tortured and forced to confess to their alleged crimes. About four hundred of them were executed. The situation worsened further after Sheng dispatched Director Lin Shuo of Internal Security to supervise the investigations into the 20th Army, led by General Shao Hua-De.

Lin, the overzealous persecutor and Sheng's handpicked advisor who had been promoted four times in a year, immediately arrested General Shao and seven of his top associates. They were mercilessly tortured day and night until they confessed to the alleged crime of being members of the Anti-Bolshevik Corps. When their wives visited their imprisoned husbands, they were also arrested and brutally tortured. Based on the confessions and information obtained by torture, some one hundred and twenty people were arrested and twenty-four of them were executed within five days.

General Shao's officers and the four thousand men of the 20th Army were outraged. Since most of them were local residents of South Jiangxi, they believed Sheng, the outsider from another province with just a few followers, was waging a vendetta against them. He had made up those false charges to purge General Shao, who was a well-regarded local hero, in order to take over control of the entire Red Army in Jiangxi. The 20th Army thus mutinied, set up its own provincial government, and declared "Down with Sheng Bao! Support Shao Huai-De!"

Their rebellion was short-lived and it was quickly put down by troops led by Tao Yin-Hu, who did his best to show whose side he was on at such a life-

and-death moment. The 20th Army's entire officer corps of eight hundred men, from ensigns to top commanders, were arrested, sent to a military court, and executed. The 20th Army was completely disbanded, and the remaining soldiers were forced to join several separate divisions of troops loyal to Sheng.

This bloody incident was followed by an even wider purge that continued for two more years across the different regional bases controlled by the Communist Party. All told, as many as seventy thousand former Red Army soldiers, officers, party members, and cadres were purged—almost the same number of casualties the enemy troops of the nationalist government had sustained during their three successive extermination campaigns against the communists in Jiangxi.

5

If General Chen was one of the two people who had mastered early twentieth-century Chinese politics, Commissar Sheng must be the other one. Both were highly ambitious, daring, and nationalistic. Both believed they could end the endless civil wars among warlords and local factions, save and unite the country, and restore China's sovereignty, independence, integrity, and glory. What distinguished them was that General Chen took a "top-down" approach to achieve these goals, while Commissar Sheng believed in a "bottom-up" one.

Obsessed with power, extremely protective of their own authority, and prone to conspiracy theories, both men were ruthless competitors in war as much as in national politics and internal party conflicts. But the similarities ended there. While General Chen was more traditional in his outlook by observing Confucianism, he was willing to heed the advice of his key aides, many of whom had Western education and connections. In contrast, Commissar Sheng had rebelled against the status quo, and he readily embraced the totalitarian part of orthodox Marxism and the overtly dogmatic concepts and bureaucratic practices of the Russians. Few people could outsmart General Chen when it comes to dealing with the Chinese warlords, urban bourgeoisie, and wealthy upper classes. For Commissar Sheng, his political advantage lay in his thorough understanding of the lower classes in China, particularly the tens of millions who made up the Chinese peasantry.

Sheng's speedy rise in the Communist Party and his ability to battle with General Chen's powerful national government depended heavily on his close ties with the rural population. Many of his colleagues had roots in rural China, but few of them had studied the peasantry as closely as he did. Still fewer of them knew how to distinguish big landlords from small ones, landlords from rich peasants, owner-peasants from semi-owner-peasants, sharecroppers from poor peasants, farm laborers from rural artisans, and landless peasants from vagrants. Whereas many, including Lenin, Stalin, Trotsky, Bukharin, and the staff at the Comintern, saw the lack of a strong proletarian force as the main weakness of a communist movement in China, Sheng was one of the few who believed that the large numbers of the peasantry could be its unique strength.

Most important, Sheng quietly separated the ideological leadership of the Chinese Communist Party from its physical composition. If the existence of a large working class was the prerequisite for a communist movement, was China ready for it while ninety percent of the population were farmers and peasants? If the majority of the party membership came from the countryside, as China's condition had dictated, how could the party truly represent the interest of the proletarians instead of the peasantry? Leadership, not the composition, of the party, Sheng insisted, was the key. As long as the party's leadership remained in the hands of the proletarians and their mentors—or, as Lenin had described, the most committed and most knowledgeable full-time professional revolutionaries—the party would fulfill its mission as prescribed by Marx.

However, an overemphasis on the role of the peasants could be as problematic as an underestimation of it. Sheng's enthusiastic assessment of the Chinese peasantry went hand in hand with his narrow understanding of intransigent "class struggle," which was always explained in a polarized dichotomy—the wealthier one's economic circumstances were, the more conservative one's political stand must be, while the poorer, the more revolutionary. Here, he made a fundamental mistake, which would cost him, the party, and the country dearly for decades to come.

Notwithstanding Sheng's high hopes for the poor peasants, who did number in the millions, he refused to concede the historical reality that the vast majority of the rural poor had actively participated in all kinds of organizations and activities—from secret societies, covert actions, conspiracies and assassinations to open rebellions, highway robberies, plundering, civil wars, violent crimes, petty transgressions, and flagrant banditry. Poverty had never guaranteed the morality of the poor's actions. The Chinese poor peasants had long played a destructive role in the past, which was not necessarily all revolutionary. In fact, they were the main source of army troops for General Chen's nationalist government as much as for Sheng's Red Army. Thus, the Chinese peasantry could be both highly "revolutionary" and actively "counterrevolutionary" at the same time, depending on who was recruiting them and who was leading them as much as who was telling the media how to describe them.

Believing that by default any class struggle in a revolution would necessarily be violent, Sheng was willing to overlook the ruthless, violent, and brutal nature of the Chinese peasantry at a time when his party needed a massive physical force to overthrow the government. This deliberate cover-up was to lead to many serious problems that neither he nor the party was ever able to resolve.

For the moment, Sheng stressed the primacy of the party's leadership since the peasantry, no matter how substantial the size, would never be able to lead a proletarian movement. Besides, he understood perfectly that, because of their scant education and serious economic constraints, the poor, illiterate Chinese peasants had never produced any advanced ideas or programs in the past except for primitive egalitarianism and embryonic social justice. Ideologically speaking, the Chinese peasants were a narrow-minded, conservative, and backward-looking class, whose awareness of the world and modern sciences was zilch and whose only knowledge and intellectual acumen were based on their local traditions and their limited understanding of China's agrarian culture and despotic history.

The pressing need for the peasantry's participation and the equally imperative need for sound leadership made the selection of appropriate party officials and effective army officers of vital importance.

Sheng's greatest assets represented both the great virtues and strengths of the Chinese peasantry, such as hard work, endurance, bravery, rebelliousness, sharp instincts, perseverance, and dogged determination. His greatest personal failings could also be traced back to the vices and intrinsic weaknesses of the very same group, such as selfishness, superstition, ignorance, narrow-mindedness, unscrupulousness, treachery, patriarchy, chauvinism, jealousy, obstinacy, conservatism, cruelty, vengefulness, and lawlessness.

As a man who was so full of himself, Sheng strongly believed in his own righteousness, although the line between his self-confidence and self-pity was thin. Sensitive to the fact that his educational credentials were not as impressive as many other party leaders, Sheng could get easily insulted whenever anyone dared to challenge his organizational authority, political judgment, and military strategies. He would never forget such an affront and would always find a way to get back at the offender. "Ten years is not long for revenge," as the villagers had often said.

Intraparty struggle was commonplace among communists, and repeated military conflicts with the nationalists only made it worse. The self-righteous Commissar Sheng believed that whoever opposed him was helping the enemy, and that his ideas were always the best for the party. Thus he, more than anyone else, deserved to be its top leader.

6

"Fatherly love can be such a strange thing," Tang Wan-Yi sighed. She had been waiting, waiting, and waiting. But there was no letter, no word from her husband.

Their three sons, seven, five, and two, were fast asleep on a single bed. She looked at them, wondering why Sheng had not returned home even once in the last three years. "Does he still love me?" Tang Wan-Yi wondered. "Even if he has been terribly busy, or even if he does not love me anymore, shouldn't he at least find time to see his boys?"

Loneliness was the saddest thing and the worst torment for the wife, who, no matter how strong she might be, would always appreciate the warmth and physical presence of the husband.

Tang had heard that communist guerrillas were planning an attack on the provincial city, which was not far from where she lived. She had hoped that Sheng would drop by for a while, just to see her and the children.

But days went by, the battle ended, and the guerrillas had withdrawn. Still, there was no news and no sight of Commissar Sheng.

Had he come with the soldiers at all? Had he been in the battle? Was he wounded? Or was he even alive? So many questions went through Tang's mind over and over again. She dared not continue thinking about them, lest these unanswered questions drive her insane.

She sat by a tiny oil lamp, feeling sad, cold, and frightened as if she were already a widow. No tears or words could comfort Tang, who felt as if her soul were leaving her body. She did not know who to turn to, seek counsel, or to receive comfort and support. If widowhood were bad, abandonment could be worse, and not knowing anything about the husband was the worst. She recalled too many tragic stories of women who had lived through a life like hers. Only they and their writings provided some consolation.

Since the time of *The Book of Songs*, women had produced some of the best poems in Chinese literature. Hundreds of male poets and authors were widely recognized for their elegant rhetoric, sophisticated diction, broad experiences, great knowledge, ornate styles, and perfect structures. Yet few of them had ever written a decent piece for their wives, and even fewer had left any record of their genuine love toward the women in their lives. No matter how much time had passed, few readers would not realize that the common thread in all the classics by female authors was their deep and profound feelings for their loved ones. They never hid their true feelings—love, longing, anxiety, anguish, sorrows, or sadness—which made their poems more human and personal, and far less pretentious, than the ones by their male counterparts.

Many verses in *The Book of Songs* were romantic poems, such as these:

Cold Is the North Wind

Cold is the north wind,
The snow falls thick.
If you are kind and love me,
take my hand and we'll go together.
You are modest, you are slow,
but oh, we must hurry and go!

Blue Blue Your Collar

Blue blue your collar,
sad sad my heart:
though I do not go to you,
why don't you send word?

Blue blue your collar,
sad sad my thoughts:
though I do not go to you,
why don't you come?

Restless, heedless,
I walk the gate tower.
One day not seeing you
is three months long.

Swift Is That Falcon

Swift is that falcon,
dark that northern wood:
I have not seen my lord,
my grieving heart is pained.
Why is it, why is it
You forget me so often!

Thick oaks grow on the mountain,
in the damp places, magnolia:
I have not seen my lord,
my grieving heart knows no joy.
Why is it, why is it
You forget me so often!

There are thick cherries on the mountain,
in the damp place, wild pear:
I have not seen my lord,
my grieving heart feels drunk.
Why is it, why is it
You forget me so often!

The stories in Chinese folk songs were overwhelmingly about love stories, such as this one:

You Told Me a Thousand Times

Didn't you tell me a thousand times on our pillow last night
that nothing can set us apart until the green mountains rot,
until a pair of scales float on water,
until the Yellow River dries to the bottom,
until stars show up in bright daylight,
and until the Big Dipper points to the south.
Apart or not, let's wait until the sun shines in midnight!

In simple language, plain style, and intimate metaphors, these nameless authors used trees, animals, rivers, mountains, household items, and natural objects and colors to stress their emotions, their commitment to the relationship, and their strong passion for their loved ones. They repeated these emotions and commitment again and again, which seemed to have become the most common theme through the ages. Tang could empathize with them. She understood, as much as these female authors did, that what a woman really wanted was not that her man should stay by her side all the time, but that he should try to respond to her emotional needs, even if only once in her lifetime. Tang felt, as any woman would, she needed that strong shoulder, that warm expression, and that explicit commitment to reassure her that she had not been forgotten, but still loved. Not receiving that reciprocal expressions of love and care would cause any woman serious grief, as the talented Li Qing-Zhao, who had lost her husband, wrote:

I look for what I miss,
I know not what it is:
I feel so sad, so drear,
So lonely, without cheer.
How hard is it
to keep me fit
in this lingering cold!

Hardly warmed up
by cup on cup
of wine so dry.

Oh! How could I
endure at dusk the drift
of wind so swift?
It breaks my heart, alas!
To see the wild geese pass,
for they are my acquaintances of old.

The ground is covered with yellow flowers
faded and fallen in showers.
Who will pick them up now?
Sitting alone at the window, how
could I but quicken
the pace of darkness which won't thicken?
On parasol-tree a fine rain drizzles
as twilight grizzles.
Oh! What can I do with a grief
beyond belief!

7

Tragic stories, painful memories. More tragic stories, more painful memories. There seemed to be no end to them, and Tang sat down to pen her thoughts about the darkest days of her life.

I have always been a very sickly child. Mother and Father thought I would not be able to survive for long. So strange that a young life could be so closely related to death from the day of her birth. Unlike other kids who were often restless, I did not like activities. I began to think a lot, almost like an adult when I was only five or six. I was particularly sad about the fate of farm animals, not understanding why people had to kill them every day. It dawned on me that every person would die too, perhaps because I was so hopelessly weak that I had always been on the brink of death all the time. But the killing of chickens, ducks, pigs, and sheep gave me nightmares, which frequently kept me awake throughout the night. I didn't understand why small boys would play with little birds, insects, frogs, and dragonflies, and sometimes even killed them for fun. They had lives too, so why such cruelty? Why did people not help these creatures live instead of speeding up their demise, and enjoying its process?

Only when I grew older did I realize that I was, in fact, afraid to see Mother watching me dying—and this awareness caused me great pain. At the same time, it was this very awareness that gave me the strength I needed to survive so that I would not die before my mother's eyes.

At sixteen, I was strong enough to leave home and go to Peking to study. I decided to start my life anew and to find a new purpose for myself. I got up early, took a cold bath, and went out for exercise every morning. I decided to strengthen my body and soul by wearing a thin jacket through the winter. I believed that self-determination and willpower could and would extend life.

Then I met him. He was so tall, so strong, and so handsome. He was the epitome of life, the personification of energy, the source of inspiration, and the fire to set my heart and spirit ablaze. I was so happy when I was with him, and he shared with me his letters, articles, and diaries. We talked about anything and everything. He often took me out for a stroll and we then walked through the small lanes and alleyways across the city several times without feeling tired or realizing the time.

Oh, heavens, how much I loved him! I said a thousand times, loud and clear, that I loved him, and that I would love him for as long as I lived.

But I was against marriage, which surprised him. I worshiped true love, and despised ceremonial marriage. The beauty of love, the most magnificent human sensation, should be the purest, I thought. Marriage was not only a social institution but also a degradation of true love.

He disagreed, insisting that marriage was naturally the final stage of true love. I resisted his idea, which I knew upset him. For a while, he stopped seeing me, which made me miserable. I began to think that he deliberately did it to win me back until one day I received a bombshell— he was dating another girl.

I was so shocked that I simply collapsed. We met again and passionately embraced one another, realizing how much we meant to each other, how much we loved each other, and how nothing or nobody could ever separate us again.

But I still had my reservations about marriage, and this time he allowed me to think it over. To be honest, my reservations about marriage continued to this day. But the death of my dear parents left me homeless and marriage seemed to be the only option I was left with.

He seemed to enjoy being married much more than I did. After our sons were born, he became busier than ever and was frequently away from home. The last time I saw him was three years ago. At first he sent short letters home, then some brief messages conveyed verbally by others. Now, I have not received any news from him for more than a year and a half.

Today is his birthday. How can I ever forget it? I cooked some special dishes tonight, and prepared the traditional long noodle soup—a must for any birthday meal since it symbolized longevity—even though he was not at home. When I went to bed alone after dinner, I could not help but burst into tears. I dared not cry all night, fearing that I might wake up the kids. Oh, heavens, how I have loved him, and how much I have missed him!

Rumors say he is sick. He always works like crazy and never stops. You will ruin your health, my dear. You are not as strong as you used to be, and you are also susceptible to diseases. Please slow down, for your sake, for me, and for your kids. May heavens protect him. Please always take good care.

I wish I could go out to find a job. If I could earn enough money every month, he would have no need to leave home again.

Yet who would hire a mother of three? And how can I go out to work while leaving the small kids at home? Can I ever be a good wife and a good mother at the same time? I love both my husband and our children, and I can't give up either one of them. I am constantly thinking and worried about them. But I can't ever satisfy all of them. What a predicament!

Oh, please, heavens, please let me know that he is fine, he is healthy, he is thinking about his kids, and he has not abandoned me. I am sad, I am sobbing, I am trembling, I can't take it anymore if I don't hear a single word from him.

Heavens, please. I love him so much, and he knows how much I love him. I don't care where he is, what he is doing, I just want to know he is still alive, he has not abandoned me and the kids.

Fatherly love is a strange thing. If he doesn't think about me, can he find time to come and see his sons?

Oh, heavens know, I love him so much. Even if he dies today, I will kiss him a thousand times, telling him that I love him and will die with him. Nothing can take him away from me. No one can stop me from loving him. I am your loving wife and you are my husband.

I might be too young to be writing my last will and testament. But, in case something terrible happens to me, I would like my sons' uncles to take care of them. Their uncles have shown so much love toward them that I have no doubt they will continue to take care of them, whatever may lie ahead.

Whoever can take this message to him is my savior.

Whoever can bring any news from him is my savior.

Oh, good heavens, how I have loved him, and how I have missed him!

The long message did not seem to be completely finished and was not signed. Nor was it clear whether it was ever delivered. But, on the back of the last sheet of paper, a few more lines appeared to be written on a separate occasion—

Cloudy days, cold winds, chilly bones,
Wayfarers, long journeys, rolling hills.
Injured foot, healed or not?
Winter clothing, prepared yet?
Go to bed alone, feeling sad?
Out of reach, out of news, anyone can help?

Give me wings, fly like a bird, searching for thou
Only to fall to the ground, broken hearted.

Your love for me never ends, as
We bond each other for this life.
Thinking about you every night,
When to have you by my side?

My love, do you know how I have missed you in silent anguish?
I screamed out your dear name in dreams, and only woke up in the
horrible long night like a lost goose.

My love, even if the universe will burn down in ashes, I will wrap around
you, laugh and kiss you in the sweetest dreams you have given me.

These fragments ended there. Tang was arrested a few months later. Her crime:
being married to communist leader Sheng Bao. A month after her arrest, Tang
was executed for her refusal to denounce her husband and to dissolve their
marriage. She was twenty-nine years old.

Chapter 14

Soviets

1

S I-TU WEN-LIANG'S WORK ETHIC WAS LEGENDARY IN THE PARTY. HE could work continuously for several days without sleeping, which often amazed and exhausted his aides. And no task would be too complicated for this genius, whose methodical mind, seamless managerial style, superb interpersonal skills, and adroit diplomacy were admired by his friends as much as they were envied by his enemies. One of the few top party officials with extensive metropolitan and overseas experience, he never expected that his first few weeks in rural Jiangxi would give him so much headache.

Insiders widely recognized Si-Tu as the gifted supervisor of party affairs—the one who held real power behind the scenes. Several leading comrades, from Lu Shi-Yan and Dong Zi-Tian to Meng Bo-Xian, had held higher offices and two envoys from the Comintern, Martin and Roy, had had more influence on policies than Si-Tu. Yet, when it came to actual operations and implementation of policies, no one could beat Si-Tu, who was undoubtedly the best and most indefatigable administrator of the organization, from its personnel issues, operational planning, external relations, and budget allocation to its covert activities. Lately, however, Si-Tu was surprised that his office had been asked to mediate several high-profile matrimonial cases, which was something he had never done before.

The first couple he had to deal with were Commissar Sheng Bao and his new wife Yu Shao-Mei.

The late Tang Wan-Yi's worst fears turned out to be true—the father of her three children, the man she had loved so much till her last breath, did abandon her after all. Only eight months after he left his family several years ago, the pragmatic Sheng moved in with the then seventeen-year-old Yu, and they had been living as husband and wife ever since.

The daughter of a wealthy landlord in Hunan Province, the tall and energetic Yu had been a social activist from her school days. She had joined the communist youth organization at fifteen and become a party member the next year. When most party members went underground after General Chen's bloody purge in Shanghai, she, one brother, and a sister had participated in an armed insurrection in their home county, which was the first armed uprising followed by the ones led by Tao Yin-Hu in the City of Nanchang and by Sheng in rural Hunan. Furthermore, the Yu siblings had close family ties with two local rebels who controlled the Cougar Mountain region along the Hunan-Jiangxi border. The three siblings had been hiding in the mountains for two months when Sheng and his failed insurrectionists retreated to the same area to escape the government's vicious retaliation, paving the way for his first meeting with Yu.

Sheng instantly fell in love with the young and lively Yu. He asked her to stay for dinner, after which they continued to talk about party matters till midnight. The next day, the commissar made the same request to have dinner with Yu, and the two came out from the bedroom together the next morning. With the besotted woman half his age standing by his side blushing, the glowing commissar proudly declared to his followers in his deep and manly voice, "Comrades, Yu Shao-Mei and I have changed our relationship from revolutionary comrades to that of wedded husband and wife!"

The overnight transformation produced blissful and explosive consequences. Commissar Sheng was obviously in more cheerful spirits than he had ever been before whenever he showed up in public. The erstwhile famous local heroine assumed the role of a dutiful housewife and dedicated personal aide, who cooked the meals, washed the dishes, and kept the private letters and official missives for the husband day in and day out. As in his previous marriage, the prowess of the commissar's virility should never be underestimated—he impregnated his young wife ten times while they were together as a couple for a decade. Within just four years of marriage, Yu had become a mother of three. Two of her babies died in infancy, and the husband wanted more, which was the reason why she had brought the commissar to see Si-Tu.

"He is a pig! And I want a divorce!" Yu shouted in front of Si-Tu and several others in the office.

"Please, Shao-Mei, please calm down." Immediately sensing a crisis, Si-Tu sprang into action. He quickly ushered everyone out, including the dejected husband, politely took Yu to an adjacent room, and soon came back with a cup of tea in his hand.

"Shao-Mei, I know you are very angry. Please, please don't be so upset. Can you please let me know what is wrong?" With these calming words, Si-Tu gently handed the tea over to Yu, and helped her to sit down.

Traditional decorum in China dictated that women should serve tea to men, the young to the old, the subordinates to the superiors, never the other way round. The fact that Si-Tu, one of the most senior and most highly respected top officials, was willing to bend backward to do just the opposite moved Yu to tears. Her anger was much deflated there and then. And, as she began to complain about her marriage life, Si-Tu patiently listened as if she were his daughter.

Two and a half hours of quiet listening and level-headed conversation were all that he needed to avert a real disaster. Yu's request for a divorce was certainly disallowed and the couple went back home with Sheng, who never thought he had done anything wrong or cared much about gender equality, feeling victorious.

What had ended this melodrama was more than skill, patience, and humility. An exemplary devotee of the organization, Si-Tu firmly believed that the happiness of Commissar Sheng, the party's top leader, was of paramount importance to its success, and worth protecting at any cost. Whatever the commissar wanted must be met, even if it meant that Yu or anyone else had to be sacrificed. For all Si-Tu's outward gentlemanly manners and genial exterior, he and Sheng shared the same conviction that in the name of the party and, for the sake of the revolution, everything else including any other individual's interests could be and should be sacrificed.

Si-Tu, in fact, was among the first one in the party to treat Sheng as a special figure by giving him an elevated status that would override all other considerations. As the chief manager of party affairs, Si-Tu believed that his fundamental duty was to protect party leaders like Sheng from harm, and he had therefore developed several hierarchical categories of loyalty—one for the general public, one for party members, and one for party bosses. Because Sheng belonged to the third category, his well-being was all-important. Party rules could be bent to accommodate his wants, and organizational principles could be manipulated to suit his needs. The Chinese Communist Party was divided into two separate entities—membership and top leadership. Si-Tu had used his great talent to make that distinction a reality, while Commissar Sheng knew about the differentiation all too well not to exploit the privileges for his own ends, often in the name of the revolution and for the sake of the proletarians.

2

Special Envoy Roy requested an urgent meeting and Si-Tu immediately granted it. After the envoy indicated that he wanted to speak to Si-Tu alone, the latter sent his aides out of the office and closed the door.

"I have been instructed to conduct an investigation on Martin and Tania." Roy's dour tone indicated how grave the matter was.

"An investigation about their…" Si-Tu, who was taken aback by the revelation, left his sentence hanging.

"About their loyalty," Roy said firmly.

"About their loyalty?" Si-Tu asked rhetorically. Having intentionally spilled the beans, Roy went on to explain that the Comintern had recently received a letter criticizing its policy toward China. The letter was signed by Tania in her personal capacity. But the Comintern suspected that Martin was the real mastermind and coauthor of the letter. The Comintern therefore ordered Roy to find out the truth. And, if Martin was indeed the real author, he and Tania would be regarded as having conspired against the Comintern's leadership. They would then be severely punished since dissenting voices, much less an opposition group, had no place in the organization.

"So, why don't you just ask the two about it?" Si-Tu pretended he did not know the answer.

"You are their longtime friend, whereas, well, you know how my relationship with the couple had soured." Roy, never the most modest person around, went as far as he could to acknowledge his dilemma—having taken over the couple's jobs, he did not want to be seen as the one responsible for prosecuting them. Roy needed Si-Tu's help to carry out the Comintern's order so he could remain in the background until the time was right.

"Okay, I will see what I can do." Si-Tu, who could read what was on Roy's mind, did not want to embarrass him by probing too much.

Roy was quick to express his gratitude even though Si-Tu warned, "I can't guarantee that I will be successful."

Like everyone else in the communist world, Si-Tu knew that the Comintern's supreme authority should never be questioned. He also knew that Stalin was conducting an unprecedented purge in Russia, and that any party member who disagreed with the party or the Comintern could be easily singled out as an enemy of the people and summarily arrested, imprisoned, or even executed. His promise to Roy could land him in a very difficult situation.

Still, Si-Tu's instincts told him otherwise. The more challenging the situation, the more satisfying the result. Si-Tu never believed that any problem could not be solved. Any unusual case only needed some unusual talent to settle it. Bold imagination was needed to pinpoint the crux of the matter and to devise an innovative solution. He enjoyed the process of solving the most difficult puzzle by exploring all feasible channels of navigation. In this case, the true authorship did not seem to be that difficult to identify at all.

When Si-Tu did have a chance to meet and talk to Martin and Tania, he quickly realized that he had a dilemma. On the one hand, he found himself agreeing with the couple in principle that the Comintern's policy toward China was unrealistic and overbearing. He was even glad that the couple had the courage to express that opinion to the Comintern. They had at least reminded the Comintern of the need to improve their assessment of the Chinese reality and to readjust their policies accordingly. On the other hand, he could not end the investigation with some ambiguous conclusion. If he chose to proclaim Martin's noninvolvement, the Comintern might suspect that he was part of a bigger conspiracy. If he were to expose Martin's role in the letter, the couple could be arrested and charged as coconspirators. Their future might be in serious jeopardy, which was not at all what Si-Tu wanted.

But Si-Tu was Si-Tu after all. Martin and Tania were stunned to hear his advice—get a divorce. Si-Tu explained that Martin should initiate the divorce to indicate that he had nothing to do with the letter, which was purely Tania's penmanship. Martin should swear that he never knew about the letter until it was read to him during Si-Tu's investigation. And he was so outraged that he could no longer live with Tania as husband and wife, since her political views were completely wrong to him. Si-Tu also suggested that Tania should write a confession, blaming her politically incorrect views on her naivety. She would take full responsibility as the sole author of the letter, and also indicate her willingness to repent and learn from her mistakes. Hopefully, these steps would minimize the damage and satisfy the arrogant bureaucrats in Moscow enough to let the matter end there.

Martin and Tania were skeptical of Si-Tu's plan. They were willing to give it a try, but wondered whether dissolving a marriage for political expediency was the only resort. Besides, marriage was a solemn spiritual matter in their custom, and how could they repair such a huge damage in the future if a divorce were rendered?

"No worry, comrades," said Si-Tu. "You are not in Rotterdam or Moscow, right? Your divorce in China would not mean a thing when you return home, would it?"

"You mean we cheat?" Martin and Tania asked.

"No, no, no! No cheating at all!" Si-Tu adamantly protested. "Only to be adaptive according to the international situation, as the great cause of the proletarians has clearly demanded."

The line between falsehood and truth, as that between honesty and deceit, was very thin in China. But it never troubled a man as sophisticated as Si-Tu, who firmly believed in the abundant utilitarian values of both falsehood and truth. Revolutionary pragmatism could be handy when one must play the roles of villain and hero in the same game. One should not be shy to tell a white lie for a glorious cause anytime.

3

A sudden change of guards threw everything off balance and Si-Tu's cunning scheme backfired.

About five years after the huge setbacks since the Shanghai massacre, the communist-led mass movement had gradually regained strength, especially in some southern provinces. In rural Jiangxi, thousands of poor peasants joined the Red Army, which, led by Sheng Bao, Tao Yin-Hu, and others, successful defeated the attacks by government troops.

Yet Moscow thought the pace of the revolution was too slow, and sent in a new team to replace both Roy and Meng Bo-Xian, who were believed to be ineffective in carrying out the Comintern's plans. Colonel Gregory was the new special envoy and, as an experienced veteran in the Russian Civil War, he would also be in charge of the military strategies for the Chinese Red Army. Mo Jia-Qi, a bright and outstanding graduate of the Russian Program, was handpicked by Stalin as the new head of the Chinese Communist Party. He would work closely with Colonel Gregory to launch a broad revolution that the country had never seen before. Also, in light of the disastrous consequences arising from Hou Shi-Suo's arrest, Moscow appointed Lin Shi-Xiong, another graduate of the Russian Program, as head of the covert action division to beef up the Chinese party's internal security.

The useless fop Roy was recalled. Blamed for being "too soft and too timid," Meng was demoted. The new team considered the guerrilla tactics Sheng had promoted "opportunist," "defeatist," and "rightist," totally inconsistent with the Comintern's goals. Stripped of his position in the Red Army, Sheng was sidelined and given a civilian post. Si-Tu was severely reprimanded. Even though he was not responsible for Hou's betrayal and even though he did everything he could to minimize the damage, several thousand party members were arrested and executed. Several hundred local offices were raided and destroyed. The party's network in the cities, built up after years of hard work, was destroyed overnight—the worst disaster the Communist Party had ever suffered. To prevent future calamities, Lin's appointment was crucial. He had extensive training in spy work and counterintelligence in Russia, and he would be working closely with Si-Tu to ensure the safety of party leaders, to expand the party's spy rings and counterintelligence forces, and to assassinate traitors. A special team hunted Hou down and killed him, along with his fourteen relatives who had some inside information about the Communist Party.

In this frantic shuffle of power, Si-Tu's clever idea of divorce did not help Martin and Tania. Lin ordered their arrest and put them in separate detention cells. It was only a year later that Si-Tu, sensing that political tensions had subsided considerably, was able to lobby for their release.

Martin and Tania knew that they were still under surveillance. To avoid suspicion, they decided to live separately. Tania went back to her old dwelling, only to find that the community was a much-changed place.

At the foothills of the sweeping Blue Grass Mountain, the familiar town Blue Grass had been transformed from a small quiet neighborhood into the busy capital of the newly formed Central Government of the Chinese Soviet Republic, modeled after the Russian Soviet Republic. Tania had never seen so many officials and public employees in such a small village, so many uniformed personnel speaking so many different dialects mixed with a strong local accent. Nor had she seen so many red flags and golden stars all over so many houses, buildings, and public places, symbolizing the communist revolution and its revolutionary regime. Whenever she walked into a government office, she could see the national emblem or national flag of this new proletarian polity hanging everywhere. Tania was told that as many as two dozen departments had been established in the town, including a brand-new national bank; the number of Red Army soldiers, stationed here and nearby, had swelled to one hundred thousand men.

Tania could hardly believe how fast residents of this once laid-back community had transformed it into a place of organized groups and activities. Boys had boy scouts, girls joined girl scouts, young adults became youth pioneers, women formed female associations, men participated in paramilitary camps, and the elderly folk set up senior clubs. Villagers were divided into cooperatives, neighborhood committees adjudicated family disputes, municipal government established home regulations, and local militia set up picket lines. A quiet farmland now boasted five schools, a military academy, two soccer teams, and fifteen mess halls. It also had a large printing press, producing several newspapers and magazines every day. Under the Department of Finance, a mint manufactured a revolutionary currency plus many types of public bonds circulating in sixty counties with a total population of more than two and a half million.

How could so much have been accomplished in such a short period of time and why would the peasants be so interested in a proletarian movement? Tania wondered. She had seen a similar scene more than fifteen years ago—during the October Revolution in Russia, where almost every place was inundated with red flags decorated with golden stars, sickles, and hammers. At that time, workers, soldiers, sailors, and city residents were rising in St. Petersburg and Moscow, whereas the Russian countryside remained apathetic. Now the opposite was happening in China, where the remote countryside was boiling and the urban centers inactive.

Tania picked up her speed as she made her way for an appointment, where she would receive her new assignment and perhaps find her answers too.

4

The failure to eliminate the communist menace troubled General Chen. The Red Army and its base in the Blue Grass region were less than three hundred miles away from the city of Nanchang, the provincial capital of Jiangxi, which was about four hundred miles to Nanjing, the seat of his national government, or four hundred and fifty miles to Shanghai, the financial capital of China.

Directing his troops from his command center in Nanchang, General Chen had two options to march down and attack the red bases in the southeastern part of Jiangxi. One was to take the road along the Fu River on the left, which was thirty miles closer to Blue Grass but more mountainous; the other was to take the road along the Gan River on the right, which had wider roads and better communication facilities. During the last three extermination campaigns, General Chen had ordered his troops to take the right-flank approach, hoping to take advantage of the transportation facilities to defeat the Red Army swiftly. At one point, the national army was no more than a few dozen miles away from Blue Grass, but failed to capture it. This time, for the fourth extermination campaign, General Chen decided to try the left-flank approach.

Jiangxi Province was famous for its mountains. The Lu Mountain, eighty miles north of Nanchang, had long been one of the most well-known summer resorts since ancient times. But the further south one traveled in the province, the more difficult and more treacherous the road conditions would become. Even though the Red Army was hiding just about two hundred miles away, the plans for its annihilation were not easily executed.

Intelligence indicated that the government had amassed nearly half a million soldiers against the communist fighting forces of seventy thousand. General Bai Yu-Xian, who had been a rival warlord just a few years ago, was appointed as the field commander. Bai was a highly experienced military tactician, whose skills were greatly admired by friends and foes alike. His recent switch of loyalty to the national government paved the way for his new appointment, even though he was not keen about the civil war. General Chen believed that the new extermination campaign would require a commander who had the knowledge and expertise to fight in the mountainous terrains in the south, and General Bai fit the bill perfectly.

Just sixty miles south of Nanchang and in a great show of force, General Bai deployed one hundred and sixty thousand of the best government troops in three columns (left, center, and right), marching in a fan-shaped offensive toward the enemy. This closely weaved operation, he hoped, would push the Red Army back into an area of no more than one hundred and twenty square miles, where his overwhelming forces could in the end trap and destroy the communists.

Now that the government troops were no more than five to six days away, the communist leaders held urgent meetings day and night to design a viable strategy to defend the territories they had fought so hard to obtain. Although Mo was the party head, he was young and had no experience in military affairs. Since the Comintern had already ordered a policy of attacking the national government with great resolve, he and Gregory would not listen to any suggestion to "retreat and lure the enemy in deep," a strategy that had been used by Commissar Sheng in the first three antiextermination campaigns. Considering the Red Army's limited strength, Tao and Si-Tu believed Sheng's tactics to be viable, but they were not tenacious enough to insist on it. They finally agreed with Mo and Gregory that a preemptive strike was necessary to stop the national troops from invading the red territories.

Led by Commander-in-Chief Tao and Commissar Si-Tu, the Red Army was organized into three legions (1st, 3rd, 5th) and four armies (11th, 12th, 21st, and 22rd). They sent twenty thousand men in six divisions from the 3rd and 5th legions—the cream of the crop—to move up north, planning to forestall the enemy's attack before they could even set foot in the red base. The six divisions waded the Fu River and quickly arrived at the outskirts of Nanfeng—a fortified township and a major stronghold on the national army's left flank.

The general attack began in the morning and lasted through the next day. Defended by five well-equipped regiments of twenty thousand men, Nanfeng was not as easily captured as the party's directives had indicated. The city walls were high and thick; with no artillery to break them, the Red Army's assaults were ineffective, while casualties were large. One division head was killed, and the attacks were stalled.

A little surprised, General Bai was quite delighted when he received the news. He had dealt with the communist forces several times in the past, which often involved a hide-and-seek game for a long time before any real fight. He never anticipated that he would discover the whereabouts of the Red Army's main force so soon and so close to his domain. Reports of the fearsome attacks confirmed his suspicions that the attackers were the best of the Red Army forces. The general immediately ordered the troops in Nanfeng to hold on at all costs, telling them that help was on the way. He ordered the two columns of his army not to continue down south any more, and redirected them to turn east to come to the rescue of Nanfeng as fast as they could. Apparently, Nanfeng had now become bait. If the Red Army kept attacking it, the general hoped, the speedy arrival of the two columns of his eighty thousand men would crush the Red Army like an ant.

The fate of the Red Army now hung on the next moves that Tao and Si-Tu would make.

The orders by Mo and Gregory from the party headquarters were unequivocal: take Nanfeng as the first key step in the antiextermination campaign. The city must be captured to stop the invasion by the government's army in its tracks. Clearly, Tao and Si-Tu knew that the Red Army, although expanded significantly in recent years, was not strong enough to fulfill that task. A protracted attack would risk the danger of being trapped in Nanfeng, while ending the attack and leaving Nanfeng for now would mean to disobey party orders, which could seriously hurt their careers. The two men had a tough choice to make.

5

On the fringes of Blue Grass and under the shade of several giant trees next to a big pond stood a modest farmhouse, and the sign on the front door said "The Media and News Press Division." Tania showed her pass to the guard and went straight to the director's office.

When Tania knocked on the door that was ajar to announce her arrival, a man with thick glasses in his thirties raised his head. He quickly stood up, walked toward her and warmly shook her hands. It was Meng Bo-Xian!

Though not close friends, they had met several times before and did not need any introduction. This first private meeting delighted them, and both were sensitive enough not to mention each other's tribulations. Tania understood that it must have been a great humiliation for Meng to have been demoted from the top party leader to a director of a news and media department in the new Chinese Soviet government.

She decided to break the ice by saying, "You have got some nice trees around here."

"Yes, yes. You mean the huge camphor trees. They are beautiful, aren't they?" Meng responded enthusiastically. "They have a distinct aroma too, which has made them quite useful."

"Really? How?" Tania was intrigued.

"Camphor oil can be extracted by steam from their fragrant branches, chipped wood, and even root stumps," Meng replied.

"Oh, that's why it's called the camphor tree," Tania was happy to make that connection. She certainly knew the use of camphor oil, as any noble person would in Russia. But she never realized it came from a tree, much less a tree in rural southern China.

"Exactly!" Meng seemed to be happy too for the tree topic had set a casual tone for their conversation.

"I have a lot to learn, it seems," Tania said merrily.

"Now, here is your *big* job," Meng took the chance to get to business and he deliberately stressed the significance of Tania's new assignment, even though he knew it was not an exciting task.

"Here is a pamphlet and you need to translate it into Russian and English in two weeks." Meng handed the publication to Tania.

The title read *The Investigations on Rural China* by Sheng Bao.

"Of course, no problem." Tania's acceptance of the mundane assignment came as a relief for Meng, who was worried that asking a former emissary to do some clerical translation work amounted to a bigger demotion than his.

"If I have any questions about the Chinese text, can I ask you?" Tania cautiously inquired for she could see that Meng was a busy man surrounded by piles of papers and documents on his desk.

"Of course, any time," responded Meng. He then went on to explain that the translations of the pamphlet would inform Moscow about the current conditions in China's countryside, where much of the revolutionary activities were taking place. The faster and more accurately the pamphlet was translated, the more it would help build a better understanding between the Chinese Communist Party and the Comintern.

Tania agreed. She was such a loyal party member and so anxious to resume working that by the end of the conversation she felt she had wasted too much time in solitary confinement for the last year. She could not wait to start working on the translations.

Tania was also personally interested to know why and how the peasantry could have played such a highly active role in the Chinese revolution, as manifested in everything she saw and everywhere she went in Blue Grass every day. From her experience, she understood that Marx and Engels believed in the dual nature of the peasantry, who were landowners and farmworkers at the same time. Suspicious of these petty bourgeoisie and their inherited conservatism, Marx and Engels seriously doubted their revolutionary potential. Their impressions and conclusions were of course based on their knowledge of the farmers in Western European countries, especially of the French farmers' role in the 1848 Revolution.

In Russia, Lenin decried the rural reform of the 1860s, describing it as a period of "the surrender of peasant land to be plundered by a handful of bloodsuckers, kulaks, and well-to-do peasants, and the surrender of the countryside to the rule of the feudal landowners." After the Bolshevik Revolution, the new government sent out soldiers to the villages to confiscate grains from the farmers to feed the starving population in the cities. Stalin had reversed Lenin's policy of forming an alliance with the middle peasants in the late 1920s. He aggressively pushed for collectivization in the countryside in the early 1930s, when the middling farmers were labeled as the "enemy of the state" and were even physically eliminated as a class. Many were exiled to remote frontiers in the Soviet Union, others to distant fringes in their respective province and still others, who numbered in the tens of thousands, were summarily arrested and executed.

Unlike these leading European communists, from Marx and Engels to Lenin and Stalin, who had strong connections to cities, Sheng had grown up in the country. As a provincial party official, he personally mobilized the peasants and turned them into a revolutionary force. Most of the soldiers he had recruited were farmers and peasants, as were most of his associates and subordinates. He had conducted extensive interviews in a dozen rural counties for months before submitting the final report of his investigations. What would he say about the Chinese peasantry? Why could they, unlike their European counterparts, be a major force in the Chinese environment? Tania could hardly wait to find out the answers.

6

The topography of elongated Jiangxi tilted from south to north. Coming down from the plateaus in southern Jiangxi to the plains to join the Yangtze River in the north, the Gan and Fu rivers as well as the main roads along their banks were the two principal transportation arteries, which had been moving cargos and passengers going north or south since ancient times. The larger and longer of the two, the Gan River lay in the western portion of the province and was separated by several ranges of high mountains from the Fu River, which ran through the eastern portion of the province. The two rivers, though highly conducive to the up and down transportation, were of little help for those travelers who must go in an eastward or westward direction. By the time General Bai's two columns of soldiers left the river valleys, rushed through the mountains and arrived at Nanfeng in the east, the Red Army had already vanished. He could not take any further action until he received some new intelligence about the adversary's whereabouts. For now, the only thing he could do was to wait.

Sensing that a dangerous net had been cast over them a few days ago, Tao and Si-Tu aborted the futile siege of Nanfeng, ending the plan for a frontal assault to block the advancing government troops. General Bai's thirty-plus divisions were a formidable force for the Red Army to confront directly, and the latter was much less likely to succeed in an all-out preemptive strike to stop them. Their instincts told Tao and Si-Tu that they must withdraw immediately and move to the mountains to wait for another opportunity, even if it meant defying the orders of Mo and Gregory.

A planned retreat was far from defeat. Tao and Si-Tu carefully directed the 11th Army as a decoy to move to Lichuan, the township forty miles further east from Nanfeng. Just a few months ago, the 1st Legion of the Red Army had infiltrated this area, and several successful battles helped them to establish the army's headquarters and training base here. At one point, the influence of the Red Army extended from Lichuan to several townships and counties. One of them was only fifteen miles to Fuzhou, where General Bai had set up his field command.

Although just seventy miles from Fuzhou, Lichuan was surprisingly inaccessible. In fact, it was only close to Fujian Province, Jiangxi's next-door neighbor. The two provinces shared some of the largest mountains in Southeastern China—an area that had long been considered the most remote of places along their joint border. Clearly, Tao and Si-Tu had used the 11th Army to distract General Bai and sent him to the mountains on a wild goose chase. All the while, they had led the rest of their main force moving down south, quietly hiding and waiting for their chance to fight back.

"All warfare is based on deception." And the key to success in guerrilla warfare was no exception, just as Sun Zi had expounded in his masterpiece *The Art of War* more than two thousand years ago. "All warfare is based on deception. Hence, when we are able to attack, we must seem unable; when using our forces, we must appear inactive; when we are near, we must make the enemy believe we are far away; when far away, we must make him believe we are near."

The plot worked. General Bai believed that the 11th Army was the communists' main force, which, after the failure to capture Nanfeng, was now escaping to the east. He ordered his troops to pursue the Red Army, and quickly set new directions for the three columns, hoping to destroy the communist force in the eastern mountains. In his haste, he did not realize that the first column on the right flank in the south was now too far away from the other two columns in the north. All the columns were moving toward the east across numerous mountain ranges, and two divisions of the first column in particular were separated by the huge range called Skylines. Although the two divisions were only ten miles apart from each other, the high hills and treacherous Skylines made it impossible for them to support each other quickly and effectively.

Behind the big rocks and tall trees, three Red Army divisions were ready for each of the two nationalist divisions, both marching along a narrow country road right into a deadly trap. At the most obscure place, called Xu village, the communists carried out a decisive ambush that ended painfully for the nationalists. The government soldiers heard gunshots over the mountains, but could not do anything to rush over to help their comrades. The three-to-one power match ended before it even started. The Red Army swiftly annihilated two government divisions, killing one division commander and capturing the other.

A furious General Bai immediately changed his tactics. To prevent the two flanks from being attacked again, he combined the previous three columns into two, and moved them closer to one other. He also transported more troops to the central column, making it more massive than ever. This revamped central column alone, General Bai hoped, would be able to penetrate deep into the heart of the communist base and destroy the Red Army soldiers wherever they were found.

The idea of reorganization was a good one, but not perfect. Reshuffling his troops had its strength and weaknesses. General Bai was so eager to find the main force of the Red Army that he was duped once again by the diversion Tao and Si-Tu had created for him. This time, he wrongly assumed that the Red Army was hiding in a county south of Lichuan. When he noticed that the Red Army had picked up its speed running down south, he ordered his troops to march faster toward the same direction as well. In so doing, he overextended his supply lines, which lagged behind twenty miles away from his main column.

Tao and Si-Tu seized the opportunity and ordered their troops to turn around quickly. They planned to ambush the rearguard of General Bai's army this time, but could not decide on where to start the attack. When Officer Yao Xi-Wa suggested a place named Wild Boulder, many disagreed.

"Wild Boulder is but three miles away from Xu village. No enemy is so stupid as to make the same mistake twice in the same area," someone argued.

"Not necessarily," Officer Yao responded. He calmly explained, "In this area there is no other alternative road, and General Bai's supply line has to pass Xu village and Wild Boulder to catch up with him. Besides, our enemy can be thinking about the same thing—that no lightning would strike twice at the same spot. Thus they might even be less guarded while passing this place."

Officer Yao was one of Tao's best soldiers. At thirty-three, he was already the commander of the 1st Legion, the best of the communist main forces. A veteran of armed struggles for nearly a decade, he was one of the ablest and most trusted officers in the Red Army. Both daring in action and methodical in planning, Yao was a widely admired military leader, affectionately called "Little Tiger" by his fellow soldiers, who loved both him and Tao Yin-Hu (meaning "Night Tiger").

Little Tiger's suggestion was no doubt an extremely audacious one, betting on the enemy's state of mind more than anything else. Tao, Si-Tu, and others debated the proposal for some time before finally deciding to take the risk. They accepted Yao's argument that the enemy would never imagine that another ambush could take place in the same area in less than three weeks.

Officer Yao's instincts proved to be right and the communist ambush was a total success. All told, the government lost three divisions and over ten thousand of its soldiers were captured. The communists collected ten thousand rifles, three hundred new German machine guns, forty artillery pieces, and other military equipment. The losses were devastating enough for General Chen to call off the extermination campaign a week later.

7

Learning and gaining knowledge could be as exhilarating as any action in the battlefield.

No sooner had Tania opened the first page of Sheng's pamphlet than she realized that she was entering a completely different world. The pamphlet was such a gem full of lively details about the Chinese countryside that even the native folk might not be fully aware of them. This was the side of China few urban dwellers or casual visitors had ever seen, and still fewer of them had ever understood. But this was also the place where the most profound social and political changes were taking place, transforming China in such a dramatic fashion that anybody who was remotely interested in the country's current affairs and her history must pay serious attention to.

Most literature on the rural population consisted of three general categories—landlords, farmers, and peasants. Village life in China was far more complicated, involving these subgroups: big landlords, medium landlords, small landlords, rich farmers, independent and self-sufficient peasants, semi-independent and self-sufficient peasants, poor peasants, farm laborers, vagrants, itinerants, and transient migrants.

Examining rural China from the lens of a revolutionary ideology, the pamphlet was certainly political in nature. It was both a propaganda tool to promote the peasants' movement for the Communist Party and a practical manual for party members to learn how to engage and organize the peasants.

Beyond that, Sheng's extensive investigations also made the booklet one of the earliest sociological descriptions of rural China, which contained a wealth of information concerning not only the diverse components of country residents but also a panoramic view of the diverse aspects of rural life, such as county government, traditional power structures, land and water transportation, postal service and communication, small businesses and handcrafts, apprenticeship system and practice, trade and commerce, homemade merchandise, local exchanges, imported foreign goods, markets and fairs, native produce, groceries and daily diet, superstition, and religious institutions. The pamphlet also covered women and children, family and marriage, kinship and filial organizations, schools and education, commons and public forestry, indigenous customs and benevolent societies, rentals, tenancy and tenants, lending practices and usury, tariffs, duties, levies, and taxation, brothels and prostitution, games, gambling, and gamblers, opium, opium dens, and opium addicts, and so on and so forth.

China's social and economic disparity shocked Tania greatly. Well-to-do landlords collected rents by the hundreds of bushels every year, while hardworking poor peasants could not feed their families. But, aside from the visible inequality common to other nations, what struck her the most was the infinite complexities of Chinese rural communities, of which the Comintern and

Moscow had little knowledge. The Marxist notion of a unified and monolithic modern class hardly existed here. Every category of the rural population from peasants to landlords consisted of many sections and subdivisions, each of which had to be considered in their own right in order to understand them properly.

The landlords did not constitute a single class but were divided into several strata. Whereas many Marxists assumed a direct link between a person's economic status and his political stance, Sheng's investigations showed a more nuanced reality. Some of the medium to large landlords were corrupt and abusive, and some were openly hostile to revolution. Yet many of them were also socially conscious—promoting local business, commerce, road construction, schools, and other public projects. Most of their children received elementary to high school and even college education, and some of these graduates became communists who resolutely rebelled against their family heritage.

To Tania's surprise, Sheng was more critical of the small to medium landlords, and his father had been one of them. This was a rising group of independent, self-sufficient, and enterprising farmers who, according to him, cared more about how to get rich than about anything else. They worked hard, saved hard, and guarded their purse strings jealously. Large and medium landlords rarely gave out any small loans since they could rarely get them back. When they did, they could charge up to a monthly interest rate of thirty percent. According to standard practice, small to medium landlords would usually charge a fifty percent monthly interest plus ten percent if the loan were not paid on time. Because of this incredible usury, poor peasants who often needed small and short-term loans hated them the most.

Perhaps echoing Stalin's hostile policies toward substantial farmers when he was implementing the collectivization program in the Soviet Union, Sheng highlighted the resentment Chinese peasants had toward their independent and self-sufficient neighbors, not the large landlords. When any land reform was underway, he purported to have found, the top two goals most peasants earnestly wanted to achieve were: an equal distribution of land and a cancellation of their debts. Both claims were targeted more at the independent and self-sufficient farmers than the large landlords.

The poor peasants' anger must be appeased and their demands met, insisted Sheng. As such, the Communist Party should never alienate the poor peasants, whose loyalty and support it needed. Otherwise the party would make the grave mistake of protecting the wrong people in the countryside.

But why were the poor peasants so important to the party? Simply put, seventy percent of the rural population were poor peasants—the largest and most likely source of manpower that the communists could rely on to build the party and its military force. Yet, poverty and destitution alone was not enough to encourage anyone to rebel or take arms, and two more conditions had to exist for the poor to become willing soldiers and active participants in the communist cause—they must feel hopelessly stranded and they must be sufficiently enticed.

For any country folk, nothing would be more enticing than landownership. Therefore, the promise of a redistribution of land for the benefit of the landless poor peasants was the most direct and effective means to lure them into the communist camp. It seemed ironic that what might actually propelled the rural poor to join the communist movement was their desire to join the middle class—the key reason that orthodox Marxists never trusted the petty bourgeoisie, whose goal in life was to become richer. But the equalization of land possession was the dream of most peasants for generations, and becoming independent landowners was *sine qua non* to the peasants' idea of paradise. The Communist Party, for the moment, was the leading force that would champion their interests and help them to fulfill their dreams.

The poor peasants only seemed to be the rural counterpart of the urban proletariat. But they were not a monolithic bloc and they could be divided into four groups. The first consisted of those semi-independent farmers with inadequate land plots, who had to rent additional parcels to make a decent living. They owned draft animals, tools, seeds, and some cash, and were therefore better off than many other peasants.

The second group owned farm animals, tools, seeds, and some capital, but did not possess any land. They had to rent to survive. Comprising forty percent of the rural population and sixty percent of the poor, these landless tenants were the largest segment of the peasantry.

Like the second group, the third category of peasants owned no land and had to rent. But, unlike the second group, they owned no farm animals and had to borrow them from someone else whenever farm work demanded. Moreover, their implements were old or broken and their funds limited.

The last group comprised the poorest, who had no land, no draft animals, and no money. The few farm implements they owned were either too old or incomplete, and they could not afford to repair the tools or acquire new ones. They did not have enough grain for the year, had to borrow from time to time, and often worked as day laborers to survive.

Not every poor peasant was actively involved in the mass movement organized by the Communist Party. As Tania was reading through the pamphlet toward the end, she came to realize that the Chinese revolution had attracted the most enthusiastic supporters from the least visible but most volatile segment of the rural population. They were not the regular community residents, rich or poor, but the transients, who had little interest in maintaining the status quo. They included itinerant tinkerers, traveling handymen, day laborers, drifters, beggars, tramps, rogues, vagabonds, and the homeless, who accounted for five percent of the total rural population, living at the bottom of society and surviving on intermittent employment and charity amid persistent bigotry and disdain.

Together with the fourth group of the peasants, they made up no more than fifteen percent of the rural population. But they were highly active in the mobilized revolution and, amazingly, occupied about fifty percent of the seats in the local soviet government. Based on his assessment of all the data, Sheng concluded that the poorer one's economic status was, the more revolutionary was one's political stance.

Chapter 15

Jolts

1

THE CENTRAL SOVIET GOVERNMENT DECLARED A GENERAL holiday to celebrate the end of the Fourth Antiextermination Campaign. The people were jubilant and the official celebration at Blue Grass attracted hundreds. Tao Yin-Hu, Si-Tu Wen-Liang, and their soldiers were given a hero's welcome. The public cheered as Si-Tu made a laudatory speech praising Commander Tao, the Red Army, and its big victory.

In a newly constructed grand auditorium, Party Leader Mo Jia-Qi and Special Envoy Gregory went up to the podium to address the exuberant crowd of two thousand men and women who had been selected from the sixty counties, which had a total population of four and a half million in the territory of thirty-two thousand square miles.

"The Red Army will be greatly expanded," Mo told the crowd. "Rural reforms will continue until land has been redistributed, wealth equalized, and the poor peasants' interests met. The exploited shall never be treaded on again. The Communist Party will lead and guide us. And we will liberate all our brothers and sisters across the nation," he said.

Gregory added, "We will not only defend our Soviet government here but also attack Nanchang and Nanjing. We will defeat those counterrevolutionaries and we will bring down the nationalist government in no time."

The energized audience responded by shouting "Long Live the Red Army! Long Live the Soviets! Long Live the Proletariat! Long Live the Poor Peasantry! Long Live the Communist Party! Down with the Reactionaries! Down with the Nationalist Government! Long Live the Liberation of the Laboring People Worldwide!"

The celebration reached its climax when Red Army soldiers brandishing newly captured weapons entered the fairground. For locals who were more familiar with knives, axes, and homemade hunting pieces, this was the first time they had seen so many brand-new rifles, shining under the sun. While the bayonet looked long and sharp, the solid and nicely grained gunstock was firm and smooth, and any touch of the metallic barrel produced a magical feel. The German-made machine guns and artillery were simply amazing, and many could not believe the sizes and enormously destructive capabilities of these advanced weapons as the soldiers proudly described their specifications.

For those young men and boys who were sufficiently impressed, dozens of recruitment counters stood nearby for them to line up and sign up for enlistment.

Few organizations in history had ever been as successful as the Chinese communists in mobilizing the masses. A master of group psychology, the party enjoyed several unique advantages and used a variety of popular techniques. Mass rallies were but one of the principal means to arouse the crowd and to shepherd it in the direction the party wanted.

The majority of peasants in China were illiterate and any attempt to engage them through a rational approach of reading, writing, or private conversation was out of the question. Mass gatherings filled with straightforward harangues, simple indoctrinations, tangible promises, brief slogans, live examples, down-to-earth explanations, visible symbols, familiar stories, and vernacular expressions were the best tools of reaching out to the peasants, whose class consciousness was more a show of emotional explosion than in-depth understanding.

Social equality, mobility, and justice could be achieved either by individual exertion or by collective action. One of the most prominent spokesmen of radical liberalism in modern Europe, Marx had dismissed the first option a long time ago while insisting on the second as the only viable solution. Although much disputed by subsequent reformists in most Western countries, his dogma provided a fitting diagnosis of the Chinese agrarian tradition, and the Chinese Communist Party embraced his conflict theory and implemented his dichotomous doctrine with absolute zest.

If the long Chinese history had ever taught the peasantry anything, it showed them that the world was always divided into "yin" and "yang," good and evil, the rich and the poor, the powerful and the powerless, which surprisingly concurred with Marx's famed assertion that "the history of all hitherto existing society is the history of class struggles." The Chinese peasantry needed no more evidence to be convinced. Their countless insurrections in the past had shown that collective action including armed rebellions had always been the only means for the poor to change their fate. The nation's pathetic social disparity only reaffirmed that Marx had discovered all the correct answers and perfect solutions to the Chinese problem.

Explaining away any social and economic problems based on the dichotomous conflict between good and evil had long been the typical mode of thinking for most Chinese, both rural and urban, and among the illiterate and the highly educated. What they needed was not a new theory but a new organization and leadership that could lead them to success.

The Chinese communists thus embraced Marxism as a new religion for the sake of China's salvation; the Communist Party was a willing instrument that would command the masses through the journey of salvation.

In the crusade they needed thousands of crusaders. Fortunately, they found them in the vast numbers of the peasantry.

To arouse the masses, propaganda and mind control were paramount, which included vilification of the rich, glorification of the poor, exaltation of absolute equality, glamorization of the party, indoctrination of communist principles, and blind worship of the party leadership.

Tania now understood that the power of the Chinese Communist Party lay in its unsurpassed ability to control the huge population of the peasantry. As an organization, the Nationalist Party never penetrated deep into the grass roots of society. By contrast, the Communist Party was constructed to get to the very bottom of society. From its Central Committee at the top national level, the organizational network of the party first went down to a series of provincial committees, which in turn led to the district and county committees. Each county committee could authorize the setting up of a branch committee at every village that had three or more members of the party.

Members of these committees at all levels could recruit new members, and the local committees especially had the responsibility to increase membership. Thus, the organization would grow like a huge mesh, ever spreading to cover as much territory as it could. The ever-growing network, however, strictly obeyed the higher offices. The centralized control gave out orders that all the lower offices must follow, making the entire organization act like a highly coordinated machine.

At Blue Grass, the hard work paid off. Out of a community of six thousand souls, one thousand men joined the Red Army. That meant one out of every three men in the village became a soldier, which effectively deprived the community of its prime farm labor. In addition, the village also had various groups made up of militia men, militia women, young pioneers, boy scouts, and girl scouts, a squad of village police and surveillance personnel, and a company of special paramilitary forces. Blue Grass not only became a place of mostly women, children, and the elderly but was also transformed into an army camp.

2

While working on the translations, Tania had listed out questions that she needed answers to better understand the original text. She went to see Meng Bo-Xian, gave him the list, and watched carefully for his reaction.

Meng patiently went over the list and said, "You seem to have three kinds of questions: the technical ones, the ones about women, and the ones about government officials. Correct?"

"That's right." Tania was pleased how quickly Meng was able to categorize her questions, which she had jotted down at random. His classification made sense, which helped to clarify her thoughts and enabled him to respond faster.

"Okay then, let's start with the first kind." Meng had circled those items that were primarily concerned with some local expressions not easily understood by outsiders. He explained,

"'The milky ones' refer to infants or small children, male or female, in rural Jiangxi dialect. This must have appeared several times when people were talking about selling their children, a heart-wrenching family tragedy for many poor people. 'Electrical oil' means battery in the vernacular. 'To eat fried pancake' insinuates that the person is taking advantage of somebody or stealing someone else's stuff. 'Daylight money' means copper or small change, which is often needed in daily exchange. The locals can grow two seasons of rice per year here, and they call the first season 'early rice' or *zao zi* and the second season 'late rice' or *fan zi*. 'Tea oil,' also called 'tree oil or wood oil,' is the eatable oil obtained from *Camellia oleifera*, which is very popular in rural Southern China, including Jiangxi. Like their cousins, the camellia flower trees, you can see them almost everywhere. The oil is produced from pressing their seeds, and is used as daily cooking oil for villagers. It's also a common commodity for the locals to exchange for cash or other merchandise. Because of its wide usage, 'an oil hill' in the local parlance often means a hill full of grown *Camellia oleifera* trees. And 'tea seeds' or 'oil seeds' often refer to the fruit of the *Camellia oleifera* trees."

Tania was enchanted. She loved to listen to these little stories, which revealed so much about the hidden nuances of the Chinese language and its intriguing regional dialects. There was always so much to learn, and it was really delightful to learn a foreign language so full of rich and subtle details of history, culture, and local customs.

Meng went on, "You have quite a few questions about women in the red base. I assume you are interested to know about their changing roles and social status in the revolution?"

"Correct," Tania said. "Sheng mentioned women numerous times in his investigations, but in a different context. I hope you can provide a little more background information."

"Yes. The issue of women is very important to us, and the Chinese Communist Party adopted a resolution on women as early as 1922 during its second national convention. For more than a decade since then, some provincial governments and the Central Soviet Government in Jiangxi have passed laws to protect women and to ensure their equal rights in society. We have abolished arranged marriages throughout the revolutionary bases. Women now enjoy the same right as men to participate in public affairs and to be elected to public offices. They have played very important roles in our local soviets and county governments. Several of them are also prominent party leaders at the provincial and national levels."

"From reading Sheng's reports, it seems that bias and discrimination against women remain strong in some places, even within the revolutionary bases." Tania said.

"True. China has a very long feudal tradition and inequality for women has deep roots in our culture and society across the nation, especially in the countryside. And our revolutionary bases are no exceptions," acknowledged Meng.

"What's the connection between the liberation of women and the proletarian revolution?" Tania asked.

"Women play a very important role in the proletarian revolution," Meng responded. "Without women's participation, as Marx and Engels pointed out, the proletariat cannot achieve its ultimate goal, which is to liberate all of the oppressed. Or, in the words of Charles Fourier, 'The degree of emancipation of woman is the natural measure of general emancipation.' The liberation of women is subject to the abolition of the capitalist private ownership system, because, in the final analysis, it is the very concept of private ownership that has turned women into men's possessions. The oppression of women will not end until private property and private ownership are abolished."

Sensing Tania's skepticism, Meng paused. "You seem to disagree."

"No, I don't disagree but I have a question." Tania said. "What does the party say about equality between the sexes?"

"Equality between the sexes will never materialize in a capitalist society. The Soviet Union has achieved real equality between men and women, which proves what Marx and Engels said—the oppression of women will not disappear as long as class oppression continues."

Tania was impressed that Meng seemed to be very familiar with the works of Marx and Engels. He quoted them often and could incorporate their statements to validate his assertions with ease. Although she felt his response was still incomplete, she decided to move on.

"What about my third set of questions, which are related to the behavior of some local government officials?" Meng was listening and Tania continued, "From reading Sheng's text, I gather that several officials of the new local revolutionary government are habitual gamblers."

"Really?" Meng was taken back. He had read Sheng's work in the past, but did not recall such details. He asked Tania to point out where she had found the passage. Tania did and Meng recognized the fact that, of the eighteen officials in a Soviet district government mentioned by Sheng, seven were habitual gamblers and one was a part-time gambler. It was Meng's turn to pause. Many party colleagues had read Sheng's pamphlet, but no one raised the same question as Tania did. Was it an anomaly, or something more serious? Meng really did not have a clear answer right away.

"You raised a good question," said he. "I am not sure how representative the situation is. But it is certainly something we need to pay attention to. If it's a special case, purely local in nature, that's one thing. But if it is more widespread, it certainly deserves our party's serious attention."

Tania understood that Meng was feeling a little awkward that he could not provide any immediate answer to her question even though he had been a top party leader for some time.

But Tania was Tania. She was a very sensitive and considerate person, and never wanted to let the host and supervisor feel bad. She took out something from her pocket, handed it to Meng, and said, "Now, my final question, which is purely personal."

"Okay, please." Meng knew Tania was trying to change the topic.

"This is, I believe, a snuff bottle made of Chinese porcelain. My question: why does it have a feminine design?"

"An interesting question. Let me see." Meng carefully held the delicate object in his hand for a minute and said, "This is not a snuff bottle but a perfume bottle or container made for ladies."

"Oh, I see. That's why the feminine design since it was never meant to be a man's object." Tania was so happy that she had finally found an explanation for the enigmatic design. She then told Meng that Martin had given her this porcelain bottle in Moscow. Martin had also told Tania the story of how he had bought it in Rotterdam when he was a boy. The same question about the design had baffled him ever since.

"What a wonderful story you have! It must be the symbol of Martin's love for you," Meng exclaimed.

Smiling, Tania said, "Now, I can let Martin know the answer, and he will be very, very pleased."

The couple had not seen each other for quite some time since the fiasco of their fake divorce, which now looked more and more like a real one. Tania hoped that this new information might help smooth out the rough patch in their relationship.

Before she left, she remembered a related question. "We—Martin and I—have always been curious why the colors of the Chinese blue-and-white porcelain can be so vibrant that no other product can match."

The ever-knowledgeable Meng beamed. He said, "The Chinese blue-and-white porcelain uses two distinctive materials. One is the extremely fine clay called Kaolinite, which is only found near the small town of Jingdezhen in Jiangxi. Used as the base, it gives the smooth and almost translucent white color of the porcelain. The other is the color pigment called cobalt blue, imported from Samarra, the ancient city in Iraq. Used as the paint, it gives the kind of brilliant deep blue glaze that no other material could duplicate. These two high-quality materials combined plus the most skilled craftsmanship have made the Chinese blue-and-white porcelain one of the most famous and most enduring products in history."

3

About six miles east of Blue Grass stood the unremarkable Lazy Mountain, which was the perfect place to escape the summer heat. Nestled behind a roll of large boulders and concealed under the bushy shade of giant firs, pines, and cypress, an abandoned temple had been converted into the residence of Comrade Sheng Bao, wife Yu Shao-Mei, their daughter Sheng Ying, and a guard squad headed by Officer Lu Di-Ping. Despite the cool environment, Sheng's mood was anything but relaxed.

A few months ago, he was dismissed from the office of commissar of the Red Army, which upset him greatly. Even though the party made him chairman of the Central Soviet government, Sheng believed he had been demoted. Managing a new administration of several dozen departments and dealing with mundane affairs from bridge repairs to regulations over domestic animals hardly thrilled him. He considered himself a military genius and his talents would be best used in devising vital strategies for the Red Army. Besides, according to his reading of Chinese history, only a successful military career would propel one to the top of any political leadership, while a good record of administrative experience would lead one to nowhere no matter how successful he had been.

Prior to his apparent demotion, Sheng had been criticized for not following the party's orders, and was particularly blamed for his dubious military tactics. The party needed someone to lead the ongoing attacks against major cities, and he was only willing to conduct guerrilla warfare in the desolate countryside. The party needed bold, forceful, and aggressive campaigns, and he was interested only in playing hide-and-seek games with the enemies. His huge ego and irritable temperament did not win him many friends, nor did his overt ambition and autocratic style gain him much sympathy among his colleagues.

Although Sheng acknowledged that the Fourth Antiextermination Campaign was a significant victory, he was not thrilled to see that most of the glory went to Tao, his one-time military protégé, who had been under Sheng's command when he was commissar of the Red Army. Neither was he happy to see that even Si-Tu had gotten a large share of the accolades. The latter, after all, was the one who had replaced him as the new commissar of the army—the worst insult Sheng had ever suffered, which he would never forget for the rest of his life.

Sheng's sentiments were highly personal, which contradicted the assumption that top communist leaders must be as holy, noble, unselfish, and altruistic as any consecrated clergyman. Many circumstances had changed and Sheng had changed along with them. He was no longer the junior member of the party, the timid outsider, and the innocent country boy. Working to mobilize the massive crowd of humble peasants, he felt like he was a giant in his home turf. Fighting in the hills and moving around the countryside, his experience in directing thousands of troops had given him unprecedented confidence that he was the chosen one to lead the army, the party, and the cause. He had gradually become accustomed to consider his future and that of the revolution as one and the same thing. As much as he needed the party, it also needed him since he was the only one representing the right path to success. Anyone who disagreed with him would be viewed as a roadblock to his ascension to power at best, if not a counterrevolutionary at worst. His rivalry with other men in the party was not personal after all, but a fight between right and wrong, good and evil, success and failure, and between life and death.

To his surprise, several associates apparently also believed that they were the chosen ones, not the incorrigible Sheng. As the rural red bases were growing in size and as the underground work in big cities had become more and more dangerous, the party headquarters was moved from Shanghai to Blue Grass in Jiangxi. For the first time in party history, the top national leadership would work side by side with the top regional leaders. The two groups did not necessarily share the same views, nor did they agree on the same policies. Different opinions and different personalities collided as important matters came up for discussions every day. Everyone insisted he was the messiah and his proposals would be the most appropriate for the party to adopt. Thus, personal differences became political and any of those differences could be viewed as a matter of life and death for the party's future.

No monolithic unity—nor absolute homogeneity and uniformity—had ever existed in any political organization. Conflicting ideas and divergent opinions were as natural as day and night, and often sorting out those differences was exactly what was required in a political process. But if the fundamental theory of a political system never accepted the legitimacy of any opposition from without, it would hardly allow any dissension from within. The colossal ideologues from Marx to Lenin were not known as accommodating revolutionaries, and the Great Purges conducted by the tyrant Stalin set a horrendous example for all the other communist organizations.

The Communist Party was one of the ugliest political machines ever invented. Without a structural framework or an institutional guarantee that would tolerate internal disagreements as part of routine political life, all bets were off and intraparty rivalries became a struggle as brutal and vile as the mortal conflict with external enemies.

Sheng now had to fight for his political survival in the presence of several powerful players—Gregory, Mo Jia-Qi, Si-Tu Wen-Liang, Tao Yin-Hu, Meng Bo-Xian, Dong Zi-Tian, and Lin Shi-Xiong. Without any visible allies, Sheng was undoubtedly the weakest among them. But his instincts told him that the more intense the competition was, the better his chances of reaching the pinnacle of power were.

For the moment, though, Sheng had no choice but to lick his wounds. Feeling dejected, he could not focus on work. He applied for sick leave and retreated to the temple with his family for an extended break. Whereas his rivals were buried in their daily grind, he used his free time to study them and contemplate his next move.

Among the seven people, Sheng analyzed, three blocs existed—the alliance between Gregory and Mo, the friendship between Dong and Meng, and the close working relationship among Si-Tu, Tao, and Lin. The main reason Sheng was often in the minority position was precisely because he always stood as a lone outlier among all of them. Their differences in educational and personal backgrounds and past experiences meant that Sheng had no trusted long-term friends and allies. He had no reliable support to count on, and he had no immediate means to break into these blocs and exert his own influence any time soon.

Strictly speaking, Gregory was not an official member of the Chinese Communist Party. But he held enormous clout over the party simply because, as the special envoy, he was the onsite overseer on behalf of the Comintern—the overlord of this national organization. His tall and strong physique and meticulously trimmed mustache impressed his Chinese colleagues, who viewed his outward appearance as authentic as his intrinsic Russianness. Eurocentric, chauvinistic, and self-centered, he never gave much thought to the meek Chinese, whose sallow faces and small bodies seemed too far removed from the conventional images of brutal warriors he used to see.

Like many Russian and European observers, Gregory believed that the Chinese did not have a soul as a nation. They were self-contented, selfish, narrow-minded, and short-sighted. They were timid and sordid as much as they were calculative and devious by nature, and would take the first chance to compromise if they could avoid fighting. The national history of the Chinese had literally ended when the last emperor of the Southern Sung dynasty lost the final battle and the country fell to the Mongols in 1278. Gregory's job in China, to put it bluntly, was to push them to fight by whatever means necessary. He was confident that with his training at the prestigious Frunze Military Academy, and with his invaluable experience in the Russian Civil War he would be the best man within the Chinese leadership to command the Red Army to victory. Most of his Chinese communist friends and high officials apparently had the same belief.

Sheng never liked Mo, who, fifteen years his junior, was nevertheless handpicked by Stalin as the official leader of the Chinese Communist Party.

He had no knowledge about the real lives in China, and his only merit was the several years he had spent in Moscow. An arrogant and naïve person, Mo could lead neither a comprehensive institution nor a fighting army. He could hold the highest office only because the Comintern was behind him. He was the Russians' puppet and Sheng, despite his humble rural background, hated to be controlled by anyone including the Russians. But the reality was that the insipid Gregory and the supercilious Mo had formed a close bond, which was exceedingly hard to break. As long as the two collaborated closely with Moscow's backing, it would be inconceivable for anyone else within the communist organization to dethrone them.

Bookish and erudite. Credulous and sentimental. Europeanized and idealistic. If similar intellectual interests and scholastic pursuits had drawn Dong and Meng closer, their shared careers in the Russian Study Program had made them good friends. Insofar as personal disposition was concerned, Meng was certainly the mellow one. He seemed rather contented and even relaxed after his demotion. He never complained about the loss of his office but worked diligently like an ant on whatever task assigned to hm. If he was not simply putting an act, Sheng thought, Meng might be a different kind of political animal—one who really did not have the burning desire to become a key figure in the party.

By contrast, Dong had four words written all over his face: "I am the leader." Proud to have been the founding organizer and the party's top-ranking official earlier than anyone else in the current leadership circle, he was overtly unhappy about his latest post in the organization. Appointed as one of the deputies in the Central Soviet Government, he believed he deserved to be treated much better. While his student Mo at the Russian Study Program had been promoted to become the party boss, Dong felt he should at least not be sidelined and relegated to become Sheng's subordinate. Perhaps because of his undisputed track record, Mo saw Dong as a formidable challenger. According to rumors, the party would soon transfer Dong to another provincial red base north of the Yangtze River, far away from Jiangxi. Thus Mo would not be obliged to meet him daily, which had caused both of them to feel uncomfortable.

One of the most intriguing personalities was Si-Tu. Widely considered the most sophisticated communist in China, Si-Tu was inscrutable as an individual. As far as Sheng could tell, Si-Tu was the slyest and the least trustworthy person he had ever worked with. One could never tell what exactly he was thinking. Si-Tu always smiled at public meetings and he was always gentle and considerate when in the company of others. But, behind closed doors, he could be as vicious, vengeful, and unforgiving as an executioner. He never appeared to be interested in power, but nothing could operate in the party without his consent. He always appeared to be even-handed, while he quietly built the largest network of followers across the red bases. He never showed any ambition to be the party's top leader, but the chatter about his suitability for the post had never ceased within the rank and file. Like it or not, if anyone aspired to lead the party, Si-Tu's acquiescence, collaboration, and support must be obtained.

Tao struck everybody as a straightforward and one-dimensional soldier whose life was made for combat, not politics. Sheng thought otherwise. He believed that Tao was as ambitious as several other top officials. He only appeared to be disinterested because he knew his strength lay in military affairs not in party politics. To become an all-rounded political leader, he needed time and experience to boost his credentials and gain wider support from more diverse constituencies within the organization. One thing for sure, Sheng thought, was that the quiet and honest Tao was not uninterested in political power. Like any skilled warrior, his simplicity and loyalty served as a mask to hide an agenda that few could yet ascertain. This could explain why Tao had never visited his former superior Sheng, who was on leave, but had instead formed such a cordial relationship with Si-Tu, who was believed to be the rising star in the party.

If Mo was Gregory's running dog, Lin was Si-Tu's. The two somehow had formed a curious friendship like two imperial scorpions dancing together; each understood perfectly how lethal the other could be. As the head of the party's special division, Si-Tu oversaw the party's spy rings and covert actions. Lin, a graduate of the Russian Study Program, went through extensive training in security and counterintelligence with the Soviet secret police. He led the Security and Covert Action Department (known to outsiders as the "Social Department") after his return from Moscow, and had worked closely with Si-Tu ever since. The two often held closed-door meetings and discussed personnel matters privy only to a handful of the party's highest officials, Sheng not included. This glaring exclusion underlined Sheng's inferior status, which pained him greatly. Frustrations such as these only hardened his resolve. He earnestly hoped that one day he could be in the same position to dictate everybody else's fate in the party. He would get there, he swore, no matter what—and how long—it would take.

4

Anticipation. Anxiety. Apprehension. Excitement. Trepidation. Tania did not know why she could be so confused this morning. Yes, she was going to see Martin for the first time in a long while. Yet she felt like a teenage girl who was about to go on her first date with her boyfriend: heart panting, face blushing, breathing faster every minute, and all that. The feeling of love was so sweet, so delightful, and so intoxicating that it could throw a person off anytime. Whether the woman was young or old, had been married or not, it could hit her with such a surprising force that she was utterly unprepared for it, and totally lost when it did.

Since Tania learned about the interesting new details of the Chinese blue-and-white porcelain from Meng, she had been thinking that she must meet Martin to let him know the real story. She recalled all the sweet moments she had with Martin in Moscow, where he gave her the exquisite porcelain bottle as a symbol of his love. She was deeply captivated by his childhood stories and was so much in love with him then. Now, the renewed understanding of this little ceramic piece seemed to have rekindled her passion for him. She could not wait to see him and tell him how much she loved him, and how much she wanted to revive their marriage. They were made for each other just as this small porcelain had carried the loving memories of them for so many years, which it would continue to do as long as they remained together like before.

To prepare for the visit, Tania asked her hostess about what to bring for the special occasion. The woman, a fervent believer in anything local, had a long list of recommendations, including navel oranges (juiciest in the world, said she), pickled meat (tastiest), gray goose (unique), Plum Mountain tea (most refreshing), Southern Jiangxi tangerine (sweetest), white lotus (most nutritious), salted duck (best dish), homemade sausages (most delicious), and Kan River wine (most enticing). The outpouring of her enthusiasm overwhelmed Tania, who eventually settled for the navel oranges, Plum Mountain tea, and some homemade sausages.

The few miles down the stream to another village was a pleasant walk, and Tania had a spring in her step, feeling as rejuvenated as she could be. The large compound where Martin lived seemed to be a much more substantial residence than the one she was living in.

A massive wall shielded the entire front of the house. Only when Tania walked around it did she realize that the impressive compound must have been an old temple or some government building. Dark gray roof tiles contrasted sharply with whitewashed sidewalls under the sun. Giant and solid double-entrance doors, oversized firewalls, tall and decorated windows, extended large eaves, several sizable courtyards, and extensive wood carvings throughout indicated that the place was anything but a regular family residence.

Apparently the compound housed multiple offices and families, and Tania did not know where to go next. A ruddy boyish soldier told her that the big foreign guy she was looking for lived at the back of the complex.

Tania hurried toward the direction given, but paused when she finally found the residence—a large room with its door, a few steps up on a stone platform, closed. Hearing some noises inside, she was about to knock but stopped. That sound of adult mischief was disturbingly familiar and Tania was afraid to confirm it. For a few seconds she froze, and a glance through the door convinced her that she must leave—Martin and a well-endowed woman were embracing and kissing each other in the room.

Disappointment. Humiliation. Regret. Sadness. Pain. Tania withdrew quietly.

On her way home, she looked at the things she had prepared only a few hours ago—a pound of navel oranges, a box of Plum Mountain tea, and a packet of homemade sausages, remembering the wonderful qualities they purported to have—the tastiest, the most refreshing, and the most delicious. Now they were all useless. She wanted to cry but no tears came out.

Maybe she had expected too much. Romance could be passionate but transient, while eternal love was rare. Any person's feelings could change and Martin was no exception, considering that they had been separated for almost two years. Still when the man Tania had loved so much for so long turned his back on her, she felt betrayed. And the pain Tania felt was as deep as her love for him.

The emotional rollercoaster overwhelmed Tania, and she felt exhausted walking back toward Blue Grass. As she was about to take a break by leaning against a big tree near the road, she heard someone calling her name.

"Tania, is that you?"

Surprised anyone would know her name in such a place, she turned around.

"Tania!"

"Zi-Tian!"

The two good friends yelled at the same time and were embracing each other the next moment.

"Tania, are you crying?" Dong asked, as concerned and caring as ever before.

"No, I am not crying. Oh, yes, yes, I am crying because I am so happy to see you." Tania corrected herself and said, "You don't know HOW happy I am to see you!"

Suddenly the melancholy vanished and Tania shot a volley of questions about Dong, his work, life, and plans. They had met a few times at various meetings during the last several years. But they were too busy to have had any chance to talk alone. Everything he said interested Tania, who only seemed to want to know even more about him.

Dong sensed something was amiss and he looked for a chance to ask about Tania, her work, life, and plans. "What goodies you are carrying? Let me help you with them."

"Oh, these are some gifts for a friend who was not at home," she replied. "Why don't you take them?"

"No, no way. You can save them for now and give them to him next time," Dong said.

"There is no next time," Tania responded to Dong, and to herself resolutely.

"I have received orders to leave Jiangxi soon," Dong told Tania.

"Really? When?"

"Very soon. I am also going to get married soon."

"Really? Congratulations! Who is the lucky girl?"

"Her name is Dai Tian. You may have met her."

"Oh, I think I know. She is a gifted writer and reporter. Very pretty," Tania recalled, delighted that the conversation had totally changed her mood. Feeling truly happy for her friend, she insisted Dong take the basket of gifts. "Now, you must have this as a wedding present. Please, please say hello to Dai Tian and warm congratulations to both of you. Bless you, my dear friend. I wish you have a very nice wedding and a safe trip to your new post."

Little did Tania knew that, from that moment on, she would not be able to see the two dearest men in her life for a very long time. Dong's next assignment would send him to another province several hundred miles from Jiangxi, and Martin would be called back to Moscow for a new mission.

5

When General Chen launched a new extermination campaign against the communist base in Jiangxi not just by gunfire but also with construction projects, Red Army Commander Tao became real worried. He believed that the enemy must have adopted a new strategy, but he was not sure what it was. His antiextermination campaign, the fifth one he had been involved with, could be tougher than ever before, and his first priority was to find out how General Chen had prepared his attacks and what he was up to.

Stinky and stuffy, the situation room at the communist headquarters was filled with the smell of cheap cigarettes and poor tobacco produced by one of the few factories the party operated. Around the big map on a massive table, Gregory, Mo, Tao, Si-Tu, Lin, and Meng were examining the situation earnestly. Intelligence said that the national government had gathered as many as one million soldiers for this new campaign, a force bigger than the first four combined. Apparently, General Chen was determined to eradicate the communist menace once and for all.

"The more the enemy wants to destroy us, the more we should fight back with unshakable will and determination," said Mo.

"Most definitely," agreed Gregory. "We are communists and we know no failure or defeat."

"What should we do to prepare ourselves?" Si-Tu asked.

"Preemptive strike! Preemptive strike!" Gregory responded.

"We have a little more than one hundred soldiers and many of them have not yet had enough time to recuperate from the battles of the last campaign," Tao reminded his colleagues.

"That's why we are called communists, aren't we?" Mo retorted.

"That's right!" Gregory joined him. "We are tireless communists, and we are fearless. No matter how large the counterrevolutionary army appears to be, we are invincible because we have Marxism, Stalin, and the Comintern behind us."

"We need ammunition. We need new and better weapons. We also need to train hundreds of our new recruits," Tao said.

"Don't worry. Support from the Soviet Union is on the way," Gregory replied confidently.

"Besides," added Mo, "we are made of special material, aren't we? We have justice, we have the right cause, and we have the support of millions. We shall succeed, and we will."

Frowning at Mo's simplistic declaration, Tao called in Staff Officer Lu Di-Ping to inform the group about the enemy's positions.

Lu saluted to the group of the party's highest officials and began speaking carefully. "Chen wants to encircle us from all four directions. For that purpose, he has organized his troops into four fronts. First, the Northern Route Army comprises thirty-three divisions; they are deployed along the Fu River. Secondly, the Southern Route Army, which is made up of eleven divisions and one independent regiment, has established its position along the border between Jiangxi and Guangdong provinces to block and even squeeze us from the south. Thirdly, the Western Route Army comprises nine divisions and three independent regiments. Their task is to block us from moving west of the Kan River. The last and the fourth front has eleven divisions and four regiments. They are assigned to prevent us from escaping to northeast Jiangxi and northwest Fujian. In sum, Chen has assembled sixty-four divisions and eight regiments, totaling one million armed men, or twice as many as he was able to mobilize during the last campaign."

"If the plan is so comprehensive, why haven't we seen any action so far?" Si-Tu asked.

"It looks like Chen has adopted a strategy of attrition this time," Officer Lu answered.

"A strategy of attrition?" Meng and Lin were puzzled.

"Yes," Lu explained, "the enemy is not in a hurry to attack us but has been proceeding very cautiously. The troops will construct a series of concrete fortifications in a given area, arrest any communists inside, and make sure of the residents' allegiance to the national government before moving forward. After they have advanced into a new area, they will repeat the same steps. Apparently, they are slowly building a chain of interconnected, well-consolidated, and ever-expanding blockages to confine, restrict, and diminish the mobility of our Red Army." Lu concluded his report and everyone in the room realized the seriousness of the situation.

"We must attack first before the enemy is ready to," Mo said loudly.

"Our troops may not be ready yet this time. Our enemy has clearly changed its tactics. We may need a new one as well," Tao cautioned.

"And we only have fifteen good divisions. It may be hard for us to prepare both our defense and offense at the same time," Si-Tu added.

"We must attack first. This was already decided at our last meeting two months ago. It has received the Comintern's approval. We can't change the plan now," Mo insisted in a firm voice.

"No one shall propose any plan similar to Sheng Bao's cowardly and escapist ideas," Gregory warned. "I remind you that the Comintern has no interest in his hide-and-seek games, and we will not listen to any excuses."

"That's right," Mo jumped in. "You have seen the results and anyone who suggests any ideas similar to that of Sheng's obsolete and defeatist tactics will be dismissed and face the appropriate disciplinary action."

Silence. Tao, Si-Tu, Meng, and Lin looked at each other. None was able and willing to argue against Gregory and Mo, even though the impracticality of their proposed strategy was clear to everybody. Not at all timid men in fighting the enemy from without, they were nevertheless too submissive to confront authoritarian figures from within. The prevailing style and firmly established tradition of this centralized organization gave enormous power only to one or two of its top leaders whose subordinates, including the highly talented Commander Tao and the highly intelligent leader Si-Tu, had long formed a habit not of independent thinking but of blind obedience. So an aggressive plan was drawn to attack several cities in the north in an attempt to forestall the nationalist extermination campaign and maybe even to defeat the enemy before it could set its foot into the red base.

6

Sitting close to a tiny oil lamp in her room, Tania held the porcelain bottle in her hand and wondered what her fate would be like if she had not run into Martin in the Senate building in the Kremlin. What if she had not received this cute little porcelain bottle as a gift? Would her life be any different? Would she still be in China now? Would she have met some other man and form a different family?

Tania knew she was subconsciously looking for excuses to escape her current distressing situation. One could never change what had happened in the past but must confront and deal with the present reality. The fact was that they had passionately loved each other. They had Peter, her dear boy, who was about ten years old now. How was he doing? What did he look like? Would he regard her as an unfit and irresponsible mother? Tania felt that she was now missing her boy more than ever; he might be the only thing left from the marriage.

The reality was, Tania realized, that Martin and she were in China to help form the Communist Party, which had developed substantially since they first arrived. Perhaps, like her Peter, this once small newborn political organ had transformed into a huge and independent body that had completely outgrown the wildest ideas they had had more than a decade ago, when they were ardent emissaries of the Comintern. The mission was accomplished, but the messenger was left abandoned. Adding insult to injury, Martin also betrayed her, the woman who seemed to have become a disposable scapegoat for everyone else.

"Was this because I grew up with the milk of a goat? Or were women forever second class to men?" Tania asked herself. "Weren't we always being used and then discarded whenever men changed their minds and hearts? What was equality between men and women? Was it really possible? Where could I find my true destiny and value in this world? Was there ever true and long-lasting love between a man and a woman? Or was I too idealistic and too impractical to ask these questions," Tania wondered.

"Ma'am, you have a visitor," said the hostess as she knocked the door.

Who could it be? And at this hour? Tania was perplexed as she opened the door.

"Yan Yan, is that really you, my dear friend?" Tania hugged her warmly and invited her in.

Nothing could heal a woman's wounds better and faster than her best and most trusted friend. The two women talked all night in their shared bed, starting from the first moment they had parted.

Tania learned that Professor Lu Shi-Yan had passed away, which did not surprise her. He had been terribly sick for a very long time. What did surprise her was that Yan had returned to nurse him until the end of his life.

"Lu Shi-Yan had found another mistress and he had betrayed you. Weren't you angry with him?" Tania asked.

"Yes, I was," said Yan.

"Then how could you go back and take care of him as if nothing had happened?"

"That's called 'fate' in China, meaning I was destined to be faithful to him even if he was not to me."

"I must confess this is completely unfathomable to me."

"Everyone has his or her fate," Yan continued, "and we must accept it without question. For example, I knew from the first time I met Lu that I was going to serve him, not he me. He was so great and smart, and I so humble and ignorant. Heavens let us meet because he needed help. And I was that help because I had been born in this life to serve him. To be his faithful servant was my fate, and I should accept my fate no matter what."

A very strange logic indeed and a fatalist idea for sure, Tania thought. But this might be the reason why Chinese women had endured so much unbearable hardship for so long. In too many instances reported by Westerners, they appeared to be meek, servile, and humble. Yet they were also incredibly kind, generous, tolerant, and strong. They could persevere to the extent that few Westerners would believe possible. They were much willing to forgive than to exact revenge. They were much purer, nobler, bolder, and more courageous than most Chinese men.

When she told Yan about what had transpired at Martin's place, Yan was totally furious. "That bastard never deserves you," shouted she.

Tania laughed for the first time in a long while. "Why?" she asked. "Should I take it as my fate?"

"No, no, no," said Yan. "You are a very special lady. You have a noble heart and the heavens will grant you a noble fate, unlike me, who only deserves a lousy one."

"Really? How so?" Tania was intrigued.

"Doubtless, you are going to meet the best man in the world; you deserve the best marriage, and you will enjoy the happiest days in your life in the future," Yan insisted like an expert fortune teller.

With that charming prediction, the two women fell into a deep slumber.

Chapter 16

Battles

1

COMMANDER TAO YIN-HU FOUND HIMSELF CAUGHT BETWEEN A rock and a hard place when he began to make plans for his new counterextermination campaign.

A graduate of a traditional military academy and a veteran of a warlord's army, Tao was not a mulish officer but a highly adaptive tactician who captured the spirit of guerrilla warfare with his mantra: "Fight if you can win, but retreat if you can't." Facing an enemy ten times the size of his troops, the professional side of Tao told him that he had to be prepared for a long and treacherous war. The suggestion by the arrogant Gregory and inexperienced Mo Jia-Qi that the extermination campaign could be ended with a swift preemptive strike was ludicrous.

But the party had issued an order of attack and the political side of Tao had no choice except to obey. Although he was the commander-in-chief of the Red Army, he was first and foremost a party member. He had sworn allegiance to the organization, which demanded his absolute loyalty and complete submission, even when he might have a different personal opinion. Party orders and policies were always paramount while his individual views were secondary, even if they were based on his sound professional judgment on military affairs.

Like throwing an egg against a rock, Tao knew the attack order was suicidal for his troops. But, since the party had decided, the only thing he could do, it seemed, was to plan the attacks in such a way that his soldiers would suffer the least. He decided to pay a visit to Commissar Si-Tu Wen-Liang.

The relationship between the commander and the commissar in the Red Army was often a tricky one. Strictly speaking, the commander held a higher rank in the military and was in charge of making combat decisions. Copied from the Russian Red Army, the role of the commissar was not as clearly defined as it should be, even though every military unit starting from the company must have one.

A post of political significance, the commissar was the chief associate of the commander and was primarily responsible for the disciplinary, educational, and propaganda matters of the troops. Yet, because he was a political appointee by the party and because of the ideological insistence on the supremacy of politics over everything else, the commissar could have greater powers and a wider influence than the commander of a military unit he had been assigned to. If a disagreement arose between him and the commander, the commissar had the power to override the commander, not the other way round.

Another open secret was that the commissar was the chief internal security officer in his unit. He had the power to inspect any soldier and officer to ascertain their loyalty to the party. If he found anything or anybody suspicious, he could start an investigation, report the case to his superiors, and even charge and punish the degenerate. This extraordinary power of control extended to the top commanding officer in the same unit, who was constantly under his commissar's watch. In other words, the commissar's real job was a party watchdog spying on every soldier and officer under his jurisdiction; any combat activity was of secondary importance to him.

The Russian Bolsheviks invented this system of dual control, political and military, which impressed General Chen during his initial visits to Russia. He was the first Chinese leader to introduce it to the nationalist army. The Chinese Communist Party quickly followed suit and the system was further perfected when Commissar Sheng Bao was in charge of the Red Army.

The system worked so well for the military in wartime that it soon became the standard organizational structure in any civilian departments and public institutions controlled by the Communist Party, such as schools, factories, banks, the police, government offices, and even nurseries, neighborhood associations, charitable institutions, and religious societies, so much so that eventually nobody living under the communist flag would not be subjected to the control of his two bosses—the professional supervisor and the party chief. As long as humans continued to congregate, no Chinese could escape this omnipresent and omnipotent grip of the dual-control system.

With so much power in his hands, Commissar Si-Tu was too experienced a politician to flaunt it openly. He remained courteous to Tao, who was five years his senior. Since seniority was very important in Chinese tradition, Si-Tu's methodical and explicit observance of the social decorum had won him much respect among the high-ranking officers in the Red Army, including Commander Tao himself.

"So good to see you, my good friend!" Hearing Tao's voice, Si-Tu rushed out from his office to greet the commander, shook his hands warmly, and allowed Tao to walk ahead of him into the office.

"Please have a seat on this chair, the most comfortable one in the room," said the commissar, adding, "Yin-Hu, you must not do this again. Next time, if you want to see me, just give me a call. I will go to see YOU immediately."

"No, no, no, Commissar. That's improper. I must come to see YOU instead." The veteran Tao knew there were two types of etiquette concerning seniority. The one for society at large was based on age, while the one within the party was based on rank. Tao could not afford to insist on the traditional one at the risk of offending the commissar, who was his boss in the party.

"Have some tea, please," the ever-polite Si-Tu said. "There must be some important matters you want to discuss."

"I was thinking about the attacks we are going to launch." Tao started speaking slowly to make sure that his statement would not arouse any suspicion. What if the commissar totally agreed with Mo and Gregory? If so, spelling out his whole plan all at once could spell disaster.

"Oh, yes, certainly, the attacks. Sure, what about them?" Si-Tu was smart enough to show his interest but not to reveal his hand.

"I was thinking, the attacks must be planned carefully so that we can implement the party's decision and protect the lives of our soldiers to the best of our ability." Tao then briefly outlined his ideas without disclosing any specifics, leaving room for him to change the direction of the conversation anytime.

"Yes, I see," said Si-Tu who understood what Tao was trying to convey immediately. "The old dog is afraid that I may report to Mo and Gregory about his scheme to circumvent the party's decision," Si-Tu told himself. But he was all smiles in front of the visitor as he said, "I agree that even as we carry out the attacks, our soldiers must also be protected."

Tao was greatly relieved that Si-Tu seemed to share his views. What the party had ordered was impractical. They had to come up with a plan to salvage the situation, and they must do it quickly. Tao let the cat out of the bag by saying, "I plan to launch the attack here—Black Dragon Crossing."

Si-Tu moved over and looked at where Tao was pointing on the map.

Tao waited as the commissar took his time to contemplate. A few minutes later the boss uttered one word: "Brilliant!"

2

"Stupid! Silly! Absurd! Preposterous!" Sheng Bao yelled and paced up and down angrily in the run-down yard of his temporary home inside the old temple.

Yu Shao-Mei nervously told Officer Lu Di-Ping that her husband had nothing against him. Sheng had been in a bad mood for quite some time since the family moved there.

Officer Lu smiled and told Yu that he understood the situation perfectly. Chairman Sheng was upset not with him but about Lu's report on the party's insistence on a preemptive strike against the approaching nationalist troops.

Lu had worked long enough with several top party leaders to understand their different styles. Chairman Sheng's audacious imagination and bewildering artistry in military stratagems; Commander Tao's patient and methodical planning in every combat, big and small; Commissar Si-Tu's amazing talents and sound diplomacy; General Secretary Mo's impressive erudition and eloquence; and Special Envoy Gregory's blunt arrogance, absurd stubbornness, and fearless determination. Lu had learned a lot from all of them, and he was now patiently waiting for Chairman Sheng to calm down.

Strangely enough, even though Sheng did not like his job in the civilian government and could care less about his title, many people and colleagues had begun to call him "Chairman Sheng Bao" and oftentimes simply "Chairman," which pleased him greatly.

He was a warrior, and he should be in the battlefield, leading the Red Army and saving it from the perils awaiting them. Instead, he was stuck in this miserable temple and had only learned through a staffer about the party's stupid strategies.

So much anger and so much frustration. So little outlet and so small an audience. Desperate, Sheng gathered Yu, daughter Sheng Ying, Officer Lu, and several off-duty guards in front of him, and began to give a lecture on what he considered to be the correct strategy under the current circumstances.

"On the surface, the number of General Chen's troops is overwhelming and, no doubt, the movement of his troops from all four directions toward the heart of our red base is threatening. Needless to say, our Red Army is facing an unprecedented and most perilous crisis. But the situation is not hopeless, nor is this the time for hasty decisions. We certainly should not take the high-risk approach of launching a direct frontal assault against the enemy when we are not ready. As many of us remember, the great master Sun Zi has said, 'Only those who understand both your enemy and yourself can succeed.' To recognize the strengths of the enemy and our own weaknesses is not a sign of frailty, but the necessary first step toward our victory. In fact, there is not one but several options we can take."

By now, Lu was not the only one intrigued; so were the guards and Yu, although the toddler Sheng Ying had fallen asleep in her mother's arms.

Delighted at the attention he was getting, Sheng continued in a more confident voice.

"Military strength is never about numbers, or numbers alone. Granted, General Chen has one million soldiers to fight against us, the largest military contingent he has been able to assemble in a decade. Yet not all his soldiers have undergone the same training and are of the same caliber. His prime forces are those national troops coming down from the north and commanded by his favorite graduates from the Huangpu Academy. They account for half of the soldiers involved in this campaign. The other half-million soldiers are either local troops or troops controlled by a few provincial warlords, such as General Dong in the east, General Tang in the west, and General Huang in the south. These warlords have never had the same goals as General Chen's. In reality, they fear us as much as General Chen, who, they believe, will deprive them of their power and territory as soon as he gets rid of us."

Sheng sipped some tea and went on.

"Because the enemies against us are never a monolithic bloc, we should find out the weakest link among them and strike at it there and then. It appears to me that General Tang in the west has only nine divisions and an independent regiment, the smallest contingent of all the extermination forces. His troops have also spread over a large area of several hundred miles. We can certainly choose him as our first target. We need to move our main forces to the west, and try to find an opportunity to strike at General Tang, instead of going along the Fu River to confront General Chen's prime troops in the north."

"That's exactly what the party has ordered Tao Yin-Hu and Si-Tu Wen-Liang to do," Officer Lu burst out.

"Exactly. That's why it's such a foolish strategy. Years of hard work will go down the drain, and hundreds of thousands of soldiers will perish for no good reason," Sheng said as he gave out a loud sigh.

"But Tao and Si-Tu have issued orders commanding the troops to move to the north," Lu said.

"They have, haven't they?" Sheng hesitated. He didn't blame the two colleagues for their actions. He knew them well, both their strengths and weaknesses. He knew it was not in their nature to fight against their party superiors. But they should have enough good sense to understand that Mo and Gregory had made a fatal mistake.

"Unfathomable. Unfathomable... unless..." Sheng paused again. Like a highly skilled chess player, Sheng had several scenarios quickly running through his head. He suddenly realized that going to the north did not have to be a bad move if Tao and Si-Tu were thinking of the same place as he was—Black Dragon Crossing. It could be a brilliant move, Sheng quietly said to himself. For the moment and for security reasons, Sheng did not disclose his thoughts, but carried on with his unfinished homily.

"Unless their true intention is something else. For example, we can break the enemy lines at some point and move our troops into the enemy's territory. We can surprise General Chen by switching positions with him. If he could take the trouble to come down from hundreds of miles away and invade our red base, why can't we march into his? And who said we have to stay here, waiting to be defeated? We don't have to run away from the nationalist troops. We can also think how to regain the initiative, turn the tables, and force the hunters to become the hunted."

Wow. Officer Lu's mouth was now wide open. He could not believe that the Chairman could come up with such an array of audacious strategies in so bleak a situation. How could he still see such a bright light amid total darkness? No wonder Sheng was a military genius. Too bad he was not leading the army, Lu lamented, but sitting here and giving a long speech not to top decision-makers but to a group comprising a woman, a girl, and low-level subordinates.

3

When a woman had passed the age of "love at first sight," getting her attention could be agonizing for many men; Gregory seemed to have been one of them. No matter what he did or how hard he tried, Tania showed little interest in him as a man, even though she gave him plenty of respect. Flattery, flirtation, small gifts, chivalry, solicitude, and even indulgence—nothing worked. He could not understand why it seemed more difficult to win a woman's heart than to break General Chen's encirclement.

For a mature and highly independent woman like Tania, she could see through a man immediately. Affectation could be her suitor's worst enemy, which would turn her off instantly. She had seen too much of society and had met too many people of all sorts to be impressed by the shallow, frivolous, pretentious, foolish, vain, talkative, or pompous. Good looks and nobility never entranced her for she was nobler and more gracious than most people, men or women. Nor would wealth, prestige, or power entice her for she had turned her back on all of them. She resolutely despised hypocrisy, arrogance, snobbishness, tardiness, filthiness, incompetence, sloth, apathy, immorality, indecency, and mediocrity, but heartily adored everything their opposite. If a man possessed none of those positive qualities, he should not even bother to approach her.

On several occasions, Yan Yan had advised her pal not to be too judgmental and condescending. "Tania, I know you are a very nice noble lady," said she. "But, in so far as dating and love are concerned, you have to lower your standards a bit."

"Yan, you are my friend, not my mother," Tania protested.

"Exactly. Because I am your friend, I am worried that you will never find a boyfriend." Yan was as stubborn as Tania was opinionated.

"No worry, Mother. I will get you one." Tania was poking fun at her friend's expense.

"Not me, YOU! You vixen!" Yan fought back.

Tania and Yan had become used to such verbal sparring for some time. They had confided in each other everything about their past and they were no longer afraid to share their deepest personal secrets and the slightest shifting emotions with one another. The trouble was that, no matter how hard Yan was trying to help Tania find a suitable man, she was as resistant as the former was persistent.

"Is anybody home?" A knock at the door.

"Yes, please." Yan rushed to open it.

"Good morning, Yan. How are you? Is Tania here?" the visitor asked.

"Yes, yes. She is." Yan ushered the man into the room and disappeared as fast as she could.

"Meng Bo-Xian. Good morning. How are you?" Tania was a little surprised. She had visited Meng's office many times, but this was the first time that he had come to see her.

Meng asked Tania about life in Blue Grass, about how the two roommates had gotten along, and whether the southern diet suited her. He seemed to be a little uneasy and Tania was not in a hurry to press him on the true purpose of his visit.

Finally, Meng took a deep breath and began. "I… I… well, on behalf… on behalf of our organization, I would, I would like to know if… if you may, if you may be… hum… hum, may be interested in Comrade Gregory… to… to… to be his fiancée, that is." Never a stutterer, Meng was greatly relieved to have completed his sentence.

"On behalf of myself, I would like to let our organization know I am not." Tania's straightforward reply surprised neither one of them. They both burst into laughter.

Curiously, as traditional marriages arranged by parents had decreased over the years, marriages arranged by the Communist Party for its leaders and army officers increased. These arranged marriages for party heads were engineered by senior officials, who, in many cases, could be the direct bosses of the women. Tania had heard several instances where young girls were persuaded to wed much older men. She therefore was not entirely surprised by Meng's inquiry.

The awkward question finally out of the way, Meng reverted to his usual relaxed self. He really did not have any other reason for the visit, but he stayed for a while, chatting with Tania.

Tania knew Meng was being polite. As one of the party's top leaders, he was a busy man and did not have to stay simply for her sake—to calm her down after the unusual request. But she enjoyed talking to him, who was such a gentle soul. She would never get tired of listening to his endless tales about China and her people, culture, and history.

Not until Meng had left did Yan return, and her first question was, "What do you think?"

"About what?" Tania sounded puzzled, although Yan wasn't sure if her friend was putting on an act.

"About him?"

"About whom?"

"Meng Bo-Xian."

"What about him?"

"What do you think about him?"

"He is a fine man and a fine leader."

"No, no, no. I know that. I mean, how do you like him?"

"I like him a lot as a friend and my boss."

"Do you like him as a person?"

"Yes, I do. He is a real gentleman, highly intelligent and very knowledgeable."

"That's all?"

"That's all."

"What about him as a man?"

"He is middle-aged, healthy, decent looking, and…"

"No, no, no! I mean what about him as your boyfriend?" Yelling, Yan could hardly play the guessing game anymore with the gal who always gave her the runaround.

"Nonsense. For your information, my dear, Comrade Meng Bo-Xian is happily married," said Tania softly as she curtseyed with her characteristic charm.

4

March. March. March. Fast. Fast. Faster.

Hiding during the day and trekking in the night, the Red Army force of twenty thousand soldiers from three directions were moving stealthily toward the north, with one goal in mind—to storm and capture Black Dragon Crossing by surprise.

At the confluence of two streams at the bottom of a broad valley, Black Dragon Crossing got its name because it controlled the pair of main roads leading to three counties, in the north, east, and south. A small ferry port with numerous warehouses along the beaches, Black Dragon Crossing had witnessed the largest buildup in history. Every day, hundreds of trucks—coming from faraway manufactories and could not proceed further due to the lack of proper roads—stopped here to drop off grain, food, medicine, blankets, camping gear, uniforms, fuel, weapons, ammunition, and equipment. Hundreds of local wagons would load them up the next day, carrying the cargos through winding roads to government soldiers stationed on the highlands. Chosen by General Chen as the launching pad of the campaigns against the communists, this obscure rural hamlet had changed into a massive supply center for the government's expedition troops.

Commander Tao's plan was to raid and destroy this supply center, cut off the support system of the nationalist troops, starve them, and deprive them of their supplies, thus compelling them to withdraw from attacking the red base.

An audacious strategy indeed. On a flat riverbank and not a military stronghold by any definition, Black Dragon Crossing was totally indefensible and extremely vulnerable to any raid. But, because of its central location, the place was surrounded by the three nearby county seats, a few dozen miles apart from each other, where General Chen's prized troops, the North Route Army, had been deploying significant military forces for months. In this narrow space of thirty square miles firmly controlled by fifteen divisions of the government's prime troops, any communist presence would be suicidal.

Commander Tao certainly understood the risks. An attack so soon and so far deep in the enemy's territory was not the best option, and he had no idea how his plan would actually play out. To further ensure his success, he plotted to throw a second punch that would be more daring than the first. He secretly ordered a small contingent of two thousand troops to leave the main column and to penetrate twenty-five miles further north into the enemy territory. Their sole mission was to attack General Chen's commanding headquarters in Fuzhou, which was lightly guarded. They would storm Chen's headquarters as soon as they arrived, and try to capture him as quickly as possible, alive or dead.

With the plan set in motion, one of the most pivotal battles in the Red Army's history would soon unfold.

The initial outcome was astonishing. Within minutes, Black Dragon Crossing went up in flames, with bullets from machine guns, hand grenades, and explosives flying everywhere. Few defenders survived the overpowering and merciless attack, which came as a complete bolt from the blue. The three companies of nationalist guards were no match for the two divisions of the communists' finest forces. Killed, wounded, or captured, the poor defense troops were wiped out within the first twenty minutes of the onslaught.

When an aide rushed in to tell General Chen what was happening at Black Dragon Crossing, he erupted, "Damned communist bastards! To hell with them!"

When reminded that thousands of his best troops were nearby, he quickly regained his composure. He ordered, "Three, no, five, no, six. Yes, SIX. Six divisions must depart immediately to save the supply center. I don't want any prisoners. I don't want any man to escape. I don't want to hear any excuses. Kill them! Kill all of them. Don't ever dare to come back until you have killed ALL those cowardly communist bastards!"

A few moments later, another aide rushed in to drop a second bombshell—an unknown number of Red Army soldiers were only two blocks away from Chen's headquarters, planning to attack the compound!

"Damned Tao Yin-Hu. I will kill you. I will definitely kill YOU, I swear!" General Chen was frantically shouting as he often did in times of frustration, as he was hastily dragged into a well-protected bunker.

Deafening gunshots. Heavy and fierce gunshots. They continued to last into the night and into eternity, so it seemed.

A few hours later the guns suddenly fell silent. General Chen came out of the cave and returned to his office, which remained intact. Guards told him that the attackers disappeared as suddenly as they had arrived.

"What's the situation at Black Dragon Crossing?" General Chen eagerly asked.

"Most of the supplies are all gone," his aide reported.

"Damn it! I want to know what happened to the communist attackers!"

"The fight is ongoing, General."

"Damn! I want to know how many of them were killed! How many! The number! I want every one of them killed, killed, killed!"

It was only a few days later that Chen's men were able to piece together the whole story. The daring raid devastated the supply center, and a huge amount of military equipment and materials had been destroyed. Tao's troops had accomplished the most amazing feat.

Beyond that, bitter reality prevailed. The rapid arrival of the nationalist troops three times the size of the Red Army surprised Tao. Their superior weapons and firepower resulted in serious causalities for the Red Army, which had no choice but to withdraw.

The plot to attack General Chen's headquarters was an outrageously bold operation. But it failed not only because of an insufficient assault force but also because of inaccurate intelligence. The expedition team had been told that Chen's headquarters was located in a church in the city. In fact, it was located in a nearby school building next to the Fu riverbank, where the general could board a gunboat anytime during an emergency.

All told, the battle at Black Dragon Crossing was a huge blow to General Chen's ego, but it did not amount to a total disaster except for the losses at the warehouses. The Red Army was fearsome but not invincible. Ironically, the loss of the supply center buoyed the morale of Chen's troops while the success of the raid disappointed his rivals. Warfare could be mysterious. No amount of preparation or methodical planning, and no masterful stratagem, would be enough to guarantee victory in the battlefield. Changing circumstances, accurate intelligence, extraordinary determination, fast adaptability, and fearless fighting spirit could all play a role, as could a small incident, plain chance, or just simple luck.

5

For the next month or so after the raid, no major action was taken by the nationalist army, which led Mo and Gregory to think that the strategy of a preemptive attack must have worked. They instructed Tao and Si-Tu to plan more aggressive attacks for more victories. But the erratic vicissitudes of war would soon show them something else.

An assiduous student of Master Sun Zi like any Chinese soldier, General Chen had learned about the paramount importance of mobility for the survival of the Red Army. The main reason his previous campaigns had failed was because he did not have an appropriate counterstrategy particularly tailored against this highly mobile and elusive enemy. He thus decided to experiment with a new strategy suggested by his German military advisors. The first phase of their proposal was primarily aimed at constraining and curtailing the Red Army's movements. After that goal had been achieved, the second phase would focus on how to fight and defeat them. Or, in General Chen's own words, "The offensive strategy of this extermination campaign should be carried out by defensive and even conservative tactics."

Thus, despite the humiliating loss at Black Dragon Crossing and despite the superior advantage his troops had over the Red Army in terms of numbers and armaments, Chen refrained from rushing into the red base immediately. He stuck to his original plan to build one fortification after another, and not to allow his troops to move forward too fast until they could secure the rear. Slowly but surely, a month had passed when his troops advanced steadily forward while the Red Army was forced to back off a few dozen miles each time. Then another month, and yet another month, the same scenario was repeated.

With no meaningful success in hand or a viable plan to break General Chen's ever-tightening encirclement, the Communist Party leaders became nervous. In contrast to the rapid expansion of the past few years, the red territory under their control was now shrinking by the day, indicating an ever-gloomier future. Complaints among the soldiers were mounting, and civilians were restless due to the strict economic embargo the national government had imposed on the red base. No trade or commerce was allowed, and neither was any exchange of goods between communities permitted. Vital necessities such as salt, grain, and medicine were extremely scarce, hurting people across the board. No one was willing to accept the currency, credit, loans, bonds, and bank notes issued by the Soviet government, since they risked the punishment of arrest, imprisonment, and even execution.

Having never felt so frustrated, incapacitated, and useless, Tao and Si-Tu suggested to Mo and Gregory that they might want to consult Sheng Bao since he was after all an experienced military leader. Gregory was adamantly against the idea, which seemed to imply that he had failed to come up with an effective counterextermination proposal as the chief strategist of the Red Army. Mo was neither entirely for nor totally against the suggestion. He proposed to send Meng to pay a visit to Sheng. Meng would be authorized to inform Sheng about the current situation and to bring back any ideas Sheng might have. In this way, the top leaders would be able to learn about Sheng's views without the humiliation of being lectured like a bunch of silly schoolboys. Meng seemed to be the right person to take on the assignment as the go-between, given that his ranking in the party hierarchy was neither too high nor too low.

Si-Tu and Tao did not understand why the situation had become so bad, while all Gregory and Mo cared about was their own face, status, and reputation. But, given the gravity of the crisis, they finally agreed with Mo's suggestion.

The meetings between Meng and Sheng were open and cordial, and each man had left a good impression on his counterpart by the time they parted. A bookish man with no overt political ambition, Meng posed no threat to any top officials of the party. He had realized a long time ago that he did not possess those necessary qualities, such as drive, authority, and cold-heartedness, to be a leader of this organization. He therefore had kept a distance from the intraparty strife as much as he could. Many saw his humility and mellowness as a serious flaw, believing that he was an unprincipled man. He remained unperturbed, thinking that he would never play party politics to compete with his colleagues. He would always follow his conscience and support anyone who would best represent the party's interests.

Meng's composed disposition and nonprejudicial attitude enabled him to see that the party badly needed Sheng's talent at this critical moment, despite his other weaknesses. Meng's even temper and natural civility infected Sheng, who became far less agitated than ever before this wise, fair-minded, perceptive, and conscientious colleague.

Looks could be deceiving. The plainly dressed and slovenly man sitting in front of Meng was also the most sensitive, most ingenious, and most cunning creature. Sheng understood instantly that Meng's visit indicated the failure of Mo and Gregory's policies. "They knew they had mistreated me, but just did not want to admit it," Sheng scorned quietly. The party, the red base, and the Red Army needed Sheng's service, and they had extended an olive branch to him by sending Meng as the middleman. Still smarting from his demotion, Sheng felt that he should have been treated much better than being visited by a lesser official. But then again, he reckoned, a visit was still a visit, which was better than nothing. Realizing the party was finally requesting his help, Sheng seized the opportunity to elaborate on his broad strategic evaluation.

He insisted that any obsession with positional warfare at the current stage would spell a dead end for the Red Army. Compared with the training, weapons, and number of the nationalist troops, the Red Army was clearly in a far inferior position, and therefore must avoid pitched battles as much as possible. This was a fundamental reality the party had to face for a very long time.

Under these circumstances, guerrilla warfare was the best approach, while the existing plans adopted by the party were impractical for the Red Army to execute at best and fatal to its survival at worst. Apparently, General Chen had already realized that the Red Army's lifeline was its mobility, and he was doing everything he could to restrict that mobility. "Yet our leaders are still obsessed with the academic notions of waging direct assault against the enemy, which has cost us dearly in the last several months. Sadly, we have lost the best opportunity to turn the tables against General Chen. He is now firmly in the driver's seat and the Red Army has become the hunted," Sheng said.

"Is there any way we can change the situation at all?" Meng asked.

"Yes, we still have a chance," Sheng responded.

For one thing, said he, the Red Army could break out of the encirclement and go up north. The communists could then create a new red base close to the Lower Yangtze Delta and directly threaten the heart of General Chen's government, forcing him to withdraw from the red base in Jiangxi. The downside of this option, said Sheng, was that the North Route Army was the strongest among Chen's troops; any attempt to break through its blockade would require exceptional planning and extraordinary courage. The cost could be very high.

The second choice, Sheng continued, was to break the encirclement on the western front, which had seen the weakest deployment of Chen's armies. In the short run, this alternative was optimal for it might save the Red Army at a relatively low military cost. "In the long run, however, this escape, if it succeeds, may have limited political potential for we will be fleeing to a much more desolate and more backward region than what we now have, making it difficult for the party to have any serious impact on the nation," Sheng added.

The third option, he explained, was to forge an alliance with the heads of the East Route Army, which primarily consisted of local troops from Fujian Province, next to Jiangxi, under the control of some provincial warlords. Historically speaking, those warlords and their soldiers were mostly interested in protecting their own interests, not in assisting Chen in his extermination campaigns. "There may be a chance that we could escape Chen's encirclement by going to the east if we could ally ourselves with the provincial leaders in Fujian. In this regard, Si-Tu Wen-Liang and Lin Shi-Xiong will be able say a lot more for they know all the secret connections our party has with the various influential personalities and factions, including those in and out of General Chen's government, army, and party."

"Whichever options the party adopts," concluded Sheng, "the enemy has already reduced the size of the red base to such an extent that the chances of winning in our own turf look extremely slim. General Chen's troops are no more than eighty miles from Blue Grass. The grand slogan of 'defending every inch of the red territory' has been proven to be impossible. We must move the fighting from within our own red base to the external lines. The party must decide on a clear and workable strategy as soon as possible to move the battles into the enemy's territory, or else we will be facing a catastrophic disaster."

6

From the fruitless way the communists had defended the red base, General Chen knew his strategy was working. He continued the harsh economic embargo and kept relentless military pressure on his foes, fully believing in the proverbial wisdom that "nothing is over until it's over." His spies told him that the Red Army was in disarray. No coherent plan was in sight and several top party leaders argued and debated day and night without reaching any conclusion. The sidelined Sheng remained in seclusion, and the strong-headed Russian advisor Gregory was still in charge, unrepentant. Perhaps for the first time in a long time, the communists finally recognized how formidable a soldier General Chen was and what a brilliant mind he possessed.

Neither Chen nor his communist foes realized that a potentially explosive condition was quietly brewing in the neighboring Fujian Province, just over the mountains east of Jiangxi. And it was all because of a legendary (or eccentric, said some) soldier General Bai Yu-Xian, who had been working on a revolution of sorts, which differed from that of either the nationalists or the communists.

A highly enigmatic figure in modern China, General Bai's pathetic family background and unfortunate childhood would embarrass the poorest members of the communists. Born into a penniless rural family, he became an orphan at five and was adopted by his peasant uncle and aunt, who treated him worse than a slave. He was the first to get up in the household, sweep the yard, feed the pigs, and cook breakfast for the family. He was always the last one to eat whatever was left after each meal, but was never allowed to sit and eat at the table. Although still a child, he worked as hard as any farmer in the field and did all kinds of farm work like any man, from handling draft animals to towing heavy cargos. He was also the last one to go to bed after he had washed the dishes, swept the floor, and cleaned up everything.

Beaten routinely by the uncle and aunt, the young Bai never spent a day without getting new wounds on his little body, arms, or face. An early eye infection had permanently damaged his vision and he could hardly see anything clearly fifty yards away. In his teens, a terrible bout of malaria almost killed him and he was thrown into the pen. Only a sow's warm belly sustained him long enough to recover. His health returned along with thousands of lice from the shitty place. As if trapped in a war zone, his whole body, from head to toe, was under endless attack by the ferocious pests. He smelled like a rotten potato and the weeping purulence all over his body sickened everyone. The uncle and aunt threw him out and never allowed him to come back.

The poor child had to beg for survival, and only he and the heavens knew how he managed to stay alive. From the time he first joined a warlord's army, he had never taken off his uniform, although he did change allegiance several times. After a doctor prescribed a pair of glasses for him, he became such a sharpshooter that no one in his battalion dared to challenge him in a shooting match. Surprisingly, this poorest of the poor was willing to defend his new masters till the end of his life. For his extraordinary valor, he quickly rose from a private to an officer and a superior sent him to attend a military academy. Sun Yat-Sen's Three Principles of the People—"people's government, people's rights, and people's welfare"—captivated him, and he joined the Nationalist Party without hesitation.

As nationalistic as General Chen, General Bai never hated the communists as much as his commander-in-chief. In his heart of hearts he perhaps still identified himself with the poor. Fellow officers recalled that he once fainted upon seeing a skinny girl in rags begging. "Would anyone care about this lass who has lost her mother at three?" They had to carry him back to the barracks.

General Bai had been Tao's classmate when both were attending the same military school. He knew Tao was a communist but they remained good friends. They later parted ways to serve in rival armies, and Bai took part in several campaigns against the Red Army, fighting against Tao's soldiers in face-to-face combat. But unlike General Chen, who portrayed the communists as cold-blooded killers and lawless bandits, General Bai believed that most communists he had known were honest, sincere, and brave patriots like he was. Committed to a militant ideology and a revolutionary approach, they were nevertheless decent and warm-blooded Chinese who were, just like him, willing to sacrifice their lives for the good of the country and for the betterment of the people.

At the same time, communist radicalism and fervent insistence on class struggle appalled Bai. For obvious reasons, he greatly doubted that the poor were truly as good as, or the rich as bad as, the communists had proclaimed them to be. His painful past and indelible experience were proof that the poor could be as cruel, ruthless, and vicious as anyone else, while many wealthy and powerful individuals had been very kind and generous to a poor boy like him. Poverty was no guarantee of virtue any more than affluence was that of wickedness. Good and decent people could be either rich or poor. Bad morals and behaviors existed not because the person was rich or poor but because those morals and actions were intrinsically bad regardless of the person's economic or financial status.

Thus, General Bai emerged as an unusual political oddity with a mixed bag of ideas and beliefs. His strong nationalism allied him with the Nationalist Party, while his heartfelt sympathy with the underprivileged enabled him to maintain a warm friendship with the communists. Undesirable and yet welcoming, uncertain and yet trusting, confused and yet respecting, Bai, suspected and accepted by both parties, allied himself back and forth between the two organizations several times, but never settled permanently with either one of them. Friends called him wise, foes considered him an opportunist, and no one could predict what he would be up to next.

The Japanese attacks on Shanghai in January 1932 changed the whole dynamic.

General Bai and his troops fearlessly defended the city but suffered great casualties. From that moment, he believed that all domestic and partisan conflicts should end, and that all Chinese should unite to defend the country against Japanese aggression. He was one of the first Chinese public figures to declare that Japan was determined to invade China, which was not a matter of "if" but "when." Japan already invaded and occupied the northeastern part of China, and installed a puppet government in Manchuria. Peking and Northern China would be Japan's next target, then Southeastern China, and soon the entire country. A small island nation with ostentatious imperial ambitions, Japan's appetite for expansion was boundless and nothing could stop its aggression except for an armed struggle.

Sickened by General Chen's continuous extermination campaigns, which had killed so many of his fellow countrymen, General Bai wanted to replace Chen's national government with his. This new government would remain true to Dr. Sun Yat-Sen's ideas by carrying out his Three Principles of the People. The new administration would be keen to get the communists on board if they wanted to.

From Fujian, where his troops stationed, General Bai sent an undercover agent to meet a representative of the Chinese Communist Party in Jiangxi. The two sides held a series of negotiations at a secret location and then signed a preliminary agreement for an alliance. A brand-new chapter in Chinese history was about to begin, and this new coalition could have delivered the much-needed salvation for the Communist Party and the Red Army. And the immediate future could have been a different story altogether had the two sides actually joined forces to stop General Chen's extermination campaign and to start a national movement against Japanese aggression.

Chapter 17

Failures

1

"SPINELESS TRAITOR! SHAMELESS SCOUNDREL! DIRTY BASTARD! Filthy son of a bitch!" General Chen's wrath terrified everyone in his office. Nobody dared to make any sound or move, watching and waiting for the general to vent all his anger until exhaustion wore him out.

The room was littered with newspaper and magazine reports—some were scattered on the desk, others covered the sofa, and still others had fallen onto the floor. None of them pleased the chief at all. One headline said, "General Bai's New Government Adopted an Open Policy against General Chen." Another read, "General Bai and the Communist Party Will Form an Anti-Chen and Anti-Japanese Alliance." A third headline printed with large letters declared that General Bai Yu-Xian had ordered his troops guarding the border to receive the Red Army, moving from Jiangxi into Fujian. Still another newspaper article had a cartoon of the vilified Chen with the caption "His bottom fell off," suggesting the collapse of the blockade he had painstakingly built over the past year during the extermination campaign against the communist rebels.

"He is ruining everything!" the furious Chen blurted out as he stormed out of his office and went straight into the bedroom.

"Darling, what's going on? Anything bothering you?" When the general was in a foul mood, his wife, Madam Chen, was the only one who could still talk to him.

The wife, whose maiden name was Shang Yu-Xi, hailed from a wealthy family. A highly intelligent and beautiful lady, Madam Chen had been educated at Wellesley College in the United States. Her charm could soothe any frustration the husband had as much as her extraordinary resourcefulness could strengthen his resolve and self-confidence.

"Look at these reports." Chen threw a bunch of papers on an elegantly carved mahogany nightstand. "The despicable Bai has declared a new government and he wants the communists to join him!"

"Let me see it." Madam Chen did not seem at all upset as she flipped through the reports. She calmly said, "No alliance is unbreakable as long as you have means to break it."

Foreign visitors had observed that, sometimes, the insipid expression on a Chinese face could be the perfect mask for some insidious scheme. For most Chinese, calculation was instinctive to them even in the most mundane daily activities, from routine personal interactions to bargaining over cabbage prices.

Political couples in particular had a favorite pastime—discussing strategies, plots, maneuvers, and tactics of all kinds. Inherited from ancient history, dramatized in literature, and embellished by popular wisdom, the never-ending interest in scheming and the national habit of calculation had long developed into a subtle yet sophisticated art form.

Confucian values stressed "virtue," "benevolence," "trust," "humility," and "propriety." While these worthy principles had shaped the outward behaviors of the Chinese for generations, they had little impact on those who were contemplating something diametrically opposite from within. What one saw as modesty from the outside could represent pride, arrogance, and aggressiveness deep down inside. If one found honesty, it could be a cover for deceit and chicanery. Where one encountered civility and righteousness, it could mean envy, ambition, lust, greed, fraud, superstition, vice, and corruption. Whenever one came across kindness and friendliness, it could mean jealousy, hatred, and hostility instead. However one might reconcile these contradictions, one would be hard pressed to find a thread of universal love and humanity—something so fundamental and yet not commonly shared in Chinese society.

Living cheek by jowl, trapped in unending poverty and demoralized by social immobility, the pragmatic Chinese perceived life as a survival of the fittest. They did not expect some fundamental change in their pathetic existence anytime soon. But they would be satisfied to presume for a brief moment that they had won a tiny battle by cheating, by gaining a slight advantage over their next-door neighbor, or by displaying ephemeral superiority to a lesser person than themselves.

Few of them ever read Master Sun Zi, and still fewer actually understood what he had meant in his masterpiece *The Art of War*. Thanks to a host of popular novels, especially *The Romance of the Three Kingdoms* and *The Water Margin*—both in the fourteenth century—and *Journey to the West* (sixteenth century), obsessive discussions on stratagem had become a common topic at private dining tables and in public bars, motels, and taverns. Those fictionalized plots against warring states had fed the imagination of millions of commoners since childhood, while those fantastic combat stories involving the conflict between the good and the bad had taught them all about life, values, behavior patterns, and survival instincts, so much so that many considered themselves well versed in both history and military tactics even though they were utterly unlettered.

Enjoyed by the elite as much as relished by the poor, the hundreds of familiar proverbs and popular maxims concerning the great variety of combat experiences had enlightened everybody to such an extent that many perceived themselves to be the best strategists on earth. Didn't Master Sun Zi say that "all warfare is based on deception?"—which provided the authentic justification for many people's elusive and deceptive character. Proclaiming to be staunch believers of Confucius, who had taught them everything about virtue, some Chinese felt no shame while plotting the deadliest schemes against each other according to what they had learned from *The Thirty-Six Stratagems*—a mysterious undated book with unknown authorship.

As much as the Italians loved their sopranos, the English Shakespeare, the Viennese Mozart, the Chinese everlasting fascination with their fabulously rich idiomatic tradition was legendary and hardly matched anywhere else. Originally described in classic texts and most often in a succinct phrase of four characters, many representative battles in real history had been popularized as colloquial summaries of ancient wisdoms concerning conflict, deception, and warfare of the past. Thus, "create something from nothing" was much more lively and stimulating to the Chinese ears than the boring word "plotting." So were "lure the tiger off its mountain lair" to the cold concept of "maneuver," "remove the firewood from under the pot" to the technical idea of "cutting off the enemy's supply lines," "disturb the water and catch a fish" to the glum suggestion of "benefiting from a deliberately created confusion," and "make a sound in the east, then strike in the west" to the flat notion of a "false attack."

Communists or nationalists, officers or soldiers, civilians or military personnel, all Chinese grew up with the same culture, history, literature, and oral traditions, and not a few of them aspired to be the next most promising warriors. General Chen and Madam Chen were no exceptions. It took them less than an hour to come up with a couple of clever ideas—one to deal with General Bai and the other the communists.

2

Sheng Bao was excited when he learned about Bai's actions. This could be a great opportunity, he thought, if the party did the right thing by sending a delegation to meet Bai to discuss terms with his new government. Sheng requested a meeting with Meng Bo-Xian, hoping to learn from him the latest developments.

Meng showed up several days later but his mood was not encouraging. He agreed with Sheng that the sudden political change in Fujian was a great opportunity for the besieged Red Army. Not having won a major battle for a long time, the Red Army had been gradually retreating while General Chen was tightening his encirclement of the red base every day. The Communist Party had lost a significant portion of its territory, leaving little room for the Red Army to maneuver or escape.

"If we can align ourselves with General Bai, we can turn the tide," said Meng.

"Yes, when General Bai stops fighting us, he will be creating a big void on the enemy's left flank. Our Red Army can march through that opening without a scratch if only we can seize the moment to strike an alliance with him," Sheng responded positively.

"Unfortunately, the party leadership doesn't seem to agree," said a disappointed Meng.

"Why?" asked a baffled Sheng. He assumed that anybody should be able to detect the golden opportunity, even if that person was not an experienced soldier.

"I am not exactly sure why," Meng confessed. "Perhaps… perhaps someone has questions about the relationship between General Bai and Tao Yin-Hu."

"Why? What about it?" Sheng was more confused.

"Tao Yin-Hu has been a personal friend of General Bai's. They both attended the same military academy and have remained friends ever since," Meng explained.

"So? That is common knowledge in the party, right?" Sheng asked again.

"Yes, it is," Meng concurred. "But, recently, there have been rumors that Tao had been making secret contacts with Bai, which alarmed some members in the party."

"Secret contacts? What do they mean? Was Tao acting on the party's behalf? Or making secret contacts on his own?" Sheng was intrigued and wanted to know more.

"The situation remains unclear. Tao insisted that he had not made any personal contacts with General Bai for a long while. But rumors say otherwise," Meng replied.

"Rumors? What rumors? Why?" Sheng believed there could be no smoke without fire.

"Some local villagers handed in several flyers the other day. These flyers told stories about some personal communication between Tao and Bai," Meng said.

"Some personal communication? What does that mean? What kind of communication?" Sheng now had more questions.

"Nobody knows for sure. Tao denies everything the flyers allege. But Si-Tu Wen-Liang, Lin Shi-Xiong, and the Security Division are investigating." Meng said.

"I can't believe it!" moaned the frustrated Sheng, hands crossing over his face. He was deeply troubled that the party was prepared to pass over a great opportunity because of a small misgiving.

Sheng and Meng began to review the chain of events, and both suspected that the rumors might have been spread by General Chen's spies. If Chen was indeed behind the rumors, he was using one of the oldest tricks from *The Thirty-Six Stratagems*—"driving a wedge between allies."

The tactic was to plant some rumor or false evidence suggesting a dubious or even disloyal behavior in the enemy camp. Hopefully, the plot would sow confusion, mistrust, and spark infighting that was severe enough to weaken the enemy's ability to fight. The most infamous instance took place when Chongzhen, the last emperor of the Ming Dynasty, was on the throne. He entrusted General Yuan with the largest number of troops to safeguard the northern frontier against the powerful Manchus. After failing several times to break through the defense, Manchurian commanders sent agents to the capital city, Peking, to spread rumors that Yuan was secretly collaborating with them. Outraged, Emperor Chongzhen recalled Yuan and, after a brief trial, sentenced him to death. The Manchus then easily stormed the poorly defended border and went on to attack the capital a month after Yuan's execution. Chongzhen committed suicide after realizing too late that his own gullible actions had destroyed one of the last defenses of his court. The Ming Dynasty, which had reigned for more than two hundred and seventy years, was then replaced by the Manchurian Qing Dynasty.

It appeared, Meng and Sheng surmised, that General Chen was trying to achieve a similar goal by adopting this "driving a wedge" tactic. Spreading the rumors could at least delay the potential alliance between General Bai and the communists. The confusion might even derail any attempts by the Red Army to escape Chen's encirclement in Jiangxi and to seek shelter under the protection of Bai's troops in Fujian.

"A cunning plan can backfire, so can a clever man be overtaken by his own cleverness." When some people indulged in calculations, they could also be oversensitive about everything around them. The reason why the "driving a wedge" tactic might have worked was simply because when high volatility combined with too much speculation and too little trust, chaos and confusion would be the most likely result. Rumors and false charges could be the last straw that broke the camel's back for the beleaguered communists.

General Chen knew that, as a longtime underground organization, the Communist Party often suspected its own members. He understood perfectly that, once the rumors were out, few would be able to figure out what the truth was. Even if the rumors were finally cleared, the opportunity of forming a grand alliance would no longer exist, which was exactly his goal.

Sheng pointed out that this could be what Chen had been thinking, and Meng agreed with him.

"What do Si-Tu and Lin say about all this?" Sheng asked again.

"They will not say anything until they have credible evidence to confirm or repudiate what the flyers have alleged," Meng responded.

"Ah, conspiracy, conspiracy! A total conspiracy!" Sheng shrieked in despair.

3

When Si-Tu's investigation finally proved Tao's innocence two weeks later, it was too late. General Bai had accepted an invitation by Madam Chen to fly to Shanghai to meet with her; she was, intelligence sources said, the true mastermind behind the "driving a wedge" tactic.

She had correctly studied the communists' vulnerability arising not only from their innocence and weaknesses but also by their exceptional revolutionary zest, where even the slightest hint of impurity could give rise to ominous suspicions. This incredible intolerance and exclusiveness, based on their puritanical beliefs, made it possible for the enemy to plant a small but poisonous seed in their organization, and the result was as Madam Chen had expected. The success of her first scheme had won precious time for General Chen to move his trusted troops into Fujian, forestalling any possible armed insurrection by General Bai. Madam Chen now went ahead to execute her second scheme, which was to disarm Bai without firing a shot by using her personal charm and beauty—another textbook application of the tactics found in *The Thirty-Six Stratagems*.

If there was any individual who truly understood Chinese politicians, Madam Chen must be the one. She saw them as hot-blooded men first and foremost, her husband included. No matter how much they insisted to the contrary and no matter how honorable they claimed to be, men were basically animals. They had carnal desires and greed in their genes, and only acquired ambition, pride, aggressiveness, and power later. Should any conflict arise between their instincts and common sense, the former would always win hands down.

General Bai could crow about his prized manliness, righteousness, and justice as much as he wanted to, but he remained an insecure little boy insofar as Madam Chen could tell. Growing up without much care and love, General Bai wanted to show that he was a caring man with a big heart—not so much to demonstrate to the outside world his righteousness but as a testimony to his inner strength and manhood. Yet the very act of switching sides before serious planning showed his immaturity. His eagerness to pull off a publicity stunt revealed his greater interest in presenting the ideal version of his public persona than in taking the concrete steps needed to implement his grandiose ideas.

"Come in please, my dear child. I have been waiting for you." The highly affectionate welcome by Madam Chen—actually two years younger than Bai—instantly reduced the stoic general to tears.

Despite his being General Chen's serious military rival, Bai had always had a soft spot for Madam Chen. For some strange reason, he thought Madam Chen was too good and too beautiful for General Chen, who was but a mediocre officer. Considering himself the true national hero, Bai had this secret fantasy of him being paired with Madam Chen, which would make them the nation's most blissful first couple.

No sooner had they sat down than servants brought tea, fruit, and biscuits to the coffee table. Madam Chen waved them away. She graciously poured the tea for him and picked up a piece of delicacy from the tray, her angelic voice chanting, "General, please be so kind as to try one. Hope it is agreeable to your taste."

Madam Chen's ivory fingers held the sweet close enough to touch his lips; her eyes were full of tenderness, and her soft fragrance was so intoxicating. Glasses falling, Bai almost dropped to his knees, his heart panting even as his brain was screaming, "What a damned beauty trap!"

The general had never been pampered this way by anyone, especially a woman. He was shaking and sweating profusely. His defense collapsed. Friends and colleagues had urged him not to come, reminding him that Madam Chen was her husband's staunchest political ally and his most gifted strategic advisor. The couple must have devised the scheme to invite Bai, who might face immediate arrest on his arrival.

Bai insisted that he had nothing to hide. He only did what he had to do to rescue the country from the abyss. He held no personal grudge against General

Chen, and he had accepted Madam Chen's invitation to prove it. In fact, he openly declared that he owed his rise in the army to General Chen, who had promoted him several times. He simply hated to see his countrymen fighting with one another while the Japanese invaders were plundering the country. So long as General Chen agreed to stop the civil war, Bai said he would be more than happy to serve the chief to fight against the Japanese.

Madam Chen was all smiles. "General Chen and I have never doubted for a moment your loyalty. Before boarding a flight to the front line, my husband left a note with these words: 'General Bai is the best brother I have ever had in my life, and I would love to see him standing side by side with me fighting against the Japanese.'"

"What can I say, madam?" Bai was fighting back his tears now. "I, Bai Yu-Xian, swear forever loyalty to you and General Chen. Believe me, madam, from now on, whoever is the foe of you and your husband shall be the mortal enemy of mine."

Thus, in less than an hour, Bai's heart melted before the hot tea and warm gaze of the madam to an extent he could have never imagined. The attempt of the alliance with the communists was aborted faster than it was first proposed. Within twenty days, Bai's mood had come full circle. His rebellious fervor vanished as quickly as it had appeared, and his dedication to General Chen's government returned as fast as a lost lamb rushing back to its mother.

4

It had been more than two hours since Tania's departure. Now almost midnight, Yan Yan was worried. A sentinel had come to their quarters earlier and said, "Director Meng Bo-Xian wanted to see you immediately." Tania left with him and had not returned since.

Yan would like to believe that this could mean that Meng indeed had some interest in Tania. Otherwise, it would be hard to fathom why they were meeting at this hour for so long. "Could that be true or is it purely my wishful thinking?" Yan could not be certain.

She did sense some uneasiness around her lately. Officers or soldiers did not seem to be as noisy and upbeat as before. Whenever some mass meeting was called, there were more sullen and grave faces than those showing jubilance and excitement. Officials and staff went in and out of their offices as usual, but they seldom stopped to chat with her as they had done in the past. Yan knew something must be going on, and she could not go to sleep until Tania returned with some answers.

The news Tania brought back was shocking—they must pack up and evacuate in the morning.

"In the morning?" Yan asked.

"Yes," Tania said.

"There are only a few hours left."

"I know that."

"Why?"

"I am not exactly sure. It is an urgent order of general evacuation."

"What is a general evacuation?"

"I am not sure."

"Can we stay?"

"No."

"Where are we going?"

"I don't know."

"For how long?"

"I don't know."

"Do we need to bring our blankets?"

"Yes."

"What about kitchen utensils?"

"No."

"Why?"

"I don't know."

Yan was very disappointed with the answers for Tania did not seem to have any further information. From the grave expression on her friend's face, Yan realized the situation must be very serious for Tania had never been this tense before. She stopped asking more questions, and the two quietly packed their belongings through the night.

It was only in the wee hours of the morning as they were waiting for some staffers to pick them up that Tania had a chance to tell Yan about what she had heard from Meng.

The antiextermination campaign had failed, and failed terribly.

Commander Tao and his troops could not hold onto the county seat, Guangchang, which was the last stronghold for the defense of Blue Grass. Located on an open plain and without a city wall, Guangchang was without doubt an impossible place to defend. And the Red Army did not have any big guns and firepower to resist the onslaught of the nationalist troops, who were aided by heavy artillery and warplanes. Despite the orders by Mo and Gregory "to defend Guangchang at all costs and to the last drop of our blood," Tao ordered a withdrawal after two days.

Closing in on their final target from all directions, the enemy now was only forty miles from Blue Grass—the capital of the red base.

"How could this happen?" Yan asked.

"I don't know."

"What did Meng say?"

"He was not sure either. Or he did not have the time to explain it last night."

"That's the best he could do?"

"No. He gave me three choices: to evacuate with the Red Army, to leave Blue Grass for another red base north of the Yangtze River, or to depart for Shanghai and then return to Russia."

"What did you say?"

"I decided on the first choice."

"Why?"

"I don't know. I just don't want to leave the people here, I think," said Tania.

5

The hastily conducted general evacuation was chaotic and disastrous.

The catastrophic failure to defend the red base triggered an unprecedented retreat, which was both poorly planned and poorly organized. The party attempted to remove the entire government, and every department took along with it all the office furniture and belongings during the evacuation. More chairs, desks, bags, trunks, and cabinets than wounded soldiers and military supplies were put on hundreds of wagons. Hundreds of footmen and porters were hired to transport documents, archives, files, papers, and office supplies, while as many were tasked with carrying grain, guns, and ammunition. Many contingents could not travel more than five miles a day for they were hauling large equipment as heavy as a gristmill, two cloth factories, several printing presses, and all the machines owned by the mint of the Central Soviet Bank.

No one knew what the destination would be, how long the journey would last, or where the retreat would finally end. For the moment, the Red Army was heading to the southwest toward the next province Hunan—the first of the thirteen provinces they would eventually trek in a year. Only then did they realize that they had accomplished a "Long March" of nearly four thousand miles on foot, which was a feat never attempted by any army in history.

Bombarded by enemy airplanes and harassed by hostile troops, the Red Army, after fleeing for forty days, had lost more than twenty thousand men by the time they reached the banks of the Xiang River. Some three hundred feet wide, the river was a major obstacle that the Red Army must pass to escape the four hundred thousand troops on their trail. It was here in this narrow corner deep in the rough southwest of China that General Chen was trying to send the last red soldier to hell and to end the communist menace once and for all.

In late November 1934, the Red Army's reconnaissance team scouted the vicinity and found a thinly defended area between two ferries controlled by provincial troops—Skinny Horseback in the north and Old Man's Foot less than six miles to the south. To secure a safe passage of the Xiang River for all the troops and personnel, the Red Army must attack the two ferries immediately and hold onto both for several days. Tao chose two of his best officers for the task—Commander Xia-Hou Ding to take Skinny Horseback and Commander Bao Feng-Nian Old Man's Foot.

The two men and their regiments dashed to their targets. Bao's men successfully attacked Old Man's Foot and secured it immediately. With the help of the locals, they quickly built a pontoon across the Xiang River. Unfortunately, no one from the Red Army came during the next twenty-four hours because the soldiers were marching too slowly, weighed down by the heavy load and equipment they were carrying. No sooner had they finally reached the east side of the Xiang River the following day than two divisions of nationalist troops arrived at Old Man's Foot on the opposite side of the river. The control of Old Man's Foot would decide who died or survived. The nationalist troops attacked the ferry with fury and at one time were no more than three hundred feet away from Bao's command center. He and his soldiers held on. They repelled the enemy's attacks repeatedly despite heavy casualties. Airplanes and artillery destroyed the pontoon not once but four times. Each time, Bao and his men managed to rebuild it with unbelievable heroism and tenacity, making sure that the party leadership and the rest of the Red Army could pass the river much faster and more safely than taking the ferryboat.

Several miles to the north, the defenses at Skinny Horseback proved to be problematic for Xia-Hou. The enemy had a stronghold guarding the ferry on each of the two ridges, separated by an open road. This opening was the only way to reach Skinny Horseback, but it was deadly for the Red Army to pass through amid the crossfire from the two hills close by. After a day's attack, Xia-Hou's soldiers were unable to overtake the two strongholds high above the ridges. Things were looking perilous. As many as five divisions of government troops were coming down the road toward Skinny Horseback from the north. If Xia-Hou could not seize this area and set up his defense, the overwhelming enemy reinforcement troops would crush his men like reeds. Worse, the enemy would then march down to Old Man's Foot in no time, and Bao would face hostile forces from two directions, making it impossible for him to defend the ferry. The nationalist soldiers could then slaughter anyone who was trying to cross the Xiang River from there. The gateway to safety would be totally blocked for the Red Army, which could be annihilated on the banks of the Xiang River.

As Xia-Hou was racking his brains for ideas, a dense fog covered the river the next morning and no one could see anything within fifty yards. His soldiers then stormed and took over the two strongholds just in time to face droves of nationalist soldiers coming down from the road. But his nightmare had only begun. The enemy's intense firepower ripped the two small hills apart, and dozens of his soldiers died in the first encounter. The tenacious Xia-Hou and his men held on, knowing that the longer they could stall the enemy, the more likely one additional red soldier could cross the Xiang River. At the cost of one-third of his forces, Officer Xia-Hou safely guarded Skinny Horseback for a day.

Under the strict orders of General Chen, Colonel Pan Jin, the field commander of the nationalist first regiment, kept on his relentless attacks. Taking advantage of the superior number of his troops, Pan also extended his lines of assault, forcing Xia-Hou to stretch his defense accordingly. Xia-Hou understood the trick but he had little choice. The overstretched defense lines serious weakened his badly battered forces, and Colonel Pan wasted no time in breaking the lines at several points. Amazingly, Xia-Hou and his highly experienced soldiers continued to resist wherever they could—shooting behind a rock, a wall, or a tree—and not giving up so quickly. Despite suffering heavy casualties, Xia-Hou held his position till at the last minute he was ordered to withdraw.

The five days of intense struggle along the Xiang River witnessed the bloodiest fight since the Red Army left Blue Grass, costing it more than thirty thousand lives. In the aftermath of the battles at Skinny Horseback and Old Man's Foot, the grounds were littered with dead bodies everywhere. At one bend downstream close to Skinny Horseback where the currents slowed, thick blood, fallen corpses, and shattered body parts turned the once clear blue Xiang River into a giant and most horrendous graveyard.

Of the eighty-seven thousand men the Red Army had when it first started the evacuation in Jiangxi in October 1934, a little more than thirty thousand were still alive after crossing the Xiang River two months later. Officers and soldiers bitterly complained about the poor leadership, and Mo Jia-Qi and Gregory could feel the heat building up on them. A deeply disturbing grassroots discontent was brewing, and top party officials realized that the army must adopt some new strategies to survive.

Chapter 18

Power

1

"YOU HAVE LET THE COOKED DUCK FLY AWAY, YOU IDIOT!" GENERAL Chen swore at General Li Hong-Tang, who had commanded the provincial troops guarding the ferries at the Xiang River.

Head down, face sallow, and hands sweating, Li clammed up and stood miserably like a chastened schoolboy, listening to the chief's searing words for a good half-hour.

Yes, the Red Army had escaped, Li conceded. But wasn't it the responsibility of the nationalist troops that were supposed to finish the job? Why blamed our provincial troops for somebody else's fault? Why were we made the scapegoats? Knowing better than to respond, Li listened quietly but hardly agreed with the wild finger-pointing and scornful charges against him.

"Okay, I guess both of us have to learn how to let go of the past. Now, what do you think the communists may do next?" Chen finally finished shouting, softened his tone, and changed the topic.

"I think the communists will try to cross the Yangtze River to the north and join forces with another Red Army force in Central China." Li responded carefully, hoping not to appear either overconfident or ignorant. He knew the chief was a temperamental man whose rage could be triggered by the slightest detection of either attribute. One must never say too much in front of Chen, lest one might outshine him. Nor should one be silent or sound timid, which would suggest indolence and uselessness. Li knew when and how to utter the right number of words so that the chief could build on them to expand HIS ideas and strategies.

"Yes, most definitely. If I were the communists, I would try as fast as I could to get across the Yangtze River and unite with the Red Army in Central China. This will give them the much-needed shelter, where they could rest and regain their strength," Chen said while looking at the huge map on the wall and, unexpectedly, agreed completely with Li's assessment.

Few people would disagree with Li, including even the least experienced in the military. Running away from Blue Grass and the red base in Jiangxi, the Red Army forces had suffered greatly. With no adequate food, stable supplies, and decent rest, they had been fighting almost nonstop for the past two months. Unless they could find some refuge, they probably could not last for another two months. Because the other Red Army unit on the left bank of the Yangtze River was the closest ally they had, the fleeing communists must have been thinking and planning to join forces with the former for some time.

The Yangtze River, ten times bigger and more powerful than the Xiang River, had never been friendly to any displaced army throughout history. Known as "The Impediment by Heaven" since antiquity, its upstream in the southwest was particularly hostile and forbidding. Running down from the snow-covered Tibetan Plateau, the Yangtze carved out its passage through a series of massive mountain ranges rising as high as four to six thousand feet. No bridge could ever be built across this giant monster, which was filled with deadly currents and mined with hidden reefs. No sizable towns existed in the region and only a handful of small ferries could be found along the banks. Powered by a crew of eight strong oarsmen, not more than two dozen people were ever allowed to board a boat each time, and ferrying a big army here in peacetime would be a monumental task, requiring weeks of good weather and substantial manpower. If guarded by troops, the treacherous waters, the rugged beaches, and the scant population along this section of the Yangtze would all make it next to impossible for the Red Army to cross.

"Never underestimate the Red Army," Chen reminded Li. "It has done some amazing things in the past, and time after time had escaped from the traps that we thought no one would be able to."

"Yes, sir," Li duly agreed. "We have locked up all the ferry boats in this area. None is allowed to sail without my permission. My troops have also set up watchtowers in every town guarded by my soldiers 24/7. No one can even get close to the riverbanks without being detected." Li then went on to provide specific details and tried to reassure his boss about his serious attitude and diligence in carrying out his assignment.

"Good to know that. But remember, we used to believe that we had done everything we could in the past, but the results somehow often turned out to be disappointing," said Chen, who then wondered why he suddenly decided to mention this unpleasant subject.

"Rest assured, sir. I will squeeze the communists this time and capture them one by one like a rat, and send all the captives to you," Li promised earnestly.

He had a good reason to do so, mainly for his own self-interest. Li knew perfectly well that the two hundred thousand soldiers under his command were not enough to guard such an extensive area along the Yangtze River. Chen had built a second line of protection by deploying four hundred thousand government troops behind Li. Ostensibly, they served as another tier of defense in case the provincial troops were not up to the task. In reality, he understood, as much as Chen did, that the real reason for the additional deployment was for the chief to watch Li closely from behind. If Li refused to fight when the Red Army showed up, Chen's soldiers would disarm him as quickly as they could. If Li did fight, it could save the lives of Chen's soldiers. If his troops failed, they would be immediately replaced by Chen's forces. Thus, Chen would kill two birds with one stone. Whichever scenario came to pass, Li would have to pay the price while Chen would rake in the benefits.

"Tell me how you plan to guard the Yangtze River," Chen went on to ask. A methodical man, he believed he was not only an expert strategist but also an experienced field commander. Never tired of details, he was concerned about the season, the water, and the terrain. The climate, the temperature, and the currents. The ferries, their sizes and distances. The guards, their numbers, their weapons, and their shifts. The local residents, their maintenance, and the communist infiltration if any. A hands-on manager, Chen never hesitated to reexamine his plans and to review those of his subordinates. He carried out onsite inspections as frequently as he dictated all battle plans. So did he change his plans, modify and revise his orders as regularly as he gave out commands.

After two hours of questions, evaluations, and deliberations, Chen seemed to be pleased with what he had heard. He then asked, "Who is in charge of the Red Army in Central China?"

"Intelligence says," Li responded, "the senior communist Dong Zi-Tian is the commissar of what they call the Second Front Army. He is one of the founding members of the Communist Party and leads an army of over one hundred thousand men."

"What about the other one?" Chen continued. "Is Tao Yin-Hu still in charge?"

"Yes and no, sir," Li replied. "Tao still holds the title of commander-in-chief of the entire Red Army units. But he does not control them alone any more than he does the Second Front Army, which has been active in a separate red base in Central China. A 'Group of Three,' as they call it, controls the Red Army, especially the Central Front Red Army or, more commonly, the First Front Red Army. The group includes Tao, Si-Tu Wen-Laing, and Mo Jia-Qi. Mo, intelligence says, is the one who makes the final decision when a political issue is involved. Si-Tu makes the final decision on any military matters."

"What an interesting arrangement! Do we know anything more about these individuals?" General Chen was genuinely curious. He did want to learn everything about the Red Army as much as about his own troops, recalling Master Sun's famed advice of "knowing yourself and your enemy ensures success every time."

"Not much so far. But we will update you if we learn anything new about them," Li said.

2

A mysterious setup to Chen's nationalists, the structure of the party bureaucracy was no less opaque and elusive to rank and file communists. Meaningful elections of any position rarely happened anywhere except for some lowest offices at the community levels, where powerful individuals and influential families controlled local affairs. Most organizational posts, including all levels of representatives, were appointed or prearranged by the party bosses.

Against such a backdrop, party representatives held a national convention once in several years when a group of Central Committee members would be selected. This National Central Committee was officially the highest authority of the party.

But with a few dozen members, the Central Committee was too big to function as an effective governing body. Besides, most of its members had to return to their provincial and local branches after the convention ended to resume their regular work, making it impossible and unsafe for the Central Committee to hold frequent meetings and exercise its powers. In fact, its first business was to vote for a political bureau—Politburo for short—which would have eleven to thirteen members.

The party's centralized power structure always worked upward like a pyramid, never downward as in shared governance. Thus, the higher the office, the fewer the leaders in charge, yet the more powerful they were. Under most circumstances, even the slimmer Politburo found it too difficult or too inconvenient to hold a full-member meeting. Thus, the Politburo's first order of business was to elect a still smaller "standing committee," comprising seven or five or sometimes even three men who would become the ultimate decision-makers.

At different times, this most powerful office of the "Standing Committee of the Political Bureau" had assumed various names, such as the Central Bureau, Politburo Standing Committee, or Central Office of the Secretariat. Its members might hold different titles as the office changed its name. They could be called members of the bureau when the Central Bureau and the Politburo were in use. But they would be called secretaries when the Central Office of the Secretariat was in vogue. No matter what their titles, those three or five or seven men were the most powerful figures in the party, who would decide all the major policies and make all the top personnel decisions for the entire organization.

Behind the scenes and behind all these standard offices, committees, and proceedings, the Comintern and Moscow always had a list of names pertaining to who would serve which of the highest posts, or who would be demoted or promoted and when—all of which were kept a secret from the rank and file or even high-ranking party officials. In the end, power always revolved around, and was concentrated in, the few who had been entrusted by the Russian communist leaders.

Thus, although Mo had spent much of his time studying in the Soviet Union, he held more power than Tao and Si-Tu, both of whom had had far more experience working inside China. In fact, Mo was the mouthpiece of Gregory just as the latter was that for the Comintern and Moscow. The young Mo ended up dominating the party even though the so-called "Group of Three" was officially in charge of party affairs. In the final analysis, however, it was Russian special envoy Gregory who was in charge of the Chinese Communist Party.

The Chinese communists' recent catastrophic failures fully exposed the ridiculous nature of the leadership structure. But changing it was not easy.

No institutional mechanism had ever existed to deal with this sort of leadership crisis. Despite the growing dissatisfaction, rank and file party members were powerless to intervene and could only complain. This acute systemic problem had its roots in the inherited Marxist theory and from the model the Chinese had copied from the Russian Bolshevik experience. Also playing a key role was the obsession with the notion of legitimacy throughout Chinese history. One of the most essential tenets of Confucianism was obedience and loyalty. The slightest hint of disloyalty and disobedience could be considered a crime as terrible as an actual rebellion. To rise and fight against any existing political authority, no matter how bad it was, was simply not in the genes of most Chinese people, no matter what their ideology was.

Political, practical, psychological, and historical obstacles abounded. Even if someone wanted to change, where would he start? The institution was a monster, which was intrinsically against change. Liberal, conservative, or radical, all big and long-established bureaucracies did not favor innovation. Any modifications could tip the fragile balance and, sometimes, the solution could be worse than the problem. If change must happen, how realistically could a minority transform itself into a majority? No one knew for sure, nor had anyone seriously tried anything—until one night when Sheng Bao visited the camp of Meng Bo-Xian.

3

All political competitions were power struggles. All elections were number games. If one needed the vote, one must know where to get it and how.

Perhaps few communists had studied how the party apparatus had been operating as closely as Sheng, whose position was not as high as he wished it was, and thus had the greatest motivation to push for change in the party. He, like everyone else, had no intention of reforming the party's basic structure. He did, more than everyone else, look forward to the forthcoming high-level meetings regarding personnel changes, which would redistribute power among top party leaders.

Sheng's position in the party had been on a steady ascent. Several years ago, at the Sixth Plenum of the Central Committee, he was elected to the much-sought-after Politburo, along with Dong Zi-Tian, Meng Bo-Xian, Mo Jia-Qi, Si-Tu Wen-Laing, Tao Yin-Hu, and Lin Shi-Xiong. Sheng's contributions in building up the Red Army were widely recognized, and he was only one step away from becoming one of the most powerful men in the Communist Party. To achieve that, he must find a way to overcome the last barrier and join the Standing Committee of the Politburo.

Three members of the Politburo—Mo, Si-Tu, and Tao—formed the Standing Committee or the Group of Three, the party's most exclusive inner circle. All of them were nominated and backed by the Comintern. It had been the standard practice that no one could be elected to the Politburo without the explicit consent of the Comintern, let alone to be elected to the Standing Committee of the Politburo. This would be an insurmountable obstacle to everyone else, but not to Comrade Sheng.

Famous for his guerrilla tactics in military affairs, the street-smart Sheng also understood how to play indirect stratagems and hold backdoor negotiations in politics, which few outsiders were privy to. Sheng correctly predicted that, as the head of the party, Mo must step down as soon as the party asked him to. Yet to try and oust him from the Politburo's Standing Committee would be too big a coup to attempt. His supporter Gregory and his longtime colleagues Si-Tu and Tao would be highly reluctant to take that critical leap, even if they agreed that Mo had made serious mistakes, resulting in heavy casualties for the Red Army and the loss of the red base. If

Sheng lobbied too hard for Mo's ouster, Gregory, Si-Tu, and Tao might start to question Sheng's real motives.

The more realistic solution, Sheng thought, would be to dethrone Mo without generating outright internal discord. Thus, it would be better to find a replacement for Mo who would be acceptable to all top officials no matter what their dispositions and inclinations were. Sheng found that person in Meng Bo-Xian.

Like him, Meng was also a Politburo member, only one step away from the coveted position in the Standing Committee. Plus, he had been the party's head for a brief period before Mo. No one would doubt his qualifications, and few would suspect his motives since Meng had been such a low-key person who had kept his good cheer whether he was promoted or demoted. He always seemed to be a likable man who was never bossy when he held the party's highest office. Nor did he behave like a disgruntled employee when he was reduced to a bystander in the party's policy-making process.

Finally and most important to Sheng, Meng was the one within the party hierarchy who was not only very familiar with Sheng's military ideas and political proposals but also highly supportive of them. Meng would be the ally Sheng needed because the former could cast the most critical vote for the latter at the upcoming elections for the party's highest positions.

Although Si-Tu and Tao would have realized by now that Mo's policies had been disastrous for the party, they probably would not rise to rebel against him. They had duly supported his policies and faithfully executed his decisions, for which they had to share some responsibility for those fiascos. Their ambivalence had made Sheng doubt whether they would support his bid for a seat in the Standing Committee.

Between the two, Si-Tu was the more pragmatic one, which was no secret in the party. He would be the first one to know which way the wind was blowing, and he would switch to the winning side in a heartbeat once he could identify it. Sheng was not so much concerned about Si-Tu as he was with Tao. A strong-willed person and as stubborn as Sheng himself, the able and experienced soldier also happened to be extremely skilled in military strategies and tactics. Tao and Sheng had competed for the leadership of the Red Army, and neither one was willing to back off from the contest voluntarily.

Lin Shi-Xiong, the last member of the Politburo, was a mysterious man. He seldom spoke at party meetings and often sounded modest when he did. Working as the head of the party's special division since his return from Moscow, he held some of the party's top secrets, and therefore was more feared than respected by his colleagues. Although lacking experience in regular party activities, such as labor agitation or peasants' movements, he had strong links with the Comintern and was much liked by the Russian communist leaders. A close friend of Mo's, his position in the party was solid.

Lin seemed to have built a close bond with Si-Tu, who had been his immediate predecessor. The two often discussed sensitive matters and classified information together, which they would never share with anyone else, including Mo and Gregory. Thus, the quiet, modest, and even reserved Lin seemed to possess powers that went beyond his official position, which had generated a mixture of envy and resentment from his colleagues.

Sheng's opinion was a little different from others. He believed in the importance of Lin's work, and thus completely understood why he had to keep his mouth shut most of the time. The party needed such a person who could safeguard the party in ways no one else could. Besides, secrecy and intelligence were of vital importance in military affairs. If Sheng rose to power, he would depend on Lin and his team of spies and special agents to provide the Red Army with accurate and timely intelligence. In this sense, Lin's support could be highly critical even though his political affiliations were unclear. Luckily, the perceptive Sheng discovered that Lin often spoke after Si-Tu at meetings, and frequently agreed with his former boss. Sheng took this as a sign that he did not have to worry about Lin for the moment. As long as he could persuade Si-Tu at some point, he probably would win Lin over as well.

Thus, if a party meeting was called right away, Sheng's promotion was not a given, nor would Mo's removal be a certainty. With the absence of Dong Zi-Tian, who was with the Second Front Red Army several hundred miles away, the only vote Sheng could count on would be Meng's, while the respective stands of Si-Tu, Tao and Lin remained uncertain and ambiguous at best, and reluctant and nonsupportive at worst.

Working within such an intricate personnel mesh and struggling to advance his political future, Sheng had to think of something else to make up for his lack of influence in the upper echelons of the party leadership—not an easy task for anyone, especially for a young man from Boxwood. Remarkably, Sheng found unexpected support not within the regular party apparatus but outside it.

4

In the most lavishly constructed building in the city of Yi, the Politburo meeting was underway and Mo felt as if he had been dragged into attending it.

"You dirty bastard, Sheng Bao," he cursed furtively. "I know your filthy little sneaky tricks, been there done that before myself," he thought. He looked around the room, and could see a difficult, embarrassing, and long session ahead of him.

Except for Dong, all the Politburo members were present, so was Special Envoy Gregory. Such a full session, which had happened only a few times since the party had given up the red base in Jiangxi, already suggested its exceptional significance. Several faces were unfamiliar to Mo and Gregory, and both understood that this was going to be an "extended session" of the Politburo. This happened when, for some compelling reasons, some nonmembers of the Politburo were invited to participate in the meeting.

All of them held high government and party posts. Most were members of the party's Central Committee but were not members of the more exclusive Politburo. Several men in uniform were not members of the Central Committee or the Politburo but were high-ranking military officers of the Red Army. Gregory did not have a clue as to who they were. Mo could identify only a few faces, such as Officer Xia-Hou Ding, commander of the First Corps, Officer Bao Feng-Nian, commander of the Fifth Corps, and Officer Lu Di-Ping, chief of staff of the Red Army.

Mo knew that this must have been Sheng's handiwork. He needed a majority but he could not get enough votes from the Politburo's sitting members. Such a scheme was nothing new; it had been repeatedly used by many aggressive party operatives, Russians and Chinese alike, and Sheng was by no means its pioneer.

Although the Politburo's nonmembers had no right to vote, they could participate in the proceedings, present their opinions, and take part in the deliberations. Most important, they could create the kind of dynamic atmosphere most conducive to the one who had invited them to come in the first place. The slightly altered but significantly augmented platform could produce amazing results not usually attainable at a regular session. Skilled party operatives frequently adopted this technique to push for their agenda and to manipulate the numbers to achieve the desired majority they wanted.

Rank and file members never cared about the distinction between a regular session of the Politburo and its extended session, whereas insiders would frequently exploit the procedural differences to legitimize those policies, programs, or personnel decisions they favored. The ability of a few ambitious leaders to engage in sophisticated manipulation without having to bother about the ignorant and clueless rank and file would characterize the power struggles at the highest level of the Communist Party for decades to come.

Realizing that he probably would not have enough votes within the Politburo, Sheng engineered his first coup within the party. He talked to Meng, secured his support, and then persuaded Si-Tu to convene an extended session of the Politburo, which would allow an overwhelming number of nonmembers to attend. He knew those discontented officials and officers would speak in his favor at the proceedings, and would therefore help him to achieve his goals.

As Sheng had expected, one participant after another spoke out as soon as the meeting began. They complained about Mo and Gregory's policies and leadership. They pointed out the critical mistakes he and Gregory had made. They particularly blamed the two men for their failure to defend and protect the Red Army, for the heavy losses at the Xiang River, and, most of all, for the lack of a clear direction from the party to save the Red Army that had been on the road for three excruciating months with no hope of victory in sight.

Mo's initial reaction was to defend his policy and leadership. Nobody listened. Those bloody losses and catastrophic failures were too obvious to deny. Reluctant at first, even Si-Tu and Tao joined the attack in the end. During a break, Mo managed to look at Gregory, who was still listening to the translations. Unfortunately, his interpreter was sick and Tania was there as a substitute. How ironic and embarrassing it must have been when Tania was translating into Russian all the blame for the recent disasters to the one who had been trying hard to win her heart. That must be the end of Gregory's courtship, Mo thought.

5

The fervent deliberations and heated criticisms inside the meeting hall notwithstanding, the worst blow to Mo and Gregory came from without—the party had lost all communications with Moscow. Just a few days ago, they received the dreadful news that General Chen's secret police had raided an underground hideout of the Communist Party in Shanghai. They captured and destroyed the only large power radio station the party had. Without it, the party had no backup radio stations powerful enough to maintain any electronic communications with the Comintern and Moscow. They also lost the codebook and trained radio operators in the raid. Other than using undercover agents and couriers on the road, they were now completely cut off from Moscow.

This bad news came at the worst moment for Mo and Gregory, whose very strength and legitimacy hinged on the authorization and directives they had received from Moscow. The same piece of news was not that bad at all for Sheng and his supporters. They were perhaps secretly delighted to see Mo and Gregory losing all contact with their powerful backers in Moscow. They now seemed free from the chains imposed by a faraway foreign authority. They could now enjoy the freedom to do whatever they wanted without worrying about external interference. Sheng would never miss this golden opportunity, Mo woefully predicted.

And he was correct. At the end of the meeting, Mo was forced to step down as the party head. Both Meng and Sheng were elected as the new members of the Standing Committee of the Politburo.

The new and enlarged Standing Committee immediately rearranged its internal structure. Two subcommittees were formed. The first included Meng, Mo and Si-Tu, and was in charge of political matters. As the new general secretary of the party, Meng was designated as the head of this group, which was responsible for the party's political decisions. The second subcommittee also included three members—Si-Tu, Tao and Sheng—who would be in charge of military matters. Si-Tu was designated as its head, and Sheng his assistant.

Mo was relieved with these changes. Even though he and Gregory were certainly sidelined, Mo was glad that Sheng was not made the party boss. He had entered the core of the party leadership for sure. But, both nominally and in substance, Sheng was only assigned as an assistant to help Si-Tu with military affairs, and it was Meng who had become the party leader.

The austere dark brown paint of the building made Mo feel depressed. According to rumors, the owner's father had a penchant for this kind of drab color because he had accumulated a huge amount of wealth by making pickles in soy bean sauce with the same color. The true story was that the owner's well-educated son had been promoted in the warlord army. He combined the family fortune and his ample military earnings to build this impressive house, spending more than twenty thousand silver dollars, which was an amazing sum in this remote and backward region of China. Unfortunately, no sooner had he finished the interior decorations of the house than the Red Army arrived. He fled the city and his elegant two-story residence became the headquarters of the Chinese Communist Party.

The sullen Mo left the meeting place and did not want to think about it anymore. He was led into a small alley to stay in a modest farmhouse. His guards told him that this was the only reasonable accommodation the security department under Lin could find for him in this old district of Yi city. The best accommodation, they said, had been allocated to Sheng and Meng, who would reside in the newer section of the city. A reclassification had already started in housing entitlement, Mo grimaced.

Little did he know that, now an inconvenience, he and Gregory would soon be sent back to Russia. Disappointment did not end there. Even the newly reorganized party leadership had little to celebrate after those carefully orchestrated proceedings. They quickly found out that Yi was a very poor place. With a population of fewer than forty thousand, it had as many hungry residents as half-naked street beggars—a situation that would not help the party to achieve its goal of establishing a new red base in this area.

After much discussion, all top leaders including Sheng agreed that the next option for the Red Army would be to move farther north as they looked for an opportunity to cross the Yangtze River to unite with Dong's Second Front

Red Army. Reports said that a large contingent of General Chen's troops were approaching the city. They had to pack and leave, fast.

6

At the foot of the Tibetan Plateau, two provinces from east to west—Guizhou and Yunnan—bordered the southern part of Sichuan, forming one of the hilliest places in China. Other than Guiyang, the capital of Guizhou, and Kunming, the capital of Yunnan, this tri-province region was thinly populated. Widely known for its huge mountains, deep gorges, and dangerous rapids, the Guizhou and Yunnan Plateau was one of the most secluded and most inaccessible regions in China. Commonly described as "an area without a flat lot of more than three feet wide, its weather not without any rain in more than three days, and its inhabitants with no more than three nickels in their pocket," this region had also been considered one of the poorest places in China.

Yi city was the last population center at the foot of those formidable mountains.

About thirty miles north of Yi, a stronghold called Loushan Pass stood in the way. Built on top of a steep hill and overlooking everything below, it was the military checkpoint that controlled the only road going in and out of the area. Locals claimed that the place was as high as no more than three inches away from the sky. "If only one soldier is on guard there," they insisted, "ten thousand men would not be able to break it."

But the Red Army had to take Loushan Pass or face the deadly prospect of being trapped in these treacherous mountains. Si-Tu, Tao, and Sheng ordered the troops to attack and they took two days to capture the stronghold. As the main column of the Red Army passed the stormed fortification of Loushan Pass, they could still smell the thick gunpowder in the air and see dead bodies lying on the roadside. Another bloody battle and high casualties for the Red Army indeed.

Complaints started to spread, alleging that the new leadership was no better than the previous one, and that all they had asked the soldiers to do was to run away from the enemies, not to fight them. The allegations hurt no one more deeply than Sheng, whose promotion was supposed to inject renewed hope into the Red Army and bring victories, not more blunders and failures. When the Red Army arrived close the next town called Skyline, Sheng decided to show his genius. He pointed out that, led by General Guo Jing, two provincial regiments of the enemy troops were pushing on so fast that they had been separated from other General Chen's troops. A deep valley outside Skyline could be an ideal place to ambush these two regiments.

Sheng's plan was approved and Tao ordered Officer Xia-Hou Ding to execute it. A day later, the three members of the military subcommittee were shocked to learn that the mission had failed and Xia-Hou's troops had suffered nearly eight hundred casualties. The enemy had in fact six regiments and the deep valley had become their strongest defense. Sheng had blown away his very first chance to shine as an exceptional military tactician.

The serious setback forced the Red Army to make another big retreat as the Group of Three ordered the troops to cross the Red River to the left and then to continue moving up toward the Yangtze River, which lay horizontally north of its tributary, the Red River.

Bad news kept coming in. Intelligence showed that Chen seemed to have predicted the Red Army's moves. He had deployed twenty-six divisions of government troops (or ten times the size of the Red Army) to seal the area. He also ordered thirty divisions of local armies from the three nearby provinces to block every possible outlet so that the Red Army would have nowhere to escape.

The communists were faced with a highly alarming situation since their troops could be trapped in this compact area of high mountains, cut by several tributaries of the mighty Yangtze. There would be little room for maneuver once the Red Army was hemmed in by one of those deep valleys.

The plight of the Red Army suddenly looked much worse after Sheng had joined the Group of Three than when it was without him. Doubts, rumors, and complaints started all over again. Even high-ranking officers began to question whether they had done the right thing to support Sheng at the meeting in Yi.

After much soul-searching, Sheng finally suggested to the Group of Three that the Red Army must stop marching forward as had been previously planned, make a one-hundred-and-eighty-degree turn around, cross the Red River again, and go back to where they had come from. Yes, they must go back to the Loushan Pass and might have to retake the city of Yi, if necessary.

A stunning proposal, to say the least, to everyone who first heard it. Mo smirked, Tao shook his head, and Si-Tu pursed his lips. Meng was trying to understand what Sheng had just said.

Truth be told, Sheng himself was not sure whether his wild stratagem would work. He was making a huge gamble, betting on his understanding of General Chen's mindset more than anything else.

Not an imaginative man, Chen was known as a circumspect and methodical commander, who would never start his final assault until he had every division of his troops in place. He was certainly planning to round up and kill communist troops between the areas west of the Red River and south of the Yangtze River, on the assumption that the real reason the Red Army had come to this region was simply because it had been preparing to cross the Yangtze River sooner or later. Thus, the only chance for the Red Army to survive was to do the exact opposite. That was, to run away from the Red River and to rush back into the areas that the nationalist troops had just left behind. Adopting these moves would totally disrupt Chen's plan, creating the much-needed confusion for the Red Army's escape.

Certainly, a great risk was involved and no one could guarantee the success of such an audacious maneuver. What if Chen had a second circle of troops behind the first? Would the Red Army be running right into another trap even after they had escaped the first? No one could answer these questions with certainty.

But Sheng had a small but significant piece of vital information that only he and the other two members of military subcommittee were privy to—a secret so sensitive that it was never made public many decades later.

From Lin Shi-Xiong, Sheng knew that two Red Army officers of the communication battalion were able to decipher the codes of some of Chen's troops. Sheng therefore could have a better sense of where Chen's troops might be moving than the general about his. Sheng's bold suggestion was thus based partly on critical intelligence, not just his imagination.

The Group of Three finally adopted Sheng's idea. For the rank and file soldiers, including many officers, the plan was just crazy. They obeyed the orders only because they had to.

But the Red Army's sudden reversal did stun Chen and his troops. They had never expected that the Red Army would dare to rush back again along the same route, attacking Loushan Pass and the city of Yi. More than two thousand government soldiers were killed in the confusion and chaos. Sheng won the first battle after his promotion, even though his nightmare was far from over.

7

"Oh, look, Bo-Xian, you have a visitor, and a beautiful one too," the relaxed Sheng Bao said to his friend cheerfully.

"Am I interrupting?" Tania asked as she entered the room and found Sheng and Meng chatting.

"No, no, no. Not at all," Sheng stood up from his chair. "I am leaving… you take care, my brother."

He patted Meng's shoulder and walked out, stretching his big chest to take in a good gulp of fresh air on this lovely morning.

"Sorry, I have interrupted your conversation," Tania apologized.

"Not at all. We have been talking all night and were finishing the discussions anyway." Meng asked Tania to sit down.

Pleasant sunshine had started to drive the mist and clouds away from the valley. But temperatures in early spring were still close to zero in this mountainous area in the early-morning hours. Meng felt the chill and got up to add some fuel to the stove, hoping to warm up the room a little more for his guest.

"Here is the translation of the document you asked for." Tania handed out a pile of papers, mostly of the proceedings of the meeting at Yi.

As he was reading them, a big piece of paper on the table attracted Tania's attention. "What is this? It looks fresh but very unusual," she asked.

"Oh, that's a poem Sheng Bao had just written." Meng did not stop reading Tania's drafts.

"A poem? Fascinating. Sheng Bao is a poet!" Tania was surprised. She picked up the piece of paper but the traditional brush handwriting bewildered her.

"What does it say? How come I can only read two or three words?" she asked.

"Sheng Bao has his style. And sometimes one has to decipher it." Meng gave a terse reply as he kept reading Tania's translated document.

"I hope you can help me," Tania requested. She held the paper up and looked at it closely, but still those large but cryptic characters escaped her.

"Now, let me see." Meng at last finished his reading and said, "The translation was good except for a few small issues, which are easy to correct."

"What does this poem say?" Tania handed the paper to Meng.

"It is about the most recent battles we had fought. But let me try to translate the verse for you first." Meng glanced through the lines quickly, thought for a few moments, and explained, "The title of the poem is 'Loushan Pass': remember the military stronghold we had taken twice in the last several weeks? Its lyrics followed the tune first created by the famous poet Li Bai in the Tang Dynasty." He then began to read,

Loushan Pass

West winds blow fiercely across the immense skies,
Wild geese cry under the frosty predawn moonlight.
Under the frosty predawn moonlight,
Soldiers' horses clatter,
As their bugles choke in tears.

Who said the great pass was as solid as iron?
We will now cross its summit in one stride.
To cross the summit in one stride,
The proud mountains are rolling like an ocean,
The wounded sun goes down in a pool of blood.

As Meng was reading the poem, Tania froze, feeling as if the dramatic images in it were in motion. She had witnessed many of those same imagines in person not long ago. Now, both the real and the poetic had come back, weaving an animated collage in front of her eyes: cold winds, sad scenes, brave warriors. Battles, horses, mountains. The sound of the bugle, the color of the sky, the bleeding of the sunset. The living, the wounded, and the dead. The insurmountable obstacles, the sweeping movement of the soldiers, the steadfast resolve, and the indomitable spirit.

"My goodness, if anyone can still compose a poem in this perilous situation, he must be a genius," said Tania, recalling that fewer than forty thousand Red

Army soldiers were still facing the approaching enemy troops of over five hundred thousand.

"Correct, we are not out of the woods yet, indeed far from it," Meng agreed. "But Sheng Bao seemed very confident, right?"

"He surely seemed so, as far as I can tell from your reading of this poem," Tania concurred.

"Yes, it is a great poem. It is also a unique piece of record in history. Artistically speaking, it is an amazing product. It has incorporated the conventional poetic style seamlessly with the revolutionary message. I love it." Meng could not hide his enthusiasm, totally overwhelmed by the absolute artistry of the poem.

Meng's mood was infectious and Tania wanted him to explain more. Many Chinese poets had written great poems with military themes in the past, Meng went on. But they often described predestined events and gloomy feelings. Sheng's poems had a broad vision concerning the communist cause and the country. His poems therefore were expressions of his political convictions and patriotism first and foremost. They also skillfully invoked classical texts and idioms of the past and cited familiar local scenes and objects of the present, making his poems vigorous, lively, and dynamic. His poems gave the reader an uplifting feeling, always upbeat, forward-looking, and optimistic, which was quite rare in traditional Chinese poetry. His ability to combine poetic imageries with revolutionary themes, to combine romanticism with idealism, was quite refreshing in Chinese literary history.

"As you may feel even from looking at his handwriting," Meng continued, "he had a free style—very free, I should say—in the way he put down his words. They seem to fly out of the paper as his emotions are pouring out from his heart. And the shapes and sizes of each of the letters followed his emotional ups and downs, which added another dimension of the dramatic force the verses had. This extremely personal style of calligraphy helped convey his views and feelings in a way no one else could. So, his lyrics, tone, style, imagery, and emotions are perfectly combined to deliver his political messages in a highly artistic piece of fewer than fifty Chinese characters."

"Wow. What a masterpiece!" Tania sighed, feeling the intensity of Meng's unconditional admiration for Sheng's poetic talent, which she had only begun to recognize.

Chapter 19

Rivers

1

I N A COUNTRY AS HUGE AS CHINA, ONE WOULD HARDLY THINK THAT several small rivers in the most remote region of the country had played a vital part in modern history.

General Chen gleefully recalled the story of the rebel leader Shi Da-Kai, who, trapped in the river system of the Southwest, was ultimately captured and executed by government troops. If this nineteenth-century episode were any guide, he would surely defeat the Red Army in the same place in no time.

Chen's communist rivals were no fools, and they were equally familiar with the same story. To avoid the same fatal mistakes made by Shi, who had been wandering and fighting alone without a base, they strived to achieve two objectives—to join forces with the Second Front Army north of the Yangtze River and to establish a new base in the Southwest. Ironically, it was precisely because they were trying so hard that their plan became visibly clear to Chen and he was able to foil it.

Under the new leadership of the Group of Three, the Red Army left the city of Yi and formed three columns marching toward the north, fully prepared to cross the Yangtze River and to carve out a territory in the southwest portion of Sichuan Province. The failure at Skyline had made Sheng suspicious. He never doubted Officer Xia-Hou Ding, who had an impeccable record in the Red Army, but he had never seen anyone defending such a small place at such a high cost, especially one guarded by a provincial unit, which tended to be sluggish and ineffective. "Is this fierce battle part of a larger plot by the enemy to keep the Red Army here while more government troops will be coming down soon to annihilate us?" he pondered.

Looking at the maps again, Sheng was stunned to realize that, starting for the next one hundred miles, only one path through a long valley would allow the Red Army to move north toward the Yangtze River as the party leaders had planned. It was exactly the same route the brave warrior Shi had taken seventy years ago, when he finally met his demise.

"This is a trap! We must leave Skyline immediately," Sheng concluded.

His gut instincts saved the Red Army and his own reputation. Once Sheng conveyed his assessment of the situation to others, they all agreed with him. The battle must stop and the Red Army must move out of the area as soon as possible.

When the exhausted and nervous soldiers from Sichuan woke up the next morning, they heard no gunshot and found no enemy in front of them.

Under the thick overnight fog, the Red Army had disappeared and waded across the Red River to the east.

2

Only several days later did Sheng, Si-Tu Wen-Liang, and Tao Yin-Hu discover how close they had been to the brink of total annihilation. The failure to take Skyline turned out to be a blessing in disguise, and the timely withdrawal to the east of the Red River had saved the Red Amy from being crushed by the fast-arriving government troops of two hundred thousand.

Reports also told them that the reason General Guo Jing and his provincial regiment had fought so fearlessly were because their boss General Liu Yi-Hao had issued strict orders to stop any Red Army soldier from entering Sichuan at all costs.

Lying southwest of China and surrounded by high mountains all around, Sichuan, known as "Heavenly Place" from ancient times, was one of the largest and most fertile provinces in the country. More than two thousand years ago, the capable Governor Li Pin had led the locals to construct the Du River Dam, which was one of the most ingenious civil engineering projects in Chinese history. Unlike most of the high dams in modern times, the modest low dam Li had designed did not stop the water but only alleviated the flood from the river by diverting its flow to irrigate hundreds of thousands acres of farmland, making the Central Plains in Sichuan one of the wealthiest, most productive, and most populous regions in China.

Liu considered Sichuan his God-given territory even though he had sworn allegiance to Chen's national government. Due to Chen's increasing pressure, Liu finally agreed a few weeks ago to send a dozen Sichuan battalions to pursue the Red Army in the neighboring Guizhou Province. Liu summoned Guo to his headquarters for a private meeting shortly before the latter assumed command of the mission.

"General Guo, you are an experienced soldier, and I have no doubt about your skills and ability to lead the fight." Liu looked at Guo's face, wondering how in the world he got the nickname "Panda," and continued, "But let me ask you about the foundation for our survival in Sichuan."

The panda-faced Guo stood up and said, "Sir, it's all because of our guns and unity."

"Okay, okay, you may sit down," waved the boss. "You are absolutely correct that guns and unity have enabled us to survive in Sichuan thus far."

"As a military commander, General Guo, you may also want to know something about politics," Liu advised.

"The reason we are able to survive till this day," he continued, "is because of the ongoing conflict between General Chen's Nationalist Party and the communists. The day this conflict ends will be the beginning of our demise. If General Chen wins the conflict, he will destroy us next. If the communists win, they will make us their next target as well. So, it is in our own interest to keep them fighting each other for as long as possible."

Guo was fascinated with the boss's outlandish theory and unusual strategy. He asked, "Then, what should I do when I lead the troops into Guizhou to fight the Red Army?"

"That's the exact reason I have called you in today for this meeting," said Liu seriously.

"Remember, the communists are weak while the nationalists have the upper hand currently. I don't want you to help General Chen to the extent that he will be able to eliminate the Red Army completely. Your job is to show our support for the national government and our anticommunism stand. That should be the core of your mission. Beyond that, don't push things too far and especially don't push the Red Army over the edge. If they disappear tomorrow, we will die soon after that."

Liu stood up and elaborated, "We know several top military officers in the Red Army have roots in Sichuan. They probably want to come back to establish a so-called red revolutionary base here in Sichuan, as they have done in Hunan and Jiangxi over the last several years. Listen! This will be the most dangerous development if they succeed. You job therefore is to prevent any Red Army soldier from entering our Sichuan at all costs."

"The most likely place where they will try to carry out their plan will be the portion of the Yangtze River right across the Red River region in Guizhou, and this area will be the one you must protect." Liu reiterated, "Remember, your primary objective is to prevent the Red Army from entering Sichuan. Once you have accomplished that goal, don't worry about where else the Red Army will go or stay. That will be the national government's problem, not our provincial administration's."

3

When insiders relayed the secret conversation between the two generals (and some believed General Liu had deliberately leaked it) to the Communist Party's top leaders, they began to hatch a brand-new audacious scheme.

Sheng was the first to recognize the impossibility of achieving the Red Army's earlier goals. As the battle at Skyline had clearly shown, the Sichuan warlord troops would fight to the end to stop the Red Army from entering their province. It would make no sense for the already weakened Red Army to continue trying, given the grave dangers ahead even if they were able to finally approach the Yangtze River.

If either going up to the north (where they had not been able to prevail at Skyline) or going back to the east (where they had suffered terribly at the Xiang River) was no longer an option, where should the Red Army go? Evidently, either south or west. For the moment, though, Sheng had to keep his plan secret, or the Red Army would perish in no time if General Chen got wind of it.

A bold and ingenious military tactician, Sheng understood that his best strategy at this moment was to keep Chen guessing. To avoid any leaks, Sheng shared his ideas with just two or three members of the Politburo's Standing Committee. For the most part, even the Red Army's most trusted officers would not know exactly where they were heading and why until much later.

4

A week after the battle at Skyline, the party decided to explore the possibility of establishing a red base south of Sichuan along the Yunnan–Guizhou border. Tao suggested that northeastern Yunnan, bordering northwestern Guizhou, might be a safe place for the Red Army to recuperate. His suggestion was adopted.

For the next two weeks the remaining Red Army of thirty thousand men were reorganized into four corps (the 1st, 3rd, 5th, and 9th) of sixteen regiments each. When the restructured Red Army marched east into Guizhou, the First Army Corps, led by Officer Xia-Hou Ding, fought several battles within five days, and won the first long-awaited victory.

Bolstered by the success, the party openly announced that it would turn the entire province of Guizhou red.

But the situation remained perilous. Chen vowed he would destroy the Red Army in this area by ordering four columns of troops, totaling four hundred men, to close in on the communists from all four directions. Considering the overwhelming odds, no one would think that the Red Army could survive for another month.

Deeply concerned, Xia-Hou telegrammed the party leaders, strongly suggesting that the Red Army should plan an attack on a township called New Market, where two divisions of Guizhou soldiers were stationed. According to his intelligence, the provincial soldiers of Guizhou were notorious opium addicts who had been lampooned by the locals as "troopers with two guns"—a rifle and an opium pipe. Their leader, Guizhou warlord Wang Xuan-Kui, was a man with few ideas. He started his career as a salt carrier in the mountains, and listened to his wife all the time. Mrs. Wang came from an extremely wealthy family. She loved political games and military stratagems more than reading literature and poetry. Often dressed in a man's suit with long pants to cover her bound feet, she rode on a sedan chair to wherever her husband's troops were going so she could advise him on military affairs every night.

Xia-Hou's urgent telegram aroused the interest of some twenty officials and officers, who happened to be holding a major meeting on the Red Army's next move. Most of them agreed with Xia-Hou for they had heard similar reports about warlord Wang, his wife, and the Guizhou soldiers. The "double-gun army" might be worthless troops, they reasoned, and yet the two divisions' ammunition and equipment would be a highly desirable prize for the Red Army.

The men in the room then turned to the Group of Three—Tao, Sheng, and Si-Tu—eager to hear their opinions. Tao agreed with the majority, thinking that an attack on New Market would be a good opportunity for the Red Army. Many in the room were visibly delighted. They respected the commander-in-chief and had followed him for years. His statement reaffirmed their views, which made them very happy since the army was going through a real rough patch.

Sheng spoke next and surprised everybody by disagreeing with the majority and Tao. Sheng agreed with some of the points they had made, such as the ineffectiveness of the Guizhou soldiers and warlord Wang's lack of military acumen. But he argued that it was not the right time to attack and New Market was not the right place either. Instead, he suggested the Red Army move in the opposite direction from New Market and attack Carpenter's Hills in the northeast instead.

"Carpenter's Hills?" someone cried out, "That's where three divisions of the government troops are!"

"Exactly." No sooner did Sheng respond than the meeting became chaotic.

"Why not attack the enemy close to us but go all those extra miles to the northeast?"

"Didn't you always say to pick the enemy's weakest link for a fight? Why go after three divisions when we can surely beat two?"

"You must be out of your mind! We had never dealt with three divisions of well-equipped nationalist troops all at once in the past. What makes you think we can do it now in our current poor condition?"

Strong opinions mixed with high emotions, and neither side was willing to concede. Sheng was repeatedly booed when he threatened to leave the meeting.

"Go ahead, leave! No one is stopping you," someone retorted from the back of the room, while others laughed.

"You will surely regret what you have said today!" the infuriated Sheng snapped back.

He had never faced such a strong opposition or been personally insulted at a high-level party meeting like this. He felt something was fishy but could not figure out why so many of his longtime associates had suddenly spoken out against him. He knew he could not possibly prevail since most of the participants were passionately against his proposal.

The emotionally exhausted Sheng threatened his opponents. "If the majority does not adopt my proposal, I will resign from the Group of Three."

To his surprise, the majority voted not only against his proposal but also to kick him out of the top decision-making body.

Devastating humiliation. Sheer agony. Deep resentment. Indescribable misery. Sheng felt like a fool and stormed out of the room.

Sheng suddenly felt isolated and abandoned by his closest associates—like Si-Tu and Tao—who had supported him not too long ago. What happened? Why? How? Sheng had no clue.

The only thing clear was that he had lost. He was nothing but a laughingstock of his comrades. He had been at the top of his career for just a short while before he was discarded like a jester.

When the troubled and angry Sheng went back to his residence, his feeble and malnourished wife Yu Shao-Mei struggled to sit up on the bed. She greeted him with the most joyful voice she could muster. "Look, you have got a beautiful new baby daughter."

It did not please Sheng, even though he knew the baby had been due soon.

Instead he exploded, as if Yu and the newborn had greatly offended him at the worst moment of his life. He shouted, "Who wants a baby now? Give her away!"

"What did you say?" Yu was stunned.

"I said give her away."

"She is YOUR daughter!"

"I know that."

"Then why? Why do you want to give your own daughter away!"

"I can't save the Red Army. How can I save my daughter?"

"Are you out of your mind? She is a newborn! How can she survive?"

"Do as I say, give her to a villager, and she will survive."

"Why?"

"I said, I can't save the Red Army. How can I save my daughter?"

"But if you can't save your own daughter, how can you save the Red Army?"

Yu fainted. The befuddled Sheng rushed out to look for help.

5

"Do you have to go, darling?" Madam Chen asked cautiously.

"Yes, I have to, my dear." General Chen's reply was no surprise. She knew that, whenever a major battle was about to take place, her husband would always head for the front line.

The general ordered his private plane to be ready to fly him out to Chongqing, the largest provincial city on the Yangtze River in Sichuan, to oversee the battle against the communists in Southwest China.

"You have deployed four hundred thousand troops. Are they enough to defeat the much weakened thirty-thousand Red Army?"

"In theory, yes; in practice, no."

"How so?"

"My dear"—the general looked into Madam Chen's sparkling eyes, smiling—"you know as much as I do that I only have four hundred thousand troops on paper. Half of them are useless provincial conscripts, led by even sillier warlords."

"You have sent your most trusted general, Pan Jin, to keep an eye on them, haven't you?" Either based on her own instincts or classified information, the madam was aware of the husband's every move.

"I wish all my officers were as intelligent as you, madam," the general said sincerely. "Unfortunately, while General Pen is an excellent field officer, he is not an acute politician. He can never outsmart those crooked warlords."

He wanted to add his favorite "son of a bitch" phrase at the end of his sentence, but stopped when the madam raised her eyebrows, her discreet sign of disapproval.

Never to miss a chance to see the country, Madam Chen expressed her wish to visit Chongqing, which the husband gladly granted.

He complained to her that, although three provinces had agreed to send their troops to fight against the Red Army, none of them wanted to finish the job.

"The old fox Liu Yi-Hao," said Chen, "has never cared about the anticommunist campaign. All he wants is to keep the communists out of Sichuan, which he controls as his exclusive domain."

"That's why he has repeatedly refused to allow the nationalist troops to enter Sichuan," Madam Chen remarked.

"Exactly," the general said. "The same thing is true of the spineless warlord Wang Xuan-Kui of Guizhou and several other similar phonies. All they are interested in is how to drive away the communists from their backyards, not how to defeat them. Therefore, no matter how good General Pan is, his one hundred thousand soldiers are far from enough to defeat the enemies and shepherd his allies at the same time."

"The communists are running for their lives, aren't they? What can thirty thousand defeated runaways do in the most remote and desolate corner of China?" Madam Chen tried to look at the bright side.

"Never underestimate those communists, especially their ringleader, Sheng Bao, never," the general said, recalling his own dealings with the communist in the past.

"Who is Sheng Bao? Is he the poor peasant from Hubei? Did he ever attend any military school?" asked the madam.

"Yes, he is the poor peasant from Hubei. And no, he never spent a single day at any military academy," replied the husband, adding, "But that's exactly the problem because I have no clue where he will strike."

"What can you do in Chongqing then?" Madam Chen was concerned.

"I don't know," her husband responded.

But he quietly turned away and murmured to himself, "I think I will kick their asses as hard as I can and drive all my troops into action. The communists will become Shi Dai-Kai the second!"

6

When Si-Tu, Tao, and Meng rushed to Sheng's residence to help, they felt deeply sorry for him, Yu, the baby, and the whole family. They were awfully ashamed of their actions just a few moments ago, which must have hurt Sheng terribly. He, after all, was trying hard, perhaps harder than anyone else, to save the Red Army from a desperate situation, while they, as his friends, had failed to offer the sort of collegial support that he needed most.

Si-Tu went to console Yu, Meng Bo-Xian looked after the baby, and Tao apologized profusely to Sheng, regretting the trio's improper behavior at the party meeting. It was a big mistake, they now agreed, that the meeting had harshly stripped Sheng of his office, and his position would be immediately restored at the very next meeting in the morning. Sheng was still upset, but he understood these colleagues never meant ill toward him or his family. Over the years, Si-Tu, Tao, and Meng had always remained his best friends and staunch supporters no matter what his official position was. During the last debate they simply happened to have opinions that were different from his, no more, no less.

Having regained his composure, Sheng helped Yu to go to bed with the baby. He returned and invited his friends to sit around a table in the adjacent hallway. He took out a map and started to explain his ideas.

"Tactically, I would agree with everyone else's assessment at the last meeting. In fact, our comrade's comments on the pros and cons concerning both New Market and Carpenter's Hills were right on the money. The key reason I favor Carpenter's Hills over New Market is more strategic than anything else."

"Our most important task right now is not about two or three enemy divisions, but about how to get out of the ever-tightening trap we are in; attacking New Market is at odds with the escape-route plan I think we must soon take."

As Si-Tu, Tao, and Meng looked on, Sheng pointed to the map, indicating to them the escape direction he had in mind. Almost immediately, they began to understand why Sheng was so vehemently against the action on New Market.

Sheng continued, "I could not be this explicit at the last meeting because secrecy is our top priority. We must not tell anyone outside this room where we are heading or what we might be doing for the next few weeks. If any of this is leaked to Chen, I am sure he will close any window of opportunity we may have to escape."

The three men looked at each other, and they nodded in unison. "Secrecy, no problem at all," one of them said.

"Now, the problem is: how can we convince our colleagues who had opposed the idea so strongly without telling them everything I had just told you?" Sheng asked.

"I promise I will try my best," Meng answered.

"I will too," echoed Tao.

"Yes, Xia-Hou's views will be very important to our top officers," Si-Tu agreed.

"Wen-Liang, do you think you can find some useful intelligence about the enemy that we can present at the next meeting to persuade our officers?" Sheng asked.

"Good idea. I will certainly check it up and I am sure I can find something," Si-Tu promised. As the *de facto* head of the party's intelligence apparatus, he had information on just about anything. Still he was a little surprised to hear that intelligence could be manipulated for internal use as well.

As the four men discussed more details into the wee hours of the morning, Sheng could feel that the worst crisis in his life, and in the history of the Red Army, had been averted.

7

Surprise, surprise. When General Chen sent government troops to reinforce General Wang's forces at New Market, the Red Army moved in the opposite direction to attack Carpenter's Hills in the northeast. Chen believed the Red

Army had made a fatal mistake by biting off more than it could chew. He telegrammed the three divisions to hold on, telling them that help was on the way.

As the reinforcement was approaching Carpenter's Hills, the Red Army disappeared. Air surveillance reported the next day that the communist soldiers showed up on the left bank of the Red River, indicating that they had apparently crossed the river for the third time the previous night.

To ascertain the true intentions of these moves by the enemy, Chen flew down from Chongqing to Guiyang, the capital city of Guizhou Province, to get even closer to the battlefield and to make sure that the local warlords were following his orders.

Ambivalent at best, Wang was nervous about Chen's visit. He knew Chen was pushing him hard to fight the Red Army to achieve two goals. Using the provincial troops to combat communists would spare Chen's troops from combat, and reduce the regional military's strength at the same time. If Wang fought hard, he would help eliminate Chen's worst enemy. If he remained half-hearted, Chen would have reason to replace Wang with his own crony, thus extending his control over Guizhou Province.

Either way, fighting the Red Army seemed to be a lose–lose proposition for Wang no matter how he looked at it. But Chen was the national president, and Wang had to welcome him with all the expected fanfare and protocol.

When General Chen and Madam Chen arrived at his military headquarters for an extraordinary visit, Wang put on a happy front as he greeted the first couple warmly. The Chens stayed for about half an hour and praised Wang's diligence and loyalty, which somehow made him sweat under his uniform.

General Chen and Madam Chen then stood up and suggested they pay a visit to Wang's wife at his residence. Overwhelmed by the honor, Wang immediately sent a messenger to inform his wife while he accompanied the first couple on the ride to his house.

Mrs. Wang was the proudest woman in town that day and for a long time after that. Never before had a national president ever visited this provincial town. Nor had any national celebrity set foot in a private household in Guizhou. Now, Mrs. Wang and her household would be honored for being the first and only local family to receive such an unprecedented visit, which would be the talk of the town for years to come.

Madam Chen was at her charming best toward Mrs. Wang, who would later gush about the first lady, including her wonderful hairstyle, glowing skin, perfect dressing, sweet perfume, friendly demeanor, astounding beauty, wide-ranging knowledge, and superb intelligence. Mrs. Wang swore to Madam Chen that the latter would be her lifelong role model.

The two men chatted for a while about the local weather and traded anecdotes until Chen mentioned toward the end of their conversation that it was perhaps time for him to go to the front line to supervise his troops. Although he had anticipated that Chen would suggest something like that, Wang was still caught off guard and could only utter one word, "Yes."

The visit was a great success. Mrs. Wang kept talking that Madam Chen had invited her for afternoon tea tomorrow, while General Wang still wondered whether he would be able to return from the front line alive after agreeing to the boss's request.

8

Unbeknown to General Chen, the surveillance reports he had received were only partially true. The Red Army had merely pretended they were moving toward the north. Once they sensed that the nationalist troops had taken the bait, they quickly made a one-hundred-and-eighty-degree turn, crossed the Red River for the fourth time, and marched down to the south.

Unpredictable in direction while small in number, decisive in action, and fast in speed, the Red Army played a great hide-and-seek game with Chen. When he finally realized their exact location, the vanguard of the Red Army had already crossed the Black River, which, less than twenty miles away, was the last defense of Quiyang, where Chen's residence was located.

By this time, Chen had sent most of the troops, regional, provincial, or national, far away to the north on a wild goose chase. Only four inexperienced local regiments were left to protect the city, whereas the rebel communists could have as many as ten regiments. They set up tents outside the city with hundreds of red flags and tall banners declaring "Storm the City of Quiyang and Capture the Felon Chen Han." A panicking Chen reached out to the closest neighbor to his left—Yunnan Province—demanding the military leaders there send as many troops as they could from the west to help defend Quiyang immediately.

As the massive contingent of three Yunnan divisions rushed to the rescue, the Red Army soldiers folded their tents and flags, quietly withdrew from the outskirts of the city, and disappeared into the east.

An overjoyed and rejuvenated Chen thanked the Yunnan divisions wholeheartedly, and then ordered them to chase and destroy the Red Army soldiers wherever they went.

No sooner had the Yunnan troops left the city of Quiyang than everyone realized that they had been duped again.

The Red Army never intended to go east. Instead, they stunned Chen and the Yunnan warlords by marching in the opposite direction to the west.

In fact, for more than a month or so, all the moves the Red Army made were deceptions.

They never intended to go north again after their failure at Skyline.

Attacking Carpenter's Hills was only to hide their true intent.

Nor did they ever intend to seize Quiyang for they had no plans to stay in the south.

They did not flee Quiyang except for the sole purpose of luring the Yunnan troops further to the east.

For more than a month the Red Army's real intention had been to cross the Yangtze River from its upper stream called Golden Dust River in the west. They were finally able to accomplish that strategic goal after Chen had ordered his troops to be moved to the north, south, and east.

9

Once they had left Quizhou Province behind, the Red Army formed three columns and marched toward the Golden Dust River as fast as they could, averaging thirty to forty miles per day on foot in the most rugged mountains of Yunnan. They clearly understood that, even though they were temporarily out of Chen's dangerous encirclement, they had no more than a few precious days to cross the river, or his ferocious troops would no doubt rush back to catch them again.

It was one of the most grueling treks the soldiers had ever taken. Yet their spirits had never been higher for they could finally see the light at the end of a long dark tunnel. Just as the Red Army was leaving the most perilous situation behind, its soldiers suddenly found a large contingent of enemy troops marching in the same direction as them just a dozen miles away in another valley.

Alarmed, the Group of Three held an emergency meeting immediately. A short conference led Si-Tu, Sheng, and Tao to conclude that the enemy was not targeting at them for no fighting formations were detected. But to have the enemy on the Red Army's tail for a prolonged period could become a serious problem, for the government troops would discover the Red Army's real purpose sooner or later. What should they do?

Si-Tu called in his aides Fang Si-Liang and Cheng Chu-Li, Sheng called in Lin Shi-Xiong, and Tao called in his chief of staff, Lu Di-Ping. Together they reexamined the intelligence more closely. Fang suggested, "Since we have cracked the code of Chen's troops, can we use it to redirect this group of enemies? Can we send a fake telegram to them?"

This was undoubtedly an extremely bold and risky suggestion that could produce unexpected consequences. If the enemy discovered the trick, the result could be deadly. But, if it succeeded, it could save the Red Army a lot of trouble, time, and resources, which would be the most desirable outcome.

The seven men pondered over the pros and cons of the idea, and decided that the benefits outweighed the risks, and thus it was definitely worth trying.

Fang immediately drafted a telegram mimicking the tone and style of General Chen's field command center, ordering the troops on the road to march in a different direction. It was then passed around for the others to read it carefully. After a few minor changes were made, the telegram was sent.

A few hours later, to everyone's relief, reports started coming in with the good news that the enemy contingent had moved away from the Red Army's forces, marching in the direction the faked telegram had specified.

No words could describe how elated Si-Tu, Sheng, Tao, and everybody else in the room were. As their aides hugged and warmly congratulated each other, the Group of Three ordered the Red Army to race speedily toward the Golden Dust River without any further delay.

Time was of the essence. From officers of all divisions to the privates, they were told that every second mattered since it could mean a difference between life and death for the entire Red Army and the future of the revolution. They must waste no time and must try to reach the banks of the Golden Dust River as soon as possible at any cost.

A special battalion composed of no one but officers was ordered to be the vanguard of the army. The Group of Three commanded them to take the ferry at the Golden Dust River and secure any boat they could find immediately.

When the main columns arrived, they were greatly disappointed to learn that only three boats had been obtained, which could take no more than a few dozen soldiers each time. At this rate, the Red Army would need a full month to cross the river, which would be suicidal for them.

This section of the Golden Dust River was peaceful but too broad to build a floating bridge. Apart from using a boat, there were no other means to cross the waters. The only other option was to use another ferry miles away in the enemy's territory.

The Group of Three, who ordered Tao to go the waterfront, insisted that a way must be found, no matter what the cost, to carry every red soldier over the river within a week.

The battalion of officers searched the riverbanks up and down for twenty miles and brought back two large boats the next day. They talked to sympathetic locals and selected from them forty strong and experienced men as crew members. These honest and sturdy volunteer boatmen promised to ferry all the red soldiers to safety day and night until they finished the job, no matter how hard it was and how long it would take.

A large kitchen and rest area were set up exclusively for these brave ferrymen, who could eat six solid meals a day and take a rest in between shifts. All troopers including officers were given an assigned number for their turn to board the boat. No one, including commanders of the army corps, was allowed to get close to the boat unless ordered to.

The red soldiers had to endure the most nerve-racking days and nights while waiting for their turn to cross the river. There was nothing they could do but to wait for the boat to come and pick them up for the opposite bank.

Waiting and more waiting. Clock ticking and heart panting. The whole operation proceeded slowly but orderly, by every minute and by the hour.

After seven anxious days and nights, the amazing local crew members made good their promise—some twenty thousand Red Army soldiers were now safely across the Golden Dust River after being ferried nonstop.

These communist soldiers were finally out of the immediate reach of Chen's troops, who had been chasing them, battering them, and threatening their very existence incessantly for the last seven incredibly brutal months.

Chapter 20
Duo

1

"I KNOW WHAT YOU ARE THINKING. I KNOW SOME OF YOU ARE SECRETLY pleased with the latest results. Remember my words today, you will pay the price soon for the Red Army will come back to haunt you no matter where you are. You will regret it. Yes, one day you will regret terribly for the huge blunder you have made today!"

Waving his fists for emphasis, General Chen ended his speech at the Regional Summit Meeting in Chongqing. He was too distraught to continue his tirade, having blasted his top officers and a group of regional commanders for the last three hours. Before heading for the door, he turned around and lashed out at them once again with an apocalyptic warning: "Mark my words, you have failed in your mission. You had four hundred thousand troops under your command, but managed to allow the communist devils of fewer than thirty thousand to vanish right before your eyes. You will pay the price. All of us will pay the price for your shameful failure!"

After the deflated chief finally disappeared behind the guarded double doors, everyone in the conference room felt more relaxed.

"Failure, yes. Disappointment, yes. Price, what price? Wasn't the Red Army out of my Quizhou now?" General Wang Xuan-Kui asked himself. If so, this should be considered a big prize he had won, not the price he had to pay.

General Bai Yu-Xian had similar thoughts. He had lost some troops in the recent clashes with Red Army forces passing through his home base, Yunnan. Now the communists would be a menace to his neighbors, and the price he had paid was worth it.

General Liu Yi-Hao was no less delighted that he held a secret meeting with General Guo Jing before heading to the front line. The provincial troops successfully defended the borders of Sichuan. Even after the enemies had crossed the Golden Dust River, Liu noticed, they headed for the neighboring Xikang Province, tiptoed along toward the north, and never bothered to confront the Sichuan troops again. Guo must have given them such a good lesson that the Red Army was likely to stay clear of Sichuan for a while.

The abundant food and drink at the reception pleased these generals, whose glasses and cheers enlivened the grand hall as the gathering recovered from its subdued state.

The burly Bai asked for a star cocktail and walked toward a big window, where several officers were talking to the tall, slim, and handsome Guo.

"General Guo, you are the hero of this campaign. Your success at Skyline was the only battle General Chen praised in his speech," one officer said.

"Not at all, not at all. Everyone did his best." Bending slightly, Guo responded modestly, mindful that jealousy among his colleagues could be his worst enemy.

"Tell us what you think about the Red Army. What it will do next?" another one asked.

"The Red Army in the south will certainly try to unite with another unit in the north," Guo said.

"The Red Army in the north? Haven't we had enough of them in the south already?" Bai cut in. Although from a different province and not Guo's direct boss, Bai held a higher rank in the army, which, he believed, gave him the authority to interrupt anyone at any time.

"Yes, the Red Army in the north," Guo politely nodded at Bai. "If you think the thirty-thousand Red Army was tough to fight, the eighty thousand in the north could be tougher."

A waiter came around with a tray and Guo picked up a glass of sherry.

"How do you know?" one officer asked.

"Because General Liu had led us to fight them a year ago. Our two hundred thousand men attacked them from not four but six directions, but we failed to capture them. The Red Army has real good soldiers," Guo said as he sipped his wine.

"Are you saying that we will never be able to defeat the communists?" Bai questioned.

"Not at all," said Guo, who had expected the question. "What I am suggesting is that we must honestly reconsider our strategies if we really want to defeat the communists."

Guo was not a conceited man. But he did consider himself a much better officer than most of the colleagues surrounding him. He noticed what Bai was having and an imported idiom came to his mind: "If one drinks a cocktail, he will swallow anything."

2

No one understood why joy turned into jealousy so quickly shortly after the First Front Red Army met with the Second Front Red Army in the barren and cold northern territory between Xikang and Sichuan provinces. For months the two armies had tried to unite, failed time and again, and lost thousands of lives in between. Yet, after they had managed to overcome incredible hardship and were finally able to join forces, the two sides found themselves at odds with each other.

The great disparity between the two Red Army forces was undeniable. After months of arduous journey and incessant fighting along the way, the exhausted First Front Army was literally in rags. Ill-fed and poorly equipped, its troops resembled a group of dirty beggars in shredded clothes and worn-out shoes.

Well-fed and far better equipped, the Second Front Army was four times the size of the First. Composed of eighty thousand proud soldiers in clean uniforms, the Second Front Army had five corps, eleven divisions, and more than thirty regiments under its command. Surrounded by this huge army, the pathetic First Front Army, numbering barely twenty thousand, had never felt this embarrassed to call themselves the Central Red Army under the direct leadership of the party's national authority.

When two stallions met, neither one would back down without putting up a fierce fight. When the egotistic Sheng Bao, the brains behind the First Front Army, met the egotistic Dong Zi-Tian, the leader of the Second Front Army, they understood each other's mentality at once and a power struggle was soon underway.

Dong never paid much attention to Sheng. When Dong achieved national fame as head of the students' union at Peking University during the May Fourth Movement, Sheng was a country boy in the city working as an obscure library assistant. When Dong assisted Professor Lu Shi-Yan to form the party and chaired its first national congress, Sheng was a dutiful follower and recording secretary at the meeting. Dong was immediately elected as one of the three national leaders, while Sheng went back to his province. When Dong was in the Soviet Union directing the prestigious Russian Study Program, Sheng was trying to survive in the mountains in Southeast China. In fact, Dong had always held a higher position in the party and had been a member of the elite Politburo long before Sheng could even attempt to become one. Most important, Moscow and the Comintern knew Dong all these years and had explicitly sanctioned his election to the top leadership position in the Politburo.

Sheng's rise in the party was largely due to his own efforts and cultivation of a support base from the bottom up in provincial and rural China. He established himself as an expert of the peasants' movement and excelled as a skilled practitioner of guerrilla warfare in the countryside. He had led the Red Army to numerous victories, which greatly expanded the territories of red bases controlled by the communists in Southern China. These interconnected steps of mobilizing the peasants and building a Red Army with a massive rural base gradually became a successful model widely adopted by other party branches in the country. Sheng's flexible military strategies saved the First Front Army at its worst moment during the Long March, and he was regarded as one of the Red Army's best military leaders. The loyalty of the First Front Army to him was unquestionable, and so was his control over it despite its current deplorable condition.

Whereas Dong's advantage lay in the overwhelming number of his rank and file soldiers, Sheng derived his strength from the policy the First Front

Army had adopted earlier on to save its officers—each had the privilege to be carried in stretchers by as many as eight soldiers. Thus, even though thousands of soldiers had lost their lives during the punishing Long March, hundreds of officers in the First Front Army survived despite enduring the same miserable ordeal. These large numbers of officers could help Sheng to expand his troops quickly once the conditions were right.

Sheng also had *de facto* control over the party apparatus. During their protracted march to safety, top party leaders including Si-Tu Wen-Liang, Tao Yin-Hu, and Meng Bo-Xian, and high army officers including Xia-Hou Ding, Bao Feng-Nian, Lu Di-Ping, and Yao Xi-Wa, had invested their trust in Sheng, and it would be extremely difficult for them to switch their allegiance, even if they had had numerous disagreements with him. In a country as traditional as China, loyalty and legitimacy was everything and nobody wanted to be ostracized by colleagues and friends.

Yet Dong saw Sheng's recent spectacular rise in the party (from an alternative member of the Politburo to the Group of Three) as his greatest vulnerability. Any change in the top party positions must obtain the Comintern's approval according to the established protocols. To have stripped the powers of Gregory and Mo Jia-Qi without consulting the Comintern and sending them back to Moscow, Dong believed, was as close to a usurpation of power as it could get. And to have Sheng elected to the Politburo's Standing Committee at a party meeting unsanctioned by the Comintern was tantamount to a coup d'état staged by Sheng and his cronies.

In typical Chinese fashion, Dong and Sheng started to play the most dangerous game in their careers, which would decide who would win the ultimate trophy of controlling the party.

Dong moved first. As the legally elected member of the Politburo, he was bitter that the party meeting at the city of Yi did not include him. Since that meeting had redistributed power without his legitimate right of participation, he demanded a more powerful and higher position in the party apparatus because of the significantly superior forces under his command. Considering Dong's demand self-serving but legitimate, Sheng's associates decided to compromise. Si-Tu gave up his position as commissar of the Red Army to Dong, who was further appeased by his appointment as vice chairman of the party's Central Committee of Military Affairs.

Rival Sheng was no doubt unhappy with Dong's gains. But he could not do anything for the moment to stop Dong's aggression. As a skilled guerilla fighter, Sheng decided to lie low for now, waiting for his chance to strike back later.

3

Cheers. Jubilance. Happiness. Friendship. The celebration party went on for hours at the headquarters of the Second Front Army. Its leader, Dong, and his wife Dai Tian hosted the party, and had invited some of their best friends to celebrate the meeting of the two armies. They included Tao, Meng, Tania, Yan Yan, and some officers and soldiers from both sides.

Tao almost broke down in tears the other day when he met Dong for the first time after their long separation. Today he was laughing and cheering as though the celebration party was the best holiday he had had in years. As the commander-in-chief of the Red Army, Tao knew, more than anyone else, how gratifying it was to see a dear friend still alive after five years of bitter fighting with the enemy. He rose and declared, "Zi-Tian, I never had a chance to be at your wedding and to congratulate you and Dai Tian in person. Now, allow me to congratulate and salute both of you. Cheers!"

"Cheers! Cheers!" The crowd responded merrily.

Meng then suggested, "Now, Zi-Tian, you got to tell us the stories about your romance with Dai Tian!"

"Yes, yes! Stories! Romance! Stories! Romance!" The crowd was excited again.

Tania and Yan noticed that the tall and well-built Dong was blushing, just like the handsome young man they had remembered, full of vigor and innocence. Yan said, "He looks so manly with his bushy hair and prominent jaws."

"He has grown a beard," Tania added.

The hesitant Dong looked at Dai, who was as helpless and bashful as he was.

"There really isn't much to tell," said Dong. "We started out simply as revolutionary friends and comrades. We just, we just fell in love naturally."

"I don't believe that a bit!" Yan screamed. "I have been your revolutionary friend for years. How come you have never fallen in love with me?"

People laughed. The embarrassed Dong looked at Dai again, who was still afraid to utter a single word, lest she become the next target of this rowdy crowd.

"The truth is… the truth is…" As one who was not used to making up stories, Dong was trying hard to come up with one quickly so he could end his misery. "The truth is that we both have the same first name. See, Zi-Tian and Dai Tian. They rhyme."

"Well, that's simply a coincidence. You must not cheat. You must tell us the truth. Nothing but the whole truth," someone said. His friends were not going to let him off the hook so easily.

"Okay, okay." Dong finally gave up. He said, "I will tell you all the details. But they are embedded in a song. So, I will sing the song and you have to figure out how it happened yourself. After the song, if you still don't know what happened, it's your problem, not mine."

Wow, Dong's friends did not see this coming, but they had no reason to refuse his terms. Besides, no one had ever heard him sing, or even knew he had such a talent. So they quietened down, waiting for him to start.

Some years ago, Dong began on a vague note, he and Dai were on a mission in a wild and remote grassland where many Tibetans lived. They stayed there for two weeks and learned this Tibetan folksong, which the musician Wang Luo-Bin later introduced to the rest of China.

The faraway place is where a pleasant girl lives.
Whenever people walk by her tent, they
always pause and turn for a second look.

Her pink little face is like the shining sun.
Her beautiful and lovely eyes
are as bright as the enchanting moonlight of the evening.

I'm willing to give up everything to go with her and the herd.
Nothing will please me more when every day
I can watch her beautiful face and gold laced robe.

How I want to be a little lamb walking by her side.
Nothing will please me more when she whips me gently,
her frisky lash touching my body over and over.

A delightful melody. A charming scene. And an adorable feeling beautifully described in sweet phrases, intimate analogies, fervent adulations, and subtle sentimentalities. The crowd was very pleased, although few of them were able to decipher how Dong and Dai got together from the lyrics.

Listening to the tone and from the way Dong was singing, Tania understood that he was deeply in love. She felt very happy for Dai, who had married such a wonderful man. She was mesmerized and decided to ask Dong to write down the lyrics for her.

Yan became motivated and started to encourage Meng to sing a song too, knowing him to be a man equal to Dong's learning and talent.

Meng vehemently declined, insisting that he had a poor voice and had never been a singer.

Soon more people were egging him on, including Dong, Dai, Tao, and Tania.

Finally, Meng said that he was willing to deal if people would allow him to tell a story instead of singing.

"It must be a love story then!" somebody yelled.

"All right, a love story," said Meng.

"Good, we now have a deal. Everyone quiet." Tao gladly used his authority to calm down the roomful of soldiers. His friend would have plenty of stories to tell and one love story should not be a problem.

In Han Dynasty, Meng began, Si-Ma Xiang-Ru, one of the most celebrated prose writers in Chinese history, was at the low point of his life. He worked as a mounted bodyguard for Emperor Jing, who cared little about his talent. He later met Emperor Liang, who appreciated his work but passed away a few years later.

The despondent Si-Ma left the court and was about to return home when he met his friend Wang Ji who was the county chief of Lin Qiong. Wang invited Si-Ma to stay in Lin Qiong by pointing out that in Si-Ma's hometown of Chengdu, Sichuan, not many of his family members and friends were still around. Thus, he would find little comfort in Chengdu if he were to return home.

Si-Ma agreed but remained dispirited. The concerned Wang then decided to arrange a party to cheer him up. Wang spread the word that the most talented prose writer was in town, and several local dignitaries gathered in Zhuo Wang-Sun's household, waiting to meet Si-Ma. Zhuo, the wealthiest man in the county, was worth millions and had had as many as eight hundred servants in the family.

When the tardy Si-Ma arrived at last, he was not impressed with the party. No scrumptious food seemed to whet his appetite, or succulent drinks his mood. In order not to embarrass the generous host and his distinguished guests, Wang brought out a qin—an ancient seven stringed musical instrument—and begged his friend to play a song. The obliging Si-Ma played the qin as he sang.

> Bird, oh, bird, flying high, flying long,
> looking for a home, looking for a confidant,
> nothing around.
>
> Bird, oh, bird, over the seas, over the mounts,
> searching for a companion, searching for a soulmate,
> no one found.
>
> Bird, oh, bird, soaring above the clouds,
> saddened with want, looking for his phoenix,
> to whom he belongs.

So impressed were the honorable host Zhuo, chief Wang, and their eminent friends that they presented more food and drinks to salute the gifted Si-Ma.

Yet no one was more enthralled than the host's young and beautiful daughter Zhuo Wen-Jun, who was hiding behind the screen. Recently widowed, she knew why Si-Ma was so melancholic, and greatly empathized with what he was trying to express in his sorrowful songs. She knew the yearning, and longed for the same kind of love, caring, and understanding as much as he did.

That night she made the most daring decision in her life that few other women in China would attempt to emulate, which was to run away with Si-Ma regardless of the consequences.

Father Zhuo was furious the next morning, vowing that he never wanted to see his daughter again for as long as he lived.

Alas, a bleak life awaited them when the runaway couple returned to Chengdu, where they found nothing except for a bare room in an empty house, just like their friend Wang had described.

Romantic love was exciting but everyday life was hard. Zhuo Wen-Jun suggested that they return to her hometown, where they could open a business with the help of the people she had known since childhood.

The reluctant prose writer agreed and the couple set up a brewery and tavern in Lin Qiong. While wife Zhuo managed the family business, Si-Ma was busy with bartending, waiting tables, running errands, and serving the patrons' needs. The wife's beauty and practical wisdom, the husband's fame and literary talent, and the couple's amazing stories and personal adventures attracted large crowds to their establishments, which became highly successful within a short period.

"Did they live happily ever after?" someone asked.

"Yes and no," answered Meng.

Urged by friends and neighbors, Zhuo Wang-Sun later accepted the marriage and gave his blessings to his daring daughter and the unexpected son-in-law. The reconciliation pleased Zhuo Wen-Jun and Si-Ma, who now could devote more time to his writing.

Then Si-Ma began to receive promotions and favors from the new emperor and his future looked brighter than ever before. But his success also led him to consider taking another woman as his concubine.

The practice was common with many Chinese men, and women, no matter how talented they were, had no power to stop it. The news shocked Zhuo Wen-Jun. Extremely saddened, she could not understand why a couple who had overcome so many prejudices and so much hardship would become estranged in times of happiness and prosperity. She composed a poem and sent it to the husband. It read,

What can be as pure as the white clouds?
What can be as bright as the shining moon?
My love for you and
Your devotion to me.

What can be more beautiful than the spring blossom?
What can be more mesmerizing than the songs I once heard?
Your love for me and
The qin you have played.

What can be more dreadful when
the clouds and the moon are gone,
when the blossom has faded, and
when the music has stopped.

The strings are broken,
My heart torn.
The mandarin ducks are still together,
The willow twigs have parted.

When the mirror is shattered,
When the morning dew has evaporated,
When my hair has turned gray,
I have no choice but to separate.

No tears to go the opposite way,
No love to gain when the heart is cold.
No need to think of me hereafter,
When both of us are growing old.

When Si-Ma read these lines, he was greatly shaken. Although not as elegant as his prose, not as lavish as his rhetoric, and not as refined as his style, Zhuo's plain words still expressed her sorrow, sadness, and determination in a powerful way. Her feelings now were as genuine as her original commitment to the marriage, which made Si-Ma feel shameful about his behavior. He gave up his plan to marry the concubine and went back home. He stayed with Zhuo Wen-Jun till the end of his life.

"Wow, what a story!" someone said.

"What a romance!" shouted another. Finding the crowd captivated by such stories, Meng suggested, "Tania, you may want to tell us a Russian story."

Those present loved the idea of something foreign. A song, a story, or a dance—anything Russian they would be glad to accept.

Tania did not at all dislike the suggestion, and she began searching her memory bank for something truly entertaining for the occasion. A few seconds later, she said, "Okay. I am so happy today to see so many friends, and I am so pleased to hear Dong Zi-Tian's song and Meng Bo-Xian's story. Now if you will permit me, I will recite a Russian poem."

"Wonderful!"

"A great idea!"

"We love it!"

"But"—Tania paused—"I will need some help. I can only recite the poem in Russian, and I need someone to translate it into Chinese."

"That should not be a problem at all. We have several Russian-speaking talents right here," someone responded.

Indeed, Dong and Meng spoke excellent Russian. Dai Tian, Tao and a number of his staff officers understood Russian to some degree. But Dong was chosen as the official translator, while others promised to help when needed.

Tania first introduced the poet, Sergei Yesenin, who was a young and relatively unknown poet to non-Russians. She recited the poem with all her tender artistry, hoping to demonstrate the poet's impressive talent after the translation was made.

The Night

When the river falls asleep,
black pines make no more sound,
nightingales no longer sing, and
long-legged crakes cease to hum.

The night falls, silence comes, and
little brooks alone chant.
Silver coating creeps over the world,
as the shadow of the moon moves on.

The Milky Way is lit,
and frosty streams drift along.
The grassland nurses new greens,
as the shadow of the moon moves on.

The night falls, silence comes, and
nature smiles in her fancy dreams.
Silver coating seals the universe,
as the shadow of the moon moves on.

Hardly familiar with the poet and poem, the crowd waited anxiously as Dong was consulting with several Russian-speaking officers about the most appropriate choice of Chinese words. When the final version of the translation was read out, they applauded and cheered. It was a beautiful poem, without pretense and pomp. But it was a poem that everyone understood perfectly. The quiet and charming scenes of the Russian landscape were visible to the listeners, who knew nature and nature's potent power from their daily experience and humble background. They needed no introduction and explanation to sympathize with the sentiments the poet had so wonderfully expressed. At the moment, they seemed to relish the poet's verses, which had miraculously made explicit the deep love and inner emotions they also had about nature and their motherland.

"What a touching piece," said Tao, while Dai warmly congratulated Tania for her poetic rendition.

"Thanks to Dong Zi-Tian and everybody else. Thank you for the wonderful translation," Tania replied sincerely for she understood how difficult it must have been to translate a poetic piece right on the spot in a few minutes.

"Tania, we want more! We want to hear more from you!" the crowd chanted.

"Yes, Tania, the poem is so beautiful. You must give us another one," Yan said while holding Tania's hand, tears filling her eyes.

"Okay, okay. Let me think of another one," said Tania, who was genuinely moved by everybody's reaction.

A few moments later, announcing this poem was by the same poet, she began:

Fresh Snow

Fresh snow under my foot as I walked,
So excited was I that my heart was panting
like the first opening of the lilies in the valley.
The road was getting dark when dusk brought out
the blue hues from the evening stars.

Was it light or darkness?
Was it the noise of the wind or birds in the forest?
Winter might not be here yet across the field,
only the flocks of white swans had covered it.

Oh, beautiful snow, the pure and vast white cloth!
The falling temperatures made my blood boil.
How I wanted to hug the white birch and
embrace her naked bosom with my body…

Tania did not finish the last stanza. She noticed some commotion in the audience, and thought that perhaps the explicit language had offended some people.

One guard rushed in and shouted in a trembling voice, "There is a bomb explosion and Comrade Sheng Bao has been badly wounded!"

The party was over and Dong, Tao, Meng, Tania, Yan, and everyone else rushed out to find out what had happened.

4

A few moments ago, an enemy airplane had flown over the camping ground of the First Front Army. It did not seem to have a special target but dropped two bombs at random before it left. One of them fell close to the tent where Sheng and his wife Yu were staying. Yu threw herself over Sheng to protect her husband when the bomb exploded. Yu was badly wounded but Sheng was not harmed. The mistaken report about Sheng being injured was due to the confusion in the immediate aftermath of the attack.

Yu's bravery resulted in such severe injuries that the doctors said it was a miracle that she was still alive. Fourteen bomb fragments were found on her back, arms, and legs, where her wounded flesh was bathed in blood. The medical team operated on her amid deplorable conditions. Regrettably, the doctors lacked the skills and equipment to take out the two last small shrapnel lodged on the back of her head. Yu was out of danger, but remained extremely weak since her health had been on a steady decline after giving birth to her daughter. Her mental health had been affected too since the baby had been given away shortly after birth. Many had seen the distraught mother on the road, wondering how and where she got the strength to keep on walking with the troops all the while. Now they began to wonder how she got the strength to risk her own life to save Sheng.

Clearly, the Red Army troops were still not safe; they were still under the enemy's air surveillance and they had to leave the area immediately. In mixed units, the First and Second Front armies took the road in two columns, marching toward the north.

The bombing incident alarmed the methodical Si-Tu, who immediately called for a meeting with Lin Shi-Xiong, Lu Di-Ping, Fang Si-Liang, and Cheng Chu-Li, asking them to tighten security measures to ensure the absolute safety of party leaders, particularly that of Sheng and Tao.

"Although the bombing incident was unexpected, we cannot afford to expose our leaders to any danger from now on," Si-Tu told his associates.

All four longtime party members swore to do their best. Lin, Fang, and Cheng, though not Lu, had had extensive security and underground experience working with Si-Tu in Shanghai for nearly a decade, and they understood the vital importance of internal security more than anyone else.

Although not a security expert, Lu had learned the importance of personal safety the hard way. Growing up in a big landowning family, he was the son of his father's ninth concubine. Since he was one of the few surviving boys among his father's numerous offspring, he aroused so much jealousy and hatred that the other concubines, led by an alpha female, conspired to kill Lu by trying to poison and strangle him. When those attempts failed, they took him into the wilderness and dumped him there. Only his mother's relentless vigilance and valiant protection saved his life.

Adolescence offered Lu neither peace nor security. When his father died, the substantial wealth he left behind became the target of competition for his numerous family members and relatives. They fought mercilessly with one another over a share of the family fortune and openly expressed their wish to see Lu dead as soon as possible. Totally disillusioned, young Lu left home and joined Sun Yet-Sen's nationalist revolution.

He rose to the rank of regiment commander before he was twenty-six and was much appreciated by his boss, who soon promoted him to be the division's staff officer. The position allowed Lu to use his acute understanding of human nature and sharp intelligence to work on sensitive military matters while providing him with plenty of protection. He also enjoyed being involved in making tactical arrangements inside the war room rather than in leading the charge on the battleground.

Although he had never participated in any direct battle, staff officer Lu had nevertheless seen enough bloodshed to know all about the fragility of life and horrors of war. Four of his superior officers were either killed or brutally murdered amid the chaos of revolution. One mutiny in his regiment had killed three dozen of its best soldiers, and he personally had uncovered several assassination plots against senior officers. Largely due to his own extraordinary vigilance and personal bodyguards' high level of alertness, Lu managed to escape four murderous attempts on his life.

Having cheated death so often throughout life, Lu's preoccupation with safety issues could not be overemphasized. With grave concerns over evil conspiracies, vicious infighting, cold-blooded murders, and treacherous assassinations never far from his mind, Lu was duly alarmed one day when Officer Kang Yi-Sheng, the head of the First Front Army's telecommunication unit, passed him a telegram.

5

"You have got to read this," Officer Kang said.

"What did it say?" Lu asked.

"It says," read the officer, "You must make sure that the plan is executed. If the First Front Army refuses, you must be ready to resolve it."

"Who sent the telegram? And to whom?" Lu questioned.

"The Red Army commissar Dong Zi-Tian sent it to his lieutenant commissar,

Wei Hao-Qin, who is here with our First Front Army." The officer added, "We just intercepted it a few minutes ago."

Lu looked at Officer Kang and suddenly asked, "Do you know Kang Yi-Jun?"

Startled, the officer said, "Kang Yi-Jun is my elder brother."

Lu instantly understood why Officer Kang had passed to him this intercepted telegram, which seemed to suggest a conspiracy. Kang Yi-Jun had worked under Commissar Dong in the Second Front Army. The two had been at loggerheads due a personality clash and policy disagreements. In his rage, Dong had ordered the brother's arrest, and the latter had suffered greatly in jail. Furious about Dong's mistreatment of his brother, Officer Kang Yi-Sheng had been planning his revenge for some time.

The feud between Dong and Sheng, and between the First Front and Second Front armies presented an unexpected opportunity. Sheng, a highly calculative and sensitive man who had become accustomed to political schemes and military stratagems, firmly believed in conspiracy theories of all kinds. He ordered Officer Kang Yi-Sheng and his unit to watch the telecommunication activities not only of the enemies but also those of the Second Front Army, which no low-ranking officer would ever dare to do without explicit orders from above.

Eager to comply, Officer Kang now had the telegram he had wished to see for some time, believing that he had uncovered a sinister scheme by Dong. Reporting this immediately, Kang hoped to be the hero in Sheng's power struggle against Dong, whom he greatly resented.

The telegram was in fact rather general. Its exact meaning was not clear and could be open to different interpretations.

Lu was not impressed, or at least not as excited as Kang was. He read the telegram again, "You must make sure that the plan is executed. If the First Front Army refuses, you must be ready to resolve it."

What was the "plan"? What did it mean to "be ready to resolve it"?

If Dong was the real mastermind of a conspiracy as Officer Kang had insinuated, Lu wondered, would he say that more clearly in his telegram? Was he trying to hide his true intentions? Or was he deliberately keeping the language vague for fear of interception?

The vague words of the telegram could be read in many ways. Since Lu could not make up his mind, he took a walk.

Lu passed by a meeting hall, where a large gathering was under way. He went in, found an empty seat, and sat near the podium where Lieutenant Commissar Wei Hao-Qin was giving a speech.

Fully devoted to the subject, Wei kept on going. Like Dong, Wei was also a university graduate and highly fluent in Russian. His specialty was Russian literature, not Russian politics. Lu looked at the speaker with an unusual interest today, and Wei's broad forehead, boyish face, and smooth skin intrigued the former.

A soldier came in and went straight to the podium. He handed a small piece of paper to Wei.

The speaker, still totally preoccupied with his topic, took a quick look at the paper and, apparently not finding anything urgent, handed it down to Lu, who was sitting near him.

Lu was stunned. It was the same telegram he had just read a few minutes ago.

The wording of the telegram was exactly the same. But, after reading it twice in ten minutes, Lu was finally able to make up his mind on what needed to be done.

Whatever the real intention behind the telegram, Lu decided to err on the side of caution by reporting it to the party leaders right away. With an old saying—"You'd rather believe its existence than its innocence"—ringing in his head, Lu put the telegram in his pocket and went straight to Sheng's tent.

6

Holding the telegram in his hand, Sheng listened quietly to Lu's report.

He then raised a question not about the telegram but about the officer who had intercepted it.

When Lu told him that the officer's name was "Kang Yi-Sheng," Sheng further asked for the exact written characters since there were so many synonyms and homonyms in the Chinese language, which could be unclear at best and confusing at worst. The stark difference in their appearances and exact meanings would not become evident until they were fully explained or clearly written in the original Chinese characters.

"'Yi' means 'to benefit,'" Lu explained, and "'Sheng' is 'holiness, or sage, or saint.'"

"You said he has a brother?" Sheng asked again.

"Yes. The brother had been arrested by Dong Zi-Tian," Lu replied.

"What's his name?"

"His name is Kang Yi-Jun."

"I bet 'Yi' means 'benefit' and 'Jun' is the word for 'monarch, or sovereign, or supreme rule.'"

"Oh, yes, they are," Lu replied. He knew that Sheng had an almost obsessive curiosity about people's names as well as their implied and explicit meanings. Silly names and wrong choice of words—such as gloominess or snake—would put him off easily. Auspicious names, felicitous choices of words, and providential implications pleased him greatly. Thank goodness, Officer Kang and his brother had good names, which Sheng appreciated. And who would not if he happened to believe that he was the sage and supreme ruler, and that one day, as the two brothers' names had shown, someone was destined to come and save him by exposing a wicked conspiracy against him?

The meeting with Sheng was surprisingly brief. Lu took less than five minutes to convince Sheng that a sinister plot against him was being carried out by Dong, who was marching with the left column (primarily composed of the Second Front Army), and his coconspirators, who were marching with the right column (primarily composed of the First Front Army).

The seriousness of the situation was not lost on Sheng, who had been suspicious of the highly ambitious Dong all along. Dong's enormous popularity among the officers and soldiers of the Second Front Army rivaled Sheng's own among the First. If their political rivalry turned into an armed confrontation, Sheng knew perfectly well that the depleted First Front Army would have no chance to defend itself against the far superior forces of the Second.

The external nemeses could be numerous, but they were never as close to him as the Second Front Army, which was right in his midst!

It was easy for Sheng to decide on his next move, based on the ancient wisdom, "If you can't fight to win, retreat."

Sheng immediately ordered Lu to instruct the party's top officials and their personal guards to leave their camps that very night without any delay and move to a safer place. No one, except the Group of Three, should know the true purpose of the sudden evacuation order until it was completely carried out.

That night, several hundred party elites and their families, top party personnel, and their bodyguards stealthily left their camping site and disappeared into the darkness. Sheng believed this was the most perilous night in his life, which was being threatened not by General Chen's government troops but by the Red Army under the control of his greatest rival, the strong-willed and fearsome Comrade Ding, who was a tough country boy like himself.

The move was so swift and so secretive that it was not until the next morning that most of the Red Army soldiers realized what had happened. The head had abandoned the body for its own sake, and Sheng asked the rest of the troops to follow him instead of Dong.

A furious Dong believed that Sheng and his tiny contingent had become deserters, and called a big rally to denounce the action. The rally turned into an emotional protest against the cowardly actions of the First Front Army and the policy of retreat that Sheng and his close associates had repeatedly adopted. Sheng, Si-Tu, and several top party leaders were denounced as traitors and expelled from the party. Dong, who appointed himself as the party's new leader, called on the Red Army to follow him to explore a different path for the future.

The telegram incident and the way the vengeful Officer Kang, the nervous staffer Lu, and the zealous Sheng had handled it triggered an unprecedented crisis, which shocked the party and the Red Army more than any of the surprise attacks the enemy troops had launched against them.

The two columns of the Red Army parted. The right column—mostly composed of the First Front Army's surviving soldiers—later followed Sheng and moved to the north. The left column—comprising mainly the Second Front Army troops—followed Dong, marching toward the west and later the south.

No one knew when and how this crisis would end. When Sheng and his followers finally ended the Long March and arrived in Shaanxi Province in Northwestern China, the troops numbered fewer than ten thousand—indicating that ninety percent of this Red Army force had lost their lives during the past year.

For the moment, they were safe but the Red Army and the Chinese Communist Party were both deeply divided. Dong stubbornly refused to recognize Sheng's authority, while Sheng had no means to force him submit.

The crisis lingered. Denounced in public, Sheng suffered a huge loss in reputation, prestige, and influence; this devastating humiliation he would never forget or forgive for the rest of his life.

Dong's plan of moving to the west and then to the south met with more failure than success. He had put all his bets on the issue of legitimacy, but he had no way of stopping Sheng from staking a claim to the party's leadership position. Nor was Dong able to weaken Sheng's control over the First Front Army. With thousands of brave soldiers and hundreds of talented officers still standing by Sheng, Dong adopted a wait-and-see strategy, hoping that maybe some miracle would happen to save him from his embarrassing dilemma.

Chapter 21

Vicissitudes

1

LYING AT THE FOOT OF THE TIBETAN PLATEAU, XIKANG PROVINCE was one of the most remote and least populated regions in China. It averaged more than ten thousand feet above sea level and was covered with numerous forbidding mountains as high as sixteen thousand feet. Local Tibetans believed that in ancient times their homeland was threatened by an evil monster, who destroyed their houses and killed their people. Encouraged by tribal leaders, many brave young men left to fight the giant monster, but none returned. One of the tribe's few remaining men vowed to defeat the beast and went into the mountains. For the next seven days and nights, the clashing of weapons and the sound of howling and screaming shook the earth until, suddenly, everything went quiet. The tribespeople then timidly went up to see what had happened. They found the slain monster, and lying next to it was their exhausted and badly mauled young tribesman, who was gasping for his last breath. The deceased hero rose to become the highest and biggest mountain in the region—the magnificent Eagle Beak—and his thirteen broken knives, swords, and axes became the thirteen peaks with names such as Bear Paw, Fox Tail, and Wolf Tooth. His copious sweat during the battle was transformed into the two main rivers of the area—the Black River to the north and the White River to the south, which flowed down from those high mountains and nursed the vast grassland where the Tibetans still lived.

The beautiful legend did not make the Red Army's task any easier. While the enemy troops were no longer on their trail, they now must climb those mountains, which were covered with snow and ice even in summer.

Most of these soldiers were from Southern China and had never seen any snow. They were utterly unprepared for the strong winds and piercing cold in the mountains during the broad daylight of August. They had no winter uniforms or shoes and no adequate supplies except for some scarves, mufflers, blankets, liquor, and hot peppers. More than half a year on the road fighting their way out of the enemy's encirclement had greatly sapped their strength. Poor nutrition and meager clothing made their journey harder than anyone could ever imagine, even though they had grown up in the harsh countryside. Every step upward became even more arduous as the air got thinner and thinner while they climbed. When exhaustion and fatigue forced some to take a rest, many of them were never able to stand up and walk again. They fainted, fell asleep, froze, and succumbed to the extreme cold.

Those who had survived that journey now faced another challenge, which was to cross the immense grassland of three hundred miles long and two hundred miles wide. The new journey was hardly as romantic as it sounded for a large portion of the six thousand square miles comprised mysterious marshes, pathless wetlands, and poisonous swamps. Few birds or animals could live in this deadly and eerily quiet environment.

The scant population of native Tibetans lived in small and scattered hamlets and depended on herds, not farming, for their livelihood. Although not necessarily hostile, most of them remained skeptical about the thousands of newly arrived armed Han intruders, who looked more like a swarm of runaway bandits than real soldiers. Pacified when told that the Red Army troops were mere passersby, some were willing to help. Since they did not produce any grain, the best they could offer were meat, cheese, milk, and barley. Some villagers helped to process the barley, make barley flour, and fry it. The fried barley flour then became the staple ration for the soldiers, and the lucky ones would have ten pounds for the week's journey.

No road existed on the massive grassland in front of the Red Army, which began its march by following the trails of the local herds. Trouble emerged as soon as the tracks ended. Too much water from the Black and White Rivers converged here and settled on this flat land for miles upon miles, only sliced by countless hidden inlets, winding coves, glittering streams, and rattling brooks, making it such an extended waterlogged and boggy place that no one could see its end.

Finding a pad of grass here or a mat of weed there was the only thing that could help one move safely forward. If one stepped onto a wrong spot, he could be sucked into the mud underneath and might never surface again. This could be particularly dangerous for those weak and sick soldiers falling behind the main column. Without the mutual assistance and collective effort in searching for the right directions, they could easily get lost and trapped—or even swallowed—by this merciless killer under their feet.

Once they had reached a high and safe ground and could finally have some rest, a new and even more serious problem emerged. Their fried barley flour, too dry to swallow, needed hot water to make it edible. Although slow-moving water was everywhere, fresh and clean water was hard to come by. The water had been stagnant in some places for hundreds of years, and much of its surface was smelly, dirty, odious, and even poisonous—which was why no birds, animals, or humans could be found in this no man's land. Even after some precious clean water was discovered, no fire could be built since there were no trees or tall plants with stems and branches that could be used as fuel.

Eating dry barley flour without any water did not matter in the end because pretty soon most soldiers had run out of their meager rations. Some started to consume the raw barley kernels, which they had not been able to process prior to the journey. The few remaining kernels would further be viewed as treasures when most soldiers had run out of everything they could eat, including the last pieces of animal bones, their leather belts, and leather laces on their shoes. Finding anything to fill their empty stomachs was a paramount but dangerous task. As many soldiers died after tasting exotic and poisonous plants as of starvation.

During the day bright sunshine warmed the feeble bodies of the badly battered and hungry soldiers. No sooner after sunset would temperatures plunge below zero. So common were showers and thunderstorms in this area in summer that they would easily spoil whatever food the Red Army soldiers still had, while the pouring rains and sometimes floods made their rest and sleep miserable at best and totally impossible at worst.

In all, the Red Army suffered the worst noncombat fatalities while crossing the grassland than at any other time and place since they started the Long March.

For the Second Front Army soldiers, this was only the beginning of their misery, because they had to go across the lifeless grassland not once but three times in the same year while climbing as many as twenty snow-covered mountains in four months. They did so only because Commissar Dong, totally engrossed in his own fancy, did not want to march alongside the First Front Army and submit himself to Sheng Bao's control.

2

Aside from their personal rivalry, Dong had good reasons to believe Sheng was on the wrong side of strategy. Going to the most desolate and poorest region of Northwestern China, Dong thought, was not the way to revitalize the communist movement, which demanded adequate resources and manpower for support. The historical Shaanxi used to be a very productive and highly dynamic kingdom, where its ruler rose to become the first emperor who defeated various hostile regional powers and united China. But centuries of warfare and other disasters thereafter had depleted its natural vegetation, and soil erosion in this province was the worst in the nation. Located on the Loess Plateau, its eroded land was a major source of the enormous quantities of sand and loess deposited into the Yellow River every year, creating a huge problem for people living downstream in Central and Eastern China. Except for some counties in the southern portion of Shaanxi, the province's general productivity was the lowest by national standards and the name of Shaanxi Province, especially Northern Shaanxi, became synonymous with drought, famine, depletion, destitution, starvation, and misery in the Chinese language.

Dong further believed that by comparison, the northern and northwestern parts of Sichuan Province were much more promising. The areas were just south of Shaanxi but had rich farmlands and a strong and vigorous population.

The Second Front Army, under his leadership, had grown eightfold from ten thousand to become the largest communist force in just three years. Dong was confident that he would be able to duplicate this amazing success, whereas Sheng's choice of impoverished Shaanxi would only end in failure.

Dong had labeled Sheng's moves as "coward escapism." To demonstrate the clear difference in his plan and strategy, Dong and other leaders of the Second Front Army decided to march in a southeast direction instead of a northwest one, to go after the enemies instead of running away from them, and to attack instead of retreat.

It was this decision that led the Second Front Army to return and cross the grassland again. After climbing a succession of snow-covered mountains bordering Xikang and Sichuan provinces, they then formed two columns, moved along the Black and White Rivers southeastward, and did not stop until they were ready to strike.

A key transport stop between the two provinces, the small town of Whetstone was chosen as their first target. No sooner had a regiment of defenders realized they were being attacked than the battle was over. The overwhelming force of the Red Army totally annihilated the regiment, captured nearly a thousand enemy soldiers, and quickly expanded the victory to three counties nearby.

The sudden reappearance of this massive Red Army and its incessant attacks at the borders shocked the Sichuan warlord Liu Yi-Hao. Reports said that the Red Army pushed on for seven days, covering one hundred and fifty miles, fighting, and winning five battles in a row. Apparently, the Red Army had not given up the attempt to enter Sichuan after all. A control freak who had been reluctant to allow the national army into his territory, General Liu wired General Chen, begging him to send government troops to defend Sichuan as soon as possible.

Greatly invigorated by the first round of successes, Dong and his top officers sent as many as fifteen regiments to capture the next target—Long Post, which was the key pass to the plains in Western Sichuan.

Only seventy miles away from the provincial capital, Chengdu, Long Post was the last fortification that no local warlord could afford to lose. Thousands upon thousands of soldiers were shipped from nearby towns around the clock to defend the stronghold day and night. Once unloaded from the trucks, soldiers were immediately sent to join the attacks against the Red Army. Close behind the marching soldiers stood the military police. They had the authority to shoot anyone including officers who slowed down the attacks or attempted to retreat without orders.

The quick sacking of Long Post gave the Second Front Army soldiers no time to celebrate. Quickly confronted with the fiercest counterattacks they had ever seen, they saw swarms of enemy soldiers marching toward them, and no one was stopping even under the continuous fire from dozens of machine guns shooting right at their faces.

The broad rice paddy fields before the trenches were piled up with dead bodies and wounded soldiers. Tanks on the ground and battle planes above, the sounds of flying bullets and the explosion of bombs and hand grenades filled the air, which were soon replaced by close combat using bayonets, knives, hands, feet, fists, and even teeth.

Based on intelligence reports, Dong and his officers learned that Liu had assembled as many as eighty regiments to recapture Long Post, totaling more than one hundred thousand men. More reinforcements, they were told, were also coming from all directions including the national government's prime division, led by General Pan Jin, one of Chen's favorite officers.

Clearly, this was not the right time or place to reenter Sichuan. Long Post was too flat to offer any serious defense and it was too close to the vital interests of the powerful enemies, local, regional, and national.

The campaign at Long Post was one of the most courageous but undoubtedly one of the most brutal fights in the history of the Red Army. To Dong's surprise, a swift and successful early attack turned into a prolonged struggle for seven days. He and his top officers had greatly overestimated their strength while severely underestimating those of their opponents. After killing fifteen thousand enemy soldiers, and losing over ten thousand of its own men, the Second Front Army withdrew, signaling that Dong's strategy had failed. The idea of going through Long Post to reestablish a red base in Sichuan did not seem any more promising than what Sheng had attempted to accomplish at Skyline in early spring.

The Second Front Army first withdrew to Whetstone and then, to foil the enemy's attempts to catch them, back into the dreaded snow-covered mountains again. To further distance the Red Army from government troops, Dong would later order the third crossing of the grassland—a grim undertaking for his battered soldiers. These decisions of going back from where they had come was an open recognition of his failed military strategy, which was a humiliating blow to Dong's ego and political ambition.

3

A telegram from Shaanxi puzzled Dong as he was pondering his next move on the journey back to Xikang. Sent by a person named Xia-Hou Dan, it read,

Comrade Zi-Tian:

[1] The Seventh Congress of the Comintern and the Chinese delegation have made many suggestions concerning the Chinese revolution, which I will now relay to you in detail.

[2] My brother, your suggestion of calling for the Seventh National Congress of the Chinese Communist Party is a valid one. The Chinese delegation to the Comintern in Moscow has drafted several proposals and resolutions. The National Congress will convene as soon as conditions allow.

[3] Internal polemics in the party should not be unduly divisive. They can exist in the party. But unity is important to the public. I shall convey this opinion to the comrades here.

[4] The Comintern has expressed views about the organizational issues of the Chinese Communist Party, viz., China is a huge country, where transportation is inconvenient, economic development is uneven, and politics varies from place to place. It will be hard for the National Central Committee of the party to micromanage everything across the board. The party therefore can organize a Northern Bureau, a Shanghai Bureau, a Northwest Bureau, and a Southwest Bureau, etc. According to different circumstances, the party's National Committee can directly control some of them, while others may allow the party's delegation to Moscow to represent them. This may be a way of achieving unity in the party for now. Please give this proposal

serious consideration, my brother, and I look forward to hearing your thoughts. The Comintern and our Chinese delegation in Moscow have great hopes for the Second Front Army. Hope to hear from you soon.

Xia-Hou Dan

"Xia-Hou Dan, Xia-Hou Dan," Dong repeated the name a few more times, and realized that he knew this person. "He must the cousin of Officer Xia-Hou Ding," Dong said.

Xia-Hou Dan had joined the party very early, had been involved in labor organizational activities for a long time, and had once met Dong in Moscow. But he was a junior member in the party apparatus, elected to be an alternate member of the party's Central Committee only a few years ago, and never held any important position in the party at the national level.

Although it sounded strange for a party member of his level to contact a Politburo member directly, a number of points in the telegram intrigued Dong.

It seemed that Xia-Hou had brought back some important news from the Comintern, which had just concluded its Seventh International Congress in Moscow. But it was unclear whether he was simply a messenger or someone with authority. It was even more questionable whether any of that authority had been granted by the party, by the party's delegation to Moscow, or by the Comintern itself.

From the language and content of the message, Xia-Hou seemed to be privy to some critical issues, controversies, and debates about some highly sensitive internal affairs of the party, such as the calling for the Seventh National Congress and the setting up of regional bureaus. Neither one of which seemed to be within the conventional ambit of an alternate member of the party's Central Committee.

Most striking, Xia-Hou attempted to establish some degree of familiarity with Dong by calling him "brother" twice in the message, even though their brief meeting in Moscow years ago hardly qualified them to be anything more than distant colleagues. Xia-Hou never worked directly under Dong, nor was the latter his boss in any capacity. There must be some compelling reason for a junior member to call a senior member "brother" twice in the same message, which was unusual in traditional Chinese social etiquette.

Yet Xia-Hou seemed to know what had been going on between Dong/ Second Front Army and Sheng/First Front Army. He even suggested the Comintern's willingness to consider the differences arising from the diverse realities of a large nation, and to satisfy the need for both institutional flexibility and cohesiveness within the organization.

Finally, he soothed Dong's ego by claiming how "the Comintern and our Chinese delegation in Moscow have great hopes for the Second Front Army," even though he provided no proof of when and where he had learned about these remarks. Xia-Hou did not and could not tell Dong that he had lived in Moscow for the last two and a half years and that he, the Comintern, and the Chinese delegation knew very little about the Second Front Army's situation. As a messenger, his main purpose in returning to China was to carry the vital codebook to reestablish telecommunications between Moscow and the Chinese Communist Party, which had been completely cut off for almost a year.

Despite these questions and doubts, Dong liked the general tenor of the message, which was gentle, respectable, and conciliatory. Although he wished he could have more clarity, Dong decided to respond to the message.

4

More anxious than Xia-Hou for the response were two men—Sheng Bao and Si-Tu Wen-Liang. For they were the ones who had carefully prepared and vetted every word in the telegram, signed it, and sent it to Dong.

Every doubt Dong had was valid. Xia-Hou had been a mere messenger whose twin mission was to communicate to China an important policy change of the Comintern and to reestablish telecommunications between the Chinese communists and Moscow by bringing back the latest codebook. In fact, when he left Moscow last summer, the First and Second Front armies were still several hundred miles apart and their respective leaders Sheng and Dong had not yet met. The Comintern had no way of foreseeing the polarization that would develop later between the two leaders and their armies, and therefore could not have authorized Xia-Hou beforehand to intervene in those political squabbles. Disguised as a fur trader, Xia-Hou was alone on the road for the next three and a half months crossing the great Gobi Desert. He knew nothing about the domestic situation in China and much less about how to deal with the convoluted intraparty strife.

Still seriously concerned about the huge military force Dong commanded, Sheng saw a possible solution in Xia-Hou. When Sheng conveyed his ideas to the intelligent Si-Tu, the latter was shocked by the audacity of it all.

"The aggressive Dong Zi-Tian," Sheng started, "will never stop until he fulfills his ambition, which is to become the leader of the party. We can never allow that to happen, can we?" He looked at Si-Tu, waiting for his answer.

Si-Tu knew that Sheng wanted to make sure where his loyalty stood. "No, no, no. Never. If he rises, we fall," he said.

Sheng grinned. He knew the answer but he wanted Si-Tu to say it in his own words. Si-Tu was such a wimp, Sheng thought, that he would never lead any charge, but always preferred to hide behind someone else. He would never be a true leader but forever remain a timid follower. As a strong man, Sheng needed followers. But he greatly despised this submissive and sycophantic man. He talked to Si-Tu a lot and consulted him often not because he liked him, but because Sheng needed to tap Si-Tu's brains to perfect his Machiavellian maneuver.

"Dong Zi-Tian only seems fearless, and likes to show that he is not afraid of anyone in the party." Sheng returned to his topic but did not make the second half of his thoughts explicit—that Dong had dared to challenge the legitimacy of Sheng's authority. "Yet he is afraid of one thing and one thing only—the Comintern."

"That's true," concurred Si-Tu half-amused. He knew that everyone, including the rascal Sheng, was afraid of the Comintern, and, when dealing with the latter, they all appeared to be as attentive, obedient, and deferential as an innocent little girl standing next to her austere grandmother.

"Therefore, if we can't convince Dong to surrender his power to us, we can use Xia-Hou to represent the Comintern to talk to him, who will surely listen this time," Sheng said calmly.

"A brilliant idea," Si-Tu almost jumped out from his seat. He knew Sheng to be good, very good in the battlefield, but never knew he could be this good in politics. "To fake the imperial order by the emperor" was a well-known stratagem in Chinese history. Yet few had actually used it in modern politics, and no revolutionary had ever been bold enough to consider its application in a communist organization.

The virtue of the scheme was immediately clear to Si-Tu, who quickly assessed the pros and cons from several angles. It was an outlandish idea for sure, but not unreasonable at the same time. Xia-Hou had just came back from Moscow. Nobody would care about the difference between a messenger and an authorized representative, since most rank and file would be in awe once they heard the word "Moscow." The faraway Second Front Army had no way to verify Xia-Hou's true status. They had no means to contact Moscow, nor did they have the latest codebook, which was now in Lin Shi-Xiong's hand.

"I think it will work," the thoughtful Si-Tu stressed. "Secrecy will be the key to success."

"Agreed. Let me put it this way," Sheng concurred with all seriousness, "no one, I mean NO ONE, should know about this except you, me, and Xia-Hou."

"Understood," said Si-Tu.

"We may have to take this secret to our graves." Sheng looked into Si-Tu eyes with his lion's gaze.

Feeling the pressure, Si-Tu was not about to waver at the final stage of the loyalty test and answered simply, "I know."

"Now, you know what to do and I will see you in two days." Sheng ended the conversation with his customary arrogance. He was a thinker, a philosopher, and a strategist. He would never involve himself directly in the nitty-gritty of the dirty work, knowing that a host of underlings would be most willing to bend over backward to accomplish that for him.

5

Bringing Xia-Hou into the fold was relatively easy. Si-Tu lauded his extraordinary solo journey from Moscow to Shaanxi and compared its completion with the great success of the Red Army's Long March, which moved Xia-Hou to tears. Si-Tu stated that the party now had a highly classified mission for him, which would need his total involvement. Xia-Hou was sworn to secrecy before he was given details of the plan.

Feeling as if the burden of the whole future of the communist movement were on his shoulders, Xia-Hou could only think about honor, glory, duty and commitment and nothing else. "Yes, yes, yes, and a thousand yeses" was his reply.

Surprisingly, a great cause justified many big and small lies and few people ever objected to them. Instead they believed lying was part of the job. If the cause was just, to lie for it must to be justifiable. Not only were they obligated to lie but the better they lied, the better they would serve the cause. A glorious cause might involve glorious lies, and only a glorious liar could serve the glorious cause gloriously. If all these were what the cause needed, so be it.

When Si-Tu and Xia-Hou sat down to compose the first telegram to Dong, it took them considerable effort to come up with a draft. They agreed on several aspects and went back and forth repeatedly to double-check whether these had been satisfied.

The first was to demonstrate the authenticity of Xia-Hou's mission—sanctioned by the Comintern—while keeping his exact authority and assignments unspecified.

The second aspect was to show Xia-Hou's neutrality in the rivalry between the First and Second Front Armies, while stressing his sympathetic views toward Dong and the Second Front Army.

The third was to offer some reconciliatory, flexible, and tantalizing proposals, while giving no indication of how to fulfill them.

And the last aspect was to praise the Second Front Army lavishly and to approach Dong with a certain degree of familiarity.

The draft was revised several times between the two, and every word was checked and double-checked with extra care. Before Si-Tu took it to Sheng for the final approval in the morning, he could not sleep and got up in the middle of the night to reexamine the text once again.

Now the small piece of paper was in Sheng's hand, and he read it slowly, making a few comments here and there.

"Do you think it will work?" he asked.

"If you think the text of the telegram is okay, the strategy should work." Si-Tu was familiar with Sheng's penchant for evasive answers. On matters as sensitive as this, he would never give a "yes" or "no" answer. He was the kind of boss who would never say explicitly that he had approved a lie. He would always let others shoulder the actual responsibility even if he was the real mastermind.

"Why?" Sheng was intrigued by Si-Tu's fast but nuanced response.

"Because I don't think Dong Zi-Tian can sniff out a good bluff," Si-Tu replied, remembering years ago how he had tricked Dong into confessing his love for Tania.

A strange recollection of a moment in time that was so sweet, so innocent, so full of mutual admiration, honesty, and love—but now it was a reconnection made under circumstances so low, so devious, and so dirty.

6

The dice had been cast and it was Dong's turn.

He telegrammed Xia-Hou:

Brother Dan:

Pleased that you are safely back home.

The opportunist and escapist political course the First Front Army has been taking must be exposed before the unity of the party can be achieved.

The Central Committee of the Chinese Communist Party here, fully supported by the Second Front Army, accepts the leadership of the Comintern.

The people you are currently with must give up their claims as the leading body of the party.

Do you have freedom of telecommunication? Please let me know directly the commands and instructions from the Comintern. We accept directives from no one but the Comintern regarding the party's internal affairs.

Dong Zi-Tian

When Xia-Hou and Si-Tu received the telegram, both were disappointed. Dong did not seem to have taken the bait, nor did he seem to be impressed by the role Xia-Hou had assumed. If anything, Dong seemed to have raised the stakes, demanding the communists in Shaanxi to stop claiming themselves as the party's central authority. There seemed to be little room left for negotiations, although the last sentence of the telegram offered a sliver of hope.

Confounded and dumbfounded, they went to see Sheng to hear his views.

Sheng held up the telegram and finished reading it in a minute. Without a word, he took out his pen and opened his inkstand. Five minutes later, he handed the draft to Xia-Hou and Si-Tu. They read it, looked at each other, and asked in unison, "Will this work?"

"It will," Sheng said with his usual confidence.

They looked at the swiftly crafted telegram again, which read:

The Second Front Army and Comrade Dong Zi-Tian:

The Comintern sent me to resolve the problems with the First and Second Armies. I have met and talked to Comrade Sheng Bao. I have with me the codebook to communicate with the Comintern in Moscow. If you have any telegrams for the Comintern, I am happy to help you with them.

Apparently, Sheng was determined to go the whole hog with his high-risk gamble.

Despite some hesitation, Xia-Hou signed the telegram and it was sent.

Then a long silence.

Xia-Hou and Si-Tu did not know what to do next. Sheng suggested a new campaign by sending a series of telegrams to high-ranking officers of the Second Front Army, praising their loyalty to the party, bragging about the bright future in Shaanxi, threatening them with disciplinary action if they did not return, and most all, strongly suggesting that the Comintern was one hundred percent behind the First Front Army.

Xia-Hou and Si-Tu learned so much from Sheng. Both knew the importance of propaganda against the enemy. But they never thought that the same tactics could be used against another group of communists whom they were calling brothers just a few days ago. Xia-Hou was particularly apprehensive. If this failed to work, he would surely become the sacrificial lamb.

To their great relief, Dong blinked.

He wired Xia-Hou, indicating that he would take the Second Front Army to Shaanxi to rejoin the First Front Army.

The undisputed prestige and authority of the Comintern, the blind faith in fellow communists' honesty, the huge pressure from his associates, and, perhaps above all, a serious underestimation of Sheng's skills and shrewd political calculations had clouded and ultimately undermined Dong's judgment.

For the first time in the party, the country boy Sheng had won a decisive victory against Dong, one of the top university graduates. But Dong would not be the last person to be outmaneuvered by Sheng. Those who had underestimated the man from Boxwood would end up regretting it in the end.

7

Two days after the First Front and Second Front Armies reunited, the party told them that a new military plan had been drawn to start a "westward campaign." The Second Army's 30th Corps was chosen to lead the crossing of the Yellow River. Less than two weeks later, the 30th Corps successfully broke the enemy's defense and moved across to the west bank of the river. Shortly after that, another two corps, the 9th and 5th, also crossed the river. Altogether, half of the Second Front Army's total forces, or twenty-one thousand, eight hundred men, including some companies of female soldiers, porters, and support staff, went westward as ordered by the party.

Dong was not allowed to go with the troops and he stayed behind with the main party apparatus, perhaps as a precautionary measure in case he and his Second Front Army got separated from the rest. A man of Dong's charisma, seniority, and prestige should never be given the power to control any army—the big lesson Sheng had learned from ancient Chinese history and from the most recent challenge posed by this formidable opponent.

The westward campaign had two strategic objectives—to expand the red base into Western China and to receive aid and supplies provided by the Soviet Union. For over two thousand years, two trading routes in the western part of the country had linked merchants, foreign and local, to Russia and Europe across the massive Eurasian landmass. Both routes constituted a major section of the famed ancient Silk Road. Extending to the extreme west but more frequently taken, one of the routes passed through Xinjiang Province, which bordered Kazakhstan—a member of the Soviet Union. Lying in the immediate west and adjacent to Shaanxi, the other route went up northward through

Ningxia Province, which was next to Mongolia—the big neighbor bordering Russia in the north and China in the south.

The two old trade routes converged not far from the place where the Red Army had crossed the Yellow River. Because several huge mountain ranges and the notorious Gobi Desert separated the two routes for more than one thousand, six hundred miles in the areas further west of the Yellow River, the Red Army would not be able to turn around and change course once it had chosen one route over the other. This Red Army, now formally called the West Army, had to decide how it should proceed, which would largely depend on which direction the Russian aid and supplies would be coming from, either through Mongolia/Gobi Desert/Ningxia or through Kazakhstan/Xinjiang.

Before Xia-Hou left Moscow, Stalin had met with him and indicated that the Chinese Red Army might approach either Xinjiang or Mongolia, suggesting that both routes could be used to ship Russian goods to China. Because of safety concerns and the secret nature of his mission, Xia-Hou himself returned to China via the desolated Gobi Desert alone. Based on common sense and historical knowledge, however, many party leaders believed that the extreme west route through Xinjiang, far wider and far better served along the way, would be more suited for transporting large quantities of goods than going through the Gobi Desert. Yet this idea was rejected by the Comintern, which compelled the Chinese Communist Party to draw a "Ningxia Plan," aimed at creating a red base in this region and receiving Russian help from this direction. The modest-sized Ningxia was right next to Shaanxi. The Comintern and Sheng did not think that the West Army would need long-term rations after crossing the Yellow River, and most of the soldiers carried a week's food supply at the most.

Two weeks later, Moscow, after obtaining more information on cross-continental travels to Asia, reversed the Comintern's orders and told the Chinese to abandon the Mongolian route in favor of the Xinjiang option. The Chinese Communist Party hastily abandoned its "Ningxia Plan" and came up with a "New Battle Plan," which would order the West Army to move deep into the west to create a safe path for Russian goods coming in from Xinjiang instead of Mongolia.

The sudden change presented huge problems for the West Army. Firstly, it was totally unprepared for this incredibly longer journey—the most direct road was one thousand, five hundred miles longer than the previous one assigned to them. Secondly, most soldiers and officers were from Southern China, who were completely unfamiliar with the new terrain they were about to enter.

One of the harshest places in China, the corridor area they now had to go through was called Dog Bone. Squeezing through a series of high mountains (the lowest was eight thousand feet) from the north to the south, the corridor was an east-and-west passage nearly six hundred miles long while its width varied from five miles at the narrowest point to between fifty and sixty miles at the widest.

So narrow and confined, so dry and windy was the corridor that it was frequented by more bandits than people, and was never promising for any large army to travel and maneuver if its soldiers didn't have any prior knowledge of the region. As the West Army pressed on, they had no base, no support, and no good intelligence. Reversing its own decision back and forth no fewer than five times, the party headquarters provided little help or guidance, asking the troops to march sometimes, to stop and wait at other times, to rush to the west right away but to move to the east soon afterward. The poor planning and frequent changes of orders and marching directions confused the West Army's leaders, who started to doubt the mission, question the strategy, and debate the correct solution.

The ones who controlled this area were the warlord Fan Jia and several of his brothers from the Fan family, who commanded as many as seventy thousand soldiers, mostly cavalry. Their familiarity with the local conditions and the swiftness of their troops on horseback cost serious trouble for the West Army's foot soldiers, who suffered great casualties in several confrontations. With supplies running low, ammunition declining fast, and wounded soldiers on the rise, the West Army realized that the best solution for them was not to tarry any longer but to fight their way out of the corridor as soon as possible. However, the party leaders once again ordered them to stop marching and to start building a red base at their location. Party leaders repeatedly and bluntly told them that no help would be sent, and that they must fight for their own survival.

Trapped in the miserable corridor like a blindfolded man in a bag, the West Army found little room to maneuver and no place to build an effective defense at several isolated small villages on the flat ground. No food, no supplies, and, finally, no bullets. Snow falling and piercing wind blowing, soldiers picked up boards and sticks and were ready to fight till the end. But their hands, fists, knives, and sticks were no match for Fan's well-equipped cavalry, who broke the communist soldiers' last defense and cut them off like dead leaves.

The West Army had covered only four hundred miles or three-fifth of the corridor five months after they had crossed the Yellow River, averaging three miles a day, mostly because of those bad planning, frequent changes, and confusing orders they received from apathetic party leaders.

As many as seven thousand red soldiers were killed in action. Of the nine thousand captured soldiers, more than five thousand were slaughtered or mutilated before they died; the rest were forced into slave labor while female soldiers were raped, forced into prostitution, and later sold as concubines. After hiding and experiencing extreme hardship in the wild high mountains for months, several hundred courageous soldiers managed to escape, and later returned to rejoin the Red Army. More than two thousand men abandoned the troops and ran away, and another two thousand or so were missing or unaccounted for. Totally annihilated, the West Army was no more— representing the Red Army's most humiliating defeat in its history.

8

Sheng, purportedly the most brilliant strategist among the communists, felt no shame over his failed leadership, which had led to the catastrophic disaster for the West Army. He covered the truth, twisted the facts, and seized the moment not to repent but to destroy his nemesis Dong.

He openly alleged that Dong's opportunist policies had misled the West Army, while Dong's escapist directives finally led to its demise.

Every action the West Army had taken was based on the orders of Sheng and his top associates, since Dong possessed no real power after the merger of the First and Second Front Armies. But he was singled out as the one to blame for his earlier mistakes in disagreeing with Sheng and, worst, for publicly challenging his authority. An eye for an eye, a tooth for a tooth, Sheng would not let him off the hook this time.

Dong was severely criticized at party meetings and was soon stripped of his high positions in the Politburo and Red Army. Demoted to a county official, he was sent to a remote small town in Shaanxi to reform himself under the close supervision of party bureaucrats.

Personal vendetta aside, the forward-thinking Sheng had deeper concerns and long-term calculations. The Soviet Union was to send six hundred tons of military supplies to help the Chinese communists. If the West Army had successfully received them, it would become the biggest star of all the Red Army forces, which was the last thing Sheng wanted to see. Furthermore, anyone with some basic military knowledge would have known that Dog Bone was not the place for a large army to stay put.

On the other hand, a successful march toward Mongolia would produce the exact opposite result; Sheng's First Front Army, already positioned closer to Mongolia than any other Red Army units, would become the biggest beneficiary of Russian aid.

Sheng's interest in the campaign quickly evaporated as soon as the Russians aborted the Mongolia plan. He never intended to assist the Second Front Army in winning the westward campaign, which would greatly enhance Dong's powers. Given what he knew about the Russians, Sheng had good reason to believe that the Comintern might well choose Dong to replace him after a clear victory for the West Army in Xinjiang.

On a bleaker note and at a more fundamental level, Sheng's earlier plan of "going north" to build a red base in Northern Shaanxi was on the brink of collapse. As Dong had argued earlier, the poor and inhospitable Northern Shaanxi was not suitable for building a base—something Sheng realized as soon as he arrived. His First Front Army managed to push into three marginal counties in Northern Shaanxi, where abject poverty and a sparse population could neither provide his troops with food, winter clothing, and warm shelter nor support the Red Army's expansion.

Finding the situation hopeless, Sheng persuaded the party to adopt his new proposal of "marching into the neighboring province Shanxi in the east," also known as the "Eastward Campaign."

Less than three months later, the campaign folded under the intense resistance of local warlords and crushing counterattacks by the nationalist government troops, which had been rushed into Shanxi.

Sheng and the First Front Army quickly withdrew and went back to Northern Shaanxi, where they had originally started the campaign.

Reinvigorated, the indefatigable General Chen deployed as many as seventy regiments, totaling two hundred and fifty thousand men, to restart his intense extermination campaign against the Red Army in Shaanxi.

The much-weakened and small First Front Army, barely twenty-thousand-strong by this time, soon ran out of food and supplies, and, even worse, ran out of a place to hide. Desperate, Sheng told the party that the Red Army might have to pack up and begin a "new long march" again. The Eastward Campaign had just failed, the West Army was gone, and the Russians did not want the Red Army to march toward Mongolia, which lay north/northwest of Shaanxi. The only direction of this "new long march" Sheng could suggest was to proceed to the south, that was, back to Sichuan, which Dong had suggested almost a year earlier.

Sheng could fail, change his mind, break his promise, and adopt someone else's idea as much as any other politician could. But, owing to his innate ambition and deeply rooted vulnerability, Sheng resented anyone talking about his frailties. As he climbed closer to the pinnacle of power in the party, he wanted people around him to think that he was special. He must appear to be brilliant all the time, destined to be their unchallenged leader. From his initial subconscious attempts to make others perceive him in the best possible light, Sheng gradually started to believe in the persona he had created, assuming that he was truly special.

Convinced he was always right and felt entitled to wield his power, Sheng would only allow others to remember what he wanted them to remember. If Dong remained in a high position in the party, he would be able to expose the convoluted happenings and murky events of this period, which mixed many communist leaders' great successes with their humiliating failures, their visionary policies with their political expediency.

But this must never happen. For the sake of his political future, Sheng felt that he must find a way to cover up all his share of failures and half-baked policies. The best way to do that was to blame all the fiascos on someone else, and the fall of the West Army presented him with a perfect opportunity. He could blame Dong and the Second Front Army for all the mistakes, and Sheng's associates, who wanted to cover their own backs, would gladly help him to accomplish that dirty task. If Sheng was always right, someone else must always be wrong. If he had to manipulate the truth and twist the facts to accomplish that, so be it. Dong was but a pawn and minor inconvenience in Sheng's road to power, to be discarded at any moment should the latter's political needs required it.

It was a sad situation that a political party could not tolerate dissenting voices from within. Even though the Chinese Communist Party had risen against enormous odds fighting against its formidable enemies from without, it had produced no theory, no foundation, no mechanism, no experience, and no vision to allow for disagreements from within.

9

The only one who felt some degree of remorse was Xia-Hou. He remained friendly with Dong, even though he never told the latter about his role in the fake telegram to lure his comrade back to the party's fold.

Xia-Hou, a loyal and obedient party member with no military experience, was later rewarded with one of the highest positions in the Red Army. Yet, poor health compelled him to retire, and he died a few years later. As Xia-Hou had promised, he never disclosed the truth to anyone about his involvement in the party's most daring political conspiracy; he took the secret to his grave.

At Xia-Hou's funeral, Sheng was one of the pallbearers leading the procession—an emphatic show of respect and gratitude that he would never bestow on any of his closest associates for the rest of his life.

The end of the West Army was not the end of the Second Front Army. As the Red Army expanded manifold for the next twenty years, more than one-third of the bravest soldiers, the most brilliant field commanders, and the most decorated military officers among all the communist forces would come from the rump of the Second Front Army.

Chapter 22

Reconciliation

1

T HE DEMISE OF THE WEST ARMY INFURIATED STALIN, WHO BEGAN to have doubts about Sheng Bao's ability. He had for a long time questioned the viability of a Chinese communist movement composed mostly of rural peasants instead of urban proletarians. And now the Chinese communists had failed to create a safe path for Russian aid to arrive in China. Was the Chinese Communist Party really a Marxist one? Or simply a group of backwoods rebels who claimed to be Marxists and Leninists? Did they truly want to follow the Comintern's lead? Or simply wanted to take advantage of the political and financial support the Soviet Union provided? Recently, several messengers from China assured the Comintern that the Chinese Red Army, led by Tao Yin-Hu and Sheng, was making significant progress. Therefore, the Seventh International Congress of the Comintern lavished praises on Sheng, whose portrait, the only one from an Asian country, was hung on a big stage with other well-known European leaders of the organization in Moscow.

But if Sheng could not handle such a small task of clearing a transport passage, how could he and the Chinese Communist Party handle more serious challenges? Stalin, who had been facing many domestic and international pressures lately, could not afford another failure like this. He decided to call in Chamberlain for a discussion.

2

Like his archrival Dong Zi-Tian, Sheng also feared Stalin and the Comintern.

Long before the Long March started, the Comintern had instructed the Chinese communists to move ahead and build new red bases in those regions in Northern China that were close to the Soviet Union. However, during the initial phase of the Long March and even after Sheng had replaced Mo Jia-Qi as one of the top party leaders at the meeting of Yi city, the Red Army took a different path—carving out territory, and settling down in every province they had entered across all the regions south of the Yangtze River.

This glaring inconsistency and the fear of Moscow's reprisal led the worried Chinese party leadership to insist on a northerly route during the second half of the Long March after they had crossed the Golden Dust River. Sheng was mindful that the Comintern still needed to approve the party meeting in Yi city and the legitimacy of its decisions, including the one on his promotion. Thus, the usually rebellious and highly opinionated Sheng was surprisingly subdued once he arrived in Northern Shaanxi. He tried to maintain a proper relationship with the Comintern, and to take every opportunity to show to Moscow that Stalin was his boss and he the faithful student and obedient disciple.

Luckily, Stalin had more urgent issues on his mind by this time and he did not push for the standard disciplinary actions to be imposed against Sheng and the Chinese Communist Party for their past transgressions. He needed their active participation in a changed environment, and how they would react to his direct orders would be the real yardstick to determine their self-proclaimed legitimacy.

To put it simply, in so far as the Eurasian giant Soviet Union was concerned, what had changed in the years following the Great Depression were the aggressive actions of Hitler's Nazi Germany to her west and a rising militarist Japan to her east. Stalin was trying all he could to avoid fighting on both fronts, and he could not achieve that goal without the help of the Chinese on the East Front.

When vital national interests were at stake, partisan disputes and ideological differences had to take a back seat. Governed by this fundamental *realpolitik*, Stalin emphatically overhauled the Comintern's international policies. Class struggle must now yield to national survival. Worldwide proletarian revolution must now be substituted by the united and popular front, which should include all classes and people of all walks of life who were willing to take part in the fight against worldwide fascism. The lofty but distant goal of communism must now be subordinated to the most immediate need of protecting the Soviet Union—the first successful socialist country and the gleaming hope for a future communist utopia.

For the moment, the Soviet Union's military was not ready to defend the nation's extended borders and to fight two wars simultaneously against Germany from the west and Japan in the east. The Russians needed time to build up their armed forces and Stalin decided to appease Hitler in Europe as much as possible, while avoiding any military confrontations with Japan in Asia as long as he could.

3

The intense rivalry between Russia and Japan over Northeast China, called Manchuria by many Westerners, went back at least thirty years earlier when the first Russo-Japanese War broke out in 1904. Japanese aggression in this area picked up speed again long before World War II started in Europe. Japan invaded and occupied Manchuria in 1931, attacked Shanghai in 1932, annexed China's Jehol Province in 1933, supported the Mongolian separatist movement in Chahar and Suiyuan provinces in 1935, and signed the Anti-Comintern Pact with Hitler's Germany in 1936. All these acts of aggression threw China into an unprecedented national crisis and created a serious threat for the Soviet Union, especially on her left flank.

If the Chinese Red Army, now in North China, could become a part of the resistance force against the Japanese aggression, the Soviet Union would surely benefit. Sending supplies to the Chinese Communist Party and helping it to strengthen the Red Army was part of the strategy. At the same time, Stalin did not want such activities getting too close to the Mongolia–Russia–China borders, which might give the Japanese troops adjacent to that region an excuse to retaliate against the Russians.

Under these circumstances, Stalin changed his mind and redirected the Chinese communists to receive aid not via the Mongolian border, but from Xinjiang Province in the far west, which was well over two thousand miles away from the Russo-Japanese rivalry in the Far East.

But the mission's failure greatly disappointed Stalin, who drafted a stern telegram that was sent to the Chinese Communist Party by the Comintern. It read,

Dear Comrades:

The recent failure of the West Army is a tragic event. We regret your inability to carry out this important mission you had promised to accomplish. It is inconsistent with your impressive record of success in the past, and a huge blow to the cause of the international revolution of the proletariat. We are looking into alternative solutions provided by other parties while considering whether to stop sending future aid to you if you believe the present situation is beyond your capacity to resolve.

The Executive Committee of the
Communist International (E.C.C.I.)

The Chinese party's Politburo immediately summoned an emergency meeting to discuss its response. The depressing message from Moscow stunned everybody, and no one wanted to be the first to talk. They looked around and laid their eyes on Sheng, the one who often had a solution in many helpless situations.

Sheng was reading an old newspaper, not entirely interested in the topic. Xi-Tu Wen-Liang attempted to engage him by offering him a cigarette, and Sheng's face lit up. "Wow, Three Castles! You have this kind of good stuff at this hour? Where did you get it?"

Everyone knew Sheng had maintained a puritanical lifestyle. He did not touch any liquor and drank only common household tea. A farmer's simple meal of steamed rice with some hot peppers was all he needed and always enjoyed. His only luxury was smoking. Not necessarily cigarettes: raw tobacco leaves would satisfy him immensely. Even when he obtained some cigarettes, especially the good ones, he would save them to entertain his guests at another time, just as most frugal and yet hospitable peasants would.

Now he gladly lit the cigarette, and said, "He is bluffing."

His colleagues were baffled. "Who? Why? How do you know?" one of them asked.

"Stalin must have drafted the telegram and he is bluffing," Sheng calmly answered.

Not an assiduous student of European history or someone who was seriously interested in any foreign culture, Sheng never went overseas like many of the top party officials did. He did read some biographies, and was a great admirer of many well-known Western rulers and leaders from Alexander, Caesar, Napoleon, Washington, and Lincoln to Peter the Great and Bismarck. He appreciated their ambitions, adored their political skills, and respected their military attainments. Most of all, he shared with them a proud nationalist spirit and an unconventional vision for the world. Standing in front a world map, Sheng could picture what might be going through Stalin's mind more easily than any of his colleagues. If that were called geopolitics, as the experts would say, he would assume the role of a great player intuitively. So inclined to think big and so accustomed to strategic planning that he could instinctively tell what must have troubled Stalin.

"The Russians are not yet ready for war, and Stalin does not want to fight Japan and Germany at the same time," explained Sheng.

"But why did he blame us for being unable to fulfill such an impossible task?" asked a perplexed comrade.

"That's because he needs us," Sheng responded confidently.

"You really think so?" another comrade echoed the doubts of those present.

"Who else in this region, in China, can help Stalin? The local warlords? Or General Chen? There are no 'other parties' and no 'alternative solutions' except for us, the communists. Stalin needs us as much as we need him," Sheng concluded firmly.

"Okay, so that's why you think the Comintern is bluffing. But how do we respond?" asked an associate, who like the rest of party officials was still reluctant to mention Stalin by name when the international organization could serve as an appropriate substitute.

The pleasant aroma from the fine-cut bright Virginia tobacco intoxicated Sheng, who had not had a chance to enjoy the taste of the well-known British brand Three Castles for a long time. Holding the cigarette he had been relishing, a few puffs of smoke came out of his mouth as Sheng got down to work. A few minutes later, an upbeat and spirited telegram was drafted. It read,

> Esteemed Comrades of the E.C.C.I.:
> We mourn the loss of the West Army as much as anyone, and regret the unfinished business deeply. But we shall never be deterred by this minor setback and will accomplish any tasks the E.C.C.I. assigns to us as completely and successfully in the future as we have done in the past. The Chinese Communist Party and our Red Army stand firmly with the Comintern and are as ready as anyone to defend our beloved Stalin and the glorious Soviet Union till the last drop of our blood.
> Any doubt of our resolve and any hesitation to trust our ability will be a grave mistake, because we don't believe there are any other people or party in China that are as both willing and able to fight for our beloved Stalin and the glorious Soviet Union as the Chinese Communist Party and our brave Red Army.
> Long live the Comintern!
> Long live the unity and solidarity of the proletarians worldwide!
> Long live the great Soviet Union!
> Long live our beloved great leader Comrade Stalin!
>   The Politburo of the Central Committee of
>   the Chinese Communist Party

"Is the language a little too strong?" someone asked.

"No. At this moment in history, Stalin wants to see a lion king, not a pathetic little lamb," Sheng responded positively as if he were Stalin's surrogate.

4

Fending off Stalin's melodramatic threat by sending a theatrical telegram was one thing; protecting the newly acquired red territory from General Chen's nasty extermination campaign was a different ball game altogether. Overwhelming in number and armaments, Chen's troops were tightening their grip daily even as the Red Army was running out of food, ammunition, and shelter. The party leadership must come up with a solution fast.

Both Sheng and Si-Tu knew that Dong and the Second Front Army used to have some secret communications with one of the local warlords in Northwest China, General Feng Zheng. In a clandestine pact, he and the Second Front Army had mutually agreed not to attack each other and to maintain a ceasefire for as long as conditions allowed. Largely because of this crucial accord, the Second Front Army avoided many unnecessary clashes and greatly expanded its size.

Sheng instructed Si-Tu to find out as quickly as possible who were involved in those negotiations, and whether the truce could be extended.

Si-Tu went to work and soon learned a funny story.

Like many of the rural poor in Shaanxi, poverty and desperation forced Feng into banditry when he was a teenager. His audacity and intelligence enabled him to rise through the ranks in a warlord's army, and he was later appointed commander of a provincial army corps. Irritable but patriotic, Feng did not want to fight in the civil war against the Red Army. Deeply disappointed that his request to confront the Japanese invaders was not granted, he was rumored to have said that he would make friends with anyone who would fight the Japanese, including the communists.

To prevent Feng from contacting the Red Army, Chen had appointed Officer Wu as an inspector, whose job was to supervise the operations of Feng's troops and stop any suspicious activities. The diligent Officer Wu always stayed with the troops day and night, which left Feng with no chance to meet the Red Army's representatives, even though he had tried to do so several times.

When news of the frustration reached the Second Front Army's Lieutenant Commissar Wei Hao-Qin, the latter decided to do something about it. His wife Han Ni was a superb folk artist, who could design and make a great variety of beautiful paper plants and flowers that would be mistaken for real ones at first glance. Wei then asked her to prepare some pretty paper-cut flowers to be used in his plan.

A few days later, Wu was told that a miracle had occurred—a dozen or so brilliant lotus flowers were blooming not on water but atop a giant tree. Intrigued by the extremely rare event, which had not happened in the area for a hundred years, Wu decided to go and have a look. Since his wife, several maids, and servants were equally excited, he allowed them to accompany him to watch this once in a lifetime sensation.

After a three-hour drive, Wu and his entourage finally stopped before an ancient tree, and their jaws dropped. For they saw a large bush of bright scarlet land lotus blooming on top of the old withered tree. Wu was so pleased with the "miracle" that he ordered his orderly to get his brush pen, ink, and paper. The excitement had unleashed the poet in him and he was not about to let such a miraculous moment pass without recording it down. As many literary geniuses had done in the past, he wanted to compose a worthy poem to commemorate this wonder. Choosing the most appropriate words and finding the right assonance took him a long while. But his wife and servants were applauding the end product of his labor, especially when a sumptuous meal with plenty of drinks was served, which continued till sunset.

By the time the exhausted team drove back to the army headquarters after watching and praising Han Ni's paper-cut flowers for hours, the peace agreement between Feng and the Second Front Army had been concluded.

The details of Si-Tu's story delighted Sheng. "A smart scheme," he said. Turning to business, he asked, "What are the terms of the agreement?"

"A mutual ceasefire and noninterference in each other's activities for as long as the political situation will allow," Si-Tu replied.

"Did Dong Zi-Tian and Wei Hao-Qin really trust the words of a warlord?" Sheng remained doubtful.

"General Feng Zheng gave them two valuable gifts to show his sincerity," Si-Tu explained.

"Sounds good," said Sheng, who was all ears.

"The first is a huge map of Northwest China, produced by the famous newspaper *China Weekly Review*. It is the first fine map of its kind printed by a Chinese company." Si-Tu paused and then added, "This is the same map that Staffer Lu Di-Ping took when we left the Second Front Army. It is now hung in your room."

"And the other gift?" An embarrassed Sheng changed the topic.

"A top-secret codebook used by General Chen's troops," Si-Tu answered.

"Oh, no wonder the Second Front Army was able to supply us with so much valuable intelligence while we were on the Long March." As one with great interest in secret codes, Sheng immediately understood how he and the First Front Army had benefited from the Second Front Army's successes.

"Yes, their intelligence was especially useful at the most pivotal moment when we were trying to figure out how to escape from the Yangtze River, Red River, and Golden Dust River regions," concurred Si-Tu, a longtime veteran in intelligence and covert operations.

"Do we know the contact who can link us up with General Feng? Is it possible for us to continue the informal alliance?" Sheng returned to his key concerns.

"Yes, we do. And I believe General Feng is willing to deal with us too."

"All right then, resume the peace talks with him as soon as possible."

5

The resumed peace talks produced some surprising results. To Sheng and Si-Tu's great delight, General Feng was no longer satisfied with just a ceasefire extension. He went further to propose a joint government with the Red Army and a "United Northwest Administration," which would be separate from General Chen's national government.

"I am sure you know something about this drastic change of stance," Sheng calmly told Si-Tu.

As one who hardly enjoyed micromanaging things, military actions excepted, Sheng knew Si-Tu was the perfect deputy to handle any assignment no matter how difficult or complicated it was. He was also aware that Si-Tu had built an extensive network of personal contacts over the years, which would serve him well under just about any circumstances. No one in the party including Sheng knew the exact size and extent of Si-Tu's network. Privately Sheng was leery that this massive network might give Si-Tu too much power and influence in the party. At the same time, he was willing to live with the situation as long as he was able to ascertain that Si-Tu was not interested in his job, and was contented to play second fiddle to Sheng. Besides, Sheng did not want to get his hands dirty. He was the leader and the strategist, and he would rather focus on the bigger and grander picture, not on the nuts and bolts of a tedious operation.

But once in a while—such as now—a curious Sheng would shoot a question or two at Si-Tu to test his honesty and loyalty.

"There is no trick. General Feng's new wife is a member of our party," Si-Tu responded matter-of-factly.

"That's all?" Sheng kept probing.

"General Feng's closest top aides and several high-ranking officers are our party members too," Si-Tu replied without divulging details.

Sheng sensed the resistance and realized he should stop asking for further details, which Si-Tu normally would not reveal for security reasons. But he could not resist asking one more question. "How many?"

A brief silence later, "Altogether, about twenty."

"Hmm," the boss responded. Was he impressed or was he displeased? Si-Tu was unable to tell. Sheng's broad face was calm but no one could tell for sure what he was thinking.

In any event, it was doubtlessly exciting news. If the Red Army and Feng's troops were to unite, they could control the vast territory in Northwest China, which would save the Red Army from the current danger. The alliance would instantly undermine Chen's extermination campaign by providing the Red Army with much-needed ammunition, food, and supplies, and by giving the communist forces access to a much larger and safer territory.

While the news might just be too good to be true, Sheng and Si-Tu wasted no time in reporting the progress to the Comintern and to seek its approval for the alliance.

The intelligence report, along with several telegrams from the Chinese Communist Party, lay on Stalin's desk. Initially he was quite amused by the professed loyalty and self-confidence the Chinese communists had demonstrated. Aides told him that, based on the writing style, they believed that Sheng must have drafted the telegram. Stalin liked what he was reading.

A strong man, Stalin was glad to have met his equal. Like Sheng, he relished tough competition both from within and without and would never retreat in the face of any challenge, no matter how formidable it might be. Reading between the lines, Stalin could see the pride, ambition, and indomitable spirit of a truepenny in remote China, which was exactly what he was looking for in times of a grave national emergency like the one the Soviet Union was facing.

But Stalin also knew that Sheng was simply trying to stay alive amid the ferocious extermination campaign waged by his archenemy General Chen. The survival of Sheng's party and that of Stalin's country were not the same thing. Different interests would create divergent paths and policies, and clashes between the two strong-willed men seemed to be all but unavoidable.

No sooner had Stalin finished reading the report than he instructed the Comintern to reject the Chinese communists' proposal for a United Northwest Administration. Such a sudden and drastic spill from the national government in China, he feared with good reasons, would probably entice the Japanese to use it as an excuse to expand the war into Northwest China. This area was too close to Russia and her ally Mongolia, where Stalin had tried very hard not to give Japan any pretext to invade.

Such a reaction surprised the members of the Chinese Communist Party's Politburo. Most of them had assumed that Stalin probably would be upset with Sheng's first ostentatious telegram but happy with his second, suggesting the possibility of a great alliance with a regional army led by Feng. What else would please Stalin, the great leader of the international proletarians, more than a huge expansion of the communist movement into Northwest China?

The arrogant but never naïve Stalin gave the Chinese the exact opposite reaction. In his book, a United Northwest Administration would escalate the ongoing civil war, and a totally disunited China wouldn't be able to resist Japanese aggression, which would only endanger the safety of the Soviet Union—the last thing Stalin wanted.

In his telegram to the Chinese Communist Party, Stalin urged its leaders to review the decisions passed at the Comintern's Seventh Congress. He also urged them to reread the August First Declaration, which he had approved. It reflected the Comintern's latest policies, and should serve as a guide for the Chinese communists to follow from now on. Read these documents, and read them carefully, he insisted.

6

In fact, the most important message Xia-Hou Dan had brought back from Moscow was for the Chinese Communist Party to understand that a united front must be formed in China to support and protect Stalin's Soviet Union.

All the final resolutions of the Comintern's Seventh Congress were related to that position, and nowhere was the message clearer than in the August First Declaration, which announced a grand program of ten new national policies approved by Stalin and the Comintern.

Sheng and all other party leaders went through the declaration several times. It was a powerful document. Sheng liked the vigorous and upbeat style of the document, which was fluid, eloquent, and passionately patriotic. Before reaching China, the declaration was translated and printed in several foreign languages including Russian and English. Sheng and Tao Yin-Hu signed the document and reissued it under their names in China several months after it was first printed in Moscow.

The only problem Sheng had with it was that the document's original author was Mo Jia-Qi—the person he had displaced at the meeting in Yi city. Now Sheng regretted allowing Mo and Gregory to return to Moscow after the meeting. He should have kept them in China, away from the Comintern and the Russians. A small miscalculation could lead to a big crisis. Once back in his power base, Mo resurrected his career. He quickly replaced the mediocre Song Pei as the head of the Chinese delegation to the Comintern.

Mo's bubbly personality, fluency in Russian and English, vast knowledge, and dynamism made him a Comintern favorite. Stalin liked this bright young man and perhaps could see him as China's leader in the future.

Out of job and out of favor, the deflated Song Pei left Moscow and embarked on the long journey back to the gloomy place called Northern Shaanxi.

The more Stalin and the Comintern liked Mo, the more troubled Sheng became. He did rise to be one of the party's powerful triumvirate and did gain significant influence in military affairs. Yet, by the expedient arrangement at the meeting of Yi city, Meng Bo-Xian was the head of the party and Si-Tu led the Group of Three, of which Sheng was an assistant to the group leader. Sheng exerted greater influence than others more because of his assertive personality than his official position.

When the Long March ended, the situation became awkward. Meng had the title, but not real power. Sheng enjoyed significant real power but did not have the official title he wanted. Keen to avoid the never-ending intraparty conflicts, Si-Tu avoided Sheng as much as possible by taking frequent road trips. But Sheng continued to feel vulnerable without Moscow's official backing. It did not escape him that the August First Declaration was originally publicized in Moscow under the name of the Central Committee of the Chinese Communist Party without his input or consent. Apparently, Moscow did not recognize him while Mo, the displaced party leader, could continue to craft policies and wield great power.

It was also clear to Sheng that Mo could do that, as well as ignore him, because Stalin and the Comintern knew Mo, who had been trained in Moscow, much better than the man from Boxwood.

What could one do when caught in a web of interwoven personal, political, and international power structures like these? Nothing much. All Sheng could do was to keep a safe distance from all of them, while recruiting more of his own followers wherever and whenever possible. A long-term strategist and skillful politician, Sheng was also an astute student of personality. He knew that Stalin was a highly suspicious man, who did not entirely trust him or Mo. Instincts told Sheng that like all politicians, Stalin was a practical man who would only recognize the one with real power in China. Thus, whoever possessed the strongest military force would ultimately receive Stalin's official recognition.

7

The failure to form the United Northwest Administration did little to dampen the patriotic fervor of General Feng, who found a kindred spirit in another young militarist, General Zhang Wu.

The eldest son of General Zhang Wei, Zhang Wu had long been designated as the heir to his father, who had once commanded the largest regional army in China. Zhang Wei, a former horse thief, ruled Northeast China with an iron hand. In the area where local bandits, the Japanese, the Russians, the disposed Manchurian royals, and Chen's national government had been competing for dominance, the father's cunning tactics and deft maneuvers had enabled him to maintain the independence of his forces and equilibrium among his enemies. But his unwillingness to collaborate with the Japanese Guandong Army, stationed in the region, led to his assassination. Zhang Wei died after several Japanese officers blew up the train he was on.

Son Zhang Wu, now 27, switched allegiance to Chen's national government. But he failed to protect his soldiers and the local population when the Guandong Army stormed his headquarters. Zhang Wu ordered a total withdrawal from the region without a fight, and since then had been carrying the guilt of a spineless traitor who had surrendered Northeast China to the Japanese, and whose failure to protect millions of innocent people had shamed the whole nation.

Eager to redeem himself and disappointed by General Feng's failure to form an alliance with the Red Army, Zhang Wu shared his frustrations with Feng. The two then decided to take matters into their own hands.

When Chen came to supervise the extermination campaign and inspect his troops in Shaanxi's capital city Sian, soldiers under the two men's command raided General Chen's residence in the suburbs, and held him hostage on the night of December 12, 1936. They declared they had no intention of harming the commander-in-chief, but did hope to persuade Chen to stop the civil war and unite all Chinese military forces to defend the country against the Japanese invasion.

The explosive event stunned China and half of the world.

8

Without its top leader, the national government in the capital city of Nanjing in Southeast China immediately split into two factions. A group of generals wanted to form an expedition army, marching toward Sian to rescue the commander-in-chief by force.

The plan terrified Madam Chen, who knew that any hasty action would further endanger her husband. If he was not already dead in the mutineers' hands, any reckless move would force them to kill him in a flash. She insisted on seeking a peaceful solution to the crisis, and was willing to board the first flight available to meet with her husband's adversaries.

The international community was also alarmed.

The United States government suggested caution and was willing to provide air transportation and communication support for any peaceable solution that satisfied all parties.

In Moscow, Stalin believed that the Chen kidnaping was another Japanese plot since a Japanese news agency was the first to report it. He was deeply worried that the hostage crisis could escalate into an all-out war at the worst time for him, and in the last place he would want to see a conflict. He decided to act immediately.

The hostage himself, president and General Chen, was furious. He had hurt his ribs and an ankle in his haste to hide during the raid. But his physical pain was nowhere near the psychological trauma and emotional anguish he had suffered. The legitimacy and dignity of his office was challenged, and he felt personally humiliated by being made prisoner by his subordinates. Throughout Chinese history, no crime was more hideous than any rebellion against the state's sovereign, whose absolute authority had been worshiped more than any other secular power or ecclesiastical institution. To rebel against him was tantamount to patricide, turning the entire foundation of Chinese society upside down.

"These bastards, they must pay! They must pay for this most reprehensible and heinous crime!" the livid Chen vowed to himself even as he remained their captive.

9

In the days following the hostage incident, the Chinese communists went through an emotional rollercoaster that they had never experienced before.

Incredulous was their initial reaction when the news first broke out. Most thought it was a mistake or a hoax. Several telegrams and confirmations later, euphoria erupted. At long last their mortal foe, the archenemy, the bloodthirsty vampire, and the brazen monster was captured. He was the butcher who had slaughtered hundreds of thousands of communists, Red Army soldiers, their family members, and their innocent neighbors. It was payback time. Thank heavens, General Chen had now been captured. Put him on trial, and sentence him to death, or let him rot in jail, but never allow him to escape this time— such were the rank and file sentiments, which were shared by Sheng Bao and other high-ranking party officials. At a big gathering of several hundred party activists, Sheng told them, "Chen Han must face trial. We will hold a public trial and he shall be brought before the court in Northern Shaanxi. He must pay for all the crimes he had committed in the last ten years!"

But a telegram from Moscow changed everything.

So unequivocal was Stalin's message that Sheng and the others were initially left speechless. Tao Yin-Hu was pacing up and down the room, scratching his head, and growling like a trapped bobcat. Only a day earlier he had learned the news and screamed, "Bravo! Kill him off! What good can be said of him? Tell the two generals immediately that the first thing to do is to kill Chen Han." Now, after reading the telegram, Tao looked like someone who had lost his soul.

The normally aloof Sheng cried out, "Everything's gone crazy. Topsy-turvy, heaven and earth have turned upside down! What will the two generals think of us if we were to reverse our support for their actions in such a short period?"

Meng Bo-Xian picked up the telegram and read it again. Yes, he thought, it would be tough to explain this one-hundred-and-eighty-degree change to anyone, given the excitement and high expectations that the incident had generated earlier.

The telegram stated:

Moscow is adamantly against the actions taken in the incident. General Chen must be kept unharmed. A peaceful solution must be found, which should guarantee a united front under General Chen's central government. The most important task for the Communist Party is to avoid a civil war. No one in China, neither General Zhang Wu nor anyone else in the Chinese Communist Party, has the same authority and ability to lead the nation in fighting against the Japanese as president and General Chen has. To find a peaceful solution to this crisis and to save General Chen from any harm will be the most critical first step in establishing a united front in China. The Chinese Communist Party must realize the vital importance of this moment, and must do all it can to push for a peaceful resolution of this incident.

The message was crystal clear—Chen should not be put on trial or punished in any way. Instead, both the two generals, Feng and Zhang, and the communists had to submit themselves to Chen, who would remain the sole national leader of all the Chinese resistance forces.

Sheng and the Politburo did not seem to have any choice. They must obey Stalin's orders or they would have to break away from the Comintern completely. They knew they could never do that because they needed the Russian military and financial support as much as they needed Moscow's political and ideological guidance.

"But ten years ago," Meng recalled, "Stalin had also told us to be patient with the nationalists and to trust General Chen. We all know what happened next. The brute killings in Shanghai and afterward ten years of bloodshed and relentless attacks on our forces and people. Can we ever trust him again even if we are willing to follow the Comintern's instructions?"

"A good question. Can we?" one said as others nodded their heads in agreement.

"I beg to differ," Sheng said as he joined the conversation. "Comrade Meng Bo-Xian has raised a very good question, and Stalin seems to have sent us the same command for the second time in our history. Can we ever trust Chen Han? No, no one, I believe, is naïve enough to think so. Comrade Meng Bo-Xian is right, and I think we have learned from the bloody experiences of the past. However, I consider the situation today to be quite different from ten years ago."

"Ten years ago," he continued, "we did not have an army but relied totally on the Northern Expedition troops controlled by the Nationalist Party and General Chen. Today, we have several army corps and plenty of skills, knowledge, and experience in building our own bases in the countryside, which can help us to expand our military forces in the future. We also have the highly valuable and extensive experience from the antiextermination campaigns and especially from our Long March. Our party and our army have learned a lot and grown a lot. We are much stronger today than ever. We are no longer a child. We are no longer as easily fooled as in the past."

Sheng sipped some water and stood up. "Most of all, our goal ten years ago was to reunite the divided country after the fall of the Qing Dynasty. Today, we are facing the unprecedented national crisis of becoming a colony of the Japanese imperialists. I think Stalin is right that we must unite under one national leader. We can't afford to prolong the civil war, or we will all become Japan's slaves."

"To form the united front and to recognize General Chen's role as the national leader is to defeat the Japanese invaders, not to give up the independence of our party or to surrender our army entirely to the nationalists. We shall firmly control our party and our military forces, and we shall continue to grow larger and stronger than ever in the days ahead."

"I must confess that I was confused and disappointed while reading the telegram for the first time. But after much thought, I think I can see great hope and opportunity in this moment of darkness. I fully support Stalin's message, which has shown us not only the right way to solve the crisis but also the right approach to ensure our success in the long run."

Sheng's upbeat speech encouraged his colleagues. After further discussions, they unanimously agreed to carry out Stalin's orders. While reporting the meeting's decision back to the Comintern, the Politburo also wired Si-Tu, the head of the communist delegation to Sian, instructing him to handle the negotiations there according to Moscow's instructions.

10

The insistence of Madam Chen, the pressure from the international community, Stalin's orders, and Si-Tu's diplomacy all contributed toward resolving the hostage incident peacefully. General Chen agreed to stop the civil war, and the Communist Party agreed to reorganize the Red Army troops under his command to form a united front against the Japanese aggressors.

General Chen returned to Nanjing safely. But he never forgave the two culprits who had threatened his life and authority. Zhang was put under house arrest for the rest of his life, while Feng was arrested and later executed in prison.

Surprisingly, the smallest and weakest player, the Chinese Communist Party, benefited the most from this unprecedented national crisis, and would soon expand greatly, just as Sheng had predicted.

Chapter 23

Darkness

1

POVERTY. HOPELESS POVERTY.

No one would understand what poverty really meant until he came face to face with the deprived population of the desolate Northern Shaanxi, where lifeless brown overwhelmed the barren landscape full of sorrow and misery.

When Dong Zi-Tian arrived in the small county of Pangolin to start his new assignment, he was shocked to see half-starved villagers hiding in their cave dwellings. A few frail and sullen men roamed the dirty streets like ghosts, while most stayed at home, especially the women, for there were not enough pants in the family for everybody to wear. Repeated drought and meager harvest yielded a lamentable amount of millet, corn, and buckwheat to fill the stomach for no more than six months, and begging was the common remedy for the rest of the year. Large-scale panhandling was thus a seasonal activity everywhere, making its appearance at a particular time of the year, just like the lunar holidays. Once the food shortage started each year, throngs of beggars would swarm every human habitat within sight, grab anything remotely edible—from leaves and household garbage to leftovers and pig feed—and stuff them in their pants, pockets, and sacks.

Dong thought his childhood was miserable enough, and hunger and deprivation had never been strangers to a lad growing up in South China. But at least fresh water was available in his hometown, while wild berries, mushrooms, and bamboo sprouts could be found in the thick bushes covering the Blue Mountains, and small fish and crabs between the rocks at the bottom of giggling streams, shy creeks, and idle ponds. Apart from the deserts, he had never known any place as arid and scorched as Northern Shaanxi, where precipitation in the best years amounted to a few inches—not enough rainfall for crops or anything else. If the neighborhood had a well of one hundred and fifty feet deep, its people would consider themselves lucky, even if the water looked muddy and tasted bitter. Some villagers had to get up at midnight to walk for miles to fetch one bucket of drinking water, because all the streams and water sources in their vicinity had dried up. Raindrops were collected and saved in pots, jars, vats, pails, and woks. People would use the top part of the collected water, and farm animals would drink the bottom part with silt. No man ever washed his face, nobody ever brushed his teeth, and no girl would ever take a bath until the day before her wedding. The place was so harsh, so poor, and so miserable for anyone that few girls would want to marry a local boy, with most of them hoping to escape somewhere far away as soon as possible.

"Drought every three years and a big disaster every five," as the locals would say about their predicament. Compounding these natural calamities were incessant fears of brutal harassment and savage attacks by bandits, which could happen at any time. Banditry was rampant across China, and nowhere was the problem worse than Northwest China, especially Northern Shaanxi. The instability of national politics, frequent changes of local government, corruption of public officials, recurring civil wars, endless famine, and natural disasters had plagued the area for decades and allowed violence and lawlessness to grow unchecked.

Highway robbers, discharged veterans, disgruntled officers, runaway debtors, unemployed laborers, thieves, reckless gamblers, rogues, opium addicts, the homeless, and even some middle-class members, such as small landlords and the educated, joined the bandits, who hid in the deep mountains during the day, and came out to plunder at night. With their bizarre long robes, short shirts, sheep skin overcoats, or military uniforms in different colors and shapes, no one would think that the bandits could fight. Nor would anyone believe that they could fight effectively, considering their antiquated weapons—from broad blades, sharp lances, and thick shields made of oxen hide from their grandfathers' generation to the assorted German rifles and Russian pistols.

But the bandits, on horseback and armed with insider's intelligence, were always well prepared to pounce on their prey, and their swift action and total secrecy ensured their frequent success. Kidnapping someone and demanding ransom was their specialty, and they would never hesitate to torture and execute any hostage whose family did not comply with their demands. Those who were forced into banditry by their circumstances believed that this was their only option: it was either starve to death or loot to live. They were also fed up with corrupt officials, social injustice, and the privileged few who never cared about the poor and the underdogs. In their eyes, robbing the haves to help the have-nots was a way to right the wrongs.

Repeated violence, mobs of bandits, bloodshed, lawlessness, fear, and instability.

Repeated drought, endless crop failures, abject poverty, mass starvation, and hopeless existence.

No matter where he turned and looked, Dong was faced with a daunting situation. His assignment required him not only to overcome those difficulties to survive but also to raise money, collect foodstuff and clothing, and purchase supplies for the expansion of the Red Army. Could there be any tougher assignment than this?

2

More than two years before World War II started in Europe in the fall of 1939, Japan had launched a full-scale attack on China. Long prepared for the final push after invading Northeast China six years earlier, Japan believed that it would not need more than three months to bring China to its knees.

General Chen instructed his foreign minister to tell Japan that the Chinese government and troops would never yield. The Chinese army would resist any Japanese aggression till the end.

He also told the troops in North China that his central government was determined to do all it could to protect the country. "We'd rather die in glory than live in dishonor, or be a shattered vessel of jade than an unbroken piece of pottery," he said, "in defending the dignity of our country and people."

Ten days after the infamous Marco Polo Bridge Incident, Chen made his stand clear in a speech at a national council meeting at Lu Mountain. Soon publicized as a declaration, he declared, "We will strive to maintain peace, if peace is still possible till the last second. But we will fight to the end to defend our country, if war is forced upon us.

"We are a weak country," he acknowledged, "and we will only survive this crisis if we are willing to fight till the end. We can't stop in the middle of the conflict, which will mean surrender. And surrender will lead to the demise of our nation. All Chinese must be clear that this is the moment when we must decide our fate. If we decide to fight, we must be prepared to accept all the sacrifices. Only when we are willing and determined to make all the sacrifices can we sustain the fight till we emerge victorious.

"Once the war starts," he went on, "there will be no division between the north and the south, no difference between the old and the young. No matter who you are, every Chinese has the duty to defend our country till the end of the war, no matter what it will cost us."

Easier said than done.

At the moment, many Chinese knew that the resistance would come at a cost. But no one could imagine that the war would ultimately take away the lives of more than twenty million Chinese, one of the highest, if not the highest, casualties in World War II.

Many Chinese also knew that the road to victory would be long and hard. But few would imagine that China would have to endure eight years of unbelievable hardship, suffering, and sacrifices until Japan finally surrendered, which marked the official end to World War II.

3

How to fight the fully prepared and well-equipped Japanese aggressors?

Many high-ranking officers and governmental officials advised Chen to focus on the north, which sounded logical because the Japanese army had started its attacks from that direction.

General Bai Yu-Xian, one of Chen's most fearsome political rivals, disagreed. He suggested striking the Japanese in Shanghai while reinforcing the Chinese troops in the north.

"Engaging the enemy on two fronts? Shouldn't this be something we should avoid now, because we are weak and the Japanese are strong?" Most generals disagreed with his proposal.

"Reality and geography. Generals, reality and geography." Bai seemed to have anticipated the questions. One of the shortest but most intelligent men in the room, he went on to explain, "The well-equipped Japanese have deployed as many as thirty to forty divisions, or six hundred to eight hundred thousand men, to attack us. They would like to finish the battle as soon as possible because Japan is a country with limited resources and manpower," Bai said.

"We have a vast territory and a huge population. But our armies are poorly trained, and we do not have the same mechanized divisions, a strong air force, and a powerful fleet as the Japanese have."

"We must not expect to stop the Japanese aggression right away. We need to prepare for the long haul, which will include a period of prolonged tug of war initially until we can turn the tide," he added.

"Fighting a two-front war seems counterintuitive in the short run, given our current military condition. But, if it stretches our resources, it will also stretch that of the Japanese army even more. Therefore, the more we can exhaust the enemy, the faster we can achieve our victory. Besides, North China is mostly plains, which will be extremely difficult to defend. If the enemy were to break our defense lines, Central China and the Yangtze River regions—the richest parts of our nation—would be totally exposed to their attacks. If we do not divert their attention and reduce their military strength now, we will give them the opportunity later to invade and attack the heart of China with their overwhelming force," Bai explained at length.

Suddenly, people realized that he had a point and his suggestion was not as outlandish as it had first appeared.

The discussions continued and people debated about the pros and cons of his plan. They could not draw any conclusion and the meeting was adjourned. Chen said he would consider all the views carefully and make his final decision the next day.

4

Following negotiations for the communists to participate in the united front, Chen allowed them to reorganize the Red Army into official divisions under the national government. Several thousand red soldiers in South China formed the Fourth Army. Those in North China formed the Eighth Army, which comprised the army headquarters, three divisions, and local affiliates, totaling forty-five thousand men.

"The united front is a huge achievement and a big step forward in the right direction in the struggle against Japanese aggression. But never forget," Sheng Bao warned his colleagues, "General Chen never really trusts us, nor can we him. We must remain vigilant and never lose control of our army."

Speaking to the troops that were about to march to the front lines, Sheng reminded the officers and soldiers again, "First of all, your most important task is to fight the Japanese invaders. But don't forget for a minute that you are the troops of the Communist Party. You also have the responsibility of spreading our message and more importantly of increasing the size of our army and expanding the number of our bases."

Amid the excitement over the great national resistance movement, several senior members and officers of the party, including Tao Yin-Hu, Si-Tu Wen-Liang, Yao Xi-Wa, and Bao Feng-Nian, urged the party to adopt swift action. Sheng resisted the idea and insisted that the small Fourth and Eighth Armies were in no position to confront the huge Japanese invading force directly. These communist troops could only play a secondary role in the government's campaigns. Familiar with Chen's military strategies, Sheng also remained skeptical whether the government's plans for pitched battles in positional warfare could work. He therefore took extra care not to allow the Communist Party's few precious divisions to participate in any large campaigns designed by General Chen, insisting that the party should have full control over its Fourth and Eighth Armies.

Throughout the war, Sheng never lost sight of what he truly wanted—which was not only to drive the Japanese invaders out of the country but also to replace Chen as China's ruling party. For that ultimate goal, he needed to protect, preserve, and expand the small number of his communist troops. Fighting against the Japanese gave him the perfect cover to do so since he could select which military campaigns he wanted the Red Army to participate in, while minimizing losses in the battles.

5

Japan focused on North China, believing that the Soviet Union was its potentially worst enemy, while Northeast China, now under the puppet government of Manchuria, was its most valuable possession.

More than seven hundred miles away from the Marco Polo Bridge in Peking's suburbs, the Chinese troops' attacks on Japanese soldiers in Shanghai surprised the Japanese government, and its imperial navy quickly got involved.

General Chen's original plan was to eliminate the three thousand Japanese marines and to destroy the Japanese fleet in the Yangtze River by a preemptive strike. Unfortunately, the plan was leaked and the Japanese fleet withdrew to international waters. The tenacious resistance of the marines reversed the early gains made in the initial stage of the Chinese attack. The anticipated surgical operation turned into a lengthy campaign.

The national government sent eighty regiments of over eight hundred thousand soldiers into the area, while the Japanese army deployed eight divisions and two brigades of some three hundred thousand men. The battle lasted for three months. The massive network of Japanese intelligence operatives combed the region and found a stretch of a thinly guarded coastal area some forty miles from the city. When the newly formed 10th Corps of the Japanese army, totaling some one hundred and twenty thousand men, landed there, the confidence of the Chinese troops was greatly shaken. The defense of the city collapsed a few days later, and Chen ordered a general withdrawal.

6

To cover the rear of the withdrawing troops, a battalion of soldiers, led by Officer Xie Jin-Yuan, remained behind to set a defense in a cement structure called Four-Bank Building. With the help of local citizens, the four hundred soldiers, claiming to be eight hundred to outsiders, withstood the Japanese attack for a week. A schoolgirl named Young Hui-Min later hung the national flag at the top of the building. Reports and pictures of the flag splashed in newspapers the next day created a national sensation. The locals cheered, "Long Live the Republic of China!" One newspaper wrote, "Our troopers are using the last bullet, the last drop of blood to stop the enemies. No one including angels in heaven will not be moved by their heroic actions. What they are doing will go down in the annals of our history as the greatest act of resistance."

Nearly one hundred thousand Japanese died and nearly a quarter of a million Chinese soldiers were either killed or wounded, including fifteen generals among the dead.

This was the first but not the last battle in which thousands upon thousands of Chinese government troops from common soldiers to high-ranking officers would make the ultimate sacrifice to defend the country.

7

Panic struck the nation's capital, Nanjing, which, lying on the same flat land of the Lower Yangtze, was less than two hundred miles away from Shanghai.

Seeking a safe shelter, the government soon moved to Chongqing in Sichuan, where the high mountains of the Southwest provided protection.

But Nanjing's citizens and soldiers were not so lucky. At least two hundred thousand of them were slaughtered, including many buried alive, after the Japanese troops sacked the city a month later. So barbaric were the Japanese atrocities that the Nanjing Massacre became one of the darkest pages in human history.

8

North China failed to defend itself. East China was under attack. Central China was in crisis.

By ten months into the war, China had lost a series of major cities including Peking, Tianjin, Tanggu, Jinan, Qingdao, Shanghai, Nanjing, and Xuzhou. The prevailing mood across the nation was as depressing as it could be.

The country badly needed a victory, and General Chen believed it could be achieved in Wuhan—the country's second largest city next to Shanghai and the commercial hub of Central China. In a broadcasted speech he told the nation and the world, "The Chinese people and government are forced to fight. The Japanese aggressors have left us with no choice. We must fight and we are determined to defend Wuhan to the end."

To stall Japan's mechanized troops coming down from the Northern Plains, Chen ordered his forces to blow off the levees of the Yellow River. The ensuing deluge ruined the lives of thousands of rural families who were caught off guard. But the roaring water flooded all the roads within three hundred miles, which delayed the movement of the Japanese troops for several months.

With the northern route full of mud and water, the enemy decided to sail along the Yangtze and attack Wuhan from the east. The Chinese troops planted hundreds of mines in the river and staunchly defended the forts along the banks. The relentless attacks and the use of poison gas by the Japanese forces broke several key defenses, and the battles continued.

As the situation became increasingly bleak, General Pan Jin from the southeast front had some good news to report. His five divisions and seven brigades of government troops trapped the 106th Corps of the Japanese Army, who had initially intended to surprise Pan from the rear. Time and again they tried to break Pan's firm grip of the area, only to have him hanging on even tighter to it each time. Desperate, the top Japanese commander of the Wuhan theater ordered two hundred officers and soldiers to be airlifted to the area to rescue their compatriots. The reinforcement troops were shot as they parachuted from the aircraft and none touched the ground alive. The week-long battle at a place called Ominous Propensity, named after a cluster of small but heavily wooded mountains, left more than ten thousand Japanese soldiers dead and almost annihilated the 106th Corps. It was one of the most devastating defeats the Japanese army suffered during the war.

As many as fifty army corps of one hundred and thirty divisions of government troops participated in the defense of Wuhan. Japan mobilized two hundred and fifty thousand troops, one hundred and twenty gunships, and three hundred planes for the offensive. After more than a hundred battles across four provinces in four months, the Japanese forces closed in on the suburbs of Wuhan and began their push for a final assault on the city from the north, east, and south.

Realizing that he risked losing his prime troops, Chen ordered them to evacuate the city. Built on the broad and open riverbanks, Wuhan offered hardly any natural defense—and another major city soon fell to the Japanese.

But the momentum of Japan's aggression had been broken, and the idea that China could be conquered in a few months proved to be wrong. As China demonstrated that it could put up a good fight, Japan was faced with the prospect of a grueling and protracted war, which the latter could ill-afford.

9

Amid the constant stream of bad news, humiliating failures, pervasive pessimism, countless tragedies, and horrendous sufferings, there were some bright spots.

After the Japanese forces occupied Northeast China a decade ago, the national government realized that North China would become its next target. To prevent the country's national treasures from the pillage of the Japanese army, the national government decided to ship the most valuable paintings, calligraphy, bronze and porcelain artifacts, and other precious antiques from the Forbidden City in Peking to a safe place out of the Japanese invaders' reach.

On the night of February 5, 1933, the city of Peking was under curfew and no one was allowed on the streets. Under the heavy protection of armed soldiers and police, about a hundred wagons left the Forbidden City and headed straight to the train station. Two trains, with two thousand crates of the treasures on board, then made their way to the south. The final destination was not even revealed to the man in charge of the packing until he was on the train.

Escorted by cavalry units along the way and guarded by soldiers with machine guns on board, the trains made no stop except for refueling. It was a nerve-racking journey, and the small team of official escorts were fully aware of the great responsibility entrusted to them, and the huge risk they were taking. Roaming warlords and armed bandits were everywhere. If they had any information of what was on the train and decided to strike, none of the government escorts would remain alive to protect the invaluable national treasures that had been collected over the centuries.

Fortunately, the trains arrived in Shanghai safely and four more shipments were made in subsequent months. All told, nineteen thousand, five hundred and fifty-seven crates of treasures found new homes for the next four years. A collection of nine hundred and eighty-four artifacts even went on display in England during the International Exhibition of Chinese Art held by the Royal Academy of Arts for three months between late 1935 and 1936. A selection of eighty was shown at Burlington House in London, creating a huge public sensation among visitors who praised their exquisite beauty, remarkable craftsmanship, and distinctive historic significance.

The excitement over the exhibition's success was quickly replaced by fear and terror when the Marco Polo Bridge Incident broke out. Some of the treasures had recently been moved to the capital city, Nanjing, for safekeeping. Now neither Shanghai nor Nanjing was safe, and these artifacts had to be transported once again somewhere far away from the conflict zone.

Despite the wartime chaos, confusion, and extreme shortage of money and manpower, the government managed to organize a grand scheme to transport and safeguard the treasures of Chinese civilization.

The plan divided the whole project into three components: the first one would take land transportation and go deep down to the remote Southwest China, the second one would sail along the Yangtze to Sichuan, and the third would travel by land to Shaanxi. A team of seven to nine people was assigned for each route, and all swore to protect the national treasures at all costs.

The dangers and risks during the journeys were countless. Fear of robbery and enemy bombing was as common as hunger, cold, broken carts, lack of funding, and exhaustion every day. Amazingly, despite the incredibly long journeys and unexpected hardships of every kind, all three teams arrived at their destinations safely. Making good on their promises, these ordinary citizens had overcome every conceivable difficulty to transport the entire collection of nineteen thousand, five hundred and fifty-seven crates of national treasures intact. Not a single piece of these items went missing or was damaged throughout the war.

10

The occupation of the North China Plain and the fall of Wuhan exposed many renowned sites of ancient Chinese civilization to the Japanese occupying troops. They included famous Anyang, Kaifeng, and Luoyang, which were older than Peking and Nanjing as the capital cities of ancient China. Across the Anyang River, rumors had it that some nearby residents had found impressive artifacts less than fifteen miles away from the village of Xiaotun, where tens of thousands of the legendary oracle bones, which contained inscriptions of some of the earliest Chinese characters, were discovered in the 1920s.

The Japanese chief of the local police in the area decided to check out the rumors. Preliminary investigations led him to a house belonging to a farmer named Wu, who showed the chief the things he had found. The chief was impressed.

But, when a group of Japanese soldiers visited the farmer's house a few days later, the artifacts were no longer there. Wu said he had sold them to an antique dealer in Peking.

The Japanese did not buy the story and suspected that Wu was hiding the treasures from them. They came three times to search his compound, each time more thoroughly than before, but found nothing.

Their suspicions turned out to be true. Earlier, in a cold spring night, Wu and his cousin had detected a hard object in the fields behind their village some forty feet under the ground. From the truncated end of the pole and from the pigment on its tip, the two men realized they had hit some treasure. They immediately asked a dozen relatives and friends for help. The buried object was too big to be pulled out of the pit before daybreak. The group dispersed.

The next night they gathered again and discovered that more manpower would be needed. The team increased to twenty, thirty, and finally forty men. Two ropes as thick as a man's wrist had broken twice, and the object still lay at the bottom of the pit. The operation was stopped.

Wu divided his men into two groups on the third night. As one group pulled the object from the top of the pit, the other shoved it from down below while shoveling earth underneath it for support every time the object had nudged up a bit. Inch by inch, the monster was finally out of the pit. It was an ancient bronze called Ding in a large rectangular-shaped manger.

Several thousand pieces of bronze had been unearthed in this region over the years and Ding, a ceremonial vessel and food container, was often found among them. But no one had ever seen such a magnificent piece weighing over one thousand, eight hundred pounds.

Too many neighbors had helped. To keep it an absolute secret was no longer possible, even though Wu had asked everyone involved to keep their mouths shut. He quickly went to purchase some miscellaneous antiques as substitutes to show to the Japanese inquisitors, while changing Ding's underground hiding place several times. The Japanese persistent interest in Wu's discovery was dangerous for him; he could be arrested and even killed any time if he continued to lie to them.

Wu buried the treasure in a new location for the last time, fled the village, and did not return to his hometown until after the war. To his great delight, the mighty implement still lay quietly under the broken manger of his run-down stable.

The resurfaced bronze finally revealed its true glory to the public. Firmly set on four rounded and powerful legs, the vessel stood more than four feet tall, three and a half feet long, and two and a half feet wide. This massive bronze was in fact an alloy of copper (eighty-five percent), tin (twelve percent), and lead (three percent), which must have required at least a ton of raw metals to be melted. Its perfect shape, stately design, and enduring durability captivated everyone. Wide ornate bands decorated the vessel's solid walls, and a tiger motif accentuated each of the two large vertical handles. Embossed "taotie" (a mystified beast) embellished the whole body and each of the four robust peg-like legs.

Nothing would vouch for the authenticity of the artifact's age more than centuries of slow oxidation of the metal amalgam, which had covered the vessel with light blue and green hues of the patina. Three words were inscribed on the interior walls of the instrument—"Hou-Mu-Wu, 後母戊," which meant "for [the king's consort] mother Wu." The bronze was thus named "Hou-Mu-Wu Ding後母戊鼎," indicating it had been designed as a food vessel in the memorial rites to honor a sovereign's mother, whose posthumous title was "Wu 戊."

Dating back to the late Shang Dynasty, about 1250 BC, it was the largest bronze in the world. Ancient bronzes found elsewhere had used the "lost-wax" process, which often produced simple-shaped small objects of thin walls, narrow bands, and very refined but low relief lines. Shang craftsmen, who had combined their knowledge of ceremonial vessels made of clay with their extensive experience in making exquisite lacquer-painted wooden prototypes, were able to cast bronze by using a "piece-mold" technique, which was uniquely Chinese.

This technique required two sets of clay molds to cast one object. Serving as the inner core, the first set was placed inside the second exterior set, which was slightly larger than the core. When the two sets were perfectly secured together in a single pattern, melted medal would be poured into the spaces between the two sets, which would cool and emerge as the final artifact. Such a process allowed craftsmen to prepare as many clay pieces as needed for a large bronze, which was particularly suited for wide, heavy, and rectangular-shaped vessels. Hou-Mu-Wu Ding had used twenty-eight pieces. They created ample space for design, of which Shang craftsmen took full advantage to demonstrate their artistic imagination while carving to prepare the clay molds. The result was that Shang metal artisans were able to cast unusually large sized bronzes with extraordinarily beautiful designs at the same time, a rare combination in ancient times.

Massive bronze productions demanded huge natural resources, fuels, foundries, transportation facilities, workspaces, huge labor supply, and an extensive administrative apparatus to manage the separate divisions of the workforce and to supervise the different stages of production. Hou-Mu-Wu Ding clearly indicated the sizable population, robust economy, and sophisticated knowledge of metalwork of the Shang Dynasty. It also suggested the high level of craftsmanship and the extraordinary requirements the royal court had demanded from its labor force. This gigantic ceremonial vessel Hou-Mu-Wu Ding was therefore one of the most visible and definitive symbols of wealth, power, and status in ancient Chinese society.

A bronze vessel of the same size had never been discovered before Wu's time or since then. The story of how it had survived the Japanese occupation became a celebrated national legend. The bronze vessel was later loaned to the national government as part of the celebrations to mark General Chen turning sixty, his first postwar birthday. Too heavy to be shipped to Taiwan after Chen fled there, the bronze became a central exhibit at China's National Museum of History.

11

The war created the worst refugee crisis in China. Running away from enemy fire in the east, hundreds of thousands of people abandoned their homes and moved west.

Few were able to count their total losses, which were beyond anything anyone had ever seen. Village after village completely destroyed. Houses burned. Men killed. Women raped. Properties looted. Rotten corpses in the fields. Whatever was salvaged was loaded onto cattle trucks, carried on bamboo poles, or put on the bony backs of the travelers. Every day filthy faces, dirty hands, crying babies, sickly elders, exhausted parents, and wounded soldiers showed up on the road. Yet, few knew of any safe places they could go to or when their miserable journey would end.

In what would be called the Chinese Dunkirk Evacuation, the Livelihood Company and its owner Lu Zuo-Fu rescued thousands of people and transported one hundred and twenty thousand tons of military materials to safety in forty days.

A highly successful businessman, Lu was the son of a poor peasant in Sichuan. He had some elementary education but learned geography, physics, mathematics, geometry, chemistry, history, and other subjects by reading. A schoolteacher and magazine editor early in his life, he was later involved in the transportation business on the Yangtze and had the largest fleet owned by a Chinese shipping company. By the time the government contacted him for help, his Livelihood Company had forty-six vessels and employed four thousand people.

Still, to ship the huge amount of military materials including metals and fuel under constant Japanese bombardment was a serious challenge, especially when the Yangtze River was about to enter its low water season. Lu worked day and night with his employees and carefully planned a schedule to ensure that the evacuation, using every ship he had, ran like clockwork.

The treacherous currents flowing in the Three Gorges on the Yangtze made night journey impossible. Shipping during the day and loading and unloading at night, Lu's vessels moved nonstop around the clock. All of his several thousand regular employees and temporary hires were divided into shifts, and no ship would stay any longer at any port than necessary for unloading, refueling, and reloading.

A month and a half later, Lu and his company not only successfully transported all the military goods as the government had requested, but also took sixty-four thousand refugees to safety—the same number of passengers that his company would normally ferry in a year.

For the amazing dedication and unbelievable efforts to help the nation, his company lost four million yuan in the operations, while one hundred and sixteen of his employees were killed and sixty-one injured.

Throughout the war, Lu and his company participated in every major battle along the Yangtze River, helping to ferry government troops and civilian refugees along the way. They transported as many as two million, seven hundred thousand troops in and out of Sichuan, the largest military mobilization in one region during the war. Lu, his employees, and hundreds more who had worked for him were the unsung heroes behind the enemy lines.

12

A successful, conscientious, and patriotic businessman, Lu was also amazingly versatile. He developed a myriad of projects related to modern sciences, sanitation, immunization, community parks, better treatment of women, urban planning, museums, libraries, sports facilities, road pavement, and railway construction. One of his key concerns was education, and Lu spent considerable time and much of his fortune to promote his hometown, Sichuan, as the new learning center. The importance of the remote inland province had grown as it played host to an increasing number of refugees from the coastal areas, and the nation's capital was moved to Chingqing, a major city in Sichuan.

Among the refugees Lu's company had helped to evacuate were various groups of government employees, school students, and college professors, who were fleeing the war-torn regions on the east coast to the safety of peaceful Sichuan. Many settled in North Boulder, a community Lu had helped create in the northwest suburbs of Chongqing. Only twenty-five miles away from the wartime capital, the pleasant environment and good public facilities quickly enticed several hundred government offices and educational institutions to move into the community. They included the National Academy of Sciences, Fudan University, the National Bureau of Translation, the National Research Institution for Agriculture, the National Research Institution for Industries, the National Geographic Research Institute, and the National Geological Research. Several thousand intellectuals and some of the best-known contemporary Chinese writers, authors, and scholars relocated to North Boulder, which became known as "capital of the capital," making it the most enlightened district to live and work during the war years.

The widening war troubled the national government deeply, and the heavy burden of resistance exhausted the nation's coffers even as its economic and financial institutions were devastated by the prolonged conflict. Despite this, the government devised a plan to protect several top universities from destruction by removing them from the war zones on the east coast to the safe havens in the west and southwest.

The universities that kept their doors open throughout the war included Peking University, Tsinghua University, Nankai University, National University in Nanjing, and Jejiang University. The government never stopped funding for these institutions, which continued to accept applications and recruit students every year. As North China became increasingly destabilized by growing Japanese aggression two years prior to the Marco Polo Bridge Incident, Peking University, Tsinghua University, and Nankai University started moving out of the area and headed for Changsha, the capital city of Hunan Province south of the Yangtze. After the war broke out and quickly spread to the south, a new plan was immediately drawn up to move their temporary campuses in Changsha, further down south in Yunnan Province.

Students, professors, staff, and their families packed again and some traveled over a thousand miles to the new site. Education continued, with the government providing financial help for those students who qualified for higher studies during the war. Students who had overcome many difficulties to attend a university were exempted from paying tuition fees and given free meals on campus. The national government wanted to make sure that these students could still graduate even amid wartime depredation and deprivation.

Living in makeshift dorms, going to tin-roofed mess halls, and running for cover during air raids, professors taught and students studied as the classes continued, libraries opened, labs functioned, services delivered, and postbaccalaureate programs offered. Graduation and commencement took place regularly over the years. Hundreds of young men and women received their hard-earned diplomas and many of China's most accomplished scholars and scientists of the twentieth century came from this generation of university graduates, including Yang Zhenning (楊振寧, physicist, Nobel Prize winner), T. D. Lee (李政道, physicist, Nobel Prize winner), Zhu Guangya (朱光亞, physicist), Ren Jiyu (任繼愈, philosopher), Zou Chenglu (鄒承魯, chemist), Wang Zengqi (汪曾祺, novelist), Nelson Ikon Wu (吳訥孫, art historian), and Ye Duzheng (葉篤正, meteorologist).

13

While taking care of those established universities, the government also had ambitious plans to expand and improve education in the west, the traditionally underdeveloped and most illiterate region in China. Funding was allocated to construct new middle schools in several provinces of the west. Support was given to Shanxi University, Sichuan University began to receive government funding, and Northwest University in Sian underwent reorganization. Appointing the renowned agriculturist Xin Shu-Zhi (辛樹幟) as president of the Agriculture College of the Northwest in Lanzhou, the capital of Gansu Province (where the West Army had met with defeat), was one of the best decisions the government had made and, under his leadership, the institution would soon become one of the best of its kind in the country.

Settling down in Northern Shaanxi gave the Communist Party the opportunity to develop its educational institutions, including a Red Army Institute (to retrain veteran Red Army officers), a Military and Political University (to train political staffers), a College of Arts (to train activists interested in arts and literature), and a University of Resistant Forces (to recruit and train personnel for the front lines). Under the agreement of the

"United Front," the party was allowed to advertise its educational programs nationwide, which attracted a wide range of applicants—refugees from the occupied regions, displaced school students from war-torn cities, girls running away from arranged marriages, young men aspiring to be soldiers, patriotic citizens determined to defend the nation, minor sons from broken families of the lower middle class, indebted small landlords, bankrupt merchants, free-spirited women seeking a new life, poor peasants' children looking for affordable education, unemployed office workers, wandering artists, struggling writers, and disillusioned intellectuals. Throngs of people, male and female, arrived at the communist base every day. Tania saw the excitement on their faces, which reminded her of how she had felt when she was first told that she would be going to China with Martin.

"They look just like you fifteen years ago, don't they?" Yan Yan asked her friend.

"No. They are way smarter than I was then," Tania answered.

A messenger came to their humble abode, a small cave carved out of a mountain side and a common form of dwelling in the region. He told Tania that party leader Meng Bo-Xian needed to see her immediately, and left.

"See. I know he is interested in you." Yan never gave up on an idea once it had taken root.

"Stop it. It's purely a meeting for official business," Tania said before she went out.

Chapter 24

Recovery

1

THE REPEATED MILITARY FAILURES TO DEFEND CHINESE CITIES reaffirmed Sheng Bao's belief that positional warfare against the Japanese offensive was not an effective strategy. The communist troops must stick to the tactics they were most familiar with—guerrilla warfare, which would be the only way to survive and succeed. The huge casualties the government troops had suffered clearly showed the danger of engaging in direct pitched battles with the enemies. Sheng was determined that this should never happen to the communist forces. The Eighth Army in the north was a minor force with fewer than fifty thousand men, and the more marginal Fourth Army in the south had fewer than ten thousand. It would be suicidal to let such a small number of troops to confront the powerful enemy prematurely. The correct strategy was, as the ancient Chinese maxim had long stated, "to hide one's capacity and bide one's time." The most important thing the communists must do, Sheng concluded, was to preserve and protect their highly valuable but limited resources and to wait patiently for their opportunities.

No matter what he had publicly promised General Chen, the national government, and the public, Sheng's secret and predetermined plan of ten percent resistance, twenty percent coping with the government, and seventy percent expansion was working. Only two years into the war, the Eighth Army increased almost threefold. If this momentum continued, Sheng envisaged, the communist troops would soon reach the million mark in the next few years—something he had always been aiming for. When Tao Yin-Hu, the commander-in-chief of the Eighth Army, and Si-Tu Wen-Liang, the principal liaison officer between the Communist Party and the nationalist government, strongly urged some serious military engagement, Sheng resisted. The size of the troops would be the party's trump card, argued Sheng, who refused to take any risk of losing them. "Go deeper behind the enemy lines into the countryside, to infiltrate the areas between the nationalist troops and the Japanese forces, continue to widen our bases and expand our army," Sheng instructed his officers. "Don't worry about the immediate gains but think long term," advised he, whose unwillingness to fight for now would pave the way for victory in the future.

2

Unbeknown to most outsiders, one of Sheng's most satisfying achievements during this period was getting married to Su Ming. A slim and vivacious woman in her early thirties with beautiful and silky long jet-black hair, the sophisticated and urbane Su was a native of North China. Her father was a bankrupt small landlord who died when she was only nine. Left with nothing, her widowed mother was hired as a washer in a big household where Su also worked as a maidservant. A tough life, hard labor, abuse, and prejudice turned her into a strong-willed girl, and she ran away to the cities to seek a better life at fifteen. She married three times and became an actress in a small theatrical company in Shanghai. She met her third husband, an actor in the same company who happened to be an undercover agent of the Communist Party. Through his introduction, Su joined the party. Mundane life and trivial quarrels soon replaced the couple's passion. They parted a few years later when the war broke out. As many thousands of patriotic and ambitious young people had done, the free-spirited Su left Shanghai for Bao An, a small town in Northern Shaanxi where the new communist headquarters was located.

Written differently in two separate characters, the "Bao" in "Sheng Bao" and "Bao An" were a pair of homonyms in Chinese. Sheng Bao's "bao" was a noun meaning treasure or preciousness. But the "bao" in Bao An was a verb, meaning to protect or defend, while "An" meant safety and peacefulness. Su liked the fortuitous but auspicious suggestions of the two names. The place, appropriately selected as the party's headquarters, must have meant to protect "Sheng Bao," to ensure his security, to provide him with tranquility, and to safeguard his serenity.

When Su told Sheng what she thought about the names and their providential implications, he was delighted. He loved the wordplay on the meanings of places and personal appellations, and was glad to know that his new wife had the same hobby.

"Do you know the story behind the phrase 'to hide one's capacity and bide one's time'?" Sheng asked.

Smart and sensitive, Su understood that this seemingly casual question could be loaded. The man she had just married was a diligent student of the past who could be testing the depth of her knowledge about classical Chinese history and literature. Any sign of ignorance might disappoint him and result in his loss of interest in her. Reminded that "to be the consort of the emperor is to be at the side of a tiger," Su responded warily.

"The story I heard often was that, during the period of 'Three Kingdoms,' Cao Cao asked Liu Bei at a banquet if he knew of any great men who might have the potential to unite China. Although extremely ambitious, Liu said he knew no one of that caliber. Raising his wine vessel, Cao pointed to Liu and himself, saying 'There are two sitting right here in this room.' The blunt statement hit the nail right on the head, except that it was a desire that Lu had tried long and hard to hide from outsiders. Frightened that he could be arrested and eliminated right away, Liu dropped his utensils onto the floor. 'Why? Are you scared?' Cao asked. 'Yes, yes, of course,' Liu replied, 'Who would not be when hearing the sound of a blasting thunder,' which happened to roll at the very moment. Thus Liu had once again managed to conceal his true ambition and stayed in Cao's camp until he found an opportunity to escape. Building up his own forces after the separation, Liu was able to challenge and compete with the once most powerful Cao."

"Hmm, a good account." Sheng seemed satisfied. "Have you heard of another version?" he kept probing.

"Another episode took place even earlier in the Spring and Autumn period," a prepared Su replied.

Gou Jian, she said, the king of Kingdom Yue, attacked Kingdom Wu and mortally wounded its king He Lü. Before the latter died, he told his son Fu Chai never to forget the archenemy Gou. Two years later, Gou learned that Fu was preparing an attack. Gou hoped to wage a preemptive strike, but his minister Wen Zhong was against it, saying their military forces were not ready. Ignoring Wen's advice, Gou started the offensive assault but was soon pushed back. This time Fu got his revenge and trapped Gou in his capital. Terrified, Gou was willing to listen to Wen, who said that several ancient kings had fallen into similar situations that became turning points in their lives. A grave crisis might not be a bad thing after all. Right now they needed to bribe Fu's chief minister Bo Bi, who might help them to reach a compromise, Wen said.

The strategy worked. Despite the furious protest by General Wu Zi-Xu who called Bo a traitor, Fu agreed to a ceasefire and took his war booty back to Wu.

The price of the compromise was humiliatingly high. Yue offered tons of gold, silver, silk, satin, and brocade as reparations to Wu, and Gou sent several thousand women to serve Fu as his mistresses.

Moreover, when Fu finally left Yue, Gou and his wife went with him as captives. The couple was given a cold stone house to live next to the grave of Fu's father He Lü. Gou worked as a stableman to feed and groom the king's horses. Whenever Fu went out, Gou must help him to mount the horse and then to sit down on an imperial wagon. Gou, the deposed king of Yue, had to walk and hold the horse for Fu wherever he was going.

Two years had passed before Fu allowed Gou to return to his homeland.

The freed Gou continued to live in a stone house, where he hung a gall from the ceilings. He tasted the gall every time before taking his meal, to remind him of the bitter and degrading experience he had endured at Fu's court.

He gave up all his past luxuries, wore coarse clothing, ate granular food, and labored in the fields with his people. His wife led women in raising silkworms to produce silk. Never before had the people rallied so faithfully in support of their king and queen. Yue became increasingly strong over the next ten years, and it eventually defeated Wu. The archenemy Fu committed suicide, and Gou was proclaimed as the overlord by all other kings of nearby kingdoms.

"Good. Very good. Very good indeed." Sheng was clearly pleased and took Su into his arms. "Do you know the third version of the story?" he spoke softly into her ear.

"There is another version?" Su's jaw dropped and her eyes opened wide in disbelief.

"Yes, there is," Sheng began. "In the early years of Western Han, the valiant cavalry of the Huns often presented a huge threat to the court. When the first emperor Gao died, his widow received a letter from the head of the Huns, demanding that she marry him. 'Your late husband and I had performed formal ceremonies to become sworn brothers. Now he is dead, and you belong to me,' he said. Widow Gao was outraged and wanted to dispatch troops to attack the insolent Huns. Her ministers said it would not be the right moment to do so since the country had just lost its king. The Huns would pay the price for the egregious offense they had committed when the time came. Widow Gao listened and wrote back, 'since I am now too old to serve Your Excellency, I have decided to send one of my daughters to comply with your wishes.' So a princess was sent, a marital liaison was secured, and the Han court gained the much-needed peace to build its strength. Fifty years later, the Huns were finally defeated, which was all due to Widow Gao's initial willingness to be patient."

"What a good story. But why do we women always have to make those sacrifices?" Su's pout amused the husband, who was not troubled at all to have ruffled her feathers.

"That's true. But sometimes someone had to make that sacrifice or progress will never be made. Don't you think so?" Sheng was pushing his body against hers.

"Did the Huns really marry their brothers' wives?" Su asked.

But before she got any answer, Sheng had thrown her onto the large earthen flatbed behind them, telling her gleefully, "I think they did. I married you after three others, didn't I?"

3

Tania could not explain why she felt the way she did every time she was about to see Meng Bo-Xian. Excitement, happiness, anticipation, anxiety, shyness, and trepidation.

Bao An, the poorest small community she had ever seen in China, had only one cross street lined with a few dozen low self-standing houses, which were still a rarity in a place completely bereft of trees. The vast majority of the residents lived in cave dwellings typical to Northern Shaanxi, the houses carved into the sides of hills and lying row after row on the terraces of the mountains.

The shallow, small, cramp, and dirty caves belonged to poor families. Yet a cave could be as big as twelve feet high, twelve feet wide, and twenty feet deep, making it a quite roomy place to live in. The single-arched entrance cave could serve as the hall, which would split at the back into one additional chamber on either side. Both chambers could be used as bedrooms, or one of them as a spare room or office. The hall was also the family kitchen, where a big earthen stove was used to cook meals and, through the flues installed underneath all the chambers, heat the "kang"—the earthen flatbed that was a ubiquitous feature not only in Northern Shaanxi but also across the countryside in North China.

Although few in number, solid caves could be dug from a stone cliff, and fancier ones belonging to substantial households could have brick-trimmed bases/floors, limestone arches, vaulted windows with intricate carvings, well-designed wood sash bars, and even beautifully decorated paper cuttings of folk art.

Against the hill, a series of caves lined up in a row on a terrace, saving the precious flat land for farming. Occasionally, the shape and size of a hill was big enough to allow a circle of caves made along the sides, leaving the middle portion open as a spacious courtyard.

Naturally insulated, a well-constructed cave dwelling was cool in summer and warm in winter. Surprisingly durable, it could last for generations, providing decent living for the rich and poor in this destitute region.

When Tania entered the hallway and walked into Meng's office to the left of the cave, she smiled.

Despite the drastic changes in location and accommodation, everything looked almost the same as when she first met him in his office in Blue Grass several years ago. Piles of papers were scattered all over the desk and the earthen bed, leaving him with almost no place to sit but on the edge of the kang.

Apparently serving as both his bedroom and office, the kang covered half of the chamber and was right next to the front window. The bright daylight cast a shadow on his papers and his face, which looked as calm and serene as ever.

"Tania, I am so glad you have come." Meng thought his greeting was warm and appropriate for the occasion.

"I am very glad to see you too," Tania responded, as she kept looking at him as if trying to figure out what had changed since their last meeting.

Unaware of the gaze, Meng continued, "The party has an important job for you."

"What is it?" Tania did not take her eyes away from Meng's face.

"To accompany Yu Shao-Mei to Moscow," Meng answered.

"Why?" Tania suddenly realized the seriousness of the conversation.

"Because Comrade Sheng Bao has married Comrade Su Ming, and… and…" Meng was searching for suitable words to continue.

"Therefore, they don't want to see her around. Is that it?" Tania interjected as she was furious.

Meng was silent for he knew Tania was right.

"Shao-Mei has been Sheng Bao's wife for ten years! She has always taken care of him and nursed him when he was terribly sick. She has given birth to his children, and suffered the loss of her daughter. Most of all, she threw her body to cover him and saved his life from the bomb explosion during the Long March! Twelve, no, fourteen, fourteen bomb fragments pierced her arms, legs, and body. She was lying in a pool of blood so he could stay alive unharmed. Two of those fragments are still lodged at the back of her head! And now Sheng has a new wife and they don't want to face her? Shame on him! Shame on them! How could they do this to her? How could anyone do anything like this?"

Tania did not know why she simply exploded on hearing the news. She did not know why she had said so much on this matter. She had met Yu several times but did not know her that well personally. But she had heard a lot about Yu's legendary career and considered her a true revolutionary heroine. In the end, it was Tania's deep sense of justice, fairness, and common decency that led to her emotional outburst against Sheng Bao and Su Ming.

Meng, after a long silence, agreed that what she had said was largely true. He told her that not a few of the party's top officials had felt the same way.

"But you dared not say that in front of Sheng Bao, right? You wanted to save your face and keep your all-men's club intact," Tania charged.

"Yes, you may say that." Meng found himself on the defensive.

"They have survived the unthinkable ordeal of the Long March, but they can't save their marriage. Why? Why?" So mournfully sad was Tania that she seemed to be howling for the loss of her own loved one.

"You are right. They have survived the Long March, but they can't save their marriage. To tell you the truth, I really have no answer," Meng confessed.

"You know the answer. You just don't want to say it. It's all because of his selfishness. Yes, it's all because of his great ambition. And you, all of you—his closest associates have allowed Sheng to run amok in pursuit of his personal ambition. You praise him as the leader, and therefore whatever he chooses to do must be good for the cause."

Hearing no response, Tania continued her tirade.

"Now you see the great injustice done to his own wife. Shouldn't this alarm you in any way? If a man can so easily abandon his devoted wife for ten years to marry another younger woman, what else would he not do?"

Meng was unable to answer.

Only an hour earlier Tania was so looking forward to the meeting. Never could have she imagined that the meeting with the one she had always enjoyed talking to would end on such a sour note. Neither one of them could even say "goodbye" to each other as they parted.

4

When the emotionally battered Tania returned home, the real lecture started.

"What? You really said all those things to him?" Yan Yan was stunned.

"Yes, I did," Tania said.

"Silly, stupid! Stupid, silly, you terrible girl!" Yan shouted at her friend. "You can never argue with your boss! How can you continue to work under him after you have humiliated him like that?"

Yan felt she had a serious responsibility to teach her friend proper Chinese etiquette. "Remember," she continued, "never argue with your boss, especially when he is a man."

"But, bless him in heaven, you always argued with Lu Shi-Yan," said Tania.

"That's different. We were husband and wife," Yan retorted.

"In your opinion, then, women have to agree with men all the time, or the subordinate has to agree with the boss, no matter what?" Tania asked.

"Oh, boy, boy. Girl, you are in big trouble!" Yan panicked.

"Why?"

"Because of what you have said. Oh, you are so stubborn. Listen to yourself!"

"Because of what I have said? Whose side are you on? Are you sympathetic toward Yu Shao-Mei or not?"

"I am, I am. I definitely am. I don't like any man, Lu Shi-Yan included, who abandoned his wife. Especially in Shao-Mei's case. She has sacrificed so much for the marriage; how could any decent man even think of abandoning her at this time when she is still suffering from her wounds?"

"So, you agree with what I said?"

"No, no, no. I mean you can't say such things to Meng Bo-Xian. He is your boss, and what you said could cause him to lose face. He will have difficulty in supervising you in the future. Plus, as we both know, his wife has long passed away. If he has had any good impressions of you, they must have vanished by now."

"No worries, my dear. I know you mean well. But I care not about the 'face' business here, nor do I care whatever impressions he may have about me. The insult to Shao-Mei should upset anyone who has a conscience. If Meng Bo-Xian thinks that's too much to take, so be it." Tania was not budging.

"I am telling you, though, the 'face' business is extremely important here. Especially for men, men of power." Yan reiterated her key point and was frustrated that her friend was not listening.

Early next morning someone came to the door knocking, "Is Tania here?"

"Yes, yes, please come in."

In came Meng, who was smiling.

"Look, Comrade Meng is here," Yan said to her roommate who remained inside and then turned to the guest.

"Tania is a very nice woman. I mean extremely nice. You can't find a nicer woman in this world. But she is indeed very upset about Yu Shao-Mei." Yan felt she had an obligation to explain and protect Tania's good reputation as if she were her daughter.

"I understand. I understand it perfectly," Meng calmly replied and Yan withdrew.

When Yan returned home about an hour later, she found her friend was in a pleasant mood. "Now, tell me what he said and why you are so happy."

"Nothing."

"Nothing? How come you are a completely different person now compared to yesterday?"

"Well, he just repeated the request and I agreed to accompany Yu Shao-Mei to Moscow."

"That's it?"

"That's it."

"Why?"

"Why? Because Yu Shao-Mei is getting very bad headaches now, and she must receive proper medical care as soon as possible."

"So you have agreed?"

"Yes, I have," Tania replied. "Oh, by the way, you need to come with me to go and see Dong Zi-Tian tomorrow."

"What? Why? Are you crazy? Hasn't he been demoted? Nobody wants to see him now." Yan was stunned again.

"That's exactly why we are going." Tania's response was as firm as her friend's protestations.

5

An endless brown sea of bald mountains extended as far as the two women could see over the horizon. Silent, quiet, and motionless. Poverty, hopeless and abject poverty had turned this immense land into a monstrous dead beast.

From the far end of their destination they heard someone singing, and the closer they walked toward the direction, the gloomier the voice sounded. Tania urged Yan to stand still to listen carefully to the lyrics, which the latter then translated:

How heartbroken when I hear you crying
    atop the opposite rim of the mountain,

So sad as we face each other so close to the edges,
but can't touch across the forbidden abyss.

The twinkling light from your cave tells me where you are
in the darkness of the evening,

But to find you during the day across the infinite plain
would be a dream in vain.

"It's Dong Zi-Tian's voice," Tania said.

"Are you sure? Why does he sound so miserable?"

"He misses his wife, who is in Moscow."

Dong was surprised and excited to see his friends coming to see him. He took them to his cave dwelling, and brought out the best thing he had to treat them—a bowl of dried dates.

"Very colorful. How come they are so small?" Yan took a red one and put it in her mouth. "Wow, it's not sweet. It's very sour!" she yelled.

Dong apologized and explained that big and regular date trees, which produced very sweet fruit, were rare in this region. Although wild and very sour, little red or yellow dates, growing in shrubs, were one of the few edible things people could find here.

"How come you have the time to visit? Tell me everything you know about the resistance," he said.

"I will soon be going to Moscow for a mission, and we are here to see if you have anything thing for your wife," Tania answered, knowing that Dai Tian had left for Moscow some time ago.

Dong's smile disappeared. He said, "Life had been very difficult for my wife since my demotion. Everyone in the party looked down on her simply because her husband had made serious mistakes. You have met Dai Tian, who has a bubbly personality. She loves the crowd. But, here, everybody was avoiding her as if she were an infectious disease. This terrible treatment hurt her deeply; it was as if she had committed some crime. She felt totally humiliated and couldn't face her colleagues and the public as usual. The ostracism had been too much and she could not stay with me anymore. So we agreed to have a divorce."

Suddenly, Tania noticed how much Dong had changed. The young, handsome, and energetic man she had known now looked like a man thirty years older than his real age. His weather-beaten face was full of wrinkles, and his hands covered with dirt and calluses. No one would imagine that he had been a Peking University graduate and, not long ago, one of the party's highest officials.

"I heard you have changed the county a lot." Tania changed the topic of their conversation. "How did you do that?"

"It's rather simple," Dong answered with pride. "The region is so poor and the economy so desolate that I just stopped the practice of land redistribution, which benefits no one."

"Why?" Tania and Yan asked.

"The land is very limited here to begin with. Most landowners are small, and most families can't make any decent living by farming. A redistribution of land will disrupt the social order, while benefiting no one, the poor peasants included."

Dong continued, "The number one issue here is the lack of underground water and low precipitation, which hinders everything in agriculture."

"So, what change did you make?" Tania was really curious for she had heard that Pangolin had increased its revenue drastically in recent months, which made for some shocking news in Northern Shaanxi.

"Dependence on land is a dead end, and the alternative option is trade. We have encouraged the locals to cultivate those indigenous plants and raise native products we could trade. Now Pangolin produces plenty of herb medicines, salt, animal fur, and coal that we can trade with other regions. We even export some of our products beyond our borders to Mongolia and Russia. Commerce and trade has helped our residents to raise their incomes, and they now even have surpluses to contribute to the support of our army and government."

"Well, it sounds like a miracle in this barren place," Yan commented.

"Not a miracle, just a realistic adjustment of policies," Dong said.

"I heard, however," Tania proceeded cautiously, "that the people here also grow poppies and trade opium. Is that true?"

"Unfortunately, it is," Dong conceded. "Growing poppies and trading opium have a long history in this region and Northwest China, and used to be the main source of revenue for both the peasant farmers and local governments. Although our party's policy is strictly against opium consumption, it's not possible to ban the opium trade completely. We have waged campaigns against smoking opium, which received strong and wide support from women, who hated to see their men become addicts. But in the interest of expediency, I must confess, we also trade opium for cash to finance our government and troops."

"Would this get you into trouble with the party?" Tania was concerned.

"I don't know. Right now the party and the troops need revenue to feed thousands of soldiers, staff, and government employees, and to purchase military supplies. They don't have the time to ask where the money came from."

"But one day they will. What will you do then?" Tania did not like Dong's attitude. He should learn from his past mistakes. He was too naïve about party politics and policies, which often shifted not according reality, but according to the needs of a few top leaders.

Dong seemed unperturbed. He was too confident about what he was doing or he simply did not care about the consequence of his actions.

"Are you sure you don't want to send some words, letter, or something to Dai Tian?" Tania felt she had to help the couple.

"No. Nothing," Dong said.

"Tell us about the songs we heard you were singing as we came," Tania asked before she and Yan were about to leave.

"Yes, tell us about them. Why are they so sad? They sounded very different from those I am used to hearing in the south," Yan said.

"Oh, yes, they are typical folksongs of the north. Very blunt, high-pitched, and often tragic in tones and lyrics, reflecting the prevailing hardships and overwhelming destitution of the region," Dong explained.

"Yes, they do sound brusque and masculine," Tania responded. "Not as soft and gentle as the ones Yan had taught me."

"That is a major difference between the folksongs of the north and those of the south," Dong agreed. "But, despite the salient dissimilarities, most of the folksongs in Northwest China are freestyle, expressed in the allegorical phrase 'Let It Fly into the Skies' or Xin-Tian-You (信天遊) in Chinese. There is no fixed way to sing any song. It's entirely up to the singer to control the tone and decide the lyrics. And any male or female, old or young, can choose any tone, fill out the lyrics, and to sing it the way they see fit."

"Okay, then, sing us another song. I would love to hear it," Yan requested.

As the two women were leaving Dong's low and humble cave, they heard a song rising from behind them. The vocal was as stunningly raucous and dreary as the lyrics were tragically sad but gripping.

Warm teardrops line after line,
Heavy memories mountain after mountain;
Arduous journeys never stop or finish,
Nor will the deep feelings I always relish.

Warm teardrops line after line,
Heavy memories mountain after mountain;
Arduous journeys never stop or finish,
Nor will the deep feelings I always relish.

Suddenly, Yan found her friend stopping in her tracks. On the very top of a mountain range Tania turned and looked back at the direction where they had come from. Tears, large drops of warm tears were running down her face as she stood frozen at the spot, looking, looking, and looking…

6

Power was a mystical possession—tantalizing when you didn't have it, but fragile and slippery when you did. No matter how powerful a person might be, the more he hoped to monopolize and keep the power to himself, the more others seemed to want to share it with him, if not to steal it from him.

Stepping out of the plane that would soon carry Yu Shao-Mei and Tania away to Moscow was Mo Jia-Qi, the last person Sheng Bao wanted to see in Bao An.

A firm shake of hands and a quick glance of each other were all it took for Sheng to realize that a new round of competition between them had started.

Fully backed by the Comintern, the resurrected Mo was as haughty as ever. Cocky and yet distinguished, his clean-shaven face, stylish suit, and symmetrically looped bowtie made him taller and more conceited than Sheng had remembered of him at the meeting in Yi city. With a perfect parting line and the short but smooth hair trimmed to the left temple, his immaculate hairstyle was enough to attract every woman in the crowd. In contrast, the scruffy attire Sheng wore and the untamed bush on his head made him look very ordinary, undistinguishable from the farmhands or day laborers around him.

Bao An, the only rural place with an airstrip, soon witnessed another excitement. Mo's reputation as the author of the August First Declaration drew huge crowds to the lecture hall, where he elaborated how the document was drafted, how it proposed the famed "Ten Fundamental Policies," how it was praised by Stalin, how it was adopted by the Comintern, and how it was printed in several foreign languages. His subsequent lecture series on "Socialism in the Soviet Union" was a sensational success, and afterwards everyone in the audience was talking about the speaker who could speak without any notes for hours on end.

At the Politburo meetings, Sheng could easily see the extra attention given to Mo by other members, something that they had always reserved for the former in the past. He could understand why. Although absent from China for some time, Mo personified the indispensable link between the Chinese Communist Party and Moscow, the Comintern, and Stalin. Everyone in the party craved for that role, but no one had the ability and access except for Mo. No one in the party including Sheng could ignore that vital connection, nor could anyone underestimate the critical authority that Mo represented. All the top brass of the party understood perfectly that none of them could ever become the party's number one leader unless he was backed by the Comintern and Stalin. As much as Sheng hated the foreign interference, he must deal with Mo carefully or risk ruining a career in which he had invested more than twenty years of his life to build up.

Sheng's dislike of Mo originated from his ambivalence toward Stalin and the Soviet Union. The Chinese Communist Party itself was a byproduct of the Bolshevik Revolution and it had relied on Russian aid to survive from day one. In the ongoing monumental task of resistance against Japanese aggression, the party badly needed the Soviet Union's continued financial support and military assistance. Sheng could not afford any action that might displease Stalin, whose decision to terminate Soviet aid would be devastating for the party and his future.

But Sheng was also keenly aware that Stalin did not fully trust him. In cultivating allies to help him defend the Soviet Union, Stalin could not see Sheng or any other Chinese communist as a viable national figure who could lead China in a nationwide campaign against the Japanese. General Chen was the only possible choice and Stalin was explicitly adamant about it.

Based on these calculations, Stalin insisted on the importance of the "united front" and stressed the submission of the Communist Party to Chen's leadership.

While accepting the "united front" as a survival tactic, Sheng never intended to relinquish his control over the party to the nationalists or to submit himself to Chen. He was thinking not only how to survive the Japanese invasion, or how to comply with Stalin's request to help the Russians, but also how to accumulate his own power for his future ascendency to national prominence.

Precisely because Stalin could see through Sheng's intentions and tricks, he had sent his faithful student Mo to Bao An to carry out his mission without compromise. Wielding the authority obtained from Moscow, Mo reiterated the Comintern's version of the "united front" and blamed Sheng for his reluctance to comply with the order. Noticing the winds had changed, Si-Tu Wen-Liang and Tao Yin-Hu jumped on Mo's bandwagon. They criticized Sheng's stubborn refusal to accept Chen as the national leader, and to participate in the active military engagement against the Japanese.

In the face of such pressures, Sheng was forced to make concessions and acknowledge his mistakes. He knew he had to face a lot of skepticism and endure a lot of abuses now before he could eventually win the power struggle. He never expected Mo, who was just as ambitious, to be his friend. But Sheng never thought that Si-Tu and Tao would switch allegiance so quickly when Mo showed up in Bao An. The biggest obstacle to his advancement, it seemed, would come from those men closest to him in the past. He must find a way to break out of this dreadful predicament.

7

Tania and Yu Shao-Mei arrived in Moscow at a time when the Soviet Union was in great turmoil.

Once upon a time, the Marx–Engels theory confidently predicted the withering away of the state and government after the proletarians had seized power. The success of the Bolshevik Revolution demonstrated the contrary. Expansion, not contraction, proved to be the case under the new regime as the

Soviet Union extended the size of its territory, multiplied the state agencies, and enlarged governmental institutions and administration. A new theory must be found to explain the apparent inconsistency. Lenin then said, "The state will not wither away under socialism, but eventually will under communism." Which, by the way, meant forever. Stalin went a step further by insisting that the machinery of the proletarian dictatorship should not be weakened but enhanced as long as capitalism existed.

Stalin's determination to preserve his autocratic control over the party at all costs, his firm grip on the state and government, pathological aversion toward political dissidents and competitors, total disregard of law and human rights, widespread use of the secret police, and hyperbolical claims in the name of the revolution led to the bloodiest purge in Russian history. The Communist Party of the Soviet Union (Bolshevik) lost one-third of its membership in the early 1930s, and it continued to drop until the end of the decade. Arrests, imprisonment, trials, and executions became so rampant that the entire country was shrouded in fear. No fewer than one and a half million people were detained, and some six to seven hundred thousand of them were shot. Among them were Marshal Mikhail Tukhachevsky and distinguished Soviet officials and intellectuals.

From the outside, the beautiful facade and the impressive columns of several major Moscow hospitals were as gorgeous and grand as ever, such as the famed Botkin Hospital close to Khodynka Field, the newly combined Municipal Hospital in Myasnitskaya Street, the classical edifice of St. Paul's Hospital in Pavlovskaya Street, the lavishly decorated Rogozhskaya Clinic in Bolshoy Rogozhsky Lane, and the plain but solemn Resurrection Hospital in Voskresensky district.

Inside those institutions, the inflexible medical staff and caustic administrators were not as hospitable as they should be. The experiences Tania had made her sick. She took Yu to several hospitals, begging doctors there to treat her friend as soon as possible, and telling them what a heroine she had been during the Long March. The response she got was that, like anyone else, they had to wait. When asked why a badly wounded heroine could not be given better and immediate treatment, the answer was that her status qualified her only as a common patient, no more, no less. "If you want her to get better and immediate treatment," they said, "change her status."

"What status?" Tania asked.

"Her political status," came the reply.

"How?"

"Go and ask those who sent you here."

"They are back in China."

"That's your problem, not ours."

"Lazy staff! Absurd dogmatists! Heartless bureaucrats! How I hate these wretched bureaucrats," the frustrated Tania said to herself. Suddenly the city she had loved so much seemed so cold, so alien, and so devoid of love, sympathy, and compassion. Why did so many behave like what Alexander Herzen had satirized about the old regime? Why did they give Maxim Gorky a reason to call them "truly Russian idiots"? What had happened to her city, to her country, she asked, not knowing that the unprecedented climate of fear and terror had made her compatriots as timid and cautious as never before.

The long and turbulent flight in the air and the frequent commute on the ground worsened Yu's health. Pale, feeble, and exhausted, she was emotionally distraught before leaving Bao An, and now she was physically distressed after a month running around from one institution to the another in Moscow. Tania became sad just by looking at Yu's traumatized, expressionless, and colorless face, which had been so beautiful and so full of life, energy, and laughter only a few years ago. "No matter what, I must never give up and I must keep on trying," Tania swore.

She went to see Song Pei, the deputy head of the Chinese Communist Party delegation to the Comintern.

"Please, you know who Yu Shao-Mei is. Please change her political status so that she can receive the immediate expert medical treatment she deserves," Tania implored the deputy.

"Well, changing her status will need the consent from the party's top leadership. Please allow me to contact them, which may take some time," Song patiently said, while knowing full well that the party's instruction had been to retain Yu's status as a common patient.

"How long should she wait?" Tania pushed for a more definitive response.

"Well, this may take a while. As you know, the communication, the deliberation, and the collaboration with our Soviet friends, everything will take time." Song was as unmoved as before.

"Why do you sound so unsympathetic?" Tania could not feign ignorance over Song's hypocrisy any longer.

"What did you say? Me? Unsympathetic? I am very sympathetic. I want to help. I swear," Song was quick to put up a defense.

"I can't believe that you are still pretending. You sly hypocrite! How I have wasted my time here in this office!" Tania stormed out.

She went straight to the Kremlin and demanded to see Mr. Chamberlain.

Not much had changed with this short, fat, and well-groomed Chamberlain, director of the Comintern's East Asia Bureau, who immediately pulled out a chair for his guest.

"Please, madam, how may I help you? It is such an honor to see you, again." Director Chamberlain was always full of charm whenever a lady showed up in his office, even though he clearly remembered the nasty critical letter to the Comintern that Tania had written with Martin.

"Very simple. You must have known that Sheng Bao's wife Yu Shao-Mei is in town, seeking medical treatment for her terrible wounds from the Long March. All the doctors and hospitals told us that she has to have an upgraded political status to receive immediate and better care. I hope you can help in this matter," Tania explained.

"Of course, madam, of course," Chamberlain began. "Any member of the Politburo, or above, of our sister party will receive special treatment."

"Yu Shao-Mei is Sheng Bao's wife. Doesn't that qualify her?" Tania asked.

"Well, it might under normal circumstances." Chamberlain gave an evasive answer.

"What do you mean?" Tania would not give up.

"Well, technically, Yu Shao-Mei is Sheng Bao's ex-wife, not his current wife." Chamberlain felt embarrassed by his own rationale.

Tania was furious. These male chauvinist pigs were playing games with her! Still, she tried to calm down and argued, "I knew quite a few females staying at the luxurious Barvikha Sanatorium who are neither war heroines nor members of any Politburo."

"My God, she has done her homework," Chamberlain said to himself. Barvikha, the high-class resort on the beautiful right bank of Moskva River, was exclusively reserved for top party elites and a few foreign guests. Where the hell did she get the information?

"That's true, madam. But they all have special connections," Chamberlain replied, beaming idiotically.

"So, a badly wounded woman and an abandoned wife of the top communist is worth nothing here, is that it?" Tania exploded.

"Madam, don't be so harsh. I will try. I will see what I can do." Chamberlain stood up to end the conversation.

8

Truth be told, Song Pei was not a bad person. Like many plain and honest countryfolk from rural China, he was tall but modest, humble but well-built, quiet and shy but strong as an ox. He worked hard all his life and was extremely loyal to the party. The organization needed members like him, hundreds of thousands of them, whose dedication, diligence, and total obedience were their common qualities. They would do anything the party asked them to do, no questions asked, no bargains negotiated, and no complaints uttered. Song was such an exemplary member whose understanding of communism was only a slight adaptation of his familiar views of Chinese society. His complete dedication to the cause led him to see the party as his only home, and its leaders his dear parents, whose instructions he, as their dutiful son, must follow to the letter.

Innocent but not blind, hardworking but not vacuous, Song sensed the winds were quietly changing within the party. He had deliberately positioned himself in such a way so that when the final showdown occurred, he would be on the winning side.

That evening after a long talk over the phone with Director Chamberlain, the sincere and indefatigable Song sat down to prepare his weekly report to Sheng Bao. He began,

I had an intense conversation with Tania today, who insisted on changing Yu Shao-Mei's political status to enable her to receive special medical and other health treatments. Her visit came as a surprise at a critical moment when I am on the delicate mission that you had assigned exclusively to me. In line with your explicit instructions, I rejected Tania's request. No negative effects should come out from her visit, which will not impact the talks I have been having with Director Chamberlain.

I just called him on the phone. Once again, Director Chamberlain has verbally agreed to push your name forward at the next leadership meeting of the Comintern. He has promised me that with your glorious experience and impeccable record, you should likely become the top choice as the official leader of the Chinese Communist Party, formally accepted and endorsed by the Comintern.

Last but not least, a new history of the Bolshevik party, personally vetted by Comrade Stalin, was recently released. A million copies have been sold within the first eight months. An English edition is in the works. Enclosed are some excerpts I translated from the Russian edition. As these extracts indicate, the Bolshevik history could be of great value to our party if we can have a Chinese edition out as soon as possible.

9

Three months later, Tania finally managed to settle Yu in a rehabilitation hospital. Doctors told her that Yu's head wounds were too deep and it was too risky for her to have another operation. They could only recommend that she be given good long-term care. She should also never suffer another emotional breakdown, they warned, which could be fatal for her fragile health.

Although Tania had tried very hard to place Yu at one of the facilities at Barvikha, the overt and implicit resistance was too much for her to overcome. The conditions at Moscow city hospitals were not ideal, but they were much better than those in Bao An. Tania had learned the hard lesson about the bloated bureaucracy and hypocrisy in the new Soviet Union and within the elaborate party apparatus. She wondered how a revolutionary government and its agencies could be so obnoxious, no better than those under the tsarist regime. She had many questions, but no answers.

A few weeks later she was on board a ship heading for New York. She had been separated from her son, Peter, for nearly fifteen years, and Mo had encouraged her, after Yu had been admitted into a Moscow hospital, to take the opportunity to visit him.

Oh, her precious baby son. How was he doing? What would he look like? Would he regard Tania as a bad mother who had forgotten about him for so many years?

Uncertainty. Tania looked forward to her new destination across the ocean amid another round of anticipation and trepidation.

Chapter 25

Resistance

1

UNDER AN ANCIENT LOOKOUT PAVILION ON THE SOUTH MOUNTAIN and over the top of several huge water pines, he could see the vast damage done to this large city across the two rivers below.

The confluence of the Yangtze River and Jialing River had nurtured the indigenous tribes of the Three Star Mountain people, who settled at what was now the city of Chongqing more than four thousand years ago. Once home to the oldest kingdoms in Southwest China, it was the most commercialized and most populous city in Sichuan Province, and now the wartime capital of China.

About six hundred miles away from the battleground in Central China and protected by the mighty Yangtze River, Chongqing seemed to be a safe place for the resistance's new national headquarters. But the government did not have an air force strong enough to protect the city. Despite massive mountain ranges in the north, east, and south, Chongqing was vulnerable to repeated Japanese air raids, which intensified after the fall of Wuhan.

The sirens had just ended, and General Chen could see, hear, and smell yet another round of appalling devastation in the city caused by the enemy's indiscriminate bombings.

The terrible residues from heavy explosions and repulsive smells of bomb powder filled the air. Hundreds of residential houses and businesses had been destroyed. Some buildings were still burning in the heart of the city between the Buddhist Temple and Coppersmith Lane, a busy commercial district he had visited only the other day. The flames and smoke were clearly visible from where Chen stood. Many civilians must have been killed or wounded for he could hear men, women, and children screaming and crying amid the utter chaos. They must have lost either their homes or loved ones, or both, the general surmised.

Chen knew those Japanese bastards were trying to bomb the city—and his government—into submission. "Over my dead body. We will continue to fight and we will never surrender. China will survive and we will succeed," he vowed to himself.

A group of his top military leaders had been working on new military strategies for several days. They must have reached a decision and it was about time for him to find out. Chen turned around and started to walk toward the underground bunker to meet with his officers.

2

Less than ten miles from downtown and named for its location on the south bank of the Yangtze River, the horseshoe-shaped South Mountain rose from one thousand, two hundred to one thousand, eight hundred feet high and was a perfect hideout from the notoriously hot and steamy downtown Chongqing in summer time. Fully grown trees, dense bamboo, and wild bushes covered the entire area of over six thousand acres, which had only one narrow and winding country road as entrance, making it a highly secluded and safe place for General Chen to set up his headquarters.

A wealthy banker used to own several buildings in this area. The government had bought and converted them for wartime use. The one closest to the pavilion was a three-story villa of bricks and wood trims, situated atop the tallest hill. A great camphor tree, "Twin Heroes," stood nearby. According to a legend, two brothers were fighting the mountain devils in ancient times. One got wounded and the other was holding him in his arms until both died.

At least seven hundred years old, the tree was sixty feet high. Its massive dark brown trunk split into two big branches, each carrying a bright, lush, and gigantic green canopy as if to provide continued safety and peace for the area.

Named after this signature tree, the Twin Heroes villa was surrounded by several additional giant fig trees, camphor trees, katsura trees, and small-leaved banyans, which hid the building so completely that no one could see it from anywhere unless he showed up before the first of the ninety-step staircase leading to the house. Bright, airy, but simply furnished, the villa was used as Chen's residence and office with a small conference room on the ground floor.

Several hundred yards down the hill to the left, Madam Chen often used a separate house as her residence, so as to give the general and his officers more privacy in his quarters during the war. Constructed on the sweeping side of a gentle knoll and aptly designed in a raised and ranch-style house against the slope in the back, the total living space of this modest residence was not any smaller than that of her husband's impressive three-story villa.

The house, with its serene and hospitable ambience, was affectionately named "Pine Court," framed and written in the general's own handwriting, for the great varieties of huge, thick, tall, and vigorous pine trees around the building. The court opened with a big wraparound and fully covered front porch lined with gray bricks and blue stone slabs. From the center of the porch, three wide granite staircases went through a series of big lush planters leading to a rare piece of flat ground, where cars could be parked. The location of her residence was a blessing for visitors because most hillside houses in this mountainous area were inaccessible to cars, including the general's villa. Everyone had to walk and climb many stairs while moving from place to place. The typical Sichuan-style "Hua-Gan," a bamboo sedan chair carried by two men, would be used sometimes when the Chens needed to go from one building to another.

Vigilantly guarded but unmarked, the war room for the military was dug deep underground in a different location far away from the first couple's residential quarters.

General Chen passed those guards, and his officers rose as he walked in.

From their expressions, the general knew the discussions were not encouraging. He asked nonetheless, "Well, gentlemen, what have you decided?"

Around the oval table twelve high-ranking officers sat quietly. No one was willing to speak first. Chen looked at his chief of staff, General Bai Yu-Xian.

Once dubbed the "Second Kong Ming," after one of the best-known and most-resourceful military strategists in Chinese history during the Three Kingdoms era, Bai had lost much of his halo after his "southern strategy" failed to repel the Japanese army. Instead, the catastrophic losses of Shanghai and Nanjing early in the war had greatly damaged his credibility, and he had since become much more cautious when advising the commander-in-chief.

Bai stood up and said, "We have come to an agreement that Changsha would be the next target of the Japanese."

"And then?" Chen wanted to hear about a plan, not a target.

"And then… and then…" Bai was looking at his colleagues for assistance. Nobody moved or said a word. "And then, we might have to withdraw." He managed to finish his sentence.

"Withdraw to where?" Chen was holding back his rising anger.

"To… to… to further south," Bai replied.

"Gentlemen, you all know we have nowhere else to withdraw." Chen finally exploded. "We have lost Wuhan. We have lost Guangzhou. We have lost Nanchang. Now you are telling me that we can't defend Changsha, the major city between Wuhan and Guangzhou. Are you suggesting that we should give up the entire South China to the enemies?"

"No, no, no, chief," Bai was shaking. "We are not planning to give up South China. We are only saying it would be hard to defend Changsha."

"What is the difference then? Not to defend Changsha *is* to give up South China!"

"We have few tanks, heavy artillery, and airplanes," someone murmured.

"And Changsha is very flat. There is no mountain, no hill in the area, which will make it very difficult to defend the city," came another rejoinder.

"I know it's hard. But is it impossible?" Chen stared at every participant and pounded the table. "I am asking, is it impossible to defend Changsha? I am sure you understand the difference!"

Silence. Absolute silence.

"What a waste of time! You have talked and talked for several days, and now all you can say is to withdraw?"

"Chief, may I say something?" General Pan Jin rose.

"Of course you may." Chen was hopeful.

All the officers in the room knew Pan was the hero at Ominous Propensity, one of the Chinese troops' few but substantial victories in this war. His success, however, had generated considerable bitterness and jealousy among his colleagues who believed that in deciding strategic matters he, as a field officer, did not have enough seniority to speak up at a meeting like this.

"Changsha can be defended." His bold statement shocked everybody, especially the older military leaders.

"How?" someone asked, apparently not wanting to be outshone.

"There are conditions, of course," Pan said.

Chen got the hint and said, "Okay, the meeting is adjourned. I will talk to all of you tomorrow at 8am, sharp!"

After everybody had left the room, Chen turned to Pan and said, "Now you can tell me what is on your mind."

3

"Welcome, general, welcome." Madam Chen stood at the double door of Pine Court as she cordially greeted General Pan.

Following the morning's military meeting, General Chen had insisted that Pan stay back for lunch.

"Thank you, madam. I am much honored." Pan saluted the first lady, knowing that the first family rarely invited anyone to have private meals with them.

"We are much honored. You are the hero of our resistance." Madam Chen took him to the dining room.

Like the rest of the house, the dining room was sparsely furnished except for the set of hardwood dining table, chairs, and serving stands.

"General, I don't know your exact taste. I usually have sandwiches, and my husband prefers rice. I know you are from Guangdong, and so I have asked the kitchen to prepare some Cantonese dishes. Hope you will like them," said Madam Chen, always the caring and thoughtful hostess.

"Thank you so much. Thank you very much, madam." Pan was much humbled. He knew the warm reception came with big responsibilities and great expectations.

"Sit down. Sit down. Don't be nervous. Let's eat." General Chen started his meal by asking the servant for the traditional preserved pickles shipped from his hometown. He could not have a meal without it.

"The soup is great. Very authentic Cantonese taste. Thank you very much, madam." Pan praised the dish that the hostess had specially ordered. The soup was actually a warm and thick porridge mixed with chopped sausages and preserved duck eggs sliced into tiny pieces—a Cantonese staple at mealtimes.

The taste of home seemed to have relaxed Pan, who knew the real conversation would only started when the boss spoke.

"Darling, you would not believe what conditions General Pan Jin had set in exchange for his promise to defend Changsha!"

"What did he ask?" The madam was curious. A hands-on manager, she always wanted to know whether her husband had made the appropriate deals in any of his appointments or negotiations.

"Madam, I have asked for the authority to command all the troops in the Changsha theater, both the forces of the central government and those of the regional units. They are all needed for the city's defense," Pan replied.

"That's understandable. One of the reasons we have failed many times in the past is because our national government had little control over the local and regional troops." A firm believer in a strong and centralized national government as much as her husband, Madam Chen tolerated no provincialism and thought the request was logical.

"Yes, I agreed. I have appointed General Pan Jin as both the supreme commander of the Changsha theater and the governor of Hunan Province, giving him all the military and civilian authority he will need to defend the city."

"Good." Madam Chen approved her husband's decision.

"Madam, I also asked—pardon me—that General Chen would not interfere with the detailed military operations once the strategy had been decided." Pan stated this with some apprehension, knowing how sensitive the issue could be for both Chens.

Madam Chen knew all about the delicate nature of military power, and how extremely protective her husband was of it. She did not say a word but looked at the man at the head of the table, waiting for his response.

It was hard. As Madam Chen and everyone around him would know, General Chen was a dedicated politician, a highly diligent and methodical commander. Whenever he was not in touch with his troops, he felt insecure or even lost if he was not on top of every military move for just a minute. He had spent his whole career building the national army, which was his power base and his life. General Chen understood clearly that micro-management was not always desirable. It could be counterproductive in the battlefield and his meticulous nature could come across as overbearing to his officers. But rational deductions and cool analysis were never enough to convince a man to change his behavior. Didn't an ancient Chinese proverb state that "dynasties may change faster than a man's behavior"? Although he conceded his style was not always suitable for the larger cause, he could not help it.

Now that Pan had formally requested his noninterference, General Chen hesitated. If he agreed to it, he did not know what it might lead to. But, if he refused to grant Pan's request, he could lose Changsha.

"Darling, I think General Pan Jin has a point. Hasn't it been our tradition in history that the field officer has the final say when the emperor is away?" Madam Chen understood why her husband hesitated and wanted to give him a nudge.

"Yes, of course, darling. I understand it, I understand it, and I understand it." General Chen agreed to the request without acknowledging it. He made a concession by recognizing the need to be flexible, while still refusing to change his management style.

4

The rise of Sheng Bao to the top of the Communist Party leadership had been the subject of many speculations and different interpretations. The truth of the matter was that it all happened at one of the most obscure and informal gatherings with the least fanfare or documentation.

Mo Jia-Qi's return from Moscow produced a surprisingly delicate equilibrium in the party's top hierarchy, which had been destabilized for more than five years since the beginning of the Long March.

Before his ouster at the city of Yi, Mo had the explicit support of the Comintern but was at the losing end when it involved the control of the Red Army. While the nonconformist Sheng had orchestrated and thus benefited from the coup at Yi city by gaining substantial influence in party and military affairs, his promotion had never been officially approved by the Comintern. Meng Bo-Xian replaced Mo as the head of the party, and was technically Sheng's boss. But Meng's modest personality and naiveté in politics were fully exploited by Sheng, who had been using him as a pawn. Meng never had any real authority in the party, and his position was also never officially sanctioned by Moscow.

An end to this unsettled situation was finally in sight when Mo informed his colleagues that Moscow had drawn up a new list of party officials and that, after this reshuffle, a new national congress would be held soon to finalize the party hierarchy.

The list selected five persons as the standing members of the Politburo: Mo Jia-Qi, Sheng Bao, Meng Bo-Xian, Si-Tu Wen-Liang, and Tao Yin-Hu. Two were named as alternate members: Lin Shi-Xiong and Song Pei. Collectively, these seven officials would form the latest leadership of the Chinese Communist Party.

Moscow had tried to be impartial. It did put Mo back at the top of the party leadership, but did not give him a more prominent role than other members. In fact, Moscow deliberately did not name a leader for the party, as it had always done previously. Based on the unsuccessful experience of the past, decision-makers in Moscow perhaps assumed that the top position might be best left to the Chinese themselves to decide. Also, out of more practical concerns, Moscow did not specify the different roles each of the Politburo members should perform, which also gave room for the Chinese themselves to sort it out.

The equilibrium was temporarily restored and all the newly nominated members (except for Song, who was in Moscow) did not disagree with the arrangement, which, rather than drastically shifted authority from one side to another, seemed to be a small but sensible readjustment of the power-sharing among the party's top leaders that had existed for half a decade.

To level the playing field was one thing, but to move forward from the new starting line was quite another. More than anybody else, Sheng wanted to make sure that he would emerge the champion in this new race. It took him a long while to figure out how to manipulate the subtle balance arranged by the Comintern so that he could use it to his advantage. Realizing that the key might lie in the way the redistribution of responsibilities in the Politburo would be carried out, he was not about to let this great opportunity slip away through his fingers.

During the difficult and penurious days in Bao An, the party did not have any designated office building. Many high-level party meetings were held wherever a good private room could be found. When Sheng suggested that the first of session of the new Politburo meet at his residence—a medium-sized cave dwelling no different from the rest in Bao An, no one had any reason to object. To prepare for the occasion, Sheng had asked Su Ming to bake some potatoes on the stove—the only luxury in the household of a high party official.

When the roomful of people sat comfortably on the heated kang and tucked into the nicely baked potatoes, they felt as cozy as they could be, especially since the nasty winds outside had chilled Bao An to sub-zero degrees. Sheng announced that he had thought about the division of work among his colleagues, and he would like to make the following suggestions:

Mo Jia-Qi, secretary of the party's Southern Bureau,

Si-Tu Wen-Liang, secretary of the party's Northern Bureau,

Tao Yin-Hu, commander-in-chief of the troops under the party's control,

Meng Bo-Xian, secretary in charge of the party's media, propaganda, and education,

Sheng Bao, secretary in charge of the party's communication and publication,

Lin Shi-Xiong, in charge of the party's internal security, and

Song Pei, head of the party's delegation in Moscow.

These suggestions seemed appropriate and harmless, and no one opposed them. The seven people would basically continue to do what they had been doing all along, and no big change seemed to be needed at this point. They unanimously accepted Sheng's simple and straightforward proposal.

5

Sheng's crafty designs surfaced not long after the "potato meeting" was over.

Meng seemed to have retained his old assignment, but he had lost the title as the party's general secretary since the meeting at Yi city. However nominal and unimportant the title might have meant to Sheng, stripping it from someone else was satisfying to him. Apparently, Meng was the first loser in this power reshuffle.

Despite Mo's ambition and strong backing from the Comintern, he was merely assigned to head a regional bureau. He was not thrilled about it, but had no reason to protest. His colleagues had argued that, after being absent from China for a long time, some ground experience might be good for him.

As for Si-Tu, the veteran official who was more senior than anyone else in the party, his new role as head of the Northern Bureau amounted to a demotion. It was a major relegation for a man of his skills and experience.

Only Tao would be doing what he had been doing all along—to serve as the commander-in-chief of the communist army.

But more critical than the separate titles and assignments was where each Politburo member would be located to carry out his duties.

Mo must go to Chongqing, where the headquarters of the Southern Bureau was.

To manage the Northern Bureau, Si-Tu must go to Shanxi Province (east of Shaanxi), where Tao must also go to take charge of the troops.

Only Meng and the alternate member Lin, neither of whom had ever posed a real threat to Sheng, would stay, with the latter at the party headquarters in Bao An.

Thus, although the five standing members of the Politburo were supposed to share power equally according to the Comintern's original intention, Sheng had already given himself more control over party affairs by sending his serious competitors far away from him.

In addition to this implicit advantage, Sheng's real authority was far more substantial than his title would suggest. He had been heading the party's committee for military affairs for a long time, and no one dared to touch that. Despite the modest title of secretary of communication and publication, he and he alone had the monopoly of any communication within the party and army, as well as all the communications with Moscow. He and he alone possessed the exclusive authority to prepare, review, and sanction all of the Politburo's major documents. Sheng's domain was in reality more far-reaching and critical than all the limited assignments of his colleagues combined. Finally, because more than half of the Politburo would be stationed far away from Bao Ann, Sheng, by default, would be heading a subcommittee to prepare for the party's next national congress. At first sight a role involving a lot of paperwork, it actually gave Sheng the opportunity to control the makeup of the party's new leadership according to his wishes, which would be of vital importance in his continuing pursuit of power.

6

Sheng's confidence in his intrinsic righteousness enabled him to justify his clandestine maneuvers, which he kept entirely to himself. A great man had to have some great secrets, he believed, which should never be shared with anyone, including his wife. "All warfare is based on deception." Master Sun Tzu's principle should never be violated.

Years of bloody fighting against armed enemies from without had hardened Sheng's heart, and the unremitting competition with political rivals from within had strengthened his resolve. Those treacherous struggles had also made him a highly suspicious person, who needed different masks for different occasions. A casual and lively communicator with commoners, he listened as carefully as he spoke before his closest peers. Telling jokes and anecdotes was a usual tactic to conceal his seriousness, just as a constant shift of topics from today's weather to ancient poetry would effectively hide his train of thoughts and clever manipulations. An enigmatic speaker, he could remain a riddle to a person even after two hours of intimate conversation.

Sheng's overt aloofness and covert chicanery intrigued one person—Lin, the Politburo's alternate member. "What a brilliant display of the 'lure the tiger out of his den' strategy at the last meeting," sighed Lin, who believed he had learned a lot about Sheng, the man and the politician. A Moscow-trained specialist in internal security, Lin could not resist the temptation of probing deeper into his boss's inner world. He knew this could be highly risky so he had to devise his own game plan.

A few days later, Lin—who was familiar with his boss's morning routine—met Sheng while the latter was taking a stroll along the bank of a quiet and shallow creek.

"Thanks for the painting by the sixth-century master Zhang Seng-Yao (張僧繇)," said Sheng.

"You are most welcome." Lin was delighted to see Sheng in a good mood.

"I heard about his legendary ability to bring a painted dragon to life by adding the pupils in its eyes. But I never knew he could draw tigers." Sheng was learned and modest at once.

"I am sure you knew. Nothing can escape your keen mind." Lin flattered the boss and said, "I was reading *Journey to the West* the other night."

Lin deliberately paused for the classic novel did mention the strategy of "lure the tiger out of its den." He wanted to see what Sheng had to say.

"Oh, wonderful. I have always liked the money king in the stories," Sheng responded.

"How about tigers?" Lin said half-jokingly.

Sheng now understood what Lin was up to. He was not about to let Lin know what was going through his mind.

"There was no tiger in the novel," he said.

"Oh, yeah, my mistake. The tigers were sent out," Lin added.

"No, there were no tigers. See this." Sheng picked up a small pebble and threw it into a lump of shrubs in the distance. A flock of quails flew away. "See, there are no tigers."

"That's because you have driven them out." Seeing Sheng was still in a relaxed mode, Lin continued their battle of wits.

"No, I did not drive them out. I just gave them some directions," Sheng replied.

Presently he saw an old and short local shepherd with a large flock of goats. "See that smart shepherd," Sheng said to Lin. "He can teach you how to keep an unruly herd together without reading *Journey to the West*."

Sheng left. Lin remained behind watching what the shepherd was doing. Nothing happened for a long while. Only now and then the old man would stand up and hurled a small clod with his long handle to keep his five dozen goats together. Sheng had taught Lin another lesson without saying what it was.

A week later, someone knocked on Lin's door in the morning. He came out and saw Su Ming was there with a scroll in her hand.

"My husband asked me to return this to you. He said thank you," the modest and shy Su said gently.

"Oh, that was a gift for Comrade Sheng Bao." Lin was surprised.

"He says it is a painting too valuable and too delicate for him to keep," Su patiently explained.

"Oh, Comrade Sheng Bao is too modest. He deserves it. He absolutely deserves it," Lin insisted.

"He had asked me to make me a copy of it by drawing," Su said.

"Oh, that's wonderful," answered Lin, who was delighted and perplexed at the same time.

7

Not until General Pan arrived in Changsha did he realize how the situation had gone from bad to worse within a few weeks.

Hundreds of thousands of refugees rushing in from many enemy-occupied territories swelled the native population, stretching local resources to the limit. Since there were not enough policemen to enforce law and order, the city was riddled with unbridled rumors, widespread chaos, and stifling defeatism.

The government had decided to adopt a "scorched earth policy" if the Japanese troops were to advance within ten miles of the city. Incompetent provincial officials hastily set up municipal procedures, and poorly organized personnel failed to ensure the proper implementation of the policy. One night, a telegraph translator working on the names of two rivers outside Changsha mistook the word "fair" for "fairy," which caused the intelligence officer who received it to panic. The correct translation should be that the Japanese army was approaching the Fair River, which was one hundred miles away from Changsha. The wrong translation put the approaching Japanese army at the Fairy River, which was only ten miles from the city.

Coincidentally, a neighborhood fire was mistaken as the signal to start the torching order hours before everything else was in place. The result was the most horrendous tragedy in memory. As much as ninety percent of residential houses, government buildings, schools, and businesses in Changsha were burned to the ground, and thousands of people lost their lives. The fire did not stop for five days, and the city's two-thousand-year heritage disappeared in the flames.

Pan was facing a ruined city even before he officially took over the reins to defend it.

8

Japanese officers had long studied Sun Tzu and they were no less fervent admirers of the master strategist than their Chinese counterparts. Several years into the war, China was still standing. General Chen's army showed no signs of giving up the fight. Compared to the isles of Japan, China was unbelievably huge and the nationalist government still controlled large portions of the country's vast territory. Frustrated but determined to gain complete control over the path through South China, the militarists in Tokyo planned to attack Changsha, break the resistance, and destroy large numbers of Chinese troops in the campaign. They selected those favorable passages by Sun Tzu to justify their full-scale aggression and pushing their troops to the limit.

Sun Tzu had said:

> To throw the troops into a position from which there is no escape and even when faced with death they will not flee. For in preparing to die, what can they not achieve? Then officers and men together put forth their utmost efforts. In a desperate situation they fear nothing; when there is no way out they stand firm. Deep in a hostile land they are bound together, and there, where there is no alternative, they will engage the enemy in hand-to-hand combat.

He had also pointed out:

> The reason the enlightened prince and the wise general can conquer the enemy whenever they move is foreknowledge. There is no place espionage is not used. And therefore only the enlightened sovereign and the worthy general who are able to use the most intelligent people as agents are certain to achieve great things.

To prepare for its aggression, nobody collected more intelligence about China than the Japanese militarist government, which had paid its consulate employees, overseas residents, civilian travelers, businessmen, merchants, and professional spies to engage in espionage activities in China for decades. Officers of the Japanese army therefore often had more accurate information about the Chinese population, better atlases about Chinese landscape, and more clearly printed-out charts and diagrams than Chinese officers, who valued the precise and highly sophisticated Japanese military maps more than any other military asset and equipment.

Lying south of the Yangtze River, Changsha, the provincial capital of Hunan Province, sat along the Xiang River, a principal tributary of the mighty Yangtze. A medium-sized city of three hundred thousand people, its famous history went back to ancient times more than two thousand, four hundred years ago and it had been a continuous human habitat since then. Linking provincial roads, shipping lines, and waterways as well as serving as a key stop on the most important railroad in South China from Wuhan to Guangzhou, Changsha had been the center of thriving business, increasing commerce, and booming education for the region in recent decades.

Passing Changsha, the lower Xiang River flowed northward to empty itself in Dongting Lake, which converged with the Yangtze. Across this broad basin, land was literally flat except for the hills and mountains rising in the distant east and west. Thus the city was highly vulnerable to attacks from the northerly direction, where the provincial highways were. Only one hundred miles away from Changsha and next to Dongting Lake, the township of Yueyang was being used as the military base for the Japanese attackers, whose tanks and trucks could make their way to Changsha on the smooth provincial highways in less than three days.

Fortunately, between Yueyang in the north and Changsha in the south, four rivers, all crisscrossing the provincial thoroughfare like a chessboard, ran horizontally from east to west to join the Xiang River. Starting from the north, they were the Fair River, Plum River, Thick Blade River, and Fairy River. To the Japanese mechanized troops, to step on the gas pedal while passing through the provincial highways might be easy. Crossing the four rivers would be another matter. Clearly, these rivers and their ferry stations would be the main roadblocks the Japanese must overcome to get to

Changsha, while the Chinese must hold onto them as the main defenses to protect the city.

Headed by Commander Okamura, the old "China hand," the Japanese 11th Army was a massive force comprising seven corps, eight hundred trucks, four hundred and fifty pieces of artillery, twenty gunships, two hundred steamboats, one hundred airplanes, and one hundred thousand men. Confident in his forces' superiority over the poorly equipped Chinese troops, Okamura believed that attacking Changsha from a northerly direction was a good strategy. His 6th Corps attacked the first Chinese stronghold at the Fair River, and the battle was on.

9

"You did well in sketching the tiger." Sheng praised the line drawings Su had made from the scroll of painting sent by Lin.

"I am glad you liked it," his wife answered gaily. She had never known she could draw and was much delighted to discover this new talent, encouraged by the husband. She regretted that she could only trace a simple outline by pencil. "I wish I could use colors. But we don't have those expensive paints as in the original," Su said.

"No need to be upset," said the husband. "That painting is not the original. Lin's is a very late copy. The sixth-century original painting was long lost. And even an ancient copy of it would be priceless. If Lin Shi-Xiong possessed one of those, he would be a very rich man, and doesn't have to be a revolutionary at all." Sheng comforted Su by laughing the matter off.

An official from the communication department came in and handed Sheng two telegrams.

The official and Su discreetly left the room. Both knew that Sheng did not like anyone to disturb him while he was dealing with classified party secrets.

The first one was from Mo in Chongqing. It read:

I recently met General Chen, who praised our participation in the United Front and our great contributions to the resistance movement against Japanese aggression. I explained to him our new policies under the United Front. He appreciated the updates and informed me about the military situation in South China, especially the ongoing campaign around Changsha. He suggested that, if our troops could take some action to engage the enemy somewhere in the north, it will be a great help for those frontline government troops that are fighting hard to defend Changsha.

Sheng did not say a word, and he opened the second one. It was from Tao and Si-Tu in Shanxi.

We are happy to report that the Eighth Army has made significant strides. Recruitment has been extremely successful in Shanxi, Hebei, and Suiyuan as our bases expanded into more than one hundred and twenty counties in these three provinces. We are confident that, with proper training, the Eighth Army, now one hundred thousand men strong, can fulfill any military tasks the party would command us to complete.

P.S. We do badly need guns and all kinds of military supplies. The sooner we can take direct action, the earlier we can seize them from the Japanese.

"Some action, direct action, any military tasks." Why did these two telegrams sound the same? Sheng wondered.

Reading between the lines, Sheng could pick up the underlying criticism. They were blaming me for the reluctance to engage the enemy. Why did they sound like the nationalists, who had ridiculed my strategy of guerrilla war as "a recipe of moving a lot without fighting"? Why hadn't they learned anything from the repeated failures of positional warfare? Why were they willing to be the mouthpiece for Chen, who never liked me in the first place?

Anger and frustration overwhelmed Sheng. He sincerely believed that he was doing everything he could to save and preserve the military forces for the future success of the communist cause, which had not been properly understood by his comrades.

He put the telegrams down on the table and raised his head. Once again his eyes were drawn to the figure of the tiger Su had copied. "What a pair of ferocious-looking eyes! What a powerful animal with brute force!"

Enlightened and inspired, Sheng calmed down. "Thank heavens I did not send Si-Tu Wen-Liang and Mo Jia-Qi to the same place. Otherwise, who knows what they may say and do together by now?" He sat down to draft his replies and said to himself, "I still like the smaller but very clever money king better than this stupid tiger."

10

The relentless attacks by the 6th Corps went on for five days. "Poor 15th Corps," General Pan said to himself, "they always got the hardest assignment from my command. I must let them rest for at least a month after this battle."

But when Pan went to the front line to inspect his troops, they told him that they found the Japanese moves suspicious. The attacks were real, but the Japanese did not seem to be in a hurry to defeat their opponents. They had the ability to force the 15th Corps to withdraw from their bunkers at the Fair River, but they always stopped short of doing so at the last minute.

About seventy miles long, the Fair River was the first major river in Northern Hunan. Less than twenty miles from Yueyang, the Japanese home base, the two-hundred-and-fifty-feet-wide and twenty-feet-deep river became the first line of defense for the Chinese troops. In the rainy season of every spring, the significant rise of precipitation would render the river impossible to cross. But, in the current dry season, the river was not a huge obstacle to the Japanese army, which had plenty of well-equipped and well-trained military engineers.

From what he could observe up close in person, Pan agreed with the assessment of his soldiers and officers. The highly experienced 6th Corps should have no problems of defeating a single Chinese corps at the Fair River within two to three days. What were they thinking after five days of fighting?

Then the reports came in and Pan realized it was all part of Okamura's strategy.

Taking the steamboats in the night across Dongting Lake, an amphibious division of Japanese soldiers had landed on the south bank of the Plum River, which was twenty miles behind the Fair River. The amphibious division immediately started the attacks from the south, while the 6th Corps resumed its assaults from the north.

The 15th Corps was in grave danger. Facing the enemy forces front and back, it was being trapped between two rivers.

Okamura, the old fox! Pan cursed. He hated to be outsmarted, but had to give credit to his opponent, who could turn the disadvantage of the rivers into his advantage.

Pan ordered the 15th Corps to withdraw to avoid annihilation.

Before the campaign, Pan and his staff had planned for the 15th Corps to withdraw at some point, because they did not believe that the first line of defense at the Fair River would be sustainable when the overwhelming Japanese forces were determined to take Changsha. Still, the withdrawal did lead to some considerable chaos along the way and even disturbance in the city.

More bad news followed. To his surprises, Pan was informed that three additional Japanese corps had started marching not from the north but from the highlands of the east, attempting to dash down into this region right between the Big Blade River and the Fairy River. These two rivers were undeniably valuable as natural barriers to fend off attacks from the north, but they were literally useless as a defense against any attacks coming from between them.

If the three Japanese corps from the east succeeded, all the Chinese defenses along the rivers would be worthless and the Japanese would soon be reaching and encircling the city of Changsha in no time.

Oh, boy, Okamura, the bastard! Now General Pan started to understand General Okamura, the strategist.

Pan knew that a frequent tactic the Japanese military, from high commanders to field officers, tended to use was to get behind the enemy lines by attacking their flanks. But, to plan and prepare such a complex operation in this wildly convoluted foreign terrain, Okamura was as bold as he was sophisticated. He must have realized the enormous difficulties to tear down four defenses by crossing four rivers in a row, and hence he had designed this two-punch strategy to get behind the Chinese lines and to render their four horizontally paralleled defenses useless.

Now that the enemy had shown its hand, it was time for Pan to execute his plans.

He commanded all his units to defend their positions as fiercely as they could. "The enemy shall pay the price for invading our land," he told the soldiers, "and we will never allow them to conquer Changsha." But, gradually, the onslaught by the massive Japanese forces was too much for Pan's units to withstand. He issued an order for his troops to withdraw. Meanwhile he gave strict orders to the 10th Corps, the final remaining force near and inside Changsha, to fight and defend the city to the last man standing. The city should never be lost to the enemies, his order stated.

The bloodiest chapter of the campaign had started. Every inch of territory was fought over along the last several dozen miles from the city. No position was taken without repeated fighting, and almost all was taken only through hand-to-hand combat.

At long last, the Japanese vanguard could see the partially fallen city walls of Changsha, which meant the beginning of tenacious and dangerous street-to-street battles inside its much-damaged neighborhoods after the ruinous fire.

Chapter 26

Shift

1

"**V**ICTORY!"
      "Bravo!"
        "Success!"
"We won!"

Chongqing exploded in joy and the crowds went wild in the streets to celebrate when news came that General Pan had successfully defended the city of Changsha. At long last, the first significant triumph in the war for the Chinese troops during a major Japanese offensive. All the terrible pain, hardships, sufferings, and losses on the arduous road of resistance were not in vain. There finally seemed to be light at the end of an extremely dark tunnel.

The strategic importance of Changsha had long convinced Pan that the Japanese must have planned to take it, regardless of the cost, to expand their occupation throughout South China. He then used the city as a bait and designed a counterstrategy accordingly. Codenamed "inferno," his plan took full advantage of the four regional rivers and carefully deployed the defensive forces in the shape of an extended web. Over forty strongholds were built, and each unit must defend its position until ordered to move.

Under heavy and repeated attacks, some of Pan's frontline troops did withdraw, which motivated Commander Okamura's soldiers to press on closer and closer to Changsha. The sight of the city further convinced them that they could break the Chinese defense as they had previously done many times at other Chinese cities.

The street battles inside the city took much longer than anyone had anticipated, and Pan's 10th Corps made good its promise to protect Changsha at all costs. Next to the burned-out buildings, near some torn-down walls, along the alleys, and behind an abandoned courtyard, the Chinese foot soldiers were surprisingly resilient and would never give up an inch without intense fighting.

Pan then set his trap. While his troops did gradually withdraw, they did so not to escape from the fight but to move to the flanks to join other enforcement units to form a new line of reserves waiting for the scheduled counterattack. As Okamura's soldiers entered the city to engage the 10th Corps, they were not aware that Pan's still larger forces, hiding in the wings, would completely surround them from behind. Instead of another big prize as the enemies had long hoped, Changsha turned into a deadly "inferno" for the Japanese in the end.

The nightmare became even worse as the Japanese troops tried to escape from the city. Many local people had helped the government troops to block roads, flood the fields, destroy bridges, and hide foodstuff and animals. Chinese artillery bombarded the fleeing Japanese, who were chased, ambushed, and attacked all the way one hundred miles back to Yueyang, where they had started the offensive two months ago.

2

"We have just received the approval from the military committee of the party's Central Committee," Commander Tao Yin-Hu told his officers, "and we shall start the attacks at 9pm tomorrow."

Tao was a practical man and no-nonsense speaker. He was interested in directing to the upcoming encounter, not in making small talk.

Si-Tu Wen-Liang rose to give an inspirational speech, the task he, as the party's head of this regional bureau, had performed many times.

"Comrades, this is the third year of our resistance and we finally have the opportunity to teach the Japanese a big lesson!" As much as anyone else in the crowd, Si-Tu had been waiting for this moment and he joined his audience in their applause.

In a firm voice and compelling body language, Si-Tu went on, "We will show our nation what we are made of! We will show to the world how patriotic Chinese will never rest until we drive the Japanese aggressors out of our country!" his enthusiastic oration continued.

After extensive investigations and discussions about the military situation in North China with their comrades, Si-Tu and Tao had decided to attack a number of enemy transportation facilities. Although the communists had greatly expanded their rural bases and drastically increased the sizes of their military units, the training of the new recruits was inadequate, the quality of equipment poor, and the real battle experience next to nil. Both men knew that in its present condition, the Eighth Army could not wage any major campaign directly against the enemy. But sitting on the sidelines and watching the nationalist troops taking action again and again had made the Eighth Army troops uneasy. They requested to engage the enemy several times and now Bao An had finally approved their plans, which made they happy, anxious, and excited.

"The main target in this campaign will be the East–West Railroad between Stone Gates and Grand Dragon. Now, Commander Tao Yin-Hu will give you the detailed instructions." Si-Tu finished his speech, and passed the stage to Tao. The meeting went on into the wee hours.

A major stop on the most important vertical artery Peking–Wuhan Railroad, the East–West Railroad connected two completely different cities one hundred and forty miles apart from each other in North China. Grand Dragon in Shanxi Province to the west was one of China's most ancient cities, whose history dated back two thousand, five hundred years. Because a large number of distinguished noblemen, princes, kings, and emperors were born and grew up in this era, it was given the most regal name to reflect the immense prestige and pride the local residents had had over the centuries. The provincial capital of Shanxi, the City of Grand Dragon, exemplified one of the most productive, highly cultivated, and wealthiest regions in North China.

Located in Hebei Province east of Shanxi, Stone Gates was a little-known hamlet that had attracted scant attention until the planners of the East–West Railroad came along about thirty years ago. They wanted to construct a terminal to connect the Peking–Wuhan Railroad in the area but did not wish to incur huge expenses by building a bridge across the nearby Hutuo River. For practical purposes, this obscure village of fewer than two hundred people on the south bank of the river was then chosen. But the place was so minuscule that it did not even have a proper name to offer the modern railroad station. Finally, some smart employee on the planning team suggested combining the names of two nearby small villages in the vicinity, Stoneville and Gatesville, thus Stone Gates, to mark the new destination. Overnight, increasing traffic and growing business transformed this teeny rural community into a booming metropolis in North China. To the surprise of many, this newest city eventually became the capital of Hebei, pushing aside a cluster of far more ancient towns and famous cities in the province.

The expansion of railroads benefited trade and businesses, but was a bane to the communists, who were fighting a guerrilla war in the region. The Japanese occupation made it worse by allowing the enemy to ship its troops faster than ever to the areas where the Eighth Army had its rural bases hidden in the mountains along the border between Shanxi and Hebei. More than anything else, Tao and Si-Tu were troubled by the Japanese control of the East–West Railroad, which had been a serious threat to the Eighth Army for a long time. Now they would finally get their chance for revenge.

Unlike all the limited maneuvers the communist troops had conducted in the past, the planned strike this time was sudden, explosive, and widespread.

Within the first few hours of the campaign, no fewer than twenty segments of the East–West Railroad were bombed. A series of guard posts and watch towers by the Japanese were stormed and then taken. For the next few days, scores of roads were turned upside down, railroad tracks removed, bridges burned, garrisons attacked, communication lines cut, grain warehouses sabotaged, mining production halted, water towers bombarded, and utility facilities destroyed. No fewer than two dozen towns and county seats occupied by Japanese troops were hit and besieged in a month.

North China had not seen such chaos since the beginning of the war.

Initial accounts were encouraging for the Eighth Army, which had never committed itself to a frontal attack this big, nor had it ever captured such large quantities of ammunition, guns, military supplies, and equipment from the enemies.

However unsupportive of the plan he might have been at the beginning, Sheng Bao was very satisfied after reading the first batch of battlefield reports. He wired Tao and Si-Tu: "Congratulations! Very pleased with the good news. Can you organize one or two more campaigns just like this one?"

Unfortunately, the news was actually too good to be all true. Originally, Tao and Si-Tu had only planned to deploy twenty regiments for the action. Incoming reports continued to add to the numbers of participating units until a staffer told them that as many as one hundred-plus regiments were fighting across the region. Apparently, the first attacks aroused the spirit of many local militias and friendly guerrillas who joined the battles in droves. The carefully orchestrated attacks and raids during the initial stage soon snowballed into an avalanche so drastic and so overwhelming that no one was able to take full control of every local action anymore.

"A battle of a hundred regiments!" The name took off faster than the instigator could pronounce it. So, the "Battle of a Hundred Regiments" it was.

As the campaign went out of control, the widespread actions and overexcitement triggered a backlash. When the Japanese assessed the damage and finally realized what was going on, they turned their attention to the north. Brutal attacks ensued to eliminate the communist menace right under their noses. Facing unprecedented difficulties to survive, the Eighth Army retreated into hiding.

3

The lovely and endless rolling hills under the crystal blue skies seemed out of this world, and the place was as quiet, surreal, and heavenly as a Christmas card with drawings of a white fence, idyllic farm, and beautiful meadow.

There were no signs of the prevailing poverty and awful ravages of war that one could see everywhere in the countryside across China. No emaciated bodies along the road, dying of starvation. No sudden gunshots and deadly military attacks. No horrifying air-raid sirens and bombing explosions. No unattended wounded soldiers and civilians begging for help. No crying babies in the arms of distraught mothers. No homeless refugees in tattered clothes with a dispirited gaze in their eyes. No appalling smells from burned-out neighborhoods. No broken stores and looted houses left by the enemies. No foreign tanks. No occupying troops.

Tania had never felt this relaxed in years until she arrived at this charming small village in upstate New York called Amsterdam. She finally met her son, eighteen-year-old Peter, who was having a break from New York City, where he was attending Columbia University. He came back to help out his foster father, Max van Aken, with some work on the family farm. Recently widowed, van Aken was a sixty-year-old grumpy man and a proud believer in hard work and self-reliance. Wielding a huge scythe to cut hay for his animals, he called President Franklin D. Roosevelt a "socialist."

"Be gentle, Papa. He is not a socialist. He is your relative. He is a typical American like anyone else." Peter handed the old man a beer, and sat down next to him at the kitchen table.

Tania adored Peter. He had grown so much and so nicely, as handsome as his father, but more congenial and milder in temperament. Intelligent, honest, direct, and yet sweet and considerate, he was such a well-balanced young man that Tania felt immensely pleased to be able to see him finally.

"Yes, he is a socialist because he has given up the principles of hard work and self-help. He wants to use the government to replace everything," insisted the unbending Mr. van Aken.

"Papa, that's easy for you to say because you are a self-sufficient farmer. What about those thousands of city folks who have lost their jobs in this prolonged economic recession?" Peter said.

"You have been corrupted by the devilish New York City," the father charged.

"You are wrong, Papa. New York is not devilish. In fact, I have a story to tell you about my recent experience in a history class," Peter responded.

"Are you switching to history? That is a useless subject," Mr. van Aken retorted in his low and stern voice.

"I know you are kidding, Pa. I am not changing my major in political science, but I have taken a history class about China this semester. And the story I heard was not about the class but about the university," Peter said soothingly to his father before starting his tale.

The reason Columbia University was one of the earliest in the United States to have shown strong interest in China and East Asia had a heartwarming personal element to it. In 1901, the university received the first endowment for

Chinese studies from Isaac Cornelius, a native of Galloway, the neighboring town adjacent to Amsterdam. He insisted that the university not use his name, but to title the endowment "The Dean Lung Professorship of Chinese."

Who was Lung? Why should he be given the distinguished honor? Well, it turned out that Lung was one of the hundreds of Chinese coolies in California, who later became Cornelius's household servant. A freshly minted graduate from Columbia, Cornelius joined the gold rush in the west and established himself as lawyer, businessman, and one-time mayor of the city of Oakland. He never married and Lung was hired to be his valet.

According to the grapevine, heavy work and a busy schedule could make the master restless and moody. One day, a pretty trivial matter touched a raw nerve and the enraged Cornelius fired Lung on the spot.

When Cornelius got up the next morning and began walking downstairs to the kitchen, he regretted his frantic rage, thinking that he must now prepare his own breakfast.

As he entered the kitchen, he was surprised to see that his breakfast—eggs, bacon, sausages, coffee, and everything else—was already on the table as usual. Lung, standing nearby, was ready to serve him.

"Why didn't you leave?" he asked.

"I knew something was irritating you, sir. You really did not mean it," Lung responded.

From that day on, Cornelius's opinion of his servant totally changed and he developed a renewed respect for this humble Chinese man, slim, calm, modest, and yet always dignified.

"What can I do for you, my friend?" the master asked him one day years later.

"I have only one wish," Lung said. "I have saved some little money in my life and I hope some university in this country could use it to help Americans understand China, Chinese history, and Chinese culture, which goes back several thousand years."

Cornelius was touched. He pledged to do all he could to help fulfill the noble wish of his modest friend, the most humble and yet most devoted person he had ever met. And on June 28, 1901, the manservant wrote this letter to the president of Columbia University:

Sir,

I enclose herewith a check of twelve thousand dollars as a contribution to the fund for Chinese learning in your university.

Respectfully,

Dean Lung

"A Chinese Person"

Accompanying this one-line statement by a common laborer/servant was his master Cornelius's own pledge, indicating that he would be willing to add his share to the fund on condition of anonymity. The fund had to be recognized as "The Dean Lung Professorship of Chinese"—the promise he had made to fulfill the big dreams of his beloved servant.

Cornelius donated three hundred thousand dollars to the fund. The Chinese government presented five thousand books as a gift to the university to help establish its Chinese collection. The German scholar Friedrich Hirth was named the first endowed chair, and since then Columbia University had had the most distinguished program of Chinese Studies in the United States.

4

When Nazi Germany attacked the Soviet Union, Sheng was concerned but not worried. The Soviet Union was three times bigger than China. Napoleon had not been able to conquer it in the past, nor would anyone in the future, he reasoned.

When Japan attacked Pearl Harbor, Sheng was not only unconcerned, but also elated. The most stupid move, thought he. Japan had won the battle but would lose the war. Japan had a hard time trying to conquer China. Now it had created a much bigger problem for itself by dragging the powerful United States into war. How could such a small country fight against three giant ones—Soviet Union, China, and United States? The alliance of the three giants would seal the fate of the Japanese aggressors. Best of all, the burden of the fighting now would be shifted to the Allies, which would allow him to preserve the strength of his communist troops for future use, Sheng concluded.

"To hide one's capacity and bide one's time": he was truly glad that he had followed the ancient wisdom in this brutal war. Indeed, nothing beat the brilliant insights their Chinese ancestors had discovered hundreds of years ago. Sheng was once again convinced that he had made a good strategic move from the beginning of the war by not participating too eagerly in any action, as Tao and Si-Tu had done. The newly formed alliance between the United States, Soviet Union, Great Britain, and China had already decided the final outcome of the war. Germany would fall and so would Japan; it was only a matter of time. Sheng now could afford to focus his attention on something more important: his personal agenda.

In a rare show of appreciation, Sheng sought the blessings of the Comintern, which, prior to its own disbandment, finally recognized his leadership position in the Chinese Communist Party. Never did Sheng feel this confident before. All his hard work, sacrifice, and insistence had been worth it. He was now the party's legitimate leader, not some substitute or temporary stand-in. No one could question his legitimacy now. He had as much backing from Moscow as Si-Tu, Mo Jia-Qi, Dong Zi-Tian, and Meng Bo-Xian used to enjoy. Most of all, unlike these people, Sheng achieved this status without leaving China at all. He was a grassroots hero. He had been a native leader fighting for his own survival for much of his adult life, and his leadership ability was finally recognized by others now.

Sheng planned to reward loyal Song Pei for his diligent work behind the scenes in Moscow, remembering the popular saying in his childhood village that a donkey would not move but for two reasons—a carrot in front of it and a whip from behind.

Also highly valuable was Song's suggestion about learning from the textbook personally vetted by Stalin, the *History of the Communist Party of the Soviet Union*. As soon as a Chinese translation became available, Sheng had gone through it more than ten times in just a few months. He loved the book whose insights were exactly what he needed most. Everything was in place now. His excitement was indescribable for Sheng believed that he had finally figured out the ultimate action that needed to be taken, which would probably be the most important step in his political career.

5

Under the ornate ceiling and a glittering chandelier, a conference was taking place in the beautiful lecture hall of the university. Peter told Tania that the next speaker would be Robert Johnson, a leading Russian specialist at Columbia University. Having not attended any academic conference for a long time, Tania anxiously waited for it to start. But two hours later, as Tania walked down the big steps in front of the university's grand main library, she felt so saddened by what she had just heard that she had to sit down on the stairs to rest.

Was it all true what he had said? The professor did warn the audience that his speech could be disturbing for some. Oh, not merely disturbing. It was sickening. Tania felt a great sense of betrayal, betrayed by the shameful act, by the propaganda, and by the brutal reality of what the party had been doing. She shared her impressions with Peter and reflected on the information she had received.

The murder of Sergei Kirov, the Bolshevik chief in Leningrad, it seemed, had led to a frenzied search for enemies from within. For several years many prominent party leaders who had been Stalin's rivals were subjected to persecutions, trials, torture, imprisonment, and executions. The big purge destroyed the lives and families of gifted party members such as Gregory Zinoviev, Lev Kamenev, Leon Trotsky, Nikolai Bukharin, Alexei Rykov, Marshal Mikhail Tukhachevsky, and hundreds more.

"How could this happen?" Tania asked Peter. "I supported the Russian Revolution for a better Russia, not for murders and destruction of people's lives."

"A revolution is not always predictable. Few can control it once it got started." Peter answered after giving it some thought.

"But this cannot be described as revolution. It is destruction and murder in the name of revolution," Tania protested.

"I really have no answer, Ma," he said.

Tania looked at Peter, whose youthful face warmed her heart. She hugged him and kissed his forehead. "Oh, my dear son, my precious little boy." Full of love and gratitude, she could see nothing more worthwhile than preserving and protecting that innocence.

"Ma'am, so pleased to have you in the audience." Someone greeted her.

"Oh, Professor Johnson, pleased to see you again." Tania stood up but felt a little dizzy.

"Are you okay, ma'am?" the professor asked.

"Yes, yes, I am okay. Just a little upset," Tania responded. "This is my son, Peter, and he is one of your students."

"Yes, he is a very good student and you must be very proud of him." Professor Johnson complimented both son and mother.

"I have a question about your lecture," Tania said. "What do you think about the Russian Revolution? Is it a bad model for other countries?"

"Well, that's a very good and important question. How about going for a cup of coffee so I can explain it to you?"

Several blocks from the campus and around the quiet corner of Riverside Drive, the three sat down at a table in a small but cozy coffee shop.

"When I first arrived in Russia in the late 1920s," Professor Johnson recalled, "the Lenin Mausoleum in Red Square already bore the hallmarks of a personality cult. While much of the exaltation was given to Lenin, the party, and the government in general, portraits of Lenin's disciples, such as those of Trotsky and Zinoviev, were commonly hung in meeting halls and official buildings. The Rykov plants and the Bukharin depots could also be found in several cities. Most people's impression about Stalin was that of a simple, accessible, and rough-hewn man. He often took a stroll outside the Kremlin without any bodyguards, and could mingle with a crowd to chat about current affairs in the streets."

"When Stalin ascended to the top, the adulation for him was encouraged, which eventually replaced all the praises given to the rest of the collective leadership. He was idolized as the single most reliable assistant to Lenin, his most dedicated student and his only trusted successor. Sometime after the 1930s, the worship of Stalin intensified, as did the persecutions of those senior party leaders who presented a threat to his power," the professor explained at length.

"So, the personality cult caused all the internal strife and persecutions in the Soviet Union?" Tania asked.

"No, ma'am. I would not go that far. Although the two could certainly be related, I don't think personality cult alone 'caused' the persecutions and purges. But I do believe that there is a proportional parallel between the degree of personality cult of one man and that of political persecutions of others," the professor replied.

"Could the same situation happen to the Chinese Communist Party?" Tania asked.

"I am not a China expert, and I really can't answer that question," Johnson confessed.

"He seemed to be very knowledgeable," Tania told Peter later.

"I told you he was good." Peter was happy that his mother seemed to be no longer in low spirits.

6

A passionate lifelong reader of everything Chinese, Sheng was hardly ever enchanted while reading a foreign book. Learning an alien language was never his strong suit, reading translations bore him easily, and keeping track of knotty European history and lengthy Romanic names gave him headaches. A self-proclaimed believer in Marxism, he was never a serious student of the works by Marx, whose voluminous publications bewildered him. Just like how a smart yet pragmatic Chinese peasant farmer would deal with everything in the household, Sheng had adopted a utilitarian approach to Marxist doctrines. He often highlighted the parts in Marx's writings he found useful, but deemphasized and even disregarded most of those he deemed useless.

If Sheng had ever gotten excited about Marxism, it must have been the moment when he read the Chinese translation of the *Communist Manifesto* for the first time more than twenty years ago. Plain, direct, defiant, rebellious, and sarcastic, this little pamphlet fueled Sheng's political ambition precisely because it had been written in the sort of combative rhetoric and militant style that the young and impressionable Chinese reader had been accustomed to.

From the outset, Marx's strong assertion on "class struggle" and his overarching claim that "the history of all existing society is the history of class struggles" not only captivated Sheng's political imagination but also supported his deductive mode of understanding, which had long been shaped by many competing schools of thought and numerous binary conventions in Chinese tradition.

Since antiquity various Chinese philosophical thinkers had developed a long line of dualistic explanations of nature and society, which underlined the enormous number of printed classical texts that had dominated Chinese political thought, social institutions, educational systems, and cultural landscape. Generation after generation was told that the secrets of the world and society could be easily summed up in a few key notions, which would shed light on how the universe operated. Representing mankind's fundamental existence in a series of opposite pairings, these notions gave birth to an all-encompassing and stratified network of guiding concepts, ideas, and beliefs by which all Chinese, men and women, would have to learn about society and their roles in it, such as heaven and earth, nature and people, fate and choice, good and evil, virtue and vice, the ruler and the ruled, loyalty and obedience, duty and harmony, male and female, old and young, life and death, this world and the afterlife.

Most outsiders regarded Confucius, the great exponent of virtue, as China's most eminent ancient philosopher and Confucianism—his teachings on how to maintain a virtuous society—the most influential philosophical system in China, which was only half or one-third true. One of the many gifted thinkers of his time, Confucius's own career as a philosopher was a failure and his ideas were not accepted by the ruling classes until two hundred and eighty years after his death. Since then, Confucianism had been promulgated as the officially sanctioned doctrine, which strongly impacted the country's political apparatus, educational system, social mores, and individual behavior.

Meanwhile, Confucius's ideological rivals—the Legalists—had also received unconditional support from the government. Their deep suspicion of human nature, strong mistrust of virtue, firm belief in tough laws, merciless application of harsh punishment, and iron grip over the population had never been questioned by any dynasty throughout Chinese history. Although all official pronouncements and ceremonies would publicly and ostentatiously propagate the moralistic tenets of Confucius whenever there was a chance, behind the gentle facade and self-righteous front were the grim and brutal Legalist practices. The longevity of the Chinese political and social structures lay in the unequivocal adoption of both Confucianism and Legalism by the government.

Between the pompous and affected Confucianism and the stern and unapologetic Legalism was the third major school of thought in Chinese society— Daoism. Literarily "the way of the cosmos," the marvelous elasticity of the Chinese written character "dao" could mean everything and nothing at the same time. It was the soothing antidote for any confused Chinese who was struggling between the morality and hypocrisy immanent in Confucianism, between the necessity and cruelty intrinsic to Legalism, or between the inherent self-contradictions, hypocrisy, duplicity, and disillusionment found in both of them.

Sensible yet mysterious, simple yet elusive, Daoism comforted those who wanted to escape from mainstream Confucianism and Legalism by ridiculing their pretensions, self-righteousness, pomposity, determinism, and positivism. After all, according to Daoism, "the way of the cosmos" did exist but no one really knew what it actually was. The harder anyone tried to codify Daoism the way the Confucians and Legalists had done it, the further away he would be from reaching the ultimate "dao." As soon as anybody assumed he knew, "dao" would escape from him completely. Skeptics loved the cynicism in Daoism, rebels its irreverence, free-thinkers its boundlessness, and fatalists its passivism. Ordinary people in particular, who were not well versed in the classics nor deep into metaphysics, adored the concept of "yin–yang" in Daoism as the two primary forces in the universe that controlled their lives and future.

Under these circumstances, Marx's insistence on class struggle added a new political dimension to the existing Chinese ideological lexicon, which had long identified the conflict of two camps as a common reality and universal truth, such as those between Confucians and Legalists, between "yin" and "yang," between good and evil, between rich and poor, between social and individual, between the powerful and the powerless, and between status quo and insurgency. More than a simple concept, Marx's summary indictment that "the history of all existing societies is the history of class struggles" reaffirmed the way of thinking that many conscientious Chinese including Sheng were most familiar with.

These indigenous aspects of Chinese tradition prepared Sheng to embrace the skimmed-through Marxist doctrines. But Marxism was more than a simple add-on to the belief system of Sheng and his generation. What further cemented Marx's absolute authenticity in their mind was the so-called "scientific" nature of his theory, which was viewed as the very antithesis of China's backwardness. Only science would transform and save China, and no pure theory could beat Marxism, which was not a fresh product from a laboratory but a science proven by the Russian Bolshevik Revolution.

Rarely preoccupied with abstractions, the typical mindset in China was big on intuitive messages and life examples. The explosive Bolshevik Revolution in backward Russia inspired those Chinese who hoped to duplicate the same in backward China. When they learned that the key to the Russian success was the Bolsheviks' resolute adoption of Marx as their spiritual leader and Marxism as their guiding principles, they were sold. From early on, progressive Russian intellectuals had been exposed to Marxism at a very high level. The first foreign edition of Marxist masterpiece *Capital* (volume one) was launched in Russia only five years after its original German edition, and fifteen years before its first English edition. The initial printing of three thousand Russian copies was completely sold out in less a year, compared to the one thousand German copies, which took five years to be sold. This systematic elucidation of his thought "was read and valued in Russia more than anywhere else," the delighted author Marx later recalled.

His close friend and collaborator Friedrich Engels invented the myth that Marx was a man of *Wissenschaft*. Amid the frantic obsession with new scientific investigations in late nineteenth-century Europe, he proclaimed that, "as Darwin discovered the laws of the development of organic nature, so Marx discovered the law of development of human history." Soon the "scientific" nature of Marxist theory would intoxicate the Russian radical mind, and the Chinese communists could not have been more thrilled when Stalin told them, in the *History of the Communist Party of the Soviet Union*, that:

> Marx and Engels, the great teachers of the proletariat, accomplished the greatest revolution in science in the middle of the nineteenth century. They converted Socialism from a utopia into a science. They made a study of capitalism, discovered the laws of its development and proved scientifically that capitalism was historically transient, just as the feudal order had been before it, and that capitalism itself prepares the conditions for its destruction.

No words could describe Sheng's ecstasy after receiving what he felt was a profound ideological revelation. The binary pattern of thought in Chinese orthodoxy fit perfectly with Marx's interpretation of society, while Marx's overestimation of the working class gave the Chinese communists much hope to wage a revolution. Succinct and yet thoroughgoing, the *Communist Manifesto* was worshiped as the sacred scriptures for communists as much as Marx as a godly figure, and the Communist Party as the Holy Grail of institutions.

7

"Is President Roosevelt a socialist?" Tania asked Professor Johnson, whom she had found to be knowledgeable but not snobbish, passionate about his expertise but gentlemanly in his disposition. Somehow she saw a little bit of Meng Bo-Xian in this American, or a little bit of Johnson in the Chinese.

"No. He is a pragmatist," the professor replied. "When capitalism is in trouble, he is willing to try something socialistic to save it, which does not mean that he is abandoning the principles of free market and capitalism. As your son, Peter, has nicely put it, Roosevelt is a typical American politician who is less dogmatic, and flexible enough to make changes when the situation demands it."

"I heard a few of his close advisors are communists," Tania said.

"No. That's not true," Johnson adamantly denied the rumors. "That's purely the scare tactics Roosevelt's political enemies have used to discredit his social and economic policies, which, in my view, are absolutely necessary to rescue the country from this terrible recession."

"Now the United States is allied with the Soviet Union to fight against worldwide fascism. I guess that will prove his policies are procommunism," Tania said as she laughed.

"Of course, he is already being attacked as a communist sympathizer." The professor smiled too.

"What's happening? What do you think about the differences between communism and capitalism?" Tania asked.

"That's a very important question, and I will try to respond briefly," said Johnson, who was impressed by her query.

He pointed out that, when Marx developed his theory of an international communist revolution, capitalism had only started to emerge in a handful of European countries, such as England, France, and Germany. Primitive capitalism did have all the ills that had sickened Marx, such as rampant greed, unbridled exploitation, and a total lack of regulations in the marketplace. His criticism of early capitalism was legitimate, said the professor. But Marx overextended his theory. He greatly overestimated the virtues of the proletariat and seriously underestimated capitalism's ability to readjust itself according to the demands of the day.

Since the time of Marx's death in the late nineteenth century, the industrial European countries and the United States had passed numerous labor laws and business regulations, which protected the interests of the working people and curtailed the wanton greed of the capitalists.

President Franklin D. Roosevelt's "New Deal" programs further enlarged the role the federal government would play in balancing both the interests of business owners and the welfare of the working class. His programs did introduce a series of policies with definite socialist characteristics, such as the Civilian Conservation Corps, the Federal Housing Administration, the Public Works Administration, the Social Security Act, and the Tennessee Valley Authority.

"In my view," the professor continued, "both the idealized communism as Marx had envisioned and the totally unrestrained capitalism in its early stage are two extremes. Both are harmful and even dangerous to the future of mankind. The good news is, however, the two systems are learning and, to some extent, are learning from each other, which is good. Because I believe uncontrolled communism will be just as bad as uncontrolled capitalism, the two systems must learn to reform and acquire better abilities to improve the lives of their own peoples."

"There will be no winners if the two systems treat each other as absolute and uncompromising enemies. But both may win if they are able to come to a middle ground where they can coexist and learn from each other," Johnson added.

"So, communism is too much centralization without competition and capitalism is too much freedom without control?" Tania tried to summarize what she had heard.

"Very much so. I don't believe there is one perfect system, either Marxist, socialist, or capitalist. The society that can consciously learn from its mistakes and keep improving the welfare of its people will win in the end, no matter what the society is called or what labels others would attach to it," Johnson calmly pointed out.

"But what about the Marxist theory of class struggle? Can that be compromised?" Tania was very curious.

"Class struggle is certainly one of the many social realities, but not the only one. Marx made at least two errors here by insisting it in his dogmatic historical materialism. One, to justify his communist revolution, he overstated the advanced qualities of the proletariat, which was the massive physical force that was supposed to play an instrumental role in the communist revolution he hoped to instigate. And, two, he confused that powerful physical potential with the advanced ideological or intellectual quality that a leading class must have in any given society."

"What do you mean by that?" Tania asked.

"It means that, to carry out any revolution, substantial manpower is needed. Marx found that in the massive numbers of the modern industrial proletarians. But they only composed a small fraction of the participants in either the Bolshevik Revolution or the Chinese communist movement. Isn't that true?" Johnson asked.

"Yes, that is true. Neither Russia nor China has a large number of industrial working class. The majority of the participants in the Chinese revolutionary movement especially have been rural peasants, not urban workers," Tania said.

"Exactly. This suggests that the leading ideas of a revolution and the principal participating class of the revolution do not have to be the same class as Marx had insisted," Johnson argued.

"Interesting."

"In fact, however industrious and honest they may be, the working classes, including the Russian factory workers and the rural laborers in China, have never been able to produce any advanced ideas for social change because of their living conditions and limited education. They have never demonstrated 'class consciousness' as Marx had hoped. The United States has the largest number of industrial workers in the world, and the best thing they did was to form the American Federation of Labor, led by the highly knowledgeable cigar-maker Samuel Gompers. This supported Lenin's assertion that, without the injection of professional revolutionaries from the intellectual class, the best scheme the working class could have was economic unionism," Johnson said.

"Are you saying the middle-class intellectuals are more advanced than the factory proletarians?"

"Precisely. Just think about Marx, Engels, and Lenin. Are they members of the working class?"

"No, they were all from middle-class families and had a good education," Tania acknowledged.

"Can you find any working-class ideas and programs more sophisticated than theirs?"

"No, I can't."

"That's why I have said that the vast physical participants in a revolution could be very different from those who formulated revolutionary ideas. Marx had confused the two as one and the same. But his own personal experience and those of the Russian and Chinese revolutionary movements have sufficiently proved the opposite."

"But, throughout history, didn't the most radical ideas always come from a few radicalized individuals, not a particular class?" Tania asked.

"That's true. But my colleague and friend Professor Edward Seymour, a distinguished labor historian, has argued that, throughout history, there have been at least three classes instead of the two as Marx had described—the upper, middle, and lower. When the upper class has become corrupt in a given society, the middle class will promote a series of radical ideas and programs to rally the lower class to overthrow the ruling upper class. After this old middle class has risen to the top, it will later become corrupt itself. And a new middle class will rise and propose a series of new revolutionary ideas and programs to rally the lower class to overthrow the old middle-class-turned-ruling elite," the professor concluded.

"So, given that class struggle is the engine of progress," commented Tania, "history is the rotation of three classes instead of two, and the middle class or the middle-class intellectuals are always the creators of new ideas, while the lower working classes, either urban or rural or both, would always provide the largest physical forces needed in any radical actions for change."

"You have encapsulated his ideas perfectly," said Professor Johnson.

"A very intriguing theory. I heard some of Roosevelt's advisors are from your Columbia faculty." Tania changed the topic.

"That's true." The professor explained, "Edward Stevenson is an economist. Paul Metcalf is a legal expert. Ross Bromfield is a specialist in international relations. They are all prominent and accomplished scholars in their respective fields. I know them and they are by no means communists. I am glad that Roosevelt is willing to listen to their counsel."

"Are they part of the 'brain trust'?" Tania asked.

"Yes, they are." The professor was delighted that Tania had done her research. "They are part of the informal advisory group that the president consults from time to time on both domestic and international issues."

"Why aren't you part of the group?" Tania wondered aloud. "The war in Europe and the alliance with the Soviet Union are highly important. I am sure the president would like to hear what you have to say about those matters."

"Oh, I am too much a scholar, not good at giving practical advice. I would rather be a good student of Russian history and culture so that people could benefit from my studies."

"Do you believe in American exceptionalism?" Tania asked suddenly.

"A big part of the New World and protected by two oceans, America is indeed in many respects very different from the Old World. But I also believe every country thinks it's special, not just America. The United States is unique and special in world history, just like Russia, China, England, and France, or even Germany and Japan, are special too. Only narrow-minded isolationists and zealous partisans would overly promote an extreme notion of national exceptionalism."

"What is your assessment of the current situation in the Soviet Union?"

"To tell you the truth, I am quite disturbed. I am reading the updated edition of the *History of the Communist Party of the Soviet Union*, which was originally edited and approved by Stalin. The book reveals a very grim history of the Bolsheviks' endless infighting. It particularly reveals how Stalin rose to power and how intraparty fights had become even worse in the last few years. I hope your experience with the Chinese Communist Party is different."

8

"Mom, you seem to be very happy today." Peter greeted Tania at the dinner table.

"Yes, I am. I had a very nice talk with Robert Johnson this afternoon." Tania sat down, her eyes gleaming with delight even though she was still panting from her trip.

"Again with that idiot?" Mr. van Aken retorted.

"Papa, be nice. Professor Johnson is a very intelligent person." Peter defended his mentor.

"Intelligent? Hmm. I am sure you have heard that 'those who can't do, teach.'" Mr. van Aken was working on a fried chicken leg, which got stuck between his back teeth.

"Teaching is an important and noble profession. Not everyone can do that," Peter disagreed.

"Well, no one has taught me anything except my father. And I think I am just fine." Mr. van Aken retired to his bedroom.

"Mom, please don't be offended. Papa is always like this," Peter comforted Tania.

"Oh, don't worry about me, Peter. You are such a gentle soul and you don't want anyone to get hurt." Tania looked at her son lovingly, wishing that every man could be as nice, gentle, and caring.

"Mom, I think Professor Johnson likes you."

"Why? Why do you say that?"

"I can tell the way he looks at you."

"Stop it! Peter, you are just a boy."

"Precisely. Because I am a boy, I know it when a boy loves a girl."

"Stop it, Peter. I am going back."

"To where? Where are you going?"

"Back to China."

"The war is still going on there."

"I know. That's the reason I can't stay here any longer. I will go back to China."

All the tranquility, peace, and domestic comfort in Amsterdam, and all the learning, knowledge, and lively conversations at Columbia, made Tania extremely happy. But beneath the glorious joyfulness was a strange feeling of uneasiness, a degree of disconnectedness, and a sense of loss. Something was troubling her, making her restless and anxious in this heavenly sanctuary. The incomparable security and comfort here in the United States were unbelievable luxuries at this time elsewhere across the globe; none of her friends in remote poor China could ever enjoy or even dream of these luxuries, which made her embarrassed. Tania now realized that she was only physically present in this picturesque upstate village. After years of hardship in that oriental country, she had become too much of a Chinese to stay here with her Peter or to chat with Professor Johnson. She felt the pull of the remote, ancient, suffering, and yet powerful nation. She belonged there. Her passion, her soul, her heart, and her friends were there, and her conscience was urging her to return "home" soon.

Chapter 27

Rectification

1

THE WEALTH OF ONE'S EXPERIENCE COULD BE A DOUBLE-EDGED sword—an incredibly valuable source of self-confidence from the past but not necessarily a trustworthy guiding light for the future.

From the sweat and toil at the obscure village of Boxwood, from the stinging scorns of those urban dwellers and university intellectuals, from the insolent abuses of the industrial workers, from the blatant mistrust and brazen insults of top party officials, from the haughty ridicules of those organizational big shots who had been overseas, from the never-ending interferences and humiliating repudiation of the Comintern, from the fierce competition for dominance in repeated intraparty strife, from the bloody struggles to save the red base at Blue Grass, and from the perilous escapes and dangerous journeys on the Long March, to the small, cold, bleak, and desolate refuge of Bao An, Sheng Bao thought that he had done it all and seen it all. That was until he read the passage in the *History of the Communist Party of the Soviet Union* that declared:

1. The U.S.S.R. had been transformed from an agrarian country into an industrial country,

2. The socialist economic system had eliminated the kulaks as a class in the sphere of agriculture,

3. The collective farm system had put an end to poverty and wants in the countryside,

4. The socialist system in industry had abolished unemployment, and

5. The victory of socialism in all branches of the national economy had abolished the exploitation of man by man.

Sheng was in awe. What a remarkable success! Was this not what a communist society should look like? The totally convinced Sheng agreed with the conclusion that "this was a tremendous, epoch-making victory of the working class and peasantry of the U.S.S.R."

Everything Sheng had experienced, every abuse he had endured, and every hardship he had overcome seemed to be worth it. The bright future, the amazing model of success in the Soviet Union seemed to be within China's reach. The only thing he needed to do was to follow the steps the Soviets had taken.

A fan of Chinese chronicles, Sheng rarely read any foreign history. But this book about the Soviet Communist Party was different. It not only showed the glorious results of a successful revolution, but all the secrets of how to get there. It was a handy manual for a person as ambitious as Sheng, who had always been eager to rise to the top while feeling that he lacked the legitimacy to rule the party. The Soviet experience—or more precisely, Stalin's experience—had clearly pointed the way through intraparty struggles. Marx's theory of class struggle had taught Sheng how to fight external enemies. Now Stalin, through this personally supervised textbook, was literally teaching Sheng how to engage in a power struggle within the party.

This was exactly what Sheng needed. He had demonstrated his talent in developing military strategies on the battleground. Yet he lacked the kind of theoretical sophistications other party leaders had acquired in Moscow and in several European countries. Many still regarded him as an accidental star from the countryside, who possessed neither the prestige nor the authenticity to lead the party. Now was the time to change this perception once and for all. Armed with the critical new insights he had obtained from the Soviet experience, the determined Sheng mapped out his plan of action. He would let the rest of his comrades know who he actually was, what he was really made of, and what he was truly capable of accomplishing.

He decided to invite Meng Bo-Xian and Lin Shi-Xiong, who had been staying at Bao An with him, to a welcome home party for the returning members of the Politburo—Tao Yin-Hu and Si-Tu Wen-Liang from Shanxi, Mo Jia-Qi from Chongqing, and Song Pei from Moscow.

2

Nothing much seemed to have changed. The plain cave dwelling Sheng Bao and Su Ming used to live remained the same, so were the well-baked potatoes—roasted, darkened, and crunchy skin on the outside while steamy, succulent, mushy, and golden inside. The atmosphere was visibly warm and cozy. A lot of small talk, exchanges, and laughs to share after a long period of separation between these officials and their friends.

When the unofficial gathering came to a close that evening, Sheng rose and said, "Comrades, it's so good to see you back here. I have been really lonely in Bao An. You are the frontline heroes of our great resistance war. Welcome back. Take a break. Take some rest. Have some good sleep, which you all well deserve. If there's anything important, we will meet again tomorrow morning to discuss it."

The officials dispersed amid a typical Bao An night under the bright moonlight—prevailing quietness wrapped by invigorating mountain air, which was extremely refreshing, intoxicating, a little nippy, but not cold.

The brawny Tao walked quickly out of Sheng's cave. Perplexed, he asked Si-Tu, "Why did Sheng Bao ask all of us to leave our posts to come back here? For a full Politburo meeting?"

"I am not sure," the usually well-informed Si-Tu replied. A highly perceptive man who could read Sheng's mind better than anyone else, he was puzzled this time. "I heard that he called us back to join a study movement," Si-Tu said.

"A study movement?" Tao loved guns, not books. He had never heard such a thing. "To study what?" he asked his colleague.

"Books relating to Marxism and Leninism," Si-Tu told the confused Tao, who then went straight back to his cave.

"How are you doing? Any news from Chongqing?" A little behind the first pair, Meng asked Mo politely as the two walked toward their caves in a different direction.

"I am doing fine, thanks." Mo replied graciously. "Chongqing still suffers from the Japanese air raids, and the damned bombings kill our citizens every day. General Chen and Madam Chen believe the Japanese real goal was to kill them, and they will not stop bombing the city until they are killed."

"That's really tragic. So, we are really lucky to be in isolated Bao An, which is poor but free from bombs," Meng responded.

"That's true. If only people here would pay a little more attention to the resistance war than to..." Mo hesitated.

"Than to what?" Meng was curious to know.

"Than to something else." Smart yet cautious, Mo did not want to make his suspicions crystal clear.

"What does that mean?" Meng was confused.

"You have been with Sheng Bao all this while in Bao An. Would you be able to tell what he is up to?" Mo redirected the question at Meng.

"He never talks to me about his plans. How would I know? What can I say?" Meng complained.

Mo knew Meng to be a highly intelligent individual with a mellowed personality, who was no match for the aggressive and calculative Sheng. He sympathized with Meng while feeling that he himself would not be able to stand up to Sheng.

"We are supposed to study Marx and Lenin from tomorrow," Mo told Meng matter-of-factly, while thinking that the one who really needed to read Marx and Lenin was Sheng, not him who had studied for several years in Moscow—the Mecca of the international communist movement and ideology.

3

The next morning, after all the Politburo members had gathered in a recently constructed conference room, Lin told the attendees, "Comrade Sheng Bao had some emergency to deal with. He asked me to make this announcement. To facilitate this important endeavor, which is called the Movement of Studying

Marxism and Leninism, a leadership group has been formed to take charge of all matters relating to the movement. It comprises Sheng Bao as the group leader, Lin Shi-Xiong and Song Pei as deputy group leaders."

Suddenly, the pieces of the puzzle began to fall into place. Sheng did not recall everyone back to Bao An for nothing. He had trapped them in this so-called "study movement" because no communist, no matter how important his position, would dare to say that he or she was not willing to study the teachings of Marx and Lenin.

For those who were not familiar with the terminology of the Chinese communists, the term "movement" must be explained.

"A movement" meant a special campaign, which originated in the military. But the Chinese communists started many types of campaigns involving massive numbers of the civilian population, such as a labor movement in the factories, a students' movement in the cities, or a peasants' movement in the countryside. "A movement" was the most common tool the Chinese Communist Party had used to accomplish its ultimate goal of social transformation, which was by definition a grassroots revolution.

But all the massive movements in the past were directed against external foes, such as hostile warlords, greedy employers, abusive landlords, corrupt administrative officials, or failing governmental policies. Sheng was the first communist leader who concocted a movement to deal with internal party affairs. He was the instigator of all subsequent political, social, and economic movements that the Chinese Communist Party would wage time and again during his lifetime.

His other dubious but equally important invention was the so-called "leadership group," and Sheng deliberately adopted a modest title to cover its immense power and insidious purpose.

Since its inception the Communist Party had been an extremely centralized institution, with the small and exclusive Politburo as its highest authority. When Sheng, without consultation and without any election process, handpicked the "leadership group for the study movement," he had also violated the last remaining rule and the most fundamental structure of the party apparatus by putting the Politburo's powers into his own hands.

Bypassing the Politburo broke the equilibrium of the collective leadership Moscow had helped to create several years ago, and hijacking the Politburo's powers allowed Sheng to become the party's overlord.

Everyone could tell that the "leadership group" was a sham. Of its two junior members, only Lin had held the post of an alternate Politburo member for more than one term. But he never said anything to offend Sheng, who, cognizant of the former's submissiveness and loyalty, had used Lin as his personal bodyguard for a long while. Although never elected to any high leadership position within the party's inner circle, Song Pei got accepted into this most powerful group largely due to his obsequious service in Moscow, which greatly boosted Sheng's personal ego. Neither Lin nor Song had the necessary seniority, experience, or willpower to compete with Sheng the strongman, the only full Politburo member in the leadership group.

Apparently, Sheng's clever design broke all the rules of the organization. His strategy allowed him to rob the Politburo of its powers, while using Lin and Song as pawns to sugarcoat his power grab.

All the rest of the Politburo's standing members—Tao, Si-Tu, Mo, and Meng—had been excluded from this "leadership group." They therefore would have no control of either how long the study movement would last or where it might be heading.

All of them were now at the mercy and whim of one person, Sheng. Empowered and protected by the "leadership group" he had personally created, he alone sat above the Politburo.

But at the moment of the announcement, the slightly altered arrangement seemed harmless, and no one realized the severity of the changes. Except for Lin and Song, who had anticipated Sheng's moves, the other Politburo members seemed to believe that the study movement might take a few days, or one or two weeks at the most. Although uncomfortable and inconvenient for the excluded top party officials, the "leadership group" was only temporary and therefore would have no reason to exist longer than a few weeks.

A huge surprise awaited everybody. The study movement went on for the next three years and Sheng gained firm control of the party by default owing to his self-appointed position as the top leader of the leadership group. The Politburo members were also in for more surprises as they began to understand what Sheng was really up to and how far he was willing to go to achieve his ambition.

4

The grand plan of the study movement was to train hundreds of thousands of party members, officials, and activists from the county level upward. After Sheng had subjected top officials to the new "leadership group," the pontiff must be able to manage the mindset of his cardinals and archbishops as well.

Members of the Politburo were then given the ambiguous task of reading not the writings by Marx and Lenin but the *History of the Communist Party of the Soviet Union*, compiled and stamped by Stalin. Weeks passed, little progress was made, participants were baffled, and Sheng sent Song to give a lecture.

"Comrades," said he, "you may wonder why you are asked to read the *History*, not any original work by Marx and Lenin. The reason is simply this: the history of the Communist Party in the Soviet Union best exemplifies the teachings of Marx and Lenin. The real-life example of the Soviet experience is better than any printed theories or analytical principles."

"But excuse me," Mo interrupted. He never liked Song, whose feeble intellect and shameless opportunism disgusted him. "Should we understand a little more about what those theories and principles are before we proceed?"

"That's true. We will study the *Communist Manifesto*, *The State and Revolution*, and *Imperialism*, *The Highest Stage of Capitalism*," Song replied.

"Why not Marx's *Capital*?" Mo was not about to give up.

"You know that's a huge book, and we don't have enough copies," said Song. "Besides, Marx's ideas and principles are embodied by the realities in the Soviet Union, which are more directly applicable to our situation."

"There are just too many Russian names, factions, disputes, and controversies to remember," Tao complained.

"That's exactly the point," Song replied. "There has been a prolonged and incessant battle between two lines of thoughts within the Russian Communist Party—the correct line represented by Lenin and Stalin, and the other opposing line represented by various internal enemies of the revolution. Lenin and his student and successor, Stalin, had fought long and hard to overcome all these evil and malicious oppositions to achieve the great successes we now see in the Soviet Union. So, the most important lesson we can learn is to gain a deep understanding of the struggles of the two lines between the Marxists and Leninists on the one side and all those sinister opponents and foolish enemies on the other. The compelling history of the struggles between the two opposing lines within the Communist Party is the true lesson of how Lenin and Stalin had transformed Marx's theory into a Soviet reality."

"Are you suggesting that any different opinion within the party can be taken as a line struggle?" Meng expressed his doubts.

"Not every different opinion constitutes a line struggle," said Song. "But, as it happens, the insistence of malicious and anti-Marxist ideas will always lead to line struggles, such as in the cases of Trotsky, Zinoviev, Kamenev, and Bukharin. Many of the leading opponents have turned out to be wicked assassins, spies, murderers, and traitors."

"Do we have enough information to confirm that? Isn't that a simplistic understanding of the situation in the Soviet Union?" Meng questioned the conclusion.

"No, that's the true reality of the Soviet experience. That's the scientific conclusions Comrade Stalin has made. And that is the lesson we must learn from them seriously," Song insisted.

5

"Reports say that some of our comrades have certain reservations about this study movement." Sheng began his talk on a grim note. The feelings of anger, indignation, and dismay were written all over his broad solemn face, making the roomful of his colleagues believe that it could be the worst day of his life.

"I would like to say that I have learned enormously from the *History of the Communist Party of the Soviet Union* more than any other Marxist literature I have read. Anyone who believes the contrary is not a faithful Marxist, not a faithful Leninist, not a faithful communist at all!"

The people in the room were shocked, but they maintained their silence.

"Some of you may think that Marxism can be found only in the printed books by Karl Marx. Whenever they talk about Marx and Marxism, they mean the thick volumes of Marx's publications. They seem to believe that the more Marxist writings they read, the more Marxist they would become. They never understand that Marxism is not a set of dead letters, nor a collection of fixed dogmas. They never understand that Marxism is alive. It lives in the daily struggles of the people. It directs their revolution, guides their journey, and helps them defeat their enemies. Marxism lives in our heart, in our blood, in our unstoppable fight for communism. Marxism is forever the enduring light in our life and revolution."

Sheng recovered from his negative emotions. His eyes lit up, his face flushed, and his voice sounded louder by the second. The listeners were visibly invigorated.

"The first day I was exposed to Marxism years ago, I took it as the ultimate scientific answer to our nation's problems. Since then I have never wavered. Today, I shall add that the Soviet Union's experience best exemplifies what a communist success would look like. To me, that is true Marxism right before our eyes—Marxism in all its most brilliant manifestation in every possible dimension. Nowhere can we learn more about Marxism than a close reading of the history of the Soviet Union. It is the place where we can find every one of the Marxist principles; that is, not only about how each of those doctrines has been written but also about how these doctrines have been implemented and transformed into reality.

"I want to be a truly dedicated and faithful student of Marxism and Leninism," said Sheng. "I hope you will too. I think I can never say that I have fully understood the most advanced science in human history, which is Marxism and Leninism. They are the most advanced social science, not because of the extensive output of their publications but because of the most amazing success now prevailing in the Soviet Union led by Comrade Stalin. I am willing to continue to learn from him, from the Soviet Union, and from its remarkable revolutionary experience. I only hope you are too."

Sheng finished his speech and left the room amid a big round of applause from his colleagues.

6

The Politburo's proud members were subdued but their doubts and skepticism lingered. Song had the unpleasant task of going back to them and hammering away the message. Besides, something would be better said indirectly by the disciples, not directly by the master himself. Song picked up from where Sheng had left.

"The Soviet experience clearly shows that the two-line struggles within a communist party would only help it to thrive, just as the intense class struggles between the proletarians and capitalists have paved the way for the triumph of the Bolshevik Revolution. In fact, the two-line struggles within the party are no more than the inevitable continuation of the class struggles from without. Lenin, Stalin, and their Marxist line have resoundingly routed their opponents and dismantled their anti-Marxist line, which made it possible for the Soviet Union to achieve all the unprecedented victories today.

"None of us," said Song, "has successfully undergone the profound transformation of a true Marxist and a pure proletarian as completely as Comrade Sheng Bao. None of us has mastered the core of Marxism and Leninism as completely as Comrade Sheng Bao. None of us can lead the party to fulfill our goals as confidently and skillfully as Comrade Sheng Bao. He is the perfect embodiment of Marxism in our Chinese experience as much as Lenin and Stalin have been for the Russians in the annals of the Soviet Union. He has represented the completely correct line of our party from its inception.

"Unlike Comrade Sheng Bao, who is from the lower-working-class family of rural China, all of us," Song said as he looked around, "have come from the bourgeois class. All of us have lingering ideas, beliefs, opinions, attitudes, habits, and sentiments from our bourgeois past. Because of our own weaknesses and biases, we have willingly or unwillingly opposed him over the years, not knowing that only his ideas and visions were the most proletarian, Marxist, and scientific. And all of us have erred at one point or another by objecting to his terrific plans and splendid strategies, which have resulted in enormous setback and damage for our party and the Red Army. We must realize our mistakes, rectify ourselves, and return to Comrade Sheng Bao's correct line. We must review our complete history to eliminate any remnants of bourgeois influences, to uphold the correct Marxist line set forth by no one but Comrade Sheng Bao."

Song reminded his listeners, "A nation and a party must have a leader. That's why the *History of the Communist Party of the Soviet Union* mentioned Lenin and Stalin more than six hundred times. It would be very hard to believe that the Russians could achieve their epic success without Lenin and Stalin.

"Similarly," stressed he, "we must recognize that Comrade Sheng Bao is the most ingenious leader of our party. He is the greatest hero of our Chinese people. He is the ultimate savior of our nation. His whole career has proved that his ideas are always correct. Whenever we followed his lead, our party won and our armed forces thrived. Whenever we deviated from his ideas and strategies, our party and army suffered."

Song then went in for the kill. "Comrade Sheng Bao is the incarnation of Marxism and Leninism in Chinese reality. He, his thoughts, ideas, and beliefs epitomize true Marxism and Leninism in the most authentic Chinese style, fully grounded in our Chinese soil and traditions while completely fitting into our unique Chinese conditions. He is the undisputed founder of our party and army. He represents the best interests of millions of the proletariat and working people. He is the embodiment of our party. His ideas and thoughts are the most valuable treasures of our cause. His leadership is the guarantee of the success of our great party and our great Chinese revolution."

7

The passionate harangue was not easy to listen to, and harder still to digest. While the lavish exaltation was stirring, its embellishments and exaggerations troubled the Politburo. All of Sheng's colleagues appreciated his special talent and great contributions to the revolution. What concerned them was the exclusive nature of Song's assertions.

Was it necessary to deify Sheng so as to solidify his leading role in the party? Politburo members knew that, like everyone else, Sheng had his great strengths and glaring weaknesses. His narrow understanding of Marxism had not broadened his mind from the restrictive confines of his rural roots. His utilitarianism in politics and romanticism in strategy had led to successes as much as failures. His penchant for traditional literature and old-fashioned history had always taken precedence over his interest in modern sciences. His heavy-handedness and enormous ego represented a patriarchal leadership style not conducive to a collegial, forward-looking, and collaborative system. His cold-heartedness, aversion to criticism, insatiable desire for power, and unmitigated duplicity under the cover of extreme self-righteousness had all the traces of an authoritarian personality, not a benevolent savior or a truly visionary hero.

To say that he had always been correct and to claim that any ideas or suggestions different from his were bourgeois or anti-Marxism would be a great distortion of the truth. Furthermore, to extol and worship him to the degree Song had propounded was to distort history; one must magnify Sheng's strengths and downplay his weaknesses, while debasing the strengths of other party leaders and exaggerating their mistakes and weaknesses. Was the party willing to embrace all these contradictions in order to elevate an essentially delusional leader to a godlike figure?

The study sessions continued without reaching a clear conclusion one way or the other. The Politburo's resistance in accepting such a demigod in their midst turned out to be much stronger than the leadership group had originally anticipated.

Sheng called an emergency meeting with Lin and Song. The report of the Politburo's lukewarm reception infuriated Sheng. "Now, we must end the study sessions and shift into the second phase of the movement," he told his deputies. "The second stage, rectification, must begin as soon as possible to step up the pressure, and force the Politburo to submit. And you"—Sheng turned to Lin— "must go and make the announcement."

The atmosphere was tense when the deputy leader walked into the conference room. An elusive, secretive, but highly powerful figure due to his closeness to Sheng, Lin had the reputation of being a bloodthirsty persecutor in the party.

He told the attendees, who used to be his superiors but were now his underlings, "The leadership group is not happy with the progress of the study movement. Now we must move into the second phase of the movement— rectification. Everyone must purge anything that is against Comrade Sheng Bao in our organization. Everyone must purge any thought that is against Comrade Sheng Bao in our minds. Everyone must purge any action that is against Comrade Sheng Bao's leadership in our party and army."

The Politburo's members noticed the way Lin talked to them. He said "everyone" must do this, must do that, excepting himself. If rectification must involve everyone, why was he exempted? Who granted him such a privilege? Why did he think he was above party rules and discipline? Yet, no one dared to speak out and the deputy leader's lecture continued, with the language and zest similar to Song's.

"Just as the Communist Party in the Soviet Union rallied around Lenin and Stalin, we must unconditionally rally around Comrade Sheng Bao and to establish his absolute leadership authority in our party if we hope to achieve communism. Comrade Sheng Bao is the future of our party. He is the savior of China. His ideas and thoughts are the incarnation of modern-day Marxism and Leninism in our revolution. And he, only he, can be the undisputed leader who will surely lead our party to success."

Participants finally realized that the real goal of the study movement was to establish Sheng as the highest and undisputed leader of the party by pressing everyone else to confess their failings and mistakes, to submit to his absolute authority, and to accept him as the Chinese incarnation of Marx and Lenin. The atmosphere suddenly changed. The conference room was no longer a warm place to congregate and discuss Marxist theories but a miserable furnace where all those present feared that Sheng's big ax might fall on them anytime.

8

"Chairman, the meetings on rectification—" No sooner did Song begin to make his report than he was interrupted by the boss.

"Wait a minute. What did you call me?" Sheng asked, as Lin sat next to him.

"I called you 'Chairman.'" Song said.

"Why? I am not one," Sheng replied.

"You will be soon," Song explained. "Once the rectification process is over, the Seventh National Congress will be called. Who else but you will be elected as chairman of our party?"

Song was thrilled that he could clearly see where the movement was heading. He wanted to be the first one to flatter Sheng with such an exciting prospect. In the past, the party had had several general secretaries, a title Sheng had long wanted to get rid of. None of the general secretaries had been able to do a good job. Sheng wanted to have a fresh start, and establish his distinctive dynasty. Like all Chinese emperors in history, he needed a new title, and Song heard him mentioning that he would prefer the designation "chairman."

But Song did not fully understand the real Sheng, who could say one thing while doing the opposite, or doing something but saying nothing. Most of all,

Sheng never liked anyone to speak *for* him. One might guess, one might surmise, one might observe, one might beat about the bush, one might serve him, one might listen to him attentively, but you should never tread Sheng's path.

Did Sheng aspire to be the party's top leader? Of course, he did. He had dreamed of holding that position for years. He hoped to rule the party. He wanted to be in total charge of the party and he enjoyed the feeling of being superior, politically and intellectually, over all his colleagues who had thought that they were better than him. Still, Sheng did not like someone else to say it, particularly Song, who was just a secondary pawn in the game. He felt his ambition and goals were somehow degraded when a lesser figure Song made such a statement.

"Never mention that again, and get on with your report," a flustered Sheng ordered.

Startled, Song's heart sank, like a dog whose greeting of his master was rewarded with a kick in the stomach. Not knowing what had made the boss unhappy suddenly, he feared that what he was about to say would make Sheng angrier still. "The rectification did not proceed smoothly," Song began timidly. "People resisted to talk about their mistakes. They either talked about them casually or did so with various excuses. They never recognized how seriously wrong they were, or how absolutely correct you had been."

"No one has said this is going to be easy," said the confident Sheng, who did not seem to be surprised or upset. "The important thing is that you should know how to break the stalemate."

"Tao Yin-Hu is the most stubborn. He has to change before everyone else will follow suit," Lin suggested, breaking his long silence. A tough person, he liked to deal with hard cases head-on.

"Tao has a lot of supporters in the army. Many generals have followed his lead for years. That's why he would not budge." Sheng could always see the bigger picture, and remained particularly cautious over anything that involved the army's personnel. He was not in any hurry to deal with the commander-in-chief.

"What about Mo Jia-Qi? Is he not the typical bookish Marxist that you had often criticized?" Song put in his two cents' worth.

"Mo is a bookish person. But his influence has decreased significantly since the Comintern's dissolution. Moscow is currently more concerned with the war than with him. His stand and attitude would count not as much in the movement now as they would have been one or two years earlier," Sheng said.

Behind those casual words and beneath his nonchalant manner, Sheng harbored a totally different view of Mo. Sheng was extremely jealous that, as the author of the August First Declaration and the instigator of the united front in China, Mo had gain a tremendous reputation at home and abroad, which greatly overshadowed his own standing. All over Bao An and many of its schools an institutions, students and young people were spellbound because the legendary Mo could dictate Marxist theories and Leninist doctrines for hours at times without looking at any notes. His classes on those Russian authors from Chernyshevsky, Plekhanov, Bakunin, Kropotkin and Tolstoy to Trotsky went on for months, drawing thousands of admirers, which significantly dwarfed those classes taught by Sheng. For a while, Sheng decided not to give a lecture anywhere Mo had been to avoid the embarrassing comparison the audiences would inevitably make afterward. Never content to be a lesser revolutionary or an inferior Marxist to anybody, Sheng had already been contemplating a secret scheme, which he would never disclose to anyone else.

"I got it." Lin agreed with Sheng's assessment and kept the discussion moving. "Personal popularity aside, Mo Jia-Qi never has strict control over any department in the party. The key figure in the movement must be Si-Tu Wen-Liang."

"You got it." Sheng was pleased that Lin often seemed to be able to anticipate who would be his archrival. "Si-Tu Wen-Liang has been at top of the party's leadership longer than anyone, myself included. He has great skills and experience. Many of our high party officials look up to him. If his attitude could change, that would make a huge difference in this campaign." Sheng stopped, he looked at the two deputies, and was apparently waiting to see which one of them was willing to take on the challenge.

Both Lin and Song knew that they were not in the same league as Si-Tu in terms of prestige, experience, and rank. Nor did they want to show their weakness and fear in front of the boss. They hesitated and Song finally said, "I will give it a try to meet with Si-Tu Wen-Liang."

Sheng smiled. The strategist and mastermind behind the movement, he controlled its direction and pace. He wanted to rake all the benefits of the movement, but he would never touch those dirty jobs and tough assignments.

The deputies must handle them, which was the exact reason for their existence. Sheng sent them away and asked his valet to get a doctor for him.

A concerned Su Ming asked, "Are you okay?"

"I am okay, just having a little stomach pain," Sheng answered.

Su quickly helped him to lie down on the kang, waiting for the doctor to arrive.

9

Song had no idea how the meeting with Si-Tu would turn out. He confided to the latter that the rectification had reached an impasse. Sheng had ordered him to find out if Si-Tu would be willing to lend a helping hand to break the awkward stalemate.

If the rule in natural selection was called "survival of the fittest" via competition, Si-Tu's philosophy of survival in this life was to make compromises. Well-grounded in the Confucian style of education and well-endowed with a great variety of tactics to handle any situation since childhood, Si-Tu had dealt with all personal relationships with the kind of ease, self-assurance, and grace that would amaze even the most gifted political fixer. His ingenuity lay in his ability to sense which way the wind was blowing faster than his other colleagues. His unique talent was to put on a different mask accordingly faster than one could blink. To survive the worst political storms in the party's history, Su-Tu had always been the first to choose the path of least resistance to protect himself, and the first to adjust his own position, instead of attempting to change that of others. Although highly intelligent and experienced, he had no desire to compete with other senior officials for dominance. While he could be highly assertive if required to protect his territory and authority, he rarely demanded more power than he needed. His first principle was always self-protection and self-preservation, not self-aggrandizement.

Unlike Sheng, who aggressively vied with everyone for superiority, power, and dominance, one of Si-Tu's cardinal beliefs was that everyone was of some use in society, no matter how obscure and how insignificant one might seemed sometimes. One person might be in power and another might be in trouble. But one day the situation could be totally reversed. Today, the person in trouble might need the help of the person in power, but tomorrow that same powerful person might need to seek help because he had fallen out of favor.

From the hesitant way Song walked in, Si-Tu knew why he had come. He warmly received the visitor and showed much deference to him as if nothing had happened between them.

Song was moved. He knew that Si-Tu had been Sheng's senior in the party for many years. But now Si-Tu had been forced to confess his mistakes, and criticize himself repeatedly before his colleagues simply because of the circumstances Sheng had created. The humiliation Si-Tu had suffered did not change him, and he remained civil, kind, and caring to all those around him. Song found a saintly quality in Si-Tu that he had never seen in Sheng.

He confessed to Si-Tu, "Unlike you and many others in the party, I have no particular talent. The only way for a mediocre person to rise in our organization is to rely on those powerful ones above me. I am ashamed that I have to flatter Sheng Bao to get ahead. But that's the only way I can have a future in this organization."

"Don't worry," Si-Tu calmly responded. "We all have our difficult times and we all have to make tough choices. I know Sheng Bao may not be perfect. But he may be the best choice we have now. Tomorrow I will go to the meeting and offer my support as you suggested." Song was extremely relieved when he heard this.

And what a support he gave! Si-Tu delivered the most heart-wrenching self-criticism and self-deprecating speech ever, which shocked his colleagues. He went back to the first day when the party was founded, and said how foolish he had been in not realizing that Sheng should have been chosen as the party leader right then. The party would have avoided many setbacks only if he and others had recognized the wonderful talent and amazing potential of the brilliant Sheng, the magnificent savior of the party and country.

Time and again, Si-Tu said, he had made many awful mistakes by not listening to Sheng's invaluable suggestions and splendid strategies, which led to the disastrous failures of the Red Army in the red bases in Jiangxi. At one point, he also made the inexcusable mistake of demoting Sheng. Si-Tu apologized sincerely for not only having deprived Sheng of the commissar's post in the Red Army but also grabbed the position for himself, which led to even greater disasters.

Those costly mistakes and painful experiences had proved that Sheng was the best, the only legitimate and the most deserving leader the party and the Red Army should have had in the first place. From now on, Si-Tu vowed, he would support Sheng as the absolute leader without any reservations. To support Sheng was to support the party. To support Sheng was to support the revolution. To support Sheng was to support the communist cause. To be against Sheng was to be against the party. To oppose Sheng was to oppose the revolution. To contradict Sheng was to harm the communist cause. To dispute Sheng was to betray Marxism, Si-Tu said.

"Long live Comrade Sheng Bao! Long live the Communist Party! Long live the Chinese revolution! Long live Marxism! Long live Sheng Bao, the incarnation of Marxism in China! Long live Shengism—Comrade Sheng Bao's correct line and his thoughts!" Arms raising high and fists over his head, Si-Tu shouted at the top of his lungs, voice creaking and tears streaming down his eyes.

Sitting in the crowd, Sheng knew Si-Tu was a good actor. An instinctively cynical and suspicious man, he could see how good the latter's performance was. He was satisfied that Si-Tu had finally submitted to his authority by openly acknowledging his mistakes. Even though he could never tell whether the actor was honest or he was simply faking it, Sheng was pleased to watch it happen in public.

The floodgates had opened. A series of high and mid-ranking officials followed suit. They started to confess their failings. They looked back at their past records, and resolutely blamed themselves for any thoughts, ideas, and actions different from those of Sheng's. They called themselves petty bourgeois, opportunistic, and anti-Marxist. They regretted for having been irreverent, ignorant, erroneous, shameful, corrupt, foolish, immature, blind, pathetic, hopeless, miserable, etc., etc.

They swore loyalty, pleaded for mercy, begged for forgiveness, vowed rectification, promised reform and purification, and craved for total transformation. They would forever be the disciples, campaigners, supporters, and defenders of Sheng, and they would remain the eternal enemies of—and would fight against—anyone who would dare to oppose Comrade Sheng. He was their most glorious champion and greatest leader, and they would forever be his dedicated, obedient, and faithful crusaders.

10

Compassion, benevolence, forgiveness, and magnanimity might be virtues for some people, but not for others. An outstanding student of history, Sheng had an elephant's memory, which was enormously helpful for his ego but a complete nightmare for others. He literally remembered everything someone had said to him or every minute incident in which the latter might have made him uncomfortable. While that person might have forgotten all about it, he remembered every detail of exactly where and when it had happened. And he would surely find a way to get back at the person one day, no matter how long that would take.

The remarkable ability of "getting back at you" was one of Sheng's most salient personal traits, perhaps inherited partially from his father's strict habit of scrupulous record-keeping, and partially from the age-old rural tradition that "every account must be squared after the autumn harvest."

Tao, the commander-in-chief of the communist forces, was unfortunately caught in this huge web of vengeance, and was shocked to learn that he had been in an "anti-Sheng Bao position" for more than ten years since the founding of the Red Army.

"You always think you are better than Comrade Sheng Bao," one officer lashed out at a public rectification meeting.

"The most recent example is that you disobeyed his orders and waged the 'one hundred regiment' campaign," yelled out another.

"Your wrong leadership has led to the contraction of our army and red bases!" a third followed.

The leadership group had encouraged army officers to attend this and other similar meetings, hoping that the pressure from a legion of those willing officers would force Tao to change his uncompromising attitude toward rectification. The energized officers started to scrutinize the commander's whole career, to recount his smallest misstep, and to blame him for all the past failures of the Red Army. And, at the same time, to attribute every success of the Red Army to the most brilliant, most illustrious, and most ingenious leadership of Comrade Sheng.

Watching many familiar faces, including his long-time subordinates Lu Di-Ping, Bao Feng-Nian, Kang Yi-Sheng, Xia-Hou Ding, and Yao Xi-Wa, in the crowd as they shouted angry slogans against their commander, Tao's heart sank. Different assessments in military affairs were commonplace. No one was a saint in a complex military campaign. Nobody was a fortune teller who could foresee everything. All that a good field commander could do was to make adjustments as the combat conditions changed.

Refusing to yield to the public pressure, Tao did something no one else dared to do. He retorted, "And if Sheng Bao's ideas and plans have always been the scientific and correct ones, why not just let him alone lead the Red Army forever?"

The crowd was amazed by his rebellious statement, but their continued shouting and yelling failed to sway Tao.

"Tao Yin-Hu is stubborn. We must find a different way to force him to submit," Sheng said as he again looked at his deputies for a solution.

The bookish Song was clueless, while Lin whispered a few words into Sheng's ear.

"Really?" Sheng asked?

"One hundred percent true," Lin assured.

"Good, let's bring that up." The boss agreed.

11

A few days later when a large session of the rectification meeting reconvened, attendees were surprised to find Dong Zi-Tian being brought before them by several armed soldiers.

Lin, siting at the head of the table, asked, "Dong Zi-Tian, did you meet Tao Yin-Hu during the Long March?"

"Yes, I did."

"When?"

"When the First and Second Armies met."

"What did you do?"

"We celebrated the meeting of the two armies."

"Comrades," Lin turned to the audience, "did you hear that? The antiparty leader Dong Zi-Tian met Tao Yin-Hu, and they celebrated his anti-Sheng Bao plot!"

"Down with Dong Zi-Tian! Down with Tao Yin-Hu! Down with anyone who is against Comrade Sheng Bao!" The conference room exploded.

No one was more stunned than Tao. Yes, he, Dong, and many others from both armies did meet and held a wonderful party to celebrate the triumphant union of the two forces. But that was after a long separation for so many good friends and comrades. That was after so many brutal fights. That was such a precious brief moment of relaxation for all the soldiers and officers who had survived so many ordeals. What was wrong with that?

"Tao Yin-Hu," Lin, sounding more like an interrogator than a moderator, pressed on. "You have always disregarded Sheng Bao's correct line and his correct orders. You met with Dong Zi-Tian, a power-hungry man. Confess, what did you two plan to do? How did you conspire to harm Comrade Sheng Bao and deprive him of the power to lead the Red Army?"

"Down with the conspirator Dong Zi-Tian! Down with his accomplice Tao Yin-Hu! Down with anyone who is against Comrade Sheng Bao! Down with anyone who is against Sheng Bao's absolutely correct revolutionary line!"

"Sheng Bao and no one but Comrade Sheng Bao is the true leader of the party!"

"Sheng Bao and no one but Comrade Sheng Bao is the true leader of our Red Army!"

"Down with anyone who dares to oppose Comrade Sheng Bao!"

"Whoever is against Sheng Bao is our common enemy!"

"Long live our party! Long live our army!"

"Long live Comrade Sheng Bao, the only true and forever great leader of our party and army!"

Speechless. Absolutely speechless. Tao could not believe what was happening before his eyes. Many high party officials and high-ranking army officers—most of whom had been his intimate friends and close associates—were becoming extremely hostile toward him. What kind of study movement was this? What kind of rectification was this? What exactly was Sheng up to? Tao had no answer.

Chapter 28

Quaternity

1

"TANIA, THANK HEAVENS, YOU ARE BACK! YOU MUST GO AND HELP Meng Bo-Xian right away!" Yan Yan was so excited to see her friend that she dragged Tania back to the door before the latter had a chance to sit down.

"Calm down, calm down, please, Yan Yan. Tell me what happened." Tania had never seen her friend this agitated and restless.

"Meng Bo-Xian is in big trouble. He has refused to criticize himself," Yan said.

"Why? Why does he have to criticize himself? What kind of trouble is he in?" Tania was more confused by the answer.

"Rectification. Rectification. Everyone has to repent and self-criticize." The friend's second answer was no clearer than the first.

Tania took Yan's arm and helped her to sit down on the kang. Over a cup of warm water, Yan explained in the best way she could, and Tania started to realize what she had been missing lately.

The study movement and rectification in Bao An had consumed everyone's energy and time for the last three years. Amid growing public pressure, most party officials and army officers had reevaluated their careers in detail, confessed all the big and small mistakes they had committed while holding opinions dissimilar to Sheng Bao's, acknowledged the absolute correctness of his line, and pledged their complete loyalty and devotion to his leadership. Even Commander Tao Yin-Hu, the most stubborn of them all, caved in when they pointed to his alleged dubious ties and suspicious engagement with Dong Zi-Tian, his former good friend, who was sinking into a frightful abyss as fast as Sheng was making his triumphant ascent.

"Silly Meng," Yan continued, "refuses to confess and refuses to declare his wrongs in the past. He has been given one more chance to speak today. You have got to see him right away. Tell him, he can't strike a rock with his head. He'd better confess and repent this time, or he will be sorry tomorrow. You are his good friend. He will listen to you. Go, please go and talk to him before it's too late."

"Okay, I will go and see what I can do." Tania reluctantly agreed. But she hardly considered herself to be the kind of persuasive person that Yan had imagined her to be, and most of all, she still did not understand what the study movement and rectification in Bao An were all about.

2

When Tania arrived at the conference room, the meeting was already underway. Meng was in the middle of his speech.

"What we have now can be called 'quaternity,' a deliberately created superstition, a personality cult, a totally anti-Marxist ideology, and a nonproletarian mythology."

A few notes in his hand, Meng went on calmly.

"Quaternity means the four misconceived and greatly exaggerated assumptions in the present personality cult. That is, (1) no one in the party but Sheng Bao can represent the true and long-term interests of the proletariat, (2) no one in the party but Sheng Bao succeeded in creating the Red Army and has successfully led our military forces, (3) no one in the party but Sheng Bao has always been holding the party's correct line, and (4) no one in the party but Sheng Bao, including his actions and ideas, is the personification of Marxism in China."

Meng stressed, "Our party's successes are due to the unwavering commitment, incessant hard work, and extraordinary sacrifices of tens of thousands of our loyal friends and dedicated comrades. The successes of our party and our military forces rely on the invaluable contributions made by tens of thousands of our rank and file soldiers and party members, including Comrade Sheng Bao, whose special talent, foresight, and wisdom have been a great asset to our cause. But, ultimately, the successes and strengths of our party lie in its honest collaboration and consistent teamwork. To credit every success to one person and to attribute every failure to others is not only illogical and incomprehensible but also utterly untrue in our history.

"For example," Meng elucidated, "Comrade Tang Shu-Hai and Professor Lu Shi-Yan's leading roles in the founding of our party cannot be denied by anyone. Even though Dong Zi-Tian did make some very serious mistakes later, his great contributions to our infant party have also been well-documented. Besides, our party was not born in a vacuum. We received enormous support and guidance from the Russian Bolsheviks, from the Communist Party of the Soviet Union, and from the Comintern.

"Similarly," Meng continued, "Comrade Si-Tu Wen-Liang and Comrade Tao Yin-Hu led the first armed rebellion initiated by our party. Their contributions to the founding of the Red Army were as great as, if not greater than, anyone else in our party. Hundreds of our dedicated party officials and thousands of our brave soldiers and army officers have died too soon, too early to be honored here today as the real founders, the real backbone of our party, army, and cause. Few of them were perfect, and many of them did make mistakes. What really matters is for us to recognize that our revolution is not a religious movement. Our party supports no superstition, be it ideological, theoretical, or personal. There has never been a demigod in our midst whose ideas and words alone can deliver salvation."

Meng explained, "China is a huge country, and the Chinese revolution is a highly complex one. No one has the silver bullet to fix all its problems. Our party's history is a combination of brilliant successes and tragic failures, and all the leading members of our party, myself included, share the joy of those successes as well as the huge responsibility for those failures.

"Some say that Comrade Sheng Bao is a military genius," continued Meng. "Military decisions and leadership, like any other decisions and leadership, require the best intelligence, wisdom, foresight, and execution that no single person can provide, no matter how smart and how experienced he is. Our history has shown that our successful strategies and tactics have been a long trial-and-error process, enriched by the countless combat experiences of many of our military personnel. Comrade Sheng Bao has undoubtedly made his great and distinctive contributions, but he also has had his shares of blunders. The terrible failure and catastrophic losses of our West Army come to mind, which were largely due to his poor planning, miscalculation, frequently changing orders, and confusing directions. I still regard Comrade Sheng Bao as a great military leader, not because he has never made any mistakes but because he is willing to adapt when circumstances change. There has never been a straight path to our victory, nor has there ever been a single military strategy that has never been changed from day one.

"I don't believe," Meng concluded, "our party will gain much by settling old scores and arguing about who was right and who was wrong in the past. In fact, I believe it will be very harmful for our party to give all the credit to one person for all the successes while blaming everyone else for all the failures. This blind personality cult would stifle any healthy debate about our policies in the future, discourage different opinions, and weaken our collective leadership. It will promote superstition in our party and among the people we are supposed to lead, which is contradictory to our goals of a revolution."

3

Never an aggressive individual, Meng had been a popular and likable person in the organization. He never sought the limelight or even enjoyed power, and was widely known as a highly knowledgeable leader who was also rather humble and modest. His surprising speech shocked the audience. For a few seconds they did not know how to react. His views were clearly at odds with the prevailing mood. But his statements sounded reasonable, not ill-conceived. Some applauded, but others screamed, "Down with Meng Bo-Xian! He refused to rectify. He's an enemy of Sheng Bao!" The crowd erupted into chaos.

Lin Shi-Xiong quickly signaled some soldiers to take Meng away.

As they rushed him out of the conference room, Meng noticed the anxiously waiting Tania. She tried to get close to him but was stopped and separated by several strong and armed guards.

"Meng…" She wanted to shout but her voice stuck in her throat. Overwhelmed with admiration, sympathy, sadness and affection, she was suddenly left speechless; only her bright eyes on that beautiful face radiated with the warmth and love that no one but the noble Tania could possess.

Meng saw it. He smiled at her as he was dragged away.

4

"What? He has been arrested?" Yan's disbelief turned into panic. "He could be tortured, and he could be killed. You must find a way to save him!"

Yan told Tania the horrible stories of how several hundred people were recently arrested, and many never came back. The two friends racked their brains and both agreed that the one person who could help them would be Si-Tu, who had tackled many knotty issues and often played the role of a neutral intermediary between friends and rivals. Tania decided to go and talk to him.

The short meeting with Si-Tu left Tania clueless. She did not understand what his lukewarm reaction meant. Maybe he was being cautious to avoid giving her false hopes. Maybe he was too reluctant to speak on behalf of Meng, whose ideas were clearly too radical in this highly charged personality-cult environment. Maybe he was too concerned about his own vulnerable position in the party, especially his tenuous and delicate relationship with Sheng.

Disappointed, Tania went to the prison where Meng was being held. She was told that no one could see him without the written permission of the leadership group.

The exhausted Tania told Yan everything after she returned. The two had a sleepless night and Tania tried to see Meng again the next morning. But she was sent away by the guards, who had been given strict orders not to allow any visitors.

It was Tania's turn to panic. Yan's fears could be true. What if Meng was tortured? What if he was secretly executed? She would never have a chance to see him again.

For the first time in her life, Tania found herself shaking as her heart wrenched with pain she had never felt before. Her longing, anxiety, grief, and the feeling of loss hurt her so much that she started sobbing.

Yan embraced her. She knew the feelings of loss and despair. She wanted to comfort her friend the best way she could. She cursed those who were hurting Meng. She cursed those who were hurting Tania. She cursed those who were hurting both of them, the nicest people she had ever known and the best friends she had ever had.

The next morning, Tania, who had somewhat regained her composure, asked Yan for a piece of cloth. She steeled herself and went to the prison again.

Tania assured the guard that she was not here to see Meng, but begged, "Please pass this small wrapping to him."

The honest and innocent guard hesitated but could not resist Tania's earnest pleas. He obliged.

When Meng opened the cloth in his cell, he saw Tania's sparkling porcelain—the tiny but most exquisite blue-and-white ceramic bottle with three glazing blue tulips on it.

5

Yan knew Tania's secret, and was glad that her friend was finally making the first move. They learned a long time ago that Meng's wife had died shortly after the Long March. Yan repeatedly told Tania that she believed they would make a good couple on the first day she saw them together. A faithful Daoist practitioner without declaring it, Yan, as most Chinese would, insisted on the importance of fate.

"You are made for each other," Yan said to Tania. "Your looks, your interests, and your temperaments suit each other perfectly. You are predestined to be a couple."

"Why did you say that? How could you tell? That's superstition," Tania answered.

"Well, in this world, you have to believe in fate sometimes." Yan tried to convince her friend.

Yan's confidence did not last long. Tania went out but did not return home that night. Then the second, and the third night. Yan got worried. She went out to ask around and heard that Tania had been arrested.

"Why? You can't find a nicer person in this world," she said.

"She is a spy," came the answer.

6

The two deputies Lin and Song Pei urged Sheng to declare both the study movement and rectification campaign a success. Si-Tu had openly confessed his mistakes, they said. Tao had never recovered from the embarrassing contact with Dong, whose diminished reputation in the party clearly showed the serious consequence of opposing Sheng. Mo Jia-Qi was incapacitated by some mysterious stomachache, with some saying that he had been poisoned by mercury in the medicine a party-assigned doctor had prescribed to him. Meng's disgruntlement was a slight anomaly that Sheng should not bother himself with, the deputies told him.

Sheng disagreed with the two men. He wanted nothing short of a total victory. He would take no prisoners. He needed confessions, submissions, and unconditional capitulation. He would not be satisfied until the last of his enemies had been crushed.

"Keep them in jail. Keep them in solitary confinement. Keep on the pressure until they submit," he ordered.

"But the war situation may quickly change, now that the United States and Great Britain have allied themselves with the Soviet Union against Nazi Germany," Lin cautiously reminded his boss.

"That's all the more reason to have a truly cohesive party and a loyal army to take part in the fight," Sheng responded.

"We are informed that Roosevelt's administration is interested in contacting our military forces in Bao An. Maybe the international tide has turned in our favor," Song added.

A close observer of international affairs, Sheng had apparently anticipated these developments. He replied, "General Chen used to say that 'the resistance against the external enemies must depend on the extermination of domestic foes first.' I would like to make a slight modification: 'the struggle against our external enemies must depend on the complete elimination of the internal enemies within our own party.'"

The rectification campaign went on relentlessly. All told, by the end of this wide-ranging political purification and organizational cleansing, everyone had been forced to confess and swear loyalty to the only party leader that the personality cult had created. Of the several thousands who had been arrested, nearly one thousand were killed, tortured, or died in prison.

Glory. Power. Control. Prestige. Legitimacy. If they had to be obtained by considerable pain, suffering, sacrifice, or collateral damage, so be it. The path to salvation was never easy, nor would it be painless—the road to the justification, glorification, and sanctification of the divine party leadership would necessarily have to be treacherous and bloody. For anyone who believed that he was the holy messiah or the glorious embodiment of the communist quaternity, his godly ascension to the highest pulpit would be worth any price.

It was not until Sheng felt absolutely certain that the much-sought-after fruit of his labor—glory, power, prestige, and legitimacy—was at long last within his reach, and that the entire party apparatus had been completely subdued did Sheng decide to call for a new national congress, which had not been held for the last seventeen years. Unanimously elected as chairman of the Chinese Communist Party this time, Sheng finally fulfilled his lifelong dream of becoming the supreme leader with immense powers in his hands.

Extremely delighted for the remarkable rise, Sheng was particularly proud that he had achieved the goals by beating all his competitors, particularly those trained and supported by Moscow. He, the native boy from rural China who had never been to a foreign land, proved to be more tenacious and formidable than anyone had anticipated.

7

"Darling, our sufferings will soon end," General Chen told Madam Chen cheerfully, feeling totally invigorated upon their return from the Cairo Conference, where the couple had met President Franklin D. Roosevelt and Prime Minister Winston Churchill.

China's importance as a major ally in Asia had been increasingly recognized by the United States. When Madam Chen toured the country and gave a historic speech before both Houses of Congress, tens of thousands Americans began to know about the war's oriental dimension, and their enthusiastic support fueled the Chinese people's resolve to fight the Japanese invaders. If American aid, loans, supplies, airplanes, pilots, and military advisors were the most visible material support the Chinese government received, Roosevelt's insistence to include General Chen to represent China as one of the four leading countries in the worldwide antifascist campaign boosted the Chinese people's morale and self-confidence. For nearly a century, China had been molested by foreign powers. Now it had a chance to join hands with the Allied nations and fight against their common enemies.

"Darling, a new delegation of American visitors will arrive in two weeks. I hope you can help arrange the reception," the general requested.

"Of course. I will be glad to meet any delegation from the United States," Madam Chen responded with a smile. A graduate from Wellesley College, she had ever regarded America as her second home. Receiving an American delegation would enhance her public image and provide her with personal joy at the same time.

8

At the meeting of the newly constituted Politburo, Sheng Bao, the proud chairman, was in a relaxed mood as he sat beside its other four members—Song (whose obsequiousness qualified him as the Chairman's right-hand man), Si-Tu (whose profuse apologies and confessions saved his seat), Tao (who gave up friendship for his post), and Lin (whose expertise the Chairman needed).

"A small group of Americans will be visiting Bao An soon. How should we prepare for it?" Si-Tu inquired.

"Diplomacy is your cup of tea. You can deal with it." The Chairman rarely cared about such trivial business.

"Diplomacy is always within the purview of the Central Committee. We are at the service of the Central Committee, and we need specific guidance so as to avoid mistakes," Si-Tu calmly replied. He knew the Chairman too well to let him off the hook easily.

When Sheng said "you can surely deal with it yourself" and when you did deal with it on your own, he would blame you for not reporting to him in the first place. If a mistake did occur in the process, he would penalize you for it. If your action turned out to be a success, he would make sure that he would be given the credit for his wise leadership. This meant that, no matter what you did, he would not be happy with your performance. To be a manservant to the king was never an easy job and Si-Tu got burned numerous times for not understanding that.

"They are American journalists. We need careful preparation to avoid negative publicity." Si-Tu hinted at the potential consequence, knowing Sheng was ever mindful about propaganda and his public persona.

"Hmm, that's true. So, give them a warm welcome and show them our best side." Sheng had finally said something concrete enough for Si-Tu to follow, even though the instruction had remained vague enough to let the boss wiggle his way out if things did not go according to his desire.

"Chairman, what do you think about Tania's petition?" Lin asked cautiously.

"It's ludicrous. She wants to marry and save Meng Bo-Xian. She thinks she is a Soviet citizen and therefore we can't harm her. I will never allow them to get married!" Sheng was adamant. Meng's searing speech still hurt him badly, for which he would never forgive or forget.

"Yes, she could be a Russian spy. She could be an American spy," Lin declared, always willing to support and even amplify the boss's vendetta. He understood perfectly what his job was, and possessed a remarkable instinct on how to accommodate the boss's prosecutorial mood.

Fed up with Lin's dirty tricks, Tao retorted, "Is there any proof of those allegations?"

"We will soon find out," Lin replied.

"Well, that may be too late now," Si-Tu chimed in.

"Why?" Always believing that he was fighting for the boss whose support he could count on, Lin demanded an answer.

"Because one of those American journalists is her son, Peter, who has requested to meet her in Bao An," explained Si-Tu.

Surprise, surprise. How did he know? Shrewd Sheng immediately reassessed several potential repercussions of this coincidence. He could detain Meng. He could arrest Tania. He could deny her petition for marriage. He could hold them as his political hostages for as long as he wanted. But he could not ignore the Americans in this war. He wanted their recognition. He needed their support. Stalin provided most of the military aid to General Chen's government and had also signed a nonaggression treaty with Japan, disengaging the Soviet Union from fighting in the Far East. The American public and Roosevelt's administration were the only potential allies the Chinese communists could hope for in their struggle against the Japanese occupation. Si-Tu was right, Sheng concluded, that it would not be a good idea to upset the American visitors at this critical moment.

"Good. This will be a great opportunity then. Tania's petition is granted. She should marry Meng Bo-Xian. And we will have a big celebration. Everyone is invited, including her son, Peter, and those American guests," the Chairman decided.

Keenly aware of the important opportunity, Sheng believed that he could take advantage of this surprise visit and turn it into good publicity. What a great media exposure it would be if he and the Chinese communists received international coverage!

Sheng's sudden reversal delighted Si-Tu, but totally deflated Lin. However difficult as it might seem to be the king's servant, to be his slave could be both bewildering and miserable.

9

Protecting the American president on his weekend trips was not any easier than ensuring his safety during his overseas flights to Casablanca or Cairo or Tehran. Like a child freed from the constraints at home, Franklin D. Roosevelt was delighted that he could finally escape the muddle at the White House. Leaving the sultry capital behind, the presidential train, which included his small entourage, headed north. Passing Baltimore, Philadelphia, and then New York, the train traveled toward Hyde Park, a hundred miles up the Hudson River, where his childhood home would provide him with the peace and serenity he badly needed for some rest away from the weighty burdens of office, which included tough domestic problems and wide-ranging international responsibilities.

The president, now in declining health, slept ten or eleven hours through the night in the thirty-five-room Big House of the family estate and was wheeled out several times a day for a breath of fresh air on top of the wooded hills overlooking the pleasant blue Hudson River below.

It was a glorious Indian summer day in this part of the country and the weather was delightfully cool and brilliant, triggering flashbacks in the sixty-something Roosevelt. He fondly recalled how, as a boy, he had cleverly maneuvered his sled, plunging down to the bottom of the bluff, walked back up to the top of the hill, and then repeated the exhilarating descent again. How mother Sara's adoring smile shone behind her gold lorgnette. How he had debated with her whether they should serve coffee or tea when the king and queen of England came to visit. Now the rose garden looked as healthy and colorful as ever before as he took an easy ride on the dirt trail. Hay still grew thick in the fields adjacent to the Albany Post Road and Roosevelt, although never the typical farmer with a long scythe in hand, hoped the good harvest would continue year after year. Unfortunately, hearing the news of his return, visitors of all ages, men and women, from neighboring communities quickly flooded the Big House, cutting short his plans for relaxation.

On the return journey, the train took an unexpected turn. It left the routine Baltimore and Ohio route, veered into the Pennsylvania-Lehigh line, and stopped at the small town of Allamuchy in New Jersey. There the president spent a few hours with a longtime friend named Lucy Rutherfurd at Tranquility Farms, her beautiful summer estate of six hundred acres. The lush foliage, the fresh garden flowers, and the delightful conversations with the hostess mesmerized the president, who was finally able to relax.

For the next several months similar arrangements were made to enable the two to meet—when Eleanor Roosevelt had left town, of course—sometimes for dinner in the president's study on the second floor of the White House, sometimes at the nicely shaded South Portico for an afternoon tea. But the more extended and most pleasant occasion was when the president went to Warm Springs, Georgia, for vacation. A rehabilitation center was built there in the 1920s after Roosevelt was stricken with polio. The natural spring waters, the mild climate, and the rustic environment captivated him, and he bought a one-thousand-seven-hundred-acre farm and designed a six-room cottage as his retreat. Painted white, the small but cozy house was surrounded by native white pines, black oaks, and red hickories. He came as many as sixteen times during his presidency and a key ingredient to his therapy might have been the fact that, only two hundred miles away, Lucy Rutherfurd and her late husband had a home in Aiken, South Carolina.

When Lucy and her daughter Anna came to visit his "Little White House," the president could not be happier. They charmed him with their sweet and cheerful presence, and he delighted them with his classy wit, charismatic humor, enigmatic allure, and boyish spirit. An acquaintance of the Rutherfurds', the artist Elizabeth Shoumatoff, was invited to paint Roosevelt's portrait, the only American in history who had been elected four times as the president of the United States.

Everything was joyous until one early Thursday afternoon, when Roosevelt felt great pain at the back of his head. A massive cerebral hemorrhage hit him unconscious, from which he never recovered.

The thirty-second American president was dead and, two hours later, his vice president, Harry S. Truman, received a call asking him to come to the White House quickly but as quietly as he could. A regular working day for the man, he put down his teacup in House speaker Sam Rayburn's hideaway office downstairs. He then went through the ground floor of the Capitol Building, passed the Crypt, got his hat from his office, raced to his long black Mercury, beat the evening traffic in the city, turned off at Pennsylvania Avenue, and stopped under the North Portico of the White House by 5:25pm. Still unaware of the grave situation, he was ushered to the second floor of the president's private quarters, instead of the Oval Office in the West Wing, as he had expected. Less than ten minutes later he finally realized what had happened, and he was sworn in as president on the same afternoon of April 12, 1945.

During the past eighty-two days serving as the vice president, Truman had met Roosevelt only twice outside of their cabinet meetings; neither one involved any discussions on important issues. Berlin fell twenty days after Truman sat in the Oval Office. One of his first tasks as the new president of the United States, was to meet with the formidable communist leader Stalin in Potsdam, Germany, ten weeks after Victory in Europe Day, better known as VE Day.

10

Although traditional wedding ceremonies were hugely elaborate events in China, they were modest affairs in Bao An for its prevailing impoverishment. The dirt walls of Meng's cave looked the same except for the paper-cutting Yan Yan had made for her friend—the big Chinese character "double happiness" in scarlet red that should never be omitted from any wedding no matter how poor one might be. After all, weddings should be as festive as they could be because they were the most important rite of passage for young people, especially the bride.

Yan helped Tania to put on her best clothes, but the latter steadfastly refused the former's attempt to give her a traditional facelift—using a cotton string to remove her facial hair. The friend insisted that it was a standard Chinese ritual for every bride.

"You are no longer a girl. The refreshed face will show that you are married so that no other men will pursue you anymore," Yan explained.

"Thanks, but no thanks," Tania said. "I am just fine with the way my face is. Besides, this is not my first marriage. No one will pursue me anyway."

"No, you are so beautiful, and no one can tell that you are married unless, of course, you do the facelift." Yan was as insistent as her friend.

"My dear, let's leave my face alone and let's go to the party." Tania dragged Yan to join the crowd waiting for the blissful celebration to start.

Just about every dignitary in the communist organization was there. Si-Tu brought a pumpkin as big as the size of a baby, which amazed everyone. "Where did you get it? I have never seen a pumpkin so big in Bao An in my life!" People asked and touched to appreciate it. Si-Tu smiled and said nothing. He bribed a nationalist officer who had smuggled it from Shanxi.

As usual, the gift from Sheng and his wife was a basin of baked potatoes, which they cheerfully distributed to every participant. Tao went to the nearby wilderness for two days and brought back a Mongolian gazelle he had shot.

The meat of the seventy-pound beast became the most sumptuous dish at the party. Song and his wife gave two new pillowcases, embroidered with a pair of charming mandarin ducks—the traditional symbol of a loving couple and harmonious marriage life. Lin's gift was a pair of pens, perfect for the two highly cultured individuals. Mo was too sick to attend but he did ask his guard to convey his best wishes. Even Dong sent someone to present two apricot-like apples to the newlyweds. He attached a note saying, "I had thought of sending a bowl of wild dates, but decided against it lest they be considered 'sour grapes.' The two apples are not fresh, and also too small and desiccated for this joyous occasion. But they are the best I could come up with. Hope you enjoy them. You are the two most wonderful people I have ever known. Warmest congratulations to you both!"

Cheers and drinks quickly filled the room and no wedding ceremony would be complete without teasing the bride and groom. "Tell us your love story!" "Tell us the secrets!" "I want to find a girl as nice as Tania some day!" The crowds went wild. They were mostly middle-ranking officials, secretaries, soldiers, and personal guards who had worked with the couple and other leading figures of the party for a long time. Intimately familiar with one another, they were glad to have this rare occasion for fun and relaxation.

"Our love is based on our shared commitment to the revolution," Meng responded in the best way he could think of, which only revealed his awkward shyness.

"We know that; it tells us nothing new," someone shouted.

"We have known each other for a long time since the days in Blue Grass." Tania tried to help, but her simple answer raised a few eyebrows.

"Aha! Blue Grass. Comrade Meng Bo-Xian was married then, weren't you?" Someone smelled something fishy.

"Shut up, you rascal! Tania and Meng Bo-Xian are the most honorable people I have ever known." Yan stood up to defend her friend.

"Well, that will depend on how the new couple will entertain us tonight," Si-Tu joked as he tried to shift the topic.

The bride and groom knew this would be coming. Meng said that he had prepared a song, "Katyusha," for them, even though he was not a good singer. It was one of the most popular songs in the Soviet Union during World War II, and it quickly spread to China. Many Russians songs sounded much better if accompanied by the accordion and Peter volunteered to play the instrument. Meng then started singing,

Apple trees and pear trees were blooming,
and river mists hovering low,
She came out and went ashore, Katyusha!
On the lofty bank, on the steep shore.

She came out and sang the song about
Her young friend, the blue eagle from the steppes
All about the one she dearly loved,
Whose letters she would treasure and hold.

Hey, a song, the song of the young girl,
Fly and go after the bright sun,
Find a soldier on the distant borderlands
Say hello from Katyusha waiting long for him.

Let him remember the young and simple maiden,
Let him hear the song she now sings,
Let him protect the motherland for sure,
As their love Katyusha will preserve.

A marching song combining patriotism and romantic love, "Katyusha" was warm, soft, resolute, and uplifting at the same time. The song was so popular in the Soviet Union that the most fearsome Russian rocket launcher was said to have been named after it. The song was also well-known among the Chinese, and many in the crowd started to sing with Meng, which gave Peter the opportunity to show off his musical skills. The lively lyrics, melodious notes, exhilarating rhyme, and energizing tempo led them to repeat it for the second time, ending the sing along on a high note. The crowd was delightfully impressed, and they turned to Tania.

Full of gratitude, Tania knew why her new husband had chosen this Russian song, which was as much for the crowd as it was for her. He sang it to please her and to console his homesick bride. He was always very considerate, very gentle. He always thought about others first, which was maybe the key reason why Tania fell in love with him. Never self-centered, he showed his love for her in his customary quietness and sometimes in indirect ways.

"I really can't sing as well as Meng does," Tania said. "So please allow me to tell you a story, a Russian tale, to be exact. And I hope you will like it."

The crowd was intrigued. Few of them had ever heard a foreign story. They stopped chattering and started listening.

"This is a story about a plant, called the Siberian dwarf cedar," Tania began. "My father, while doing hard labor in Siberia, had met a guy named Nicholas Ivanovich, who was much stronger than he was. They worked in the mines, the hardest work under the most horrendous conditions. One day, they were assigned to collect cedar needles in the mountains. And here is the story my father told me."

The hills glistened white with a tinge of blue—like loaves of sugar. Round and bare of forest, they were smothered with a layer of dense snow compacted by the winds. In the ravines the snow was deep and firm; a man could stand on it. But on the slopes it swelled up in enormous blisters. These were shrubs of the Siberian dwarf cedar, which lay flat on the ground to hibernate through the winter—even before the first snow fell. They were what we had come for.

Of all northern trees, I loved the dwarf cedar most of all.

I had long since come to understand and appreciate the enviable haste with which poor northern nature shared its meager wealth with equally indigent man, blossoming for him every variety of flower. There were times when everything bloomed in a single week and when only a month after the beginning of summer the almost never setting sun would make the mountains flame red with cowberries and then darken with their deep blue. Rowan shrubs hung heavy with full, watery berries—so low you didn't even have to raise your hand. Only the petals of the mountain sweet-brier smelled like flowers here. All the others exuded a sense of dampness, a swampy odor, and this seemed appropriate to the spring silence, both of the birch and the larch forest whose branches slowly clothed themselves in green needles. The sweet-brier clung to its fruit right into winter and from under the snow stretched out to us in its wrinkled, meaty berries whose thick violet skin concealed a dark yellow flesh. I knew of the playful vines, which again and again changed their color in spring from dark rose to orange to pale green, as if they were stretched with dyed kidskin. The slender fingers of the larch with their green fingernails seemed to grope everywhere, and the omnipresent, oily fireweed carpeted the scenes of former forest blazes. All this was exquisite, trusting, boisterous, rushed; but all this was in summer when dull green grass mixed with the glaze of mossy boulders that gleamed in the sun and seemed not gray or brown, but green.

In winter it all disappeared, covered with crusty snow cast into the ravines by the winds and beaten down so hard that to climb upward a man had to hack steps in the snow with an ax. Everything was so naked that a person in the forest could be seen half a mile away. And only one tree was always green, always alive—the dwarf cedar. The tree was a weatherman. Two or three days before the first snow in the cloudless heat of fall when no one wanted even to think of the oncoming winter, the dwarf cedar would suddenly stretch out its enormous five-yard paws on the ground, lightly bend its straight, black, two-fist-thick trunk, and lie prone on the earth. A day or two would pass and a cloud would appear; toward evening a snowstorm would begin. And if in the late fall low, gray snow clouds would gather accompanied by a cold wind and the dwarf cedar did not lie down, one could be sure that no snow would fall.

Toward the end of March or in April, when there was still no trace of spring and the air was dry and rarefied as in winter, the dwarf cedar would suddenly rise up, shaking the snow from its reddish-green clothing. In a day or two the wind would shift, and warm streams of air would usher in spring.

The dwarf cedar was a very precise instrument, sensitive to the point where it sometimes deceived itself, rising during a lengthy period of thaw. But it would hurriedly lie back in the snow before the cold returned. Sometimes we would make a hot campfire in the morning to last till evening so we could warm our hands and feet. We would heap on as many logs as possible and set off to work. In two or three hours the dwarf cedar would stretch its branches out from under the snow and slowly right itself, thinking that spring had arrived. But, before the fire could even go out, the tree would again lie back into the snow.

Winter here is two-toned: a high pale-blue sky and the white ground. Spring would lay bare the dirty yellow rags of fall, and the earth would be clothed in this beggar's garb for a long time—until the new greenery would gather its strength and begin to blossom furiously. In the midst of this pitiless winter and gloomy spring, the dwarf cedar would gleam blindingly green and clear. Moreover, tiny cedar nuts grew on it, and this delicacy was shared by people, birds, bears, squirrels, and chipmunks.

I had never before worked in gangs that gathered dwarf cedar needles. We did everything by hand, plucking the green, dry needles and stuffing them into sacks; in the evening we handed them over to the foreman. The needles were hauled away to a mysterious "vitamin factory" where they were boiled down to a dark yellow viscous extract with an inexpressibly repulsive taste.

Before each dinner this extract had to be drunk or eaten—in whatever way a person could manage. Its taste spoiled not only one's dinner, but supper as well, and many considered this "treatment" a supplementary means of camp discipline. But without a shot-glass of this medicine it was impossible to get dinner in the cafeteria; the rule was strictly enforced.

Scurvy was everywhere and dwarf cedar was the only medically approved cure. It was ultimately proved that this preparation was completely ineffective in curing scurvy and the "vitamin factory" was closed.

Nevertheless, faith conquered all, and at the time many drunk the stinking abomination, went away spitting, but eventually recovered from scurvy. Or they didn't recover. Or they didn't drink it and recovered anyway.

The instructions prescribed cedar needles as the only source of vitamin C.

"Needle-picking" was considered not just an easy job, but the easiest of all. Moreover, it didn't require the presence of a guard.

After many months of work in the icy mines where every sparklingly frozen stone burned the hands, after the clicks of rifle bolts, the barking dogs, the swearing of the overseers behind our backs, needle-picking was an enormous pleasure, physically felt with every exhausted muscle. Needle-gatherers were sent out after the others, while it was still dark.

It was a marvelous feeling to warm your hands against the can with the smoldering logs and slowly set out for the seemingly unattainable peaks, to climb higher and higher, constantly aware of your own solitariness and the deep winter silence of the mountains. It was as if everything evil in the world had been snuffed out and only you and your companion existed in this narrow, dark, endless path in the snow, leading upward into the mountains.

My companion watched my slow movements disapprovingly. He had been gathering cedar needles for a long time and correctly saw in me a weak, clumsy partner. Work was done in pairs, and the "wage" was divided fifty–fifty.

"I'll chop and you pick," he said. "And get moving, or we won't fill our quota. I don't want to have to go back to the mines."

He chopped down a few branches and dragged an enormous pile of green paws to the fire. I broke off the smaller branches and, starting from the top of each branch, pulled off the needles together with the bark. They look liked green fringe.

"You'll have to work faster," said my companion, returning with a new armload.

I could see that the work was not going well, but I couldn't work faster. There was ringing in my ears, and my fingers, frostbitten at the beginning of winter, ached with a familiar dull pain. I yanked at the needles, broke entire branches into smaller pieces without stripping the bark, and stuffed the product into the sack. The sack wouldn't fill. Before the fire rose a mountain of stripped branches that looked like washed bones, but the sack kept swelling and swelling and accepting new armfuls of needles.

My companion sat down next to me, and the work went faster.

"It's time to go," he said suddenly. "Or else we'll miss supper. We haven't got enough here for the quota." He took a large stone from the ashes of the fire, and shoved it into the sack. "Now we've met our quota," he said.

I stood up, scattered the burning branches, and kicked snow on to the red coals. The fire hissed and went out, and it immediately became cold. It was clear that evening was close. My companion helped me heave the sack onto my back. I staggered under its weight.

"Try dragging it," my companion said. "After all, we're going downhill, not up."

We barely arrived in time to get our soup. No meat or vegetables were given for such light work.

Tania ended the story, and everyone was dumbstruck. It was such a compelling story, strikingly beautiful and profoundly sad at once. It took everybody to a remote land, extremely harsh, cold, forbidden, and yet imbued with the enormous strength, power, and endurance of the insuppressible human spirit. The wedding guests were completely mesmerized and they started applauding.

Peter was moved too. As a boy, he never had the chance to listen to his mom telling him any bedtime stories. But he thoroughly enjoyed this one. He understood the hard times his mom and her parents had gone through and he could now clearly see what great a mother he had.

"I would like to read a poem for my parents, if I may," Peter stepped forward.

This was totally unexpected. "Of course, you may," Tania and Meng looked at Peter adoringly.

The crowd got even more excited. Most of them had never been to a foreign country. They had heard a Russian song, a Russian story. Now they were going to hear an American poem, something that they had never even dreamed of.

"Okay, I will now recite the poem and request that my mom and papa translate it into Chinese for everyone." Peter then began, "The poem is titled 'Thinking,' or more popularly known as 'The Man Who Thinks He Can.' It was written early in the century by a very obscure poet named Walter D. Wintle, of whom very little is known."

If you think you are beaten, you are;
If you think you dare not, you don't.
If you'd like to win, but you think you can't,
It is almost a cinch that you won't.

If you think you'll lose, you're lost;
For out of the world we find
Success begins with a fellow's will
It's all in the state of mind.

If you think you're outclassed, you are;
You've got to think high to rise.
You've got to be sure of yourself before
You can ever win the prize.

Life's battles don't always go
To the stronger or faster man;
But sooner or later the man who wins
Is the one who thinks he can!

When in the next few minutes the crowd heard the translations, they exploded into loud cheers and applause. Yan cheered the hardest, evidently one of the happiest in the crowd. Full of tears, she was as moved, excited, and joyous as her dear friend Tania, her husband Meng, and their son, Peter. "Good heavens," she prayed, "please, please bless this wonderful new family. May happiness and good fortune always be with them."

11

War generated its own rationale and would only follow the course formulated by the circumstances of its own time, not affected by the emotions, opinions, or judgments of either previous or later generations.

On the day the Allied forces declared victory in Europe, the Battle of Okinawa had already been underway for more than a month. This bloodiest campaign in the Asian Pacific Theater did not end until a month and a half later in mid-June, and it cost the Americans the lives of twelve thousand, five hundred servicemen, or twenty-seven deaths per square mile, to win the small island. The top brass had not anticipated such a brutal fight, with them projecting that a quick capture of Okinawa would provide the Americans with a crucial military base to launch attacks on the Japanese mainland. The awful losses had a sobering effect on them, and they now believed that, at this ominous rate, the final assault on the mainland could cost the lives of as many as one million men, which would be more than double the number of all the casualties the United States had suffered in Europe and elsewhere throughout World War II. Obviously, something must be done to avert such a horrendous prospect.

Unaware of the "Manhattan Project" while he was vice president, Truman was not briefed about its existence until twelve days after becoming president. He was anxiously waiting for the results of the first atomic bomb test, codenamed "Trinity," which was scheduled to take place on July 16, 1945, a day before the Potsdam Conference. But the complete report did not reach the president until five days later, in which the man in charge of the project, General Leslie R. Groves, wrote, "The test was successful beyond the most optimistic expectations of anyone."

Immensely pleased, President Truman, now a changed man, went for the conference's evening session with fresh vigor and great confidence. He stood firm against Russian demands in the negotiations, and insisted on them making good their promise that they would open a second front against the Japanese. The invasion of the Japanese mainland was scheduled in November 1945. While the president had hoped to secure a Soviet declaration of war against Japan at Potsdam, Truman in the end decided not to request their help after the successful bomb test. Japan would surrender before long and Stalin should not be allowed to get too much of the action.

Immediate preparations were made to use the new weapon based on plans unanimously agreed by a top-secret government committee (including three eminent scientists, two of whom were university presidents from Harvard and MIT) and its advisory panel of four prominent nuclear physicists as early as May, right after VE Day.

On August 6, the first atomic bomb was dropped and Hiroshima was destroyed. In his public statement, Truman warned that "a rain of ruin from the air" would fall on Japan if it did not surrender.

Two days later shortly before midnight, the Soviet Union declared war on Japan.

The next morning, on August 9, a second atomic bomb was dropped on Nagasaki. Truman declared:

The world will note that the first atomic bomb was dropped on Hiroshima, a military base. That was because we wished in this first attack to avoid, insofar as possible, the killing of civilians. But that attack is only a warning of things to come. If Japan does not surrender, bombs will have to be dropped on her war industries and, unfortunately, thousands of civilian lives will be lost. I urge Japanese civilians to leave industrial cities immediately, and save themselves from destruction.

We have used it against those who attacked us without warning at Pearl Harbor, against those who have starved and beaten and executed American prisoners of war, against those who have abandoned all pretense of obeying international laws of warfare. We have used it in order to shorten the agony of war, in order to save the lives of thousands and thousands of young Americans.

We shall continue to use it until we completely destroy Japan's power to make war. Only a Japanese surrender will stop us.

Japan surrendered on August 15, citing, among others, that "the enemy has begun to employ a new and most cruel bomb, the power of which to do damage is, indeed, incalculable."

World War II, the most brutal and ruinous war in human history finally came to an end.

Chapter 29

Civil War

1

"So, WHAT DO YOU THINK ABOUT YOUR TRIP HERE?" TANIA ASKED Peter, who was about to leave Bao An and return to the United States soon.

"It has been a wonderful trip. I have learned so much, which would have never happened if I had remained in New York," Peter answered enthusiastically.

"Please tell us what impressed you the most," Meng Bo-Xian chimed in.

"I must say the sheer size and diversity of the country," Peter said. "Back home, few people know where China is and how big it is. Most Americans believe America is the biggest country in the world, not knowing that several countries are bigger, including China. If people have heard anything about China at all, they tend to imagine it as a mystical and faraway land."

He continued, "When I traveled across the country, I saw so many people in different regions, with different backgrounds and education, and different livelihood and aspirations. I realized one thing—that China's problems must be resolved by the Chinese themselves. Any outside forces, no matter how powerful, would not be able to solve the problems for China."

"Part of the problem comes from the complex domestic situation, right? Such as the Nationalist Party and the Chinese Communist Party having different agendas," Meng said.

"That's true. I found both parties have been locked into their separate ideologies, which could lead to open conflict sooner or later," Peter said.

Tania and Meng looked at Peter; both were impressed but not surprised by the statement. They asked, "Why?"

The young man said, "From what I have read about General Chen and Sheng Bao and from what I could observe up close at their respective press conferences and media interviews, I think they are two fruits from the same tree—the tree of the long Chinese tradition and its rich culture. Each believes that only he can best represent the interests of the people, and that only his party represents the future of the country. This clearly shows they are on a collision course."

"I am surprised that you have such a pessimistic view," Meng remarked.

"No, I am not pessimistic. I am just being realistic," Peter said.

"A typical American trait, I suppose," Tania said.

"Well, maybe that is true. But I don't think it's necessarily a negative quality. People need ideas and sometimes maybe even ideals. But they need to be realistic as well," Peter responded.

"So, tell us how you come to this 'realistic' conclusion?" Tania asked.

"You see, the Communist Party is unlike any opposition party in the West. Although still regional in scope in various parts of the nation, it is a *de facto* form of government on its own. It has built a sizable army, established grassroots organizations, created administrative institutions, controlled extensive territory, run separate economic activities, and even printed its own currency. I don't believe the party that has initiated all those policies and established all those practices would be satisfied simply with a few seats in the national government. Do you?" Peter asked.

Tania and Meng looked at each other and said, "No, we don't."

"So, it's very clear to me that your party, the Communist Party, will compete for national power with General Chen, who will also never give up his authority. Am I correct?" Peter asked.

His parents had to agree with him and said, "Yes."

"If a civil war is inevitable, which party will win?" Tania asked.

"A strong nationalist, General Chen believes that he is destined to unify the country and to lead China's only legitimate central government. He may make some concessions but he does not seem to be willing to share his power with the Communist Party," Peter observed.

"Sheng Bao is an equally strong-willed person, who will never stop fighting for power and dominance because of his ideological convictions," Peter went on. "At the moment, General Chen has the superior forces, but many of his government officials and military officers have become corrupt after the Japanese surrender. They are more concerned with collecting bribes to satisfy their self-interests than dealing with the nation's urgent economic and social problems.

"Precisely because the Communist Party is currently the underdog, it is much more unified and more frugal, and more dynamic and upbeat, than General Chen's party. In fact, I believe that your party has a better chance of winning only if you play the cards right," Peter predicted.

"I never knew that you are this much into politics," Tania said, approvingly.

"I am not into politics. I am just interested in making my own observations," Peter said.

"Do young Americans like to think and analyze things as independently as you do?" Meng was curious. He now clearly liked Peter, whose inquisitive mind and even-handed analysis impressed him.

"Not everyone. But some do," Peter said.

"But here is the tough question. What do you think about the American government and the Russian government—what would they do with China given its current situation?" asked Tania, who felt very proud of her son. His sensible mind and clear articulation pleased her enormously. Like any mother who would love to see a bright son, she liked to hear her young boy talking even more. She enjoyed every minute of the conversation with him and saw in him a mature, thoughtful, and upright man, the kind of man she definitely adored and loved.

"Well, no offense, Mom, I have to say that Stalin's government has an imperialist ambition to expand its power and influence in Asia. And China unfortunately will fall under that influence and dominance."

Peter explained, "Russia has been expanding into the northeastern part of China since the last century. A few hours before the U.S. dropped the second atomic bomb, more than one and a half million Russian Red Army troops attacked Manchuria simultaneously on three fronts from the west, north, and east, and the Japanese Kwantung Army was crushed in a month. The end of World War II and Japan's defeat gave Stalin the perfect opportunity to regain control of this area, where Russia has several key interests, such as the Chinese Eastern Railroad, the Southern Manchurian Railroad, Port Arthur and Dairen on the Liaodong Peninsula, and cities like Harbin, Shenyang, and Changchun. All of them are strategically important to the Russian expansion in the Far East, including their long-term goal to establish and preserve ice-free ocean ports in Asia.

"Considering these interests and goals," continued Peter, "the Soviet Union would need the collaboration of a legitimate Chinese government. Thus, Stalin, a shrewd player of the power game, will work with General Chen. Meanwhile, the belief in a worldwide proletarian revolution, fostered by Marxist communist ideology, also allows Stalin to support the efforts by the Chinese Communist Party to advance its cause in the country. The ideological Stalin does not seem to have any problem with playing the dual roles of a leading promoter of communist causes and an imperial expansionist at the same time."

"What would the U.S. government do then?" Meng asked.

"Truman's administration would have to make some tough choices. Due to the overwhelming public pressure to demobilize after the war, it can't support an all-out civil war in China, nor can it totally abandon the country. So, the administration is adopting a middle-of-the-road approach that, as General George Marshall is doing right now, is to try to negotiate peace between the Chinese Communist and Nationalist Parties. I don't think this will work. And the U.S. will be blamed by both the nationalists and the communists in the end," Peter grimly predicted.

"Why?"

"Because American politicians are too naïve. They know little about Chinese history and have no idea of how complicated the reality in China is today."

"Sounds like you should serve in the State Department," Meng joked.

"No, no, no. I am just an intern newspaperman. I can't be a diplomat." Peter laughed.

"Oh, Peter, I am so glad that you are here. Both Meng and I are very happy that you could attend our wedding and gave us that wonderful recitation." Tania hugged and kissed Peter.

"Mom, and Meng," said Peter, "that was the happiest time in my life. I am so glad that I could be at your wedding ceremony, which was truly the highlight of my trip to China."

2

Was Peter correct? Had China really produced two iron-willed strongmen who had been focusing on exactly the same goal in their careers? Were they born from the tree of the same tradition, as Peter said? Or they were like a pair of twin brothers, who could read each other's mind—each wanted to rule China alone, and neither one of them wanted to share power with his rival brother?

General Chen regretted his decision almost as soon as his delegates had signed the peace accord with the communist delegation two months after the Japanese surrender. He clearly understood Sheng's grand political objectives as much as Sheng knew about his—neither of them would stop fighting until the other guy was dead. Both wanted to unify China and each wanted to rule the country alone on his own terms.

The Chinese civil war was one between two ambitious brothers and two competing forces, and neither of them had the willingness, experience, or political foresight to consider an alternative, peaceful, and more forward-looking solution to their conflicting political goals and interests.

What bolstered their ideological conviction was the two men's faith in themselves—each considered himself to be a pretty good military strategist.

With a mighty force of as many as three million troops under his command, General Chen was confident that he would prevail. He had beaten most of the rivals within his Nationalist Party, outmaneuvered and defeated all the warlords, and survived the worst attacks by the Japanese. He led the Chinese resistance war, and was widely recognized by the international community as one of the major Allied leaders against fascism during World War II. He now also had the Americans' strong military and financial support. Chen had no reason to doubt his future as the undisputed leader of a reunited China.

3

Although he controlled only a million troops, Sheng was no less confident. He used to have a minuscule force of fewer than a thousand, but survived more ordeals and perilous situations in the battlefield than any other military leader in recent memory. His strength, besides the singularity of his ideological commitment, lay in his intuitive and yet perceptive understanding of Chinese military affairs.

One could almost imagine that the fearsome and dogged fight between Sheng and Chen was, at an implicit level, an equally fearsome and dogged competition between two schools of thought—one by the old Chinese master Sun Zi and the other by his more modern German counterpart Carl von Clausewitz.

Sun Zi was one of the few ancient Chinese thinkers who had written a cohesive theory in thirteen chapters to expound his philosophy before his death. Those chapters were later found, compiled, and issued in a single volume titled *Sun Zi's Military Stratagems* in the early Chinese editions. But it was the English translation with the modified title *The Art of War* that actually better captured the essence and spirit of his work.

A true mastermind and an imaginative strategist, Sun Zi treated war more as an art than a science. He was certainly one of the first in history to reveal the connection between warfare and politics. He was no doubt one of the first to elucidate the various principles and diverse rubrics of combat activities, such as organization, training, leadership, and discipline. He was also one of the first to articulate explicitly several universal rules of war that had long been tacitly practiced, such as "all war is based on deception," the importance of intelligence and espionage, and "knowing both yourself and your enemy is the basis for victory."

But his most important contribution was his clear depiction of the elusiveness, unpredictability, ever-changing nature, fast-evolving circumstances, infinite uncertainties, and inherent volatility of war. Throughout his discussions, Sun Zi repeatedly warned of these elements by emphasizing the concept of "shi" (the state, position, and momentum of an army, sometimes translated into "energy" in some English text)—a highly fluid and adaptable Chinese notion but alas very poorly understood by outsiders.

That was why war was an art, not a science, which demanded the best imagination to win, above and beyond the most methodical calculations about soldiers, numbers, equipment, formations, and deployment. Not everyone could fully understand his text no matter how many times they might have read it. He was speaking to the best and the most creative minds, not to a bookish student or university pedant.

One of the gifted minds who truly understood the ancient philosopher's message, Sheng mastered not only Sun Zi's specific principles but also the essence of the art—the daring imagination, the unconventional way of thinking, and the immense creativity and risk-taking ventures any form of warfare would demand.

Chen, on the other hand, received his military education and training in Japan, and served in the Imperial Japanese Army (molded in the Prussian and German tradition) and was influenced by several German military advisors. Chen was a good cadet but not an imaginative and bold strategist. He could be a good pupil of Carl von Clausewitz, who excelled in sophisticated compartmentalization of modern warfare, but not a good disciple of Sun Zi, who constantly challenged one's mind and creativity.

Dogmatic, inflexible, hesitant, and insecure, Chen was a competent commander in the fight against the warlords, but not good enough to fight the formidable Sheng head-on.

Shortly after World War II ended, Chen published the *Manual for the Extermination of the Communist Menace*, which was a reprint of his brief discourse on the same topic more than a decade earlier. While he still saw his opponents as scattered and unruly bandits, the communist troops had multiplied more than three dozen times over the years, and had improved and changed their tactics significantly, a reality the general would come to realize very soon.

4

General Chen woke up in the middle of the night, yelling.

"What happened, dear? You are sweating?" Madam Chen was concerned.

"I… I had a nightmare," said the general.

"A nightmare? Why? Everything should be okay, dear." Madam Chen was surprised to hear it. The general rarely had any nightmares when they moved to Chongqing and faced the Japanese bombings every day. Now the Japanese were defeated and they had moved back to Nanjing, the general seemed to have more worries on his mind.

"The communists... the communists..." murmured the general. "They attacked us! They attacked this presidential palace!"

Finally realizing what had been bothering the husband, Madam Chen said, "Darling, there is no communist attack. We are okay. They are isolated in remote and poor Shaanxi. Don't worry."

"You don't understand," the general was now fully awake. "Deceitful. Despicable. Most treacherous. They are more difficult to deal with than the Japanese."

"But you had a military conference with the generals, didn't you? They must have strategies," Madam Chen said, although she knew her husband had never fully trusted his officers.

"Yes, we did. Yes, we did." General Chen went on to recount the meeting.

Most of his top officers agreed that the nationalist troops had the advantage of a vertical plan, controlling all the major transportation and communication lines from the north to the south. The enemies tried to cut through this vertical plan by a horizontal plan pushing from Bao An in the west to the eastern seaboard.

"Good analysis. What is the strategy then?" Madam Chen inquired.

"Here is the problem. General Bai Yu-Xian proposed a plan to attack the communists in the east," General Chen explain. "But General Pan Jin proposed a plan to attack the communists in the west."

"What do you think and what did you decide then?" Madam Chen asked.

"I... well..." the general responded, "I thought both plans were good. But the generals believe we don't have enough troops to conduct two campaigns at the same time."

"Our forces are three times as big as the communists', correct?" Madam Chen had been involved in so many discussions about national affairs that she was as much on top of military intelligence as her husband was.

"Yes, we are. The ratio is three million to one million. But," the general cautioned, "the communists are extremely tough to deal with. They used to have much fewer troops in the past, and yet we were unable to eradicate them with an army tenfold bigger than theirs. A three-to-one ratio today is not a big advantage."

"Then choose one plan and postpone the other," suggested the madam.

"Yes, that's what the meeting decided. We will adopt the 'east plan,'" answered the general.

"Good. So, let the generals carry out the plan then." Madam Chen was tired and she hoped the general would allow his subordinates to handle the details.

"But I am having second thoughts now," the general told his wife. "Maybe General Pan is right. 'To catch the bandits, catch their ringleaders first.' His 'west plan' is a good one. Yes, yes, I must call General Bai right away."

"Darling, it's midnight. You can call your chief of staff in the morning," a drowsy Madam Chen advised.

General Chen had already put on his robe over his pajamas and went out to make the call in the adjacent room.

When he returned to the bedroom, Madam Chen was already fast asleep. Lying on the bed and yet too stirred up to go back to sleep right away, he went through some scenarios once more. Then he became restless again. Maybe the decision of the conference was correct? Maybe he should not have changed his mind in such a haste? What if Bai's "east plan" was more attainable? Maybe he could put off Pan's "west plan" for the moment until he had a better idea whether the "east plan" would work out. Maybe…

Much troubled, General Chen got up, quietly put on his robe again, and went out to make a second phone call.

Several hours later in the morning, General Chen called Bai one more time, telling the chief of staff that the absolute final decision was to prepare for both the "east and west campaigns" immediately.

5

The conclusion of a top military meeting in Bao An did not satisfy Tao Yin-Hu completely. He did not disagree with the decisions made, but the lack of a more comprehensive view of the civil war troubled him.

The meeting took place under somber circumstances. Stalin suddenly changed his mind about the military equipment surrendered by the Japanese troops in Manchuria, which he had promised to deliver to the Chinese Communist Party. Sheng Bao and the Politburo members called in the top army officers for counsel.

Song Pei outlined the situation they were facing. "Our plan to take Manchuria may be delayed due to the Russians' reluctance to let us control the region. Meanwhile, the nationalist troops have been moving into position on two fronts: the east and west. According to our intelligence, Chen Han is planning one–two punch attacks against us anytime now. Please share your thoughts on how we should react."

Officer Xia-Hou Ding said, "Manchuria in the northeast is the area we must have. It is rich in natural resources, farm products, and industrial output. It is right next to the Soviet Union and can provide a broad base for our troops. From our current locations, we are closer to that region than the nationalist troops. We must take advantage of the situation, send out troops there as quickly as we can. We may have issues with the Russians, but we belong to the same communist camp. We must have their help, even if it means negotiating with them."

The chief of staff, Lu Di-Ping, agreed. He said, "No region under our current control is as rich and productive as Manchuria. The numerous industries and railroads, developed by the Russians and Japanese, are absolutely necessary for our future expansion. The region is least damaged through the last war because it was under the direct occupation of the Japanese Kwantung Army. So, if we can control Manchuria, it will become our solid base for our future actions by supplying new recruits, abundant foodstuff, ammunition plants, and transportation facilities we badly need."

"Now, if we agree to take Manchuria," said Sheng after seeing that most attendees were of the same mind, "who is going lead the operation?"

"I will," said Officer Xia-Hou, who seemed to have thought about the matter and anticipated the question.

"Are you sure?" Si-Tu Wen-Liang asked. "You are from the south and Manchuria is extremely cold."

"Yes, are you sure? We heard spittle freezes in midair there in wintertime," Yao Xi-Wa warned.

"No problem at all," said Xia-Hou. "Most of us are from the south, aren't we? And most of us had never seen snow until we were on the road during the Long March."

"That's true. We are glad that Officer Xia-Hou Ding is going to take charge of the mission," Sheng said and then asked, "What about the one–two punch attacks?"

"The planned attack on Bao An is certainly aimed at destroying our party headquarters here." Tao was the first to respond.

"Yes, this is a very vicious move. Shaanxi is a very poor place, and can't provide strong and prolonged defense." Several Politburo members agreed with Tao's assessment.

"But if we lose Bao An, it will give Chen Han a major publicity coup," someone said.

"What about the eastern front, then?" asked Sheng, who preferred to have an overall assessment before making any specific decision.

"The eastern front is our weakest link, where we have far fewer troops and very limited bases," Lu explained. "Besides, many of our soldiers on the eastern front are new recruits and our bases have only been developed lately."

"So, Chen Han must have known that he has chosen very good targets for his attacks," Song commented.

"That's true. Chen Han has done his homework by choosing these two places," concurred Sheng.

"If we don't want to lose in these two campaigns, who wants to lead them?" he asked.

"I will go back and lead the eastern front," said Yao, who was the commanding officer of that region.

"I will lead the western front defense," Bao Feng-Nian said.

The Politburo was pleased that the meeting went well and all the major issues were settled. The meeting was then adjourned. Yet something seemed to be missing, which bothered Tao. He was not sure what exactly it was. While he felt obliged to keep examining the situation more carefully, he was also concerned with how he should present his ideas to the Politburo.

6

Post–World War II China was the battleground of four factions that were playing a delicate but dangerous balancing game—the Soviet Union, the United States, the Chinese nationalists, and the Chinese communists.

The U.S. and the U.S.S.R., the two international superpowers, had just come out from a bloody war. Their wartime alliance quickly disintegrated as their separate interests propelled them to compete for dominance in Europe. As the "iron curtain," in the words of Winston Churchill, descended across the European continent, their rivalry in China became further complicated.

The mighty Soviet Red Army entered Manchuria from three directions in the final days of the war and quickly subdued the Kwantung Army—the last Japanese strategic reserve of one million soldiers who did not put up any fight after the Japanese government decided to surrender.

The United States, though pleased with the war's end, was deeply disturbed to see the aggressive expansion of Soviet influence in East Asia, from Xinjiang, Mongolia, Manchuria, and Korea to the Kuril Islands and the Liaodong Peninsula. Claiming "war booty," the Russians were dismantling factories in Manchuria and transporting industrial material and equipment worth as much as eight hundred and fifty-eight million U.S. dollars back to Russia. Worse of all, the several thousand warplanes, tanks, artillery pieces, and tons of ammunition they had obtained from the surrender of the Kwantung Army would fall into the hands of the Chinese communists if the Russians decided to support them.

The instigator behind the scenes, Stalin, knew what he wanted and how to play the game well. Flexing his muscles wherever he could, he extorted as much as he could from anyone he wanted—Truman, General Chen, or Sheng Bao. But Stalin was shrewd enough not to make any reckless move that would trigger a direct military confrontation with the Americans in Asia. Hence, the hostility between the Chinese nationalists led by Chen and the communists led by Sheng offered the Russians, who continued to befriend with both, a perfect chance to extract as many concessions as possible from China by playing off one side against the other. Meanwhile, the master player was also careful not to let their conflict get out of hand. As long as the Chinese belligerents kept fighting with each other, a divided and chaotic China would serve as a buffer between the United States and Russia, reducing the potential of an open hostility between the two super powers. In the end, whoever were to win the civil war, either the nationalists or the communists, they would continue to need Russian support and Russia's interests in China would still be protected.

Caught in the middle of this convoluted web of the big powers' rivalry, the native sons Chen and Sheng were understandably frustrated and felt powerless, because neither one of these strong-minded leaders was able to act independently—General Chen needed Washington's backing as much as Sheng couldn't do without Moscow's. The challenge for both of them was to see who could make use of the other players better so as to achieve his own agenda in this twisted quadruple game.

For the same reason, they resented foreign interference. Chen viewed the U.S. government as hypocritical, always talking about democracy, alliance, free elections, and all that stuff. The U.S. wanted to bridge the insurmountable gap between the Communist and Nationalist Parties, which was complete naiveté at best or a total waste of time at worst. The communists would never give up fighting. They wanted power and they wanted to finish off their enemies, no matter how enthusiastically they talked about a "coalition government."

Sheng loved the rhetoric of "democracy," and used it relentlessly to attack Chen and his government. He listened to the Russians, tolerated their abuses, and begged for the leftovers from their enormous military arsenal in Manchuria, even as he made preparations to attack Chen's troops.

7

"Anyone here has heard about the Chinese go master Wu Qing-Yuan?" Tao asked his Politburo colleagues who were seated at the conference table.

"Why?" Most of them did know the name, but they asked anyway.

"I was thinking about a fantastic game he had played in Japan when he was just nineteen," Tao recalled. "Some say that was the greatest game of the century."

"Yes, yes. I remember. That must be the game he played in 1933 against Hoju Tamura (or Honinbo Shusai), the title holder of the Honinbo—the highest honor a go player may achieve in Japan at the time," Lin Shi-Xiong, a serious lover of the game, enthusiastically responded.

"So ironic that they played the game of go when a real war was taking place between Japan and China," Sheng commented.

"Because of that," Si-Tu Wen-Liang added, "Wu was frequently harassed in Japan."

"Do you want to recommend the game of go to the Politburo?" Song Pei joked, knowing the usually reticent general must have a good reason to mention it at such a high-level meeting.

"The opening of that game struck me as brilliant," Tao explained.

"Yes, yes." Lin, considering himself an expert on this story, took it upon himself to provide the details.

"You see, for this intricate yet highly flexible game, a normal opening in go involves some standard steps, each of which is called a 'ply,'" Lin said. For those very experienced contestants, the serious competition would not begin until each player had placed some fifteen to twenty plies.

Wu's first three plies shocked the world of professional go players because he put his first three black stones in places that no one else had ever done—(1) at the spot of the upper right-hand corner, where it was one grid removed from the standard one, (2) at the lower left-hand corner, which rarely happened as a countermove to where the rival, Shusai, had put down his first white stone, and (3) right at the center of the board, which had never been attempted by anyone in the past.

Because of these highly unconventional positions, each of the three black stones presented a disturbing puzzle to the opponent and collectively, the three stones had formed a formidable line of threat wherever anyone looked across the game board.

"Deeply disconcerted by these opening steps, Shusai had a very hard time figuring out what his opponent was up to and he remained in an awkward, hesitant, and reactive position throughout the game. Totally unexpected and completely unconventional, Wu's astonishing new method of opening steps revolutionized go, and he rose to become the reigning champion of the game for years to come." Lin gleefully concluded his account.

"But I heard Wu lost the game. Is that true?" Sheng asked.

"Yes, he did." Fearing he might have been promoting the wrong hero in front of the boss, who was not into those trivial games, Lin quickly explained,

"He lost by a small margin of two points. And that was only because Shusai had stopped the game thirteen times and requested a recess to consult with his disciples, whenever the pressure on him became too much. The game lasted three months and Wu was literally fighting a group of Japanese players, not just the Honinbo."

"What a shame and what a sham," said Si-Tu.

"Despite his loss, his message remains loud and clear," Tao said.

"Explain what you mean," Song demanded.

"The message is that we can't passively react to what may happen to us. We need to find a way to surprise our enemies, to disrupt their plans, and to force them to play the game on our terms, not theirs," Tao replied.

"That's easier said than done, General Tao," said Song. "How can we lead the game in our current weak position?"

"I have been thinking that Chen Han's strategy is to force us to stretch our limited resources to defend our two bases in opposing directions. What we decided last night was to react according to his plans. What if we can turn the tables and force him to respond to our plans?"

"That's a good idea. But how?" Lin asked.

"Chen has forced us to take defensive positions in our revolutionary bases in the east and west. What if we could force him to take a defensive position in his own territory instead?" Tao hinted.

"Wait a second," chimed in Sheng, who could sense a great prospect that had not been discussed before. "Please elaborate."

"As all of us have agreed, Chen has planned a one–two punch campaign against us on our interior lines. If he plans to attack us from the east and the west, why can't we learn from Wu Qing-Yuan to move into the exterior lines of Chen's territory and attack his center before he realizes it?" Tao stated calmly.

His bold proposal impressed everyone.

Sheng was the first to see the brilliance of the idea. Yes, yes, the enemy had exposed its soft underbelly when Chen divided his troops to trap the communists in two different locations far apart from each other. "Attack his center before he realizes it!" This daring move would surely turn the tables, and the attackers would become the ones under attack. A superb idea!

"A great suggestion," Si-Tu praised. "Chen wants to brandish his two arms to beat us, but we will strike his unprotected belly hard instead."

"Yes, that is the idea," Tao agreed. "It will enable us to push the battle into the nationalist-occupied territory, and to lessen the threat to our own bases on the interior lines significantly. That is, an offensive–defensive strategy."

"The key, then, is to choose where to strike and who to lead such an important mission. Let us talk more about this," Sheng told his colleagues.

8

"I don't like it. I don't like it at all!" Yan complained to Tania.

"Why? You don't like to come with me?" a smiling Tania teased her.

"You know what I mean," Yan said. "I have never been upset with you, my friend. I just don't like them to separate you and your husband. Why can't they send someone else instead of him to the Central Plains? Or why can't they send someone else instead of you to the Northeast? You are a couple. How can they do this to you two?"

"Please stop it, Yan. Stop complaining. You know how difficult our situation is. Our bases are under attack from multiple directions, and many are risking their lives to defend us. We can't refuse the party's assignments just because we are married." Tania was all sincere in her explanation.

"But why can't they send you on the same mission instead of sending the two of you to different locations more than a thousand miles apart?" Yan did not yield.

"The Northeast expedition needs to make frequent contacts with the Soviet Red Army, and they need people who can speak Russian," Tania patiently explained, "That is why not only I but also Dong Zi-Tian and Mo Jia-Qi are going."

"Then why not Meng Bo-Xian? He speaks perfect Russian too, doesn't he?" Yan seemed to have more reason to stick to her opinion. "It must be jealousy. Yes, yes. They must be jealous. You both speak Russian and you are happily married. They just don't want to see you together as a sweet couple working as a team."

"True. Many good men can't marry in this terrible long war," Tania conceded. "Meng and I are the few lucky ones who can form a family. But you must also remember that Meng has sharply criticized the organized personality cult in a speech not long ago. He was arrested and stripped of all his positions in the party as a result. He has been completely sidelined since then until a few days ago, when General Tao Yin-Hu threw Meng a lifeline."

"Do you know how grateful we are," Tania continued, "when Meng and I heard that General Tao had insisted on taking Meng as the commissar or the chief political officer of the troops that he would command for the march to the Central Plains? General Tao is giving Meng a second chance to work for the party again. He is taking the great risk of offending Chairman Sheng to help Meng. How could we refuse his enormous kindness and betray his trust?"

"That may be true. But I still think the decision to send you to another part of the country is a complete mistake." Yan never gave up if she believed it was her duty to defend someone in any way she could. She might be simple-minded, but she knew right from wrong. Once she had decided to be Tania's loyal friend, she would forever remain true to her obligations to protect and defend her dear friend.

"It's quite all right. We are not teenagers, and neither is this our first marriage. We can handle this separation." Tania tried to assure the friend and comfort herself.

"You can handle it? Let me see," Yan said in all seriousness as she looked straight into Tania's eyes. As she expected, she found traces of pain and sadness in that pair of beautiful hazel eyes.

"See, what did I say? No woman likes to be separated from her husband. Women suffer a lot more in separation than men do. How can they do this to you?"

"Yan, calm down. Calm down please." Even though her heart was aching, Tania could still see the bigger picture. "So many are suffering from starvation, homelessness, and death in this terrible civil war. A brief period of separation is the least we could endure for the sake of the revolution. Besides, you now have a chance to stay with me. Do you want to keep whining, or are you coming with me or not?" she asked Yan.

That did it. Nothing would make Yan happier than being together with Tania.

"Of course, I am going with you!" Yan was all smiling now, "I never said I was not coming. I only wanted to stress that Meng Bo-Xian should be coming with you too."

"You silly, naughty girl! If he is coming with me, where will you stay?" Tania quipped.

"Well, then, let him sleep in the adjacent office and we two can sleep in the bedroom together as we used to," Yan answered.

"In your dreams," said Tania, gently knocking the friend's forehead.

9

Feeling safe, secure, peaceful, and completely free of all worries, she was holding his arm, walking with him, and letting him take her wherever he wanted. For a woman, she believed, lying in her man's arms was the most wonderful place to be in the whole world. They had talked for so long all around the hills they passed, and still seemed to have more to say until Meng stopped on a ridge. The sun was setting and a gentle mist was rising in the valley.

"Meng, you must take care of yourself on the march," Tania said. She knew she should call him "Bo-Xian" by now according to tradition. But she preferred calling him "Meng," which sounded special. And he was special because he was hers.

"I know. You must take care of yourself too on the journey to Manchuria." Meng then said, "Do you remember the day when you suddenly took me to a pigpen?"

"Of course, I remember. A sow was giving birth and eventually delivered fourteen piglets; can you believe it?" Tania cheerfully recalled.

"Then what did you do?" Meng asked.

"Then what did I do?" Tania repeated but did not answer the question.

"You shoved a boiled egg in my hand and ran away," Meng said.

"Did I?" Only pretending to be surprised, Tania was glad that Meng remembered the first token of affection that she had ever given to a man after Martin.

Love was such a private, unexplainable, and tender feeling between two individuals that the more delicate the expression, the sweeter the memory, no matter how subtle, how transient, and how inconspicuous the gesture might have been, or no matter where, when, and how the first spark had been lit.

"I think it was the talented Chinese female artist Lin Hui-Yin who said, 'to produce an impression takes a few seconds, but to relish its memory is to last a lifetime,"' Tania remarked, totally rapt in the warm and innocent moment of the past when they were alone for the first time, next to a pigpen notwithstanding.

"So true and very well stated. Lin was very gifted, and as talented as her famous husband, the architect Liang Si-Cheng," Meng agreed. "I have made something for you," he said and took out a small wooden box and handed it to Tania.

It was a tiny box, carefully made but not yet painted; Tania could hold it in one hand. "I did not know you are a craftsman," she opened the lid and saw her porcelain bottle in it.

"We are leaving tomorrow morning. I believe we will have many tough battles ahead. The ceramic is too fragile for me to carry, and I will never forgive myself if it is damaged in any way. I have made this box for you so that you can keep it safely, although I didn't have time to finish the paint." Meng explained.

He did not mention that they would have to march for nearly five hundred miles before reaching the mountains, nor did he elaborate on the serious dangers he and his soldiers would be facing—marching through the flat plains, without bases and supplies, where the nationalist troops would certainly attack them.

He was always thoughtful and considerate. He cared more about Tania's feelings than his own safety. He expressed his concerns by his deeds, and he always thought how to best treasure and protect the person he deeply loved.

Tania found a piece of paper inside the box and she took it out. It was a poem and she read it softly:

The clearest cloud in the skies
is not as pure as your little ceramic.
The brightest blue oceans
can't match the fires the three tulips provide.
No one is closer to my heart
than Tania, my dearly beloved bride.

"Oh, Meng, my dear Meng, you are so sweet." Tania threw her arms around the husband's neck and kissed him all over his face passionately. "I love you! I love you! I love you so much, my dear!" she said.

Chapter 30

Novelty

1

EAST, EAST, EAST. MARCH, MARCH, MARCH.

For more than a month Tania had followed the troops rushing over the mountains in Shaanxi and across the Northern Plains. Determined to beat the nationalist troops and take possession of Manchuria first, they did not stop anywhere until they finally arrived at the Majestic Fort, the first grand garrison of the Great Wall at its eastern beginning, which was the last township in Northern China and the first major pass into Manchuria in the Northeast.

Luckily, the railroads were intact and the soldiers gladly jumped onto the train cars to rest their exhausted bodies.

Tania and Dong Zi-Tian sat face to face next to each other, starting to recall how familiar the scene was. Tania had traveled along this same route from Russia to China with Martin many years ago, and Dong had taken this route too but in the opposite direction, from China to Russia to study in Moscow. They jokingly said that the greatest achievement of the substandard imperial Russian Trans-Siberian Railroad was to bring Marxism and Bolshevism to China.

The steam puffs from the engine and the clattering sound from the piston reminded them of *Anna Karenina*, in which Leo Tolstoy described the slow arrival of the passenger train that brought the eponymous heroine to the train station, where Alexei Vronsky stole a glance at her for the first time. The greasy smell from the bottom of the car, the rhythmic wobbling of the train, and the slow pace of the movement also reminded them of the night Tania and Dong boarded a similar train to visit Tolstoy's estate near the small town of Tula.

Now everything seemed to have come a full circle. The tired soldiers sleeping all around them, they sat so close to one another, feeling like the whole rolling, dark, and tired world outside was theirs. Behind his dirty uniform, wrinkled face, and callous hands, Tania saw the young, innocent, and caring Dong, her good and dear friend. He looked into Tania's sweet face with the same adoring gaze he had always had for her and said, "I can't believe that we still have a chance to meet and talk like this."

"Yes, what a rare opportunity. Tell me everything, please, everything about what has been happening with you," Tania said earnestly.

"You know my situation, and nothing much has changed. But I did receive a letter from Dai Tian."

Tania knew that the bubbly reporter Dai had married Dong but they got divorced after his demotion. She asked delicately, "What about the letter, what did she say?"

Dong then told Tania his ex-wife's story.

Growing up in a noble and privileged family, Dai had excellent education but refused the marriage the parents had arranged for her. She fell passionately in love with a young artist and ran away with him—only to discover two years later that he had married her only for her family's money. Furious, she left him and started to make a living on her own, mainly through freelance writing until she was hired as a reporter.

Contrary to her lively outward appearance and seemingly carefree personality, Dai was a very sensitive young woman who was deeply concerned about social justice and extremely serious about the sanctity of marriage. "When I got demoted, she was very upset, thinking that I had not only betrayed the cause but also tarnished our marriage," Dong said.

"I must admit that by making frequent excuses for my busy work," continued Dong, "I had not been the good, considerate, patient, and caring husband that

I was supposed to be. I was particularly not in a good mood in those days after the demotion. I yelled at her and often argued loudly with her, letting my own frustrations and anger get out of hand, which hurt her greatly."

"She asked for a divorce and I agreed, thinking this would end the misery for both of us."

Dong continued, "You see, unlike in the West, the public presumption of 'guilty by association' is very strong in China, where the penal code of ancient courts routinely punished the offender as well as his kin, beginning with the Qin Dynasty more than two thousand years ago. Even today, people often assume that a criminal's close relatives must have done something wrong to facilitate his crime, even though they may have absolutely nothing to do with the offense.

"This can be extremely harsh for anyone to bear, especially for those who are totally innocent. Yet this is the tradition that we have to live with. I can certainly understand the enormous psychological burden and social pressures that Dai, who was such a delicate and sensitive woman, had to face daily during that period. She suffered greatly not due to any fault of hers, but simply because she was married to me. I alone had made those big mistakes in the party, and I could not bear to see my dear wife in such terrible and prolonged pain."

Tania began to understand the great emotional quandary and complex cultural entanglement behind Dong's story. "What happened then?" she asked.

"She said in her letter that she wanted us to get back together again," Dong answered.

"Well, that's wonderful!" Tania was surprised to hear it and asked, "What led her to change her mind?"

"Her travel experiences, her travel experiences," Dong said as he read Dai's letter.

According to Dai, while she was in Moscow, she had a chance to visit Yu Shao-Mei in the hospital, and was outraged to learn that Sheng Bao had divorced his ailing wife to marry another woman after the Long March. Dai had met the couple in Blue Grass, and personally witnessed how Yu had been a dutiful wife and dedicated mother to their small children. How could Sheng, such a high party official, so heartlessly abandon his wife, who had been there for him through thick and thin?

After blaming Sheng for treating Yu the way he did, Dai started to reflect on her own actions. In her letter, Dai shared the thoughts that went through her mind as she reexamined the circumstances that led to her divorce with Dong. "Did I abandon my husband when he needed me the most? Good heavens, how could I leave him just because of some social pressure? How could I lose faith in him, whom I had loved so dearly?" With these troubling thoughts and questions, Dai then went to England.

There she encountered a few similar stories. Several married Chinese students in Europe had abandoned either their husbands or wives back in China to be with their newfound lovers in a foreign land. What was love? What was marriage? Dai was confused. Could love ever be as pure and noble as extolled in literature? Could a marriage ever last forever? Could a man and a woman ever be as faithful to one another as portrayed in those romantic legends? Dai could not find the answers until one day she met Lilian, a Chinese female dancer living in London.

At twenty-three, Lilian was the best female dancer China had ever seen in modern times. She had fallen madly in love with an Austrian artist, Wally, who was already engaged to a French girl, Simone. Despite Lilian's passionate pursuit, her efforts came to naught, and Wally married Simone. Soon World War II broke out, and Lilian left England to lead a dance troupe traveling all over Southeast Asia to raise money for the resistance movements in China. Years passed before she learned that Simone had died and Wally was terribly sick and all alone. She rushed back to London, found her lover, and nursed him till the day he died in her arms. She was asked, "Was it worth it? You had waited for him all your life and what you received in the end was a few months with an old man who was at death's door?"

"It was worth every minute," Lilian replied. "Once you have fallen in love with the great ocean, how could you love a river or a pond?"

"You are my ocean," Dai told Dong in the letter, "and I deeply regret leaving you. Please, please forgive me for my mistake. I believe I have now a much better understanding about love and marriage. I am no longer the naïve girl I was a few years ago. I will come back to you, I swear. And I hope to marry you again when we meet. As long as you don't mind my past, I will never ever leave you again."

"So, what should I do?" Dong asked.

"Apparently, Dai still loves you. She is such a lovely girl with such a wonderful soul. Do you still love her?" Tania asked.

"Yes, I do."

"Then marry her, of course, the moment she comes back to meet you!"

2

No matter what happened and no matter where the party set up its headquarters, Sheng Bao would spend at least several hours a day at the communication center, where all the intelligence would come in through the wires and where all the party orders would be signed and sent out. More than anyone else in the organization, he understood the cardinal rule that if knowledge was power, as the erudite Englishman Francis Bacon had insisted, whosoever possessed intelligence would have the upper hand.

For this reason, he strictly limited the other Politburo members' access to intelligence. All of them would receive news and intelligence pertinent only to their assigned areas of responsibility, while only Sheng could have unlimited access to all top-secret intelligence and communications across the board. In the meantime, all outgoing telegrams in the party's name could not be processed without his signature, and no major party instructions and communications would be complete without his consent. By the same token, only Sheng could make any direct telecommunication with Moscow and all other Politburo members would only get to hear about news from Moscow through him.

Military plans, operations, appointments, and directives, in particular, had long been considered Sheng's exclusive sphere, which he guarded jealously. Any high-ranking party officials and any high-ranking army officers who ever dared to enter this domain would promptly be identified as a great threat, if not an actual challenge, to Sheng and his authority.

Today, Sheng was in a good mood. News from several fronts seemed to have pleased him.

The one from Manchuria read, "Significant progress has been made. The Russian Red Army has finally allowed us to take over large quantities of military equipment from the Kwantung Army, which are enough to arm five of our divisions."

"Tell them," Sheng instructed Lu Di-Ping, "that's not enough! We need more. We need more weapons and military equipment to arm ten... hmm not ten but fifteen... no, no, no, not fifteen but twenty. Yes, yes, twenty!—twenty of our divisions! Ask them to go back to the Russians, to press them, and to press them hard on this. They should not relent until the Russians agreed to our demands."

The wire sent by Officer Bao Feng-Xian from the western front was encouraging. He reported that his troops were leading the nationalist expedition army on a wild goose chase in Northern Shaanxi, where the harsh weather, punitive terrain, and hopelessly long and difficult supply lines had exhausted and starved his enemies.

"Great! Tell him to look for a chance to teach them a lesson," Sheng told Lu.

"Understood," the dutiful chief of staff replied.

"I mean Officer Bao must come up with a battle plan that will annihilate—I emphasize *that must annihilate*—at least a division of Chen Han's troops."

"Yes!" Lu said.

"In addition, Officer Bao must take action to destroy Chen's western campaign completely within the next three months," continued the confident Sheng.

Officer Yao Xi-Wa reported that the eastern front was still locked in an intense tug-of-war battle with General Pan Jin, whose troops had moved very aggressively into the communist bases.

"Wire Officer Yao not to be afraid." Sheng instructed Lu to draft a reply. "Tell him that he can continue to withdraw further into the north where the mountainous areas will eventually become a problem for Pan. Remember, the further away you move, the more Pan will be forced to stretch his forces thin, and hence there will be a greater chance that his weaknesses will surface. Officer Yao's opportunity for counterattacks will come in the end as long as he keeps his forces intact by continuous moving."

What really concerned Sheng was how Tao Yin-Hu's troops were doing. The daring move into the enemy's territory had never been tried before, and fighting on the flat plains had never been the communists' strength. Every small advance was precious, and not a single day would pass without the Politburo asking for the latest update on the Red Army's march to the Central Plains.

The first several weeks were especially critical, and no one knew whether they could survive this unprecedented expedition.

Lu handed to Sheng the latest wire signed by Tao and Meng Bo-Xian, which said that their troops had broken the nationalist defenses along the Yellow River.

"Thank goodness." Sheng was greatly relieved. Crossing the Yellow River was the most dangerous obstacle the communist troops had to face on the march. If they had been unable to break the enemy's defenses and move over to the southern bank, they could have been trapped in the north and the entire mission would have fallen apart.

As planned, the telegram continued, they had started marching southeastward toward the Great Divide—the big mountain range that separated the Hui River in the north from the Yangtze River in the south. They fully anticipated more tough fights along the way for the next one hundred and fifty miles, because General Chen would never allow any hostile army to settle in an area so close to his bases along the Lower Yangtze River.

"Tell them," Sheng dictated, "the Central Committee is very pleased to hear the critical progress you have made. You have successfully completed the first stage of action we had planned. The second phase can be more difficult and we trust your leadership and the fortitude of our soldiers to reach the Great Divide safely."

Indeed, other than verbal encouragement, Sheng had little to offer. As everyone else at the party headquarters, he could only pray for the safe journey of Tao, Meng, and their soldiers.

A couple of hours after sunset, Sheng finally left the communication center and returned to his cave dwelling. He found Su Ming in the midst of writing something on her small desk on the kang.

"What are you doing?" He was curious.

"I am playing a game," she said.

"A game? What game?" the perplexed Sheng asked.

"Look at this." Su handed the husband a newspaper—the party's official organ, *Liberation*.

"What about it?" Sheng still did not get it.

"Not the front page. Look, here," Su helped. "Look at the announcement on the literary page."

"Oh, I found it." Sheng read, "Reports say that Lu Sun had cut short his visit to Bao An. Whoever knows his whereabouts or the reasons for his early departure please write to the editor of this page."

"The first ten best answers will receive prizes," Sun could not help but finish reading the last sentence of the announcement.

"So, you are writing your answer now?" Sheng asked.

"Yes, yes," Su happily replied. "I am writing my answer now and I may just receive a top prize tomorrow."

"How childish!" Sheng said, shaking his head. He could tell that some editors had injected the fun element to enliven the tone of the official publication. But, still, everybody must have known that it was a simple diversion because the famous writer Lu Sun had died more than a decade ago. His visit and departure were pure fiction. A game was just a game, he thought, which was never as worthwhile a pursuit as reading intelligence reports and military wires, as far as Sheng was concerned.

3

"No, I don't have any more troops to send to you! You must find a way to defend yourselves!" General Chen angrily ended the phone conversation. It was the fifth in a row from his subordinates, all asking for more support and reinforcements.

From early on, the two-fronted attacks of his aggressive campaigns had somehow turned into a hide-and-seek game, and General Chen found his plans upended as his attacking troops were increasingly being attacked. Now it seemed likely that neither of the campaigns had any chance of success, nor could his troops withstand the communist onslaughts much longer.

"So, what do you have to say about the situation?" the general asked Bai Yu-Xian, who had been called in for emergency consultation.

A cautious man, the chief of staff knew that Chen was tormented to see his military plans falling apart. He had ignored Bai's advice that the national government did not have sufficient military strength to wage two campaigns simultaneously. He should have listened to Bai's advice to choose one direction to attack, instead of spreading his forces thin, which allowed the communists to deal with them one by one. The boss was on the edge and could explode any time. The chief of staff did not want to be at the receiving end of Chen's dreadful rage.

"The situation is not going as well as we had planned," Bai calmly responded. "Nor is it as bad as those officers have portrayed. We do have some reserves, which, however, can only help our troops on one front."

Bai paused as he waited for Chen's reaction. He did not want to put his head on the chopping block by being the one to decide which front should be saved or sacrificed.

General Chen knew what Bai was thinking, and held his tongue as well.

Eventually, Bai took the safer route by saying that it was better to send reinforcements to rescue the troops on the eastern front led by General Pan Jin, who was Chen's favorite officer.

His suggestion was accepted and Bai was relieved that he had made the right bet.

"But we can't do this anymore!" Chen yelled. He was not done yet. "We can't let Sheng Bao and the communists dictate our actions. We must do something to break this vicious circle," he said angrily.

"Yes, we are in a passive–reactive mode. The communists' sudden push into the Central Plains has given us a big headache. It has totally disrupted our plans. We are stretched extremely thin on the eastern and western fronts. Now we have to seriously consider how to protect our center, which is where the heart of our transportation, industry, finance, and communication systems is," concurred Bai.

"I don't need an explanation. I need a solution, a solution!" Chen interjected.

"I do have two suggestions," said Bai, who had come prepared.

"Really? Let's talk about them," Chen was a bit surprised, thinking that this old fox always had some ideas whenever circumstances got tough; no wonder he had been called a master strategist.

"Well, suggestion number one must be kept absolutely secret," Bai whispered. "It is to send an undercover special force to Shaanxi to locate the communists' headquarters, and try to catch or kill Sheng Bao."

Chen liked the idea and asked, "What's suggestion number two?"

"Propose a truce, which will give us time to regroup." Bai again paused, waiting for the boss to react.

Chen knew this was the so-called defensive–offensive strategy, the opposite of the communists' offensive–defensive. This might break Sheng's momentum and give the national government some breathing space, which would allow Chen to take advantage of the transportation systems under his control to reconfigure his troops.

"But would the communists agree to a truce? Sheng Bao would certainly know what we are up to," Chen cautioned.

"Yes, you are right. Sheng is no fool. But he might take the bait this time," Bai replied with an air of confidence.

"Why?"

"Because the truce suggestion will not come from us but from a third party."

"A third party?"

"Yes, I have been approached by Gan Zu-Xun, who knows several top communist leaders, including Sheng Bao and Si-Tu Wen-Liang. Gan is willing to serve as a messenger between our Nationalist Party and the communists."

"Hmm, let me think about it." Bai could tell that the boss was seriously interested in the plan.

4

Within days, General Chen's secret plans were the subject of a top party meeting convened by Sheng. All Politburo members were present, except for Tao, who was on the front line with the troops.

"Si-Tu Wen-Liang's intelligence division is as effective as ever," Sheng praised, "and we know Chen's next steps even before many of his top officials got wind of it."

"It's all due to the correct leadership of the Chairman and the Politburo," Si-Tu, who controlled the party's far-reaching spy network, said modestly. He knew Sheng could be both lavish with his praise and still extremely sensitive about being outshone by anyone.

"So how should we respond to Chen's plans?" Song Pei asked.

"If Chen is sending an undercover detachment to attack us, we can organize a special force to trap them," Lin suggested.

Sheng and others liked the idea. Covert action was Lin's specialty, and it was better to let him to handle the situation.

"What about the ceasefire proposal, which will be sent to us soon," Sheng asked while looking at Si-Tu.

Si-Tu got the hint. He had known Gan Zu-Xun better and longer than anyone else in the room, and he was obliged to meet him since he was in charge of the party's external affairs.

"I can meet with Gan. But I need specific instructions from the Politburo," Si-Tu said.

"The first is certainly to know his real intentions," Song said.

"Finding out all the terms of the truce is important," Lin added.

"Do not say 'yes' or 'no' right away," Sheng joined in. "Never underestimate Chen Han's cunning. He is creating a diversion, playing a game, or adopting delaying tactics. He never wants real peace and we will never be duped. But we will play the game with him as long as it's needed."

"I suspect that Gan will most likely propose a joint national administration of sorts," Si-Tu pointed out, "that is, a shared government between communists, nationalists, and some third force, based on what he has learned about Western-style democracy in the United States."

"If that is the case," he continued, "if that is Gan's basis for a truce, what would be our response?"

A really tough question to answer, and no one in the room was able to suggest anything immediately. For all the long, rich, and complex history China had had, the concept of a shared government was never part of its experience, political, social, or cultural. Ruled by successive dynasties until recently, the Chinese people had only known monarchies and emperors, tolerated despotism and tyrants, endured dictatorships and authoritarianism, accepted abuses and corruption, and supported centralized government for centuries. Obedience and loyalty had been the cornerstones of China's value system, which shaped not only political institutions and social behaviors but also literary styles and cultural patterns. Old-fashioned dynastic stories passed down through generations in classical poetry, drama, music, and fiction. Teaching both the young and old, rich and poor alike, about the importance of how the collective should maintain the status quo, the prevailing Chinese educational system had been a perfect grinding machine to crush any individualistic thinking. Civil rights, elections, and public participation had never been any part of the inherited tradition, or any part of the contemporary popular experience.

Trained and influenced under these conditions, members of the Chinese Communist Party readily accepted the Russian style of a one-party system with a heavy-handed central governing body. No Chinese communist leader had enough knowledge about the Western form of electoral government, nor were they ever prepared to create one in the future.

Always eager to show his ideological purity, Lin broke the silence. "We believe in what Lenin has called 'proletarian dictatorship,' correct? If so, any talk about Western democracy would be anti-Marxism. Right?"

"I think we can respond to that positively." Sheng's statement surprised his colleagues, as could be seen by their puzzled expressions.

Considering it to be not a policy shift but a new dimension of his grand stratagem, Sheng explained, "We are communists. We certainly don't believe that Western stuff and capitalist crap. But, as a tactic, we may use it to our advantage. Right now, our number one enemy is Chen and we have no reason to push the third political force away. If we can use it to weaken the nationalists' one-party rule, why not?"

"Please remember," Sheng continued, "we are waging an unprecedented revolution in a big, backward country. We are still small and weak, compared to Chen's army and his government. We need every potential ally we can get to fight against his dictatorship. If Gan or any third-party spokesperson is willing to talk to us, we have no reason not to meet and listen to them."

"So, you are saying that we will join a coalition government with the nationalists and the third party?" asked Song, who was voicing aloud Lin's thoughts too.

"For the moment, yes," said Sheng, who quickly added, "which doesn't mean forever."

5

The minute Su saw her husband walking in, she greeted him with a sense of pride and enthusiasm, "Look! I won a prize!"

Sheng looked at the newspaper she had passed to him, and the proud wife pointed to the fine print on the entertainment page: Third Prize Winner Su Ming.

The list was a long one and the response to the editor's question seemed to be overwhelming. What Sheng saw was a selection from the first round of answers.

"A few days ago we posted the following," the editors said. "Reports say that Lu Sun had cut short his visit to Bao An. Whoever knows his whereabouts or the reasons for his early departure please write to the editors of this page.

"Today we have selected from the multitude of our readers' letters a small sampling of the answers, viz.,

"He left Bao An because it's too cold for him.

"Sitting on the kang was never his strength.

"He left because no one here understood his eccentric satire. (2nd Prize)

"He was told to quit writing essays and to learn carpentry instead.

"'Politics has killed literature and literary criticism,' said he.

"He refused to head the College of Lu Xun Studies.

"He could not substitute millet for rice in his diet.

"The quality of tobacco here was too poor for him.

"Despite repeated invitations, he declined to join the party.

"Everything was perfect here and he found nothing to criticize. (1st Prize)

"He needed a new haircut.

"He had a hard time learning how to use his left hand to write.

"He had lost his donkey, which was tired of carrying him around every day.

"The withdrawal of dining privileges with the top elites stunned him.

"His former students had become his boss.

"Too difficult for him to accept that the organization was more important than him.

"He did not like having to salute every captain he met in the morning.

"The ubiquitous brownness confused his sense of direction.

"He was too lazy and hated morning exercises.

"Long lectures, ideological indoctrination, and strict discipline bored him.

"He injured his hand while taking notes, writing reports, and composing apologies.

"Rumors say he had talked to many college students (all young females).

"He was too short to be a soldier.

"His mustache was out of style.

"He would not look good in a uniform.

"He could not handle a gun.

"No interpreter was able to translate his words into the Shaanxi dialect. (3rd Prize)

"More theaters in Shanghai than canteens in Bao An.

"Loud folk songs here drove him crazy.

"He failed to meet his quota for digging carrots.

"He lost a tooth while chewing on sorghum.

"He wanted to serve the people, but didn't know how to write about them.

"He never took an oath and must be an unfaithful person.

"An arrogant, snobbish, and self-centered individual.

"Once a bourgeois, always a bourgeois.

"He thought he was hired as a teacher of literature, not a dancing instructor.

"Too sentimental, too self-indulgent, too opinionated."

Reading the responses with Sheng, Su laughed from time to time. Sheng seemed to be amused at the beginning, but he soon frowned. "Guard," he shouted, "let Lin Shi-Xiong know that I must see him the first thing tomorrow morning."

6

"How are you?" "How have you been?" They quickly greeted each other and sat down.

"You have not changed much," Si-Tu said softly, looking across the table at the man who still appeared as young, fresh-faced, and dapper as twenty years ago. Clean-shaven, he was confident but not haughty. His navy pinstripe suit on the slim body gave him a nice shape and erect posture, revealing his good health and abundant energy. Fanciful but not overly expensive, the two-toned lace-up shoes with clear stitches were formal and indicative of good taste.

"You have changed a lot," said his guest, Gan, who skipped completely the Chinese etiquette of complimenting the host's youth, health, wealth, happiness, good looks, etc.

Si-Tu laughed, "After twenty years in the woods, mountains, and underground activities, few people would remain the same." His once round and boyish face was now gaunt, with a chiseled chin, distinguished cheeks, and a firm forehead. Not every Chinese man would look good in a Western suit. But he, a handsome person in his early forties with thick black hair and beard, would have looked attractive and sophisticated if he chose to wear it. Si-Tu deliberately put on a worn uniform without any medals and insignias, while still looking neat, smart, and vigorous.

"I know you are here to propose a truce," Si-Tu opened the talks.

"I know you have a lot of doubts and reservations about my proposal." Gan's reply was as direct as Si-Tu's opening statement.

"China is at a crossroad and we are facing two choices: Chen Han's or ours," Si-Tu said.

"That's why I am here. There is a third choice, which is not violence and war but peace," Gan said.

"We have always wanted peace but we have been repeatedly cheated by Chen, who will never stop fighting us until he has wiped us out," Si-Tu vied.

"But you have the same belief about Chen, right? That is, you will never stop fighting until you have wiped him out," Gan responded.

"We will sit down and talk when Chen is willing to do the same," Si-Tu changed his tone but not his fundamental position.

"That's exactly the problem in this country. Everyone blames the other party, and no one will take the initiative to move in a direction that will be better for the nation," Gan remarked.

"You do sound like a third party of outsiders. But China is not America," Si-Tu quipped.

"The United States used to be a British colony." Gan understood the host's insinuation but he was not about to give up. "And yet it has chosen a different path after independence."

"But it couldn't avoid a bloody civil war, could it?" Si-Tu thought he knew as much about American history as his counterpart, the Stanford graduate in political science.

"That's true. But that was more than eight decades ago. I think we can do better if we have the vision and courage to do what we can today." Gan was not going to allow Si-Tu beat him in his area of specialization.

"I agree. And for that goal, don't you think Chen and his government have the responsibility of giving up the idea of killing all our communists?" Si-Tu asked.

"Certainly. I will convey the message to General Chen. But I can't speak for him or his party. And I would only suggest that you and your party should give up the idea of killing all the nationalists as well. We are all Chinese. We have suffered long enough and the terrible civil war has got to stop."

Gan went on, "I believe China is on the threshold of a new era. After a century of domestic turmoil and foreign invasions, China can have a much brighter future if we—the current generation of Chinese—have the vision to break the country's vicious circle of violence and war, and to give peace, reconciliation, and democracy a chance. You, Sheng Bao, and Mr. Chen are patriots. You are all brave and heroic nationalists, and all of you only want the best for the country. Why can't you give up the mutual suspicions and hatred of the past? If your two parties can do that, you can save the lives of millions of innocent people, and you can put China on a completely different path than what those dynastic rulers, regional warlords, and foreign aggressors had done to this nation over the decades. Together you can build a truly strong and proud China that every citizen will love and appreciate for generations to come."

For a moment, Si-Tu was actually moved. He could see Gan's sincerity, which surprised him a little. He had expected Gan to be snobbish and arrogant, just like many Chinese students who returned from overseas. They believed that they had seen the world and exposed to the most sophisticated European cultures or the finest American universities. They felt superior to their countrymen, including even those graduates from the most prestigious educational institutions in big Chinese cities. They thought they knew better than average Chinese, and were more than willing to teach them a thing or two about how things should be done in the way they had learned elsewhere. They were completely out of touch with Chinese reality, and only believed that they had all the right answers to China's ills.

Gan seemed to be different. Although a lady's man as far as Si-Tu could remember, he seemed to have changed a lot. Si-Tu did not know the reason for the change, but he was willing to listen and find out more about Gan.

Taking a recess, the two men relaxed and adopted a more personal approach to their negotiations.

Si-Tu told Gan about the excruciating pains and losses the Communist Party had suffered, the remarkable recoveries it made, and the upbeat prospect for its future.

Gan related his disappointing experience in working with General Yan, the warlord in Shanxi. He downplayed the influence the general's multifaceted diplomacy had had on him, even though he confessed that the general's skills and ability to "dance on three eggs [the Japanese, the nationalists, and the communists] in Shanxi during the war" still amazed him. But he had enjoyed his stay in the United States, especially his college days at Stanford University, then a fairly obscure institution in the western state California, under its official but rather cumbersome name of Leland Stanford Junior University.

Yes, no Chinese community had ever held a democratic town meeting, Gan acknowledged. No officials were elected to run government. Few had read Plato, Locke, Rousseau, Mill, Montesquieu, or Shaftesbury. Few political organizations ever had a chance to campaign and compete for public office. Few citizens were ever truly protected by law. Few of them had enjoyed human rights or freedom of the press. But now could be the time to do so, to reverse the trend that had stifled the Chinese people for generations.

Western democracy might not solve every problem in China, Gan conceded. But it was worth giving democracy a try, especially when the country wanted so much to end the civil war. Insofar as he knew, Gan continued, democracy was messy and ineffective in many ways. But one thing democracy was undoubtedly superior to other political systems was the fact that it relied on the rule of law and provided fundamental liberties and freedoms to all citizens. Most of all, it would gradually change hostile enemies into competitors, which would in turn allow for a peaceful transfer of power from one party to another, or from one generation to the next.

Such a peaceful environment was perhaps what China needed the most. The Communist and Nationalist Parties certainly represented two very important spectrums of national interests. But the military hostilities, which had plagued the nation for too long, had exacerbated their differences while downplaying their similarities. Peace and unity would highlight their commonalities, and therefore could create a far better environment conducive to both parties to advance their programs while avoiding the ravages of war and the loss of human lives.

Competing for public support over their respective national agendas, the two main parties could, along with third parties, share the operations of the government under a democratic framework. Thus all of them could join forces to open a brand-new chapter in history. China could restore its greatness by drastically reducing the chances of violence and bloodshed in the future, which would be the most significant achievement any political party could hope to accomplish in Chinese history.

7

Not long after Si-Tu's initial contact with Gan, the Politburo held a meeting to decide on several urgent issues.

Sheng told his colleagues that he had received new instructions from Moscow, which encouraged the Chinese Communist Party to accept the invitation to form a joint government with Chen's Nationalist Party.

"It's good that we have anticipated this change. Good that Si-Tu Wen-Liang has already met with Gan Zu-Xun." Whenever the thoughts of a subordinate were in sync with the boss's, Song Pei was always the first to feel gratified.

Si-Tu, although glad that his meeting with Gan had not been a waste of time, was more inclined to find out the real reason behind Moscow's insistence on peace and negotiations. "Why would Stalin want to support a joint government," said he, "when we now have a chance to defeat Chen and build a completely new communist government?"

Apparently intrigued by the same question, Sheng responded, "Perhaps Stalin is afraid that the Chinese civil war could get out of hand. If that's case, the United States could get involved. And, if the United States gets involved, it could threaten the peaceful reconstruction of the postwar Soviet Union."

"Yes, yes. That must be the case. That must be what Stalin is thinking," Lin quickly agreed before others did.

As Sheng looked around at the faces of his Politburo colleagues, who were nodding their heads, he said, "Okay, if that is the case and since that is what Moscow wants, why don't we just comply?" He then instructed them, "We will conduct a big publicity campaign to broadcast our support for joint government, democracy, peace, unity, general elections, and all that stuff."

"Another Sun Zi tactic of 'making a feint to the east while attacking the west'?" Si-Tu remarked, smiling.

Sheng smirked but did not answer. He then asked Lin a different question. "What have you found out about those who were behind the newspaper quiz on the literary page?"

"The investigation is still ongoing," replied Lin. "We know the editor used the pen name 'Wild Lily.' We will surely get to the bottom of the case soon."

"'Wild Lily.' 'Wild Lily,'" repeated Sheng. "Hmm, let me know, immediately, the real identity of the person or persons once you could determine it."

"Yes, I will," said Lin resolutely.

"It's a mess! It's a disaster! Extremely vulgar and offensive, openly irreverent and rebellious, that so-called entertainment could appear in our official organ *Liberation*!" Sheng was furious. He reminded the meeting of what had happened recently and asked for their reactions.

All the Politburo members said they had seen the question and answers, but viewed them as harmless pranks by some young people.

"You are too naïve," Sheng told them. "This is no entertainment at all! This is pure profanity! This is a declaration of war against party authority! This is an open attack against our literary giant Lu Xun. This is scandalous, and totally blasphemous—desecrating our party's image and authority. We must deal with this incident seriously."

"Very seriously," the determined Sheng repeated.

Chapter 31

Denigration

1

"**D**ICTATOR!" "TYRANT!" "TOTALITARIANISM!" "ONE-PARTY RULE!" The stunned General Chen could not believe what he was reading in the newspapers.

"This must be Sheng Bao's dirty tricks," he told Madam Chen.

"Then you must respond in kind," said she.

"Respond, yes. But how—now that Mr. Hu is dead?" General Chen hesitated, which was uncharacteristic of him.

Madam Chen had heard the sad news that Mr. Hu, General Chen's longtime secretary and speechwriter, committed suicide recently. Duan Lin-Yu, the director of the Counterintelligence Office, discovered that there were communist spies in Mr. Hu's family. Both his daughter and son-in-law were undercover communist agents. General Chen informed his gifted spokesman about the intelligence findings, but assured Mr. Hu that he would remain a close friend and personal aide. But the shocking news devastated Mr. Hu, who was so humiliated by what he deemed as a serious breach of trust that he could no longer face his boss.

"Why can't Duan stop these abhorrent communist infiltrations?" Madam Chen asked.

"Well, Duan is no match for the communist spymaster Si-Tu Wen-Liang, who controls God knows how many spies in our camp. Sheng Bao will have access to our top-secret plans before many of our own high officials even know about them," the disheartened General Chen acknowledged.

"But you can't give up. You are the national leader and you have to fight no matter how difficult the situation is," Madam Chen encouraged him.

"Yes, I know. Thank you, my dear, for always being here for me, no matter what." The general was truly grateful that he had always been able to count on Madam Chen's unconditional support throughout his career.

But the situation somehow looked more ominous this time. Even though the communists did not have those military airplanes in the sky and armored tanks on the ground, as the Japanese troops had in the last resistance war, they seemed to pose an even more dangerous threat, and their strength seemed to be far greater than their sheer number would suggest. This was an all-out war for sure, General Chen realized.

For years the communists had greatly mobilized the poor in the countryside, promised them land reforms, and recruited thousands of them to join their ranks. On the espionage front, they had employed hundreds of spies to collect sensitive military, political, and financial information from every division of General Chen's troops and every department of his government. The intelligence and clandestine activities alone would add enormous strength to the communists. Even as they reached out on the diplomatic front for support from the Soviet Union, which had been their traditional ally for several decades, the communists also learned to influence public opinion in the United States, hoping to gain sympathy from the most powerful Western nation. For that purpose, they had carefully opened a new front by orchestrating a media campaign that labeled General Chen as the villain while portraying the Communist Party as the true believer in democracy.

2

Far from being cheap talk, propaganda was a wonderful tool, and no war was ever conducted without it. A combatant could advertise anything he wanted at a particular point in time, only to do something completely different later on. Depending on the purpose, he could leak, falsify, and withhold some information, while exaggerating some other details. He could misinform and manufacture white lies if lying could conceal the truth about his military strength or the lack of it. He would try as much as he could to exploit his enemy's weaknesses, deny the truth, hide the reality, implement harassing tactics, adopt deceptive strategies, create confusion and mayhem, invent false attacks, and stretch the enemy's resources to the limit by forcing them to defend themselves on all fronts. Didn't the master Sun Zi say "when he prepares everywhere he will be weak everywhere"?

Propaganda could embolden a leader's troops and confuse his enemies. Although an indirect means and a nonphysical tactic, propaganda could help significantly influence the dynamics of a military confrontation, or, as Sun Zi put it, "Generally, in battle, use the normal or direct force to engage; use the extraordinary or indirect to win." Well-planned propaganda was therefore of special importance in warfare, and lying, deceiving, and projecting fictitious images of both the combatant and his enemies were always critical components of wartime publicity campaigns. The uniqueness of communist propaganda was not that the party leaders never lied but that they lied based on the convenient moral justification that they were doing it not for the self-interests of the few but for the long-term interests of the proletarian, for the fundamental benefits of the millions of working people, for the bright future of the entire nation, and for the glorious success of the communist cause worldwide.

General Chen was no fool and he could feel the heat of a virulent media campaign against him lately. Some reports exposed the scandalous corruption in his government. Others blamed the government for its wrong economic and financial policies. Many publications reported the hardship and widespread discontent in the country, urging for an end to the civil war and calling for the establishment of an inclusive and united government.

"Sheng Bao must have been the mastermind behind all this. But Gan Zu-Xun is helping the communists! His party has much influence over those newspaper editors, those so-called intellectuals and the so-called third-party supporters!" General Chen's ingrained disdain for the educated was only slightly less than Sheng's.

"Darling, you can't afford to alienate them, even if you dislike them," Madam Chen gently advised the husband, whose overconfidence in his military prowess concerned her as much as his underestimation of the media's power and influence.

"I know that. But I don't understand why those college students and city folks are never happy. I have called for a general election, I have invited the third party to join the national government, and I have even allowed the Communist Party to participate. What else do they want? I think the bottom line is that they want to replace me with Sheng Bao, which I will never allow," General Chen said firmly.

3

The media campaign was relentless. A sharp and vigorous freestyle essayist, Sheng displayed his talent in the newspapers as fully as he did on the battleground. Under his orders, the communist propaganda machine published editorial after editorial, condemning Chen's one-party rule and praising Western-style democracy.

One of the most frequent topics was their unabashed flattery of the American system, such as this one:

Ode to America

We praise the United States—the beacon of modern democracy. We celebrate the Fourth of July—the birth of this independent and great nation. Each year on this day, every kind and honest person on earth would feel happy for science and democracy have taken roots in the New World since the day of her birth. Some one hundred and seventy years later, the shining light from the Statue of Liberty illuminates the darkest corners in the world, bringing warmth and hope to all people around the globe.

From our childhood, we have held a special affinity for the United States, whose great leaders George Washington, Thomas Jefferson, Abraham Lincoln, and Franklin D. Roosevelt are our heroes, and whose famous authors such as Mark Twain, Walt Whitman, and Ralph Waldo Emerson have educated our generation. They have taught us about the dignity of humanity and the pricelessness of freedom. Most important, they have taught us how to resist dictatorship and totalitarianism in a country without any democratic tradition.

America and China are oceans apart. Only a handful of us would be fortunate enough to have any direct contact with each other. But the Pacific Ocean will not be a barrier between our two nations, nor will it stop the friendly exchanges of our two peoples. In our current ordeal, we look up to the United States for hope and direction. When the day comes after we have defeated fascism, we will rebuild our country on the basis of science and democracy, just like what the United States had done after achieving her independence. The great principles of American democracy have already taken root in our heart, and American science and technology will help millions of the soon-to-be-liberated Chinese to build a new, strong, and democratic China in the future.

Long live the Fourth of July! Love live democratic America! Long live the war for Chinese independence and democracy!

4

Meng Bo-Xian was much encouraged after reading those prodemocracy editorials. He thought Sheng and the Politburo finally had a change of heart, reversing the nondemocratic trend of promoting a personality cult. He sent the newspaper clippings to Tania, hoping to share the good news with her.

Tania was equally excited when she read a report of a long interview with Sheng by the American columnist James Sudbury. Part of their conversation went as follows:

Q.   At a recent government reception, Madam Chen remarked that democracy is on the rise internationally, and that democracy is much needed in China as well. What is your comment?

A.   She is absolutely correct. In today's world two systems are competing for dominance—democracy and fascism, and no middle ground exists. China, like the rest of the world, certainly wants democracy, not fascism.

Q.   At the practical level, do you think democracy can materialize in China?

A.   Yes, of course. Madam Chen has said that a democratic government will fulfill the popular wishes once the government knows what those wishes are. Two points may be added here. One is the people must be allowed to speak out so that the government can understand what they are thinking. The second is that government must be responsive to the public's demands. Without the two specific steps, democracy is just empty talk.

Q.   Some people here and many in the West believe that the literacy rate in China is too low for the population to embrace the democratic form of government, something that the Chinese people have never experienced before.

A.   The concerns you mentioned are real. Many think today's China is not ready for democracy, and it has to wait for many years until the majority of the population has reached the level of education close to that in the Western countries, or democracy will have no chance of success in China. True, eighty percent of Chinese can't even write their own names now. True, when the literacy rate is much improved, democracy will thrive. But let me tell you how we conduct elections in many rural villages in our revolutionary bases. We allow those who can write to specify on their ballots whom they wish to vote for. We also allow those who are illiterate to vote by putting a bean into one of the bowls behind the candidates, who are sitting with their backs toward the voters. In the end, those candidates with the highest number of beans and ballots will be elected. See, the processes can be improvised and democracy can be practiced if we give it a chance.

Q.   That's an interesting technique. I think some ancient Native American tribes have also used the same method in their elections. But democracy is more than elections. Can you tell me how the democratic process has helped in public life in areas under your control?

A.   A good question. I was once told about a village chief who had
been leading the village for many years. He used to believe that
the villagers were like his subjects, and often forced them to do
things for him whenever the county government assigned him
new tasks. Villagers complained that some of the tasks were
unrealistic and could not be finished on time. He then attended
a training class on how to improve leadership style, where he
learned the importance of public opinion, open dialogue, and
patient persuasion. He realized that heavy-handed tactics and
blunt demands were often counterproductive. But active public
involvement could help accomplish those official tasks, and
prove to be far more effective than what he had imagined. A
small but substantial change in leadership style had benefited
this village head a lot. When similar methods are more widely
adopted, they will help hundreds of thousands of our local
leaders and public officials to improve their work.

Q.   Pleased to know that. Most Americans are concerned about the
nature of communism and communists. What are your thoughts
about the relationship between China and the United States in
the future?

A.   Communism is our ideology and faith, just as capitalism and
Christianity are yours. But we are also fair-minded realists just
as President Franklin D. Roosevelt had been a great fair-minded
and realistic statesman. China not only needs democracy, we
also need modernization and industrial technology. We need
close collaboration with the United States, which, more than
any other country, can provide that assistance to us. China must
modernize and modernization is based on capital investment
and market economy. America can provide both and China will
welcome its support. American businesspeople need not worry
about us. We want close collaboration with America. We don't
fear the influence of American democracy, and the American
public should not worry about us.

5

"Tania, you have a visitor," Yan reluctantly told her friend.

She was of course very familiar with Dong Zi-Tian, who had visited Tania at her dwelling several times in recent months. Yan somehow felt a little uneasy about these visits, suspecting that Dong was secretly pursuing Tania while her husband was away. An intimate friend and vigilant observer, Yan had known Tania long enough to suspect that she might have some reciprocal feelings for Dong, which began to concern her since Yan strongly believed in chastity.

"Look what's in this Shanghai newspaper, *The Daily Telegram*!" Dong showed a roll of newspaper to Tania as soon as he entered the room.

"Democracy and Freedom of the Press," Tania read from one of the headlines.

"Yes, yes. That's the piece you must read," the enthusiastic Dong responded as the despondent Yan realized that he apparently had no intention of leaving anytime soon.

A big wood-burning stove heated the room nicely. To make himself more comfortable, Dong took off his thick overcoat and sat on the kang, which was larger and warmer than those commonly found in Shaanxi. Nothing could make a man feel more satisfied than sitting so cozily next to the woman he liked, particularly in such a terrible winter day in Northeast China—it was minus thirty degrees centigrade outside.

"When is this guy going to leave?" Yan moaned, while Tania seemed totally oblivious to her friend's annoyance.

Tania then began to read the article on democracy and freedom of the press:

Throughout history we have seen the rulers in a single person, a single family, or a single party. They have deprived the people of the right to govern and silenced their voices to preserve the exclusive ruling authority for themselves. Kings, emperors, monarchs, tyrants, totalitarians, and dictators would never allow the freedom of the press, which could challenge their government and threaten their absolute power.

Democracy is the rule of the people. They have the right to criticize government policies and are allowed to form different parties and organizations to compete for power. Neither one of these rights could be realized without the freedom of the press, which includes the right to free speech and independent opinions, and the abolition of censorship.

Simply put, if the strict controls over intellectual thought and public opinions have been one of the grim hallmarks of rule by a single person, a single family, or a single party, freedom of the press will be one of the first prerequisites for modern democracy.

Does China need democracy? The answer is certainly "yes." The democratic countries of the United States and Great Britain have defeated fascism and totalitarianism in WWII. They will continue to lead the rest of the world toward a more democratic direction. If China doesn't want to be left behind, it must swim with the tide, not against it.

Our great founding father Sun Yet-Sen had pointed out more than twenty years ago that the concepts of freedom, equality, and justice could be found in ancient Chinese philosophy. But those sporadic ideas and fragmentary thoughts have not been fused into one dominant school of thought in our tradition, much less have they evolved into an accepted form of official programs or social institutions. To achieve democracy under these conditions, China has to overcome several serious obstacles.

The first of these is to realize that democracy is far more than a political institution, even though it has been frequently defined by its elective and representative form of government. Democracy must also be a way of life that encompasses a society's legal apparatus, value systems, and political and social behaviors of its citizens. It particularly has to include the four fundamental freedoms that U.S. President Franklin D. Roosevelt had so clearly articulated—freedom of speech, freedom of worship, freedom from want, and freedom from fear.

Democracy and freedom of the press have to go hand in hand. Freedom of speech, freedom of peaceful assembly, freedom of thought, freedom of expression, and freedom of the media are the necessary preconditions of a democracy. No democracy can emerge or survive without freedom, just as no living creature can breathe without air. Precisely because of that, they are the very antithesis of universal conformity in the passt, under which any critical attitudes, divergent opinions, different viewpoints, creative suggestions, alternative approaches, and unconventional proposals had been branded as heretical in China for three thousand years. Thus, in the push for freedom today, every small step requires extraordinary efforts to break away from governmental suppression and to break down the deeply rooted resistance from old traditions.

Since the May Fourth Movement the progressive intellectuals in China have been fighting for democracy for almost three decades. But the principle of freedom of the press has yet to take root, as the government continues to control and censor the media, and attack independent-minded journalists. And freedom of the press is not possible without the rule of law. Without the just protection of the law, the individual rulers, be it an autocrat, an iron-fisted ruler, a warlord, or a one-party leader, will continue to rule as he pleases. Freedom of the press will evaporate in a flash. Thus, in the next issue we will discuss "Freedom of the Press and the Rule of Law."

6

"It is a very good article. Thanks for bringing it to me," Tania said to Dong, who smiled while listening to her sweet voice.

"You are most welcome. I am glad that you like it," said he.

"Who do you think the author is?" she asked.

"I think Gan Zu-Xun wrote it," he answered.

"Oh, I see." Tania's face darkened as she had a sudden flashback of a past incident.

"Do you know him?" Dong asked carefully, noticing Tania's mood had changed.

"Maybe, maybe," Tania responded vaguely.

When Yan finally saw Dong off, she noticed Tania was still in a pensive mood. "What happened?" she asked. "Did he say anything to upset you?"

"No, not at all," Tania said absent-mindedly. "He has asked me to attend his wedding."

That evening, Tania woke up and grabbed Yan, yelling, "Yes, yes. It's him!"

"What are you saying? Who did you find? Who is him?" The stunned Yan was totally confused.

"Gan Zu-Xun. Gan Zu-Xun—the man who kidnapped and sold me in Shanghai!" Tania said.

7

Although it had been seriously damaged and had not been maintained for a long time, the Saint Sophia Cathedral was still the most impressive structure in the city of Harbin. Today, many soldiers came early in the morning to sweep the grounds and decorate the interior, preparing for the wedding ceremony of their top regional leader, Dong Zi-Tian, and his wife, Dai Tian.

"Good heavens, I have never seen anything like this!" Yan cried out when she and Tania turned at the corner of Toulong Street, facing the grandiose building, the largest Russian Orthodox church in the Far East.

No Chinese city today, big or small, would be complete without having Christian churches, which were introduced by foreigners. Some were built by the Catholics, others by thrifty Protestant denominations. Plain in design and small in scale, most of them could hold no more than a few hundred worshipers. There were exceptions, although they were found only in urban centers. The largest and most elaborate church in Shanghai, for example, the Holy Trinity Cathedral (Anglican), at one hundred and fifty feet long and fifty feet wide, could seat two thousand people.

Growing up and living in the south for most of her life, Yan never expected to see any church building that could be bigger and more beautiful than the ones she had seen in Shanghai. Now, right in the heart of this remote city in cold and forbidden Northeastern China, the massive and colorful cathedral stunned her, when she only vaguely remembered one dreary and small Orthodox church in Shanghai.

Luckily, she had Tania, who felt so much at home watching this grand Russian revival church. Since the ceremony was yet to start, the two women took the time to take a stroll around the building.

Constructed on a foundation in the shape of a Greek cross, Tania explained to Yan, an Orthodox church was usually more compact than, or not as elongated as, a Catholic one, which was often built in the shape of a Roman cross. Covering nearly eight thousand square feet, the nave of this church must be able to hold at least two thousand people, making it almost as big as the Holy Trinity Cathedral in Shanghai, the most cosmopolitan city in Asia. Not a small feat in this less-populated part of China.

The most striking feature of this Russian church must be its colors. However brilliantly designed and well-constructed, the exteriors of most other Christian churches looked grayish, solemn, and monotone in color. By contrast, Russian Orthodox churches were known for the outlandish display of a great variety of bright colors. Saint Basil's Cathedral in Moscow was a prime example, whose multicolored domes, roofs, walls, and exteriors made it look like a doll's house rather than a house of worship. Even many far smaller and very obscure Russian churches were awash with a great variety of bold colors.

This Saint Sophia Cathedral in Harbin, said Tania, could have been modeled after Christ the Savior Cathedral in Borki, a tiny village of a few thousand souls in Ukraine. Yet the design of the church was as sophisticated and colorful as many other major Orthodox church buildings across Russia.

"The locals had told me that the original building of Saint Sophia was a wooden structure," Tania continued. "It was rebuilt twenty years later and highly influenced by the Byzantine revival style of the time. If I remember correctly," said she, "a number of famous Russian architects from David Grimm to Vasily Kosyakov had developed a new type of structure, incorporating the typical single-dome Byzantine cathedral with four symmetrical apses that became standard in the 1880s and 1890s. From the exterior shape of this church before us, we could see the influences of David Grimm's St. Alexander Nevsky Military Cathedral of Tiflis in Georgia, Vasily Kosyakov single-dome Astrakhan church and its copy at Kamianets-Podilskyi in Ukraine.

"But, it seems to me, another prototype of the current building could be the Alexander Nevsky Cathedral in Baku in Azerbaijan, the largest church in the Caucasus. Designed by the German architect Robert Marfeld and his Polish student Józef Gosławski, the church was constructed between 1888 and 1898. Unfortunately, it was destroyed during Stalin's antireligious movement in the 1930s," Tania continued. "Ironically, we can trace back some remarkable features of that Russian church from this Chinese model in front of us.

"You see, dominating the skyline is the golden Russian Orthodox cross, also known as the Suppedaneum or Patriarchal cross, which has three horizontal crossbeams instead of one or two on a Roman cross. Right under the cross and extending thirty feet in diameter, the huge bulging green dome looks exactly like what most Chinese have called it—a giant onion, which is as common as the Patriarchal cross in any Russian churches."

"But there are five crosses on the building," said Yan.

"Good point," responded the friend. "Whereas a typical Roman church has one big cross, most grand Russian churches will have multiple ascending crosses, which is another visual distinction of an Orthodox house of worship."

Tania then asked, "What do you think about the western portion of the church, where the second tallest cross is?"

"It looks like a huge ship made of millions of dark red bricks," answered Yan.

"Yes. Symbolizing Noah's Ark, the ship-shaped structure is common in church buildings. And the tall and impressive tent-like bell tower, on which the second golden cross sits, is distinctive of a Russian church," explained Tania.

"Hmm, interesting. I really like it." Hardly a regular churchgoer, Yan nevertheless really appreciated the information Tania had provided. The more Yan listened to her calm and peaceful voice, the more she regarded Tania as not only her best friend but also the most pious person she had ever met.

The two walked up the stairs of the wide porch and entered, under the vaulted archway of thick moldings, the huge front portal made of fine redbrick tracery, which was as elaborate as those found in many big Gothic churches. Passing the narthex, what opened to them was indeed the spacious rectangular nave, which could no doubt hold two thousand parishioners.

Sadly, stripped of all its valuables, the church interior looked awful. The altar, the templon, the choros chandelier, and the icon stand had all disappeared. Fragmented frescoes disfigured most of the paintings. Discolored paints were peeling everywhere from the columns, walls, railings, and ceilings. All the cleaning the soldiers did in the morning cleared away some dust, but did little to change the deplorable status of the stripped-bare church.

Standing close to the now-demolished sanctuary, the two women bathed in the rays of the pleasant winter sunshine coming through the huge sixteen vertical windows surrounding the steady polygon drum, which supported the heavy dome from high above.

It was an extremely serene but magnificent feeling except that there was no church music, no sermon, no hymns, no prayers, no ribbons of bluish incense curling in the air, no panels of the beautiful yet mystical iconostasis—no sound, no image, and no movement.

Solemnly and deeply overwhelmed, the two women quietly walked around. Both were totally enthralled in this abandoned and yet holy environment until Yan said, "There are no seats or pews here. Are they pillaged too?"

"No." Tania smiled kindly. "Unlike the Christian churches, an Orthodox church does not provide any seating. Every believer shall stand equally before God."

"How sad to see such a gorgeous church being plundered," said Yan.

"'But the poor mansion offers thee its best,'" replied Tania, quoting the American poet Julia Ward Howe.

8

"What happened to the ceremony?" Even Tania had become impatient after an hour of waiting inside the cathedral.

Just as Yan, who had not wanted to attend the wedding in the first place, was planning to leave the church with Tania, a guard rushed into the building and announced loudly, "The wedding ceremony has been cancelled. Everybody can leave now."

"What? Why? What happened? Why is it cancelled?" Tania, shocked, hastily asked the guard.

The soldier looked around for a few seconds to make sure that no one was close by. Lowering his voice as much as he could, he said, "Dai Tian was arrested this morning by two internal security officials."

"What? Why?" both women cried out.

9

Several days later when Tania returned home, she told Yan, "You need to help me pack."

"Why?"

"Because Dong Zi-Tian needs help."

"You want to help him, again?"

"I mean Dai Tian needs help."

"I know she had been arrested. But why can't Dong help?"

"Because there is a war going on. As everyone knows, Dong is the top civilian leader here in the Northeast. Tens of thousands of soldiers must have food, shelter, supplies, and medical care every day, which he must provide. He can't leave and he will not leave."

"Then why not someone else? Why you? Dong married Dai, not you, correct?"

"That's correct. But I am his friend."

"Dong should have a lot of friends. Why not them? Why you?"

"Because few of them want to speak up on this sensitive matter."

"Cowards, spineless chickens! How can those guys call themselves 'men' when they would not help a friend in trouble?"

"Well, things may be more complicated than that."

"Tania, you are very nice and you are a true friend."

"Don't say that. I am not sure if my trip will really help."

"So, tell me what you plan to do to help Dai?"

"That's a secret."

"Really? But I am your friend."

"A secret is a secret, even to a friend."

"Oh, I am your friend no more?"

"Hey, you said the opposite just a second ago!"

"That's because you are Dong's friend, not mine! Ha, ha, ha…"

"Your naughty girl, I should teach you a lesson about good friendship!"

Finger fighting, chuckling, and giggling ensued as the two women fell to the kang.

10

It was hard to believe that only a few months ago she had boarded the train with Dong, chatting and talking all through the cold evening. Now, she was on the same train, but alone and headed in the opposite direction.

The several feet of snow on the ground had finally begun to thaw. Spring was in the air and the strongest trees sprouted little green buds so tiny that only the most active birds could detect.

Feeling the warm air and watching the pleasant scene outside the train did little to calm Tania, wrenched in pain.

Dong told her that Dai had used the pseudonym of "Wild Lily" to publish some humorous piece in *Liberation*. It greatly offended Sheng Bao, who ordered her arrest.

Tania promised Dong that she would talk to Si-Tu Wen-Liang to see whether he could help.

Dong doubted it would work. But he had no better idea and eventually agreed that Tania should give it a try.

Dong also told Tania another piece of shocking news—Martin, who had returned to the Soviet Union some years ago, had been arrested and was now being held in a labor camp.

Tania begged Dong to make sure the report was accurate, and he confirmed it was. According to intelligence reports, Martin was in the notorious hard labor camp Kolyma in northeastern Siberia. It was one of hundreds of concentration camps under the infamous Soviet gulag system, far away from the heart of the Soviet Union but close to China's Northeast.

Never had Tania been this restless on a journey. Two people's lives now depended on her mission, while she had no idea at all whether it would succeed.

"I must see Si-Tu as soon as possible. I must meet him and implore him to help," Tania said repeatedly to herself.

With nothing to calm herself down, she took out a piece of paper from an envelope of documents Dong had handed to her before she left. It seemed to be an official party directive, which began:

I am greatly disturbed by the recent publication in our official organ *Liberation*, which had ridiculed the great literary giant Lu Xun and our party's leadership role in art and literature. It is a serious political incident and every branch office within our organization, especially the propaganda department, must stop similar incidents from happening again in the future. For that purpose, I want to make clear five key points in this directive that must be implemented immediately throughout the party.

First, party leaders must realize that our revolution cannot succeed without effective propaganda, and that no propaganda can be effective without the participation of the educated.

Since thousands of new recruits from the illiterate lower classes comprise the majority of the rank and file, not only must we develop effective propaganda programs to recruit them, we must also wage frequent and effective propaganda campaigns to unify their goals, focus their attention, raise their morale, keep up their fighting spirit, and teach them discipline and skills; every step of which requires the knowledge and action of the educated. To ignore their important role in this prolonged and difficult revolutionary war will be a big mistake for our party.

Second, party leaders must understand that art and literature are anything but tools in the present revolution.

The so-called "art for art's sake" has never existed in history; it is a false claim by the bourgeoisie. In any stratified society, the ruling class has its art and the working class has its own. The educated members of our party in general and those artists, writers, journalists, teachers, musicians, and performers in particular are from the bourgeois class. What they have been most familiar with is bourgeois art and literature. Even though thousands of them have joined our party, their ideas, values, tastes, habits, interests, and standards of judgment remain more of the middle and lower middle classes, rather than those of the urban laborers and rural peasants.

Therefore, if art and literature are tools in the revolutionary cause, the artists, writers, and other educated persons must be willing to become the tool for the cause and for the party. They must undergo a complete ideological transformation before they could conform to the party's needs and to serve the party's cause. Therefore, to replace the old bourgeois ideology of the artists, writers, and other educated personnel with the new proletarian and Marxist ideology is a serious task our party must undertake.

Third, party leaders must understand that "art for the people" is our fervent belief and principle, which shall be used to judge all art and literature produced in our camps in the future.

Who are the people? They are the millions coming from the hardworking classes. Hundreds of thousands of our brave soldiers are the people. Tens of thousands of our loyal party members and officials are the people.

The bourgeoisie have created a myth of "apolitical art and pure literature." But we openly declare that people and politics shall always come first and foremost in evaluating any art and literature.

Does your art serve the people? Do people like the novels you write, the music you compose, or the plays you perform? If the answers are in the affirmative, your art and literature are correct and good. If the answers are in the negative, your art and literature are wrong and bad.

Yes, in our camp and for the success of our revolutionary war, there are the right and good—and the wrong and bad—categories of art and literature.

Our proletarian judgment of good and bad and our political standards for right and wrong always override any artistic tastes and supersede any literary criteria.

All forms of working-class art and literature are of the right type, no matter how rustic, primitive, and elementary they appear.

All forms of bourgeois art and literature are of the wrong type, no matter how advanced and sophisticated they look.

The standard and the only standard to judge between the good and bad, between the right and wrong, is to see whether or not any piece of art or literature would be accepted by the working class, our soldiers, and our party members and officials.

Those accepted by the people shall be considered the right form of art and literature.

Those praised by the bourgeoisie will always be the wrong form of art and literature.

Our party's task is always to promote the right form of art and literature and to suppress the wrong form of art and literature, wherever and whenever they are detected.

Fourth, party leaders must be aware that a major battleground is between conformity and creativity, between collectivity and individuality, and between our party's insistence on class struggle and the so-called universal concept of humanity.

Marxism and Leninism did not deny individual creativity offhand. What our party stresses is that creativity and individuality can't survive in this world without a cause. Every artist and writer must decide whether they are going to use their individual talent and creativity to serve the handful of bourgeoisie or the vast proletariat.

If they decide to serve the vast proletariat and the people's cause, they must obey the party's rules and discipline, they must learn from the people about their wants and needs, they must give up their selfish desires and interests, and they must subject themselves to the collective interests and needs of our party.

In our struggle to overthrow the reactionary government, we must defeat the big bourgeoisie who have supported this government. We must also reform the artists and writers who largely belong to various groups of lower to middle classes.

The reform of those limited number but educated bourgeoisie in our ranks is a class struggle in a different form.

Members of the lower to middle classes have only two choices—they can follow the wealthy bourgeoisie to preserve the corrupt government, or they can follow our Communist Party and the vast working people to topple it. No middle ground exists in today's China, and they must make a conscious choice one way or the other.

For those members of the lower to middle classes who have chosen to join our camp, they must give up the great variety of wrong ideas and habits they had inherited from the corrupt wealthy middle class. They must realize that the struggle between bourgeois selfishness/individualism and communist collectivism/group interests will never end until they totally give up their arrogance, irreverence, and self-centeredness, and until they totally and willingly adhere to our party rules and discipline. Until then they will always remain the allies of the middle class in our camp, i.e., the potential enemies of the proletarians.

Lastly, all our party members and officials must recognize that the bottom-line question we are facing in the present situation is whether we will allow the bourgeois members in our party to lead us, or we the proletarians to lead them.

Whether willingly or otherwise, the unreformed, semi-reformed artists and writers had mocked our great proletarian icon Lu Xun, ridiculed our party leadership, belittled the working-class members of our party, disparaged our brave soldiers, vilified the glorious people, denigrated our revolutionary bases, and rendered great damage to our great cause.

We must not remain silent. We must react. We must fight back. We must win this battle in art and literature, just as we have won hundreds of times in the battlefield.

Let us unite with the Communist Party to create the true proletarian art and literature for a new China!

After reading the document, Tania's heart sunk. She could tell that Sheng must have written this directive, suggesting that he was taking a personal interest in the matter. What Dai had said or written must have greatly offended him. The attempt to free her from jail at this juncture would be an uphill battle to say the least, or absolutely impossible at worst, unless someone could persuade Sheng to change his mind.

"No matter what lies ahead, I must try my best," Tania said to herself.

Chapter 32

Debate

1

T HE BIG ROLLING HILLS FROM THE WEST FINALLY CAME TO AN END, merging with the vast alluvial North China Plain in the east, thanks to the enormous sediments deposited by the mischievous Yellow River for thousands of years. Nestled in one of the last few valleys and hiding behind a saddle-shaped mountain crest, the tiny village of Saddle Slope was a quiet and pleasant rural community of one hundred families.

After scouting around for a suitable and safe place close to the front lines for a long time, Sheng Bao and his Politburo members had secretly left isolated Shaanxi and moved here to set up the communist headquarters, where they could better direct the war.

The offensive against the nationalist army in the civil war had gained momentum and was developing in the communists' favor. General Chen's reactive tactic of "dual-front attacks" was not working and the communist troops were winning in both the Northeast and the West. The audacious and surprise move to plunge deep into Central China had completely disrupted General Chen's strategy, and he suddenly found himself increasingly on the defensive. In an attempt to protect every urban and commercial center under the nationalists' possession, his forces were stretched too thin and their numerical advantage dissipated at a much faster rate than he was able to replenish the lost soldiers. For the first time in his illustrious military career, the ever-vigorous, powerful, and self-assured General Chen was staring defeat in the face.

The mood at Saddle Slope was jubilant. The soothing and moist spring air from the plains, the clear and chuckling downstream brooks, and the lively hues of youthful green sprouting in the fields added much joy to the group of newcomers to the village, who had been stuck in the cold, colorless, and desolate Shaanxi for more than a decade. Reviewing reports, conducting meetings, making phone calls, drafting commands, and sending telegrams to subordinates across the country, Sheng and the Politburo members were busier than ever. They knew that victory was in sight, and everyone was filled with unprecedented energy, confidence, and enthusiasm.

2

Tania's arrival attracted much attention from the villagers, who had never seen a Russian woman. When she told them that as a baby she had survived on the milk from a goat provided by a Chinese farmer, they laughed heartily, believing her to be one of their own. They stuffed her lodging with the best things they could offer a friendly guest—flour, beans, eggs, walnuts, peanuts, and apples. Still too poor to have any meat at this time of the year, the locals did present a few special products from the region. Some women encouraged her to try a cone-shaped fruit, which was brilliantly golden and yet extremely soft and spongy. It tasted surprisingly great, almost like ice-cream because it was so sweet and cold.

"What is it?" Tania asked.

"A persimmon," they replied.

"I think a persimmon can be very astringent," she said.

"That's true until we let it freeze outside overnight for several days," one villager said, drawing laughter all around.

The pleasant mutual introductions and warm conversations temporarily eased Tania's anxiety. She wanted to see Si-Tu Wen-Liang immediately, but was told that he had been very busy lately. She had to wait until further notice to meet with him.

Well, it looked like she just had to be patient. She took out some papers to read, but could not concentrate. She did not know how long she had to wait or what the delay could mean for Dai Tian and Martin's fate. Frustrated, she took out a pen and began to write a letter to her son.

My dear Peter,

I hope this letter finds you well. How is your new position with the faculty at the State University at Albany?

Two days ago I arrived at a charming village called Saddle Slope in Hebei Province, which I had never visited. Its landscape is beautiful and the weather pleasant. I have really started to appreciate China's diversity after living in Blue Grass in the south, Bao An in the west, Harbin in the northeast, and now Saddle Slope in the north. It is next to the great and fertile North China Plain, which looked so well cultivated, so big and almost endless as my train passed it the other day.

Oh, how I hope the civil war will end soon and these gentle and most friendly people here can return to their normal lives. Some villagers told me that their ancestors came from Shandong Province in the east some four hundred years ago after another terrible civil war in the Ming Dynasty. Poor China seemed to have been riddled with war and violence, and generations of her people have suffered long and hard as a result.

Several articles intrigued me lately. I have enclosed two of them— "Democracy and the Freedom of the Press" and "Democracy and the Rule of Law." I hope you can let me know your opinion after reading them. As for myself, I am ambivalent. Since I know the character of the author and his past, I pretty much doubt his personal integrity and sincerity. Yet his articles make sense. Which is why I am torn between the person and his work. I had hoped to see some consistency between the two; but perhaps I should understand that the real world rarely offers any consistency in human nature and behavior, right? You know America better than anyone I know, and you must let me know what you think about the writings (and how I can better deal with such complexities).

I am here on a personal trip, which can be very important to you too. But the ongoing warfare has postponed the meeting I am expecting. I pray it will happen soon. Until then I hope you will stay healthy and happy. Love you and hundreds of kisses!

Mom

3

No, he was not pleased, not pleased at all.

Just as everything was going his way and just as Sheng felt that everything was going according to plan, Tao Yin-Hu's blunt rejection irritated him. Sheng's past record had led him to believe that he was a military genius. Also convinced were all his colleagues who had idolized him as a master of military tactics. "All of his colleagues" except for Tao.

"What is the purpose of his telegram? What does it mean? Why this rejection? Why this suggestion of 'reconsideration'? What is the motive behind his action? Specifically, why such a response at this most critical moment of our struggle?"

Sheng kept asking himself these questions repeatedly, while pacing in a small room that had been converted from a farmer's residence into his office.

The mild climate and rich source of local timber prompted a practical style of housing. Rectangular in shape and modest in height and size, the brownish farmhouses were the familiar, inexpensive, but sturdy and well-insulated dwelling structures in rural Hebei. Most of them were built on thick and solidly tamped clay walls, and the ubiquitous coat of lime and cement slurry gave the universal exterior brown color to those houses. Generally speaking, a single central purlin, two beams (front and back), and a row of common rafters would be used to support a flat roof, which was not elegant yet adequate for shelter against the limited rain and snow in the area. Housewives frequently used the spacious and convenient flat rooftop to sun grains, vegetables, clothing, blankets, and other household items on a warm and clear day.

Large wood-framed rectangular windows with grid patterns were standard, but few were installed with glass. Like bricks and tiles, glass was a luxurious building material and only the big and wealthy landlords could afford it.

Common households used window paper—good families used the bright and smooth white Korean paper made of mulberry barks, while average families used coarse and semitransparent paper made of rugs. Inside the house, the large kitchen stove was connected to the kang, just like the rest of the farmhouses in the north. But most families also had a second earth stove attached to the main room's exterior walls. This outdoor stove would be used to cook meals (for people or pigs) in the hot summer days so as to reduce the excessive heat inside the house.

Many families had an enclosed courtyard, complete with a pagoda tree and some fruit trees, such as date, cherry, peach, pear, or persimmon. When members of the household gathered under the tree blossoms in springtime, it would be the happiest moment for the family.

Passing the small wooden door over several steps, the Politburo members entered the tidy compound where Sheng lived.

"Chairman, look, the pagoda tree in your yard is sprouting!" Lin Shi-Xiong announced.

"The apricot is about to bloom!" Si-Tu said.

Coming from behind, Song Pei remarked, "What a nice yard! What a beautiful morning!"

All of them were in a good mood as they walked over a brick path and entered Sheng's house, which, different from other' residences, had a slightly raised stone foundation—a sign of a decent abode in this region.

Not at all interested in the frivolous compliments and niceties, Sheng greeted them by waving a telegram in front of them, "Look, Tao Yin-Hu disagreed with my plan!"

His visitors' smiles disappeared. They hovered around Sheng to read that telegram, and quickly realized their dilemma. Both Sheng and Tao were equally gifted, experienced, highly confident, and headstrong. Neither one would change his mind when their views clashed. As their colleagues, those present did not want to see a rift in the top leadership, especially on matters as vital as military strategies. But, as their longtime friends, they also knew how difficult it would be to reconcile the two.

"Should we overrule his opinion and proceed with our decision made at the last meeting?" Lin asked cautiously, looking at Sheng.

Sheng was thinking and did not reply immediately.

Si-Tu, noticing Sheng's frustration and hesitation, suggested, "Why don't we postpone the final decision?"

"But postpone for how long?" Song asked before Sheng could respond.

"I was thinking," Si-Tu said in his usual calm manner, "that we can recall Tao to come here and explain his ideas in person before the Politburo."

"That will take a long time," Lin complained.

"Yes, this will take some time. But do you want us to implement a major military decision for our troops without the consent of their commander-in-chief?" Si-Tu responded gently.

People in the room knew Si-Tu had made a good point and they looked at Sheng. He, though never liked to be overshadowed, knew that Si-Tu was right. The party could not afford to make a critical decision on the eve of a major offensive without the commander-in-chief's support.

"Okay," said Sheng. "Let's telegram Tao asking him to return as soon as possible and to explain to us his serious objections to our plans."

"He better has a good explanation, or it will be a huge waste of our time," Lin added.

4

"Darling, is there something troubling you?" asked a concerned Madam Chen.

"Never mind, never mind. You go back to sleep," the general answered.

"No, I won't unless you tell me the problem," the madam insisted, knowing that her husband would give in.

"Okay, okay, I tell you," General Chen said. No matter how fearless they were in the battlefield, few Chinese generals could resist the charm of their wives and General Chen was no exception.

After Xia-Hou Ding's troops swept the Northeast, he was poised to come down south of the Great Wall to seize several major cities in Northern China, and Peking and Tianjin would be his principal targets.

General Chen certainly wanted to defend Peking. If this ancient capital and the largest city in the north was lost to the communists, he would certainly suffer a big humiliation as a national leader. While he could never allow that to happen, the general had a tough time deciding who could defend the city better—General Yan Shu or General Pan Jin.

"General Yan Shu. Definitely General Yan," said Madam Chen confidently.

"Why?" the husband asked.

"Because General Yan is a northerner and he knows the conditions there much better than General Pan, a southerner."

"But everybody regards General Yan as a sly old fox. You know how he has been playing a two-faced game with me for years, right? How can I trust him this time?"

"Precisely. If he can play the game with you, he can do it with the communists as well."

"Hmm, that's a thought. But I still don't trust Yan since he could very well make deals with the communists behind my back."

"Then send the best intelligence officer to keep an eye on him."

"Yes, yes. I will certainly do that."

The general seemed to be in a better mood now. He turned to his wife and asked, "So, tell me why you recommended General Yan, not General Pan."

"I have told you already," said the madam.

"Yes, you did tell me the reason for choosing General Yan. But you did not tell me why you *did not* choose General Pan," the husband stressed.

Madam Chen know she would have to come clean since her husband was no fool and his suspicious mind could easily detect if she was hiding something from him. She confessed, "Okay, I will be frank. Both of us know that General Pan is our best field officer. He should be in charge of the defense of Southern China, where our real base is. Peking is a great city. But it should not be the main focus of your defense, unlike Shanghai and Nanjing, which should always be your priority."

"I agree with you completely," admitted the general, "for I have been toying with the same ideas for a while. But I could not make a final decision until now. I am so glad that you confirmed what I had been thinking. I always trust your instincts better than mine."

5

Tania finally got a chance to meet Si-Tu. He patiently listened to her two requests and promised immediately to help with Martin's case. He said he would contact the party's liaison official in Moscow, who would make a special request for Martin's release. Once he received any news, he promised that he would let Tania know.

As for Dai's case, he expressed his doubts. "Did you read Sheng Bao's Five-Point Directive?" he asked.

"Yes, I did," said Tania.

"The Chairman has made it very clear that literary expressions like Dai Tian's in *Liberation* are detrimental to our revolutionary cause," Si-Tu explained.

"I thought we supported the freedom of expression, as the series of editorials in our official publications had openly stated not long ago, didn't we?" Tania asked.

"Yes, we did. But we also believe, as Sheng has pointed out, that all expressions represent the interests of a class. Some expressions are proletarian, and some are bourgeois. We can't allow bourgeois ideas and expressions to appear in our publications freely, can we?" Si-Tu responded.

"That's a serious charge. Is there any evidence that Dai's opinions were bourgeois? If so, who made the charge?" Tania asked.

Hearing no answer, she further asked, "Even if her opinions are considered improper, she did not commit a crime, did she? And why was she arrested simply for some light-hearted casual comments in the newspaper?"

The normally eloquent Si-Tu could not answer Tania's questions. He covered his embarrassment by saying that he would get more details from those who were in charge of the case.

Tania decided not to push him any further. She knew the circumstances of Dai's arrest could be more complicated than she was able to tell, and she did not want to lose Si-Tu's sympathy, who could be her only hope to save Dai.

Tania left Si-Tu's brownish house with a heavy heart and a sense of despair. She was not sure what the future had in store for either Martin or Dai, and the feeling of uncertainty made her feel terrible. All of a sudden, she remembered the phrase "no freedom or liberty could exist without the protection of the law."

"Who said that? Where did I read it?" Tania asked herself as she went back home.

"I got it!" she said later, smiling as she entered her room, "I read it in 'Democracy and the Rule of Law' by Gan Zu-Xun, the man I really loathe."

6

The tension in the conference room was palpable when Sheng did not say anything but kept on smoking.

Tao Yin-Hu, who had taken the floor, thanked the Politburo for giving him the chance to present his ideas in person. "Telegraph is a great modern technological advancement. But sometimes it is still inadequate in explaining complex situations," he laughed, alone. Every other member was as quiet as Sheng.

"The Politburo's intention to push our troops southward deeper than ever before is a bold design," Tao began. "I can see the strength of this plan, which could further disrupt the government's defenses by creating more chaos in the extensive territory under the nationalists' control than Chen Han could have ever imagined."

"However, I have several concerns about the proposed plan," he continued. "First of all, to send thousands of our troops across the Yangtze River is a huge and unprecedented undertaking. Our foot soldiers have little training and experience in sailing. Most of them are from the dry land of the north. Few of them could handle a boat or know how to swim. To prepare them for the crossing will take a much longer period than the time-frame outlined in the plan."

"Second, even after successfully crossing the Yangtze River, they will be faced with an environment and climate they are completely unfamiliar with. For more than a decade, our attention and military action had focused on the north, where our bases were and where our soldiers and officers had grown up. The plan is now to move a large portion of our forces south of the Yangtze River, where diseases, supplies, and care for the wounded will pose serious problems for our expedition army. But Chen's troops will enjoy all the advantages we lack, and are just waiting to fight us—a scenario Master Sun Zi had long warned of: 'Move not unless you see an advantage.' He specifically pointed out that 'whoever is first in the field and awaits the coming of the enemy will be fresh for the fight; whoever is second in the field and has to hasten to battle will arrive exhausted.' I am afraid that the planned expedition will give Chen's troops the advantage of 'first in the field,' which will be hard for our soldiers to overcome after crossing the Yangtze River while having no base of support in the south."

Tao added, "Thirdly and perhaps the most important, even if everything were to work out as planned, I still prefer most of the major fights in the future to be confined largely to the north of the Yangtze River, not south of it. The Yangtze River region and especially the Lower Yangtze River Delta is the most fertile and most productive region in China, not to mention home to prosperous urban centers like Shanghai, Nanjing, and Hangzhou. Even during the last resistance struggle against the Japanese, unlike the war-torn north, this region remained largely intact, which will be enormously beneficial to us when we come to power. If we extend the battle fronts across the Yangtze River too soon, we will be doing a real disservice to ourselves, because the subsequent warfare may destroy the vital agricultural, industrial, commercial, and financial infrastructure that we will need later. Therefore, we will benefit a great deal if we can refrain from moving into the south at this point—I wish to repeat that I have never said that we should never march across the Yangtze River, which we will definitely do sometime in the near future, but definitely not right now—when the government's massive forces are still powerful. We better find a way to annihilate them here in the north instead of pushing them to the south where intense fighting is going to destroy the last of our country's most developed regions."

Tao sounded reasonable and his detailed explanation went down well with Song, Si-Tu, and Lin. They seemed to agree with his opinion, and his third consideration especially seemed to be more farsighted than their original proposal. But they did not want to jump on Tao's bandwagon yet before Sheng said anything. They had to give him a chance to respond first since he was the one who had first proposed the plan to cross the Yangtze.

The early inspiration for Sheng's original plan was instinctively daring, audacious and downright prodigious in imagination, scale, and determination. He had envisioned that, if crossing the Yellow River had totally disrupted the enemy's strategy, another similar move of crossing the Yangtze River would surely put the last nail in Chen's coffin. Overly enthusiastic and largely persuaded by absolute tactical terms, Sheng failed to pay attention to the practical dimensions of the operation, or the grave sequential impacts of the move. Tao's objections clearly reminded him of those serious implications, which he began to see now.

Sheng suddenly felt chills run down his spine, as he realized how fortunate it was for the Politburo to have given Tao a chance to speak out before it was too late.

Crushing his cigarette butt in the ashtray, Sheng stood up and said, "Well done, Tao Yin-Hu. Now we have learned so much from your observations, we will certainly review and revise the original plan. Why don't Wen-Liang take you to your residence to have some well-deserved rest? And we shall resume our meeting tomorrow."

So the meeting ended without a conclusion one way or the other.

A fundamental principle for a leader was never to admit his mistake in public. He might change, repent, or regret. But he must never show such contrition to his associates, and certainly not to the public, since it would jeopardize the leader's reputation and undermine his authority.

Sheng had believed in this principle for a long time and had perfected the skill of not admitting his mistakes so well that none of his colleagues could ever recall a time when he had apologized for anything.

Just as Tao was about to leave the room, Sheng casually asked, "Can we really win if the most horrendous battle were to take place north of the Yangtze River?"

Tao understood why Sheng asked the question. North of the Yangtze River was where the great North China Plain lay. The communist troops, first rising from the mountains twenty years ago and still relying heavily on the mountains for shelter, protection, and popular support, had thus far avoided fighting on the plains. To suggest that they should confront the nationalist forces head-on in the vast open field was an extremely daring idea.

Tao thought for a few seconds and replied, "Yes."

7

"General, the situation in Jinan is not promising. I suggest we withdraw from there and use the troops to form stronger defenses in Xuzhou, which is vital to protecting our capital, Nanjing," General Bai Yu-Xian said as he concluded one of the grimmest battlefield reports to his boss. Full of trepidation, he waited for a thunderous response from General Chen.

The boss, surprisingly, remained calm and kept looking at the huge wall map in the military room. No words, no moves, no emotions.

About five minutes later, Chen turned around and said to his timid chief of staff, "No, we will defend Jinan. We will never give up Jinan, which is less than two hundred miles from Xuzhou. If we lose Jinan, we can't defend Xuzhou, which is only one hundred and seventy miles from Nanjing. If we can't defend Xuzhou, we can't save the capital."

"General Bai, relax," the boss went on. "Remember we defeated a group of ferocious warlords in the same place years ago? I am sure we can beat the communists here again this time."

"Yes, we did. But times have changed and the communists are not the warlords. They have the support of millions of the poor in the country," said Bai as softly as he could.

"But they don't have heavy artillery and tanks, do they?" Chen quipped.

"No, they don't," Bai admitted.

"Jinan is the largest city in Shandong Province. The multilayered defense is two hundred and thirty miles wide and ten miles deep. How can the poorly equipped communist troops break that? Their sheer numbers don't count here. But weapons and determination do." Brimming with confidence, Chen continued to enumerate the reasons why Jinan could be defended and therefore should not be surrendered to the communists so early in the game.

"Inflexible, dogmatic, stubborn, arrogant, vain, highly egoistic, and opinionated," Bai said to himself as he left the self-indulgent boss in the office, feeling totally depressed.

Several decisions by General Chen, made over Bai's objections, greatly disappointed the chief of staff. The first was to wage the "two-fronted" attacks simultaneously against the communist bases, which split the government forces and seriously weakened the effectiveness of the operations. The second was to appoint the sly Yan Shu to head the defense of Peking, which surprised just about everyone who knew him, the former crafty warlord in Shanxi.

Now Chen had rejected Bai's suggestion to withdraw from Jinan. Chen had this firm conviction that a defense was a defense, which must be conducted at all costs and at all times. He did not understand that defense could be flexible, and that there was a difference between passive and active defense. Yes, the communists did not have heavy artillery and tanks, Bai noted. But that made them more agile and more unpredictable. They would exploit any opening if the nationalist troops stretched themselves too thin in trying to defend Jinan. To withdraw the troops from Jinan and to use them to consolidate the defense around Xuzhou was to drastically reduce the area the nationalists must defend, which would in turn greatly reduce the chances of the communist troops sneaking through. Individually, the various nationalist units would have a much smaller area to protect while collectively, they would have a much better chance of supporting one another in the event of an emergency, Bai had told his boss.

Unfortunately, Chen did not listen. No, he was not even willing to listen. His mind was already set and he had decided he would defend every city that the communists planned to attack. He would never back down and he would never ever show his weakness.

This might be good as a political maneuver, but not as a military tactic. He could win the battle but lose the war. Or, even worse, he could lose both the battle and the war.

The shrewd, experienced, and highly perceptive Bai could not bear to think any further. By the time his limousine took him home, he had already made up his mind that he would resign as Chen's chief of staff.

8

Her son's letter gave Tania such joy that she could not help but read it immediately.

Dear Mom,

So happy to receive your letter and I am very pleased to let you know that I am enjoying my current teaching position at SUNY Albany very much. Although most of my students know little about China, just like I was a few years ago, I try to share my understanding of the country with them as much as I could. Learning is always a journey, isn't it? And I think the journey will never end. I am still learning and I will always enjoy that journey.

I am closer to home now and Papa said "hi" to you, as did Professor Robert Johnson.

Thanks for sending the two articles and I read them with great interest. I think the author has captured the notions of democracy, freedom of the press, and the rule of law very well. He seems to be a very knowledgeable person who must have had considerable insights into American society, politics, and history. My reservation is less about his pertinent delineations of those Western concepts than about the context of those concepts.

Western democracy in general and the American system in particular did not come out of a vacuum. The English Magna Carta was written in 1215, or roughly during the Southern Sung Dynasty in China. It was a compromise between King John and his lords, who were granted certain legal rights in exchange for their support of him. It was only over the centuries that those rights and liberties of protecting the nobles were gradually extended to the general population in England. A similar situation happened in the United States. The first elective House of Burgesses was established in Virginia in 1619, the first governor of the Massachusetts Bay Company was elected in 1629, and all local public offices were elected annually in Massachusetts for the next fifty years after 1630. These events were taking place before the Manchurians defeated the last emperor of the Ming Dynasty and established the Qing Dynasty in 1644.

What I am trying to say is that introducing those Western ideas and concepts is useful, but to put them into practice and to experience them in real life will be even more critical. Even the English and the American public would not have known what to do with democracy and freedom if they had not had centuries of personal experiences in participating in town meetings, political debates, election processes, dissemination of popular publications, and other public activities. Since the May Fourth Movement the Chinese intellectuals have talked about the notions of "science," "democracy," and "freedom." But little has changed in the country, perhaps less because of the absence of those notions than because of a lack of step-by-step practice and realistic personal involvement in exercising those ideas and concepts. This is certainly not the fault of the intellectuals but that of the politicians.

I am not sure about the exact complexities you are facing. I do agree, though, that ideally there should be much more consistency between a person's inner character and his outward behaviors. Yet that's not commonly found in our world, is it? In my usual pragmatic manner, I would only suggest that, if we can't have purity, we'd better learn how to deal with the complexities.

I am sure this is not the answer you had expected. But your question did remind me of the challenge every reasonable person has to face: where to draw the line in a complex situation. To deal with a single issue, one needs to see at least two sides. And to differentiate the two by a straight declaration of black and white, good and evil, is perhaps the simplest way of thinking, which ignores the vast gray areas between the two extremes.

But what if there are two overlapping and sometimes conflicting issues? Then one has to come up with an appropriate assessment from at least four dimensions. Most important, where do those dimensions start, how to draw the lines, where each of them may stop, and to what extent those lines, points, and dimensions may overlap or diverge? Unless one has a clear idea about these questions, one can't really say that he understands any complex issues.

I think it was Alexander Hamilton who said, "As too much power leads to despotism, too little leads to anarchy, and both eventually to the ruin of the people." Power and liberty are both needed. The emphasis on authority and the insistence on freedom are not in themselves automatically good or evil. They seem to be an inseparable pair and they do overlap and shift their respective positions from time to time. It's therefore the degree of power and the extent of freedom, too much or too little, which would make them acceptable or unacceptable.

The real world is always complex and intriguing. But that is why we are constantly probing—the reasonable people are constantly studying our world, and testing the limits, boundaries, and validity of our ideas and actions, from the noblest to the most obscure.

Love you ever so much,

Peter

"My Peter can be both philosophical and methodical," smiled Tania as she finished reading the letter. Nothing could please her more as a mother than to see her son maturing into such a thoughtful and level-headed person. She even noticed the influence of Professor Johnson, who had warned about the dangers of extremism.

"Too much power is tyranny. Too much freedom is anarchy," she repeated. "Hmm, interesting. Never thought about it that way."

Bang! Bang! Bang! Knocks on the door.

"Tania, you got to help us!" "No, no. You got to help this poor baby." "Yes, yes, you got to help this poor girl. She is dying!"

Several neighbors rushed in and they shouted loudly over each other.

"Stop, stop, please! I can't hear you if you all talk at the same time," said Tania. "Slow down, slow down, please. Now, let one person talk so that I can understand what's going on."

A few minutes later, Tania finally got the full story. The neighbors found an abandoned infant girl, who had been left in the streets. It was no secret that many traditional families preferred boys over girls and the infanticide rate of girls was notoriously high in rural China. This unwanted baby was just one of the thousands of innocent victims.

Tania looked at the infant's almost colorless face, her tiny fingers, and her pallid lips, longing for a little warmth and for a single drop of milk. Suddenly Tania felt like she was looking at a mirror of yesteryear, when she was a desperate newborn, struggling to survive in this cold and strange world.

"I will take care of her and I will raise her as my own daughter," Tania told the villagers, who were greatly relieved.

9

The attacks on Jinan started. What troubled the nationalist defenders was that they did not know which direction the communist main attacks were coming from.

A river ran right through the middle of the city, dividing it into the eastern and western portions. Both were protected by extensive exterior installations including bunkers, barbed wire, mines, trenches, and moats. The only difference between the two parts was that the western portion, which was close to an airfield, had the military commanding center and many government offices, while the eastern portion had more residential buildings, marketplaces, and businesses.

The question of where to launch the main attacks had also baffled Tao Yin-Hu, Meng Bo-Xian, and their officers as well, and Tao did not make his final decision until the last minute. When Bao Feng-Nian was given the secondary task of assisting the attacks from the east, he was deeply upset. He secretly changed the order, saying that another eastern attack would be led by him, which would not be any less severe than the one from the west.

Thus, when the battle began, the gunfire surprised the defenders because the attacks sounded equally intense from both east and west, contrary to the anticipation that the western side would be the main target. Two days into the fighting, the attackers suddenly halted their action. When it resumed, the most severe assaults were directed against the east and southeast. Confirmed by air surveillance, General Chen allowed the field commander to move his reserves from the city's west to the east to deal with the ferocious engagement there.

No sooner had these moves been completed than a new round of massive attacks started from all directions. The communist troops quickly occupied the airfield, cutting the city from any possible support or escape from the west. Bao's troops destroyed the exterior defenses of the east, reached the city walls in no time, ready to attack the inner city at any moment.

The panicking nationalist soldiers used the one-hundred-feet-high walls for their final defense where, from top to bottom, three layers of shooting positions had been built to kill anyone attempting to get close.

But the brick walls failed to stop Bao's valiant soldiers, whose relentless and fearless onslaughts eventually broke the nationalist troops' defense in twenty-four hours. The city of Jinan was captured in nine days, an amazing feat that surprised the two archrivals, Chen and Sheng, alike.

Greatly encouraged by the latest success, Sheng, Tao, and the communists became bolder. While still in a state of shock, Chen's real nightmare had just begun.

Sometime earlier during the fight, three government army units (the 2nd, 7th, and 12th) had left Xuzhou for Jinan. Before they could rescue the nationalist forces there, they were in danger of becoming targets themselves. Assuming that the defense of Jinan could last at least several months, Chen had sent these three units with the aim of trapping Tao's forces around Jinan. Although the city had now fallen, Chen was still hoping that the three units of more than three hundred thousand soldiers might still have a chance of beating some communist troops in the area.

The failure to order the three army units to return to Xuzhou as quickly as possible proved to be costly. The razor-sharp Tao immediately found the enemy's vulnerable spot that he had been looking for. He ordered six corps to isolate one of the three nationalist units, which had broken away from the rest of their main forces. Trapped in a small village, the 7th Army of one hundred thousand men was annihilated in two weeks. The swift, decisive, and surgical action shocked everyone because the battle took place less than forty miles from Xuzhou and all of Chen's field generals failed to come to those soldiers' rescue. They had all turned into cowards in the face of the communists' unrelenting attacks.

The furious Chen decided to do something. He called in General Bai and flattered the latter by praising him as the best strategist he had ever known—in the hope that Bai would agree to become the commander in charge of Xuzhou's defense. Bai politely declined the offer. He had worked with Chen long enough to know that it was impossible for any single officer to reverse the current tides of war.

The dejected Chen could not fathom why his eight hundred thousand soldiers in and around Xuzhou could not beat Tao's six hundred thousand. The government forces obviously had the numerical supremacy. But how could the communists win? Yes, yes, they lacked courageous and competent leaders, Chen concluded. He called in General Pan Jin and had a heart-to-heart talk with his favorite officer. Fortunately, Pan agreed with the boss and promised decisive action in the field.

Although victorious in recent campaigns, Tao remained level-headed. He understood perfectly that the dynamics of the war could change any time, and that the tenacity of his opponents should never be underestimated. Tao then changed his tactics and laid a trap for another enemy unit, which was duped, not because it was too timid but because it was too bold and aggressive. As a growing number of military units were becoming reluctant to engage the communist troops, Pan, the proud commander of the 12th Army, led his one hundred and twenty thousand soldiers marching fearlessly into battle, only to get ensnared in the trap that Tao had prepared for him. Just as Tao was about to order the final assault, Sheng telegrammed him, ordering him to hold his fire.

10

The armed confrontation in the north had reached a crucial stage. General Yan Shu, the commander of the nationalist forces in Peking, expressed his willingness to talk to his counterpart Xia-Hou Ding, the communist commanding officer, whose soldiers, one million strong, had imposed a watertight siege on the ancient city. Chen's disastrous failures in the Xuzhou area had led Yan to have some serious doubts on whether he should continue to fight for his boss.

Sheng directed Tao to hold off his final attack against the 12th Army, because he wanted to delude Chen into believing that his campaign to protect Xuzhou was far from over, and that his dogged efforts to reverse the situation were not yet hopeless. If Pan's 12th Army were to be eliminated as quickly as the 7th Army, Chen might order Yan to withdraw from Peking immediately. The communists would then have to fight him and his six hundred thousand men at another time and location, which might not be as advantageous to the communist forces as the current situation. Besides, if the battle for the city really started, Peking and all its priceless ancient treasures would go up in flames. That would be an irreversible and most devastating loss for the nation, no matter which political party survived the campaign.

The initial contact came and went, with the highly capricious Yan playing the same hide-and-seek game with his communist adversaries that he had done so many times in the past with his diverse enemies, be they local, regional, national, or international.

Days passed, and Yan was still wavering between a total capitulation and a conditioned compromise. Sheng called a Politburo meeting to discuss the situation.

All members agreed that, since Peking was such a historic city, it was worth the wait for its eventual peaceful capture. Meanwhile, they also agreed that they should not be fooled by the wily Yan, who could be using delaying tactics.

They needed to obtain some reliable insights into Yan the person and his true intentions in order to evaluate the whole situation properly.

Si-Tu suggested, "Gan Zu-Xun used to work for Yan Shu for several years. He might have some intimate and useful knowledge about the man, his character and behavior."

"Yes, that would be great if it is true." "Why don't you arrange a meeting with Gan to find out?" Both thrilled about the potential breakthrough, Song and Lin responded almost simultaneously.

Si-Tu was more than willing to act on the idea immediately, but he did not say anything. Characteristically, he never attempted to hog the limelight at any high-level meeting, nor would he ever assume that he would be the one to make the final decision. He simply waited patiently for the reaction from Chairman Sheng, the most important authority in the meeting.

Fully aware of Gan's background and political views, Sheng thought about the proposal and its ramifications for a while, and then said to Si-Tu, "Okay, you may arrange a meeting with Gan."

11

Tania had almost lost hope when, one day, she was suddenly summoned to see Si-Tu.

The two greeted each other and Si-Tu seemed to have reverted to his gentle, charming, warm, and courteous self, qualities that he had possessed since his youth.

"I heard that you had adopted a little girl." He started by making a polite inquiry.

"Yes, I did," Tania replied.

"What's her name, if I may ask?"

"She doesn't have a name yet. I am waiting for her father, Meng Bo-Xian, to name her when he returns," Tania said calmly.

Si-Tu sensed the underlying dissatisfaction, and changed the topic quietly. "I heard negotiations have been going on between our troops and Yan Shu, the nationalist officer in charge of the defense of Peking."

"Yes, I heard the rumors too," Tania responded.

"No, they are not rumors. There are indeed secret negotiations underway," Si-Tu gently corrected her statement.

"Oh, okay, yes. But, then, I am not sure why you have asked me to come here? I do not know anything about those negotiations." Totally confused, Tania did not understand why the highly sensitive negotiations between two armies should involve her in any way.

"Now, the thing is this." Supplied with some new information from Gan, Si-Tu began to reveal the true purpose of their meeting. "According to our intelligence, although Yan has nine wives, he has a half-sister, who is extremely close to him and who basically takes care of all his personal matters. Those close to Yan believe that this half-sister is highly influential when it comes to helping him make decisions. We would like to find someone who may have access to this woman. And we now know that Dai Tian knows this woman very well. They were classmates in the same girls' school when they were young and have remained close friends since."

Now Tania finally realized why she had been summoned for this meeting. The party now needed Dai, who might be employed as a go-between in the negotiations.

She did not say anything, thinking that it was better to let Dai decide for herself whether she was willing to take the assignment.

"What do you want me to do?" Tania asked.

"We have talked to Dai. But she seemed to be reluctant to accept the mission. So, so I hope you could talk to her and let her know how much you and Dong Zi-Tian are keen to get her out of jail." Si-Tu now revealed his cards.

"I am not sure I can do this. It's better to let Dai Tian and Dong Zi-Tian decide." Tania hesitated.

"But that will be too late. We can't wait. We need Dai and her active participation right away. Otherwise, once the fight starts, hundreds of thousands of soldiers' lives will be lost. You know how beautiful Peking is. If our soldiers begin to attack the city, not only will civilian lives be in jeopardy but the whole city could be ruined in no time!" Si-Tu stressed.

"But what about the charges against Dai? What about her arrest? Shouldn't she be cleared of those charges before she started working for the party again?" Tania asked.

"Of course, of course. Those charges will be dropped. Her record will be as clean as a whistle. Everything will be reset and the party will still trust her; it will be as if nothing, nothing has ever happened," Si-Tu spoke without so much as a blink, and his resolute attitude was infectious.

"Are you sure? Do you promise?" Tania asked again.

"I am sure. Totally. Absolutely. One hundred percent. I promise," he reaffirmed.

"Fine, I trust your words and I will talk to her," Tania said.

12

When an edifice was crumbling, hardly anything could stop it.

The twenty-day ceasefire gave the 12th Army a chance to breathe but not to escape. Its demise came quickly when Tao's troops resumed their attacks. Its commander and the famed war hero Pan was captured, much to the chagrin of Chen, who had placed such high hopes in him.

Intelligence and spy rings contributed to the astonishing success of the communists as much as anything else. Of the half-million nationalist soldiers who were defeated during the campaigns in Xuzhou, a fifth defected to the communist side. Even the cunning General Yan eventually gave up after the communist leaders had found out and accepted his one and only condition for surrender: that they preserve his dignity by not treating him like a common captive.

The surrender of Peking and the final victory at Xuzhou eliminated the last roadblocks for the communist troops to sweep through the remaining areas north of the Yangtze River. No one, including General Chen, could deny now that the communists' rise to power was no longer a question of if, but when.

Chapter 33

Korea

1

N O ONE WAS HAPPIER ABOUT TANIA'S ADOPTED BABY GIRL THAN Yan, who instantly assumed the role of her rightful guardian and natural godparent. Her fervent insistence persuaded Tania to hold a party today for the baby's "drawing the lot" ceremony on her first birthday.

"You know, this ceremony is most important for the baby," Yan told her friend seriously.

"Really? This is the tenth time you are telling me that," Tania replied, although her tone suggested she was not uninterested.

"Of course. It concerns her future happiness. Well, for that matter, it concerns your future too, because no parents would not care about the future of their children. Don't you think so?" the self-assured Yan asked earnestly, thinking she was highlighting a principle that Tania could hardly deny.

"That's true. But there are different ways to care for the future of the young. Don't you agree?" Tania responded indirectly.

"I do. And the only way I will know is to see how she would perform in today's 'drawing her lot' ceremony," Yan said with great delight and in even greater anticipation than Tania and the baby.

"Congratulations on her first birthday!" Dai Tian was the first to arrive and she could not wait to take over the baby from Yan's protective and reluctant arms. "What's her name?" she asked while kissing the baby's adorable rosy face.

"Her name is Xi," the proud mother said.

"Which 'Xi' is that?" asked Dong Zi-Tian, who had just walked in.

"Let the father explain." Tania turned to her husband.

"'Xi' as the word 'rare' ('shao') and 'hope' ('xiwang')," answered Meng Bo-Xian, who had entered the living room to greet their friends.

"Oh, what a striking name for the baby!" Dai praised.

"So appropriate of the moment she came to this family," Dong agreed.

"Hello everyone! And happy birthday to our little girl!" Tao Yin-Hu rushed in and put a small hat on Meng Xi's head.

"Well, a cute tiger-shaped baby cap!" Dai cried out again.

"Look at the red, golden, and black colors! The tiger even has whiskers! Thanks; it's very beautiful," Tania said.

"Now, will everyone come here and see what our baby girl will choose for her future?" Yan invited the guests to a big table, on which assorted objects had been laid in a circle.

She put Xi down in the middle of the circle. Everybody remained still and quiet. According to tradition, the object the baby would first pick up and hold on for a few moments would symbolize her future.

Some pens and pencils (a future writer), writing brushes (scholar), crayons (artist), a small dictionary (professor), a ruler (mechanic), a pair of small sneakers (traveler), a ball (athlete), a lipstick (actress), a harmonica (musician), a pair of stethoscopes (doctor), a piece of celery ("qin cai," diligence) and even a few money bills (wealth) were spread in front the girl. She touched several objects but did not hold onto them long enough to be considered her definitive choice. At last, she picked up a miniature abacus. From the way she enjoyed playing with it, Yan declared that the abacus was her chosen destiny.

"So, you will have an accountant in the family," Tao joked.

"This means that you will never have to worry about your business, my friend!" Dong teased Meng, whom he knew had never cared about business or money.

Noticing that Yan seemed unhappy and Tania perplexed, Dai went up to them and said, "Hey, this girl will grow up extremely smart, intelligent, well-disciplined, and methodical about details."

"Yes, yes, just like her mother and father!" Yan's face suddenly brightened. She brought out a big customary flour cake she had carefully prepared for the occasion. "Have some, have some. Thank you for coming," said she, who was now very pleased with how the ceremony had turned out.

A soldier hurried in and whispered a few words to Tao.

"I must leave for an urgent meeting. Thanks for the cake and I might just need to borrow your accountant in the future." Tao kissed the baby once more and quickly left with the soldier.

"You have a nice home," Dong looked around and commented.

"I know a much nicer place just around the corner. Want to go and have a look?" Meng said to his friends.

2

The peaceful settlement with Yan Shu allowed the communist troops, now called the People's Liberation Army (PLA), to capture Peking without a shot. Unlike many big cities and small towns across the country, which had suffered great damage in the worst civil war in history, this ancient city remained intact and was quickly chosen as the capital of the new People's Republic of China in 1949.

Selecting the best property in the heart of the city, the Chinese Communist Party established its headquarters and the central government in the old imperial palace, named Abundance, which had been the site of lavish regal gardens next to the enormous and priceless Forbidden City. Sheng (now both chairman of the party and president of the regime), members of the Politburo, their guards, and some high-ranking officials and top administrative offices moved into the complex, where they would rule China as a new generation of its proud occupants.

Feeling uncomfortable or inconvenient, some chose not to live in that compound. Meng and Tania's residence was located in a small alley close to a main street called Xisi. It was a major intersection in the northwestern part of the city—one of the principal business districts in the four corners in Peking.

Their house was a modified traditional courtyard, small but adequate for the family of four. What impressed Dong and Dai the most was that one of their side walls in the yard was extraordinarily tall, grand, and solid, which was at odds with the inconspicuous style and material used in the rest of the house.

"Why is this wall so big?" they asked.

"We'll go and find out," Meng answered.

He took the group out for a short stroll before making a quick turn at the end of the alley. Before them were three massive masonry gates lined on one side of the busy intersection.

"A Buddhist temple!" Dong recognized it immediately.

"Exactly. The three gates, homophonic to the sound of 'mountain gates,' is a distinctive structure of a Buddhist temple in China," Meng explained to Tania.

"Interesting. A temple right in the middle of the downtown business district," his wife commented.

"That's why they felt the need to erect the massive gates to separate the temple from this temporal world," Dai remarked.

It was late afternoon and most people were about to go home for dinner. The temple was unguarded and the group walked in. Several monks in the yard continued with their rituals, seemingly undistracted by visitors whom they must have seen every day.

"Royal Decreed Guangji Monastery," Dai read from the golden inscriptions over the stone portal.

"Was the court really involved in building this monastery?" Tania asked.

"It could have been. The court's support may take many forms, money, land, or some exclusive privilege or special gift. We will find out soon," Meng said.

Dai added, "Originally, Buddhism was a foreign import, which presented a challenge to Chinese authorities and institutions. Early Buddhists had been severely persecuted and many Buddhist temples confiscated. To secure at least some type of formal government backing was thus very important for their survival."

"Even in the form of a name?" Tania persisted.

"Yes, an honored name granted by the emperor alone would oblige assailants to think twice before attacking the temple," Dai affirmed.

"Great." Looking at the scale and layout of the structure, Dong said, "This must be one of the eight famous monasteries in the inner city of Peking. I studied at Peking University, but never had a chance to see this one before."

"Yes, Peking has so many ancient treasures, and this is just a small example. About seven hundred years ago this temple was first built in a small village then in the western suburbs of Yuan Da Du, the eastern capital of the Mongol empire, from which the modern city of Peking developed." Meng continued with the introduction as they strolled into the first courtyard of this huge Buddhist monastery.

Standing right in front of them were a bell tower to the right and a drum tower to the left, which Tania easily recognized. She had seen similar towers in several old Chinese cities. Although most of them were much bigger and taller than the ones here, Tania was able to appreciate their detailed structures because they were only two stories high. Built for a local neighborhood temple, they were the cutest pair of bell and drum towers she had ever seen.

"Are these the original buildings from the eleventh century?" she asked.

"No. They had been destroyed and rebuilt no fewer than five times, I believe," Meng responded.

"Yes, it would have been a miracle if they had survived all the frequent wars, violence, and natural disasters in the past," agreed Dong.

"Indeed. We must thank Dai Tian for her efforts in the negotiations, which allowed our troops to secure this city in one piece. Otherwise, we might not be able to see this temple today," Meng told Dai.

"And I also have Tania to thank for saving me from a life in jail," said Dai as she hugged Tania, who had become her dearest friend since her release from prison.

"Oh, please stop it! I want to know more stories about these fantastic buildings. I have been to many churches, but only a few Buddhist monasteries," Tania tried to refocus the group's attention.

"Zi-Tian, you were a Buddhist monk at one time. You tell us the stories," Meng teased his friend.

"Well, when I was as poor as a church mouse in my childhood, as the Westerners used to say, I took shelter in an abandoned monastery as a beggar. That's the extent of my Buddhist experience," Dong confessed. He seemed to be delighted to have the chance to relax and to spend time with Dai and his good friends without thinking about his heavy workload.

This "great heavenly hall," said he, was dedicated to Maitreya Buddha and his four brave and fierce-looking warrior-protectors. The first major building in a Buddhist temple, its standard size was three rooms in length and one room in width, or about ninety by twenty feet.

As they entered the hall, a surprised Dong said, "This is the most unusual Maitreya Buddha I have ever seen. Most of us are familiar with the fat-bellied Buddha, half-naked and with a broad smile on his face. A symbol of tolerance, benevolence, and good-heartedness, he was the one who would take care of the sick and the poor and who, it is said, has given us the most widely celebrated nationwide holiday—the Chinese New Year."

"This Buddha, however," continued he, "was cast in bronze, slim and fully clothed. The right leg down from the lotus base: he sat half cross-legged, unlike the ones we commonly see that are fully cross-legged. I think this bronze had captured the earlier and more authentic version of Maitreya Buddha before he was Sinicized."

"A very good point," said Meng.

"Interesting," added Dai and Tania.

The second and main courtyard had four huge pagoda trees that were at least several hundred years old. Their thick and extended canopies covered almost the entire courtyard, giving it a feeling of serenity, security, and reassurance. Several visitors were praying before a giant bronze incense burner, which stood upright almost fifteen feet tall in the middle of the four trees.

"This place reminds me of the Third College of Peking University." The beautiful layout and the tranquility of the courtyard mesmerized Dong.

"Yes, it does remind me of the western portion of the university, where you took me and Martin to see the performances," Tania agreed.

What a pleasant flashback. What a memorable moment from the distant past.

"I am sorry to hear that Martin is still interned in a hard labor camp," Dai told Tania, almost feeling guilty that she had gained her freedom.

"Don't worry. Si-Tu has told me 'things are making progress,'" Tania comforted Dai.

The main hall, called Da Xiong Dian (Hall of the Big Hero) measured one hundred feet long and fifty feet wide, said the diligent docent Dong.

"That means it's five rooms in length and three rooms in width," Tania observed.

"Exactly." Dong was delighted that Tania had quickly learned the old-fashioned Chinese way of describing the measurements of a large building.

Da Xiong Dian was decorated with statues and paintings. The place to pay tribute to Gautama Buddha, visitors would come here to pray and residential monks would burn incense all day long. Although all of the icons and images were foreign to Tania, the buffs of smoke, light fragrance, and quiet hymns reminded her of what she would encounter inside any Orthodox church. Behind the main altar, a most impressive painting was hung, from top to bottom about eighteen feet tall and thirty-four feet wide.

After talking to a monk, Meng informed the group that this painting was commissioned by Emperor Qianlong for his mother's birthday. The artist was Fuwen, who used not a brush but a finger to paint this remarkable picture. It depicted the moment when Gautama Buddha was preaching, and hundreds of different lay and mystical characters were listening. The entire drawing was sketched with a brownish color and nothing else, making it extremely simple, and yet consistently impressive and moving. It was the only painting of its kind that had survived today.

The friends were very pleased to have a chance to view this highly treasured art piece. As they moved to the third and last courtyard, they discovered that it housed the monastery's extensive manuscript collections, numbering more than one hundred thousand volumes. But it was not open to visitors.

Feeling very satisfied with the tour, they were about to turn around and leave when Meng said to them, "Did you notice something?"

"What, where?" they asked.

"Look, over there." Meng pointed to a corner of the last building in the back.

The large traditional tiled roof was lined with decorative glazed elves. Several huge and extensive pine branches stretched out to the outside beyond the courtyard's side walls.

"Oh, I know it! That must be where your house is located!" Dai yelled.

"Yes, I see. So you are the next-door neighbor to this beautiful monastery." Dong also realized the connection.

"Yes, indeed," Meng acknowledged.

"Then, you better behave. Or the Buddha will punish you if you mistreat Tania!" Dong teased his friend.

3

The two men were smart. They could see through knotty issues in seconds.

Both loved power, authority, control, duplicity, manipulation, or anything that gave them great prestige and ideological righteousness.

Both were big gamblers on strategy. They could come up with audacious schemes and intricate tactics way beyond what any of their fellow politician could imagine.

Both were ambitious. Their competitiveness, ego, drive, energy, and vanity could be overwhelming for anyone else, but never enough for themselves.

Both were ruthless. Once they had set their goals, they would strike, dispose, or kill anyone in their way. They must achieve those goals no matter the cost, even if tens of thousands of lives might perish.

Both had to win, had to be the best, and had to remain at the pinnacle of supreme leadership until the end of their careers.

Both shared all the good, bad, or necessary qualities of a zealous revolutionary. The only problem was that they were not enemies, but fervent believers in the same camp of communism.

Precisely because they shared so many of the same ideological principles and personal traits, they pretended to like each other even as they competed not only for dominance in the communist world, but also for that in international affairs.

They were lying to each other all the time. They lied in person, behind each other's back, to the media, to their own organization, to their own people, and to the general public.

This odd pair of comrades-in-arms were known to the outside world as Stalin and Sheng Bao.

Stalin never liked Sheng. By nature a headstrong demagogue, he could smell an equally strong-willed ideologue hundreds of miles away. Worse, Stalin's version of Marxism was not the same product as the one Shang had manufactured. He therefore had variously labeled Sheng an imitator, a fake, an opportunist, a pretender, and an imposter.

Suspicious of Sheng and his background, Stalin felt the pressure and threat from this rising star of a big communist party next door, who could challenge his pristine Bolshevik reputation and absolute authority that he had carefully built in the international communist movement over several decades. Stalin never believed that Sheng, a peasant farmer with some high school education and without any Comintern tutelage, could ever become a real Marxist. Stalin was particularly upset that Sheng had managed to exclude many Russian advisors and Russian-trained Chinese officials from the Chinese Communist Party's top leadership. Like General Chen, Stalin concluded, Sheng must be another militant Chinese nationalist, whom he had encountered far too often in the past.

Deep down in his heart, Stalin never considered those Chinese, communist or not, to be his equals. The national interests of the Soviet Union should always supersede those of any other nation's. In this regard Stalin had a real advantage over Sheng. As leader of a developing but still struggling country, Sheng could never claim that China's national interests were aligned with those of the international communist movement. But, as a longtime leader of the established Soviet Union and of the worldwide communist organizations, Stalin could make such a claim, which he did all the time. He could use either General Chen or Sheng or even the entire Chinese nation as his pawn on the international stage in ways the Chinese leaders, nationalist or communist, could not.

In the end, not matter how egoistic or self-confident he was, Sheng realized that he could not escape the deeply embarrassing situation of being one of Stalin's many hangers-on. Stalin had control over Sheng's fate and the future of China, not the other way round. The gulf between a developing country and a mighty superpower was too obvious to ignore; so was the great disparity between an obscure regional representative and a widely recognized international leader. As a consequence, Sheng would suffer more personal insults and psychological trauma than he had ever anticipated long after he had finally reached the pinnacle of power within his own party and within China.

Two months after the communists founded the People's Republic of China in October 1949, Sheng paid a visit to Moscow. It was the first time that he had ever set his foot in a foreign land, which proved to be such an unpleasant personal experience that he would complain about it repeatedly years later, even though the trip was publicly pronounced as a huge success in the Chinese media.

In fact, Sheng had considered visiting either the United States or Soviet Union. Stalin, after all, did not want to see the Chinese communist troops winning over the whole country. Taking the two Germanys and the two Koreas after WWII as a model, he particularly wanted Sheng to stop sending his army across the Yangtze River, which would allow General Chen's nationalist government to maintain its rule in South China while the communists could control North China. Sheng considered Stalin's divisive proposal preposterous at best and a complete sellout of his party and leadership at worst. When the nationalist government lost the capital of Nanjing to the communists and escaped to Guangzhou in the south, the Soviet embassy fled with it while the United States embassy remained in Nanjing. Sheng could read those diplomatic signs, thinking that, if Stalin could waver between him and Chen, he should be able to choose his allies too.

But Sheng's attempt to play the tantalizing power game with the American devils angered Stalin, who believed himself to be the master of such a sport. He was not about to let this affront go easily.

When Sheng's train arrived in Moscow on a frigid December day after a ten-day journey, two Soviet officials far below his rank walked up to greet him. The Chinese delegation was then escorted to an old municipal building, where a welcome ceremony was held. Only later did someone tell Sheng that the place had been used to receive insignificant foreign guests from noncommunist countries. Deeply hurt, Sheng's ordeal had only started.

On Stalin's seventieth birthday, which was the ostensible purpose of Sheng's visit, the Chinese delegation was grouped with that of the Bulgarians at the Bolshoi Theater for the celebration. Although it had been arranged according to the Russian alphabetic order, the face-conscious Chinese were not happy at all to be treated as a member of the minor league. Not even the neoclassical facade of the grand royal theater, the iconic architecture of the building, the beautifully cast quadriga, and the magnificent balconies and exquisite interior could make up for their disappointment.

Sheng took several doses of atropine to keep his head from spinning, but managed to summon his strength to praise the "great leader and teacher" Stalin. As the lavish reception and sumptuous Russian dinner went on and on, Sheng, who had been used to the simple life and rustic diet, found no pleasure in either. The fact that Stalin sat on his immediate right pleased Sheng little, for the two men barely talked to each other throughout the evening. Even the official photos of the two showed their solemn and emotionless faces; it was as if they were both attending not a birthday party but someone's funeral.

After the banquet was over, Stalin sent Sheng back to a cozy but isolated dacha, but then avoided meeting his Chinese guest for a month. The devastated Sheng was furious and threatened to leave Moscow if nothing was done. Stalin eventually received him, feeling that Sheng had by now learned his appropriate place. The Chinese delegation signed a treaty of friendship, alliance, and mutual assistance with Moscow, which tied China to the communist giant. The cost of such a partnership was enormous, as Sheng and other Chinese would soon realize. All along Stalin had held all the cards close to his chest, and China was one of them.

4

About four months after the Sino-Soviet treaty was signed, the Korean War broke out when, in an attempt to unify the country, the North Korean army invaded South Korea. A United Nations military force was immediately deployed to assist the South Koreans to repel the invaders. Knowing that the act of aggression would attract widespread international condemnation, the shrewd North Korean leader, Kim Il-Sung, had sought Stalin's prior approval before attacking the south. While watching the situation unfold from the sidelines, the calculative Stalin was not willing to commit any Russian troops to help Kim. With the Cold War in full swing, and the Soviet Union fighting for dominance in Europe and locked in a nuclear arms race with the United States, Stalin needed an armed conflict far away in Asia to divert the West's attention, but at the same time did not want to get personally embroiled in it. Instead, he correctly anticipated that Sheng, given his ego and militancy, would do the job for him by getting China involved in the Korean War.

While emboldened by the fast dismantling of General Chen's government, the proud Sheng suddenly realized that he was facing a big dilemma. He had tried long and hard to prove his loyalty to Stalin, who was now asking him to wage war against the UN forces led by the Russians' archenemy, the United States, in the Korean Peninsula. Should he refuse, all his tireless efforts to obtain Stalin's approval would be in vain. Stalin would have all the more reason to downgrade his status in the international communist movement. However, no matter how eager Sheng was to comply with Stalin's request and to prove his loyalty once again in this international crisis, most of his colleagues did not share his views. They did not think that China could afford a military adventure in Korea when the Chinese troops were still recovering from the just-ended bloody civil war. In South, Southwest, and Northwest China, fighting against the remnants of General Chen's troops, various armed resistance groups, and local bandits still continued. China badly needed a break from armed conflict to emerge from the war ruins and rejuvenate its domestic economy. Only then could it stand up on its own two feet again.

If anyone should get involved, the Politburo members suggested, it should be Stalin, who had encouraged Kim to attack South Korea in the first place.

Given the overwhelming opposition, Sheng knew that his political future, not only as a strong Chinese communist leader but also as a rising international player, was on the line. If he backed down, he would immediately be seen as a weakling, and would never be forgiven by the merciless Stalin, who had been suspicious about his true character from the start. Sheng was not about to do anything that would jeopardize his reputation in Moscow.

Thus, even though the debate was on Korea, the bottom line was whose interests should prevail—the country's or Sheng's? Against the rest of his colleagues' counsel—and against the country's interests—Sheng decided to intervene in the Korean War.

If the powerful Stalin was not willing to confront the Americans, China's involvement could be a great opportunity for him to rise on the international stage, so reasoned Shang, whose defiant ambition should never be underestimated.

5

If uncertainty, volatility, change, and drastic turnarounds had been part and parcel of all warfare, they were even more so during the first six months of the Korean War. Two days after Kim's all-out offensive across the 38th Parallel, the ill-prepared South Korean government evacuated from the capital city, Seoul. Within just two months, the deeply demoralized South Korean troops were trapped in a small area around the port of Pusan on the southeastern tip of the Korean Peninsula, where they attempted to hold the last defensive line of no more than one hundred and forty miles.

Despite the considerable assistance provided by the UN forces, even the most sympathetic observers believed that the South Koreans could not survive this frightful nightmare for long. Suddenly on September 15, 1950, U.S. General Douglas MacArthur completely reversed the situation by ordering a surprise amphibious invasion of the port of Inchon, then a little-protected small city along the coast of Northwest Korea. Effectively cutting Kim's forces and supply lines into pieces right in the middle, the daring and successful operation was followed by a series of dazzling advances. Within two weeks MacArthur's soldiers recaptured Seoul. Pyongyang, the capital of North Korea, fell into his hands in a month. Immediately afterward his troops continued to march one hundred and fifty miles further north toward the Yalu River, which was the border between North Korea and China. Retreating all the way from the south, Kim and his shattered troops could do nothing to stop the Americans except to try and save their own lives.

These outlandish actions and startling accomplishments grabbed newspaper headlines around the globe, and MacArthur boasted that the American and other UN soldiers could expect to go home by Christmas when this nuisance named the "Korean War" would be finished at the point where it had all started. Unbeknown to him and the American military intelligence, some two hundred thousand Chinese government troops (many veterans of the civil war), disguised as "volunteer soldiers," had quietly moved across the Yalu on the same night that he captured Pyongyang.

These twenty divisions of Chinese military forces hid during the day and marched in the night, totally undetected by the American and UN forces. In fact, they moved so stealthily—without using any telephones or telecommunication—that they did not know any other unit's position apart from their own. Tao Yin-Hu, their commander-in-chief, accompanied by one driver, two guards, and an aide, went so fast in his jeep that he almost ran right into the vanguard of a rapidly approaching South Korean regiment from the opposite direction.

6

Some sixty miles south into North Korean territory, the Chinese troops had eyed their first target in a small town called White Clouds.

Located atop one of the ubiquitous mountains in Northwest Korea, White Clouds controlled a critical path leading to the Chinese border along the Yalu River to the north. Behind the hills and around a river bend, it served as a forward defense area after its recent capture by South Korea's 1st Army Division—one of the advanced troops sent by MacArthur to round up all the remaining North Korean forces north of Pyongyang, and to secure a major hydraulic dam and power station on the Yalu.

Totally unaware of the danger ahead of them, the 1st Army Division ordered three battalions to leave White Clouds and move forward as planned. Two Chinese divisions had laid an ambush for the South Korean soldiers, who were completely caught off guard by the sudden attack. Even as they hurriedly put up a defense, the South Koreans thought their attackers were part of a pathetic ragtag group of defeated North Korean soldiers. Unfortunately for the South Koreans, the joint UN forces—having moved too fast and been spread too thin over the last eight weeks—had left a number of gaps along the way. One of them proved to be fatal to the three South Korean battalions, whose left wing was exposed to the enemy for a void of several miles between them and the friendly forces of the U.S. Army 24th Division.

Tao saw his chance immediately and ordered Bao Feng-Nian to lead another division to join in the kill. Piercing through the gap and encircling the South Koreans from behind, Bao's overwhelming forces, along with two other Chinese divisions, smashed and then sliced the entrapped Korean troopers into three separate sections, and the terrible slaughter began.

Desperate, the South Korean battalion officers sent out urgent calls for help. Still unclear about who the enemies were and where they came from, the commander of the U.S. Army 24th Division dispatched an infantry battalion for the rescue. Before they could even reach the site of the ambush, the American infantry battalion itself was trapped by another Chinese division under the command of Tao, who had anticipated this American reaction a few days earlier.

Absolute secrecy, stealth movement, carefully planned ambush, element of surprise, and resoluteness—these were the ingredients of their successful attacks for a force who had no superior weapons or equipment but only superiority in numbers. "To seize one enemy and to kill another on the way"— these were the common techniques the Chinese communists had perfected for years in their prolonged and treacherous civil war. Now Tao, Bao, and their fellow officers and soldiers had a chance to apply the same tactics to their new enemies.

7

What shocked military historians was not the catastrophic losses of several battalions, or the sudden disappearance of the enemy forces right after their attacks. What truly surprised them was the American military's stubborn refusal to recognize the astonishing fact that the intense combat at White Clouds was proof that tens of thousands of Chinese regular troops had entered the war.

Several captured Chinese soldiers had told their captors about the Chinese involvement in the war and some high-ranking officers of the South Korean 1st Army Division had also warned their commander of the joint forces. But MacArthur did not believe it. The legendary warrior from West Point, hero of the two world wars, the victor over Japan, the champion of the Pacific, the savior of South Korea, and the supreme commander of the UN forces, the five-star American general did not think anyone would dare to challenge him in the battlefield, where his formidable reputation alone should be enough to deter any of his potential enemies—Korean nationalists, Russian communists, and especially the poorly trained and woefully equipped Chinese guerrillas from the other side of the Yalu River. When President Harry Truman had asked him about the possibility of a Chinese military intervention ten days earlier, the proud general replied, "Then there would be the greatest slaughter."

MacArthur's arrogance was matched only by his ignorance. One month after the encounter at White Clouds, two of his field officers ordered their units to keep moving north without taking the necessary precautions—the 8th Army advanced upward along the western side of the Korean Peninsula, while the 10th Army Corps pressed on toward the Yalu along the eastern side of Korea. This one–two punch offensive strategy in the shape of a clamp would certainly destroy Kim and obliterate the North Korean forces once and for all, so the thinking went.

A perfect plan except that the Baekdu Mountain lay in the middle of the peninsula, dividing the two armies into two separate operations rather than connecting them as mutually supportive forces in one campaign.

For the moment, though, the soldiers were enjoying the warm turkey, mashed potatoes, and sweet pumpkin pies for their delicious Thanksgiving dinner before starting their scheduled march the next morning.

Then it was White Clouds all over again. With bugles blaring, a great multitude of Chinese troops struck the 8th Army only a day after it started to move. Thousands of Chinese soldiers, armed with burp guns, hand grenades, and satchel charges, swarmed the American positions. Several American units were overrun, destroyed, or fell into disarray. The Chinese communist onslaught took MacArthur and the UN forces completely by surprise and almost instantly changed the tide of the war. Soon, the 8th Army was in a headlong retreat southward.

What happened in the west did not seem to trouble the 10th Army Corps in the east. It proceeded according to a previous plan that divided the forces into two columns—one spearheaded by the 1st Marine Division to the left side of the Changjin Reservoir, and the other by the 31st Regimental Combat Team, comprising elements of the 7th Infantry Division, to the right side of the same lake. Separated by this huge body of water, the two columns had little inkling of the crisis awaiting them.

Thinly populated, the Changjin Reservoir region had the worst terrain for conducting a Western-style offensive campaign, where thick woods, tall trees, and big rocks served as ideal locations for an ambush. Poor roads, narrow bridges, winding creeks, and marshlands easily slowed down the movement of tanks, artillery, trucks, and heavy equipment, which provided Chinese foot soldiers with the perfect opportunity to catch up and confront their mechanized enemies.

After the commander of the 31st Regiment had sent out a reconnaissance platoon to scout around for nemeses in the area, none of its members returned. (All of them, it was learned later, had been either killed or captured by the Chinese troops.) The disappearance of the reconnaissance team was made worse by the fact that no landlines were set up. Radio communications between the different units were poor at best, or simply nonexistent. These untoward circumstances proved to be extremely damaging to the 31st Regiment Combat

Team, which had been hastily assembled with many components from diverse units of the army whose collaborating experience was nil.

Three Chinese divisions stormed the 1st Marine Division in the west, while one division attacked the 31st Regiment Combat Team in the east. The unsuspecting American soldiers fought back valiantly, although inadequate preparation, rugged terrain, poor communications, and bad logistics were costing them dearly. The unrelenting assaults continued through the night, when the Chinese soldiers' blowing bugles and wild screaming sounded even more terrifying than they did in the day.

The nightmare eased somewhat at sunrise, when the Chinese stopped their attacks for fear of the American air attacks. The commander of the 10th Army Corps flew in and reiterated his orders, "We're going all the way to the Yalu. Don't let a bunch of Chinese laundrymen stop you." His officers and ground troops had no choice but to keep on fighting the impossible fight.

When it all ended, the 1st Marine Division, although severely bruised, managed to break the enemy's trap, while the 31st Regiment Combat Team, after losing two of its top commanders and several hundred soldiers, was annihilated. The ambitious expedition began on a festive Thanksgiving note but ended on the coldest Christmas day in fifty years at Hungnam, the seaport on the east coast of the Korean Peninsula, where the last American foot soldier was evacuated from the battlefield. Or, as MacArthur would finally acknowledge, "this is now a totally new war in Korea."

8

Top Chinese leaders watched with trepidation the unfolding events in Korea, and were overjoyed by the latest developments of the war.

Feeling vindicated, Sheng was jubilant. A communist rebel for thirty years, his combat experiences dominated his life, which had shaped his mind more than any standard textbook on Marxism. The military victories over the nationalist government in 1949 convinced him that, if he could lead one million troops to defeat General Chen's three million, nothing else on the battleground could stop him from winning.

The initial encounters with the mighty U.S. army and the UN forces in Korea further reinforced his most cherished principles, which included a unique form of military romanticism. The politically conscious Sheng had always intended to save the oppressed, and by liberating the underdogs his military romanticism was in sync with his political ambitions. The weak force could beat a superior one, he had often insisted. Since the poor soldier's morale or his inner strength was more important than his external or material condition, concluded Sheng, man could beat weapons. More precisely, the ultimate decisive factor in the battlefield lay in people, not in any military technology or modern armaments, including the newly emerged nuclear weapons.

Furthermore, because the internal, emotional, and psychological elements were so important in warfare, propaganda would be decisively vital to mobilize the masses, assemble great armies, ensure their unity, focus their attention on their singular tasks, and maintain their fighting spirit and self-confidence. War would always incur sacrifices and lead to ruins. But, any cost would be worth it for the sake of the ultimate victory, no matter how high the price might be and no matter how devastating it might look for the moment, , including the losses of territory, possessions, and human lives.

And, last but not least, no one could see the ultimate victory better than the Communist Party, no one could design the best strategy to achieve the ultimate victory better than the party's central leadership, and no one among the top party leaders had the best insights and unparalleled experience to formulate that strategy better than Sheng himself. Thus in the fighting against either General Chen's nationalist troops or the U.S.-led UN forces or any domestic or foreign enemy, the absolute belief in communism, the absolute obedience to the party's leadership, and, most important, the absolute trust in Sheng's vision and strategy must be unconditional and absolutely necessary for any successful military campaigns.

When Sheng reviewed the recent military actions in Korea, he saw no reason not to conclude that his whole career had best exemplified this truism. To believe in him was to believe in the ultimate success of the party, no matter what powerful enemy the party was facing. To follow Sheng's leadership every step of the way was tantamount to marching toward the final and most glorious triumph of the Chinese revolution and perhaps even that of worldwide communism.

From the recent events in Korea, Sheng had also learned a great deal. Even if he were faced with overwhelming opposition from his closest colleagues, he could somehow still pull it off. He won and the whole country did not know a thing about how the Korean War started or why China had to get involved in the first place. And it proved to be an extraordinarily successful propaganda campaign and an extraordinarily successful personal gamble in his political career. His position, power, and prestige had been consolidated to such a degree that no one in the party, not even the majority of its top leaders, could force him to change his opinions. Once he had set his mind on something, his decision would be the party's policy. His determination would set the course and everyone else must follow. A victorious start at first sight but a precarious path to take from the beginning.

9

Less sanguine and upbeat was Tao Yin-Hu, who had seen first-hand the dark side of the Chinese campaign and the unprecedented carnage of the military conflict in Korea.

"Congratulations on your victories!" Sheng warmly greeted Tao as the latter walked into the Chairman's new office and residence called the Garden of Lilacs in the finest courtyard in the beautiful imperial compound Abundance.

"I am afraid that there is not much to congratulate." The commander-in-chief sounded less chirpy than Sheng.

The last engagement had cost a staggering seventy-five thousand casualties, or about one-third of the total forces under Tao's command. His 9th Army Corps of one hundred and fifty thousand men on the east front, for example, confronted the U.S. 10th Army's one hundred thousand men in the Changjin Reservoir region. The 9th Corps had trapped the U.S. 1st Marine Division of twenty-five thousand men, and was able to penetrate and break it into several sections. Yet, for the next two weeks, three armies of the 9th Corps could not defeat the 1st Marine Division, whose superior weapons and firepower ensured that the entrenched marines were largely unharmed. Despite the intense fighting for another two weeks, the 1st Marine Division broke away and withdrew safely to Hamhung and its port city of Hungnam, a major supply center on the east coast of North Korea some seventy miles south of the Changjin Reservoir.

Tao recounted, "At one point, my soldiers from the 9th Corps blew up a major bridge to block the marines' retreat, only to see the bridge repaired overnight. They blew it up again, and the same thing happened the next day. The soldiers finally blew up the entire foundation and supporting columns of the bridge. Two days later, the American air force lifted a prefabricated bridge from Japan and dropped it to the site. The marine engineers quickly set it up and our soldiers could only watch, in total amazement, the 1st Marine Division crossing the new bridge unscathed.

"At Hamhung, five divisions of the 9th Corps attacked the city repeatedly for nine days to no avail. Our light weapons and inferior firepower simply could not penetrate the city or its port; both were protected by heavy bombings and artillery of the enemy forces from land, sea, and air in the surrounding areas. In the end, the 1st Marine Division and several other units pulled off their most successful evacuation. As many as one hundred and five thousand combat personnel, including several thousand of the wounded, seventeen thousand vehicles, three hundred and fifty thousand tons of military equipment and supplies, plus ninety-eight thousand Korean civilians, were shipped out from Hungnam on nearly two hundred vessels; all the while we simply had no means to stop them. The rest of the food, medicine, supplies, and heavy equipment, which the Americans could not carry with them, were blown up right before the eyes of our soldiers, who desperately needed them but were utterly powerless to save them from the massive explosions and scorching fires," Tao continued at length.

"So, what are you saying?" Sheng's smile disappeared. He had quietly started smoking while listening to Tao's report.

"We must have better equipment, better weapons to continue the fight. We need more and much-improved military support in all areas than what we have now, such as ammunition, new weapons, better medical service, better transportation, better air cover, and stronger artillery support," Tao stated. "Patriotism and the revolutionary spirit are important. But they are not enough to defeat the enemy, who are armed to the teeth. We have lost too many brave soldiers who were using ridiculously outdated Japanese Type 38 rifles against carbines, hand grenades against tanks, and 122mm howitzer against 155mm field guns. This simply cannot continue!" Tao proclaimed.

The self-conceited and complacent Sheng was not prepared to hear this torrent of criticism, complaints, and gripes. He remained silent and kept on smoking.

Tao went on. "We must also have much better food supplies, warm clothing, tents, shoes, blankets, sleeping bags, medicine, doctors, trucks, and transportation vehicles. Thousands, yes, thousands of our soldiers froze to death. Hundreds of thousands of them suffered hunger, cold, and malnutrition. Hundreds of them had to sleep in the snow for days on end. Hundreds of them did not have a warm meal for weeks, and only survived on frozen potatoes. Tens of hundreds could not receive prompt and proper medical care when they were wounded, and hundreds of them—yes, hundreds of them—died as a result."

"So, what should we do?" Sheng had to ask a question to break up the depressing conversation.

"You know the old saying as much as anyone else, 'Before moving your troops, provide them with supplies.' I strongly suggest that we speed up our military and civilian production to support the war. I also strongly suggest that the leadership in Northeast China be strengthened to take full charge of this endeavor, since they are right next door to North Korea across the Yalu."

"How can we do that?" Sensing Tao had more on his mind, Sheng asked again.

"I think Dong Zi-Tian would be the best choice for the role," Tao replied.

Sheng seemed to have known that this would be coming. The ever-suspicious Lin had informed the Chairman that Tao was getting unusually close to Dong. Not long ago, he, Dong, and Dai visited Meng and Tania, ostensibly to attend their baby's "drawing the lot" ceremony. Sources said that they had a "very good time" together.

Sheng did not respond to Tao's suggestion immediately but picked up another cigarette.

"After the Japanese surrender, Dong led the reconstruction in Northeast China, which provided the best civilian and military support in our fight against Chen. I think he will do great this time again, if given the chance," Tao said and then discreetly waited for Sheng to respond.

Any personnel decision regarding the senior party leadership was a highly sensitive matter, especially when it pertained to the very top post in the northeastern region, which had become the backbone of China's industrial and agricultural bases under the new communist government since the end of the civil war.

Sheng clearly understood the economic significance and the military implications of Tao's recommendation. What he was thinking went far beyond that. What if Dong succeeded again? Would he become too powerful in the party again? What if he did bounce back and started to outshine others? What if…

The Chairman cut short his train of his thoughts and said to Tao, "Okay, let's assign Dong to take charge of this important task."

Chapter 34

Reconstruction

1

WITH THE OPPORTUNITY AND AUTHORITY GIVEN TO HIM, DONG Zi-Tian not only fulfilled his mission but also exceeded all expectations.

Before they left for Korea, the Northeast had provided Tao Yin-Hu's troops with two thousand, six hundred rifles, five hundred artillery pieces, two hundred trucks, four thousand barrels of fuel, and two thousand horses. A special command center and three transport routes were established to ensure the supplies would reach soldiers in the battlefront. Working day and night, as many as six thousand personnel were tasked with transporting the supplies, ammunition, and equipment to the war zone. For the first few months of the fighting, one hundred and seventy thousand tons of food, four hundred tons of cooking oil, nine hundred and twenty tons of dried vegetables, more than two billion bullets, nearly six million, seven hundred thousand rounds of ammunition, two hundred and ninety thousand barrels of gasoline, and two hundred and seven tons of medicine were shipped across the Yalu River.

But Dong knew these supplies were still not enough. He could see how badly Tao and his soldiers needed faster and better support while fighting against an overwhelmingly powerful, well-organized, and superbly equipped enemy force.

Reversing the national trend of demobilization at the end of the civil war, Dong expanded the regional military factories from five to twenty, which comprised a workforce of four hundred and twenty thousand, or about one-half of all the skilled employees of the military industry in China at the time. They repaired three hundred airplanes, two thousand, four hundred engines, and three thousand cannons during the first two years, in addition to making tons of other weapons and munitions.

Realizing from combat reports that tanks and armored vehicles presented one of the worst threats to soldiers, Dong ordered service engineers and technicians to come up with a solution in three months. The result was the Chinese 57mm and 90mm rocket launchers, derived from the captured U.S. "bazooka" rocket launchers.

But, more than weapons and supplies, Dong clearly understood that, without a solid industrial foundation, no one could win in this modern warfare. Only a well-developed economy could produce the real military might Tao's army needed to face the American and UN forces.

A no-nonsense leader, Dong implemented several measures that quickly ramped up industrial production. As one of the most senior veterans of the communist organization who had long been marginalized, he appreciated the second chance to prove his loyalty to the party and to demonstrate to his friends that he had not been beaten. He was still the vigorous, gifted, creative, upbeat, and daring individual who was never afraid of any challenges.

He formed the Economic Council of the Northeast, which had broad powers to decide on major economic and financial policies in the region. As its director, Dong mobilized the whole party apparatus to focus on how to raise industrial productivity and agricultural output of the five provinces (later merged into three) in the Northeast. He had a clear goal in mind: to bring to the levels of production, trade, and consumption to new historical heights in three years.

Dong knew full well the importance of trading in economic life, and turned his region's proximity to the Soviet Union to his advantage. The Russians loved the produce, grain, foodstuff, tea, cloths, furs, shoes, and minerals from China. Dong secured a trading agreement with the Soviet government and ordered the opening of all the border towns for trade. His strategy was to exchange local farm and handicraft products for manufactured goods, and the revenues generated from trading would be used immediately to buy heavy machinery or equipment, and to improve the transportation facilities and industrial infrastructure of the region.

Rich soil, adequate sunshine, and plenty of precipitation had made Northeast China famous for its high-quality wheat, soybeans, sorghum, corn, potatoes, beets, rapeseed, and hemp. Widespread land reforms and drastically reduced farm taxes lowered the burdens of the farmers, whose productive energy propelled the regional agricultural production to a new historical high in two years. Tons of grain and other farm products fed the urban population, supported a large segment of the Chinese troops, and generated an unprecedented amount of trade and foreign currency surplus, the likes of which the region had not seen for decades. Similarly, consumer expenditure rose threefold, and regional gross domestic product increased one hundred and seventy percent.

As an organization largely composed of rural members, however, the party had little experience in managing large-scale industries, even though some party officials were familiar with old-fashioned agrarian production, trade, and handicraft. Dong decided to learn from the Russians.

He invited Russian expert advisors and technical personnel to assist him, and greatly admired the Soviet model of a planned economy with a strong emphasis on heavy industries. He disagreed with those colleagues who thought a communist-owned factory should be run by a team of party officials who were no experts in factory work. He strongly insisted that the factory head— the most experienced and knowledgeable professional of the production line— should be in full charge of all the industrial operations, which was the standard practice in the Soviet Union.

The Korean War stimulated the economic growth and industrialization process in the Northeast. Its increased industrial capacity and robust agricultural productivity led China's efforts in supporting her troops in Korea. No fewer than one hundred and fifteen thousand tons of munitions alone were shipped to the front lines in the first fourteen months of the war. Tens of millions of civilians contributed time, money, and manpower to the war effort, and no fewer than two hundred thousand local residents of the Northeast went across the Yalu as noncombatant transporters, cooks, stretcher carriers, guards, nurses, and caretakers to assist their fellow countrymen fighting in Korea.

2

Sheng Bao could not understand why Tao did not seem to be keen to launch another offensive, building on the momentum of the communists' success in the initial campaign.

Four years ago, the communist troops were able, in a few months, to decimate twenty-five brigades of General Chen Han's forces, or as many as thirty thousand men. Now Sheng saw no reason why Tao should hesitate when asked to annihilate only "ten to twenty thousand U.S. and puppet troops" in a new offensive. "More troops are not really needed," he wired Tao, "until the final decisive campaign."

Whereas the sudden and early Chinese intervention greatly surprised General Douglas MacArthur, the laudable performance of the Chinese military greatly encouraged Kim Il-Sung, who desperately wanted to restore his government. Still dreaming of a fully unified country under his rule, he cajoled Sheng into joining hands so that they could drive the American and UN forces out of the Korean Peninsula altogether. Sheng shared Kim's goal, which was buttressed by his unwavering conviction that the "subjective" element in war was more powerful than the "objective." He had already shocked the Americans and impressed Stalin, and was persuaded by Kim's flattery. Why not push the envelope? From what Sheng could observe so far into the war, the heavily armed Americans had a lot of steel but little spirit. China could certainly win the war because its poorly equipped troops were the exact opposite—little steel but a lot of spirit. The confident Sheng had no doubt that the Chinese "spirit" could triumph over the American "steel."

"If our forces spend the entire winter resting and reorganizing," Sheng warned Tao, "it would cause the capitalist countries to speculate about our intentions and cause the friendly nations to distrust us." Winning another offensive, he emphasized, would "strike a new blow at the imperialists." Under pressure and unable to persuade the Chairman to change his mind, Tao had no choice but to move ahead with Sheng's plan. Hoping to secure an even greater numerical advantage over the enemies, he increased the size of his forces by sixty percent with the deployment of six additional army units. The total number of his soldiers rose to nearly half a million men divided into forty-eight divisions, up from thirty. He then directed his officers to plan for the next phase of the conflict.

3

The car, sent by Si-Tu, fetched Tania and Meng from their home on a cool early-spring evening. It made a left-hand turn at the intersection of Xisi and proceeded straight to the east. Few residents in Peking owned a car, and most of them used a bicycle for commuting. Except for a few municipal buses, the streets were largely empty and the city was already in a sleeping mode at dusk. Very few stores would remain open after dark, and bars and the nightlife were nonexistent.

Still noticeable under the twilight were the large slogans posted on many walls along the streets, stating "Fight against the U.S. and Defend China," "Support the Brave Soldiers of Our Chinese Volunteers' Army," "Long Live the People's Republic of China," and "Long Live the Chinese Communist Party!" No pedestrian could possibly miss these slogans, written in the stern-looking and four-squared ideographic characters, each of which, brush-painted in rich black ink, was as big as a sizable pumpkin.

Writing slogans and putting them up for public display were commonplace in China, made popular by the mass movements the Communist Party had frequently engaged in both rural and urban areas. Sponsored by different businesses, work units, or individuals, they were the first signs that a significant public campaign was underway. The party's propaganda department would issue specific guidelines to all factories, stores, schools, and villages, which, led by the party's local branch offices, would respond immediately by posting those big-character slogans in the public domain to demonstrate how faithful they were to the party's call and how enthusiastic they were in supporting the official policies.

The implicit competition among the sponsors to demonstrate their loyalty and commitment notwithstanding, slogan writing and posting could also be a spectacular demonstration of public art. Walking through the streets was like visiting a grand museum, and the ancient writing techniques had been aptly transformed into the most inexpensive tools of instant propaganda and fast dissemination. To grab the visitors' attention, some of the exhibits demonstrated their splendid skills of calligraphy, churning out the stupendous characters with prodigious energy and sensational outpourings. Some competed by size and stretched each individual character to more than six feet tall, standing upright like a row of young warriors lining up for their daily inspection. Those who had neither calligraphy talent nor massiveness to show employed a great variety of colors and shapes of the papers, which rendered the ongoing messages as fun to browse through as it was pleasant to read them.

In less than ten minutes, the car made a right-hand turn and soon disappeared behind a big ornamental gate to the left with a huge national emblem on the imposing portal. This broad and quiet tree-lined street was the west entrance of the party and central government's giant compound Abundance. Protected by twenty-foot-high by five-foot-thick gray walls and guarded by armed sentries round the clock, the place was as mysterious to any out-of-towners as to the nearby residents.

A few hundred yards to the immediate left from the gate, the office and residence of Si-Tu Wen-Liang, now the new government's first premier, occupied the northwest corner of the compound. The car stopped at the door of the courtyard house named Pavilion of White Garlands.

The garden of a Qing Dynasty prince, the courtyard was not the top choice of residence in Abundance. Broken tiles, discoloration, and falling paints appeared everywhere, and the building looked old and decrepit. In fact, Si-Tu had lived in the Garden of Lilacs before Sheng, whose residence was then in the suburbs of Peking. After the Chairman finally decided to move into Peking's inner city, Si-Tu's sharp instincts told him that he'd better yield the best place in Abundance to the most powerful man in the party and country.

With a sizable courtyard in front and another in the back, the Pavilion of White Garlands, when the repairs were done, was not a bad choice at all. Having housed the State Council and the municipal administration of Peking under the old regime, the compound continued to serve the new government by providing no fewer than a dozen rooms at the sides, protecting the main office in the backyard, and giving the new premier all the security and tranquility needed to carry out his duties.

Si-Tu's wife Hong Shi-Mei came out, greeting, "How are you? So good to see you both." She shook the couple's hands warmly and took Tania and Meng into the reception room.

A southern belle of considerable charm, the stylish Hong was as much a narcissist as some middle-aged women could be. Deeply concerned with her image in public, the first question she always asked in the morning was how she looked. She believed that, as the premier's wife, she had the huge responsibility of maintaining the dignity of her husband's office. Because of her low-ranking status within the organization, the party had assigned her no more task than to take care of Si-Tu's domestic life. This, however, would not stop her from assuming a greater self-importance.

"How do I look?" she asked Tania, whose opinions about makeup and beauty Hong took most seriously, even though the Russian rarely wore any makeup.

"You look marvelous today," said Tania as she would always do whenever the two met.

"Don't you think that I have gained some weight?" Hong asked again.

"No, nonsense. Not at all! You look just like the same young girl I first met twenty years ago," Tania insisted, even as she felt embarrassed that she had now acquired the Chinese trait of obsequiousness.

"Oh, I am sorry. Wen-Liang is having a meeting and he will be a few minutes late. Please sit down. Tea?" Hong turned to direct a servant to get the drinks.

4

Crossing the 38th Parallel into South Korean territory and, in particular, the seizure of Seoul left the Chinese leaders in Peking dizzy with success. *The People's Daily*, the official organ of the Communist Party, issued an editorial claiming, "The recovery of Seoul had proven once again the invincibility of the Chinese Volunteers' Army. The absolute superiority of U.S. air, tank and artillery forces has been proven useless in both the defensive and offensive battles against the great Chinese and North Korean troops."

Determined to drive the enemy out to the sea, Sheng wanted to conclude the war quickly and pushed for a new round of offensive, which deeply troubled Tao. He told the field officers, "They only pay attention to our success in the battlefield and have no idea of the price we had to pay or the difficulties we faced."

In a series of telegrams to the Chairman in Peking, Tao reported that, after three offensive operations in a row during the last several months, his troops had been stretched to the limit. "We are still inferior to the enemy in terms of equipment and technology," he said. "Our troops are experiencing combat fatigue and serious shortage of food, ammunition, medicine, and other supplies. Most of all, without air support, our greatly extended transportation lines are under constant and severe attacks by enemy bombs and airplanes. Large casualties have reduced our combat capacity and the recruitment and training of young soldiers will take time. We are suffering from an acute shortage of manpower, which had only been our advantage not too long ago.

"The enemies," the commander continued, "still have a well-equipped force of two hundred and thirty thousand men in their established defensive positions. They enjoy much shorter supply lines and maintain tremendous mobility, provided by mechanized transportation and protected by heavy artillery. They have also learned our strategies from the recent battles and have changed their tactics accordingly in their offensive campaigns. To prevent us from separating their troops through any gaps, they had been advancing slowly side by side to keep in constant contact with one another and not to allow any unit to move too far ahead of others. Thus they were able to provide better mutual support to their units now than the past, making our efforts to isolate any of them more difficult than just a month ago."

Tao added, "We have long lost the secrecy and surprise element we had had in the early stages of the war. Hiding the movement of any large troops is no longer possible. The narrowness of the Korean Peninsula and its mountainous terrain further reduce the chances of long-distance and large-scale maneuvers that, no matter how well designed and cleverly disguised, will be detectable by the enemy's reconnaissance abilities and advanced intelligence-collecting technology.

"If we do want to wage another offensive," Tao insisted, "I will need more reinforcements and my soldiers will definitely need time to rest, resupply, and reorganize. It may take at least two to three months for my troops to be combat ready."

Sheng was not pleased to hear Tao's rambling, not pleased at all. According to his estimation, a clear victory over the U.S. and UN forces would be ideal. Nothing would prove his prowess and greatness more than a decisive battle that would drive the enemy out of the Korean Peninsula once and for all. If that were unattainable, some offensive that could annihilate a large number of enemy forces could also prove his brilliance, suggesting that "men" could indeed beat "weapons." Tao must be getting old and timid. He had missed the best opportunity to destroy the enemy, and his hesitance allowed the enemy to recuperate.

Sheng believed that he had given Tao more than enough chances and options to win the war. But the latter was not willing to listen, and instead was making all kinds of complaints in every communication. Combat fatigue, time out, supplies, equipment, protection, and all the rest. Where was his energy? Where was his vision? Where was the amazing courage, imagination, and creativity that he used to possess?

Sheng was seriously thinking of replacing Tao. But he had no suitable candidate for the position. Most of the military's top brass remained lukewarm about the war, and Tao was one of the handful senior officers whom Sheng had to rely on.

For the moment, Sheng concluded that he'd better listen to Tao and try to persuade him to hold on to the 38th Parallel as a last resort. Never would Sheng allow the enemy to recapture Seoul and cross the line.

Thus decided, Sheng wired Tao, urging him to come back to Peking to plan for the next phase of action.

5

"Ha, ha! Look who is here!" The characteristic laughter of Si-Tu Wen-Liang hit them as Tania and Meng were about to have their first sip of tea.

In walked Si-Tu and Martin!

Even though Meng and Tania had been informed about this meeting, Tania still felt overwhelmed and began to cry uncontrollably.

So many years had separated the two, and so many happy, regrettable, sad, and yet precious memories.

They walked toward each other, held hands and looked into each other's eyes.

Too many past encounters raced through their minds. About the big stairs where they ran into each other in the Kremlin? The first cup of coffee they drank together? The first moment Martin laid his eyes on Tania?

Or the letter they had composed together to send to the Comintern? The first peek Tania had of Martin with another woman?

The treacherous journeys on the Long March? Or the backbreaking toil in the cold, hard labor camps in Siberia?

But the past was now past and it was better to let it pass.

"Shall we sit down and have dinner?" Si-Tu suggested.

"Yes, yes. Let's sit down and eat," agreed his wife, Hong, who took the opportunity to explain. "In this wartime austerity, Wen-Liang has paid for this meal, and will not charge the government a cent even though this is part of his official duty."

"You don't have to mention it, Shi-Mei. All of us have been good friends for decades, haven't we?" Si-Tu looked at Tania, Martin, and Meng, and they all nodded heartily.

The hot meal soon eased the initial awkwardness.

"How is Peter?" Martin asked Tania.

"Oh, he is quite a handsome man now. The Red Scare McCarthy created has forced the university to suspend his teaching position in Albany. So he has returned to Amsterdam to manage Max's farm. He is doing okay, but poor Max has unfortunately passed away. A rough but very kind man," Tania said.

"What's your plan next?" she asked cautiously, saddened to see his evidently shrunken body and the loss of the sheen of his youth and energy.

"I think I will go back to Rotterdam," Martin responded. "I heard that you have adopted a baby girl."

"Yes, yes. Her name is Meng Xi, which means rare and precious." Tania's face lit up, talking about the girl. "She crawled to pick up an abacus when she was a year old. And now she can stand up and run. Would you believe it?"

"How do you like your new position?" Tactfully redirecting the conversation, the ever-anxious Si-Tu turned to Meng, noticing that childless Hong was not thrilled about the topics of children or child-rearing.

"I like it. In fact, I like it very much," Meng replied in all honesty. A man of his experience and seniority, he was surely qualified to hold just about any top position in the new government. Yet, because he had seriously offended Sheng, he was appointed to head an obscure bureau of translations.

But, as someone with no ego and desire to have a high profile or power, Meng was truly contented with what he was doing. With fewer administrative responsibilities, he was having a lot of time to read and think about the issues he would prefer to focus on.

"Good. Really good to hear it. But, as I have told you, do let me know anytime if you need my help." Si-Tu then turned to Martin.

"I know you have decided to go back to Rotterdam, a choice I respect. But keep in touch and do come and visit us when you have the time." Si-Tu hugged Martin warmly. The two men began to get emotional as they embraced each other.

"Before you go, though, I would like to present you with this gift as a small token on behalf of the Chinese Communist Party and the Chinese government, to thank you for your many significant contributions to the Chinese revolution."

Si-Tu, followed by the others, took Martin to a nearby table and opened a delicately carved wooden case.

In the case was a pair of two big shining plates made of the finest blue-and-white Chinese porcelain they had ever seen.

When Martin looked at the smooth, bright, and exquisite ceramic plates, he could not hold back his tears, murmuring, "Thank you, thank you so much for such a beautiful gift. I am truly honored. This is absolutely the most splendid blue-and-white ceramic I have ever seen in my life!" he told Si-Tu.

Then Martin turned to the rest and explained, "You see, the plate on the right depicts the St. Lawrence Church in Rotterdam in its full glory of the past, while the plate on the left depicts the same but dreadfully bombed St. Lawrence Church standing alone in the totally demolished downtown Rotterdam after the Nazis' 1940 Blitz."

"Well, tell us the stories," the premier said, as the others nodded to express their interest.

As if taking a stroll down the hometown alleys of his youth, Martin started, "St. Lawrence Church has been the most prominent landmark in Rotterdam for three centuries. Inspired by the New Church of our neighbor Delft, which can be seen in a rare landscape painting by the Delft native Johannes Vermeer, the church was constructed on a standard platform in the shape of an elongated cross facing the west."

"Although a Gothic church in style, it has followed the native Dutch tradition and possesses a more frugal exterior than those grand Catholic cathedrals. Look, it does not have the traceries and window planes as intricate as those found in Notre-Dame. Nor does it have any statues and figurines so eminently featured in the Chartres Cathedral. Rising almost three hundred feet high, it is a simple but dignified church with a plain brick facade and a single public entrance in the front. Looking from the above, it is a typical cross-shaped building. With the north and south transepts, the two-hundred-foot nave to the west and the massive ambulatory to the east formed a perfect cross, where a turret sits in the middle of the roof."

"The church looks somehow truncated," said Meng.

"Yes, you are right," Martin replied. "The church never built a spire and its bell tower has a disastrous history. Originally a wooden structure for a fifth floor, it collapsed many years later and was never raised again. Now the top fourth floor serves as the bell tower."

"The last time I saw this great church in one piece," continued Martin, "was in the painting by Hendrik Johannes (Jan Hendrik) Weissenbruch. Although he was better known for his watercolors and rural landscapes, his early painting of the St. Lawrence Church was perhaps the best record we ever had about the church exteriors since the church has become a shadow of itself after the war."

"The church still looks massive," Tania commented.

"Yes. Measuring five hundred feet long and two hundred and fifty feet wide, it has remained the largest public structure in Rotterdam," Martin said.

"What a pity. What a beautiful church! And look at the damage: it's real sad," said Tania, as she and Meng compared the two plates depicting the same church under completely different circumstances.

"I am deeply impressed and moved that the Chinese craftsmen have captured the magnificent medieval building so well. Look at its beautiful lines and details here. And look at the depiction of all the rubbish and wreckage around it—this church is now the only sixteenth-century building left in the city after the war." Martin was again choked with emotion.

"I am confident that the people of Rotterdam will rebuild the St. Lawrence Church. This great church and its full glory shall be restored in no time." Si-Tu comforted Martin, shaking his hand and patting him on the back.

6

He was furious. For the last several days Tao had met with various officials in Peking, telling them his needs on the battlefront. Everyone was warm, cordial, attentive, and polite, but nobody gave him a clear answer as how to fulfill those needs. They said they would report his requests to their bosses, they would deliberate as soon as they received the instructions from their bosses, and they would do their best to meet his demands. But nobody could tell him exactly when and how any of his needs would be fulfilled.

Tao went to see Vice President Song Pei, who was second only to Sheng in the government's chain of command. Song immediately called the premier, telling him that the commander-in-chief was in town, and would need his assistance.

Putting down the phone, Song said to Tao, "The premier and his assistants will see you at the meeting hall of the Central Military Commission in one hour."

"Another meeting? Another place? Why is the bureaucracy here more damned complex than the logistics in Korea?" The commander stormed out.

It took twenty minutes for Tao's driver to find out where the meeting hall was, for the party's military commission had several offices spread across the city. Coming out of the Abundance compound, heading north and then east, the driver finally dropped Tao off at the place called Three Gates, where the meeting hall was.

The roomful of high-ranking officials and generals stood up to welcome Tao, shaking his hand and calling him the "war hero." He shrugged it off and announced impatiently, "Our soldiers are bleeding. They are using their bodies to protect the nation, facing the overwhelming firepower of the enemy. I can't let this continue, nor can you. Here is what I need. I need more divisions, more weapons, more food, more uniforms and warm clothing, more air support, more artillery, more tanks, more medical units, more surgical instruments and medicine, more nurses, more mobile tents, more rear support service, more supplies, more trucks, and more equipment. And you must let me know right here and now when I can get them!"

Silence. The dumbfounded participants in the hall did not know how to respond to the stern Tao, whose grim statements diametrically contradicted what the official media had told them every day.

Si-To, who knew it was his responsibility to reduce the tension in the room, stood up and said, "Comrade Tao Yin-Hu is our most experienced and most revered general. What he said is highly important and every department in our administration shall fully support the war efforts. Now, looking at the list of his requests, who will speak first?"

The Korean War had put a tremendous burden on the nation. As the premier who controlled all the county's economic data, Si-Tu knew better than anyone else about China's actual economic and military strengths and weaknesses. But he preferred not to say "yes" or "no" immediately. He would rather allow the department heads to present their views first before he would proceed any further. He understood that many departments had tried their best to meet the demands of the war. But China had just ended its own civil war, which had destroyed much of the country's economic capacity. Hunger, poverty, social unrest, and natural disasters still haunted the nation, which had not had a strong industrial infrastructure to begin with.

"Shortage of manpower is a serious problem for both the army and civilians," one provincial head stated. "In my region, tens of thousands of young men have been recruited by the army, and women, children, the weak-bodied, and the elderly have to pick up the slack in the fields."

"In the cities, however, things are not that easy," a head of an urban department continued. "Training new employees will take time, and productivity will be affected once many skilled workers are redeployed for weapons production."

"We have supported the war in Korea by providing the best weapons we have in our units under my command," said a high-ranking military officer. "That is, at the expense of reducing the defense capacity of the troops in my military region."

"We lack the ability to produce trucks and mobile vehicles. To put it bluntly, we don't have the technology, facilities, skills, and experienced workforce to manufacture any trucks and mobile vehicles; we can only repair some of them," declared the head of transportation.

"Our railroad workers have been working around the clock to make sure the supply lines move smoothly. But the enemy's heavy bombardment has given us a lot of problems, such as stoppage, delays, and widespread damage. But we have tried out best to overcome those difficulties and to ensure our soldiers receive what they need," the railroad department reported.

"If we can't produce all the weapons, artillery, airplanes, equipment, and ammunitions, why can't we buy them from someone else?" one official asked.

"We are buying them already," the head of trade and finance department responded. "Despite our extremely limited foreign currency reserves, we are purchasing as many weapons as we can. The Western countries certainly will not sell any military equipment to us. We have to buy them from the Russians. Believe me, they are not cheap. Nor would I recommend sustaining a war by buying military supplies from others. The daily cost of this war is enormous. The number of munitions alone, including bullets, artillery shells, explosives, and cartridges, is in the millions, and we have not even included the cost of heavy weapons, airplanes, transportation, and medical supplies."

The meeting went on for another three hours without any clear conclusion, and Tao's heart sank further by the minute.

Back in his hotel, the tormented Tao tossed and turned in bed all night, searching for a solution.

Unlike the military struggles against Chen in the past, the challenges of the current campaign in Korea were far too many, and the cost far too staggering. The enemy forces had absolute air and naval superiority, and their firepower had prevented Tao's troops from capturing their heavy equipment. The most visible disparity was the poor weapons of the Chinese infantry soldiers, whose rifles came in all shapes and sizes. Still using a great variety of guns left by the Japanese in World War II, provided by the Russians, or captured from the U.S. and UN forces, the Chinese troops needed different supplies of guns and munitions for different models made in different eras with different sizes and calibers. This single complexity presented a huge problem to the rear support service and its various transportation units. Confusing directives, mismatches between demand and supply, and low stockpiles frequently delayed the combat readiness of the soldiers on the battlefront.

Even with their clear superiority in numbers, Tao's poorly armed soldiers had not been able to overrun a U.S. unit above the level of a battalion. At one point, they did defeat three battalions, which amounted to a regiment. They even killed the regiment officer and captured the regiment flag. But the three battalions belonged to two different regiments, which, strictly speaking, did not mean that they had totally annihilated a standard regiment in its full capacity. Even when facing a single U.S. battalion, the poorly equipped Chinese troops would have a very hard time defeating the enemies despite their overwhelming numbers.

The U.S. and UN forces still had at least twenty-five infantry divisions alone (not counting their artillery and mechanized units), and annihilating any one of them would not be as easy as Sheng and Kim Il-Sung had predicted.

Tens of thousands of Chinese soldiers had died in the last few engagements. Nearly half of them died not in combat but because of cold, starvation, diseases, frostbites, and wounds that were not treated properly and immediately.

These serious problems of weapons, equipment, and supplies had to be corrected before Tao and his field officers could launch the next offensive. But these problems were not properly understood back home.

Tao did not return to Peking simply to ask for more of everything. He needed to change the outdated views of the Chinese leaders on how to conduct modern warfare in a foreign land.

He woke up his driver at daybreak and ordered to be taken to Abundance. He must see Sheng, the only one who could reverse the situation.

When the car stopped at the Garden of Lilacs, a guard said to them, "The Chairman has just gone to bed, and no one can disturb him."

"I know the Chairman has the habit of working in the night and sleeping during the day. But this is a military emergency. I must see him right away," Tao explained.

"The Chairman has just taken some sleeping pills. He can't be disturbed. He would not be able to talk even if—" the guard insisted.

That did it. So angry was Tao that he shoved the guard aside and pushed the door wide open.

The next second, he was in the middle of the yard, yelling at the top of his lungs, "Sheng Bao, get up, get up! My soldiers are dying! I must talk to you!"

7

The idea of a picnic in the suburbs greatly pleased Yan, whose lovely image of spring had been ruined by the terrible daily winds and dust flying everywhere in Peking. Normally in the south at this time of the year, ordinary villagers could enjoy the first picks of green tea and the first crops of delicate vegetables of the new season. Here in the capital city in the north, the low clouds and gray skies were as depressing as wintertime, and the outdoor frosty air almost suffocated her. Worst, the smells of animal dung in the streets mixing with rotten airborne dirt, partially burned gasoline from buses, and fluttering coal powder and wasted wood ashes from the alleys had become so nauseating for Yan that she desperately wanted to escape from the city.

Meng Xi was equally excited as she watched Yan prepare the picnic goodies, especially the delicious pickled eggs and homemade sausages that were usually available only during weekends and holidays.

Everything sounded good and looked good until Yan learned that Tania had invited Dong Zi-Tian and Dai Tian to come.

"I thought it was going to be a family picnic," Yan grumbled.

"It *is* a family picnic. Dong, Dai, and we are a family, aren't we?" Tania said.

Yan's discomfort, however, vanished as soon as the team arrived at Cherry Valley, fifteen miles northwest of the city. A lesser known scenic location outside Peking, where the Forbidden City, Great Wall, Summer Palace, and dozens of famous royal sites and ancient parks attracted vacationers and tourists from near and far, Cherry Valley had remained under the radar, where only some informed local residents would visit occasionally.

Lined with cherries, peaches, apricots, dates, apples, and persimmons, the whole valley was an enormous orchard beaming under the pleasant spring sunshine and blanketed in blossoms. Hot pink was the color of the cherry flowers, rose the peaches, white the apricots, green the dates, bright pink the apples, and yellow the persimmons. The delightful layers of colors, the sweet smells of flowers, and the humming sound of swarms of dedicated working honey bees led Yan to believe that spring was finally here.

"A big boulder over there!" Xi exclaimed, pointing to a flat black stone in the shape of a gold nugget extended like an elongated small mountain.

"Believe it or not, that boulder is called 'Great Gem Stone,'" explained Dong, who had been here before. "Legend says that this stone has inspired Cao Xueqin, when he was broke and hiding here, to write his masterpiece *Dream of the Red Chamber*, which was originally titled *The Story of the Stone*."

"That's interesting," said Tania, who had read the Chinese classic.

With a stream of crystal-clear spring water flowing down the mountain as a backdrop, the group sat on grass next to the big boulder and started to devour the lovely lunch Yan had prepared.

"Congratulations, Zi-Tian! Congratulations on your new position!" Meng announced to the group.

"Yes, yes. Congratulations!" Tania joined in the cheers.

"Congratulations too! I am so happy for you, Zi-Tian!" added Dai, who looked at her husband adoringly.

"Thank you, thank you all very much," Dong said modestly. "I can't be happier than sharing this moment with you, my friends. And I thank you for your unfailing support of me over the years from the bottom of my heart."

Yan finally got it. The picnic was not for the family but to celebrate Dong's promotion. From the group's conversation, Yan learned that he had been appointed to head a new National Economic Planning Council, which had greater powers than the premier's State Council. Also, as the country's vice president, Dong would report directly to Sheng, which meant that his authority would be equal to, if not greater than, the one held by Song, the other vice president.

Big deal, Yan thought. This was what politics was all about. Sometimes you got promoted. Sometimes you got demoted. Life was like a rollercoaster and Dong's career was a perfect example. No so long ago he was ruthlessly discarded like a piece of trash. Look at him now—happy, exuberant, upbeat, and even ambitious. Look at Dai and even Tania; they had suddenly turned into starry-eyed young girls flattering the victorious prince, and in awe of his newfound power and prestige.

Politics. Hopeless politics. Yan concluded.

"Thank you, Yan. The meal is simply delicious," Dong and Meng said to her in near unison.

"Yes, very delicious. I haven't had a good meal like this in months," praised Dai.

"Well, then, you should come and visit us more often," Tania responded.

"Yes, yes. Please come and visit us, and I will cook anything you want," Yan told Dai.

"Dong, no matter what a fantastic husband you are, I will not invite you," Yan said to herself while smiling at him.

Unbeknown to her and many Chinese citizens, Sheng had handpicked Dong to coordinate the nationwide war effort, believing that Song and Si-Tu had been slow and ineffective. They did not support the military intervention in the first place, and remained lukewarm as the war in Korea continued. The displeased Chairman was adamant that he would not to allow such weak and ineffectual leadership to ruin his great struggle against the American imperialists overseas.

"Let's go and see another rarity," suggested Dong. "Just around that slope in the next valley, a grove of dawn redwood has survived for millions of years. Scientists call them the 'living fossils in botany.' Their leaves can change color in the fall, although not as brilliant as the famed maple and sycamore trees in the nearby Fragrant Mountains. Deciduous, they must be sprouting now in spring."

8

The attacks launched by Tao and his field officers encountered setbacks from the start. The ten new divisions they requested had arrived, but adding more troops helped little in the battles.

The enemy's well-supported formations and heavily protected positions were not easy to overcome with the inferior weapons Tao's troops had. Poor intelligence and miscalculation also led to mishaps.

Two army corps differed in their assessments of which enemy units they should attack first. The debate and indecision slowed down their own movements, which gave the American troops the opportunity to mount a swift and powerful counterattack.

Utterly unprepared, the two columns of Chinese troops could have been completely cut off from one another had Tao not realized the immense danger and ordered a timely retreat.

In the chaos, one infantry division was fully cut off and absolutely decimated, while the final casualties of the campaign amounted to eighty-five thousand. Seoul fell into the enemy's hands once again, which was widely publicized as a significant U.S. and UN victory.

A livid Sheng blamed Tao's poor planning and indecisive leadership for the failure. "You should have attacked the enemy a lot earlier," lectured the Chairman. "But you insisted on more time to 'rest, resupply, and reorganize.' You allowed the enemy to consolidate its position, which made it difficult for our troops to make any headway," Sheng said.

The Chairman's tirades aside, Tao now realized that the U.S. and UN forces would never allow North Korea to recapture Seoul. Truman relieved General MacArthur of his command, signaling that the U.S. mission was to preserve the South Korean government, not to cross the Yalu. The best the Chinese forces could do was to persuade the North Koreans to accept the reality.

The despondent Kim did not agree, and kept trying to move his troops south of the 38th Parallel. But, each time he did, he was pushed back by the U.S. and UN forces.

With both sides feeling exhausted by the prolonged conflict, the belligerents agreed to discuss a ceasefire. Although several bloody ground battles broke out in the next two years, a demarcation line began to take shape in the area where the Chinese had launched their last major offensive.

An armistice was signed in 1953, which restored the status quo of the prewar divide roughly along the 38th Parallel, with the North Koreans suffering a net loss of one thousand, five hundred square miles in territory. Kim's wanton and ultimately unsuccessful attacks since 1950 had cost more deaths and devastation for the Korean people than they had suffered in World War II.

To save Kim's regime, China had deployed sixty infantry divisions, other troops and civilians totaling nearly two million personnel, but suffered half a million casualties (including the ones killed in action, wounded, captured, and missing). This amounted to a greater loss ratio than it had suffered during the bloodiest campaigns against Chen in the Chinese civil war.

Chapter 35

Stratagem

1

MEETINGS, MEETINGS, AND MORE MEETINGS! NO ONE COULD tell Song Pei when, why, and how the party had become an institution of meetings, a prevailing reality the entire nation humbly accepted. His life was consumed by meetings—an astonishing variety of them. There were Politburo meetings, high-level private meetings, committee meetings, department meetings, division meetings, council meetings, and board meetings, as well as regional, national, and international meetings. There were annual meetings, quarterly meetings, monthly meetings, bi-weekly meetings, weekly meetings, daily meetings, and evening meetings, not counting, of course, the number of special meetings that could be squeezed at a moment's notice whenever there was a chance.

Also emergency meetings, natural disaster relief meetings, and negotiations with foreign delegations. Members and representatives of constituencies, industries, businesses, associations, unions, clubs, offices and societies, and a great many heads of governmental agencies, came to see Song all the time, demanding a meeting with him.

Then there was the diverse range of issues he had to deal with, from politics, national defense, economy, diplomacy, and personnel appointments to newspaper headlines, tomorrow's editorials, and the sizes of the Chairman's official portraits. From signing the death sentences of counterrevolutionaries to the establishment of a national network of security and police forces. From the regulations on where citizens could or couldn't reside to the guidelines on what intellectuals could or couldn't write or talk about. From the sort of publications that should be banned to the type of entertainment that should be allowed. From the selection of nursery rhymes and school textbooks to the decision on currency exchange rates and farm prices. From the appointment of every officeholder at the provincial level to the redeployment of more than three thousand county heads.

Since the party made every major decision the country must follow and since Sheng Bao only cared about long-term strategies, Song and Si-Tu Wen-Liang were the ones to carry out whatever policies Sheng and the party had decided on, except for those related to military affairs. This awesome responsibility required a lot of work and skills. Si-Tu thrived on complexity, while Song was sick and tired of it.

Not a well-organized and effective leader, Song never enjoyed handling governmental affairs or administrative issues. He was a mediocre thinker who indulged in contemplation. A product of China's orthodox education, Song had lost his imagination and creativity a long time ago. His training in Russia taught him how to please his superior whoever the person might be, but not much else. His specialty was how to become a loyal subject and, once he had achieved that, he had no energy or motivation to do anything more.

The second-in-command in the party and government, Song enjoyed his high position and prestige. But he lacked the required skills and great ideas to run the party apparatus and the nation's business smoothly. Sheng's sudden appointment of Dong Zi-Tian, previously his mortal enemy, to one of the top positions in the nation deeply worried Song. He immediately feared that the erratic Sheng was dissatisfied with his work, and that he might even be removed from his current position.

How could Song protect himself? How could he prevent himself from falling out of Sheng's favor, as many had experienced in the past? If that were to happen, Song would lose everything—position, power, prestige, money, and influence. He would end up a nobody.

Clearly, whatever the party had given him, it could easily take that all away anytime.

Nobody but Sheng could determine Song's fate. To survive, he had to follow those conventions, the footsteps, and the path that the institution had long established. He was one of the highest officials in the party and one of its most subservient and powerless slaves. He had to follow the orders of his iron-fisted master and obey his will, which was the only way to survive in the party.

When Marx theorized that a "public ownership" under a proletarian regime could be the panacea for all the evils of private property, he never anticipated the cost or what building his dream world would entail. Lenin's partisan theory and the Bolshevik Revolution launched that journey to a communist utopia, which the Chinese revolutionaries closely followed later. The Chinese party-state also invented an all-encompassing bureaucratic machine in the name of "public ownership" that Marx and Lenin would have never imagined.

The surprising separation of Marx's utopianism from its real-life application would result in stark alienation, deprivation, disparity, and polarization in any communist state. The public ownership was a sham when the party ruled the entire population with supreme and absolute authority. The rank and file of the party became totally irrelevant when the party leadership claimed to be the omnipotent head, while the entire membership the mindless body. Furthermore, when the whole party and its top leadership insisted on the infallibility of their beloved Chairman, he became simultaneously the *sine qua non* of the party, the people, the proletarians, the working class, the general will, the best interest of the nation, the embodiment of Marxism, the triumph of the Chinese revolution, and the truth of the universe. When push came to shove, nobody's opinions but his mattered. He controlled the Politburo, terrorized his colleagues, and destroyed his rivals. He owned the organization, the people, their lives, and their future. The same Marxist belief and communist system had managed to convert the glorious "public ownership" into one person's possession—with the nation's property and authority all centralized in the hands of a single individual—the red emperor!

Sitting atop that machine and next to the pinnacle of power, however, was not as comfortable as one might assume. Highly diligent but not clever enough to manage well the myriad day-to-day affairs, Song felt overwhelmed. He had little time to study the intricate party politics and dreaded the intraparty games, plots, and intrigues. A terrible feeling of vulnerability haunted him often. Thus, Song's uppermost priorities were not how to improve his effectiveness but how to survive the never-ending internal strives and, most of all, how to please his master. He searched his soul and composed a heartfelt essay—to reassure himself and to appease Sheng—under the catchy title of "Confucianism and the Chinese Communist." Dedicated to the beloved Chairman, it read in part,

> Our Chinese Communist Party is the most wonderful amalgamation of two best traditions in the world—the Confucian heritage from our three-thousand-year-old history, and Marxism and Leninism from modern Europe.
>
> If Marxist and Leninist communism has provided us with faith— the only true faith and belief system in the world—Confucius has taught us how to be the loyal and perpetual devotees to that faith and creed.
>
> The great Marx has created for us a profound theory and world-shattering ideology, and Confucianism has shown us how to be humble, dutiful, and persistent students of that grand theory, and how to worship that divine ideology as we have always behaved before any royal authority.
>
> If Lenin has told us how to build a powerful partisan apparatus, the deeply rooted Confucian tradition of self-restraint and self-righteousness readily transforms us into stalwart disciples devoting to nothing else but that great institution.
>
> If the party has told us that Marxism and Leninism serve as everlasting beacons to the proletarians worldwide, Confucianism has taught us how to follow its light without any question or deviation.
>
> Whereas Marxism and Leninism have aroused our zest, passion, energy, and great sense of mission, Confucianism has given us the distinctively Chinese style of obedience, submissiveness, discipline, cohesiveness, commitment, diligence, endurance, and perseverance the party must have.

When Marxism and Leninism have been proclaimed to be a universal truth and a science, Confucianism is the perfect vehicle for disseminating them.

The world has never seen any radicalism, militancy, and rebellious spirit more powerful than the ones fanned by Marxism and Leninism. The greatest virtue of Confucianism is its remarkable elasticity in justifying any authority, which has enabled us to worship that intoxicating appeal and power of communism.

International communists find no authority but Marxism, no idol but Marx. Confucian Marxists recognize no authority but the present-day Marxism with Chinese characteristics, no saint but the saintly Sheng Bao, no idol but their dearly beloved party apparatus, no God but the godly Chairman Sheng.

Marxism and Leninism promote a grand cause, and Confucianism preaches how to make grand sacrifices for the cause. Communism needs blind faith and total obedience, which are among the most splendid teachings of Confucianism.

The Communist Party needs no individuality but conformity, and Confucianism specializes in that by subjecting everyone to the interests of others' from the day the person was born.

Marxist and Leninist communism would find no better audience than in the Orient, where the hallmark of Confucian virtue has been its unparalleled potential to produce generations of Chinese communist crusaders.

After Song had completed the last sentence, he was not entirely satisfied with it. So he went on to write a more suitable conclusion:

Marxism and Leninism represent the best new religion we have ever acquired and Confucianism is the best ancient religion we have ever inherited.

The great Chinese revolution, born out of a combination of the two religions, would liberate the poor and eradicate poverty and inequality, which has been the dreams of millions of Chinese for centuries.

Integrating communism with Confucianism, or communism with Chinese characteristics, has led to great successes in the past. Further integration between the two would guarantee even greater successes in the future.

The combined forces of communism and Confucianism will ultimately transform China into a perfect society—one that has all the virtues of communism and Confucianism, but without any of the vices of the old regime and capitalism.

Long live communism!

Long live Confucianism!

Love live their lovely offspring—the Chinese Communist Party!

Now, Song felt much relieved after he had done his best to profess his complete loyalty and faithfulness to the party, to the communist cause, and to his beloved heritage. He would be as submissive as a dutiful schoolboy in praising the Marxist ideology while as pious as a churchgoer worshiping at God's altar. He called in his secretary to make copies for other party leaders, and he planned to present a signed copy to his boss, Sheng.

2

Famous for its exquisite royal gardens and courtyards, the Abundance compound also had a handful of modern structures to accommodate a different generation of communist leaders. Located on a spacious ground to the west side of the compound, this new building's large windows and heavy furniture clearly showed the officeholder's status. But the lack of a personal touch and carefully arranged furnishings gave the visitor a feeling of emptiness in an office so big and stately.

This was not the first time that Si-Tu had come to meet Vice Chairman Song, and he did not notice anything special other than Song's dark overcoat hanging on a tall mahogany rack, looking almost like the owner's shadow behind his desk.

The conversation started with some daily administrative stuff, and Si-Tu was not surprised when the topic was raised by the person sitting opposite him; Si-Tu's own reaction was as warm, friendly, respectful, and firm as ever, while sending a noncommittal and cryptic expression at the same time.

No sooner had Song hinted his suspicion about Dong's recent promotion than he regretted it. "Si-Tu Wen-Liang, the sly fox in the party. Who knows what he would do tomorrow, now that he knows what I am thinking," said Song to himself, who was not sure whether he should end or continue the meeting.

Anxiously waiting for a response, he froze in the chair, sweat droplets oozing from his large nose. Si-Tu's short pause and a gentle smile made Song relaxed a little.

"You see," began Si-Tu, "Dong's position is not as threatening as it seems. His last big promotion was largely based on his efforts to support the Korean War. Now the war is over and his importance will diminish as Sheng will shift his attention to other areas of interests," Si-Tu explained.

"But Sheng did promote him over you and me," Song pointed out. "Sheng now trusts him more than either one of us."

"On the surface, yes. But not in reality," Si-Tu replied.

"How do you know?" A practical person without much experience in infighting at the highest level, Song was not convinced.

"Hardly anything would remain the same for long, nor would Sheng's new fancy," Si-Tu calmly responded.

His confidence puzzled Song, who had dropped to third place in the government behind Sheng and Dong, even though he still held the second-highest position in the party's Politburo.

Why was Si-Tu not concerned? He had dropped further, to fourth place in the government as a result of Dong's promotion. Song did not understand.

The key difference between the two men was that Si-Tu could read Sheng far better than Song. In fact, no one in the party could understand Sheng inside out better than Si-Tu, who had worked side by side with him much longer than Song did.

Si-Tu had learned long ago about a cardinal aspect of Sheng's personality: His trust in anyone was precarious, while his suspicion of everyone was perpetual.

In terms of education, talent, skills, experience, seniority, personal charm and sophistication, Si-Tu was superior to Sheng, and was also more popular than him. But Si-Tu was a perfect product of Confucianism; he valued the qualities of virtue, modesty, and faithfulness to the king as dearly as his own honor. A son of a landlord and official under the old regime, he could never overcome his inferiority complex to compete confidently with Sheng, the son of a peasant farmer. A small difference in terms of social status but a huge and most serious concern in a proletarian movement, which judged the inherent quality of a person by looking at his birth—the poorer his family background, the more revolutionary he would be, while the wealthier his family was, the less revolutionary he must remain.

It did not take long for a man of Si-Tu's intelligence to find his niche in the party. Dutifully supporting Sheng as the number one leader, Si-Tu made preserving his personal purity and reputable public image his top priority, while considering his absolute loyalty to Sheng as the most salient manifestation of that purity and credibility.

Top leaders in the party also had a similar inferiority complex like Si-Tu, since most of them, including Song, came from slightly wealthier families than Sheng's—except for Dong, who could be uncompromising and fearless in challenging Sheng's authority and legitimacy.

But Si-Tu knew Dong and Sheng too well—both their strengths and weaknesses—not to see that the former was no match for the latter.

Although both grew up in the countryside, campus life had changed Dong into a starry-eyed idealist, whereas Sheng, who had fought his way through the jungles, had remained a street-smart manipulator who was willing to do anything to achieve his goals. Dong was a bookish revolutionary, while Sheng was an iron-fisted dictator. Dong was a hands-on operative whose life had been preoccupied with one task after another, leaving him little time to think about anything else. But Sheng was a strategist, who spent most of his time thinking and designing his stratagems, while evaluating the weaknesses of his foes as thoroughly as no one could.

Fundamentally, Sheng was a highly suspicious person who would never fully trust anyone who had opposed him. This suspicious nature, according to Si-Tu's observation, had grown even stronger as Sheng rose steadily up the party hierarchy and became most powerful.

Si-Tu therefore did not believe for a minute that, significant as it was, Dong's promotion amounted to a complete reversal of Sheng's opinion of him. That promotion could even be a sinister trap that he had laid deliberately for the unsuspecting Dong, who was once the most formidable challenger to Sheng's authority.

"What shall we do then?" Song asked.

Si-Tu did not like the word "we"—it was as if he were concocting some covert scheme with the mediocre Song. No, he would never do anything like that. Or, to put it more precisely, he would never leave any trace of doing something that might arouse Sheng's suspicions later. (Be aware, Si-Tu knew perfectly well that every guard, secretary, nurse, cook, maid, or servant in this government compound would report anything, suspicious or not, to Sheng.) The Chairman would never allow any conspiracy to be hatched behind his back. Factionalism had no place in the party, he insisted, even though he himself was a master at playing off one faction against another in the party.

"Since the Chairman now wields enormous power and carries great responsibilities, he needs the best protection that can guarantee his absolute safety. If any weakness can be detected and needs to be corrected to improve his protection or to eliminate his misgivings, I think the Chairman will greatly appreciate the feedback," Si-Tu gave his suggestion without offering any specifics, hoping that the pathetic Song would get it.

"Boy, isn't he smart? I hope he will never use his brains against me someday. Then I will be dead for sure," Song said to himself as he courteously escorted the premier out of his office.

3

Stalin's death in 1953, shortly before the Korean War ended, shook the communist world in a way that few people had anticipated.

Beneath the public mourning and laudatory commemorations, an intense power struggle was underway, ending with the execution of security chief Lavrentiy Beria not long afterward, and the rise of Nikita Khrushchev as the new first secretary of the Communist Party of the Soviet Union.

Sympathetic, apathetic, awakened, vigilant, sanguine, and even energized, Sheng's varied reactions to the events surpassed everyone else's.

The passing of Stalin, the most powerful man in the communist world for thirty years, reminded Sheng of his own mortality. Now, at sixty, he had reached that stage of life widely considered "old" in the Chinese tradition. Suffering from migraines and sleepless nights more frequently than before, his concerns about a successor intensified.

Stalin's death also ended the era of his overreaching power and extensive influence in Chinese affairs, which Sheng had long resented but could do nothing about it. Nobody could boss Sheng around from now on, for his seniority and experience in the international communist movement was second to none, including Khrushchev. The Chinese Communist Party was suddenly no longer a minor but a major league member, and perhaps even a coleader with its Russian counterpart.

More importantly, Sheng saw an extraordinary new opportunity available to no one but him. When he was left alone in the empty hotel in Moscow during his maiden visit to the Soviet Union, Sheng recalled, he visited several factories in the city, where some huge billboards attracted his attention. On those gigantic cement walls, colossal portraits of Marx, Engels, Lenin, and Stalin were painted against a sea of red flags, signifying the four great leaders of the international communist movement. Now, all four of them were dead; who would be the next one to lead the movement?

Whenever Sheng considered this question, he could not help but think of himself. Who else in the communist camp possessed the same experience and successful record as he did? Khrushchev was but a regional commissar during World War II. How could he compete with Sheng, who had led a brutal war in the jungles ten years earlier?

To become the undisputed leader of the communist world was his next goal. Thus decided, the ever-ambitious Sheng felt a sense of contentment. He would be remembered not simply as a hero of China but a world hero, the fifth portrait in that gigantic billboard, to be worshiped and revered forever as an Asian leader who was able to stand as an equal alongside four famous Europeans.

4

Power and privilege needed distinctive rankings to classify, positive hierarchies to crystalize, and rigorous structures to solidify.

Although only a few years into the new communist era, increasing governmental bureaucratization and compartmentalization had made collective intimacy, friendly access, and revolutionary camaraderie things of the past. After the success of the revolution, no one, not even the highest officials in the party, could meet the Chairman as often as they wished. Heavily guarded, the massive royal palace Abundance and the most forbidden Garden of Lilacs elicited fear and awe, which was a far cry from the humble caves in the dirty streets of Bao An, where many soldiers or civilians, old or young, men or women, could step into them for a visit anytime. And a visitor should not expect the Chairman and his wife to bring out their freshly baked potatoes to treat guests like they used to in the past; rules, restrictions, and protocols now placed a limit on who could see him, and where, when, and for how long.

Today, the conversations at two brief meetings had raised Sheng's eyebrows—one with Su Ming and the other with Lin Shi-Xiong.

Su told him that she had recently seen a movie called *The Villager*. Based on a real story during the late Qing Dynasty, the film was about a poor peasant who lost the girl he loved to a wicked landlord, who had cheated them by forging a legal document that they were unable to read or understand. The incident hurt the peasant so badly that he decided to build a school to teach poor children how to read and write. Convinced that literacy was the way to salvation, he worked hard and even became a beggar for the next twenty years to save every penny for the future school, and he eventually succeeded in building one.

"It was a good movie, very touching," said Su, who even recited the lyrics of its theme song, "The Running Streams":

The moon rises bright and clear,
I yearn my love in the mountain.
My love is like the moon in heaven,
Alas, my love.

The streams run at mountain's foot,
The moon shines on the slope,
reminding me of my love.
The breeze reaches the slope,
Alas, my love.

May the breeze carry my words to my love,
The moon rises bright,
The stream runs brisk.
My love is like the moon in heaven,
It reminds me of my love.

Alas, the clear mountain.
Alas, the running streams.
Alas, my love.

"Hmm, a romantic story and a romantic love song," the Chairman said as he watched Su leave his office. Since sentimentality was never his strong suit, he did not make any further comment but decided to conduct some investigation.

The affinity between Sheng and Lin was forged more out of mutual disrespect than mutual esteem.

Lin know perfectly well what his job was: to take care of the dirty aspects of politics. After all, somebody had to do it. Being a professional, it was his duty to protect the boss. He wanted to do a good job and not to overlook anything that might be potentially harmful to the boss. No more, no less. His pride in his job, or his remorse in doing it, was no different from that of other professionals.

Spying on his closest colleagues for decades was not something Sheng would ever brag about publicly. But, to maintain his supreme authority, he had to do it. To be more precise, Sheng never considered the preservation of his absolute power to be selfish but done in the best interests of the party, people, proletariat, and revolutionary cause, and for the ultimate success of international communism. Tantamount to safeguarding the successful regime of the Chinese Communist Party itself, any means to achieve such an altruistic goal were as justifiable as any tactics, overt or covert, were permissible.

Lin's report was brief, discreet, and to the point. He merely informed Sheng that the newly promoted Dong had been unusually active around the capital, visiting his old friends and accepting the congratulations from his legion of former subordinates. His rise seemed to have attracted the attention of Moscow. Several members of the Soviet embassy had invited Dong to official functions, and some might even have held private meetings with him.

Paradoxically, the highly centralized political structure in China was as extremely fragile as it was exceedingly powerful. Like the gigantesque web of a spider, the slightest vibration at any point of the web would instantly alarm its owner. As soon as Sheng detected that vibration, his revolutionary instincts would kick in as if his whole house were under attack.

Sheng thanked Lin for his report, and began to look into his options on how to deal with the vibration.

5

The ultimate difference between an ordinary leader and a great one was purely innate and subjective insofar as Sheng could tell. Not a single day of his life had been easy. From the endless toil under the scorching sun in the paddy fields of his hometown to the humiliating visits to the factory plant in Wuhan, from the hiding grounds in the wooded mountains in Jiangxi to the desperate escapes on the road during the Long March, and from the few hundred armed men under his command to the million soldiers during the civil war, he had survived, succeeded, and excelled. Against all odds, Sheng had defeated all his opponents, won some of the most spectacular military victories over his archrival Chen Han in four years, and even halted the military advance instigated by the American-led UN forces in Korea.

If Sheng had proved to be the unquestionable victor on the battleground, what else could stop him from achieving more triumphs in any other field? Would reconstruction, economic development, and social reform be any more difficult than those hundreds of life-and-death military campaigns he had been involved in? He did not think so.

His remarkable personal experience and stellar record, which was as long and extensive as that of anyone else's in the party, seemed to suggest that his ideas, skills, and designs for winning military struggles could be easily replicated for any social reforms, political campaigns, and economic expansion with equal success.

As far as the confident Sheng was concerned nothing—be it rebuilding China's economy or pushing for land reforms, collective movement, urbanization, and industrial development—would be unattainable if only the party would continue to follow his leadership, which would no doubt bring China even bigger success and greater prosperity in all areas. And the key here was for the party to embrace his exceptional vision, resolute courage, and wise policies. Great leadership was everything and Sheng, the proven leader of the past, would be China's only true champion for its future.

Unfortunately, many of his colleagues became timid, cautious, and even conservative after the party had established the new government of the People's Republic of China. They, including Vice Chairman Song and Premier Si-Tu, complained about all kinds of difficulties and made all kinds of excuses, attempting to slow down the speed of the socialist reforms he had wanted to implement.

"Those who have become complacent bureaucrats, managers, supervisors, and administrators will never be real leaders," scorned Sheng, who felt more than ever before that he, as the only visionary communist leader, had the responsibility to lead his colleagues and the party to achieve the most glorious destiny preordained by Marx and Marxism.

He deliberately promoted Dong, whose positive attitude and energetic actions in the Northeast were exactly what was lacking in the rest of the national leadership. Sheng had hoped that this promotion would jolt Song and Si-Tu, who would follow Dong's example to speed up the social and economic reforms under their jurisdictions.

Lin's report, Sheng believed, was as much about Dong's activity as it was about Song and Si-Tu's displeasure with this dark horse. They must have been deeply concerned that Dong might one day replace them in the national government, and they certainly were not happy at all about this new superstar who had posed a serious challenge to their powers in the central administration.

The three senior officials represented three powerful factions of the party. Dong was very popular in the Northeast, and many officials in Northwest China and many officers of the old Second Red Army still admired him greatly. Si-Tu's supporters included those who had worked with him in Shanghai and when he was the bureau chief in Central China. Song had been the chief of Northern China, where he had built up his strength and following. Both Si-Tu and Song greatly expanded their reach in the new central government by appointing their favorites as top department heads.

The three factions were roughly equal in size and importance, while Si-Tu and Song had a clear advantage in the central government. The balance ultimately hinged on Sheng, whose attitude and inclination could make or break any of them. He, of course, would love to see these subordinates split into factions, which would then need him to be their arbiter.

For the moment, though, the veteran tactician was not in any rush to make a final decision. He needed Dong's enthusiasm and energy as much as he had to rely on Si-Tu's skills and Song's control over the country's immense bureaucracy. He was willing to play a wait-and-see game.

6

To say that the communist world was completely stunned by Khrushchev's secret speech was an understatement.

At the Twentieth National Congress of the Soviet Communist Party, the first secretary gave a four-hour speech at a secret session on March 24 and 25, 1956. He berated Stalin for his brutal purges of the party and the Red Army in the 1930s and for the wanton excesses of his personality cult.

Excluded from the session and not fully informed of the contents of the speech until after the event, the Chinese Communist Party was as shocked as other communist parties in both East and West. After the initial confusion, Sheng made known to the Soviets his real views about their late leader.

He talked to the Soviet ambassador in Peking for three hours, complaining about Stalin's mistreatment of him as if he had been one of the worst victims under Stalin's regime. He was no doubt against the personality cult—the un-Marxist practice exposed by the courageous and honest Russian Communist Party, a move he fully supported.

Riding with the tide of de-Stalinization, Sheng believed that he could take advantage of the popular sentiment for progress, which might force his unwilling colleagues to step up their action. Announcing a policy of "letting a hundred flowers blossom and a hundred schools of thought compete" in China, Sheng wasted no time in appealing to the party's rank and file and the general population to raise their voices and offer suggestions on how to help the party leadership improve its work.

It was an unusual situation to the average Chinese, who had never been invited to criticize their superiors and government officials, or to participate in discussions of issues of national significance. Most were reluctant to speak out for fear of retribution. Things slowly started to change only when top officials went public, declaring that the people's government was all sincere in working with citizens from all walks of life to improve the workings of the party and the government.

7

The limited access to information and strict media controls deepened the public's curiosity. Many wanted to know exactly what had happened in the Soviet Union, what Stalin had actually done, what Khrushchev had said about him, and why. News reports by Chinese media agencies were fragmented, while information from foreign news organizations was not available to average citizens.

Meng Bo-Xian's seniority in the party entitled him to receive regular updates. And he asked Yan Yan to let him know as soon as they arrived. Mostly compilations of reports, comments, and articles selected from Western newspapers and translated into Chinese, these updates reflected the mood and speculations of the foreign media rather than insiders' accounts of the event.

The package Tania brought home one day shattered everything. Sent by Martin, it was a copy of Khrushchev's speech, which Tania and Meng perused together overnight. Its contents left them heartbroken and tears were running down their faces; the couple simply could not believe what they had just read. Tania was in Moscow during the period mentioned in the speech, when she was accompanying Yu Shao-Mei for treatment. She had sensed that something was terribly wrong, but did not realize the extent of the horrors until now.

It was determined that, of the one hundred and thirty-nine members and candidates of the Central Committee who were elected at the 17th Congress in 1934, ninety-eight persons, i.e., seventy percent, were arrested and shot (mostly in 1937–1938).

The same fate also fell on the majority of the delegates to the 17th Party Congress. Of the one thousand, nine hundred and sixty-six delegates with either voting or advisory rights, one thousand, one hundred and eight persons—more than a majority—were arrested on charges of antirevolutionary crimes.

We should recall that the 17th Party Congress is known historically as the Congress of Victors. Delegates to the Congress were active participants in the building of our socialist state; in the prerevolutionary years, many of them suffered and fought for party interests through their underground activities and participation in the civil war. They fought their enemies valiantly, and often fearlessly stared into the face of death.

The vicious campaign began with the People's Commissariat for Internal Affairs (or NKVD) preparing the lists of persons whose cases were under the jurisdiction of the Military Collegium and whose sentences were prepared in advance. Yezhov would send these [execution] lists to Stalin personally for his approval. In 1937–1938, three hundred and eighty-three such lists containing the names of thousands of Party, Soviet, Komsomol (the All-Union Leninist Young Communist League), Army, and economic workers were sent to Stalin. He approved these lists.

A large number of these cases are being reviewed now. A great many are being voided because they are baseless and falsified. Suffice it to say that from 1954 to the present time, the Military Collegium of the Supreme Court has rehabilitated seven thousand, six hundred and seventy-nine persons, many of whom have been rehabilitated posthumously.

Mass arrests of party, Soviet, economic and military workers caused tremendous harm to our country and to the cause of socialist advancement.

Mass repressions had a negative impact on the moral-political condition of the party, created a situation of uncertainty, contributed to the spreading of unhealthy rumors, and sowed distrust among communists. All sorts of slanderers and careerists were active.

Resolutions of the January 1938 Central Committee Plenum brought some measure of improvement to Party organizations. However, widespread repression also occurred in 1938.

Only because our party has at its disposal such great moral-political strength that it is able to survive the difficult events in 1937–1938 and to educate new cadres. There is, however, no doubt that our forward march toward socialism and toward the preparation of the country's defense would have been much more successful were it not for the tremendous loss the cadres suffered as a result of the baseless and false mass repression in 1937–1938.

As if what they had read were not dreadful enough, a small note attached by Martin at the end further revealed:

Sources say that the purge of the Red Army and the navy included three marshals, thirteen commanders, eight admirals, fifty army corps commanders, and one hundred and fifty division commanders.

In the same period of the late 1930s, an antikulak campaign persecuted fifty-seven thousand people, and forty-eight thousand of them were executed.

No fewer than one hundred thousand Orthodox Church believers were arrested, and close to thirty thousand of them were clergymen.

Some two thousand writers, intellectuals, and artists were imprisoned and one thousand, five hundred died in prisons and concentration camps.

Those nearly four hundred lists Stalin personally signed in 1937 and 1938 authorized the execution of some forty thousand people, and about ninety percent of these were confirmed to have been shot.

In all, it is estimated that more than one and a half million people were detained, arrested, or persecuted under the Great Terror. Of them, nearly six hundred and eighty-two thousand were shot.

8

What could be worse than those tragic deaths and horrifying news? They all sounded so terrible but at the same time seemed to be something from the distant past, as if from the darkest days of the tsarist era.

Not long afterwards, on one rainy night, someone came knocking at the door. It was Dai Tian and Yan Yan brought the totally drenched woman into the living room.

When Tania and Meng rushed in to greet her, they found Dai curled in a small sofa, weeping uncontrollably despite Yan's attempts to comfort her.

"Tell me, my dear, why, what is going on?" Tania asked.

"He... he... Zi-Tian is dead!" Dai cried out loud.

Chapter 36

Rightists

1

H UMANS WERE COMPLEX CREATURES AND THE CHINESE PEASANT had his share of duplicity and contradictions. His legendary hard work and endurance were the backbone of the nation as much as his ignorance and narrow-mindedness were barriers to its progress. Unbelievably tough and resilient in the face of physical hardships, he could be extremely sensitive and vulnerable about his public image, face, name, and reputation.

If he did not hold any political power, he could be the most gregarious and carefree person anyone could ever meet—friendly, warm, honest, affable, and open-minded.

If he gained any authority, his possessive instincts instantly took over. He would fight to preserve his power as doggedly as any frugal, inflexible, vigilant, and insecure small landowner, who would protect and preserve the last piece of his hard-earned property to the hilt.

Docile but irritable, calm but impetuous, relaxed but insecure, unsophisticated and unpredictable, innocent and treacherous, harmless and deceitful, all at the same time, his mellowness, easygoing ways, and cheerful attitude could turn into bloodthirsty fury, tyrannical violence, merciless vengeance, and sheer brutality in seconds.

Sharing power in any democratic process made no sense for him, who had never had any experience nor any belief in the rule of law. No match for the fables he had learned from the beloved Chinese classical novels; those foreign concepts and alien practices could hardly teach him anything more about politics than the several thousand years of rule by either king, emperor, regent, warlord, president, despot, general, or chairman.

Nurtured by the same experience, tradition, and mentality as Sheng Bao, his colleagues assumed their appropriate positions around him as his dutiful ministers, obedient subordinates, and faithful subjects, who valued their self-preservation in his court more than anything else.

Since the party was the country and since the Chairman was the party, they argued, loyalty to the Chairman was the same as loyalty to the party and country. To preserve and protect the Chairman's authority was to preserve the power and integrity of the party and nation.

If the Chairman ruled the nation and if his agenda dominated the party, any deviation from his ideas would post a threat to his authority. And the most serious challenge now would come more from within the party than from without. If intraparty conflict was his worst nightmare and if any suspicious activities of his closest colleagues in the Politburo could trigger a grave crisis, the Chairman had the prerogative to use any means to eliminate his potential rival within the top party leadership.

When Sheng directed the Politburo members to look into Dong Zi-Tian's "mistakes," they were as enthusiastic as those valiant Roman gladiators who were ready to slaughter the caged beast in the Colosseum.

"Dong Zi-Tian has always had personal ambitions since the days of the Long March," Song, who was chairing the meeting, said as he looked at the accused.

"I would say," joined Si-Tu, "since the first day the party was founded."

"Yes, yes. He always thought he was better than everybody else, even wiser and smarter than our great leader Comrade Sheng Bao," agreed Song.

"He believed he could replace Song Pei and me as the top official in the government"—Si-Tu went on the offensive—"by hatching an insidious plot with his followers."

"His ultimate goal was to replace the Chairman and to become the head of state himself," Song elaborated.

Both he and Si-Tu knew they could say anything they wanted at this exclusive meeting, because no one would be able to confirm the validity of any of the allegations made here. A top-secret meeting of this sort was to pave the way for the final punishment—from demotion to expulsion from the party—of anyone who had offended the Chairman; he wanted to ascertain the crime, not the evidence of it.

At an implicit level, the same meeting was also a highly important occasion for everyone to demonstrate his innocence and express his absolute loyalty to Sheng and his policies. No official minutes of the meeting would be kept except for one copy, made exclusively for the Chairman, of the full transcript of every participant's statements. Since he was never present at such a meeting, the Chairman must know who had said what so that he could scrutinize everyone's attitude. He would then lock the copy in his personal safe for his future use, a dreaded practice since the information could be used against anyone who might have disagreed with him. The Chairman's personal safe had kept the top-secret and most personal documents of all high-ranking party leaders, whose life, fate, and future were all locked up in that steel box. These documents could help refresh the Chairman's elephant memory whenever he needed the records to use the subordinates' past behavior against themselves.

"Hold on for a moment please." Tao Yin-Hu could not remain silent anymore. "Sheng Bao promoted Dong Zi-Tian over you two. Why has it become his fault or his ambition to replace you?"

"Comrade Sheng has told us that Dong had the ambition to replace us. Are you suggesting that our great Chairman is lying?" Song responded.

"I never said to replace either one of you." The disheartened Dong finally opened his mouth. "I only said that the chairmanship may be rotated while the Chairman is on vacation."

"See, he admitted he had ambitions," Song pressed on.

"I only made a suggestion at the time when the Chairman was soliciting suggestions as to what should be done while he was on vacation," Dong tried to defend himself.

"But how do you explain your secret meetings with Russian officials?" Lin Shi-Xiong suddenly jumped in, believing he had the smoking gun. He knew the Chairman was extremely sensitive about anyone seeking Russian support behind his back. Dong's sound knowledge of the Russian language and the Russians' great fondness of him had been Sheng's biggest bugbears for the longest time.

"Those were not secret meetings. The Soviet Union offered us extensive trade deals, financial aid packages, and military support programs during the Korean War. Those communications were absolutely necessary to ensure our troops receive adequate equipment and support throughout the war," Dong responded.

"Yes, the Northeast shouldered the largest burden of supporting our troops in the Korean War. Dong had made enormous contributions to that effort, and his frequent contacts and communications with the Russians were absolutely essential for that success," Tao concurred.

"Reports say that he had discussed the list of members of the next Politburo. Would this not be proof of his ambition and conspiracy?" Lin insisted.

"That's a lie. I have never discussed such a list with anyone!" Dong yelled out.

"My reports are never wrong," said the hard-nosed Lin, who was all confident and unforgiving.

"I will challenge, face to face, the person who made this allegation," Dong protested.

"That will not be up to you to decide. This committee will handle all the charges against you," declared Song, who was so relieved that Sheng had finally put him in the driver's seat. He could have been sitting on the same defendant's bench just as Dong was now if only Sheng had decided to support Dong over Song. The Chairman must have realized that in the end what he really needed was not talent, innovation, and energy but faithfulness, obedience, and mediocrity.

Calmer than Song, Si-Tu could see the endgame already. The Chairman had clearly made up his mind to abandon Dong. Lin's accusations were lethal, because Si-Tu understood better than anyone how deeply distrustful Sheng could be. Si-Tu's clever hints to Song to spread rumors and to arouse the Chairman's suspicions about Dong seemed to have worked. For the second time in his life, Si-Tu concocted a dirty scheme to undermine Dong. He did it with trepidation the first time. Now he was doing it with great skill and perfect ease.

To Song and Si-Tu's surprise, Dong stubbornly denied all the allegations against him despite the enormous pressure exerted by the Politburo. When they reported the impasse to Sheng, the Chairman ordered Dong to be declared an "antiparty conspirator," who was to be held in temporary custody by the security forces of Abundance.

Two weeks into his detention, Dai Tian was told that her husband had committed suicide.

2

"From what I have seen, *The Villager* is a terrible movie," Sheng told Su Ming in a chiding tone. "It is a reactionary propaganda film that lauds reformers and vilifies the revolutionaries. It insinuates that our great armed struggle is not as important as a little neighborhood school, that thousands of our Red Army soldiers are not as heroic as a village scrounger."

"I am so sorry. I am so wrong. I truly apologize." The frightened Su had heard about her husband's infamous wrath, which could send the most senior party leader or the most decorated general to jail. Now she deeply regretted that she had ever attempted to please Sheng by making a foray into the murky world of entertainment.

"You are innocent. You are too inexperienced to know the intricacies of class struggle." The husband's comforting words moved Su to tears. What else would a faithful wife want but her man's heartwarming sensitivity, congenial understanding, and timely expression of affection?

"What can I do to correct my mistakes?" she asked earnestly. A highly intelligent woman, Su believed that she had the ability to regain Sheng's trust, if only she were given the chance.

"Don't worry about it." Not magnanimous by nature, Sheng was, however, very forgiving toward his wife this time. He explained, "Contrary to the belief of many of our party members, class struggle is getting more intense and more extensive after the liberation than before it. As true communists, we must be prepared to face this new phase of class struggle wherever and whenever it appears."

Su's face turned red. She was excited. She knew that the Chairman had long contemplated the question of class struggle in the post-liberation era.

But this was the first time that he had expressed his idea so explicitly to someone else. Sheng had told her that no one in the past had provided a clear answer to this important issue, including the great teachers Marx, Engels, Lenin, and Stalin. She was so proud to be the first person to be privy to this profound new revelation. Although she did not participate much in the past revolutionary activities, she was willing to devote herself to this new phase of class struggle that the Chairman, her dear husband, had so plainly illuminated.

"I must have read the *Communist Manifesto* no fewer than two hundred times by now and I reread it several times lately," Sheng continued.

"Marx and Engels created the theory of an international proletarian revolution based on their analysis of class struggles of traditional societies. Lenin and Stalin had applied that theory and created the first country under the rules of a communist party, called the proletarian dictatorship. But none of them had the opportunity to advance that theory to the next level, which should address the entirely new development of class struggle *after* the communist state and the proletarian dictatorship have been established."

The profundity of the issue and the exciting prospect of a potential new discovery captivated Sheng, whose eyes were shining and voice was rising.

"If the international communist movement is to move forward, a new Marxist and Leninist theory must respond to the question of how to continue class struggle under the proletarian dictatorship, which is but the transitional stage to communism," said he.

"I am so excited to hear this. And I believe you are absolutely correct. What can I do to help? I want to be part of this continuous revolution!" Su responded excitedly.

"Good. It is a continuous revolution and I like the characterization." Sheng was pleased that Su had understood his ideas quickly and accepted them completely. He wished his Politburo colleagues could behave in the same way.

"Okay, if you really want to participate, why not start with an investigation. That is, you can lead a team to investigate *The Villager*—who made it, what are the social and political backgrounds of the director, playwright, producer, actors and actresses, and why they are more sympathetic toward the reformers than the revolutionaries," Sheng suggested.

"That's a great idea. I have always been interested in the movie industry." Su was very pleased. A real trooper, she started to plan her course of action right away.

3

"I can't believe it. I don't believe Zi-Tian would ever commit suicide," Dai said to Tania and Meng, who tried to comfort her as best as they could whenever she came to visit following Dong's death.

"No, I don't believe it either. Zi-Tian was a very strong and very optimistic person," Tania agreed.

"Did you notice anything unusual during his detention?" Meng asked.

"I knew he was very upset writing his apologies and self-criticisms. But nothing abnormal. He told me that he had had much worse experience in the past, and I believe him. But I was only allowed to see him twice in detention, and I am not clear about what really happened in his cell during the last days of his life," Dai said.

"Did you ask his guards? Or did any party leader tell you anything?" Meng asked again.

"Lu Di-Ping was in charge of the security and Song Pei was in charge of the investigation. Neither one told me much other than to say that Zi-Tian had committed suicide, which reaffirmed his crime as an 'antiparty conspirator,'" Dai replied.

"That's crazy. Haven't we learned anything from Stalin's horrific purges?" Tania was indignant. "What about Si-Tu Wen-Liang? He usually would have some insights?" she asked, still believing the premier to be the one who could answer even the toughest questions.

"No, not this time. He has not been forthcoming lately, and never told me anything about what happened at the last Politburo meeting that Zi-Tian attended," Dai recalled.

"Oh, what about Tao Yin-Hu? He has been highly appreciative of Zi-Tian and his work," suggested Meng.

"Yes, General Tao had been very kind and said a lot of good things about Zi-Tian. But he told me that he really did not know anything after Zi-Tian was detained by the security forces under Lu Di-Ping," Dai explained.

"It seems that Lu Di-Ping, Song Pei, Si-Tu Wen-Liang, and certainly Lin Shi-Xiong know the truth. In a case like this, the more reluctant a person is to talk, the more likely he knows more than he professes," Meng speculated.

"I don't care. I will continue to investigate until I get to the bottom of it! I will find out the whole story, I will find out the whole truth, and I will prove Zi-Tian's innocence." Dai cried as she uttered those last few words. A flood of emotions—love, sorrow, affection, regret, and determination—overwhelmed her. "If I could not be by your side as much as I should have while you were alive," she vowed, "I would forever love you and remain your dearest and most faithful wife till I die."

As Tania took Dai into her arms, Yan Yan walked into the living room.

"Have some tea, please, Dai Tian. I have added some honey and hope you will like it," she said softly.

Yan had changed. She had been surprisingly gentle and cordial toward Dai whenever she visited them after her husband's death. Maybe, as the self-appointed guardian, Yan no longer saw Dong as a distraction in Tania's life. Or maybe, as a woman, she had an instinctive affinity with Dai over her tragic loss and suffering. Or maybe both her secret relief and great sympathy had quietly transformed her into a genuine friend and most caring comforter of Dai's.

"Thanks, Yan. The tea is very nice," Dai said.

"Oh, I am so glad that you like it. I will make you some more if you want." The flattered Yan was smiling all over, and she was apparently prepared to do anything to please the guest. Yan was the kind of person who did not expect much in return; she only wanted to give.

"No, thanks, Yan. I am fine. I am really fine, thanks."

Dai's polite words moved Yan, who was completely overwhelmed whenever anyone treated her kindly as an equal human being, not as a maidservant.

"Listen, my dear. You come here every day and I will make you the best tea you would ever want."

"Thanks, Yan. You are such a nice person."

"No, please don't say that anymore. You poor girl. You take care, Okay? I will always be here for you. Trust me."

Yan hugged Dai with all the love she had to give. The next thing Tania and Meng noticed was the two women in each other's arms, sharing their tears.

4

Sitting on a raised and capacious stone platform, the grand, tall, and brightly painted Scarlet Hall was the most conspicuous building in Abundance. Converted into a convention hall, it had been used to hold some of the most important party meetings since liberation.

The crowd gathered here today must have been very different from the kind that the staff and guards working in Abundance were used to seeing. Not the regular high-ranking party officials, provincial leaders, nor soldiers' representatives, workers, and peasant farmers, they were instead a group of university professors, intellectuals, scientists, engineers, writers, authors, journalists, editors, movie directors, artists, musicians, performers, and entertainers. Also present were a few dozen former Nationalist Party officials, Chen Han's generals, and the third-party organizers who had accepted communist rule by participating in the new government.

Song Pei, who was chairing the meeting, went up to the podium to speak.

"Friends and comrades, we are here today to announce an important policy that, I believe, concerns everyone here and the future of our nation as well. Now, let's welcome our premier, Comrade Si-Tu Wen-Liang, to make the announcement."

"Friends and comrades," the premier said, "on behalf of the Central Committee of the Chinese Communist Party and on behalf of the Central National Government, I announce the policy of the 'Hundred Schools of Thought' and the 'Blossom of a Hundred Flowers.'"

"This means that our party encourages the freedom of thought and healthy intellectual debates and artistic pursuits in all areas of our nation's economic, political, cultural, educational, literary, and entertainment activities.

"We especially welcome any suggestions including open criticisms about the Communist Party, which will help us improve our efforts in striving for greater socialist success that can be shared by all our citizens."

The brief announcement surprised the audience, who had been accustomed to receive orders from the party apparatus, not to make their own individual choices and proposals. As a class of teenage schoolchildren would often do in front of their solemn teacher, those present broke into small groups and started to chatter, gossip, and poke fun at one another without speaking out.

"Is the party leadership really sincere about the new policy?" A voice rose from the left side of the auditorium.

"Comrade Mo Jia-Qi raised a good question." Si-Tu immediately recognized the speaker, who used to be his colleague in the top party leadership but was now reduced to a pathetic and marginalized government employee. In his typical gentlemanly civility, the premier went on to explain, "The party is committed to create a democratic environment where people will feel free to express their ideas and pursue their creativity."

"I hope this is not Sheng Bao's tactic of 'politeness first and retaliation later,'" Mo quipped.

"Not at all," responded the perpetually composed Si-Tu. "Comrade Sheng Bao is a great strategist. But that tactic was used against armed enemies from without, not against friends and citizens from within our own camp."

"Can the third party raise questions to challenge the ruling party?" asked Gan Zu-Xun, representing the constituency of several groups of clubs, associations, and societies that had no affiliation with either the Nationalist or the Communist Parties in the civil war.

"Yes, certainly. The reason why we allow the third party to continue to exist after the end of the civil war is to give its members the opportunity to participate in governing, including the right to watch and criticize the Communist Party," Si-Tu replied. "We have had a long history of working with many parties and organizations under the united front. We shall continue to work with any parties and organizations that are willing to work with us to build a new, stronger, and more prosperous China."

"From what I have observed, Sheng Bao is not a person who can take criticisms easily. He craves personal greatness and success. He has never been known to have a liking for freedom of expression or democracy. Would that be a problem in the policy you have just pronounced?"

Looking over the crowd, Si-Tu realized the speaker was Pan Jin, the nationalist general who had fought many tough battles against the Red Army and the Japanese. He came from the same countryside as Sheng, and therefore knew a lot more details of the Chairman's personal habits and personality than many other delegates.

"General Pan is a brave soldier and we greatly respect his stellar military record," Si-Tu responded slowly and carefully. "General Pan must know as much as anyone that you need a fervent spirit to win in the battlefield. I think both General Pan and our Comrade Sheng possess that steel will and invincible spirit in their military careers. But Comrade Sheng is also a visionary leader, who knows the importance of working with people of all persuasions and from all walks of life. In fact, the policy I just announced was first proposed by Comrade Sheng himself, who, I am sure, will uphold this open policy toward all our friends for years to come."

"The new policy sounds very good. But what about the 'Five-Point Directive' Comrade Sheng issued about a decade ago? Is there any discrepancy between the two policies? If so, which one will prevail?" asked a woman from the delegation representing the media and publishing sector.

Si-Tu traced the voice and found it was from Dai Tian, who, if his memory served him well, was working as a senior reporter and editor with a provincial newspaper.

"There is no discrepancy between the two policies. The 'Five-Point Directive' was made in the war years, when our party needed to fight against armed enemies. The document therefore highlighted the purpose and unity that our communist members from the educated and artistic community must observe at that time. The new policy of 'let a hundred flowers blossom and a hundred schools of thought compete' is meant for the current era of peaceful economic development. The two policies speak for the different needs of different eras, and the new policy is certainly better suited for the needs of not only Communist Party members but also today's vast majority of intellectuals, artists, writers, and creative people of all sorts."

Song concluded the meeting by saying, "I think the premier has answered the questions very well. I would only add that our Communist Party is prepared to review our policies and activities to correct the corrosive habits of dogmatism, bureaucracy, hedonism, waste, and extravagance in our party. After the Soviet Communist Party held its 20th National Congress, many countries and people around the world were concerned with the issue of personality cult. I can tell you unequivocally today that our Chinese Communist Party is committed to preventing those tragic events in the Soviet Union from happening here in China. Our party is firmly against personality cult. We will continue our good revolutionary tradition of mass movement and mass line. Today's announcement is a clear indication of our firm belief in how to build a democratic China. We sincerely invite all of you, including those of your friends and comrades who are not here today, to join us on the new journey of building a great modern China."

5

The announcement at Scarlet Hall triggered an avalanche of views and opinions that shocked the nation.

One outspoken critic was the fearless Pan, who said, "After the liberation, the Communist Party has gradually become the people's boss, and yesterday's great call for 'serving the country' has turned into a hollow slogan today. Party members consider themselves the privileged few who have founded the nation, and therefore deserve special treatment. They monopolize power, indulge in extravagance, and consider themselves above the law. Boasting the party's 'greatness, glory, and correctness,' they put themselves above the country and people, as if the 'party is the country, the state is the party.' Because only the Communist Party has the complete authority to make any critical decisions on all matters, nonparty members and noncommunist organizations are never trusted or consulted.

"For the past few years since liberation," he went on, "no real socialist democratic practices have been implemented except for some token measures, which are not democratic at all or even close to the false democratic practices in the capitalist countries. The constitution has become a dead letter, and the party does not pay any attention to it. On the surface a general election and a united front do exist. But no nonparty people could hold any leadership roles with real authority. The Communist Party dictates everything. The twelve million-member party controls a country of six hundred million citizens. If you are not a party member, you only have the obligation to implement the party's resolutions, without having the right to participate in the decision-making process. The party is the overlord, holding the Marxist–Leninist bible in one hand and wielding the mighty sword of the state with the other. Whoever dares to raise objections will either be arrested or branded with the label of an 'anti-Marxist–Leninist' on his forehead. The election is only a sham, representing no one but the will of the party. Average citizens know nothing about how officials are elected, who they are, and why they are qualified to represent the people. When the general population has no right to free assembly, free association, free publication, and free expression, how can one say that the people are the masters of the country? This violation of basic human rights and destruction of the rule of law must be stopped."

Pan called on the Communist Party's top leader to come down from his throne to observe the real lives of the people. He called on the Chairman and the party to reform the government and to establish a real democratic state by granting the people the freedom of speech and by recognizing their fundamental human rights.

Similar sentiments and comments echoed throughout the country.

Mo suggested setting up a national institution of research for political reforms, where researchers, political scientists, government experts, veteran politicians, and experienced public figures would be recruited to work out a roadmap for a new democratic China. Governmental reforms, said he, should be an open process that welcomed the voices of the people, not a highly guarded party secret in the hands of a few.

Gan reiterated his longtime interest in freedom of expression and the rule of law. In an article in a national newspaper, he wrote,

The 20th National Congress of the Communist Party of the Soviet Union has clearly showed that the Soviet model has problems. The Chinese Communist Party should come out with its own ideas to deal with the problems in the international communist movement.

Democracy or how to realize modern democracy is one of the major problems the Soviet Union has not been able to resolve.

In the Soviet Union, the proletarian dictatorship has changed into the party's dictatorship, party dictatorship into the dictatorship of a few, and a privileged few into a totalitarian dictatorship of a single person.

From the National Central Committee to a small village, the party controls too much, leaving no room for autonomy and flexibility. The higher the party leaders rise, the harder they fall. Because those in power have formed a single class, they would not consider anything else but their own interests. They think alike and behave alike. They have no independence or the ability to stand on their own feet. Once Stalin falls, everyone goes down with him.

In Western countries such as England, France, and the United States, administrations change as frequently as people change their shirts. Yet society remains stable whether the government changes or not. Our problem is not that our leaders are unwise, but that we have not discover the peaceful solutions to our internal political differences due to the Marxist brand of authoritarianism we had inherited from the Soviet model.

The essence of democracy lies in freedom of expression and freedom of the press. Our newspapers are not allowed to discuss political issues. Freedom of expression does not exist. The people should have the right to comment and evaluate the activities and policies of their leaders, which would enhance their ability to select the appropriate officials.

If capitalist and imperialist countries can allow the free flow of information, why can't we do the same to allow free speech and freedom of the press?

We can learn something from the principles of "checks and balances" and "judiciary independence" under the capitalist system. Our current problem is too much "trivial social democracy" and too little "important political democracy."

The party Central Committee controls too much, and has kept the population ignorant.

The political system the Soviet Union has passed down to us is too inflexible, restrictive, and not responsive to change. The Chairman has enjoyed great prestige, which is a product of the past but increasingly promoted by personality cult. I hope the Chairman can use his great power and prestige to provide the answers on how to build a healthy socialist democracy based on freedom of expression and the rule of law.

Speeches and sentiments like this captivated the nation, which was on the brink of a huge explosion. Party officials watched the situation nervously, especially those at top of the hierarchy.

6

The Korean War. Stalin's death. Khrushchev's secret speech. Now the Hungarian revolution involving no fewer than one hundred thousand people flooding the streets of Budapest.

The film *The Villager*. Dong Zi-Tian's death. The first five-year plan. The collective reforms. The return of Tao Yin-Hu from Korea. Now the charges of dictatorship and totalitarianism from individuals, newspapers, and various organizations.

Feeling inundated, Sheng needed to escape from his office and take a stroll.

Leaving the Garden of Lilacs, he paused, not knowing which way to turn. Right in front of him was one large lake, around which the compound Abundance was located. If he turned to the right, he would have to pass several courtyards to the west side of the lake, where other Politburo members lived. It was better not to see them before the upcoming meeting, he thought.

If he turned to the left, the road along the south side of the lake, which was the size of one hundred and twenty football fields, would soon lead him to the island of the South Palace, where a young emperor of the Qing Dynasty died after he was allegedly poisoned by his mother. Not exactly a suitable place for the Chairman to be this evening, when he had too many things on his mind.

He made the left turn, passed the road to the island, and kept walking on a bridge until he reached the east bank of the lake. Rarely would any party officials come here, where a number of barracks housed the guards and servants.

Sheng slowed down and strolled along the well-maintained road next to the lake. His bodyguards kept a discreet distance of fifty feet behind him. Regulation number one of the compound prohibited anyone, including the staff, from approaching the Chairman or other top party leaders even if they could see them walking by.

A pleasant and peaceful October evening.

"They blamed me for ruling like an emperor," Sheng Bao complained to himself. "Do they know what they are talking about? Did they know how many emperors, princes, and royals have died in these picturesque royal gardens? Did they know how much blood has been shed in the Forbidden City next door? Plots, murders, conspiracies, intrigues, usurpations, coups d'état, manipulations, you name it. Is it easy to be an emperor even if you are given all the powers and authority? Do they know how many people are plotting to take my place every day? Do they know how difficult it is to protect and preserve my position even years after the liberation?"

Sheng arrived at a small unassuming pavilion named "Graceful Waters," which was constructed on a tiny piece of dry land. Standing under it, he could see the night lights blinking across the lake and feel the calm waters at his feet. A beautiful, quiet, and pleasant evening, he thought.

"The return of Tao Yin-Hu from Korea. The return of Tao Yin-Hu from Korea." The Chairman needed to consider his next move. The real reason why Sheng had eventually decided to sacrifice Dong was because of Tao, whose triumphant return after the ceasefire in Korea had generated a lot of excitement in the country. Instincts told him that a close collaboration between Dong and Tao, who made for a perfect combination, would be more threatening to his power than a tenuous alliance between Song and Si-Tu, who were much more submissive, indecisive, opportunistic, and manageable.

Tao was a war hero, who commanded enormous prestige in the military. Sheng had to find a way to counterbalance his growing popularity among the troops, over which the Chairman had always believed that he should have absolute control.

The next Politburo meeting would formally decide Tao's new appointment, and few would doubt that he would be the national defense minister. What could be done to limit his influence in an inconspicuous manner? The Chairman had weighed several options, but none satisfied him completely.

Then he remembered the poem in the ancient *Book of Songs*:

When a crane cries at the Nine Swamps
Its voice is heard in the wild.
A fish can plunge deep into the pool
Or rest upon the shoals.
Pleasant is that man's garden
Where the hardwood trees are planted;
But beneath them, only litter.
There are other hills whose stones
Are good for grinding tools.

When a crane cries at the Nine Swamps
Its voice is heard in Heaven.
A fish can rest upon the shoals
Or plunge deep into the pool.
Pleasant is that man's garden
Where the hardwood trees are planted;
But beneath them are only husks.
There are other hills whose stones
Are good for working jade.

The Chairman knew that Tao had several talented officers, such as Bao Feng-Nian, Xia-Hou Ding, and Yao Xi-Wa. "Some of them should be willing to collaborate with me if they were given the appropriate incentives," Sheng mused. He decided to call in Lin when he returned to his Garden of Lilacs.

October was the best month of the year in Peking. Almost every day was refreshingly clean, bright, sweet, and airy. A great variety of seasonal fruit, vegetables, and produce stocked the market, which delighted the snobbiest patrons and the most discriminating customers. For those city dwellers who had heard of the brilliant foliage of acres after acres of sycamore, maple, and smoke trees changing colors from green to yellow, red, and gold in the surrounding mountains of the suburbs, the consistent blue skies and mild temperatures of the fall never failed to encourage them to get out of the city to see it for themselves.

But the air was now getting chilly by the minute over the massive body of silent water in the darkness.

Sheng's personal guards had thoughtfully summoned his limousine driver to be on standby, and the car, stealthily parked next to the pavilion of Graceful Waters, was ready to carry the Chairman back to his residence anytime.

7

Hardly had a week passed by in Abundance without a Politburo meeting since Khrushchev had made his secret speech earlier in the year. No meeting was tenser and more disturbing than the present one, as the Politburo members examined several photos lying on the table, showing security forces opening fire and widespread unrest in the streets of Budapest, the capital of Hungary, a satellite country under the control of the Soviet Union since after World War II.

"This violent counterrevolution must be stopped!" said an indignant Sheng.

"Sources say that Khrushchev has decided to pull out the Soviet troops from Hungary," reported Song.

"What?" Those present—Si-Tu, Tao and Lin—were shocked.

"No, no, no, no! They can't do that!" yelled the agitated Chairman. "Somebody must tell the Soviets that, if they withdraw now, they will betray the Hungarian people. No communist should abandon socialist Hungary, unless he is prepared to be the eternal sinner."

As the meeting continued, Sheng glanced over some of the photos once more. Appalled, disgusted, and even personally hurt, he ended up being reticent but restless for the rest of the meeting.

Those photos showed a series of disturbing images, including one where a giant bronze statue of Stalin was pulled down in Budapest, its head chopped off and mutilated, and the severed body dragged through the streets in broad daylight.

For all the fierce battles Sheng had fought, and for all the tragic deaths he had seen, none had horrified him more than these few photos of the vandalized statue of a much-revered or feared communist leader. The Chairman had never been afraid of death, and he had experienced some of the most perilous military situations in his life—even though he had never carried a gun, or even shot at anyone. What upset Sheng tremendously was the way those Hungarian rebels had desecrated Stalin's statue—symbolizing the greatest humiliation of a most powerful man.

The death of a person, no matter how evil he might have been, should settle all accounts and end all hatred. Any mutilation of the body amounted to the worst form of disrespect in Chinese tradition, which could cause unease even among the most sympathetic onlookers.

Sheng was suddenly reminded of the possibility that, one day, a mob could treat him the same way as the Hungarian protestors had treated Stalin's statue— cutting up his body and dragging it through the streets. Such a gruesome scenario could not be ruled out in the near future if Sheng failed to choose a suitable successor, one who would faithfully protect and preserve his legacy.

"Look at what's going on in Hungary! Those damned counterrevolutionaries! It's all Khrushchev's fault! Look at what his secret speech has done to the legacy of Stalin! Look at the irrevocable damage the Soviet Union has done to the international communist cause!" The more the Chairman reviewed the situation, the more outraged he became. Sullen and depressed, he lit his fifth cigarette of the day.

Following the Hungarian revolution, the repugnant thoughts of body mutilations, despicable betrayals, worthless successors, vicious rebellions, and unrelenting rioters would haunt Sheng for years to come. Unable to shake off those horrific images of Stalin's massive statue being smashed and dragged through the streets, Sheng solemnly pledged to himself that, as long as he was alive, he would do everything possible to avoid a similar fate.

"Chairman, the meeting has reached a tentative decision." Si-Tu gently roused Sheng, who appeared lost in his thoughts.

"Oh, yes, yes. What do we have now?" The Chairman managed to pull himself together quickly.

"We have decided to send a delegation to Moscow immediately to inform the Russian leaders of our decision," Song replied.

"Good. Who will go?" asked Sheng.

"I will go," said Song.

"I will go too, if needed," Si-Tu volunteered. As the premier, he had always been in charge of the Department of Foreign Affairs and he was not about to cede control of his turf to Song, who, although not a competent administrator, was still a serious rival within the party.

"Good." The Chairman thought for a minute. "Why don't both of you go? Song will deliver the message personally to the Russians and the premier can stay behind to make sure that the Russians will send their troops back to Budapest."

"Understood," Song and Si-Tu responded.

That settled, the Chairman asked, "We do have one last item on the agenda, which is to appoint Tao Yin-Hu as our defense minister. Any objections?"

"No, not at all. General Tao has led our troops against the Americans in Korea. Who can better serve our Defense Department than him?" someone said, as others nodded in agreement.

"Then I would like to make a minor suggestion." Sheng tried to sound as casual as he could. "I would like to suggest that General Xia-Hou Ding be appointed as chief of staff of the armed forces to assist General Tao. And, to better coordinate the increasingly heavy workload our central committee has to handle, I would also like to suggest that General Xia-Hou Ding be appointed as secretary-general of the secretariat under the Politburo. Any ideas, comments, or suggestions?"

The Chairman's proposal caught them by surprise, coming at the tail end of the meeting. But, since the top leaders had been in harmonious agreement all along, and since the suggested appointment could indeed alleviate the Politburo's workload, no one was in the mood to let the meeting continue any longer by a lengthy deliberation.

"Yes, yes, no problem."

"General Xia-Hou Ding's distinguished career is known to all of us."

"Good suggestion."

"Wise choice."

Seemingly casual but in fact carefully calculated, Sheng's proposal was unanimously adopted.

A month later, new secretary-general Xia-Hou made his first report to the Chairman and the Politburo, viz.:

Protected by more than two hundred tanks, two hundred thousand Russian troops marched into Hungary, crushed the rebellion against Soviet domination, and rounded up its Hungarian supporters. Seven thousand, eight hundred people died, twelve thousand were wounded, thirty thousand were arrested and persecuted, several hundred ring leaders were executed, and two hundred and fifty thousand people fled the country. The chief conspirator, Imre Nagy, and fourteen associates, who had sought refuge in the Yugoslav embassy, were later arrested and charged with treason. Nagy and two other defendants were later executed.

Chapter 37

Leaps

1

TANIA NERVOUSLY ENTERED THE WARD IN ROTTERDAM WHERE Martin had been hospitalized for a month. Peter, who had arrived several days earlier, told her that the chances of recovery were not promising. His poor heart condition, made worse by the harsh incarceration he had suffered in Siberia, was wearing him down rapidly. Curled like a baby under the blanket, Martin was asleep, but Tania could feel his response to her touch even though his eyes remained close. It was as if he knew his girl had come to see him for the last time. Tania could sense that he was at peace with himself and ready to leave this world.

Peter took Tania out of the ward, and found a couch at the corner of the hall for them to sit down.

"How are you, my dear?" Tania asked, looking earnestly into the face of the man who looked so much like his father.

"I am fine. I am really fine. How about you, Mom?" Peter said.

"Oh, I am good. And so are Meng Bo-Xian, Meng Xi, and Yan Yan. Yes, everyone in the family is fine." For some reason, Tania started to sob even though everyone was fine in the family.

Peter put his right hand on Tania's shoulder to comfort her. "Dad said the other day that he was concerned about you, and that you have been under a lot of pressure lately."

"No, not at all," she replied.

"Mom, you don't have to hide anything. I have heard about what's happening in China," Peter persisted.

"No, don't listen to all that propaganda. Everything is okay in the family," assured Tania.

"But is the country all right?" Peter probed further.

"Of course! The country is doing great!" Tania replied.

"Great? What about—"

Peter attempted to dig further but was interrupted by a nurse, yelling, "Martin's family, come in quickly!"

Several nurses and a doctor hovered over Martin, trying to revive him. Tania and Peter rushed to his bedside. He was wheezing as he tried to utter some words, but neither one of them could figure out what he was saying. Martin drew his last breath, and the medical team slowly stepped back from the bed.

2

So, this was the place where it all began for Martin—Rotterdam was still a noisy port, with ships and trains coming in and out of waterways, canals, and railways all the time. But the 1940 Blitz had completely destroyed the old town, wiping out all the historic buildings and structures that could have shown visitors the city's glorious past. Tania and Peter stopped by the scaffolding site of the St. Lawrence Church in Cathedral Square next to the Delft Canal, and wished the rebuilt church could be as grandiose as its original self.

"This church must have been very beautiful before, and the porcelain plates the premier gave Martin are masterpieces," Peter recalled, having seen the Chinese state gift at his late father's house.

"They certainly are." Tania pondered for a while and suddenly she shouted, "The antique shop, the antique shop! Yes, yes. 'Antique' and 'shop'—those must be the last two words that Martin said!" She slowly mimicked the movement of his mouth to pronounce the syllables.

Peter realized his mother was right. "Yes, yes, he seemed to have said 'antique shop.' But what antique shop? Which one?" said the puzzled son.

"It does not matter," Tania replied. "Martin told me a long time ago how he had bought the tiny blue-and-white ceramic bottle at a corner store when he was a boy, using his monthly allowance, a real extravagant purchase in those days. Now, the antique shop must have been destroyed in the war as the rest of the city was callously bombed. What mattered was the memory he still had, still treasured until the last moment of his life."

Peter hugged Tania, "Mom, you are a very lucky woman. He still loved you and he still cared about you."

"Yes, he was a nice man and you had a very good father," Tania agreed. "How do you like your new teaching position?"

"I like it and I am glad McCarthyism and the Red Scare are over. Father told me that the intellectuals in China were under close scrutiny recently. Is that true?" Peter asked.

"Yes, it is true," Tania acknowledged, as if Martin's passing had allowed her to face a different challenge in her own life.

"Isn't China a country that greatly reveres learning and knowledge? Why have Chinese intellectuals suffered more than their counterparts in the West?" Peter asked.

"I asked Meng the same question, and his reply was 'tradition,'" Tania answered.

"Tradition? What does that mean?" said Peter, who was reminded of the book by his esteemed colleague and historian Richard Hofstadter, *Anti-Intellectualism in American Life*.

"Some two thousand years ago, Qin Shi Huang, the first emperor of China, executed several thousand scholars and burned tens of thousands of books to preserve his power. A terrible tragedy to the nation and an appalling instance in Chinese political history," explained Tania, who had learned the story from Meng.

"But the intelligentsia has been considered the mainstay of the country throughout history, hasn't it?" asked Peter.

"Yes," Tania responded. "But the problem is that the intelligentsia and officialdom are but the two sides of the same coin in China."

"Why?"

"Because, under Confucianism, the highest aspiration of the educated is not to become scientists, engineers, doctors, or lawyers but to become office holders in government. Learning in traditional China is synonymous with observing ancient moral codes, following established protocols in government, and most important, maintaining the status quo. Young students are taught not to develop their own potential by exploring truth or discovering new knowledge but instead to memorize by heart the millions of creeds and conventions buried in the old classics. Tens of thousands of them would spend the best years of their lives to prepare for the county, provincial, and national exams, hoping one day their well-adopted conformity would be recognized by the court. They are content to become a perfect devotee of the orthodoxy in order to be accepted into government bureaucracy. In this sense, China does not have the same class of intelligentsia as Socrates personified in the West. Except for a few extraordinary individuals, the educated Chinese are unimaginative government servants, not independent or creative thinkers."

"Why then should the government have any reason to fear and persecute them?" Peter wondered aloud.

"A good question. The reason is that only a fraction of the educated can be selected into the privileged group of government officials, while the vast majority of the learned would remain disenfranchised civilians or relegated bystanders. For the longest time, the powerful ruling elites have been preoccupied with the multiple threats of invasion, rebellion, or political conspiracy. Thus, the educated, sophisticated, but restless members of society would become the rulers' worst enemies if they were to collaborate with potential invaders, rebels, or conspirators. The rationale seems to be that 'if you don't serve me, you must be against me.' The ruling class therefore has been extremely suspicious about those gifted and cultured people, whose ideas frequently deviated from orthodoxy. How to control their minds, how to suppress those heretics, and how to eradicate those most dangerous nemeses wherever they are found, either inside or outside government, have been some of the most serious concerns of all Chinese rulers in history," Tania shared at length.

"Really?"

"Some of the most shocking and notorious cases involved the so-called 'literary crimes' during the last Qing Dynasty, when hundreds of intellectuals were arrested and executed. Informants alleged that they had found insidious innuendos against the royal authorities hidden in some essays or poems, which later turned out to be complete fabrications or hoaxes," Tania said.

"That's real tragic. Let's hope the Communist Party will not follow in those imperial rulers' footsteps," Peter said.

"I hope so too," Tania said. "How interesting that we are discussing China and Chinese tradition on the bank of the New Maas River in downtown Rotterdam." Turning to a happier subject, she asked: "How is Lynda?"

"She is fine," a smiling Peter said of his wife.

"Does she like Berkeley? Or do you miss New York?"

"Well, I would say we like both places," responded Peter, who had accepted a faculty position in the Political Science Department of the University of California, Berkeley.

"So, you are both New Yorkers and Californians?" Tania joked.

"I guess so," Peter said. "Oh, here is a letter that Martin left for you."

Tania opened the envelope. In it was a hastily scrambled message that appeared to be an outline of Martin's last thoughts on nine questions:

Why has a worldwide proletarian revolution failed to occur as promised by Marx?

Why the widespread development of democratic socialism in Western Europe?

Why the rise and fall of Stalinism in the Soviet Union?

Why the never-ending intraparty strife in a communist party?

Why the brutal suppression of the Hungarian revolution?

Why the "new class" as in Milovan Djilas's book?

Are these the personality problems of the leaders?

Are these the institutional problems of the party structure?

Are these the ideological problems of the inherited *isms*?

"Father said he did not have any satisfactory answers to these questions, but he hoped you will someday," Peter told Tania.

"I am not sure that I can find out all the answers. But I will try and I need your help too," she replied.

3

The mood at the Politburo meeting was jubilant. The Chairman's big and puffed face was radiating with satisfaction. "Xia-Hou Ding, tell us the result," he said loudly.

A robust and well-built man, Xia-Hou had been one of the top military officers since the earliest days of the Red Army. On that smooth and oval-shaped head, his stoic expression gave little away, whereas his sharp nose suggested intelligence and his protruded eyebrows determination. Despite his extensive combat experience under enormously harsh conditions, he had never been sick in the past thirty years. The secret was that, rain or shine, he would take a cold shower every morning, noon, and afternoon. A methodical tactician and a man of a few words, his success lay in the fact that he would never strike at the enemy until he had worked out the smallest details of a campaign—sometimes down to the position and movement of a single platoon.

Not much taller than when he was sitting down, Xia-Hou stood up and proclaimed, "The Anti-Rightist Movement has been a complete success. Half a million rightists have been identified; they had either expressed antisocialism or anti-Communist Party opinions. They will receive due punishment ranging from demotion and expulsion from their workplaces to being sent to hard labor camps."

Sheng Bao had estimated the number of rightists to be between one and ten percent of the nation's educated population. Xia-Hou put it at five percent, making it appear as if he was taking a middle-of-the-road approach. But the Chairman knew that Xia-Hou was not the simple-minded straight shooter many thought he was, and understood the game the officer was playing.

"I heard a significant percentage of them comprised university professors, scientists, engineers, publishers, writers, editors, and journalists. Is that correct?" the Chairman interrupted.

"Yes, that is correct," Xia-Hou dutifully replied.

Visibly delighted, the Chairman thought it appropriate to make a statement at the expense of his victims. His enemies had branded him variously as bandit, rebel, murderer, thug, insurrectionist, outlaw—all of which he accepted with a certain degree of pride. But the one thing that hurt Sheng's ego badly was to be ridiculed as "lowly educated." "See, those so-called intellectuals wanted us to adopt the capitalist system of elections and freedom of the press. They sought to overthrow our party and government. Many dared to question our leadership in those higher educational institutions, in the arts, literature, and science. Look again and see who is now leading whom? A humble and poor school student like me is today still in control of these great and famous intellectuals!"

Sheng beamed with pride, while his fellow Politburo members indulged him by smiling and grinning.

"Yes, yes. They must have realized by now what the Marxist and Leninist proletarian dictatorship really means," Song said servilely.

"These highly educated intellectuals must be wondering how they ended up being trapped by our Chairman's inconspicuous 'passive-defensive' strategy," added Si-Tu, who had a predilection for nifty political maneuvers, especially a highly calculated but understated one.

"Another half a million individuals have been classified as harmful members of our socialist society, ranging from persons with slight rightist inclinations to those with the most dangerous rightist tendencies. These classifications will be documented and put in their personnel files permanently. They shall receive further punishment in due time, from demotion to expulsion." Xia-Hou concluded the first part of his report.

"I would say the Chairman's tactic of 'luring a snake from its lair' was most brilliant, and has led to the great success of our Anti-Rightist Movement," praised Song.

"Yes, the strategy of 'round up the whole gang at one fell swoop' was undeniably as critical as in any battles against the nationalist Chen Han," Xia-Hou enthusiastically agreed, making no distinction between fighting against armed enemy troops and defenseless civilians.

"A small trick. A small trick. Our communists are not afraid of any opposition and confrontation, either the ones with machine guns or the ones with pencils and pens," said Sheng, who was brimming with confidence and satisfaction. "Whoever wants to challenge my authority, I will send them to hell," he continued under his breath.

"A few disgruntled professors, writers, novelists, editors, artists, and performers are no match for the masses, who will always side with us. A public meeting of a thousand will teach them a good lesson. An angry crowd of ten thousand will scare them to hell. Besides, what do I fear about the wicked but silly and weak intelligentsia? They have never had deep roots on the ground. They live in ivory towers. They do not know the peasants. They do not know the workers. They do not know the soldiers. The only thing they know are the few books they had read in New York, Moscow, or Berlin. In fact, in the United States they are called eggheads. How could these eggheads fight against our party and our People's Liberation Army?"

Casual, earthy, and randomly sentimental, Sheng's rambling resonated with his Politburo colleagues, who applauded him to show their appreciation of his great leadership and red-hot revolutionary spirit.

"If push comes to shove," the resolute Chairman declared, "I can always go back to the mountains to restart my guerrilla war and rebuild my revolutionary bases in the countryside."

Although the last part of his speech seemed to be sheer exaggeration and even unnecessary, those words were not uttered without purpose. Sheng wanted to intimidate those within the party, his colleagues, as much as he had terrorized those from without, like the intelligentsia—to ensure that no one would ever dare to challenge his power and authority. And he was completely prepared to launch another civil war to preserve them if need be.

After he had looked around the conference table to ascertain that every participant had gotten his message, he moved to another topic.

"I heard we have some collateral damage and fatalities," the Chairman half-joked, as he couldn't help himself from using language that was more suitable for the battlefield.

"Yes, Chairman." Xia-Hou proceeded to report on another aspect of the campaign. "Some three thousand party members made serious mistakes in this movement, and one hundred and fifty high-ranking officials in twelve provinces have also committed rightist crimes by supporting various capitalist propositions. They will receive punishment ranging from being stripped of their leadership positions to expulsion from the party."

"These rotten snakes, turncoats, spies, renegades, and apostates. They are worse than those rightist middle-class intelligentsia." Still haunted by the Hungarian revolution, the Chairman was especially wary of internal enemies, who could be time-bombs within the organization. Any of the party's top leaders could become the next Imre Nagy during a crisis, he feared. "They are the worst enemies of the party. They are cancerous. Their punishment must be severe and merciless," the Chairman instructed.

"Yes, yes. They will be sent to labor camps, which are more dreadful than prisons." Xia-Hou immediately wrote down the Chairman's orders.

He then said, "A final question—what about the punishment for Meng Bo-Xian, who has been very sympathetic toward those rightists?"

Sheng seemed to be prepared for this and turned to Tao Yin-Hu. "You two are good friends. Why don't you pay him a visit?"

"All right," calmly replied Tao, who knew that Sheng remained suspicious of him. The Chairman intended to test his loyalty by observing Tao's handling of Meng's case—he was one of the tens of thousands who had been rounded up in this Anti-Rightist Movement. But Tao thought he had nothing to fear and would be glad to visit his friend as ordered by Sheng.

"Very good. Good job. Xia-Hou Ding, you did not disappoint me." The Chairman rarely praised anyone, and this was one of the rare occasions when he publicly lauded someone's performance.

Xia-Hou kept his excitement in check. He sat down quietly, knowing that, as the most junior member, his duty was to listen, not to speak too much at such a serious meeting.

"Now, I have a favor to ask," said the Chairman, as always in control of the agenda.

"My erratic headaches have turned into regular migraines. I sincerely hope this meeting will release me from the duty as the country's president." He added, "I propose Comrade Song Pei to assume that position."

"No, no, no. The Chairman is always our great leader and the nation's great president." Song humbly refused, even though Sheng had spoken to him about the matter beforehand.

The back and forth between "yes" and "no," all the conceivable pros and cons, the strong insistence on resigning, the equally fervent refusal to accept it, and the hyper-ritualistic politeness continued for the next twenty minutes until everyone recognized that all the mandatory conventions had been faithfully adhered to.

So, the next president was decided. Song would become the new head of state without anyone outside the meeting room knowing about it. Released from his perfunctory duties and ceremonial role, Sheng would take on his favorite position of working behind closed doors to draw up great plans for China and for himself.

4

When Tania returned home from Rotterdam, nothing was recognizable in the capital. Loudspeakers, big-character posters, upbeat music, and the deafening sounds of gongs and drums filled broad streets and small alleys alike. "The Party's General Line Is to Construct Our Socialist Society with Great Output, Stride, Efficiency, and Economy," official signs, slogans, broadcasts, and newspaper headlines reminded the residents time and again. Visibly different from the plain style of the populace, teams of young performers put on nice makeup and colorful clothes. Touring every neighborhood, these propaganda squadrons danced and played revolutionary music, encouraging residents and passersby to participate in the latest campaigns of the Great Leap Forward. Large crowds, huge excitement, high expectations, and the sea of red flags had transformed Peking into a gigantic army camp fully galvanized and ready to act.

"Where is Bo-Xian?" Tania asked as she entered the house.

"He has been charged as a rightist, stripped of his office, and sent to the countryside to work as a brickmaker," Yan Yan answered.

"Where is Meng Xi?"

"She is on a field trip with her classmates to round up sparrows in the countryside."

"Sparrows in the fields? Why?"

"Because, along with rats, flies, and mosquitoes, household sparrows have been identified as one of the four pests targeted by a national hygiene campaign for their extermination."

"Any news from Dai Tian?"

"She's in deep trouble. As a result of her outspokenness in the last few months, she is no longer the senior editor at her newspaper, and has been assigned to conduct some field reporting in the distant poor hinterlands."

"Where are you going with the metal pots and pans?"

"Our neighborhood furnace needs them."

"Neighborhood furnace? What neighborhood furnace?"

"Each ward in the city has built a backyard furnace. And ours is to produce the first steel tonight!" Off Yan went after the bizarre response.

The baffled Tania sat down. She picked up some papers from a pile of official newspapers and party documents, hoping that reading them might shed some light on what was happening.

Frankly, the history of the Communist Party had been one of endless crusades—massive demonstrations, big or small uprisings, organized rebellions, recruitment drives, internal rectifications, land reform programs, the Korean War, collectivization campaigns, "letting a hundred flowers blossom and a hundred schools of thought contend," and the nationwide Anti-Rightist Movement. But none of these could compare with the energy and magnitude of the Great Leap Forward, which had seized the entire nation's imagination in a way never seen before.

The mastermind of this unprecedented mobilization was once again the Chairman. Only two years earlier, Song Pei and Si-Tu Wen-Liang had produced a similar plan for substantial economic expansion within fifteen to seventeen years, which was a very ambitious target. Not happy with the timeline, Sheng ridiculed Song and Si-Tu's proposal "as too cautious, timid, conservative, and backward-looking as if women with bound feet."

Sheng vowed to catch up with the industrial output of Great Britain in ten years, while surpassing that of the United States in fifteen. Astonishingly, the Chairman continued to revise his own timeline several times in the next few months and finally claimed that China would beat the steel production of Great Britain in three years and that of the United States in seven.

The available statistics showed, Tania recalled, the country had produced five million tons of steel last year in 1957. Song and Si-Tu's goal was to double that amount in twelve months, which was already extremely aggressive. Sheng's sweeping revision was to triple China's annual production of steel in a year, which would be regarded as impossible by any rational economist around the world.

Where did the enthusiasm come from? Was it the result of overconfidence? Why such insane economic goals? What would be the cost? And where would this extremely zealous campaign lead to?

Troubled by these vexing questions, Tania decided to visit Meng to get some answers.

5

Choice. Life is all about choices, right or wrong, good or bad, expedient or deliberate, selfish or noble. Sometimes, those choices were voluntary. Sometimes, they were forced upon a person. Sometimes, the person could be extremely proud about his choices, while other times embarrassed by them. Either way, a person's life was determined by his choices and their consequences.

The moment Tania arrived, she knew this must be an exclusive place where no women were to be found.

On the left bank of a river, a small village sat at the mouth of a valley, with sprawling fields in front and rolling hills at the back. Less than one hundred miles from the capital, the village of Broken Kiln had a celebrated past. It used to be a royal facility and produced fine ceramics for no one but the court. Dynastic cycles came and went, and the kiln lost its privilege because the style and color of its products were no long wanted. Devastated local craftsman shifted to produce other varnished artifacts, but the quality of glaze they managed to create was too poor to compete in the market. The kiln folded when all the workmen left.

Some two hundred years later, along came an old and crippled man, who recognized the potential of the ancient but deserted kiln. The clear water, the desirable quality of the local soil, and the abundant trees in the nearby hills would make a perfect site for the manufacture of tiles. No one remembered exactly when tile making had to make way for brick production, which had remained the most famous local product for generations.

Normally, no women would walk into the compound where men, laboring under grueling conditions and high temperatures, were often thinly clothed if not almost naked, while a strong local superstition alleged that a female presence would make the bricks brittle.

The villagers at Broken Kiln had never seen any government official higher than a district head. They promptly treated Meng with deference, believing that the senior position he used to hold automatically entitled him to everything he wanted, including a spousal visit, which was not allowed to other laborers.

A few weeks of work at the kiln had converted Meng into a passionate brickmaker. As soon as Tania sat down on a small kang in his dorm, he could not help but share the excitement of his newly acquired knowledge.

"Many outsiders believe that we must have some secret recipe in our brick making," said Meng. "In fact, honesty and hard work are the only things we need. We do have desirable local soil that has the perfect quality for making bricks. But before it could be used, the smooth, gray clay has to be laid in the open and turned back and forth regularly every day for up to five years. The four seasons every year and the hot and cold temperatures from day to day, month to month, break the soil so completely that all the particles of the earth reach a total consistency in firmness and moistness."

He continued, "Once the earth is mixed with water into dough, it has to sit for another seven days, which allows a new consistency to set in. With as much precision as sheer force, the workmen press the stabilized dough through a heavy wooden mode to cut out a brick. Lying for another day or two, each fresh brick is arranged in the kiln by a specialist, who ensures that all the bricks will be placed in such a way as to receive the same temperature in the heating process. The master craftsman then starts the fire and watches the rise of the temperature closely. Like all brick kilns, ours can rise up to one thousand or one thousand, two hundred degrees. Experience will be the only reliable barometer here because the quality of the fuel, the humidity of the season, and the changing elements of day and night can easily alter the temperature inside the kiln.

"When after four to five days the master craftsman orders to put out the fire, we will climb on top of the kiln to spread water slowly and evenly, helping the inside to cool. How much water should be used and how much steam should be generated are entirely up to the master craftsman's judgment and expertise. The kiln cannot be opened until he says so, and no brick will become our final product until it is thoroughly dried by wind under a specially covered shelter for a week.

"In flawless form and consistency, every brick from our kiln is the best building material in any construction. Depending on the different sizes the customers have ordered, the bricks can weigh from thirty-five to one hundred pounds. Every corner and every line of the brick is perfectly aligned in straight ninety degrees no matter from what point you begin to measure. Our beautiful bricks are known for their smooth blue hues, rock-solid bodies, and impeccable shapes. Most of all, they can produce a pleasant metallic sound when knocked, which no any other brickmakers can replicate." Meng concluded his detailed explanation.

"Well, you sound like a master brickmaker already," said an amazed Tania.

Never a pessimistic person, Meng showed no signs of depression or self-pity in this hard labor camp. Although totally obsessed with his new job and new knowledge, the harsh life had taken a toll on his appearance. Scorched by the sun and blazing flames of the kiln and perpetually sweating, Meng had aged considerably, with visible wrinkles on his face and large bruises and calluses on his hands. He had also lost a lot of weight and now looked like a withered carrot. But Meng still managed to smile as he did not want Tania to feel sad. He had always cared more about her than himself.

As she gazed at Meng, Tania had a flashback to a scene from her past—it was as if she were looking at Dong Zi-Tian in the wild and impoverished mountains in Shaanxi years ago. What a strange similarity. What a strikingly similar experience, she thought.

6

A month earlier, Tao had gone to see Meng, to inform the latter that Sheng was outraged by his strong criticisms of him, the party, and the government. The Chairman had called Meng a rightist, and the Politburo had agreed on three possible kinds of punishment for him—submit an unreserved apology, get demoted, or be sent to a hard labor camp.

"So, the Chairman wanted you to deliver the message. And of course he wanted to know my reaction from your report," Meng had then told Tao. "I will choose hard labor."

The two friends had shaken hands and exchanged smiles. Tao had known that Meng would never apologize, while Meng had hoped that his decision would not only allow him to keep his conscience clear but also reduce Sheng's suspicions of his friend Tao.

"I knew you have information for me. But we have to talk about how to make bricks. Someone must be watching and we need to be careful," Meng explained as he hugged Tania in his dark and cold bedroom.

"I know," said she, who enjoyed putting her head against his chest.

"It was good that you could see Martin before he passed away. How is Peter?" Meng asked.

"He has moved to California with his wife Lynda. He loves his new teaching position at UC Berkeley."

"But Martin did leave some questions, which I think you may have some answers." To ensure that she would not leave any paper trail, Tania told her husband the nine questions verbally.

"Hmm, these are important but huge questions. I have to think carefully before I can answer them," Meng responded.

"I also don't understand why there is a need for the current Great Leap Forward campaign, and why the excessive targets for economic development," Tania shared what had been bothering her.

Meng thought for a while and said, "I think it could be more than economics."

"What then besides economics?" she asked.

"As you have correctly pointed out, the goal set by Song and Si-Tu was very high. To double our steel production in one year would be a great, if not impossible achievement under any circumstances," Meng said.

"But I don't see any domestic imperative to triple that output, which would be, yes, as you have said, a madness," he went on. "The armed conflict between us and the nationalists during the civil war was a life-and-death issue, which had to be resolved one way or the other. But an unrealistic timeline for economic progress can be counterproductive, especially when we don't have much experience and expertise in this area. Unless the Chairman is under the impression that economic expansion can be achieved by using the same tactics for military confrontation, in which you can wage one campaign after another and keep assaulting the enemies until they collapse."

"Yes, I think so too. The Soviet Union has made serious blunders in economic policies even with many specially trained experts and highly educated professionals," said Tania.

"A good point," concurred Meng, who suddenly seemed to have discovered some clue to the puzzle. He contemplated for a few moments and then yelled out, "Yes, yes, it must have something to do with the Soviet model and experience."

"Why? Why would the Great Leap Forward have anything to do with the Soviet Union?" Tania was more confused than ever.

"If what I have observed is correct, I think the connection can be the following," Meng said calmly. He went on to share with Tania his analysis:

The death of Stalin ushered in a brand-new era of international communism. Personal grudges and old complaints against the deceased notwithstanding, Sheng realized that he had the potential to become the next Lenin or Marx on the global stage of the proletarian movement. Perhaps rather incidental and tenuous from the beginning, this rare and exciting ambition gradually crystallized as he watched the handful of rival candidates closely. Despite the great prestige many Soviet leaders had, for example, Khrushchev was no more senior or experienced than Sheng in the international communist movement.

Based on an implicit understanding, the Soviet Union would lead the revolution in Europe, while China did so in Asia. But Khrushchev's secret speech, the decline of Stalinism, and the Soviet actions in postwar Poland and Hungary had undermined the Russian leader's authority and reputation. The expulsion of Yugoslav leader Tito from the communist camp and the failure of the Polish and Hungarian uprisings reaffirmed the need for a strong international leader in the communist world. Sheng believed that his firm stand and active involvement in Eastern European affairs had enhanced his reputation beyond Asia.

But, to become the legitimate successor to Marx and Lenin, his achievements in diplomacy and international relations were not enough. Sheng must accomplish something grand, unique, and outstanding; he surveyed the revolutionary landscape.

The armed struggle he led in China was spectacular, but the Bolsheviks had done that in 1917, in their civil war, and in World War II.

The Chinese land reforms and collectivization movement were impressive, but the Soviet Union had championed those programs and achieved those objectives a long time ago.

China was at the historic juncture of becoming a modern industrial society, which was again more or less a copy of the Soviet model of a planned socialist economy.

Sheng realized that, to fulfill his newfound potential as the preeminent leader of the communist world, he must accomplish something distinctively Chinese. His achievement must also be universally significant so that communists worldwide would recognize his greatness second only to Marx or Lenin.

What uniquely Chinese characteristics could he bring into the lexicon of international communism?

A militant peasant rebellion—the most radical form of revolution?

A tight party apparatus—the most centralized form of bureaucratization?

A new style of personality cult—the epitome of dictatorship and authoritarianism?

Deeply embedded in the native Chinese experience, these examples did not have a wide appeal that the Chairman could brag about in front of a world audience.

Too many years in the isolated countryside, too much focus on those pragmatic applications of communist doctrines, but too little time, preparation, and opportunity to formulate his own distinct philosophy. Never before had Sheng been so frustrated at his lack of theoretical attainment, which might have produced his own brand of ideology as grand and everlasting as Marx and Lenin had done.

A rural and underdeveloped nation, China had little to offer except for its large number of citizens, in whom Sheng finally found his leverage.

Yes, indeed, the sheer size of the inhabitants in China was unmatched in the world.

Mass campaigns, mass movements, mass mobilizations, mass recruitment, mass participation, and the party's mass line—they were all uniquely Chinese.

The party could not survive without the multitudes, and the Chairman's most splendid talent was to mobilize and manipulate them.

The extraordinary size of the Chinese population might not change the innate nature of communism, but it could introduce to that revolution a preponderant momentum—the scale, speed, and impact of which the world had never seen before.

This greatest collective movement in history, which would captivate a quarter of the world's population, could not be achieved until the Chairman, who had been the undisputed master manipulator of the masses, lent his hand.

Yes, with more than six hundred million Chinese galvanized by the party to support him, the Chairman would be able build a socialist–communist society bigger, faster, more substantial, more popular, more decisive, and more dynamic than the Soviet Union had ever been able to demonstrate.

His Chinese model of revolution would then beat, outshine, and outpace the Soviet model. This unprecedented achievement would no doubt put Sheng on the throne of the international communist movement. The proletarians around the world would recognize his greatness. He would then become the first non-European to be in the company of such giant figures as Marx and Lenin.

Ambition was a strange medicine, which could alter a person completely. The more tantalizing the ambition was, the more catastrophic the consequence would be. Sheng's newfound aspirations started to consume him, and would eventually drive him over the edge.

However dedicated internationalists they had been, Song and Si-Tu were content with their existing roles as China's national leaders. Struggling with his mundane duties, Song wished to have no extra responsibilities. The tactful and gregarious Si-Tu, often preoccupied by daily businesses with various departments, knew his limits and had no desire to compete for global fame. Neither of the two men would need any new earth-shaking success to further their careers beyond the national borders.

But the highly motivated Sheng needed one that could shake not only China but also the world. He therefore drove Song and Si-Tu crazy, blaming them for their slow pace and conservative plans for economic growth, even though the targets they had set for China were already highly unrealistic.

What the zealous Chairman demanded was speed and scale—faster speed, bigger scale, the faster the better, and the bigger the better, which was now known as the Great Leap Forward. He badly needed this new record of success. At sixty-five, he was racing against time. Before his demise, he wished to see the day when he would rise to the pinnacle of prestige and power, not just in China but also in the communist world.

As Sheng often did in formulating a military stratagem, he would not consider the costs involved, no matter how devastating an impact the campaign might have on human lives and the economy. Once he had set his goals, he would never give up until he prevailed. This dogged determination and fierce fighting spirit could be a strength in military actions, but not necessarily in economic planning.

The Chairman might have mistakenly assumed that nothing could be more challenging for him than to be tested in the battlefield. But, in reality, economic, financial, and productive operations could be far more difficult to plan and manage. The large number of intricate complexities, multiple sectors, hidden costs, diverse influences, overlapping dimensions, and invisible variables could easily outnumber those complications in any military campaign.

Meng concluded his patient analysis by saying, "The repercussions of an economic catastrophe might not be visible or felt by us at the moment. In the end, we may all have to pay for Sheng's grandiose ambitions."

Meng's dire prediction stunned Tania. A highly pessimistic view from a usually optimistic person. Tania did not know whether she should agree or disagree with him.

7

"Tania, I have some important news to tell you," said Dai Tian as she grabbed Tania's hand and led her to a chair in the living room.

Tania had just returned home from Broken Kiln and found her friend quivering with both fear and excitement.

"What important news? Is it good or bad?" asked Tania, who was delighted to see Dai.

"I have learned how Dong Zi-Tian was shot," Dai said, her voice shaking as if overwhelmed by her discovery.

"What? Didn't they tell you that Zi-Tian had committed suicide?" It was Tania's turn to be shocked.

"Yes, they did. But I learned the truth from another source recently," Dai said.

"What source? Is it reliable?" Tania asked.

"Yes, very credible. Han Jian, the person who talked to me, was one of the two guards at the place where Zi-Tian had been detained," Dai explained.

"What happened then?"

Dai continued, "On the morning of Zi-Tian's death, Lu Di-Ping and two guards came. Lu Di-Ping asked Han to stay behind to guard the door, as he and the other soldier went in. Han soon heard a quarrel breaking out inside. Zi-Tian said he must see the Chairman to ask the latter to clear his name. Lu told Zi-Tian the Chairman was too busy dealing with urgent matters, and had no time to meet someone like him. Zi-Tian must have gotten very angry at this point, for Han heard the sound of fistfight followed by 'bang!'—a gunshot—a few seconds later. He rushed in, and saw smoke coming out from the other guard's pistol. The room was filled with the foul smell of gunpowder, Zi-Tian was lying on the floor in a pool of blood, and a bullet had pierced his heart. Lu warned the two soldiers not to say anything to anyone and rushed to report the incident to Sheng Bao."

"Now I remember, there has never been a coroner's report on Zi-Tian's death," Tania said.

"No, not even a coroner's report," confirmed Dai.

"How could we find hard evidence to prove the soldier's story? They could deny the account by insisting that it's all hearsay," Tania wondered.

"Yes, that's the problem. I don't know what to do, and I don't know who to believe." The confused, tormented, and heartbroken Dai began to sob.

"My dear friend, my poor girl," Tania embraced Dai. She looked at Dai's pale face, pretty yet wretched, wondering how to get to the bottom of Dong's death.

Chapter 38

Bounds

1

"YOU ARE RIGHT, CHAIRMAN. PREPARATIONS FOR THE MOVIE *THE Villager* started before 1949. Many of its crew members—the producer, director, screenwriter, actors, and actresses—had ties with the old regime, and some of them were Nationalist Party members. No wonder it was a bad reactionary movie," Su Ming reported to Sheng Bao after her team had completed its investigation.

"Hmm, very good. What else have you learned?" the Chairman asked, pleased to hear the results of Su's mission.

"I now know that 'art for art's sake' doesn't exist. Promoting reforms rather than revolution, extolling reformers and denigrating revolutionaries, the movie has been capitalist propaganda all along," Su answered with confidence.

"How so?" the Chairman probed.

"Well, as you have said, the value of an art lies in whether or not it can contribute to the proletarian cause. The more it can serve the cause, the more valuable the product is. But, if it does a disservice to the cause, it is counterrevolutionary art, no matter how artistic it is," Su replied.

"Yes, 'art for art's sake' is bogus. Only two kinds of art exist—proletarian or capitalist. You know why?" the Chairman said.

"Why?" Su asked.

"Because the proletarian and the capitalists are the two principal antagonists in our society. Any art, either a movie, a play, a painting, or a novel, will take a stand—either for us the proletarians against the capitalists, or for the capitalists against our proletarians. There is no middle ground in this fight," he explained.

"You are absolutely correct, Chairman."

"No, no, no. It's not me, but Marx, Karl Marx. He pointed out in the *Communist Manifesto* that all human history is a history of class struggle—a tenet I have never forgotten since I first read it almost forty years ago," the Chairman said, with a tinge of nostalgia.

His enthusiastic yet sentimental voice was infectious. Su was in awe for she had never seen the Chairman this emotional. His fervent conviction, total dedication, and one hundred percent pure Marxist beliefs overwhelmed her, and she felt so proud and so fortunate to be his wife. Su vowed to herself that she would forever stand by his side, to protect this great Marxist, this great leader of the Chinese proletarians, and the world's greatest communist hero.

"Any news lately?" Sheng's question brought Su out of her reverie.

"Oh, in a recent article a university professor claims that our country's population is too big, and that the yearly growth rate of two to three out of every thousand is too fast. If the government does not control the birth rate through appropriate family planning programs, the national population could explode to two billion within fifty years, which will be extremely hard for the country to support," said Su.

"Yeah, I heard the news too," he said, nodding. "Those big arrogant capitalist intellectuals would never miss a chance to teach us something. They always believe they are smarter than we are. They are always questioning and challenging our ability to govern. They never understand that the real strength of our party comes from the people—the bigger their number, I believe, the better it is for the country. In the past, tens of millions of Chinese had followed our lead to take down the nationalist government. They now continue to follow us to build a wonderful socialist and communist society that they have dreamed of for generations. The larger the population the country has today, the more massive following we can expect to command tomorrow. The more massive participation in the Great Leap Forward, the sooner China will be the first to witness the triumphant success of communism. What could be wrong with that?" the determined Chairman asked.

2

Sheng was elated as he left the capital to visit the countryside. According to a populist phrase, "The people are the water, and the party is the fish." The unequivocal belief in such mutual dependency was reiterated in the organizational tenet of "faith in the people and faith in the party," which appeared as big-character slogans in many places across the country. They provided the Chairman with the immense reassurance he was looking for.

He had not felt this reinvigorated for a long while since he moved into the royal compound in Peking, where he had been surrounded by red tape and unimaginative bureaucrats. All he could hear was negativity, cynicism, caution, and warnings. "No, no, no, you can't do this." "No, no, no, you can't do that." "It's too fast." "It's too risky." "It's too bold." "It's too uncertain." "It's too premature." Sheng was sick and tired of such pessimistic mentality.

"Where is the revolutionary spirit? Where is the can-do attitude we used to possess in the trying times of guerrilla war when we had nothing? Now we have finally achieved power and have all the national resources at our disposal, and yet they are telling me we can't do much?" Strongly skeptical of what he had been told, the Chairman decided to flee from the suffocating capital city and to see for himself what was really going on in the country.

Since Sheng dreaded flying and was deeply concerned about his safety, he boarded his special train, which would take him anywhere he wanted to go. The vast green North China Plain welcomed him with the first breath of fresh air. In the dew-soaked farm field, the Chairman's arrival attracted huge crowds and local officials could not wait to tell him some good news.

"Our wheat production is three hundred bushels per acre this year, which is five times that of last year!" reported one.

"Our corn production is five hundred bushels per acre this year—three times that of last year!" said another.

"Why has productivity increased so much?" asked the Chairman, who felt vindicated by the reports.

"Socialism and collectivization have all the answers," replied one.

"The party's correct policies and your great leadership," another chimed in.

"So, the Great Leap Forward is correct?" Sheng tested the crowd.

"Of course." "The most appropriate!" "An absolute must!" "A great success!" His audience cheered.

"What do peasants like the most?" The Chairman had always cared about the opinions of the lower strata in society.

"They love the people's commune. They especially like the public mess hall, where you can eat as much as you can and whenever you want," came the answer.

"So, the people's commune is a desirable new institution? And the public mess hall a good idea?" The delighted Chairman needed to hear direct confirmation.

"No question at all. The people's commune is a great idea and the public mess hall is most wonderful!" the enthusiastic crowd responded in unison.

"The mess hall frees housewives from working in the kitchen," one woman said.

"So much grain is in storage, we don't know what to do with it," one official added.

"Great! Long live the people's commune! And everybody can have five meals a day at the public mess hall then!" suggested the exuberant Chairman, who had never felt this pleased before.

"Long live the people's commune! Love live the Communist Party! Love live the great Chairman Sheng Bao!" the ecstatic crowd cried at the top of their lungs.

Sheng was deeply touched. His strategies had worked. If party leaders resisted his ideas, his last resort was to appeal to the people directly. He could always count on their support because his prestige would always prevail. Any opposition against him would fade away before the populace who worshiped him as a demigod.

Surrounded by the adoring masses, Sheng remained humble before them and insisted, "People are the real heroes. The masses will always win." He led the crowd to shout, "People and only the people are the real engine of history!"—even though he did not believe for a minute in any of the words uttered.

3

A letter from Yao Xi-Wa deeply troubled Tao Yin-Hu, who could not sleep after reading it.

Nicknamed "Little Tiger," Yao had been his favorite officer in the army for thirty years. Tao trusted him but still could not believe what the letter had said.

Recently I had a chance to go back to my hometown in the countryside of Jiangxi and saw swarms of people working in the fields. When asked what they were doing, they said they were launching an artificial satellite.

"A manmade satellite?" I was surprised.

"Yes, yes. All of our neighbors are launching satellites every day. We are working to launch ours tomorrow," one said.

"A satellite can be launched in the fields?" I asked.

"Of course. One neighborly commune launched one the other day, claiming to have produced eighteen thousand pounds of paddy rice per acre, which was a satellite!" another villager answered.

"But that was beaten two days later by the satellite launched by another commune, which was twenty-five thousand pounds per acre," someone else said.

"So, a satellite refers to the highest yield of rice you can produce," I said.

"Yes, yes. But it can be the record production of anything. A wheat satellite is six thousand pounds an acre. A pumpkin satellite is three thousand pounds. A champion pig is five thousand pounds. A cotton king is as big as a tree..." They went on and on.

Is this the Great Leap Forward? I asked myself. Most of us who had grown up in the countryside knew how much an acre could produce. A yield of six thousand pounds of rough rice would be considered a very good year for a top producing acreage. Unless there was some miracle, a yield three or four times of that in such a short period was really mind-boggling.

I saw they were carrying loads of rice crops into the same paddy field and asked, "Are you faking it?"

"We don't care. Nobody cares. The county heads will be coming tomorrow to weigh the yield. What they need are numbers, nothing else," they said.

So shocked was I that I was literally speechless.

Is this what we really want? We have set up high goals for economic advancement, which is perfectly fine. But can we really achieve them by making up those incredible numbers? If the average villagers care less, what about those officials? Do they care? Or do they report those numbers to the central government, which will, in turn, use those highly inflated numbers to make national economic plans?

Tao had heard similar rumors in recent months about the exaggeration of economic achievements, including false reports and misleading statistics. He conveyed those concerns to Song Pei and Si-Tu Wen-Liang, thinking they would take care of the problems. After all, Tao was the defense secretary and he did not want to be seen as interfering with something that was not under his jurisdiction.

The part of Yao's letter that troubled Tao most was his final paragraph:

If this had happened during a war, thousands of our soldiers would have died because of the wrong information. In our party, false reports have never been tolerated in war, nor should they be in peacetime.

Tao decided that he would personally investigate the situation to ascertain if there was any truth in what Yao had said.

4

The world had never seen an institution as omnipresent and omnipotent as the Chinese Communist Party, nor had the ubiquitous churches of any ancient world religions ever possessed the same degree of power and dominance as this modern colossal organism. Adding one million new members every year since 1949, the party membership ballooned to thirteen million in a decade—greater than the populations of the Netherlands or Australia. If the party were a nation, it would have been one of the largest on earth.

Only veteran party members were allowed to hold the top post in any head office, be it administrative, military, economic, commercial, civil, educational, or cultural. A party committee of three to five officials controlled everything everywhere, from a small elementary school to a large corporation, from an urban shoe factory to a tiny village in the wilderness, from a newspaper publishing house to a squadron of foot soldiers, from a research institute to a dancing company, from a state postal office to any police force. And the network of seven hundred thousand village committees, forty thousand township committees, two thousand county committees, six hundred city committees, and thirty provincial committees controlled the lives of the entire population.

Sitting on top of the immense bureaucracy, the party's Central Committee and its three most active branch offices—the organization, propaganda, and united front departments—controlled the operations of the party and the few hundred high-ranking officials of those committees and departments controlled the decision-making processes of the whole organization. In the end, of course, the five members of the Politburo, especially the Chairman, were the real party bosses, controlling all the appointments, promotions, demotions, and dismissals of the top senior officials.

Unity, conformity, and efficiency were the strengths of this empire, which could mobilize the citizenry to focus on a single task faster than any other nation or institution could. But the top-down organization tolerated no dissenting opinions or criticisms, which were regarded as the worst internal threats to the party's authority, unanimity, and cohesiveness. If Sheng, the red emperor, enjoyed adulation and flattery and frowned on associates who disagreed with him, he was only personifying this mammoth institution, which thrived on strict party discipline and monopolization of power in the hands of party elites.

Since his demotion after the death of Dong Zi-Tian, Lu Di-Ping had been thinking about how to regain his previous position in Abundance. Strictly speaking, Lu should not really complain about his "demotion," since his new appointment as the first secretary of the party committee of Henan Province amounted to just a slap on the wrist. His ranking and remuneration remained the same, and his position as provincial secretary (only thirty were available) was one of highest in the country, next only to those department heads of the central government. His transfer was less a demotion than a horizontal move from one high government post to another. But, since any position in the central government in the capital carried much more prestige than a provincial one, and since his old job in Abundance was one of the most coveted in the party, Lu felt that he had been made the scapegoat for Dong's death, which he believed had been much desired by the Chairman.

As any obedient party member who clearly understood how the system worked, all Lu could do was to hold his tongue, lick his wounds, and wait for the next chance. Once someone like Lu had become part of this massive machine, it would control his life, never the other way round. Unless he sought self-destruction, he must find a way to ingratiate himself with the boss, the only one who could reverse his fortune.

The Great Leap Forward presented such an opportunity and Lu was determined not to let it pass. He rallied the party members under his domain and urged them to fulfill the great Chairman's dream of bold social change and rapid economic development.

"Artificial satellites! I want a record-breaking satellite in every field. I want people's communes in all the counties. I want backyard furnaces built everywhere. I want the best results, I want exceptional achievements, and I don't care what you have to do to get them!" he yelled at his subordinates, who ran like hell to demand the same from their subordinates.

As much as the Chairman's wishes were like royal decrees to the party, the first secretary's desires were like military orders in Lu's province.

The chain of command extended to every party committee in all local organizations, schools, banks, plants, workplaces, businesses, communities, and villages, and a massive movement of human action spread across Henan like no one had ever seen.

Brilliant performance and splendid news poured in.

According to initial feedback, the best wheat production jumped from two hundred and seventy bushels per acre to four hundred and sixty bushels, then to six hundred bushels, and finally to nine hundred and fifty bushels in a month!

The yield of sesame seeds increased seventy times to six hundred and seventy bushels an acre, while that of corn, sorghum, millet, and soybeans one hundred times!

Fully anticipating that the total annual yield would triple, the exuberant Lu wired Peking, "The Chairman's prediction that the output of farm products would increase by leaps and bounds in the near future has been realized in my province."

Meanwhile, he informed the party's Central Committee that eight counties in Henan Province had the capacity to produce one thousand tons of iron daily, and that the highest was more than four thousand tons a day.

Soon *The People's Daily*, the party's official organ, published an editorial "congratulating Henan Province for becoming the first province in the country to achieve a record production of eighteen thousand tons of iron made by backyard furnaces in a single day."

Within three months of the time when the first commune was established, ninety-five percent of rural families had formed one thousand, three hundred and thirty-five communes. All public mess halls were open and free, and some peasants received partial salaries.

No one was happier than the Chairman when he heard the exciting news. He told top party officials, "Henan can be a good model. If Henan can do it, so can the rest of the country."

Lu was thrilled. He knew that orthodox Marxism had anticipated a transitional period from socialism to communism. But no one, not even the first socialist country, the Soviet Union, knew how long the transition would last. If China were to discover a different but speedy path from socialism to communism that the Soviet experience had yet to show, the Chairman would no doubt become the greatest leader of the international communist movement. Willing to bet his career on Sheng's majestic ambition, Lu vowed to lead the charge in the Chairman's latest campaign. Even though the Russian Bolsheviks had pioneered the first socialist revolution in one country and even though no Marxist theorist knew when, where, and how communism would ultimately come, the dedicated and fearless Lu moved ahead of the pack, boasting that "one province can achieve communism" and that "Henan will achieve communism in four years."

When zest, euphoria, and ambition gripped powerful leaders, the mobilized masses fell under the spell of their grand experiment. Based on the only experience he was familiar with, Lu divided the population into army corps and turned Henan into a boot camp. A typical county would have ninety regiments, three hundred battalions, and one thousand companies. Since more than seventy percent of the rural population ate at the one thousand, six hundred public mess halls, the county administration could direct them to any project that the provincial head Lu wanted, anywhere anytime. As many as ten million laborers were deployed to build irrigation systems, fifteen million on summer antidrought campaigns, and another fifteen million on the construction of nine reservoirs.

"Great!" said the Chairman. "We have defeated Chen Han's eight million troops in the civil war. Now that thousands upon thousands of people are aroused to rally behind us once more, nothing can stop us on the road to communism."

The magnitude of the immense Chinese multitude was undoubtedly impressive if anyone were able to mobilize them. How could the firm, confident, and optimistic Sheng not visualize those throngs of people joining him as rank and file soldiers in the unprecedented battle he had designed? How could anyone not be excited to see that the perfect Marxist society was finally rising in China in Asia, not in the Soviet Union in Europe? He told the party, "Only two years ago, I suggested that we ought to find a better and faster way to develop our socialist society than what the Soviet model had shown. We then declared the goal of producing more steel than Great Britain and the United States within a dozen years. In fact, our true purpose is to surpass the Soviet Union and to introduce something most profound to the international communist movement."

"The Russians have relied on technology and experts, and have adopted a top-down approach since the Bolshevik Revolution in 1917. But we are different." The Chairman went on, "No matter how intense and how perilous those military conflicts of the past had been, our party's mass line has withstood the test of time and has always proven to be victorious. This unique revolutionary experience is our most valuable asset and our best solution to any economic problems and challenges we are facing today.

"Our approach is the bottom-up one, firmly guided by our party's mass line," said Sheng. "Massive mobilization is the key to transforming our socialist society into a communist one on the largest scale and at the fastest speed the world has ever seen. The people's commune is our invention, which has all the promise to lead China into communism before the Russians.

"Think about it!" The ecstatic Chairman was beaming with confidence, pride, and excitement, "We, the Chinese Communist Party, will fulfill Marx's dream in ways that neither the Russians nor the communists in any other countries could have ever imagined. We shall be the pioneers in leading the world into the ever-blissful paradise of global communism!"

5

The more places Tao visited on his tour around the country, the deeper his heart sank.

At a small village where he had stayed during one of the final campaigns in the civil war, he could not believe what he saw. Under siege in irking silence, no household was cooking at mealtime or making any noise. The local residents had stripped the last skins from the elms (believed to be oily and eatable) for food, and some had even dug out the roots. Exposed to the sun, the giant but naked trees were dying as if they had been mutilated and cut into pieces by fleeing robbers. A horrific rotten smell filled the air, coming from a nearby filthy pond, which had been drained to catch every fish and crab in it. The sounds of birds, dogs, chicken, and other animals, often heard in a peaceful village, were nonexistent. Most likely, they had been caught, eaten, or had run away from this repulsive place.

Looking at the dishes on the table—a small bowl of watery porridge mixed with chopped cabbages and two steamed shriveled sweet potatoes, Tao could not eat.

Deeply apologetic, an elderly village head humbly admitted that these few items were the best he could find for Tao. Most families in the area had left the village some time ago to beg for food elsewhere, he said.

So many villagers were facing starvation and so many local communities were in disarray. "I have not seen anything like this even in wartime," Tao told himself. He did not know how to reconcile what he was witnessing in the country with what he was hearing from the party leadership.

Out of nowhere, three small boys and two little girls showed up to stare at his table from an open window. They looked hardly human—their desperate eyes, battered faces, shredded clothes, and skeletal bodies made them look like a group of terrified teeny animals.

"Go away!" the old man yelled, feeling embarrassed that Tao had witness such an unpleasant scene.

"Don't say that to the children." Tao stopped him and took the food to the window. "Are you hungry? Now, take these. Take them all."

In a split second, the children snatched the food and ran away as fast as they could, fearing the man might change his mind.

"Why is there such a serious shortage of food? You have some great harvest this year, haven't you?" Tao asked.

"The harvest was okay. But the officials from local to county administrations have greatly exaggerated the output. As a result, our quotas to sell grains this year were twice as high as in the past. The official quotas are mandatory and we have to sell most of our grains to the government. Now we are left with not enough food to last for the whole year. Most families have a shortfall of several months, and many families were completely out of provisions a few months ago," the village head explained.

"Did you say that officials had exaggerated the harvest numbers?" Tao asked for confirmation.

"Well, they exaggerated a lot of things." Realizing his slip of the tongue, the old man tried to cover it up by insisting that the officials did that with good intentions.

"What else have they exaggerated?" the enraged Tao kept pressing.

"Well, reports like the record output, record participation, record benefit, and record success." Now feeling trapped between a rock and a hard place, the old man sounded evasive.

"Okay then, tell me what numbers I can trust." Tao could sense the man's reluctance to tell the truth, and decided to cut to the chase.

Silence.

Embarrassing silence.

Not a word on the subject, and both men understood what it meant.

"You have the public mess hall, don't you? You can go there to eat, right?" Tao decided to change the topic.

"The public mess hall was closed down a long time ago after the commune ran out of food and grains. Free meals lasted only a few months, and there had been a great deal of abuse and waste."

"The residents chose to build the public mess hall and join the commune, isn't that correct?" Tao asked again.

"Well, yes and no. We really didn't know what a commune was and why we had to have it. Officials said it was a good idea. So we let it happen."

Tao was now as deeply disturbed as he was confused. He did not know why, where, and how it went so wrong. The whole party overwhelmingly supported the Great Leap Forward. The mass line and public mobilization had worked so well, enabling the party to mobilize not just a few millions but the entire population. Yet people were starving and the newly created institutions were failing. Was it due to misinformation from the locals? Was it due to the unrealistic demands from the national leadership? Was it the exaggerations by the county, regional, and provincial officials? Was it the ever-expanding goals set by the party? Was it the fault of the public mess halls? Was it the weaknesses of the people's communes?

To find satisfactory answers to these knotty questions, Tao decided to dig deeper for more information. Only correct and reliable information would help him to assess the situation correctly.

6

No one understood the vital importance of accurate national statistics better than Si-Tu Wen-Liang, who, working in his quiet office in the Garden of White Garlands, would receive a great variety of updated reports every week.

One morning, a city announced a new "satellite," saying that it had produced some one million tons of iron in one day. Surprised by this astounding figure, the premier asked a secretary to check it out. He reported that three to four tons of iron ore, two to three tons of coke, and more than ten tons of limestone and other materials were needed to produce one ton of iron at a normal plant. The city, which was small and not known to have any industrial facility, expertise, or resources, must have transported some fifteen million tons of materials to its site to produce one million tons of iron, which was utterly impossible.

Yet, eager to demonstrate one's unflagging dedication to fast-track communism, such wild claims happened so frequently that many started to ignore the basic need to verify their credibility.

Under the Chairman's insistence that steel was the key to industrial development, achieving that goal became a national obsession. Few understood the technological expertise and heavy equipment that steel-making would demand. Steel could not be produced directly from iron ores, much less by any backyard furnace. Besides, the quality of pig iron made by those backyard furnaces was so poor that it was worthless. Farmers had no idea of how to distinguish a real iron ore from a colored rock. Yet millions of them were driven to the mountains to find the mineral for months on end. Acres of forestry were destroyed to make fuel for the backyard furnaces, which was a terrible environmental disaster. The more time, money, and manpower any local administration spent on this crazy mission, the more financial losses and material wastes it would incur.

If no one else knew the truth, Si-Tu did, since he had to provide four billion yuan from the national treasury to help compensate the ridiculous losses by his ignorant but overzealous subordinates. Not counting the expenses on manpower, this singular crusade for steel production alone had cost the nation more than thirty billion yuan during the Great Leap Forward.

Official newspapers and the propaganda department continued to run enthusiastic editorials with such headlines as "Long Live the Party's General Line," "Long Live the Great Leap Forward," "Long Live the People's Commune," "The Land Can Produce as Much as You Can Imagine," "To Light the Skies with Fires and to Build Blast Furnaces From Scratch," "The Public Mess Halls Are the Best," "Dare to Think, Dare to Do, and Dare to Achieve 2,000 Bushels of Sweet Potatoes Per Acre," "The Meat of One Pig Can Feed a Commune for Half a Year," "You Need a Ladder to Pick Up the Flowers from a Cotton Tree," "A Day Equals Twenty Years, and Communism Is Just Around the Corner," "Long Live the Public Mess Hall," "Iron Bowl and Free Meals Are What Communism Is All About!"

At the provincial level, Henan spent three hundred million yuan and mobilized fifteen million rural laborers to construct irrigation systems. Only one-fifth of the projects was completed. Because of serious mistakes in design, some dams had to be blown up immediately after construction. Instead of benefiting the local peasants, several newly dug canals ruined their livelihood because they used the waters from the Yellow River, which badly salinized the farmlands.

In Northwest China, the party committee of Gansu Province decided to build a grand canal system that would bring water to the drought-ridden region on the Loess Plateau. The main canal, one thousand, one hundred and fifty kilometers long, should be forty meters wide at the top, sixteen meters wide at the bottom, and six meters deep. With fifteen additional branch canals, the total length of the new system would be three thousand, five hundred kilometers, which could irrigate two and a half million acres of land. Along the way two reservoirs would be built and two dozen power stations would be constructed. When the entire project was finished, it would benefit the four million people in the twenty poorest counties in the nation.

Designed to finish in four years, the project was launched with one hundred thousand laborers sent off to the construction site amid much fanfare, which also attracted national attention. Hundreds of delegates from other provinces came to visit and some national conferences were held here, propagating the belief that the project had not only a national significance but also an international one.

The central government invested one hundred and sixty million yuan on the project. The provincial administration spent sixty million yuan and ninety-seven million pounds of grain to support the massive labor force working on the site.

Unfortunately, the project that had promised so much was abandoned within two years due to a gross underestimation of its engineering complexities as well as a gross overestimation of its possible benefits. Not a single acre was irrigated after all the short-lived excitement, wide-ranging publicity, and colossal expenses.

More troubles were yet to come for Si-Tu. Unofficial information indicated that shortage of grain and starvation in the Sunshine District of Henan was so bad that villagers resorted to cannibalism.

The tragic news stunned the premier, who decided to keep it a top party secret. Any information relating to the incident would be made available only to the Chairman and the Politburo members.

Keenly aware of the extreme sensitivity of the case and of the strong resistance from various departments, Si-Tu immediately assigned two of his longtime assistants, Fang Si-Liang and Cheng Chu-Li, to lead a team of specially selected officials from the central government to investigate the situation. A month later they reported that the death toll in eighteen counties amounted to one million, or one-eighth of the population in the region. Unlike many impoverished communities in China, the Sunshine District was a prosperous area well known for its advanced farming. Such a horrendous tragedy was doubly puzzling because the region was also one of the earliest red bases, which had produced thousands of communist soldiers and hundreds of high-ranking Red Army officers. During the worst decade of the civil war, about one hundred thousand people had died in the same region, a small fraction of the current extremely high death rate in peacetime.

A key reason for the disaster was the widespread practice of reporting artificially inflated statistics. Dedicated to the speedy realization of communism, the party leaders of the region intentionally exaggerated their harvest figures to impress the provincial officials, who had been hard pressed to achieve higher targets after attending national meetings at the capital. Exaggeration, cheating, falsified numbers, and fabricated reporting became commonplace in governmental data collection, making official records totally unreliable.

Although in the Sunshine District the total regional output of grain for the year was no more than one hundred and eighty thousand tons, the figure swelled to two hundred and fifty thousand, three hundred and twenty-five thousand, six hundred and fifty thousand, and finally one million, two hundred thousand tons by the time the report reached the offices of provincial administration. Compared with the previous year, the actual output of the region had decreased by forty percent, but local peasants received a mandatory quota from the government to produce a grain output that was two and a half times larger!

These grossly distorted figures satisfied the egos of those local, county, and provincial officials, while inflicting a devastating blow on the common people's lives and grassroots communities. Apart from seeds and animal feeds, the yearly ration a peasant could have was one hundred and eighty pounds of raw grain, barely enough for six months!

If lying and cheating were bad, the government policy of mandatory collection of grain was harsher. If the three thousand public mess halls were totally useless, and if the grandiose public irrigation projects and thousands of backyard furnaces led to little benefit but astronomical expenses, what was even worse was that starving peasants were banned from leaving their community. No migration was allowed, not even panhandling in the vicinity of one's residence, because officials were fearful that outsiders might realize the truth, exposing their gross incompetence, negligence, and irresponsibility. Anyone who attempted to flee from their hometown would be beaten, arrested, and sent back, even though there was no relief from the famine in sight.

Si-Tu was furious. He could not believe why straightforward information, reliable data, and simple reality had become more difficult to obtain in peacetime than in the past, when the party had been facing mortal enemies. What had gone wrong? Yet, as the nation's premier, he must shoulder the blame for such appalling regional disasters, starvation, and cannibalism. He decided to do something.

7

The meeting was visibly uncomfortable for both men.

"Chairman, too many local officials have made false reports to boost their records. They have faked the figures of some supposedly unprecedented harvests, which led to the government's overcollection of the grains the peasants actually had," Tao said, his face sullen as if to reflect his grim mood.

"Slow down, slow down," the Chairman said. "Cigarette?"

"No, thanks." The general continued, "Starvation has occurred in several provinces, and many people are dying. We need to do something."

"So, what do you suggest?" said the Chairman, as he held a cigarette in his mouth and then inhaled the smoke slowly but deeply into his lungs.

"Our goals for this year may be too high. We may want to change our targets to make them more attainable," Tao suggested.

"Are you saying that the Great Leap Forward is wrong?" The Chairman sounded alarmed while exhaling for several seconds.

"No, no, no. The Great Leap Forward is not wrong, only the haste of it all," the general replied.

"But the essence of the Great Leap Forward *is* its speed," snapped the Chairman.

"As in war, speed is important. But speed is not everything. Unrelenting speed can be counterproductive sometimes," Tao insisted.

"So, what is the proper speed according to your opinion?" the Chairman asked, picking up another cigarette.

"We may want to review and revise the figures we have set for this year, and maybe for the next few years as well," Tao replied.

"All right, let me think about it," the Chairman responded, reaching out for the ashtray.

Tao left the Chairman's office without a clear idea of what the latter was really thinking. He felt that the meeting was too brief to enable him to explain himself clearly. "The issues are too important to be ignored, and I need to do something tonight to explain my ideas more fully," Tao said to himself.

8

The conversation between the two men was nerve-racking.

"Starvation? Are you sure?" Song Pei began.

"Yes. The investigation team reported that one million have perished in Sunshine District," replied Si-Tu.

"Really?" Song said before pausing.

Si-Tu understood the implicit question behind the pause, adding, "The report is reliable. Two of my most dependable aides led the investigation."

"What about the other regions?" asked Song.

"I have yet to receive reports from several provinces, especially Shandong, Gansu, and Sichuan. The investigations are ongoing," Si-Tu said.

"Has there really been cannibalism? Is it really that bad?" Song finally raised the most dreaded question, and anxiously waited for the premier's answer.

"Yes. More than one hundred cases did happen in Sunshine District," Si-Tu responded with a pained look on his face.

"Oh, good heavens!" Song yelled out. Visibly shaken and saddened, his voice cracked as he asked, "What can we do?"

"We need to convince the Chairman to slow down."

"That will not be easy."

"Then, more people will die and…"

"I know, I know, more cases of cannibalism could happen, which could be most damaging to the party's reputation and to ours," Song admitted.

Although he was not the mastermind of the ongoing campaign, he was the president of the country. The fact that thousands of innocent people had died under his watch in peacetime deeply troubled Song. The public would blame him for the tragedy, and he would not be able to shun his responsibility.

"The current speed is not workable. We must do something, and we need to talk to the Chairman, no matter what," Song said, as Si-Tu nodded in agreement.

9

Throughout his career, Sheng had thrived on challenges—the bigger, the better.

A master strategist, he practiced preemptive strikes as much as he was adept at launching stealthy counterattacks. He had survived on these tactics through protracted warfare and scored considerable successes, making him believe that the same tactics were applicable in domestic affairs and intraparty relations.

Although Sheng had been at the pinnacle of power for more than a decade, he had a penchant for adopting a defensive stance whenever his judgment or decision was first questioned. Only later would he respond to anyone who had dared to criticize him with a well-calculated vengeance that could be as lethal as a coiled cobra suddenly releasing itself into the air and injecting into the victim its deadliest venom.

The political stratagem of this sort satisfied his huge ego and conceited conscience. His purported innocence spoke of his moral contemptuousness. His professed "defensive" and "reactive" actions justified his mortal attacks. He loved to complain about his "vulnerability," to expose the dissenters' "wantonness," and to elaborate on the popular and legitimate support he received from the masses, especially the poor and downtrodden.

Using cleverly disguised but meaningless rhetoric, he was never tired of highlighting the sharp contrast between the high status of his detractors and the lowliness of his background and education. He, the humbled, the chastened, the less polished, the less intellectual, and the defenseless, had repeatedly fallen victim to the upper class, the bourgeois, and their sophisticated professors and students returning from overseas. He, the underdog, the rustic, the vilified, and the victimized, must fight back for survival, for justice, for the happiness of the masses, and for the ever-glorious cause of communism. The only thing he needed to do was to identify his enemies.

When members of the party's central committee were called to meet in Shanghai, they were apprehensive after hearing that the Chairman was in a sour mood. Rumors said that he was very upset because this year's economic targets would not be met despite enormous efforts by all the countrymen. Not an encouraging sign for this gathering.

"Many believed that the Great Leap Forward was a mistake!" The Chairman opened the meeting with a grim statement.

"They doubted our party's mass line and our steadfast determination to achieve great successes. They questioned our ability to lead, they doubted the great ingenuity and unbridled energy of our people, and they have forgotten that class struggle remains the most fundamental issue in our society." The Chairman sipped some tea.

"They are the rightists in our party. They represent the interests of the bourgeois, not those of the working classes. They want to forestall our march toward the dream of great communism by dismissing our ability to compete with our domestic and international enemies. They believe they are better than the party, smarter than the current leadership. They want to change the course of our party. They want to overturn the correct line of our party!"

Waving a document in his hand, the Chairman went on, "A few days ago, I received this letter from General Tao Yin-Hu. Now every one of you has a copy of it. I hope you will read it carefully, and detect those sinister conspirators behind it.

"We are facing a serious new battle between two camps: the Marxist and the revisionist. I trust the party will make a correct choice as to which camp you should follow and whose political line you should adopt.

"If no one believes in me anymore, I am willing to resign and I will go back to the mountains. I will begin to build revolutionary bases and recruit a new red army to start all over again if necessary!"

His furious warnings echoed throughout the large auditorium and the speechless audience was left dumbfounded. None of them was willing to think about the frightful consequences lurking behind Sheng's apocalyptic proclamations.

As the bewildered delegates looked at each other, not knowing what to do next, the haughty Chairman stormed out of the meeting hall, confident that he had staged one of his most brilliant performances.

Chapter 39

Storms

1

WHAT WAS IT? AN ULTIMATUM? WAS HE BLUFFING? FOR WHAT?
At whom?

Sheng Bao's fury, cryptic language, and outrageous manner
left the Central Committee wondering what his game plan was. But one thing
was clear—the Chairman had found in Tao Yin-Hu his archetypal enemy.

When the party head threw someone into the dungeon, those who had
been with the organization long enough knew that a merciless slaughter would
ensue.

A pivotal moment in Tao's life as much as that in everybody else's, the
one hundred-plus members of the Central Committee were holding their
breath, knowing perfectly that only some dramatic shift of pinion could
save the general's career. They must be very careful about what they would
say next.

If one or two Politburo members would stand up to tell the truth, if
some members of the Central Committee would follow their conscience to
acknowledge the plight of the country, if the majority of the same committee
would think how to protect the interests of the people, not their own offices

and the salaries they were receiving from the party, the meeting could have proceeded in a very different direction.

Alas, no mechanism had been set up to allow any of the above to happen. A well-oiled machine, the party had been operating in a top-down fashion since its inception, and the organization had produced a membership to follow orders, not to think. In particular, the Chairman's will and authority had been viewed as absolute, while loyalty and conformity must always prevail. Individual opinions and candid discussions had been shunned, and over the decades, the institution had suppressed all the oppositions and criticisms every time they surfaced.

Unwilling and unable to stand by Tao, officials from the highest ranks started to accuse him in ways that they believed would please Sheng.

The winds had changed, and so had the atmosphere in the auditorium. Nothing could escape the sensitive Si-Tu Wen-Liang, whose intimate knowledge of the party's internal affairs instinctively took control over his mind, body, and behavior. He was the first to stand up, professing his gratitude to the Chairman, whose wisdom and foresight had saved him from falling for Tao's wicked conspiracy. Si-Tu was secretly glad that he had not rushed to report to Sheng about the events in Sunshine District.

"This sly Si-Tu," Song Pei thought, "he never wanted to take the lead in anything, always trying to hide behind someone else. He wanted me to tell the bad news to Sheng to save his ass. Real son of a—"

But now was not the time for Song to show his contempt for Si-Tu, who was about to end his pretentious and tearful confession after rambling for two and a half hours. Song quickly rose and pounded the desk in front of him, charging that Tao had been plotting against the Chairman since the days in Bao An. "We knew he was against the Rectification Movement. We knew he was against the Chairman in the Battles of One Hundred Battalions. We knew he was against the Chairman in the Korean War. He has been a rightist fighting against our great Chairman all along in his career!"

The outrageous charges angered Yao Xi-Wa. An officer under the general's command all his life, he could not tolerate the brazen slander against Tao anymore. Shooting up from his chair, the brave officer shouted, "Are you out of your mind? General Tao Yin-Hu has been one of our most dedicated soldiers since the beginning of the revolution! He—"

Before Yao could utter another word, four armed soldiers rushed out, pressed him down, and promptly arrested him.

Sitting next to Song and Si-Tu in the front row on the raised platform, Lin Shi-Xiong had been closely watching everyone below in the large meeting hall. The Chairman had given him strict orders the previous night to report everybody's reaction to his earlier speech and to arrest anyone who dared to say anything on Tao's behalf.

No more explanation was needed on what the Chairman really wanted from the party apparatus. His blazing wrath, Si-Tu's speedy capitulation, Song's explosive charges, and Yao's instant arrest made it crystal clear what members of the Central Committee must do. They quickly surrendered to Sheng's will.

2

"No, you can't say that about your Uncle Tao, who has been very nice to you," Yan Yan attempted to calm Meng Xi down. She did not know why the teenager seemed so restless today after returning from school, when it used to be a delightful and relaxing time for her.

"Why not? He is antiparty, anti-Chairman. He is an enemy of the people," Xi replied.

"Stop it! You don't know anything about Uncle Tao. He held you in his arms when you were little." Baffled at her shocking allegations, Yan tried to reason with the agitated girl.

"No, he is not my uncle. I don't have an uncle like him. He is bad. He is an enemy of the people, and he is the enemy of our great party!" the adamant Xi protested.

Yan was speechless. She did not know where the appalling accusations had come from, and her futile efforts to convince a girl only a fraction of her age frustrated her. Fortunately, she saw Tania walking in and said, "Look, you must tell Xi that Tao is a good man. He is not an enemy of the people."

"What's going on?" said a surprised Tania.

"Our teacher told us today that Tao had been plotting against the party and our great Chairman. Thanks to the wisdom of our party leadership, his wicked conspiracy was exposed. He and his evil conspirators have been arrested," Xi reported, beaming with childish innocence.

Tania looked at her confident daughter and then at the dejected Yan, shaking her head in despair. What a sad day, she thought. She had just come back from Broken Kiln and must now deal with this. Her heart was broken, again.

"Now, darling," Tania said, struggling to be as calm as possible, "please listen to me. You are too young to understand the whole story, and you haven't seen the whole picture yet. I will explain to you someday, okay? For the moment, no matter what others have told you, please remember that Uncle Tao is not a bad person."

"But… but… our teacher told us about him, reading from the newspapers right in front of everybody in our class." Xi was confused.

"I am sure he did. But, believe me, you are not old enough to understand this very complex matter. Do you trust Mom?" Tania asked.

"Yes, I do," Xi murmured although she was still confused.

"All right, now go to bed. We will talk about this later, okay?" Tania took Xi to her room.

"You did not see Bo-Xian?" Yan asked Tania when she returned to the living room, although she already knew the answer from Tania's disheartened expression.

"No. They told me that he had been transferred to an unknown location according to orders."

"Why?" Yan asked.

"They did not explain. They just said that they did everything according to orders," Tania said.

"What are you going to do?" Yan asked, saddened to see Tania in pain, which had become all too familiar for her two friends in the last several years.

"I will continue to try until I find him," Tania replied in her characteristic gentle but firm voice.

Yan felt useless and she hated it. She wanted to help. She wanted to comfort Tania. But she didn't know how. She had never been interested in any party politics. But the situations did look more alarming than the ones she had experienced in the past. She did not understand why Meng Bo-Xian, Tao Yin-Hu, and Dong Zi-Tian, who had devoted their lives to the revolution, would be treated more harshly after the liberation than before it. Maybe she was getting old, and maybe things were becoming too complicated for her, as much as it was for Xi, to comprehend. She went into the kitchen to make a new pot of tea for Tania.

That evening Tania, sitting by herself, reviewed the series of recent events and suspected that Meng's disappearance might have something to do with Tao's case. The party authorities knew that the two were close friends who had supported each other through thick and thin. As a precaution, the Chairman could have ordered Meng's relocation to keep a closer watch over him.

Where could she find out some reliable information about where Meng was detained? Who could help her to see him again?

It did not take long for Tania to realize that her options were limited, if nonexistent. She could not call on Si-Tu as easily as in the past, since access to his office in Abundance was now strictly controlled. Dong was dead and Dai Tian was away. Tao had fallen from grace and even his close friend General Yao was arrested. Tania had no one to turn to for help and, worst, most party officials did not even want to see her, lest any contact arouse the suspicions of the distrustful Chairman and his vigilant security personnel under the eagle-eyed Lin.

She now totally understood why Dai had been so depressed years ago in Bao An. The enormity of her grief, the suffocating frustration, and hopeless isolation made Tania felt like she was about to explode—and she knew she needed to find an outlet for those feelings. She needed to cry. But she resisted, resisted, and she didn't. Finally she took out a piece of paper and began writing a letter to her husband.

My dear Bo-Xian,

I am so sad these days and don't know who to turn for counsel. I am writing to you, thinking you are the only one who can hear my sorrows and understand my grief. The worst torment for a woman is to be separated her from her husband. The deeper their love is, the worse the torment. And how I hate it.

Right now, loneliness and darkness are my worst nightmares.

My dear and dearest Bo-Xian, you are my man, and I am your woman. My love for you has never been as passionate as now. Even though I can't meet and see you anytime soon, my love for you will only grow stronger every day.

My longing for you will never end until the day I see you again.

I love you so much and I need to see you, touch you, kiss you, hug you, and to feel you are next to me.

I need to hear you breathing. I need to smell your unique scent to know you are by my side.

I need to see your face. I need to touch your hands. I need to kiss your eyes to make sure you are here with me. I need to embrace you to enjoy the warmth, the care, and the caress you have always given me. I need your kisses to feel safe and to sleep tight.

Oh, I love you so much and I love you with all my heart and soul.

You have told me many touching stories about several Chinese female poets. They composed heart-wrenching poems, when left lonely at home while their husbands were away. How those poems you have showed me expressed the same feelings I now have! Listen, here is one from the *Book of Odes*:

My Lord's Gone to Service
My lord's gone to service,
I don't know for how long.
When will he come home?
The chickens roost in their nooks,
it's the evening of the day
and the sheep and cows come down.
My lord's gone to service—
how can I not think of him?

My lord's gone to service,
not for a day, nor for a month.
When will I see him again?
The chickens roost on their perches,
it's the evening of the day
and the sheep and cows make their way down.
My lord's gone to service—
May he never hunger or thirst!

And I agree with you that Li Qing-Zhao's poems are among the finest examples of ancient Chinese poetry. Her amazing sensitivity, felicitous choice of words, flawless composition, and the splendid fluidity of her style have made her poems the most beautiful and most moving.

Slow, Slow Tune
I look for what I miss,
I know not what it is:
I feel so sad, so drear,
so lonely, without cheer.
How hard is it
to keep me fit
in this lingering cold!
Hardly warmed up
by cup on cup
of wine so dry.
Oh! How could I
endure at dusk the drift
of wind so swift?
It breaks my heart, alas!
to see the wild geese pass,
for they are my acquaintances of old.

The ground is covered with yellow flowers
Faded and fallen in showers.
Who will pick them up now?
Sitting alone at the window, how
could I but quicken while
the pace of darkness won't thicken?
On parasol-trees a fine rain drizzles
as twilight grizzles.
Oh! What can I do with a grief
beyond belief!

I wish I could write some similar verses as beautiful as these female poets had done in the distant past. But, even if I don't have their poetic talents, my heart stands by every word they have said. And my feelings and my love are as strong as theirs.

Sadly, some women think of leaving their men when they are in trouble. Some may even think about a divorce.

Believe me, I will never do that.

No matter where you are and no matter what lies ahead, I will never leave you. I am so madly in love with you and I am always yours.

Tania stopped writing, and read the lines she had put down. She smiled at the melancholy and could not believe that she had written a love letter at this stage of her life. Maybe the separation had made her realize how deeply she loved Meng. And she was glad that her passion for her husband had renewed her strength and given her hope at a time when she needed them the most. No longer as sad as she was a few hours earlier, Tania went on to write:

I read several books recently, which you may be interested to know— Yevgeny Zamyatin's *We*, Aldous Huxley's *Brave New World* and *Brave New World Revised*, and George Orwell's *Animal Farm* and *Nineteen Eighty-Four*. They are among the books Martin had collected in his library (perhaps with some input from Peter).

I must confess that I haven't read so many dystopian books in succession. They did sound pessimistic, but they also made sense. I like Zamyatin's warning of any attempt to "integrate completely the colossal equation of the universe." Or "Yes: to unbend the wild curve, to straighten it tangentially, asymptotically, to flatten it to an undeviating line. Because the line of One State is a straight line. The great, divine, precise, wise straight line—the wisest of all lines…"

Does that ring a bell? A bold, fascinating, and remarkably realistic prediction for a man writing in 1920.

I did not realize that Zamyatin's fiction had influenced Huxley and Orwell, especially the latter's *Nineteen Eighty-Four*, which seemed all the more pertinent now when he described "Big Brother," "newspeak," "double-think," and particularly "thought police" and "thought crimes."

Interestingly, some biographer described George Orwell as a "tall and spindly fellow," whose early career in Burma was shockingly similar to that of Martin's when he was a young man working in Java.

On balance, however, I am equally concerned about what Huxley had pointed out about "propaganda in a democratic society." He wrote, and I completely agree with him, that "human beings are a good deal less rational and innately just than the optimists of the eighteenth century supposed."

His next statement, in my view, was as prophetic as the allegorical stories written by either Zamyatin or Orwell. He wrote,

"Democratic institutions are devices for reconciling social order with individual freedom and initiative, and for making the immediate power of a country's rulers subject to the ultimate power of the ruled. The fact that, in Western Europe and America, these devices have worked, all things considered, not too badly is proof enough that the eighteenth-century optimists were not entirely wrong. Given a fair chance, human beings can govern themselves, and govern themselves better, though perhaps with less mechanical efficiency, than they can be governed by 'authorities independent of their will.' Given a fair chance, I repeat; for the fair chance is an indispensable prerequisite. No people that pass abruptly from a state of subservience under the rule of despot to the completely unfamiliar state of political independence can be said to have a fair chance of making democratic institutions work. Again, no people in a precarious economic condition have a fair chance of being able to govern themselves democratically."

Oh, how we need this "fair chance" in China now more than ever.

Oh, how I wish I can discuss all these matters with you. How I wish I can hear your voice and listen to your opinions.

You always think on your own. You always make your independent judgment. That's why I love you so much.

You think, and you are never afraid of speaking your mind. You are a real man, a true human being who is always faithful to your own conscience. I love you so much. My kisses and eternal love for you...

Your forever passionate Tania

Tania knew that she could not send this letter out. She didn't know where to send it even if she wanted to. The mail could be easily intercepted, which would not be safe for both of them, even if it could reach him.

But she felt much better now. She felt she had talked to Meng, shared her thoughts, ideas, and feelings with him, which was most important.

She decided that she would continue to write to her husband until the day she could finally reunite with him.

3

Frankly speaking, Sheng Bao never liked Shanghai—the birthplace of the party that he had presided over—and kept a firm grip on—for years. He did not know a single industrial worker from this famous metropolis, nor did he have any interest in any of its modern but imported amenities. Theater, opera, music, movies, dramas, art exhibitions, or any stage performances rarely attracted his attention, while requests from fancy hotels, restaurants, sports facilities, and grand edifices for his patronage were simply rejected. He preferred a solid wooden bed over a Simmons mattress, a bowl of steamed rice over a delicate French dish, a cup of strong tea over a glass of exotic whisky, the traditional Chinese clothing over suit and tie, and simple handmade sandals over a pair of dress shoes from Italy.

Despite his misgivings about the city, a recent newspaper article authored by the Shanghai party secretary had aroused the interest of the Chairman, who invited the official for a talk. A chance to meet the Chairman was a great honor for any regional head who would definitely take advantage of such a rare opportunity.

Kang Yi-Sheng, the party secretary of Shanghai, was an old acquaintance of the Chairman's from the days of the Long March. No one in the party could receive any important assignment without Sheng's scrutiny and consent, and Kang's appointment to lead the largest city in China clearly showed the Chairman's liking of him. But, like all regional administrators, Kang still wanted more and hoped to be promoted to the national government in Peking, where the most powerful and most prestigious positions existed. The only way he could do that was to impress the Chairman, attract his attention, and gain his endorsement.

"You wrote a good article on promoting the new achievements of the last thirteen years," the Chairman said.

"It's all because of your great leadership, Chairman," Kang responded modestly.

"Su Ming, did you read the article?" asked the Chairman, who had deliberately brought his wife to meet today's guests.

"Yes, I did, Chairman. I learned a lot from the article," Su replied in a similar modest fashion.

"Oh, no, no, no. I have much to learn from Comrade Su." Kang's voice was humbler still; he would never dare to say anything that would displease the husband or the wife.

"We both remember how you had warned us of the enemy retaliation in peacetime," added the evening's other guest, Bao Feng-Nian, the party chief of the East Bureau, which oversaw Shanghai.

"Yes, the recent attacks by Tao and company were a perfect example. I am glad you stood firm in this battle," said the Chairman, looking at the faces of his guests.

"We vow to defend our Chairman anywhere, anytime," Bao and Kang swore in unison.

"Good, good to know where your loyalty lies." Sheng was pleased and relaxed.

Sensing his chance, Kang said, "Chairman, I noticed that you had reminded us of class struggle on a number of occasions since liberation. Such reminders may benefit the party even more if you could compile your directives in a single volume."

"Oh? Go on," Sheng was intrigued.

"See, right after liberation, you detected the enemy's plot behind the movie *The Villager*. During the Anti-Rightist Movement, you pointed out the evil intentions of those bourgeois intellectuals to undermine our communist leadership. Most recently, you exposed the conspiracy within the party led by Tao. Your vision, wisdom, and foresight have protected our great nation," Kang elaborated.

"Hmm," Sheng was thinking as he smoked his cigarette.

"Yes, you have averted one disaster after another and kept our country and government safe," Su said.

"You have made great new contributions to Marxism and Leninism," Bao praised.

"You truly think so?" the Chairman asked slowly.

"Yes, yes," they reassured him.

Could they actually see something that he could not? No, no one could outsmart the Chairman, not even his most devoted supporters. For quite some time Sheng had pondered on his grand theory of class struggle in the post-liberation era, which, he believed, would set a new milestone in the worldwide proletarian movement. But he had been so preoccupied with the practical aspects of running the party and nation that he did not have the time to focus on his theoretical task. At a deeper level, the lack of his intellectual sophistication and academic rigor also held him back, since Sheng felt that he was unable to proceed even if he wanted to. Buried in reports and meetings, the Chairman had written countless piecemeal comments, summaries, instructions, orders, policies, and newspaper editorials. But he had not produced anything substantial or systematic for a decade. The proud Sheng was afraid to acknowledge that he needed help. He needed a reliable hand who was knowledgeable and skillful enough to assist him in completing the task.

That was why Sheng had invited the two men after reading the newspaper article—he wanted to test their loyalty once more before making a decision.

"All right, if you all agree. Bao and Kang, why don't you two start work on the project? Remember, this must be kept in absolute secrecy. If you need anything or have any questions, do contact Su. She will be the liaison between us," the Chairman ordered.

"Of course, wonderful," said Kang, who was as elated as Bao. They were entrusted with this unbelievable assignment directly by the first family. Nothing could beat this honor and no other party official could compete with them career-wise anymore.

"The Chairman wants you to stay for dinner," Su rose and said. "We always have simple meals. But he has asked the kitchen to add two dishes tonight—one sweet and sour fish from the West Lake and the other Dong Po meat. We hope these typical southern dishes will suit your taste."

Su's words and the Chairman's hospitality overwhelmed the guests, who knew that nothing could top the honor of an intimate dinner with Sheng and his wife in their private residence.

The lovely dinner proceeded well on the night of the Chairman's seventieth birthday.

4

The fall of General Tao, one of the most prominent founders of communist China, terrorized the party. No one dared to question the Great Leap Forward any more after the Chairman showed that he was willing to strike back even at his closest associate for expressing a different opinion. The frantic movement continued and the tragedies that Dai Tian witnessed in several provinces were beyond description.

Fearful of any reprimand from their superiors, local officials faked numbers to satisfy whatever record output the higher authorities wanted. In less than two months, the publicly announced output of raw rice purportedly had risen nineteenfold in separate locations, from twenty-one thousand pounds per acre to thirty-seven thousand pounds, sixty thousand pounds, sixty-nine thousand pounds, one hundred and one thousand pounds, one hundred and seven thousand pounds, two hundred and forty-three thousand pounds, two hundred and eighty-eight thousand pounds and finally to an astonishing three hundred and ninety-eight thousand, eight hundred and eighty-four pounds (or one hundred and eighty-one tons) per acre which anyone with any elementary knowledge of farm work would know was utterly impossible to achieve. County and provincial officials were thrilled with these dazzling results. Some so-called scientists, willing to serve the government, insisted that, given nature's potential abundance, famers had plenty of room to increase their productivity still further.

All of those figures had been fabricated. Dai was told that a common scheme was to move nearby rice plants to a single field during the evening if the harvest of the acreage were scheduled for inspection next morning. At one village, county officials saw a massive throng of local villagers waiting to help with the inspection process. They did not realize that those peasants—some six thousands of them, many from nearby communities—who carried rice to be weighed at the front of the line would return to the end of the queue with the same rice to be weighed again and again until sunset. The simple plot worked because the waiting line was simply stretched too long for the outside officials, busy with the scales for hours, to distinguish (or unwilling to distinguish) between those whose rice had been weighed and the ones who had not. In another village, a diligent provincial head decided to examine the result in person to prevent any fraud and the final tally of nineteen thousand, eight hundred pounds of wheat per acre seemed to be acceptable to him, not knowing that the locals had stuffed two-thirds of the grain (thirteen thousand, two hundred pounds) inside the threshing machine the night before he came.

Thus, the Chairman wanted a Great Leap Forward and he got it, alas a fraudulent one.

Between being branded antiparty rightists and making a "great leap forward," most government officials, high or low, chose the latter and routinely inflated their actual harvest by two to three times, believing that they were contributing to the party's most glorious cause. A county produced seventy-two thousand tons of grain but reported one hundred and twenty-eight thousand, five hundred tons. Another county produced seventy-seven thousand tons but reported two hundred and two thousand, five hundred tons. A province produced three and a half million tons but reported seven and a half million tons.

While these highly exaggerated reports earned officials lavish praises from the party leadership, they were made at the expense of the peasants, who were forced to sell more grains to the government than they actually had. In one province, grain production declined by twenty percent from 1957 to 1960. Meanwhile, because of the falsified reports, the new quotas for peasants to sell their grains to the government increased by ten to fifteen percent annually for three years, reducing the average possession of yearly grains in the hands of individual peasants from six hundred and fifty pounds in 1957 to five hundred and thirty pounds in 1959 and four hundred and seventy-five pounds in 1960. Such a sharp decline alone had created a severe food shortage, and three million people across the province were facing starvation.

In fact, hundreds of thousands of able-bodied peasants were sent to work on public projects, to cut trees in the mountains, and to join the frenzied army making iron in backyard furnaces, resulting in a great shortage of manpower in the fields. The enormous pressure for high yield led to the belief that close planting was the solution. But the practice was taken to extreme lengths that some farmlands turned into impenetrable jungles, which must be fanned day and night for oxygen. In the end, dismayed peasants found no grain but only tall grasses in an experiment gone astray.

The most gut-wrenching stories Dai heard were of widespread hunger and starvation.

Small children said that they were like dogs and pigs fighting over the last bit of food with their siblings. "I cried at every mealtime when there was really nothing but boiled water in the cooking pot," one boy told her. "All I did every day was sniffing for food everywhere like an animal. One day, mother split a rotten sweet potato for us, four boys and girls. I believed that my sister had gotten the larger piece, and grabbed hers, only to find that mine was bigger. So I tossed it back and snatched my original share from my sister's hand. Mother beat me, saying that she should not have given birth to such a useless, greedy, and heartless boy. All of us wept."

"We ate everything," every adult Dai met would say to her, which included herbs, flowers, young shoots, sprouts, buds; tree leaves, barks, roots; grass in the fields, grass behind the walls, grass on roofs; clay, coal (and the right kind could be chewy and tasty if anyone would believe it); mice, lizards, frogs, snakes, earthworms, and insects; any crumbs of bran, cotton seeds, rape seeds, corn stems, sorghum stalks, and rice husks. Many found food substitutes in microorganisms growing on straw, seaweed, cotton batting, molasses, distiller's grains, animal feed, animal dung, and even bird droppings.

People were so hungry all the time that many had edemas. So deprived of nutrients and so weak were their bodies that their stomachs and legs became translucent, and many could see their intestines twisting under the skin. Dai had seen them in droves, and the sight made her feel like she was hallucinating. Their bone-dry faces sunk like an empty bucket and their eyes looked like dead fish. All the ribs were exposed like an open book. Their two temples had turned into deep concavities that a pigeon egg could fill the hole on each of them. The deformation of the lower bodies—due to severe and prolonged deprivation of proteins—made for a ghastly sight. Their calves, full of tissue fluids, first swelled to become as big as their thighs, but might shrink to become as thin as a weed a few days later. No one could live long after undergoing the same process several times.

Edema did lead to death when hunger persisted. In one province, three hundred and eighty-eight thousand had edemas and thirty-nine thousand, seven hundred and twelve died in one year. Hundreds of thousands of women had uterine prolapse, and were unable to give birth during this period of massive starvation.

Visiting the province was like stepping into a surreal world, everything was at a standstill, no sound, no bark, no animal, and no movement. Hundreds of ravenous men, women, boys, and girls lay on the ground like skeletons. When a few of them had the last energy to move, they drifted like ghosts.

The same devastation occurred in town after town, village after village, which Dai visited.

To conceal the failures, officials often hid the true number of deaths. One of the national model communes reported to have lost six hundred lives, which later turned out to be four thousand. One county reported eighteen thousand deaths, later revised to eighty thousand. Another county reported thirty thousand, later found to be over one hundred thousand. Still another county admitted three hundred and eighty thousand, later raised to four hundred and eighty thousand, only to be determined at one million in the end.

It was far worse at the village levels where starvation had taken away as high as twenty, thirty, forty, and even fifty percent of the local population. Hundreds fled to beg elsewhere, while dozens of households perished because everyone in the family had passed away. Too many were dying and the rest were too weak to move. Wild dogs fought over the dead bodies, and scattered their bones. The carnage was too terrible to watch or describe.

So many people died that the numbers of villages shrunk. In one county where more than one hundred and twenty thousand people died, the number of villages dropped from five thousand, four hundred and eighty-nine to four thousand, eight hundred and five. Remote and poor areas suffered even more. In a county of two hundred thousand in the Northwest, one-third of the population died, two thousand, one hundred and sixty-eight families were completely wiped out, eleven thousand, nine hundred and forty people fled, and one thousand, two hundred and twenty-one children became orphans. About six hundred thousand acres of farmland were abandoned, thirty-three thousand farm animals died, forty thousand sheep were slaughtered, and almost no pigs, dogs, cats, or chickens could be found. Official reports conceded that no place had a bleaker situation than this county, where fifty thousand houses were in ruins, two hundred and seventy thousand trees were cut, most schools and factories were closed, and agriculture came to a grinding halt.

Although not always true, the rumors of cannibalism did involve real cases. "When you see so many people lying everywhere," an old man told Dai, "on the kang, against the wall, in the ditches, under a tree, or clinging to a hill, you can't tell who is dead and who's alive. You don't have to fear the dead for they could move no more. But you have to keep an eye on those who are still living—they might catch, kill, and eat you."

"In my village," another told her, "people went to see one man repeatedly, praying for mercy not to eat the bodies of their loved ones. They paid him with whatever valuables they still had, but to no avail. The man took their gifts, cut, and ate the flesh of the corpses anyway."

"One day some smoke was coming out from a chimney," a local official told her, "which I had not seen for a long time in this famine. I went into the house and a woman was cooking at the stove. Before she could stand up, I went up, opened the lid, and saw a human leg in the pot. I could never forget the shocking and confused expression on her face."

At least six provinces had a death toll of between two hundred thousand and nine hundred thousand people in three years. Fatalities in eight other provinces amounted to sixteen and a half million. The exact death toll (not counting the stillbirths) was not known, although estimates ranged from twenty-five to thirty million, the highest in peacetime in Chinese history.

5

Exceptionally frugal in managing the family budget, Yan thought that she had handled the recent food crisis well. Faced with a depleted vegetable market, she did not throw away the bottom stalks of the cabbage but instead put them in water, and used the sprouts as salads for weeks to come. By doing so she believed that she had committed a sinful act because, in Southern China, the inability to obtain a great variety of fresh produce would be considered a housewife's most embarrassing failure. As many urban dwellers in Peking had been doing, she also learned how to bake soybean cakes, which she later mixed with corn, and to grow chlorella in bottled water for food supplements. She even learned to identify some Northern weeds and plants that could be added to the family diet, such as willow twigs, flowers of pagoda trees, leaves and buds of Chinese elm, red-toon shoots, bur-clovers, goosefoot, sow thistles, pigweed, and the "shepherd's purse." Her proudest achievement was to use three ounces of clean rice to make three pounds of steamed rice using a neighbor's recipe. The secret was to let the rice soak and dry first, to add water before steaming for just a few minutes, and then to repeat the same steps for the half-cooked rice twice or even three times until the rice expanded like cauliflowers when fully cooked.

Shocked by Dai's stories, Yan insisted that she stay for dinner as if the reporter were in danger of starvation. Dai laughed, saying, "I am quite all right. Because of the government's different policies toward cities, urban residents fare far better than the rural population this time. Peking, which has always enjoyed special treatment, is most isolated than all other places from the nationwide problems of starvation and food shortages."

"Come, have some ribbon fish—the only meat I can find in the market." Yan treated Dai with extra care at the dining table, considering the guest a heroine who had dared to visit those suffering towns and villages.

After listening to what her friend had detailed all afternoon, Tania wanted to ascertain the truth once more, "Is the situation really that bad?"

"Yes, our teacher told us," Xi chipped in, "poor weather, severe drought, and natural disasters are to be blamed for the situation."

"There has hardly been a perfect climate or any perfect year for our nation this big throughout history, and we have always experienced some bad weather conditions somewhere across the land every year. But the scale and severity of the ongoing starvation I have witnessed is absolutely true, and the situation is an unprecedented manmade disaster," Dai responded.

Reflecting on Dai's clarification, Tania whispered, almost to herself, "If all that is true, General Tao's warning would have been correct all along."

"Mommy, why are you always willing to defend those antiparty rightists?" Xi yelled out.

"Xi, we can think about and discuss issues calmly. And we should allow everyone to express their views and there is no need to yell," Tania replied.

"I don't know. Your opinions always seem to be different from the party's." The daughter was not happy with the mother.

"Xi, we all try to understand the situation and to better serve our people; many of them are suffering greatly," Dai explained to the girl.

"I know. But… but…" Xi was struggling to reconcile the different messages she was receiving at home with those from her school.

"Okay, Xi, you need to finish your dinner and complete your homework," Yan suggested.

Dai waited until they had left the dining room. She turned to Tania, "I believe that I have seen the Chinese Gulag camps."

"What?" Tania was dumbfounded. "Could there be worse stories than those of starvation?"

"When I was traveling in the Northwest, I heard about a labor camp called Quail Nest in a desolate county next to the Gobi Desert," Dai began.

"The labor camp used to be a prison for four hundred inmates. After the Anti-Rightist Movement, two thousand, four hundred rightists replaced the convicts and the prison was turned into a labor camp. Obviously, the old facilities could not hold that many new arrivals, who had to dig caves in the vicinity as their shelters."

Dai added: "As you know, that region was further west from Shaanxi. One of the harshest terrains in China, Quail Nest was actually very close to the Dog Bone Corridor, where the West Army had met its demise. The place had no vegetation but puncture vines so full of thorny nutlets like thumbtacks that locals called them 'devil's weed.' It was one of the few plants, like wild onion, salt cedar, bindweed, needle grass, sea buckthorn, and desert poplar that had the tenacity to survive in the extreme climate of little precipitation in summer but extremely windy and cold in winter.

"Although not sentenced by any court or convicted of any criminal activity, those rightists were treated as felons, with heavy labor being as much as a form of punishment as it was a means of keeping them there. Housing construction was soon followed by large field projects, which were intended to build conduits to irrigate the bleak terrains or, more ostensibly, to turn the arid wasteland into farms. The toil was as boundless as it was useless. Big sandstorms buried the ditches as quickly as they had appeared, and no amount of water was in sight to bleach the saline soil any time soon. But the quota was twenty-five cubic yards a day per person, which was enough to fill a thirty-ton dump truck. No one could fulfill the quota by working less than twelve hours; sometimes standing in salty waters, it could take fourteen hours or more. The harsh working conditions were meant to punish the denigrated rightists and reduce them to slaves."

She continued, "The misery only got worse amid the food shortage. While the work schedule remained the same, their daily rations were cut first from one and a half pounds to one pound a day, and then to a few ounces. No one cared about these rightists, who had been treated worse than common criminals only because the party leaders had ordered it. No camp officials were willing to help improve their pitiful conditions.

"Poor people, they ate any weeds, barks, roots, and plant seeds they could find. They looked for rodents, caught lizards and snakes, but some died from eating them raw. A group of nine inmates stole a big sack of potatoes, and each of the ecstatic men ate almost twenty pounds. Shortly afterward one died from eating too much too fast. The next morning, another man was searching for leftovers to suppress his own hunger from the dead man's stinky discharge.

"Despite the persistent hunger, nobody wanted to die. An old man found a piece of animal bone in the desert but feared it might not be safe to eat. He built a fire to bake the bone until it produced particles of yellow powder. He collected the powder and put it in his mouth, and found the taste agreeable. He then started to gather animal bones whenever and wherever he could, recommending to others that animal carcasses could save human lives.

"But tragedy struck, and the feeble-bodied died every day. Under the most despicable conditions of cold, starvation, and diseases without any help or proper treatment, two thousands of those enslaved rightists perished within three years, and only a few hundred survived. The death toll rose so fast that there were not enough healthy men to bury the dead in graves. One woman, who traveled two thousand miles from Shanghai, came to Quail Nest to see her husband. The inmates told her that he had just passed away a few hours earlier. When she ran out to look for the body, she saw several wild dogs tearing it apart. She collapsed."

6

"This is awful, insane!" Tania cried out.

"I know. It is a real catastrophe, a human catastrophe," Dai agreed.

Tania suddenly remembered something and asked, "You mentioned that the labor camp Quail Nest was near the Dog Bone Corridor, where the West

Army had been deployed. Anything thing new from Han Jian, who was witness to Dong's death?"

Dai, who had anticipated the question, burst into tears as she said, "He is dead."

"What? Why? How?" Tania was in shock again.

Before Dai could explain, there was a knock on the door.

Two plainclothes policemen entered the house and demanded, "Who is Dai?"

"I am," said she.

"You are under arrest."

Chapter 40

Games

1

As had been aptly stated in *Animal Farm*, "All animals are equal but some animals are more equal than others."

The communist society replaced the old ruling class with its own, creating a new political order and social stratification firmly grounded in a one-party system. Since the party was a pyramidal institution, the social divide it had created adopted the same pattern. At every school, village, or workplace, no administrative post would be given to anyone who was not a party member. Party affiliation was the exclusive permit to occupy any office in any field across the board, giving party members a special status over ordinary citizens. The higher one rose within the party, the more powerful and prestigious governing posts one could expect to obtain. More than any other social distinction, the party's top leadership positions were the most sought-after appointments within the organization. At every level, local, county, regional, provincial, departmental, and national, the party chief could have up to more than a dozen deputies. But everyone understood that those deputies did not matter, because it was the number one party principal who possessed all the *de facto* powers.

The higher one climbed up the institutional ladder, the fewer senior posts would be available. This pyramid organization and its highly compartmentalized power structure bred a new type of intraparty competition, which intensified whenever there were positions to be filled. Because the party had no rival in the nation and never held any real elections, because all key positions were appointed, because party membership was for life, and because nobody would retire after they had won the hard-fought leadership appointments, the desire to rise in the institution forced aspiring men and women to seek patronage. Their bosses' favor would be critical to their career advancement, while the former's disapproval would decidedly end anyone's dream of getting further ahead within the organization.

An implicit but inevitable outcome of this internally charged rivalry was that, if anyone wanted to move up, somebody had to come down.

2

As usual, the Politburo meeting began in the early evening and ended at 10pm, which suited the Chairman's timetable. He would continue to work through the night and go to sleep in the morning.

Also as in the past, the Chairman proposed the agenda and controlled the proceedings of the meeting. It went well. By default, Xia-Hou Ding attended every Politburo meeting in his capacity as its secretary. His diligence and effectiveness had pleased the members, who agreed to accept him as a candidate member. Lin Shi-Xiong was formally promoted from an alternate member to a full member of the Politburo, replacing the dismissed Tao Yin-Hu, who was now under house arrest.

Another major development, in accordance with Sheng's wishes, was the formation of a committee called the "study group" comprising Lin (director), Su Ming (deputy director), and three members—Si-Tu Wen-Liang, Bao Feng-Nian, and Kang Yi-Sheng. Under the Politburo's direction, the Chairman explained, this committee was assigned to review a document, submitted by the East Bureau, titled *Class Struggle and the Proletarian Revolution in Socialist China*.

Sheng was disappointed, however, that his last suggestion to reappoint Lu Di-Ping to a central government post was not accepted. Song Pei pointed out that Lu had falsified many accounts to boost his record during the Great Leap Forward, which had a devastating impact on his province. Several million people had died of widespread famine and starvation, and cannibalism had also taken place in a number of counties, which was too appalling for any government official to overlook. "History will condemn us for this horrendous crime," said he. "Someone has to take responsibility for it."

Si-Tu and Xia-Hou had read the same reports concerning Lu's performance, and they agreed with Song. A promotion of Lu at this point, they hinted, would send a wrong message to the nation, which had only recently terminated the costly Great Leap Forward.

No matter how much the Chairman had wanted to support Lu, it seemed clear that Sheng was a minority in this issue. He withdrew his proposal. "You win some and lose some," he consoled himself. But there was also something else besides Lu's case that was inexplicably troubling him. The more Sheng thought about it, the more it vexed him.

Sitting before the massive desk piled with books, Sheng picked up a volume of the *Comprehensive References to Government*. A set of two hundred and ninety-four volumes in three million words, the *Comprehensive References* was compiled by China's distinguished historian and scholar Si-Ma Guang in the eleventh century. By detailing the dynastic stories spanning one thousand, three hundred and sixty-two years, from 403 BC to AD 959, Si-Ma had hoped that later rulers could use them as a guide on how to govern the country by drawing lessons from both the successes and failures of the past. Sheng loved these books so much that he had perused them no fewer than seventeen times. To help modern readers who were less familiar with the ancient literary style, he had ordered a group of twenty specialists to produce an annotated edition, which had been printed several times in recent years.

Savoring every narrative by the gifted pen of Si-Ma, Sheng moved to a comfortable rocking chair and began to enjoy his most relaxing pastime.

Xun Yue (AD 148–209, scholar, thinker, and historian) once remarked that the key approach to victorious strategies involved the correct assessment of three elements—form, motion, and disposition.

"Form" meant the overall trend of winning or losing. "Motion" meant the swift flexibility and adroit adaptability while facing a fast-changing situation. "Disposition" meant the weakness or strength of one's resolve and commitment.

The distinctive nature of each of the three elements required different skills and methods to assess them. Therefore, using the same strategies to deal with seemingly comparable events could produce dissimilar consequences.

About four hundred years ago, Advisors Zhang Er and Chen Yu encouraged the rebel leader Chen Sheng to restore the six kingdoms to attract supporters, which he did and succeeded. Years later Advisor Li Shi-Qui advised the same to Prince Liu Bang, head of Kingdom Han, who failed in his mission. The reason was that everybody hated the Qin Dynasty, which had invaded and crushed the six small kingdoms. The deposed lords and princes wanted to regain their power and repossess their territories, which was exactly what Zhang Er and Chen Yu had advised Chen Sheng to do. But Prince Liu Bang was facing a nation divided by two major factions; few people were willing to bet on his success, which led to the failure of his strategy. Moreover, Chen Sheng enticed his supporters by granting land that did not belong to him to begin with. He was using somebody else's land to obtain support, which was truly a good bargain. Prince Liu Bang was distributing his own possessions in exchange for sympathy and support from those who had remained lukewarm to his cause. Clearly, using the same strategy did not work in Liu Bang's case because his enemies showed no signs of being defeated easily.

When the battle between Kingdom Qin and Kingdom Zhao was underway, Song Yi advised Xiang Yu, head of Kingdom Chu, to take a wait-and-see position and not to attack Qin until it had been weakened. Xiang Yu did not listen but killed the advisor. When Bian Zhuang-Zi was about to fight with two tigers, Guan Shu-Zi urged him not to enter the fight until the two tigers wounded themselves first in their fight over a buffalo. Bian Zhuang-Zi listened and caught the two tigers in the end. It seemed that the same advice had produced two different endings. The examples showed the importance of adopting different moves in dealing with different scenarios. When Xiang Yu led Chu to join Zhao in the campaign against Qin, no middle ground existed. He could not wait and watch his ally Zhao fight alone in the life-and-death battle against Qin, or else Xiang would have been killed after Qin annihilated Zhao. Under another set of circumstances where no serious crisis arose, the conflict between two powerful kingdoms might not necessarily mean the demise of one or the other. If this was the case, the imperative was to be patient, to wait for the right moment, to withdraw if the situation demanded it, or to attack if the opportunity arose. Patience, flexibility, adaptability, and decisiveness were the keys to ultimate victories.

When the army of Kingdom Han assaulted that of Zhao, Commander Han Xin positioned his soldiers next to the banks of a river, which was an apparently vulnerable position. But the enemy troops could not defeat him. When Liu Bang, the ruler of Kingdom Han, stationed his army on the banks of the Sui River, he was defeated by Xiang Yu who drove many of his soldiers into the river and killed them. Why the difference? Han Xin deployed the best of his troops near a river so that the soldiers had no place to escape but to fight for their lives. His enemies noticed the vulnerability, relaxed, and underestimated their opponents' resolve. When a desperate army engaged a relaxed one, the former would win. When Chu lost the capital city Peng to Liu Bang, Xiang Yu and all his soldiers were outraged. They were determined to take the capital back, whereas Liu Bang and his troops let their guard down to hold various parties to celebrate their victory. When an idle army faced a highly determined one, the latter would win. Similar locations would not decide the outcome of a battle, but discipline, focus, resolve, and determination would.

Thus it could be surmised that strategies should not be predetermined, because unpredictable motions and changes were constant. The most critical prerequisite was always to be prepared to adapt to shifting circumstances while deciding the appropriate strategies.

So familiar was Sheng with these lines that he could recite many of his favorite passages verbatim. These masterfully composed classics, he believed, were simply beautiful, heavenly, and enlightening. He never had a more congenial companion or a wiser advisor than those divine authors in history. A new reading of their familiar chapters never failed to refresh his mind, uplift his spirit, and sooth his pride every time.

The Chairman's encyclopedic knowledge of traditional Chinese politics and insatiable interest in the Chinese printed records had enticed him to go back again and again, searching for insights and nourishment from those classical Chinese masterpieces, rather than from the translated foreign publications by Plato, Rousseau, Hegel, Mill, or even Marx. The impeccable language, tantalizing stories, and indescribable excitement found in the works of Si-Ma and countless other native writers enchanted Sheng. He felt he had met those historical figures, knew their faces, understood their careers, shared their glories and frustrations, and would love to talk to and consult with them. He was certain that he could freely mingle with these famed ancients who would not mind but even welcomed his presence.

Sheng noticed that many influential leaders including emperors, kings, generals, and even rebel chiefs in Chinese history had also been brilliant military strategists. Not a few of them had come from a humble background with little education. But their enigmatic ability to rally the troops, firm grip on their subordinates, ingenious battle plans, steely resolve, and extraordinary valor had made them successful rulers of the country. No politicians could rule China without the military, Sheng concluded, nor could any military leaders, no matter how great they might have been, govern China without a fair amount of political wisdom. Much of Sheng's pride and self-confidence lay as much in his thorough understanding of political stratagems as in his extensive experience in military affairs.

Looking back at history, domestic and foreign, Sheng could find few names who could match his credentials. He had commanded an army of six million troops, a figure that even Alexander, Caesar, and Genghis Khan could not possibly rival. He had launched no fewer than four hundred battles in his life and lost only a handful of them. The last major campaigns he and his comrades had strategized in the late 1940s decimated more enemy troops than the military giants Washington, Napoleon, Wellington, Lee, Grant, Marshall, Eisenhower, Zhukov, and even Stalin, could ever imagined.

Such a lifelong record of great personal achievements made Sheng particularly cherish those wide-ranging tactical maneuvers and intense military battles that Si-Ma had artfully elucidated in *Comprehensive References*. For the immensely enriching tradition Sheng had inherited, he was no doubt a great twentieth-century leader living in the past. A born superhero, he thrived in the battlefield, which had made him feel forever young, vigorous, and unstoppable. If he had been invincible in war, he would be unbeatable anywhere on any stage in any theater of action, the Chairman believed.

3

Although Song Pei had been to the same building countless of times, he could be easily lost in it without an escort.

The Great Hall of the People, sitting on the west side of Tiananmen Square at the heart of the capital, was the largest office building in China. Completed within ten months, it was one of the monumental landmarks constructed in Peking during the Great Leap Forward. Measuring six hundred and seventy-five feet wide and one thousand, one hundred feet long, the massive neoclassical complex boasted forty-two acres of office space, which had been used exclusively for the central government since 1959, the tenth anniversary of the republic.

With no residential homes, business premises, or traffic nearby, the area was exceptionally quiet in the evening. Only the few lights on top of the building illuminated this mammoth structure, supported by one hundred and thirty-four pillars all around the sixteen-foot-high granite foundation. At the main entrance on the east side, each of the twelve bluish-gray marble columns was six and a half feet in diameter and eighty-two feet tall, giving the soaring one-hundred-and-fifty-three-foot, four-story edifice a clean, simple, but dignified facade.

In the area larger than the total usable space of the Forbidden City, this single modern structure was the site of the central administration's state waiting hall, greeting hall, reception hall, banquet hall, meeting hall, main hall, friendship hall, and many dozens of government office areas. Led by his aide, Song passed the red-carpeted hallways, ornate passages, and marbled staircases, heading straight to the western section of the building where, he had been told, he would find the premier.

Inside the Grand Meeting Hall, Si-Tu was conversing with a group of people standing next to the raised stage occupying the entire front portion of the great hall, bigger than a standard basketball court. Song took a back seat on the second floor and watched. He had something to discuss with the premier, but was not in any hurry. Glad to have a chance to sit down and take a breather from his heavily packed daily schedule, Song waited for the premier to take a recess.

Lit by five hundred lights circling around a giant bright crimson star at the center of the domed ceiling, the Grand Meeting Hall was truly magnificent. With a capacity of ten thousand seats on three levels, its hugely sweeping wood-paneled platform alone would comfortably sit as many as five hundred people in leather chairs with all the modern amenities associated with working desks in front of everyone.

But tonight the hall was filled with a pleasant fragrance coming from a unique group of visitors. Unlike those highly selective delegations of the party organizations in the past, they were some three thousand, five hundred elegantly dressed dancers, singers, choir members, musicians, composers, writers, poets, choreographers, actors, actresses, conductors, directors, and stage designers. Acting as the director-in-chief, Si-Tu was working on the largest theatrical production the nation had ever seen—a musical called *The East Is Red*.

With the musical meant to celebrate the upcoming national holidays, those involved in the project had less than two months to complete their rehearsals. Talking, waving his arms, listening patiently to his audience, and responding resolutely to their big and small questions, the tireless Si-Tu was as energetic and upbeat as ever.

"Poor Wen-Liang," Song said to himself, "at sixty-five, he still pretends he is a man of eighteen, a young actor. Maybe, his most suitable profession is not politics but the theater."

"Everybody, please listen," Si-Tu shouted. "We need to rehearse once more the changes we have just made." Everybody stood quietly listening to the premier, who told the performers how honored he was to work with such an extremely talented and dedicated group of artists. But he reminded them that they did not have the luxury of time. They had to design, improvise, test, revise, and practice over and over again until they could achieve perfection in these last few days before the actual performance.

The lights dimmed, music filled the air, and the rehearsal started.

The storyline was familiar to Song—about the rise of the Communist Party, the long struggle for liberation, and, most important, the preeminent role Sheng had played from the beginning till the end.

The whole production, divided into six acts, had thirty songs and twenty dance items, all interconnected with the theme of praising the party as China's savior, and the Chairman the greatest liberator. Each act, song, and dance was to extol his unmatched wisdom, vision, and leadership. His achievements were unprecedented, while the party's loyalty to him absolute, the nation's gratitude to him unlimited, and the people's love of him unbounded.

For the next three hours, Si-Tu hummed the tunes with the orchestra, watched the moves of the dancers, modified the tones of the singers, conversed with stage managers, opted for different shades and lights from the electrical control board, and proposed alterations to the clothing and makeup of the performers.

"About twenty years ago," Song reflected, "I raised the concept of 'Sheng's thoughts' but Si-Tu was not enthusiastic about it. Look at him tonight; what he is doing is absolutely remarkable. One has to admit the premier does everything in style and with great finesse."

The rehearsal did not end until midnight, when Song finally had a chance to sit down with Si-Tu in a special kitchen downstairs.

"Sorry I was not able to talk to you during the rehearsal," Si-Tu apologized, handing a small bowl of hot "hun-dun" or delicate southern-style dumplings to the president.

"That's all right. Nothing urgent. I heard you have kept some records on the total death toll in those disaster-stricken provinces in the last few years," Song said.

"Records? No, I don't have them anymore."

"Really? Who has them now?"

"No, no one has them."

"Why? How come?"

"I ordered them destroyed."

"What? Did Sheng know this?"

"No, no need to let him know," the premier answered. "It's in the best interests of all us," said he.

4

Bravo! He had hit the jackpot! His gamble had paid off.

Recently handpicked to serve in the "study group," the jubilant General Bao Feng-Nian had more to celebrate tonight. He allowed himself to drink a small glass of the famous liquor Maotai before going to bed.

Unlike many officer friends who had fought with him for several decades, Bao had never drunk or smoked in his long and distinguished military career. But today was different. His article, "Long Live the People's War," was published, in bold letters, on page one of the party newspaper, *The People's Daily*, which was the most influential paper in China. He was confident that, tomorrow, every newspaper and every major publication in the nation would do the same and carry his article on their front pages, as they had always copied what *The People's Daily* was doing. His article would be the talk of the town, of the country, and maybe even of the world, he predicted.

A discreet and modest man on the surface, the highly perceptive Bao had detected some subtle changes within the party's central leadership for a while. An astute student of traditional politics as much as of military tactics, he noticed not only the visible differences between Sheng and Tao but also the gradually diverging opinions between Sheng and Song. He believed that he had an opportunity to do something ahead of everyone else, which would certainly please the Chairman. Bao decided to write the article to praise Sheng's military strategies openly at a time when some top leaders were questioning the practicality of the Chairman's ideas and policies.

The brilliant move enabled the general to kill several birds with one stone. The fifteen-page article flattered Sheng by mentioning his name seventy-three times, which clearly demonstrated Bao's unadulterated loyalty to the great Chairman. The general knew that Shang had felt vulnerable after Stalin's death, especially after Khrushchev's secret speech. He needed support and reassurance—especially from the military. Bao's lavish praises provided exactly what the Chairman wanted at this critical moment in both men's careers—one was deeply concerned with how to preserve his legacy, while the other saw a good chance to move ahead.

As Sheng's domestic policies in the Great Leap Forward had led to criticisms in the party, the article reaffirmed the absolute correctness of Sheng's line by highlighting the Chairman's great military successes in the past. It also stressed the intensified threats from American imperialism and Soviet revisionism worldwide, suggesting the absolute need to preserve and continue the Chairman's great leadership today.

Although Sheng had been playing a less conspicuous role in the government's day-to-day operations, the article hailed his status as a true world-class leader. His bold strategy of leading the communist troops from the backward countryside to defeat enemies in advanced urban centers had guided the Chinese revolution to its successful conclusion. This unprecedented achievement opened a new chapter in the history of the international proletarian movement by giving hope to millions of people across Asia, Africa, and Latin America in their brave rural struggles against the mighty imperial powers of the West.

General Bao had seen the beaming eyes of Ernesto "Che" Guevara when the guerrilla war hero from the Western Hemisphere came to meet the Chairman at his Garden of Lilacs in Abundance. Hundreds of thousands of revolutionaries in the Third World now looked up to China and Sheng as their role models, and the Chairman was the greatest contemporary leader of the international communist revolution. With great ingenuity and creativity, Sheng advanced Marxism to a new phase superseding what Lenin had achieved early in the twentieth century. In other words, the Chairman was the greatest Marxist alive. He was not only the undisputed leader of the Chinese revolution, but also that of the world proletarian movement. Bao knew enough about Sheng's egoism to predict that the Chairman would love to hear this affirmation, and that he would never be tired of hearing others repeating it publicly.

Ostensibly, however, Bao was a professional soldier, not a writer. He actually did not compose the article himself but had sought help from other members of the "study group." Lin and Kang, in particular, were known in the party as skilled authors and sharp observers, and the two men delighted the general with their great expertise and enthusiasm. "We have a perfect alliance between the military and the literary," Su jokingly said during one private reception. Bao smiled. He understood her insinuation and he valued the alliance more than he was willing to say out loud.

5

"Patience, flexibility, adaptability, and decisiveness are the keys to ultimate victory." The words came out of Sheng's mouth even though his eyes were closed.

"Chairman, wake up. Chairman, please wake up," said Su gently, having just returned home.

"Patience is the key," the half-asleep Sheng continued to mumble.

"Chairman, you need to wake up or you will catch a cold." Su tried once more to wake up the husband.

For the first time, she realized that Sheng was getting old. His body was slumped in the rocking chair, massive yet motionless. His mouth was wide open on that big plump face, drooling and snoring.

"Chairman, wake up, please. You need to go to bed to sleep," Su repeated herself for the third time, and was ready to call the servants for help. She was too small to carry the Chairman.

"Oh, I must have fallen asleep." Sheng finally woke up.

"Yes, you have. I told you that your work habits are not healthy, not healthy at all," Su complained.

"Well, old habits die hard, I guess. What do you have for me?" Sheng asked. From the day he managed to put the wife in the "study group," she had become the unofficial but sole liaison between him and the Politburo, even though she had never been elected or held any important office in the party or government.

"Here are the seventh draft of the *Proletarian Revolution* by the 'study group,' a copy of *Long Live the People's War* by General Bao Feng-Nian, and the printed program of *The East Is Red* sent by Premier Si-Tu Wen-Liang," Su answered.

"That's all?" Sheng seemed to be expecting more.

"Oh, yes. President Song Pei has submitted his revised *Confucianism and the Chinese Communist* for your review," Su added.

"Okay, leave them on the desk and you may go to sleep." Sheng rose and was about to resume his work.

"It's getting late. In fact, it's four in the morning already. You better stop working and come with me too," Su suggested.

"You go, you go. I have things to do," Sheng insisted.

No one could argue with the Chairman, and Su left.

Looking at several documents lying on his desk, Sheng lit a cigarette and expressed no interest in them; he despised them all.

"They know I am getting old and looking for a successor. Each of these people tries to impress me, hoping I will favor him instead of someone else." A man who had never fully trusted any of his colleagues, Sheng said to himself.

Philosophically speaking, Lin and Su, the two leaders of the "study group," and to a lesser degree Kang, understood Sheng's ideas best. Expecting certain returns, of course, they strongly supported his vision of a Chinese-style Marxist revolution, and were willing to support him in any way they could to realize his vision. Unfortunately, they had mostly worked behind the scenes and lacked national exposure, stature, and authority. The ideological side of the Chairman trusted these group members more than anyone else. But his practical side warned him that the leadership of this "study group" had a long way to go to establish its own credibility and authority before the party and nation.

Premier Si-Tu was too smart not to know that he was no more than a figurehead in the "study group," which was purely a tool of the Chairman's. He never interfered with what the Chairman wanted the "study group" to accomplish. But Si-Tu had his own way of competing with other group members, and the theatrical production of *The East Is Red* was meant to showcase Si-Tu's talent and loyalty.

The only problem was Sheng's mercurial temperament. Like a sly peasant who only looked innocent, nobody could tell what the Chairman was really thinking. When someone was frank with him, Sheng would interpret it as irreverence. When the person praised him, he would say "no personal worship." When the same person stopped praising him, Sheng would suspect that the former was plotting against him. That was exactly why the more artful the premier's production became, the more the Chairman doubted the true intentions behind the musical extravaganza. In fact, the premier's seniority, intelligence, sophistication, and increasing popularity (now even among the artists and the educated, the Chairman noticed) made him most qualified to be a good national leader. This development left Sheng displeased and deeply concerned.

Sheng's liking for General Bao went back to their Red Army years, and it was only partially due to the general's own merits. Sheng, the master politician, understood more than anyone else that the essence of Chinese politics was all about who controlled the military. All party politics came down to personnel appointments, and the principal way for the Chairman to exercise his control was through a trusted deputy. Although Sheng valued the general's extensive military experience, expertise, and talent, he was not sure about the latter's potential in politics. The general had never demonstrated any interest and skill in any field beyond military operations. Besides, a firm military leader could pose a threat when his power became too great, something that the highly vigilant Chairman was sensitive about. When needed, the pragmatic Sheng could make use of the war hero Tao just as readily as the paranoid Sheng could sack the general when he sensed that the latter had become a threat. Paradoxically, the more the Chairman needed a strong military leader, the more fearful and wary he would become. The deeper he understood how old-fashioned Chinese politics worked, the more dilemmas he would create for himself.

A fearless rebel by nature and a ruthless revolutionary for life, Sheng never liked the condescending, authoritarian, conformist, dogmatic, conservative, hypocritical, superficial, affected, and moralistic teachings of Confucianism, which he believed had always served the interests of the ruling classes. Yet he would like the rest of his party to behave exactly as Confucius had admonished them, which was to obey the Chairman's authority as subserviently as the Chinese population had done to a king, an emperor, or a monarch. He viewed, with good reason, that Song's *Confucianism and the Chinese Communist* was dull, boring, and totally devoid of imagination and innovation. As a national leader, didn't Song have anything better to do than revising his pathetically outdated piece? What the Chairman needed was energy, speed, class struggle, a great leap forward, and another brand-new revolution, not any of those old clichés of Confucius. Song's ardent desire to please Sheng only resulted in his stronger disdain for the former.

All the headaches and misgivings aside, the Chairman understood that the older he grew, the more urgent it was for him to decide on a successor.

No Chinese officials had ever dealt with the question of leadership succession openly in practice or theory; the only experience they knew was through brutal intraparty strife. Once the one-party system was firmly established, no other alternative seemed available for the nation. Stalin's death reminded Sheng of the potential problem of succession, and he then arranged for Song to be the president as the successor waiting in the wings. Nevertheless, only a few years into the arrangement, problems started to crop up. Not pleased with the progress the new administration had made, the Chairman jumped from the back seat to the front, pushing Song and Si-Tu to speed up their actions to a degree that both men were reluctant to accept.

Disasters ensued in the Great Leap Forward and Song's explicit warnings alarmed the Chairman. Didn't he say in front of the full Politburo that "somebody has to take responsibility for it"? What did he mean by that? Who did he have in mind? Song could have very well meant him, thought Sheng, even though he was only pretending to blame Lu, who, everyone knew, was the Chairman's protégée. Looking back now, a shiver started to run down his spine. Sheng vowed that he would never become another Stalin, allowing another Khrushchev to destroy his hard-earned reputation and lifelong achievements. He must adopt a new strategy.

Whereas Marxist principles and Soviet experience had provided no clear solutions to the situation, ideological barriers banned anyone from looking beyond the communist lexicon for any alternatives. Pressed for answers but limited in options, Sheng did something he had always done—seek wisdom from the inexhaustible sources of Chinese political history and ancient classics.

He picked up another favorite tome, *An Analogy of Seven Strategists*, and turned to the sections on the principles of ruling and commanding. According to those ancient sages, the qualities of a capable king were very similar to those of a good field commander. For they stated,

A monarch should act like a great mountain, and his ministers could only look up to him but never see the top. The monarch should keep all his plans and options to himself, and his ministers would never find out how deep his bottom line is, as if in a mysterious abyss.

A benevolent king should rule his kingdom like the heavenly dragon, staying high above in the clouds and watching in all directions clearly and carefully. He may show part of his body, but never the totality of his designs and tactics, which should remain as unpredictable as the infinite skies and as unfathomably deep as the abyss.

No principle is more important for the field commander than his exclusive authority to make the most critical decisions on his own. If he can, he will be able to act without external interference, coming and going at will, moving freely, and conducting all the campaigns he wants. Emperor Huang has said, "Pure concentration and exclusiveness are the only ways to approach the fundamental laws of the universe, most likely to a heavenly state. The command of this ability can catch the opportunities others can't, produce favorable conditions for you, not others. Thus, a wise king should grant this to his marshal who could excise this authority to achieve his exclusive potential."

The wisest man is the one nobody can tell his wisdom, the best strategist is the one nobody can see his tactics, the bravest man is the one nobody finds him brave, and the man with the biggest interest is the one nobody can detect his self-interest.

If winning is important to the general, patience and secrecy are most critical to strategic planning as much as surprise is to military maneuvers, and unpredictability is to battle designs.

Never justify the most important decisions, never reveal the most important elements in maneuvers. If decisions are that important, brief explanations will be inadequate. If the maneuvers are so sophisticated, nobody needs to understand the details. Coming by surprise, leaving without a trace, everything decided by the general alone without any restraint from others. These are the keys to command an army.

Sheng could not agree more with what those ancient authorities had so clearly articulated, nor did he ever doubt that he alone was the incarnation of the king, who also personified the supreme military commander. These exclusive roles required him to protect the kingdom as much as his grave responsibilities demanded absolute secrecy and decisiveness. He alone was responsible for the kingdom's well-being, and he alone would decide its most enduring policies, which he would not share with anyone. Anyone.

6

A major intersection in the city, the name Xisi (literally, "west" and "four") originally meant the West Market in the capital. A big transport center for horses, sheep, cows, and camels from the Mongolian grasslands, one street here had been named Sheep Trading Road and the other Horse Trading Road as early as the Yuan Dynasty. As transport and travel activities grew, local inns, taverns, bars, restaurants, warehouses, and forage facilities began sprouting along the roads. The Ming and Qing Dynasties saw further development when the city's consumption of coal increased steadily and the black substance had to be carried by teams of camels passing through this area. Busy traffic, various exchanges, and increasing volumes of business and trade attracted more merchants to set up shop in the vicinity, selling tea, silk, cloths, shoes, clocks, watches, and jewelry. Blacksmiths, repairmen, tinkers, and wagoners opened their workstations along the sidewalks, as did bankers, pharmacists, doctors, tobacconists, vendors, and entertainers with their companies, offices, clinics, shops, stands, and stalls.

Originally a marker of a particular neighborhood, an elaborate archway was built at each of the four major intersections (northeast, southeast, northwest, and southwest) in the inner city of Peking. At the center of the northwestern quarter of the city, now called Xisi, a group of four grand and beautiful archways formed a square to face four directions, and each of the archways allowed one of the four streets to pass and meet at the center. Supported by tall and strong wooden pillars of two to three stories high, each archway was highly ornamental, stood on carved stone bases, and had lacquered rooftops with flying eaves. Three arched open spaces lined below on every side in all four directions, allowing pedestrians and carts to go through. These four-hundred-year-old structures became obstacles to modern traffic, and were removed as the widening of the city streets took place in the early 1950s. Only the colorless term Xisi reminded those who cared to recall its much more glamorous original name—Western Marketplace at the Four Archways.

Yan Yan loved to take a stroll here every day, especially when she was able to persuade Tania to come along with her.

Xisi looked heavenly and smelled liked a paradise for anyone who enjoyed those fresh and colorful produce and assorted local delicacies.

Some small eateries and food stalls, which used to be far numerous next to the archways, were still surviving. They sold tasty breakfast porridge, crispy pancakes, cornmeal soup, soybean flour cakes, fresh tofu, beef stew, juicy lamb, fried meat balls, homemade sausages, spicy noodles, and a great variety of sweets, satisfying those budget-conscious customers whose discerning palates made it difficult for them to resist good food.

The worst of the food shortage seemed to have passed and many shops and venders had restocked their shelves. Yan paused before a counter, looking at a basket of bright radishes.

"Sweeter and crisper than pears. Unbeatable and the best radish there is!" a vigorous salesman shouted cheerfully.

The smooth skin, the beautiful green color, and the consistent cylinder shape of the radishes intrigued Yan, who hesitated.

"Want to have a taste? Please, please feel free to take a piece." The young vendor had already cut one open, showing the excellent juicy flesh, which was as bright and smooth as a piece of translucent jade. "Very sweet and crisp, I promise," said he.

As Yan finally agreed to try one, she noticed that Tania had left. Where did she go? Yan started to look around.

Across the street, Tania had walked toward the place she liked the most—a bookstore.

Standing close to the sidewalks right next to the intersection, a pair of corner buildings conspicuously represented a bygone era by their colors, shape, and style.

Locals said that these two buildings were among the few remaining structures constructed toward the end of Empress Dowager Cixi's reign. Her courtiers had hope to hold a huge official ceremony to celebrate her sixtieth birthday by renovating the grand Summer Palace in the suburbs, and by constructing a series of welcome stations all the way along the route from the Forbidden City to the Summer Palace. That ceremonial journey was planned to pass Xisi, where the two corner buildings were to be erected as a pair of those special stations. The money for those extravagant plans was said to have been skimmed from the budget for the royal navy, which was then facing serious challenges from the Japanese fleet in the East China Sea. When news came that the Chinese navy had suffered a devastating defeat in the First Sino-Japanese War, a nationwide outrage forced the court to downscale the dowager's birthday festivities. Many projects were cancelled. The corner buildings at Xisi survived the ax, but they appeared a lot less grandiose than they had been initially intended.

The two-story welcome stations, which did look modest, were certainly smaller than the palace buildings inside the Forbidden City. Still, they were far larger and taller than any of the best civilian housing nearby. The massive and stately tile roofs made it difficult for anyone to miss the impressive royal facade. The solid walls, steady posts, side-by-side balconies on the second level, and scarlet window panels throughout outshone all of the low gray houses around them.

After the fall of the Qing Dynasty, the building on the east side of the street became a bank office and the other, on the west side, was converted into an official bookstore after the communist takeover.

This store, because of its size and convenient location, had become the largest and most popular bookshop in the capital city for nearly a decade. Living just around the corner of the same neighborhood, Tania loved to stop by the store whenever she had a chance. She knew most of the employees here, who also got to know her when Meng Bo-Xing, and sometimes Dong Zi-Tian and Tao Yin-Hu accompanied her to the store.

Unlike in the past, Tania did not ask "what's new" this time. On the big flat counter in the center and on several bookcases against the back walls, prominently displayed was the booklet *Long Live the People's War* by Bao. Never before had Tania seen such a prominent display for a single publication, except when a new title of Sheng's work was released.

When Yan entered the door, Tania was about to pay for her purchase.

"Why did you buy ten copies?" Yan asked.

"It must be a very important work. I am sure some of my friends would like to have one," Tania replied.

"Do I get a copy? Am I included as your friend?" teased Yan, who did not enjoy reading, even though she had learned enough vocabulary to read.

"Of course, you are. And we can read together too." Finding her friend frowning, Tania added, "How about I take you to a new place?"

"New place? Where? Tell me, I love to go anywhere with you." Yan got excited.

"Well, you will see. It's not far from here at all," Tania said.

7

August was a notoriously hot and humid month in Peking. Luckily, after leaving Xisi eastward, the street was only a short distance away before it came to a "T." Turning right would connect them to a boulevard leading to several famous places in the next mile or two, including the North Gate of Abundance, North Sea Park, Forbidden City, and the Royal Garden.

Turning left would lead them to a quiet lane named West Alleyway of the Imperial Walls.

When it was first constructed centuries ago, the one-hundred-and-eighty-acre Forbidden City had its own special district, which was about four times as big as the compound of the royal palace itself. Enclosed by protective walls, this special district housed many parks, temples, ceremonial sites, production and storage facilities, and supply centers for the exclusive use of the royal family. After the fall of the last Qing Dynasty, the special district was abolished and its land was opened for civilian use. Most of the protective walls were also demolished, and the leveled streets were named Alleyways of the Imperial Walls to signify its past.

One section, the West Alleyway of the Imperial Walls, was not a broad street; only its regal name might seduce casual pedestrians into thinking that it was much grander than it actually looked. Since it had been close to the royal palace, many traditional and influential families lived here. Walking three or four blocks up the alley, Tania and Yan came to a courtyard compound. Yan could tell the importance of this place simply by looking at the tall and windowless walls of seamless gray bricks, which extended several hundred yards in both directions.

The two women stopped before an enclosed doorway, and Tania pressed the bell.

Half of a young man's face appeared behind a peephole window. "What do you want?"

"I would like to see General Bao Feng-Nian," Tania said.

"Who are you?" The guard was suspicious.

"My name is Tania, an old friend of his," she said.

"Okay, please wait." He disappeared.

Now Yan knew why Tania had taken her here. She wanted to find out about Meng's whereabouts, and was hoping that his old colleague Bao might be of help.

"Are you sure that Bao can help?" Yan asked.

"I don't know. But I have to try," Tania answered.

They did not have to wait for too long before the guard returned.

"I am sorry, lady. The general is out for a meeting and I don't know when he will be back." His tone was no longer unwelcoming, although the gist of his message suggested otherwise.

"All right then, thanks," Tania said.

Silence except for the incessant loud noises from the impatient cicadas perching high above in the giant poplar trees.

"I knew it. These heartless opportunist people. They always hide behind the walls. They can't even bring themselves to the door and tell you what they think face to face." Yan was upset.

"That's understandable. We are different people now. No one wants to be seen with the wife of an incarcerated rightist," Tania said calmly, albeit with a tinge of regret.

"Look, look at what I have got!" Yan changed the topic.

"A raw radish?" Tania was surprised. "It must taste awful."

"No, no, no, no. This is a very famous radish, the most authentic one called 'jade radish' from Tianjin, the best in the world. Emperors and royalty savored it in the past. It's unbelievably sweet and crisp. Better than a pear. Please taste some," the saleswoman in Yan now insisted.

"Here on the street? No. I promise I will try it with Xi at home," Tania said.

8

Inside his large office, Bao pushed a bottom on the desk and spoke through the intercom, "Ask Number 5 to come to my office."

A middle-aged man in civilian clothing showed up a few seconds later.

"Go and pay a visit to this woman, and tell her what I am going to say next." Bao pulled out a photo of Tania from a drawer and laid it on the desk.

"Yes, Chief," the man answered.

Chapter 41

Flames

1

I DEAS, ACTIONS, AND CONSEQUENCES—EVERYDAY EXISTENCES AND commonsense logic. Ideas produced actions, and actions consequences. Good ideas might lead to good actions, and good actions to good consequences, while bad ideas might lead to bad actions and bad consequences. Extreme ideas would produce extreme actions, and extreme actions extreme consequences.

Commonplace? So they seemed.

Nothing moved in a straight line in human behavior. What about a mixed idea? A shifting idea? A controversial idea? A minority's idea? A dangerous idea wrapped in a fabulous cover? A popular yet erroneous idea? A self-righteous idea based on bigotry? A sugar-coated idea with deadly intentions? A lofty but impractical idea? A lovely utopian idea without foundation? A revolutionary idea never tested? A grandiose idea purely fabricated? An overwhelmingly powerful idea not yet investigated, deliberated, or contested?

In an autocratic environment, serious problems would inevitably arise when nobody except one man was able to propose, evaluate, challenge, or control the ideas.

787

And that man saw conflict as the panacea for all society's problems, no matter how much pain the conflict would inflict on the people.

He viewed the total destruction of any opposition as the prerequisite for his version of progress.

He served the people, whose well-being only he understood and whose future was always subject to his self-interest.

He trusted and empowered the masses, who were capable of both heroic and criminal acts.

He claimed to be the visionary leader of the modern proletariat while many of his basic ideas and ideals had originated from the ancient agrarian past.

He deceived, attacked, and manipulated his colleagues, who repeatedly became his tools, pawns, and preys.

He desired to build an ideal society of the purest, fairest, most just, and the most egalitarian via the only approach he knew best—class conflict in the style of a military campaign.

With all the ideological, political, and military authority vested in himself, the Chairman could do anything at will, and no one in the party or country could question or stop him.

Now, he was ready to review his battle plans for the last time before striking.

2

Sitting in her living room, Tania thought she had seen the man a long time ago, but could not recall when or where. From the way he sat, she deduced that he was a veteran soldier, even though his large and strong body was clad in the currently ubiquitous plain blue attire.

"My boss has asked me to tell you," the man with the code name Number 5 started, "that you should stop looking for Meng Bo-Xian."

"Why? He is my husband. I must find him," Tania said.

"My boss said that he had been sent to the Purple Prison, the top security jail for political prisoners in the country," No. 5 answered.

"Who is your boss? How does he know?" Tania asked.

"You went to visit him the other day. I am sure you know who he is, and I need to say no more," No. 5 briefly responded, trusting that the reference to his boss could explain everything.

Oh, that must be General Bao Feng-Nian, Tania concluded. Happy to have finally received some information, she asked, "When can I see my husband?"

"My boss said that you had better not try to contact him for now, which would make his case even worse," the man replied.

"But I need to see him. I must see him. I need to know that he is alive and well," Tania insisted.

"In that case, I can pass him a letter from you. Please don't tell this to anyone. My boss never instructed me to do so. This can make him look very bad if it becomes public."

"Of course, of course. I understand. Please wait for a few while and I will write a quick note to my husband."

Tania went to another room. Yan came in to refill the tea pot with some hot water. Minutes later, Tania came back with a packet in her hand.

"Please give this packet to Bo-Xian. It has my letter and some personal things, which my husband often uses."

"All right. I will bring your packet to him as soon as I can."

"Thank you so much. I really appreciate it."

"You are very welcome. I also have a personal suggestion; hope you don't mind."

"No, I don't. Please say it."

"You have a friend Dai Tian, correct?"

"Yes, I do. I have lost contact with her lately as well."

"She has been sent to a labor camp called Quail Nest in—"

"What? I know that horrible place. Hundreds of people have died there. Why?"

"She is believed to have been investigating the death of Dong Zi-Tian."

"What's wrong with that? He was her husband."

"But she was also collecting materials to write Dong's biography."

"Anything wrong with that?"

"Yes. Dong and his career have been one of the most sensitive issues in the party. Her plan to write his biography is considered an attempt to rewrite party history, which will pose a serious threat to the current party leadership."

"Unbelievable. She may simply want to keep her personal memories of her beloved husband."

"No. Nothing is personal here. Everything is political."

"Even personal reminiscences?"

"Yes. Definitely. I therefore strongly urge you not to contact Dai, which could hurt you and your husband."

The man left and Tania sat in her chair, contemplating.

Yan came in and said, "I know who he is."

"Who?" said Tania absent-mindedly.

"The man who just left."

"Who is he? How do you know?" Tania was surprised.

"Remember, when we were in Shanghai many years ago, he stopped by the party headquarters several times. I suspected then that he could have been a secret courier or agent working for the party. His name is Li Fan."

"Oh, yes. Now I remember. No wonder he looked familiar. It must have been him," Tania agreed, feeling delighted that Li was willing to help in her moment of great need.

"I will visit Dai," she told Yan.

"What? Didn't Li Fan tell you not to contact her anymore? It could hurt both you and Bo-Xian," Yan protested. She knew too much about the notorious practice of implicating innocent people in China to allow her friend to get involved.

"No. I must go and see Dai. I am her only friend and relative in this world now. I can't leave her alone in the labor camp," Tania insisted.

"Then I will go with you," Yan suggested.

"No, you can't. Xi needs you. She can't be left alone here."

"So, when are you leaving?" Yan could not find a good reason to change Tania's mind.

"Tomorrow."

3

With the exception of Si-Tu Wen-Liang, who was attending a state event, the "study group" held a meeting in Abundance to finalize its document.

"The seventh draft is a big improvement and it reads much better than the earlier ones. I like the document as a whole, but am not sure about the term 'permanent revolution.' Why does it sound so familiar?" the Chairman asked.

"Well, we were debating about it too. Marx, Engels, Lenin, and Trotsky had all used the same term. But in a different context, of course," Lin Shi-Xiong replied. Considered one of the party's top experts in Marxist publications, he was the authority to address this sort of theoretical or stylistic hurdles.

"Yes. By 'permanent revolution,' Marx meant to say that the proletarians must push the revolution beyond what the petty bourgeois class was able to achieve," said Su Ming, who was apparently pleased to show off her knowledge in front of the group.

"By 'permanent revolution,' Trotsky meant to say that the Russian proletariat must hold onto the leadership role and resist the pressures from international enemies to carry out a thorough revolution. In other words, to make the Russian Revolution the prologue to a worldwide revolution," Kang Yi-Sheng added.

"It seems my theory deals with a different stage of the proletarian revolution." Sheng Bao spoke slowly but clearly. "Marx raised the notion of 'permanent revolution' at a time when a proletarian revolution was not yet imminent. Trotsky used the term during the initial stages of the Russian Revolution in the early 1900s. I developed my theory long after our liberation. Therefore, a different expression must be found to distinguish my ideas from theirs. I especially don't want to be lumped with Trotsky."

"Yes, yes, we must do that," Bao Feng-Nian agreed completely but he, a general not a scholar, provided no concrete input to the discussion.

"How about 'continuous revolution'?" suggested Kang, pleased to be able to offer a new terminology.

"Should it be 'continuing revolution'?" Su countered.

"Hmm, 'continuous revolution' or 'continuing revolution.' They both sound fine to me. What do you think?" Sheng asked Lin, who was gratified that the Chairman was willing to solicit his opinion on the matter.

Lin personally believed "continuous revolution" to be the better term. But, aware that his choice might upset Su, he answered, "Yes, I agree both terms are acceptable."

"But a little bit too long, isn't it, if we use the whole phrase—the 'theory of continuous or continuing revolution under the dictatorship of the proletariat'?" In any message to the masses, Bao always preferred simplicity over wordiness.

"How about 'eternal revolution'?" Sheng proposed.

"Oh, yes. That's a good idea," the delightful Su responded.

"Yes, yes. That's a brilliant idea. It conveys the same meaning as 'continuous revolution' but avoids using the same term by either Marx or Trotsky." Lin was lavish as ever in praising the Chairman.

"Revolutionaries around the world are looking for a great new leader, and our Chairman's grand theory of 'eternal revolution' shows that he is that new master," declared the astute Bao.

"Yes, both Eduard Bernstein's old revisionism and Nikita Khrushchev's new revisionism are dead. From Nelson Mandela in South Africa to Ernesto 'Che' Guevara in Latin America, from Vietnam, Cambodia, Laos, and the Philippines, from Northern Ireland and Colombia to Chile and Nicaragua, revolutionary fighters cannot wait to embrace an updated Marxist theory to guide their uprisings. Our Chairman's theory of 'eternal revolution' is the greatest revolutionary philosophy today," Lin elaborated.

"All right then, that's settled—'Eternal Revolution' it is," Sheng announced. "Tomorrow we will present the final version of our document on 'Eternal Revolution' for adoption at the Politburo meeting. The meeting will formally pass a resolution to launch the Great Proletarian Cultural Revolution, which we have been preparing for more than a year. This 'study group' will also be elevated to the 'leadership group,' which will be in charge of all matters relating to the Great Proletarian Cultural Revolution."

Sheng paused and looked around earnestly, "You will be the proud champions of the first Great Proletarian Cultural Revolution in human history, and you will be remembered as the greatest and most dedicated crusaders in the international proletarian movement."

"Thanks, Chairman. I swear that I will remain loyal to you, our great Chairman, till the end of my life," Bao said.

"Me too. I will be your most loyal soldier in this unprecedented historic revolution," Su said.

"Not matter what lies ahead, we all swear absolute loyalty to no one but our great Chairman till the end of our lives," Lin and Kang concurred.

4

The official announcement came like a bombshell for the nation. Like millions of citizens, Tania had heard about it over and over again throughout the day at bus stops, ticket booths, and train stations, and now the announcement was made yet again through a loudspeaker inside the passenger car of her train:

> Initiated and led by our great leader Chairman Sheng Bao, the Great Proletarian Cultural Revolution is here upon us. A brand-new phase of class struggle, this Great Proletarian Cultural Revolution will eradicate all the evil capitalists, their corrupt ideas, and their wicked agents who have been hiding like cancers in our society. Our struggle against them is part and parcel of the eternal revolution our great Chairman has taught us since liberation. Our dedication to the eternal revolution will consolidate our socialist success of today and guarantee the arrival of communism tomorrow.

The message was followed by a long list of goals and targets of the revolution, and the broadcast on the train only ended at sunset.

A deep sense of sadness overcame Tania, who had never felt this lonely and depressed before. All her loved ones were either dead or imprisoned. Yan had to stay behind with Xi, and Tania had to take this lonesome train journey to faraway Quail Nest. The slow train ride reminded her so much about the past, and of her sweet and youthful memories, including those of Dong. Now, he was no more. Now, she was on her way to search for his grieving widow. Subconsciously, Tania had mixed feelings upon hearing about Dai's detention. Although sad and worried that her friend had been thrown into a notorious labor camp, Tania was heartened to know that Dai had also been working on Dong's biography. She hoped that she could meet Dai soon and share the intimate stories of Dong's life, which for some reason had stayed with her all these years.

Memories. Strange and mixed memories. Sweet, bitter, sad, and tragic memories. Tender, congenial, and heartwarming memories. Inspiring, estimable, heart-wrenching, inexplicable, and irrepressible memories. "Why do humans have these feelings, sentiments, memories, and desires?" she asked herself. A question she found no answer on the hard bench of the moving train.

But the repeated monotonous announcement weighed on her mind. Tania wondered whether she could continue to protect that tiny but precious space in her heart, and whether her personal sentiments could be viewed as "corrupt capitalist ideas" soon to be eradicated from this world. Amid the dark and constant motions of the train, Tania could hear the weighty sound of metal wheels rolling across the tracks as if to remind her of "eternal revolution," "class struggle," "antirightists," "insidious capitalist agents," and "total eradication."

Dai had told her, Tania recalled, that for more than a decade, a slew of big and small political movements had always been intertwined with economic development, and the model of class struggle had often been adopted as the guiding principle to regulate productive processes. Take the Sunshine District in Henan Province, for example, where the last famine had hit the hardest; many officials had doubts about the Great Leap Forward and some resisted the attempts to fabricate productivity records. But they were singled out and labeled as "antiparty," "anti–party line," and "anti–party leader" rightists. A large number of provincial and regional officials were severely criticized and summarily fired or demoted. As many as seventy thousand so-called rightists were unmasked, one hundred thousand alleged conspirators discovered, and two hundred thousand local officials implicated. Such a strong backlash suppressed any healthy discussions about party policies and silenced those who might have some good opinions on how to develop the nation's economy.

The great famine cost the lives of one million people in the Sunshine District, or about one-eighth of its population, a catastrophic calamity ten times worse than the devastation it had suffered during a decade of civil war. A manmade tragedy and a failure of party policy notwithstanding, Sheng insisted that the fiasco happened because local residents had failed to carry out his plans for a complete revolution. After reading the reports of official investigations, he asserted that the high death toll was a clear sign of retaliation by the wealthy class, whose members viewed the communist state as their enemy after it stripped them of their power and property after the liberation. Deceitful counterrevolutionaries must have taken control over the villages, and cunning landlords must have infiltrated the government by marrying off their daughters to party leaders, Sheng claimed. If the enemy's contemptible retaliation were the root cause of the famine, the proletarians would have no other choice for salvation except a resolute counteroffensive.

The Chairman whitewashed the party leadership's wrongdoings, and his directives allowed government officials to shift all blame to the locals. They conducted a campaign to round up suspects, vowing to arrest all those counterrevolutionaries and imprison and kill all those class enemies. A massive prosecution team of four thousand members descended on the district, singled out one hundred thousand people, and detained eight thousand suspects including forty ranking regional and county officials. Labeled as "corrupted" or "rightists" or "turncoats," some three hundred were arrested, more than eight hundred were either fired or demoted. Several thousand village councils underwent drastic changes. In one county, it was believed, half of the communes had been corrupted, as were seventy to eighty percent of the local village organizations and production units. As the Chairman had wisely predicted, the fight was indeed a life-and-death struggle between the "reds" and the "whites," those government prosecutors positively concluded.

It was a cool morning two days later when the chugging train slowly came to a halt at the final destination at the edge of the Gobi—an eerily quiet place without any trace of life except for the endless sea of sand. The next eight miles of the journey on foot took Tania the entire day to complete. At the entrance of Quail Nest stood a run-down shed made of a few dark and dirty shingles, which were at odds with its desolate but ubiquitously yellowish surroundings. It must be a luxury to stay in any manmade structure here, Tania thought.

A man on duty, short, withered, and hunchbacked, grudgingly asked Tania what she wanted.

"To see my friend Dai Tian."

"What's your name?"

"Tania."

No soon had she uttered the word than two armed guards mysteriously showed up from behind the door, yelling, "You are under arrest."

5

"Why are you back so early today?" Yan was surprised to see Xi coming home at midday. "All classes have been cancelled. We are in a revolution now," Xi answered.

"A revolution? What revolution?"

"A Great Cultural Revolution."

"What does that mean?"

"I don't know. We have no classes anymore."

"Where are your teachers? Where have they gone to?"

"They are not going anywhere. They have stopped teaching to carry out revolutionary activities at school."

"What revolutionary activities can a school have?"

"A lot. To investigate school leaders, to expose their corrupt activities, and to reform the educational system."

"What will you do then?"

"I will go to the streets and participate in the revolution."

"Revolution in the streets?"

"Yes, of course. There are parades, meetings, demonstrations, protests, music, songs, loudspeakers, and big-character posters everywhere. I want to be a part of that."

"Sounds exciting but confusing," Yan confessed. At her age, she had seen too many revolutionary movements to be excited.

"Where are father's old uniforms?" Xi asked.

"What uniforms?"

"You know, the uniforms he used to wear as an officer. You have kept them somewhere, haven't you?"

"Yes, I have. But they are too big for you. Why do you need them anyway?"

"Well, all the Red Guards wear them and I would like to have one too."

"What is a Red Guard?"

"The Red Guards are the loyal soldiers of the Chairman. They are the vanguard of the Great Cultural Revolution."

"Are you one of them?"

"No, they said I can't because my father is a rightist. But I can dress up and pretend to be a Red Guard. Nobody can tell I am not one when I am wearing father's uniform."

"I told you, they are too big for you to wear."

"You know how to alter clothes right? You have always made beautiful clothes for me and Mom. I know you are the best tailor in our family."

"And the only tailor in this family, I should say."

"Yes, yes. I agree. Please, dear Yan, I need my uniform desperately. Please, please help me."

"Okay, okay, my little princess. I will alter one of your dad's uniforms for you."

Two hours later, a glowing and delighted Xi appeared in the living room, clad in the green military uniform that her father used to wear. It was a little discolored, but Xi liked that even more for the faded color, like that of an antique, reflected the authenticity of the attire better than a brand-new one.

"You look good, like a pro." Yan was about to say "like a young woman" but decided against it.

"How does it fit?" Looking at a mirror, Xi was quite satisfied with her transformed image—she looked like a real soldier, not a schoolgirl any more. But she wanted confirmation from an adult.

"Yes, yes, it fits you perfectly. You look just like a young soldier," Yan reassured her.

"All right. I am leaving. I am going out to join the revolution. No need to wait for me at dinner."

"What time will you come home? How long will you stay in the streets?"

"I don't know. As long as the revolution lasts," Xi said as she disappeared through the door.

"Don't be back too late. I will wait up for you," Yan shouted at the teenage girl, who was enthralled by the idea of becoming a great revolutionary.

6

It was a restless—no, torturous—night for Si-Tu, who had been reading several top-secret files at his desk.

Sitting in his office in the Pavilion of White Garlands next to the northwest corner of Abundance, he could hear intense noises from the nearby streets outside the compound—shouting, yelling, and passionate revolutionary songs from a steady stream of demonstrators all day long. Obviously, the Great Proletarian Cultural Revolution had unleashed tremendous energy and attracted massive popular participation as Sheng had wanted. That the Chairman's new Cultural Revolution would be an unprecedented mass movement was crystal clear to the premier, who needed to find an appropriate response to this phenomenal event, which was not as easy as it might seem.

One of the top-ranking officials in the party and government, Si-Tu had survived many ups and downs. He knew of too many intraparty conflicts that had brought down one powerful and bright leader after another. He did not want to become one of them. He needed a strategy. But, before he could achieve that, he needed to know Sheng's true intentions behind this dazzling movement.

Schooled in the same Marxist–Leninist ideology, Si-Tu understood Sheng's broad rationale for the Cultural Revolution. It originated from the conviction that classes and class struggle still and would continue to exist in a socialist society long after the Communist Party had risen to power. When the Soviet Union under Khrushchev took a revisionist turn, Sheng had become deeply concerned with how to keep the revolutionary flames burning in China and across the globe. The existence of conspiracies and imperialist infiltrations in Eastern Europe further alarmed the Chairman, who was determined not to allow both his political and personal legacies to be altered in any way by his successors or adversaries.

But who could they be? Prepared by Sheng and his "leadership group," the party's latest public announcement had explicitly stated,

They simply deny thousands of years of human history as a history of class struggle. They deny the class struggle of the proletariat against the bourgeoisie, deny the proletarian revolution against the bourgeoisie, and deny the proletarian dictatorship against the bourgeoisie. On the contrary, they are the faithful running dogs of the bourgeois class and imperialism. Our fight with them is a life-and-death struggle.

A group of bourgeois agents and counterrevolutionary revisionists have been hiding in our government, army, and various cultural departments. As soon as the right moment comes, they will seize power and subvert the dictatorship of the proletariat in favor of the bourgeois. Some of them have been discovered, some have not, and some have even become our trusted successors, just like Khrushchev and his ilk. They are now lying low by our side. Our party committees at all levels must pay full attention to this matter.

Evidently, the Chairman believed in the widespread existence of these "secret bourgeois agents" and "capitalist running dogs" inside the party. He must also have identified those within the party's top leadership. Or else he would not have needed to start the Cultural Revolution, which was but his tactic to ensnare them all at once.

If nobody else knew who exactly those top "agents and running dogs" might be, Si-Tu did.

Sheng was apparently angry at Song, something the perceptive Si-Tu had noticed for some time. Experience had taught him that, once somebody had run afoul of Sheng, nobody in the party could save him. Therefore, Si-Tu's first instinct was not how to save Song but himself.

Even though Song's imminent fall did not trouble the premier, he was concerned about its repercussions. What if Song's political demise produced a domino effect? Who else would be implicated then?

The premier had a close working relationship with Song, who, as the nation's president, had been his direct boss for many years. How could Si-Tu survive Sheng's ax this time? How could he explain convincingly to the Chairman that he knew nothing about the "bourgeois running dog" even though they had been working together daily for years?

"I will repent, I will confess, and I will be willing to be the first senior party official to expose Song," Si-Tu decided. "As soon as Sheng hands down his sentence, I will kneel and beg for Sheng's mercy, if necessary. I will swear to him that I have no ambition in the party. I have never attempted any office other than the one given by the Chairman. I will swear that I have always been and will forever be the most faithful soldier to fight for the Chairman for as long as I live."

Having prepared his contingency plan, Si-Tu could breathe a little easier and relaxed. He picked up the last piece of document from the pile, thinking that he could finish his work in a few minutes. It was an appointment letter, and his face immediately turned as white as the paper.

Signed by the "leadership group," it read, "Si-Tu Wen-Liang will head the official investigation into the crimes that Song Pei has committed against the party, the nation, and Chairman Sheng Bao."

"Bastards! They don't want my confession. They want *me* to be in charge of the execution!" Si-Tu swore under his breath, even as he quickly began a new round of mental calculation on how to survive this latest political manipulation.

"You think you are smart by preparing Plan 'B,' but Sheng had thought about it long before you did," the premier chided himself as he wiped his forehead with a handkerchief. "He wants to keep you on a short leash. He has seen through your brain and knows precisely what your next move is going to be. You are his pawn, you are his prey, and you are his slave—all at once. He will never allow you to run away. He has set up both the game and the rules of the game. He has also decided on your role in the game. And you have no way of escaping his absolute control," Si-Tu sadly concluded, "as long as you belong to his party."

7

The young and upbeat Xi had never felt this free before. No school, no class, no teachers, no parents, no curfews, no homework, no examinations, and not even a Yan to nag at her. All public buses and trolleys were free for anyone wearing an authentic army uniform since the conductor automatically assumed the former must be a Red Guard. A youngster in uniform could hail a truck or hitchhike any automobile by telling the driver that he or she had to take care of some urgent revolutionary business somewhere in the city. Xi's discolored uniform was her best protection, business card, and passport at this pivotal moment of a momentous revolution.

Years of indoctrination in school had transformed Xi, still a teenager, into a dedicated revolutionary, a passionate supporter of the party and the great Chairman, and a tenacious fighter for the proletariat and communism. She had missed too many great opportunities in the past, such as the Anti-Japanese War and the civil war against the nationalists. She vowed not to miss this one or she would regret it for the rest of her life.

A short bus ride took her to the Southwest Marketplace, where she saw a large crowd. Pushing through the throng, she found a team of Red Guards interrogating several pedestrians.

"Which family are you from? What kind of job does your father have?" a girl Red Guard asked a young man, pointing at his face.

Despite repeated propaganda, the party's reliance on the masses was in reality never unconditional. Based on the Chairman's doctrine of perpetual antagonism between classes, the government had since the liberation divided the nation's population into two principal subdivisions—the "red" and "black" sectors. Class consciousness was believed to be hereditary from one generation to the next in both categories, making a continuous vigilance by the "red" camp against the "black" one necessary.

Favored by the authorities, the "red" sector included five categories of people: workers, poor and lower-middle-class peasants, revolutionary soldiers, revolutionary officials, and descendants of revolutionary martyrs. Considered trustworthy and loyal to the communist regime, anyone born from one of these families would automatically receive preferential consideration in employment, promotion, or admission to good schools and universities.

At the opposite end of the spectrum, anyone born into any of the five "black" categories (landlords, rich farmers, counterrevolutionaries, bad elements and transgressors, and rightists) would forever be stigmatized in every social and political aspect of life. Under constant suspicion and mistrust, they were treated as second-class citizens at best and perpetual criminals at worst.

Because the Chairman had initiated the Cultural Revolution to unleash a new round of class antagonism from top to bottom, the Red Guards were obsessed with distinguishing friends from foes. The simplest way to do this was to find out about one's family background, which was often the first intimidating question many people had to answer day and night.

"My family is all working class," the young man quivered as he replied, not knowing why he was being targeted. Fearing that a simple response might not be enough to dispel his interrogator's nagging suspicions, he elaborated, "My father is a factory worker, and so are my uncle, my elder sister, my cousin, my grandfather, my fiancée, my future mother-in-law, and—"

"Stop!" the girl Red Guard shouted. "Look at your hair! See how long it is! Parting to the right, not to the left. Definitely a counterrevolutionary style! Greasy, smelly, and ugly. You are a disgrace to the working class, whose members always have short haircuts!"

"All right, all right. I will change, I promise I will cut my hair as soon as I get home." The young man felt deeply embarrassed at having tarnished the purity of the great proletariat.

"Why wait? Why don't we have a total transformation right here and now?" A boy Red Guard came forward with a huge pair of tailor's scissors in hand.

Before the young man could say anything, his head was swiftly sheared like a sheep.

The girl Red Guard yelled to the crowd, "Our Great Cultural Revolution is to eradicate all the old customs, old culture, old habits, and old ideas, and to replace them with our new customs, new culture, new habits, and new ideas of the great selfless proletariat!"

"Down with capitalist haircuts! Long live the revolutionary hairstyles!" her audience responded boisterously.

The next one in line went up, pleading, "Esteemed Red Guard Comrades, I know I have made a terrible mistake. I should not have worn this dirty bourgeois dress today, and I promise to throw it away myself when I get home."

Xi saw a woman in her forties talking, and she was wearing an exquisite silk cheongsam with the distinct high neck and a sexy slit revealing her long legs.

"All right. You are smart. Never wear this dirty and obscene stuff again in public!" Several Red Guards surrounded her, and one of them quickly painted a big scarlet cross on her chest, while another's scissors mowed through her newly permed long hair.

Tears in her eyes, she pressed through the hostile crowd as they shouted at her, "Down with the 'Old Fours' of the bourgeois! Long live the Great Proletarian Cultural Revolution! Long live the dictatorship of the proletariat!"

The interrogations went on and on, directed at anybody suspected of having a bourgeois taste or style. A young man's pants were believed to be too narrow, a woman's skirt too short and too colorful, and an elderly man's dress shoes too pointed. All items were promptly ruined, to the dismay of their owners but to the great satisfaction of the young Red Guards and the onlookers.

Xi thought she had seen enough street justice at one spot, and decided to continue her adventure.

Frantic actions, passionate beliefs, lofty slogans, red flags, gigantic posters, and fast-moving multitudes besieged the city, where hundreds of thousands of innocent schoolchildren and university students, freed from school, became the perfect tools for the Chairman's Great Proletarian Cultural Revolution. Lured by his personal mystique and encouraged by his personal approval, they formed a militant organization—the Red Guards, and turned the capital city into the first battleground as they strived to implement the Chairman's glorious principles of "Eternal Revolution."

Not far away from a major thoroughfare, a huge bonfire attracted Xi's attention. She rushed there, only to see several dozens of Red Guards tossing hundreds of rare books, valuable paintings, fashionable clothing, hardwood furniture, and expensive jewelry into the flames.

Ancient temples were looted. Artistic wooden panels were taken down and torched. Giant statues were smashed. Historic monuments and tombs were demolished. Everything old must be destroyed. Every sign of the past must be replaced. Thus, the Concord Hospital was renamed "Anti-Imperialist Hospital," the street leading to the Soviet embassy was changed to "Anti-Revisionist Street," and the Royal Garden now became the "Working Class Garden."

At "Old Harmony," the famed Peking Duck Restaurant, a group of Red Guards were asking why its one-hundred-year-old sign was still hanging. The manager replied that the restaurant was no longer a private establishment; it had been nationalized many years ago. His explanation cut no ice with the Red Guards. Off they went to drag down the heavy wooden panel, and hammered it into pieces. The ransack continued as the Red Guards scratched every old painting and sign in the dining hall, replacing them with huge posters of Chairman Sheng's portrait and his revolutionary slogans. One of them read,

> People around the world unite to defeat American invaders and their running dogs! People around the world must have courage, dare to fight, and never be afraid of any difficulties. If they push forward, generation after generation, the world shall be theirs. All the demons and beasts will be destroyed!

The next morning, the restaurant reopened with a smashing revolutionary flare. Waiters and waitresses dressed up like Red Guards, and welcomed passersby with the greetings not of "How are you" or "How may we help you," but of "What about your family background?" The terrified patrons fled as fast as they could.

Xi's next encounter was a bloody scene that was totally devoid of hilarity. Inside the compound of a large courtyard house, a group of Red Guards were beating the elderly owners, forcing the couple to disclose their evil conspiracy against the state. They kneeled and begged for mercy, but to no avail. Fists, leather belts, baseball bats, and metal pipes rained down on them repeatedly and mercilessly. Load after load of personal possessions, clothing, books, jewelry, paintings, and other valuables were cleared from the rooms, dumped in the front yard, and then set on fire before a rowdy crowd of Red Guards, nearby residents, and passersby.

The breathless old man fainted several times, and his wife pleaded for mercy. She vowed that they harbored no ill-intentions toward the new government, and that they had donated all their factories, facilities, and stocks to the country. The only thing left was the monthly interest they received from the banks.

"Interest? You still receive interest in this day and age under socialism?" A boy hit the man with a large spade. He fell to the ground, and his wife collapsed.

"Is he dead?" a girl Red Guard asked, looking at the lifeless body.

"These capitalist running dogs die every day," the boy answered casually.

"What should we do then?"

"We can just stop a truck and haul the corpse to a crematory."

8

Three days of wandering had exhausted Xi, who was both tired and sickened by what she had witnessed. Were all those actions revolutionary? Was this what the Great Cultural Revolution all about? She had questions but no answers.

Trying to find her way back home gave her another headache. Walls of big-character posters covered every street in the whole city. She could hardly recognize many of the familiar alleys, places, buildings, and neighborhoods of the past. She struggled to get home, hoping to sleep for the next three days. "Where have you been?" A woman stopped her at the door. "Who are you?" Xi was surprised.

"I am your neighbor."

"Why are you here?"

"Because no one lives here anymore."

"What? What do you mean?"

Xi went into the house and saw it was empty.

"Why? Where is Yan Yan? Where is my mom?"

"Your mom has been arrested and Yan is dead."

"What? What did you say?" Xi was dumbfounded.

The neighbor explained that two policemen came the other day to inform Yan about Tania's arrest. A group of Red Guards then stormed the house, proclaiming its residents to be rightist criminals. When Yan argued with them, they started to beat her.

Then another group of Red Guards from Peking University came in, and said that Yan was the widow of Professor Lu Shi-Yan, the notorious opponent of the Chairman's in the early years.

"She has been the enemy of the party!"

"She had been the enemy of our great leader Chairman Sheng Bao!"

"She is the worst enemy of the proletariat!"

They shouted and the beating resumed, and poor Yan was dead within a couple of hours.

To demonstrate the completeness of the "Eternal Revolution," anyone who had disagreed with the Chairman must have been a counterrevolutionary. To justify the Chairman's greatness, every party official's life must be thoroughly scrutinized and totally rewritten. The name of Lu Shi-Yan, whose prominent career contradicted the official textbook, must be expunged from memory. Thousands more senior party member would face the same tragic path and brutal persecution. Yet the innocent Yan fell victim to the frantic attempts to reinvent communist history only because of her selfless dedication to her husband.

Suddenly, Xi's world was turned upside down. She was not a Red Guard. She never was from the start, but had earnestly fantasized about becoming one. And this was what she received in return. An orphan created by violence, lawlessness, and revolution, she must now survive on her own.

Looking at the few chairs and tables around the house, she remembered how happy her family used to be, when Mom, Dad, and the sweet Yan were with her. She could not believe that it was only a few days ago that she had walked out of the door, feeling totally liberated. Now she missed her mom, dad, and Yan terribly. She wished to see Mom and Dad. She needed their kisses. She needed their care. She wished her adoring Yan was still around to groom her, chastise her, argue with her, dine with her, and cuddle her.

All that warmth, tenderness, care, and love was now gone.

Chapter 42

Fiascos

1

SONG PEI KNEW THAT SHENG BAO WAS DETERMINED TO GET RID OF him this time. Although disappointed, he was not upset. Never the smartest or the most effective among the top-ranking officials, Song had nevertheless worked diligently for the party from its inception, contributing all that he could to build the organization. He had held many important posts and was responsible for the new government's development and the nation's reconstruction. He had served the Chairman faithfully and labored hard to promote his rise to power. He had made wrong judgments and mistakes, but harbored no malice against anyone. He had tried to be a model party member, based on the standard Confucian education he had received like everyone else of his generation. Didn't Confucius say, "Let the king be the king, the minister the minister, the father the father, and the son the son?" These fundamental precepts and social divide had controlled Chinese society for two thousand years, and the dutiful Song was not about to change his Confucian mindset overnight. If the boss did not want his service anymore, Song was prepared to leave quietly, even if that would mean an end to his political career.

The problem was that Sheng did not simply want to let him go quietly. He had identified Song as the archenemy who, as the nation's president, commanded much support within the government. The officials followed his orders while resisting the Chairman's ideas and programs; thus, nothing short of a total annihilation of Song and his followers would satisfy the furious Sheng.

In fact, Sheng had greatly exaggerated the differences between him and Song. The two men had embraced the same ideology, believed in the same doctrine, belonged to the same organization, and been committed to the same goals for more than four decades. But Sheng violated his own promise to stay behind the scenes to focus on strategic issues, while allowing President Song to handle the day-to-day operations of the government with Premier Si-Tu Wen-Liang. Instead the Chairman romanticized the socialist process and set fantastic goals, which clashed with Song and Si-Tu's realistic understanding of progress. He misconstrued their hesitance as disruptive and even hostile to his ambitious objectives. Meanwhile, Sheng's increasing concerns over his grip on power and his highly cherished concept of class struggle compelled him to look for a deadly enemy to justify the need for his "Eternal Revolution." His skewed views of the world originated from his own extremist theory, and the only reason Song appeared to be Satan was because Sheng had used a distorted lens to demonize his own handpicked head of state and successor to his own dynasty.

Song, a chief target of the Cultural Revolution and an unfortunate victim of Sheng's "Eternal Revolution," did occasionally disagree with the Chairman. Those disagreements should be commonplace among members of any political organization, except that the Chairman believed that he was always in the right. Overly confident about his righteousness and overly underestimating the virtues of others, the Chairman confused the differences between fundamentals and technicalities, strategy and implementation, principles and tactics, substance and approach, direction and speed, and honest opinions and hostile attacks. Increasingly paranoid about being marginalized, Sheng launched the Cultural Revolution, which gave him the much-needed excuse to leapfrog to the front of the national leadership and take over the reins. Reclaiming his so-called flagging power with vengeance, the Chairman declared that all those policy differences between him and Song amounted to a life-and-death struggle between the proletariat and the bourgeois.

Highly personal at first glance, the head-on clash between the two most powerful men indicated how deeply they had been trapped by the same ideology, same party structure, and same political system that both men had wholeheartedly helped to construct. Debates, quarrels, discord, divisions, friction, and even factions were never anomalies in any political organization of a modern society. Working with the same people for nearly half a century within one institution, it would be surprising if some of the individual disputes did not escalate into serious conflicts. But the problem was that the party's revolutionary ideology, institutional infrastructure, and political framework had never provided any mechanism to settle those differences in a peaceable manner. Both men were locked in the same system they had created, and the only way they could settle their differences was through a deadly intraparty struggle. A one-party system and an authoritarian apparatus for as long as anyone could remember, the Communist Party had not only created its worst enemy from within but also expedited the most brutal infighting in any modern political organization.

From Marx, Lenin, and Stalin to the ambitious Sheng, none of them had ever faced the conundrum squarely even as each of them had contributed to the systemic problem. The first and most basic flaw was the claim that Marx's political economy and his revolutionary theory of communism constituted an infallible science and a universal truth. This assertion was routinely wielded as the magic wand to stamp out any views that differed even slightly from orthodoxy, labeling them as anti-Marxist, antiproletarian, revisionist, or counterrevolutionary. The academic and inquisitive sides of Marxism aside, the pragmatic and dogmatic aspects of Marxism had become the most powerful secular religion ever created in human history. Worshiped as the only truth and completely scientific, this ideological absolutism stifled the mind, prohibited freedom of thought, and had been repeatedly used to silence any internal critics and to label dissidents and nonconformists as heretics, conspirators, turncoats, apostates, or enemies of the people.

Even if a portion of Marx's ideas were applicable under certain circumstances, who would be entitled to say so since this secular church had no ordained clergy? The answer lay in the leadership of the Communist Party while the rank and file had no knowledge or power to decide on these theoretical matters, just as no parishioners had ever decided on any doctrines for the Catholic Church.

In the end, the final judgment of who was a true Marxist and who was not lay entirely in the hands of those who held the greatest power, no different from the kind of power wielded by bishops, archbishops, cardinals, and popes in Catholicism. To win any debate in the party and to have ultimate power in the party were but two sides of the same coin. The winners would always proclaim the success of Marxism on behalf of the proletariat even though the latter had no idea about what was going on. The losers would always be declared the enemies of the people, rightists, bourgeois agents, capitalist running dogs, or any other nasty names the winners cared to invent.

Marxism, one of many alternative social theories of the nineteenth century, had been transformed into a blind dogma that would radicalize not only society but also the party apparatus. An institution committed to revolution not reform and a party that recognized no law but brute power would apply the same principles to its internal operations. As an organization that had grown through intense warfare and was committed to violence, the Communist Party structure was intrinsically unable and unwilling to deal with any political controversy from within, other than through a ruthless internal fight.

The higher the power structure went, the fewer the players would remain, and the more likely that any delicate personal differences would develop into an open confrontation for dominance. Inevitably, this internal conflict would lead to the fall of one faction and the rise of another. The theory of class struggle was only a convenient tool to vilify the defeated faction, while exalting the winning bloc. Some communists would kill other communists no less resolutely than their external enemies would. Until some new theory could rise and until some new structural changes could be implemented, the intraparty conflict would continue and someone, no matter how high his office might have been and no matter how much he had done for the party, would continue to be made the scapegoat for the fundamental flaws that the institution had inherited from its inception.

Song realized that his doomsday loomed. He pleaded for a meeting with the Chairman, hoping to mend fences for the last time. He was told that the Chairman had left town. After Sheng had set up all the traps, he had no interest to meet with the victim and hear his pathetic pleas anymore. Besides, the Chairman would never touch a weapon, or kill anyone by his own hand. He left that to the one who could better handle the case than anyone else in the party—the premier.

The next morning when Song opened the front door of his residence in Abundance, Si-Tu walked in. "President Song, let me introduce to you"—the premier pointed to the large crowd behind him—"these young revolutionaries from schools and universities who are here to help you."

Shouting "Down with the capitalist Song Pei" and "Long live the great Chairman Sheng Bao," hundreds of Red Guards rushed in and Song knew that his worst nightmare had begun.

It was not until six hours later that the badly abused, brutally beaten, and deeply humiliated Song returned to his office. His clothes were torn, face swollen, nose bleeding, shoes missing, and splashed ink stains, eggshells, and tomato juice all over his body. He was outraged. Looking at a copy of the *Constitution of the People's Republic of China* on his desk, which had his signature of approval only a few years ago, he started to write a resignation letter to the Chairman, stating that, stripped of the basic rights of freedom and legal protection, he no longer possessed any capacity to execute his duties as the president of the nation.

2

Momentous, patriotic, and heroic, as well as volatile, chaotic, and dynamic, a great revolution called for great participation and generated great excitement. The blazing flames of the Cultural Revolution consumed everyone in the capital and would soon spread to the rest of the country. Deeply infected, Xi decided not to stay at home but to plunge into the chaos by boarding a train to Shanghai to explore the most thrilling event in life.

Sheng Bao and the "leadership group" highly recommended four main methods—"public meetings, open expressions, large-character posters, and big debates"—to get the population involved, which were only partially successful at the beginning of the Cultural Revolution. While universities and schools in Peking got an early start, nationwide reactions were uneven at best and lukewarm at worst. The Chairman's orders must be faithfully executed across the board and the revolution must reach every corner of China. Thousands of devout Red Guards, blessed to have been received by the Chairman in Tiananmen Square in the summer of 1966, willingly became the imperial messengers, taking the trains to all major cities to spread the revolution. With the Chairman's consent, the government stopped charging fees on the national transportation system and introduced a massive scheme called "travel without bounds." Tens of thousands of young people and Red Guards took the trains, buses, and vessels, traveling around the country and promoting the revolution, all for free!

Excitement replaced sadness as soon as Xi boarded a train. She sat among young boys and girls about her age, and listened to them discussing all night long about their great responsibilities to fan the revolutionary flames in Shanghai— home of the proletariat and the birthplace of the Chinese Communist Party.

Linked by dark tunnels and narrow pathways, Shanghai's small, overcrowded terminal and its decrepit facilities disappointed Xi, who had expected to see a more impressive introduction to the largest metropolis in the nation. Talking to the locals and observing the way they behaved, Xi thought they were more like petty bourgeois than the valiant proletarians she had read about in school textbooks.

Most of its residents were more interested in what was going on in their immediate and uneventful neighborhood than in what was happening in the faraway and noisy capital. Frugality, not revolt, was decidedly a universal virtue here, and every man and woman seemed more economically savvy than politically inclined. They cared less about who might be the most dangerous class enemy inside the government than about how to get a good bargain while buying morning groceries at the marketplace. They could spend hours debating how to save a penny in bus fares, but were genuinely surprised and speechless when asked to name the party leaders of the municipality. Like most Chinese, urban or rural, they drank tea, loved gossip, played poker, enjoyed majiang, and cared little about the great revolution that had descended upon them no matter how many times the official propaganda machines had reminded them.

Months of national agitation and propagation produced no rebels but a handful of cases where a few local factory hands voiced some mild criticisms about their managers. Shipyard workers, steel workers, textile workers, railroad workers, consumer-goods factory workers, and municipal transportation employees numbered more than two million in Shanghai. Yet they, the supposed vanguard and leading class of the revolution, remained as disinterested as the rest of the general population.

Descending from the capital and carrying the decrees of the "leadership group," the militant Red Guards of Peking came not a moment too soon, and managed to motivate the mighty local industrial workforce to assemble a rebel group of fifty thousand employees from four hundred and seventy factories in two weeks. But the conservative labor organizations quickly swelled to eight hundred thousand members, who were as willing to defend the established authorities as the rebel group was ready to oust them. Adding to the mix was the quarter-million temporary and short-term laborers, who were also organized as a third column to fight for their economic protection, benefit, and improvement.

Despite the official claims of socialist justice and equality, the stratification of Chinese society had more layers and permanent social gaps than an outsider could imagine. A national registration system, the origins of which could be traced back to two thousand years ago, divided the population into two distinctive categories—urban residents and rural inhabitants. The urban population was protected by the government, which gave city dwellers many benefits ranging from food supplies, education, employment, salary, job security, and paid holidays to health care and retirement. The rural population had to fend for themselves, and, except for rudimentary care, they could not expect the government to give them any salary, jobs, education, retirement, or medical benefits.

Each family and every person's identification in the registration system was permanent and inheritable. The sons and daughters of a rural villager could not move into a town or city to live, where no food, shelter, job, or education would be provided to any rural person. If one had been born a rural inhabitant, his children and children's children would forever stay that way unless enlistment or acceptance into a university might temporarily change one's status.

Within the urban population, differences between large cities and medium and small ones would further determine the benefits one could expect to receive. The most desirable places to live in the nation were Peking and Shanghai, for both offered high salaries and good benefits. Meanwhile, the smaller and the more remote the urban area was in any province and county, the fewer and poorer benefits would be available. For instance, even though they were administered as the metropolis's suburbs, employees in several rural counties adjacent to Shanghai received salaries three times lower than their counterparts inside the city districts.

Of all the privileged urban residents, government officials had the most secure jobs and greatest benefits. Government-owned factories provided higher pay, as well as more skilled and more prestigious jobs than local businesses and collectives. At the lower rungs of the social ladder, temporary positions in the city including construction and cleaning work were usually filled by migrant workers from the countryside, who would earn considerably lower wages than regular employees of state-owned enterprises. They could be fired without any reason, and received no health care and retirement benefits from the government. No wonder the first public announcement of the organization of temporary workers demanded not "eternal revolution" but the "dignity of man."

From reading a large-character poster, Xi learned for the first time the term "six–four" laborers, which she had never heard before. "What is that?" she asked several bystanders. One of them told her that, when a rural laborer was hired to work on some urban project, he had to give sixty percent of his income to the collective unit he belonged to in his village, while keeping the forty percent for himself. No teacher at her school had taught her anything about this.

Growing up in a comfortable family in the nation's capital, Xi now realized that ordinary people at the bottom of society must have been working very hard, a lot harder than she had ever imagined, to make a living. She sensed the social and economic complexities, which were hardly as clear-cut as the school textbooks had taught her. Not everything was black and white, and especially not so when dealing with so many diverse social groups and their interests, frustrations, desires, ambitions, and aspirations. The proliferation of conflicting opinions, demands, and slogans were extremely confusing for her. Yet, Xi felt that she was beginning to learn something that perhaps she would have never discovered if she had stayed at home in Peking. Still deeply baffled with all the information she had received, she was glad that she had at least taken the plunge.

At the corner of a major interception and behind a registration table, a big-poster announcement caught her eye, saying that a new labor organization would be holding its inaugural meeting the next morning. A team of young women came by, proudly marching, singing, and shouting slogans in Xi's direction. From their plain clothing, abundant energy, and robust bodies, she thought that they were a group of migrant rural laborers working in this metropolis. Could they be a group of those "six–four" laborers? She was captivated and was about to greet them to inquire further when she saw a person in uniform walking fast toward her.

"This person must know me. Who is he?" Xi quickly racked her brain. As the person got closer, she recognized him. "He must be the guy Mom and Yan called No. 5."

When he reached her side, Li Fan whispered firmly into her ear, "Don't look around. You must follow me now."

Xi left the registration table and followed him.

3

At the most disastrous meeting he had ever had with the "leadership group," the Chairman was so livid that his face turned purple. He promptly adjourned the meeting and went home.

Sitting in his big and bright office in the new residential hall called the "Swimming Pool" in Abundance, which had been built to satisfy his desire to swim day or night any time of the year, Sheng called in the premier.

"What the hell is Song doing these days?" The Chairman's harsh voice was intimidating.

"He has been writing apologies, confessions, and self-criticisms," Si-Tu replied dutifully.

"What did he say about his wicked plot against me?"

"Well, not so much about his plot than about his mistakes."

"Hmm, mistakes? Who would believe that? He is still defending himself by hiding his crimes. I knew it. I knew it. He would never surrender, he would always resist, and he would always lie. He is a fake, a true-blue capitalist. How is the investigation going about his traitorous behavior in jail in the 1930s?"

"It's still ongoing."

"You need to speed up the investigation. I strongly suspect that he had betrayed the party back then."

"Yes, yes. I will investigate that carefully."

"I must have the final report in two months, before the party's next national congress, understand?"

"Yes, yes, I will have it ready then."

Si-Tu left quietly. He knew that the Chairman wanted to seal Song's fate once and for all by labeling him a traitor, the worst crime for a party member. At this point, the premier did not care what Sheng wanted to do with Song. Shortly after he was publicly brutalized by the Red Guards, Song was arrested and sent to a top-secret location in the countryside, where he, deprived of the basic necessities, became extremely sick and was now struggling to survive. No one cut his hair or fingernails. He was too feeble to get up and wash himself, and had been excreting in bed for months, which made his room smell worse than a jail cell for a common criminal.

The premier, who had arranged everything according to Sheng's wishes, knew about the awful situation and was told that the ousted president was like a forlorn corpse, and could die at any moment. Imitating the cold-hearted Chairman, the premier remained as unaffected as a loyal servant should. He could not and would not care. What Si-Tu wanted the most was to end his own ordeal as soon as possible in this hellish "Eternal Revolution." Thus, he would not say anything to Sheng about Song's wretched plight, nor would he utter any objection no matter what the Chairman ordered him to do about the incarcerated president.

Sheng called in Lin Shi-Xiong next and asked, "What is the latest report from your source?"

Lin, who had planted a mole, understood exactly what the Chairman's coded words meant and said, "The source said that the general's health is not improving. His addiction to drugs has rendered him rather weak day or night. He can't be exposed to light and he can't tolerate any noise. He can't concentrate on anything for more than an hour."

"Pathetic. Hopeless," scorned Sheng.

"But my source also reported," stressed Lin, "that the general has been reading Zeng Guo-Fan lately."

"Really? General Bao Feng-Nian is interested in history and literature now?" the intrigued Chairman asked.

Lin immediately withdrew, noticing that the Chairman wanted to be left alone as he reached out for the pack of cigarettes next to a large tea mug on the desk.

"Have I opened a Pandora's box?" Sheng slowly inhaled and contemplated.

No sooner had he officially announced his plan to remove Song from power than the scramble for the replacement began, which led to an intense quarrel at the last meeting of the "leadership group."

General Bao, of course, thought he was the obvious choice. Not only had he been one of the most senior and most decorated war heroes in the party; he was also the one who had promoted Sheng's leading role on the world stage in the widely publicized article "Long Live the People's War." The Communist Party could not have succeeded in winning national power without Bao's enormous sacrifices and significant contributions, nor could the Chairman continue his legacy without his abiding devotion and loyalty. A strong proponent of personality cult, Bao was the brains behind the *Little Red Book*, a compilation of Sheng's most popular quotations. Printed in millions of copies, it was now the authoritative bible for every Chinese and many believers in guerrilla warfare around the globe. Most of all, Bao understood that the crafty Sheng would never be able to strike at Song, who had the full backing of the civil service, without the general's explicit promise of loyalty and support on behalf of the military.

Acting in unison for the moment, Lin Shi-Xiong, Su Ming, and Kang Yi-Sheng claimed the moral high ground by insisting on the ideological affinity they had shared with the Chairman for decades. Impressive as it was, the article on the people's war was a product of their efforts, not the general's, the trio claimed. Indeed, no one in the party, and no one in the world for that matter, understood the Chairman's ideas, philosophy, strategies, and aspirations as thoroughly as they did. And one of them was his spouse, who had shared the same bed with him for years. Good heavens, who could be that close to the great Sheng and claim that he or she was a more faithful disciple of the Chairman's? The mantle of leadership clearly belonged to Su and her closest allies, Lin and Kang, their argument went.

"You don't have any experience in running the country," argued Bao, who never had any regard for women in general, and Su in particular.

"You don't know a thing about Marx and Marxism," retorted Kang, who considered himself well versed in philosophy, history, literature, and military affairs.

"Stop throwing mud at each other. I need constructive suggestions, not meaningless insults and sarcasm!" Frustrated, Sheng shouted at the group, something he rarely did.

"We need a new president of the nation," Bao proposed.

"No, not a good idea. Keeping the same title would remind people of the deposed one," responded Lin.

"How about a vice chairman of the party, second-in-command," Su suggested.

"That is a good idea. Su will be the best candidate," Kang attempted to flatter both the wife and husband.

"A couple at the two top positions in the nation? That would not look good to the people," Bao snapped at the obsequious suggestion.

"Well, you haven't said a word in this discussion. What do you think, Wen-Liang?" the Chairman asked.

"A replacement for the top position in the government is a most serious matter. Since we don't have a consensus right now, why don't we mull over it and come back to discuss the matter again after we can have more input and have given it greater consideration?" Si-Tu calmly said.

"That old fox," Su protested after everyone else had left the meeting hall. "He always pretends that he does not care at all about the top position. In fact, he knows that he is a strong contender for the position given his broad administrative experience. Besides, he has many old friends and colleagues in the government, who would surely lobby for his promotion behind the scenes."

Sheng agreed with his wife. A highly ambitious and skeptical person, he never believed that the extremely intelligent Si-Tu could ever be as totally disinterested in the presidency's post as he appeared to be. Holding various high positions, he had been the second or third most powerful man in the party for as long as Sheng could remember. Right now, there was only just one post between him and the Chairman. Why would he not be interested? Sheng could not fathom it. And, the more reticent Si-Tu was on this topic, the more Sheng doubted his true ambition and motives. For the moment, however, Sheng did not like any of those ideas raised at the "leadership group" meeting. He wanted no new president, or a new vice chairperson. He had to think about the situation clearly and design his plan carefully before he could make his next move.

4

Xi did not know why she felt compelled to follow and listen to No. 5, whose seriousness, age, and uniform accorded him unexplainable authority.

Li Fan told her that she must leave Shanghai immediately, since major unrest was about to break out. "You better go home as soon as possible," said he.

"I have no home anymore. Father is in jail, Mother is arrested, and Yan is dead," she said.

"I will try to find your mom, and will let you know as soon as I have any information," Li assured her.

"But how and when?" asked the skeptical girl.

"Don't worry about that. Just go, leave this place quickly," he insisted.

That night Xi took a train departing for the South. Two days later, she learned the shocking news that the first armed clash had taken place in Shanghai. As many as one hundred thousand armed members of a militant labor association attacked another revolutionary labor organization, whose members were trapped in an office building. After five hours of fighting, the latter's defense collapsed. About ninety men were wounded, two hundred and forty group leaders arrested, and the remaining twenty thousand rank and file surrendered the building.

Just as Xi was feeling relieved that she had been forewarned of the armed confrontation, the train stopped at a small, obscure station. Railroad employees informed the passengers that large-scale violence and armed skirmishes had broken out at numerous places in the region, all in the name of revolution and the dictatorship of the proletariat. Cut off from supplies and threatened by perilous conditions along the tracks, the train, like several others, suspended its service, leaving passengers hopelessly stranded at the station. No departure time could be set until the volatile situation eased for the train to continue the journey safely.

Completely caught off guard, passengers started to panic. Limited food and water supplies at the desolate station made many sick, and Xi barely survived the first two days by chewing on a piece of biscuit. When the sun rose on the third day, Xi knew it was going to be another day of misery. The rising heat in the day and the freezing cold at night tormented the stranded passengers, especially the feeble, elderly, and children.

Leaning against an iron railing and beset by hunger, Xi was thinking hard how to alleviate her predicament when she heard someone reading,

There is an ancient Chinese fable called *The Foolish Old Man Who Removed the Mountains*. It tells of an old man who lived in northern China long, long ago and was known as the Foolish Old Man of the

North Mountain. His house faced south and beyond his doorway stood two great peaks, Taihang and Wangwu, which obstructed the way.

"Who has the energy to read such stuff now, which is taken from the *Little Red Book*?" Xi wondered. She turned around and saw a boy sitting and reading on the other side of the fence.

The boy, Xi soon learned, was from Guangzhou. He wore a uniform similar to Xi's but with an authentic Red Guard armband, which she did not have.

"You must be a Red Guard." Xi tried to make small talk.

"Well. Sort of," the boy said as he continued reading.

"I need some help," said Xi as she changed tack.

"Like what?" The boy finally raised his head.

"Could you take this money and food coupon to buy some cookies for me?" Through the railing Xi handed a one-yuan bill and the coupon, which was an official voucher required for the purchase of any grain and food including snacks and biscuits at any shop or restaurant anywhere in the country.

"All right. I will." The boy took the money and coupon and left.

Almost immediately Xi regretted her action. She didn't know anything about him. What if he did not come back? She wouldn't be able to see or find him again. For the next hour, fear replaced her hunger until the boy finally showed up.

"Sorry to have kept you waiting," he apologized, wiping his sweaty forehead. "All shops around the station had sold out their cookies. I had to run down several blocks to the business district to find them. Here is the bag of cookies, and the change and remainder of the food coupon. Please count them to see if they are correct." He then sat down and picked up where he had left from his book.

"What an honest and nice boy," Xi said as she began telling the boy about why she had left home and how she got stuck here.

The boy responded with his stories and, three hours later, the intimate exchanges turned two complete strangers into fast friends. He was from Guangzhou, which was where Xi had wanted to go. So they decided to go together.

5

The ouster of Song, now languishing in jail, had created a political vacuum that Sheng deliberately left unfilled. He believed that he had made a serious mistake by giving up part of his power too early to another person, who eventually became his archenemy. Although this unfortunate episode was largely a result of his own paranoia and extremist theory, Sheng was determined not to make the same mistake twice. He vowed that he would never share his power with anyone else, nor would he ever surrender his ultimate authority until the day of his death.

To always be in the driver's seat and to keep all the cards to himself till the end were the two cardinal principles that the Chairman never disclosed to anyone, even as he talked about the importance of succession from time to time. No one except Si-Tu could see through Sheng's veiled plan to cling to power, which was why the premier had kept silent about who should replace Song. Like the selection of a crown prince whose future was entirely in the hands of the king, the second-in-command or the chief-in-waiting next to the fickle and irritable Chairman must be the most difficult position in the party; the astute premier would never want that post even if it were given to him. In addition, he and Sheng were about the same age. His energy and health had been declining as much as Sheng's, and Si-Tu had no interest and desire to compete for a post that clearly should go to someone from the younger generation. Bao Feng-Nian and Su Ming were much younger, and the premier was willing to watch from the sidelines the latest race for power.

Ecstatic that they had made vital contributions to Song's fall and Sheng's unprecedented preeminence, both Bao and Su believed that they deserved some reward from the Chairman. They did not realize that they were playing a highly dangerous game with the most powerful and skilled political operator, and any misstep could be fatal to their own well-being.

For the moment, though, Sheng was content with the cat-and-mouse game by balancing three blocs within the "leadership group"—the military faction represented by Bao, the ideological faction represented by Lin, Su and Kang, and the administrative faction represented by Si-Tu. Considering these divisions to be the "separation of powers," Sheng was pleased with his masterful scheme of "checks and balances" among the three factions, where no one but he pulled all the strings with one hand while keeping all his vassals on a separate leash with the other. Since the Cultural Revolution targeted the administrative faction, Sheng knew that the timid Si-Tu was much subdued. When talking to the other two factions separately, he deliberately made each of them feel that he or she was his favorite and most trusted heir. But Sheng would never let his guard down, nor would he ever allow them to form an alliance against him. He would do everything possible to keep all three factions in his tight grip and to use each of them to carry out his objectives while maintaining his absolute authority intact.

What inadvertently upset the delicate equilibrium was not any domestic situation but a series of international events. When Sino-Russian relations deteriorated in the late 1950s, the Chinese government was increasingly alarmed by intelligence reports that the Soviet Union had steadily increased its military presence in the Far East. Signed in 1966 (the same year the Cultural Revolution started), a pact between the Soviet Union and the Mongolian People's Republic allowed the Russians to send a dozen divisions into the areas north of the Chinese border. The eight tank and armored divisions had a striking distance of one to two hundred miles, which meant that Peking, just five hundred miles away, was dangerously under their threat. Any Soviet ground attack could reach the Chinese capital in a week, a bomber in an hour, and a nuclear missile in a few minutes.

In the face of the Soviet military buildup, Sheng had no choice but to rely on Bao for border security. The general was authorized to take all steps necessary to reinforce national defense in the northern regions next to the Soviet Union. Sheng also promised him the title of vice chairman of the party, signaling to the "leadership group" that Bao had been chosen as the Chairman's successor. The unexpected decision made the ideological faction unhappy, but they had no credentials to challenge General Bao's extensive experience in handling military affairs and border safety.

A new balance ensued, with the military faction evidently advancing ahead in the game.

To make sure his plan seemed all natural and necessary to the public and to distract the enemy, the Chairman engineered a border crisis at Damansky Island, one thousand, two hundred miles away from Peking, in the remote Northeast, where three hundred Chinese soldiers ambushed thirty Russian border patrols. Coming less than two weeks before a scheduled party national convention, the incident generated strong anti-Soviet sentiments, and created a grave sense of military crisis in the nation.

As the party's official congress was to put the final stamp on the decisions the Chairman had already made, he wanted everything to be perfect. Sheng was determined that the new congress must showcase the great unity and success under his undisputed leadership.

He checked with the premier once more about the investigation into Song's case. "What is the conclusion about his conduct in jail?" the Chairman asked.

"As you predicted, the evidence shows that Song Pei betrayed the party in the 1930s, when he was under arrest," Si-Tu answered without missing a beat, knowing full well that all the charges and evidence had been fabricated.

"Have you signed the final report of the investigation?" Sheng was not about to skip any minute detail, or to allow the shrewd premier to deny his role in this dirty business in the future.

"Yes, I have," Si-Tu replied.

"Let me see it," the Chairman said.

"Here it is." Si-Tu was as cool as a cucumber, while saying to himself, "Damn, he is scrupulous."

"Great. Everything seems to be in good order and we can now go the Great Hall of the People to convene the historic meeting and to celebrate the Great Proletarian Cultural Revolution's big success." The Chairman was obviously in good spirits as the premier helped him to stand up.

6

Xi had the boy as her traveling companion for only a few days, and the two parted as soon as they arrived in Guangzhou. Not the idyllic city she had hoped, Guangzhou in the south was under a siege more terrible than the one in Shanghai on the east coast. Rumors had it that several hundred convicts had escaped from prison in the suburbs, and were planning to ransack the city at any moment.

In a place where law and order had completely broken down and where anarchy and mob rule prevailed, helpless civilians could only live in fear and terror. They closed shops early, locked up fences, organized teams of neighborhood watch, and began to patrol the streets day and night. Any stranger in the community would arouse instant suspicion, and any suspects, migrants, visitors, or persons with unfamiliar looks and deformities were interrogated and quarantined immediately.

Too often vigilantism had become synonymous with violence and crimes, and Guangzhou was no exception. From the winding streets to the dark allies, from the business districts to the suburbs, and from the corners of local parks to the empty lots adjacent to the cinemas, new dead bodies were found every morning, sometimes in the dozens. Some of them were hanged on trees, some were dumped in ditches; while some might indeed have been criminals, most were totally innocent people. Deeply sickening and disturbing as they were, the random executions were nowhere close to the damage caused by the organized confrontations between opposing groups, factions, societies, and associations. All of them claimed to be the purer revolutionaries and the more faithful students of the great Chairman than their rivals, with each charging the rest as the most despicable capitalist running dogs. For these antagonists, only the battleground could determine who were the true revolutionaries and who were the imposters.

The bloodshed at the power station and the provincial union headquarters in Guangzhou were the worst Xi had ever seen. Whereas wood sticks, baseball bats, and leather belts had been used in the armed fights in Shanghai, the clashing organizations here used knives, spears, axes, sharpened steel pipes, army rifles, machine guns, hand grenades, mortars, and even cannons. The attacks and counterattacks lasted for days, cement buildings were shattered, dozens of people killed, and hundreds badly wounded. Quoting the Chairman's words from the war years, those proud revolutionaries who had survived the slaughter continued to shout, "Hundreds of thousands of revolutionary martyrs, for the sake of the people, have died before us. Let us rise from their pool of blood, hoist their flags, and keep on marching forward!"

Enough was enough. Xi decided to leave the chaotic Guangzhou as soon as she could. But where would she go? The whole country was engulfed in the flames of revolution. Fired by the eternal commitment to class struggle, every community, school, business, factory, county, town, and village was split between the so-called revolutionaries and counterrevolutionaries, between radicals and conservatives, and between rebels and conformists. Peers, coworkers, colleagues, and classmates turned into hostile adversaries. Acquaintances, friends, neighbors, and relatives became foes. Even family members, parents and children, husbands and wives became suspicious of, and turned against, each other. The Chairman's "Eternal Revolution" turned China upside down, destroying its very social and moral fabric. The nation was consumed by an unprecedented political civil war, and Sheng's totally erroneous theory and dirty manipulation had led to the worst human tragedy the country had ever seen.

The most direct way for Xi to return to Peking was to take a train through Wuhan in Central China. But Wuhan was having the worst armed standoff in the country at the moment. Split between two powerful factions, each over a million strong, the city was under siege by armed rebels and their supporters. Still not satisfied and totally committed to expanding the turmoil further, one faction screamed out for more conflict, insisting that "the deeper, wider, madder, more violent, and more chaotic the turmoil goes, the better." Supported by local troops with weapons drawn while patrolling the streets, the other faction vowed to annihilate any antagonists.

To appease the situation in Wuhan, the "leadership group" sent a work team, whose members were immediately detained and harassed. One was thrown into a truck, interrogated for several days, and badly beaten in a hidden location. His rescuers later found him with a broken leg. Staying in the same luxurious compound no more than a few hundred yards from the work team, the Chairman, who had made a secret and impromptu stop in the city for a quick swim in the nearby Yangtze River, fled the scene by taking an airplane, a first for him.

The city had spiraled out of control. Since neither the "leadership group" nor the Chairman had any idea of how to put Humpty-Dumpty back together again, Xi decided it was better to avoid Wuhan at all costs.

The train detour Xi took, passing through Guangxi and Sichuan Provinces in the Southwest, brought her closer to death than anywhere else she had been. No fewer than one thousand, five hundred people were killed in the riots in the provincial capital of Guangxi, where more than eight thousand were arrested, three thousand houses burned down, fifty thousand became homeless, and the loss of property amounted to six hundred million yuan. In the wake of the devastation, an additional one hundred and eighty thousand people were persecuted for involvement in the riots, and five thousand committed suicide. Even more appalling, savage cannibalism cost the lives of more than four hundred people in forty counties in the province. This horrifying episode was made worse only by the fact that some government officials simply turned a blind eye.

Atrocious and sadistic, the conflict in Sichuan was just as bloody and violent as that in Guangxi, because heavy military weapons were used in the riots. Preparing for war since the early 1960s, the Chairman had decided to build a "Third Front" by moving many defense installations from the coastal areas to the hinterland Sichuan. In the provincial capital, Chengdu, thousands of highly trained industrial workers, ironically labeled "conservatives," were trapped in several buildings at a nationally owned airplane factory. Tens of thousands of their antagonists, including many teenagers, adopted a human wave strategy and repeatedly assaulted the buildings with stones, sticks, and sheer brawn. When the defense of the buildings began to crumble, the industrial workers shot the attackers using handguns, rifles, and machine guns. The fighting in Chongqing, the most populous city of Sichuan, escalated into an all-out war, employing every kind of weaponry the region was able to produce, including rifles, machine guns, tanks, artilleries, and even warships.

Bloodshed, pure bloodshed, engulfed the most zealous among the warring factions but, too often, unsuspecting civilians, naïve schoolchildren, and innocent bystanders were not spared in crossfire.

What was happening to the country? Xi wondered. Why were people attacking people? They had been neighbors, friends, and coworkers only yesterday. Why did they suddenly become deadly enemies? Why were there so much malice, hatred, vengeance, cruelty, violence, and killing? Why was any weapon ever needed in this Cultural Revolution? She had no answers.

When she finally escaped from Sichuan and reached Xian in Shaanxi, Xi remembered that Bao An was less than two hundred miles away. Why not visit the famed red base where father and mother got married? It would be wonderful to search for the romantic memories of her parents and to rediscover what they had experienced when they were young, she supposed.

Hundreds of visitors had similar ideas. Most came by bus, while some were on foot, marching on the same dirt road toward the same destination with the same anticipation and excitement as Xi had. Bright red flags, big-character posters, deafening sounds of gongs and drums, and colorful local dance troupes welcomed them to Bao An, which had become one of the most visited holy shrines during the Cultural Revolution. The cave dwellings looked antiquated and poor, and the landscape of the Loess Plateau impressed them as extremely grand but barren. Yet the memories and the revolutionary spirit, taught by every school across the nation, seemed most alive here, preserved in the historic buildings, evident in every piece of old furniture, sewn on big red banners, aired through loudspeakers, painted in slogans on the walls, and repeated by the captions underlining each of the black-and-white photos in all the exhibits in the area.

Xi stopped by a small tavern, hoping to take a short break for some refreshments. No sooner had she sat down than a dozen people encircled her, begging for food. Startled, she, who had never seen so many dirty paupers in absolute rags, did not know what to do. Before she knew it, two boys grabbed the dish she had ordered and fled, while another man ran away with the bowl of millet she had not touched. Furious, she ran after them but was stopped by an old man at the door.

"My girl, it's useless to chase them," said he. "The local government has banned begging a long time ago. But every month, several hundred beggars and vagabonds are captured and sent to detention centers. See what happened to your meal? They will be back, and they will always come back to beg and steal no matter what."

"What a shame! How come this can happen?" Xi asked.

"No food. With only a few hundred pounds of grains per person every year, people never have enough to eat. They live like pigs, and consume everything from grain, bran, husk, and chaff to weeds and leaves. When these things are gone, they have to beg year after year."

"But people have been liberated for nearly twenty years, haven't they? Can't someone do anything to improve the situation?"

"Liberation yes. Good life, no. Poor harvest hits us every year and begging has become a pattern here."

"Improve the land. Increase productivity then."

"Well, our first job right now is the Cultural Revolution. The revolution will solve all the problems we have."

"Can revolution produce a good harvest?"

"I have no clue."

Chapter 43

Reckoning

1

IN THE BRILLIANTLY ILLUMINATED GREAT HALL OF THE PEOPLE, delegates to the party's National Congress were on their feet, eagerly waiting for the Chairman to give his final remarks to wrap up the session. The proud Sheng Bao, radiant and exuberant, rose from his chair at the center of the stage. He had achieved all that he wanted by starting the Cultural Revolution—first to depose Song Pei, now officially expelled from the party for his betrayal of the Chairman, and second to install General Bao Feng-Nian as the new successor, who would now hold the title of vice chairman. After looking at, clapping with, and waving to the cheering audience for a good five minutes, Sheng announced in his strong Southern drawl, stressing every vowel and consonant, "Comrades, we have had a great and successful meeting, and I hereby declare that this National Congress is adjourned."

As the music "The East Is Red" began to fill the hall via the loudspeakers, the several thousand enthusiastic delegates, filled with passionate tears, love, dedication, and excitement, shouted,

"Long Live Our Great Leader Chairman Sheng Bao! Ten Thousand Years! Ten Thousand Years! Ten Thousand Years!"

"Long Live Our Beloved Vice Chairman! Good Health! Good Health! Good Health!"

"Long Live the Great Proletarian Cultural Revolution!"

"Long Live the Great Proletarian Dictatorship!"

"Long Live the Great Chinese Communist Party!"

"Long Live Great Marxism!"

"Long Live Great…"

"Great…"

"Long Live…"

Nauseous and tired, Sheng left the big stage and the thunderous screaming behind; he had more important matters to deal with than listening to the repeated roaring clichés.

2

Late that evening, as he was being driven back to Abundance in his special black limousine, a gift from the Russians, Sheng, all alone in the back seat, felt that the more power he had, the more isolated he had become. Everything in the party depended on his decision, and he had long been used to this exclusive and reclusive process formulated by his awesome dominance and by the fear and deference others had of him. His word was law, his wish public policy, and his fury someone's misery. The process satisfied his enormous ego and forced him to think deeply and plan early for every step he was about to take. He enjoyed this intense mental exercise, believing it to be his greatest strength and privilege. But it could also generate headaches for, if no one else participated in the process, there would be nobody to share the responsibility with. He alone must shoulder both the triumph and failure, the glory and criticism, and the burden and risk of the same process. Besides, however much he believed in his ability to control everything, the gravity of issues facing him never receded.

Powerful politicians could detect the ambitions of their rivals from miles away as much as sensitive people could discern the idiosyncrasies of others from tiny clues and casual observations. Sheng, who had a flair for such things, first became alarmed when he heard that Bao was reading Zeng Guo-Fan. General Zeng was the preeminent military strongman, tactician, politician,

Confucian scholar, and moral philosopher during the last Qing Dynasty, the role model for all subsequent regional warlords, and the patron saint of such leading court ministers as Li Hong-Zhang and Zuo Zong-Tang. General Zeng's voluminous writings had been essential reading for many aspiring military personnel and experienced politicians alike for decades.

Himself a professed admirer of Zeng since childhood, Sheng instantly understood why Bao was reading the general's works. None of the senior career officers under the Chairman were interested in reading, especially the classics. Clearly, Bao was not simply interested in military affairs, reasoned the Chairman; he must also be deeply obsessed with politics now. This could be a significant evolution for a professional soldier. Sheng himself had undergone the same transformation during the earlier part of his career, and was therefore not surprised that Bao was doing the same homework. But the general's newfound passion also raised a red flag. "He is young and I am old. What if he can't wait? What if he is no longer contented with the existing high position he has, and what if he is preparing to replace me as the top leader?" the ever-wary and vigilant Sheng mused.

The more Sheng thought about it, the more uneasy he became. Bao was a renowned war hero and an exceptional military commander. Reining in him, now the second most powerful man in the nation, would not be as easy as keeping either President Song or Premier Si-Tu under control. Bao had a lot of admirers and commanded enormous prestige in the military. If push came to shove, the fight for ultimate dominance could lead to a full-fledged civil war.

"Calm down, calm down. As long as I keep thinking, I will find a way to deal with him," the self-assured and crafty Sheng told himself.

3

One morning, a few months after her return from Bao An, Xi heard a knock on the door. She could not believe her eyes when she opened it: Tania was standing before her.

Mother and daughter hugged and cried in each other's arms.

"I thought that I would never see you again, Mom." Tears in her eyes, Xi lay in Tania's embrace, savoring every second of their reunion.

"Oh, my dear, how I have missed you. Look at you, how you have grown!" Gazing at her from head to toe, Tania kissed Xi's face, lips, and eyes, giving her all the motherly love she had been missing the last couple of years.

"It's a pity Father and Yan are not here tonight," Xi said.

"Yes, dear, we miss them so terribly," agreed Tania.

They then talked for hours, sharing their experiences into the wee hours of the morning. So much to talk about, so much to share, so much to learn, and so much love between mother and daughter.

"We need to find Father," Tania said, and they both believed that Lin Fan might be the one who could help them.

Suddenly, a loud knock on the door startled them.

"Who is it?" Tania asked.

"It's Li Fan," came the reply.

The two women could not believe their ears. Xi ran for the door and they could hear Li's voice even before he entered the room. "You must come with me immediately."

"Who? Which one?" the women asked.

"I mean both of you. Please be quick," said he.

"Why? Why both of us? Where are we going?" Tania and Xi were equally surprised.

"Premier Si-Tu Wen-Liang is waiting to see you both right now," he replied.

"What?" they yelled.

4

"Tania, it has been a long time." Clasping her hands, the premier greeted his old friend as if they had parted only last week.

"Please sit down, make yourselves comfortable. And you must be Meng Xi, the darling daughter of Bo-Xian's. What a lovely young woman!" Si-Tu's personal charm, infectious warmth, and spontaneous friendliness were all too familiar for Tania, and they seemed every bit as genuine as they had been many years ago.

"How are you doing? Tell me everything." The premier sounded as if he had reserved the whole morning for Tania and Xi. But the more courteous he was toward his guests, the more it made Tania uneasy.

"You must have some very important things to discuss with me," Tania decided to cut to the chase.

"I knew it, I knew it," laughed the premier, who had expected Tania to waste no time getting down to business. "Have you heard anything from Peter lately?" he asked.

"We have had no communication for several years, as you might have guessed," replied Tania. "The Cultural Revolution has stopped all mail from the U.S. and interrupted everything."

"Would you want to write a letter to him, if I say that he will have no problem receiving it?" the premier asked.

"Of course, I would love to write to my son and I would love to hear from him." Tania was thrilled.

"Are you sure that Peter can get my letter?" Still a little puzzled by the sudden favor and knowing perfectly well how strict the government censorship was, Tania asked again.

"Yes, yes. You have my word as the premier and as your old friend. I guarantee that Peter will receive your letter," promised Si-Tu.

"May I ask a favor then," Tania said.

"Of course, please," said the premier.

"I need to know where my Bo-Xian is. I have not seen him for almost five years. I don't know where he is. I don't know whether he is alive or dead. Our daughter and I must see him as soon as possible," implored Tania.

"All right, all right. I understand. Li Fan, why don't you take it from here and do not stop until you find Bo-Xian. Tell everyone and anyone you meet that this is a direct order from me and from the Chairman himself."

The atmosphere became more relaxed until Xi said suddenly to the premier, "Why is there so much killing around the country?"

Tania was instantly apprehensive about his reaction.

"Well, I understand what you are saying." Amazingly, Si-Tu did not seem to be offended, or even surprised by the blunt question. He dropped his head and sighed, "Very sad, very tragic, isn't it?"

5

After mother and daughter returned home, Tania opened an envelope that Li had been instructed to pass to her. Tears immediately ran down her face.

"What happened, Mom?" Xi quickly rushed to comfort Tania.

"Read it, read this letter," Tania handed the paper to Xi. It was a letter from Peter, dated and signed several years ago. It began,

Dear Mom,

By the time you receive this letter, you will have already become a grandma of a beautiful girl, whose name is also Tania.

She was born yesterday, weighing six pounds and nine ounces. She is very healthy, vigorous and so is mother Lynda. Hope this letter finds you, Bo-Xian, Yan Yan, and Meng Xi well. But please don't be disappointed when you find out that Tania Jr. may have dark curly hair and sparkling green eyes.

Love,

Lynda, Peter, and Little Tania

"Oh, hurray, I have a cousin now!" Xi yelled as she jumped up and down, full of childish joy and excitement.

"No, darling," Tania laughed. "You are an aunt now and Tania Jr. is your niece, not your cousin."

"Okay, I am going to write a very long letter to my cute darling little niece, telling her everything about China," Xi said with all seriousness, fetching a pen and paper from her desk.

"A good idea, but don't be long-winded in your first message to a baby. You will have plenty to say to each other in the future." The indulging parent watched Aunt Xi, who was now writing as diligently and seriously as never before.

Tania's face flushed with all the sweet tenderness, great joy, and profound love of a mother and a first-time grandmother.

6

The new strategy the unscrupulous Sheng had devised was proceeding slowly but decisively. If Bao thought he was smart, the Chairman was ten times smarter. To disarm the general, Sheng was careful not to irritate him in any way. Instead, he asked Su to visit the general often, inquire about his health, and take time to be photographed with Bao when his schedule permitted. Several of the photos were later printed prominently in official publications, giving the public the signal that the first and second families were in perfect harmony and had great mutual respect for each other.

Behind the scenes, Sheng was quietly getting involved in a geopolitical game that was bigger than the ambitious Bao could ever imagine.

Since the end of World War II China had been caught in the crossfire of the Cold War between the Soviet Union and the United States—the two real superpowers in terms of opposing ideologies and military forces. No matter what political party was in power, the Chinese government had to choose sides, which made many citizens feel humiliated. China was a huge country with a great heritage and pride, and the subjugation to some foreign powers indicated that China was no longer the center of the universe, as generations of Chinese had been told. Reality was harsh. A country as big as China had to find an ally to survive in this modern era of global competition, acting no differently from what its small neighbors had been doing for centuries.

Sheng's communist government had allied itself with the Russians in 1950, but the alliance was never as solid as the two communist giants had claimed. Their increasing friction led to an open split in the 1960s. Now that the United States was bogged down in the quagmire in Vietnam, Sheng saw a chance to extend an olive branch to the American government, hoping to play one superpower off against the other. If the threat from the Soviet Union had boosted the role of the party's military faction, Sheng was now willing to embark on a bigger gamble by engaging the United States in a three-sided power game.

President Richard Nixon and his national security advisor, Dr. Henry Kissinger, were excited about the prospect of a thaw with communist China. When Nixon had been running for the presidency, he had outlined his views of American foreign policy, in an article titled "Asia after Vietnam" in *Foreign*

Affairs magazine, in which he pointed out, "Any American policy toward Asia must urgently come to grips with the reality of China… Taking the long view," he went on, "we simply cannot afford to leave China forever outside the family of nations, there to nurture its fantasies, cherish its hates and threaten its neighbors. There is no place on this small planet for a billion of its potentially most able people to live in angry isolation." Ten days after Nixon became president, he wrote to Kissinger to explore the "possibilities of rapprochement with the Chinese."

The move, the two agreed, should be kept utterly secret and nothing about this new approach should be leaked to the media. Daring, venturesome, manipulative, and heavy-handed in global strategy while ambitious and egoistic in personality, both Nixon and Kissinger enjoyed the clandestine high-powered diplomacy as much as Sheng, who happened to share the same global aspirations and individual traits as his American counterpart.

Using the premier and his administrative faction to flirt with the Americans helped the Chairman to rebalance the power structure in the party. All the classified arrangements and communications with the U.S. government were directly handled by the premier and his Foreign Ministry, leaving the military and ideological factions out of the loop.

Thus, the Chairman managed to regain control over everything, just when Bao thought that he, the designated crown prince, could act as the top leader. In fact, the general's eagerness to initiate a major military action for national defense only aroused Sheng's suspicions. According to the established protocol, no one, no matter how high his rank might be in the military, could move a platoon of soldiers unless he had received explicit permission from Sheng, who was also chairman of the party's military committee—the military's highest authority. When Bao, acting as the second-in-command, ordered a full-scale alert for all army units along the Sino-Russian border, the Chairman was furious. He believed this could be a dress rehearsal for Bao and his supporters, whom he suspected of plotting a coup against him.

When a year later Bao and his followers insisted on reinstating the office of the presidency, Sheng, convinced that the real goal was to relegate him, unequivocally rejected the proposal by saying "over my dead body." Only then did Bao realize that he had been used as a pawn in the Chairman's plot against Song. Sheng had never completely trusted Bao as his heir.

7

Sheng's audacious balancing game and his renewed interest in the United States required Si-Tu to work hard on the diplomatic front, and the premier in turn found that Tania's family ties could be used to improve unofficial communications with the American establishment.

Every letter from Peter and his family would bring Tania and Xi great joy. Lined with exotic stamps and labels, the package often contained much information from the outside world, which fueled Xi's interest in the English language.

One day, Li came to visit them with the sad news that Meng had died two years ago in jail. The cause of his death was unclear, although all three understood that the lack of official explanation had become all too common for too many families these days. Li brought back the few personal belongings that Meng had left, including the blue-and-white ceramic bottle and the wooden container he had made for it.

Holding the small, unpainted, and crude box, Tania cried all night despite Xi's tireless efforts to console her.

"It was made by his own hand. It was made by his own hand," Tania repeated to Xi again and again, while gently touching and stroking the box with her fingers as if to search for her husband's.

This was the second terrible loss for them. The first was Yan's tragic death. She had been such a beautiful soul, who had never hurt anyone in her life but had always given all of herself to others. Tania had never met a purer, wittier, more innocent, more upright, more honest, and more courageous person than Yan, who was more than a friend, confidant, and sister to her. She had been Tania's moral compass and backbone.

And now the devastating news of Meng's death. Tania had hoped that, with the slowly changing political climate, she might have a chance to be reunited with her husband. All that dream was now shattered. The meeting with him at Broken Kiln would forever remain their last memories together. How she now wished that she could have stayed one or two more days with him, helped to cook some additional meals for him, kissed him more, embraced him tighter, and received his warmth and love a little longer.

All that was gone. All that was left were memories.

Xi hugged her mom, telling Tania not to cry any more. They would always be together, and she would love her mother with all her heart and soul. She could never replace father, but she would try to be the best daughter a mother could have, Xi promised Tania.

Heartbroken, the two fell asleep, emotionally and physically exhausted.

8

"Mommy, who is Li Fan? Why does he know so much? Why is his life as knotty as his name?" Xi asked, trying to divert Tania's sadness. The word "fan" could mean "complexity" or "multiplicity" in Chinese.

"Well, he does seem to be a mysterious person and I don't know the full story. What I do know comes from the bits and pieces of information that I had managed to gather," Tania said as she began to share with Xi what she knew about Li.

Originally named Lin Shuo, Li Fan, a senior party member whose acquaintance with Sheng went back several decades, had a lot of insider information about the Red Army's early development. He worked closely with Sheng in the red bases and contributed to their expansion. Because of his seniority, extensive experience in internal security, and wide-ranging connections in the party hierarchy, he had worked on various highly classified missions for the national government and for the party's Central Committee under the direct command of top officials including Sheng, Song, Si-Tu, Bao, and Lin Shi-Xiong. Sometimes, Li worked as an agent, a double-agent, and even a triple-agent, although fortunately he still managed to keep a decent conscience. Some suspected that this unusual combination could be due to a change of heart after witnessing the terrible persecutions in the Red Army in the late 1920s.

"Although he never told me directly," said Tania, "he did seem to be disenchanted with the frequent intraparty conflicts. It was in fact very dangerous for him to help me to make contact with your father. But he managed to keep it a secret when I asked him to pass a packet to your father in jail, including this little ceramic bottle."

"Here, look at it. It is still intact," Tania continued as she passed Xi the bottle.

"Most amazing. Look at the wooden box made by your father. He might have a scholarly appearance, but was actually quite dexterous with his hands. He could have been a good carpenter, you know. Now, look at the box closely; you will find a secret chamber at the bottom. Open it, yes, open it carefully from here. Do you see something inside? Yes, that's the last message your father had written in jail. That's the most important legacy he has left for you, me, and the world. They were his answers to the nine questions I had raised the last time I saw him.

"Only Heaven knows under what condition had my dear Bo-Xian managed to write down his thoughts in jail before he passed away. This must be his most significant piece of writing. I will make several copies for safekeeping. And you, Xi, remember that you first mission in life is to pass your father's handwritten work to Peter. Tell him to find a way to publish it and let the world know about his father's last words."

"Yes, Mom. I understand," Xi answered. At that moment, she felt that she was no longer an innocent girl. She had grown up, she had become her mom's confidant, and she must begin to face the real world. No matter what might lie ahead, she must carry out her mission for the sake of her mom, dad, and their unwavering love toward each other.

9

Frustration, sheer frustration engulfed the ideological faction. Lin Shi-Xiong, Su Ming, and Kang Yi-Sheng had no power to direct the military or control the Foreign Ministry. They felt that they had been completely left out of the Chairman's recent maneuvers.

"We can't let this continue," yelled Su, who, like an agitated feline, was determined to get back into the game.

"Yes, sure. But how?" Kang asked.

"Well, we do things our way and we are the best in our business, aren't we?" responded Lin who slyly blinked his eye.

"Oh, I get it. Words can be more powerful than bullets." The sharp Su instantly got the hint by Lin, who controlled a vast network of spies and informants across the country.

Since Lin had collected all kinds of insider information about every high-ranking official in the party, the three quickly worked out the details. The next day a classified document was delivered to the Chairman.

Sheng opened the envelope and read,

Top Secret

A report on General Bao Feng-Nian's latest statements and opinions concerning the Chairman:

"Sheng often makes up statements about what you stand for, and then will criticize them as if they were your own views. If you have no opinion, he will create one for you. Must be very careful about this tactic of his.

"Sheng needs coddling. When he has all that attention and pampering, he will not make a fuss. He needs constant praise, not criticism. He can never handle different opinions. So long as someone points out his creativity, success, and political brilliance before he does, he will have no need to be belligerent.

"He worships himself. He is self-obsessed. He believes in personality cult. All successes belong to him, and all failures to others.

"If you say 'A,' he will say 'B.' Never speak before he does.

"What he is most concerned about is whether he will have the majority during any vote.

"Vindictive. He can be jealous of other people's capabilities, and hopes to get all the credit.

"His tactics to deal with foes are limitless, such as 'lure the snake from its den,' 'peel the onion,' 'be a patient fisherman,' 'transport stones and sand and mix them,' 'crack a hole in the wall,' and 'say something then deny it later.' He is very unpredictable. Deviant, elusive, and insecure, he never keeps his word.

"Temperamental, erratic, and impetuous, his rage is disgraceful and awful.

"He resents different opinions, but loves flattery. Highly suspicious, he changes his mind without warning. Never trust what he says. He covers his punch with damask.

"He is aging fast and becoming more doubtful of everybody by the day.

"He is a loner. He does not need anyone, and he may not have anyone in the end.

"For the moment though, agree with everything he says. He is the boss. He represents the masses, who worship him. To side with him is to side with the majority."

Livid, Sheng's face turned pale, as his blood ran cold. General Bao had worked with him for four decades and certainly knew about the most intimate details of the boss's life and personality. Sheng knew that all those things that had been said about him were true. But the astute observations and acute depictions were like a sword piercing him from behind. Sheng was furious, feeling insulted and betrayed. Bao would pay for what he had done, the Chairman vowed.

10

It was the darkest and most depressing day in Si-Tu's life. It was the worst and most painful decision he had made in his career. Once again the premier realized how malignant the two cancers had become, and he was unable to eradicate either of them.

Blood had been found in his urine sometime last year, and he was diagnosed with bladder cancer. His doctors believed that, if treated immediately, he would have a good chance of a full recovery. But the Chairman disagreed, insisting that the premier should not be told of the diagnosis or his treatment options. Because Si-Tu was a Politburo member, any medical treatment must be approved by the Chairman. Considering his role as the premier, the Politburo agreed with the Chairman by suggesting a conservative medical approach. The cost of the delay was deadly. The bleeding worsened and the cancer spread to other organs even after Si-Tu underwent several surgeries many months later.

The struggle with bodily cancer was exhausting and painful. Grappling with political cancer was even worse for the premier.

After his sudden tour to inspect various military command centers around the country, Sheng returned to the capital, confident that he had obtained explicit promises of loyalty and support by the regional commanders. Now he was ready to arrest the isolated Bao, charging him with conspiracy and treason.

Under the cover of the night, however, Bao and his wife and son escaped the capital, fleeing in a car toward the military airport, where the general's special airplane awaited them.

Sheng immediately called and ordered Si-Tu that the group should never be allowed to flee, alive or dead.

Everything was moving so fast. What could he do? The premier had only a couple of hours to decide.

Rising by the second, the stakes were too high for everyone and the fallout would be an unprecedented disaster.

If Bao did escape, it would be the most devastating blow to the Chairman and his ego. It would also be the most disgraceful event for the country, whose number two man in government had become a fugitive. Likewise, it would be definitive proof of the failure of the Cultural Revolution, which had been in shambles for several years.

The clock was ticking. "Why me? Why not someone else? Why not Sheng himself?" the tormented Si-Tu moaned, while thinking fast for a solution at this extremely tense moment.

But the premier had some special genes in his blood. He excelled under pressure. He always believed that there must be a solution to every situation, no matter what. He had grown up amid all sorts of challenges and difficulties. He could handle all kinds of pressures and emergencies. Nothing was unsolvable as long as he was willing to put his mind to it. Truly, the premier was a genius—he could always find a solution to resolve any unsolvable problem.

The only trouble he had was the conflict between his pragmatism and his conscience, his loyalty to the Chairman and his sense of justice, his inclination to obey and his tolerance of dissent. No one understood the superbly talented premier better than Sheng. He gave the strict orders to Si-Tu because he knew exactly where the premier's deeply hidden weaknesses lay. Between loyalty and justice, between obedience and objection, and between the Chairman's command and his own conscience, Si-Tu would always choose the former and forsake the latter, no matter how painful such choices might be.

As Sheng had predicted, however tormented the premier must have felt, he eventually picked up the emergency telephone. He made a direct call to the military airport and, in the name of the Chairman and the party, ordered the commander to install a device onto the special airplane Bao and his family were planning to board.

A few hours later, the aircraft took off and then exploded in midair five hundred miles away from Peking.

Si-Tu drunk a whole bottle of strong liquor and cried like a baby.

A few moments later he pulled himself together, and went to tell Sheng that the airplane crashed after suffering a mechanical failure in mid-flight. No one on the plane survived.

A faint sneer went across the Chairman's face.

11

"You don't love me anymore! In fact, you have never really loved me at all!" Su shouted at the dejected Sheng, whose credibility had been gravely shaken lately. No matter what the party was telling the public, the shocking news of Bao and his family's fatal bid to escape cast great doubts about the real objectives of the Cultural Revolution, which had caused incessant chaos, disasters, sacrifices, and deaths. The sudden and ghastly demise of Sheng's handpicked successor only showed that the fanatical movement had hit a dead end. Where was the revolution going from here? No one had any answers, including the Chairman, who had single-handedly started it in the first place. The worldwide negative reactions to the Bao incident and the public's increasing cynicism of the revolutionary movement had taken a visible toll on the aging Chairman, who tried to maintain his calm facade. But the wife's rants went on and on.

"You made me a big promise, didn't you? Where is it now? Ha, where is your big promise? You tell *me* where it is. You gave the position of vice chairman to Bao Feng-Nian, that idiot. See what happened! What about me now? What do I get from your big proletarian struggle? What has your great 'Eternal Revolution' done for me?"

Politics was a double-edged sword, which could bring out the best and the worst of people. Not an overtly aggressive person by nature, Su, thanks to the indelible lessons Sheng had taught her, gradually became obsessed with her own self-importance as she was dragged deeper and deeper into the secretive and ugly affairs of the party. Watching Sheng's every move closely, she had quickly learned how to bargain for her share in the game. The husband was not getting any younger, reasoned Su, so she must secure what she deserved in the post-Bao reshuffle, or she could lose everything should Sheng suddenly die. He had suffered several strokes, and no one knew how long he could last.

"Please, I did promise you a good future. But look at your own manners: who will listen to you when you behave like this?" Sheng defended himself by pointing out the wife's failings. How she had changed! When she first arrived in Bao An decades ago, she was an innocent girl. Look at her now, a despicable shrew, he cursed silently.

"Don't blame it on me. I know your tricks. Don't ever think that they will work on me. I am not Song Pei. I am not Bao Feng-Nian. I am not Si-Tu Wen-Liang! I am not afraid of you!"

Indeed, like many husbands who appeared formidable in front of their colleagues at work, they could be extremely timid and helpless when facing their wives. Sheng, the most powerful man in China, was such a pathetic husband. A giant of six foot five, he could be ruthless and could kill at will. But he could not stand up against his wife, a small and frail woman of five foot three.

"Look at the newspapers. Look at the pictures of Si-Tu Wen-Liang. They are here and there, everywhere, every day, in all the newspapers these days. With Henry Kissinger, with Richard Nixon, with William Rogers, with Alexander Haig, with James Reston, with… Where is my picture? Where are my photos in public?" Su dumped all the jealousy, anger, and frustration on the husband.

"The premier was conducting diplomatic negotiations. He was signing international accords and meeting with foreign news corps. You are not a diplomat, and therefore you were not there," argued the Chairman.

"Okay, okay. I am not a diplomat. I can't be there. But what is THIS?" Su hurled a stack of photos on the desk.

Sheng took a peek and froze.

"These are the photos of Yu Shao-Mei, your second wife, if I am not mistaken. I know where she is. I know who took her back from Russia and escorted her to China. You must decide who you want to be with: me or her?" A woman as crafty and strong-willed as Sheng himself, Su knew how to handle her man. His vulnerability was her strength, and she was prepared to exploit her advantage to the fullest.

"Well, tell me. You want to get back with her or you want me?" she demanded.

"You, of course, you." The Chairman was completed deflated.

"Good. You have made the correct choice. Now, the second but more important question, do you plan to fulfill your promise or not, and when?" Su spoke like the real boss in the room.

"Yes, I will fulfill the promise I have made, I swear. But I do need time," replied the defeated Sheng, who had suffered all kinds of verbal abuse whenever he met his wife in private for the last several months.

All right. The threat seemed to have worked and Su did not want to push her luck too far. She received the reassurance from the husband that was the real reason for bullying him in the first place. Contented, she stormed out of Sheng's office as suddenly as she had barged in an hour earlier.

Sheng now regretted that he had promised Su a high position when he needed all the support he could muster to expel Song. He never thought Su, an apolitical person just a few years ago, would become such a fearsome political animal. He had no idea what had changed. But he had to face the reality that, once he had started the game, he could not stop; he must keep all the factions contented, balanced, and under control.

12

Her quarrelsome and insufferable nature notwithstanding, Su's complaints did remind Sheng that the administrative faction was getting too much attention these days. Premier Si-Tu had indeed been in the international limelight a lot since Kissinger's first secret trip to China, followed by President Nixon's highly publicized state visit.

Fearful that the resurrected Si-Tu and his administrative faction would follow Bao's steps in challenging his authority, the Chairman decided to turn up the heat on them and he sent the ones who would be the ideal executioners to do the job.

For the next three months, the remaining members of the "leadership group," namely Lin, Su, and Kang, conducted closed-door meetings session after session to crush the premier by labeling him as a coward, deserter, and a capitulator who had ceded China's national interests to the imperialist Americans.

Believing that the classy and slick premier was the number one obstacle to her rise to power, Su led the charge with vengeance. She threw all the mud that she could find at the premier, who was still under cancer treatment, as those secret long meetings had been designed to torture him. One day the hostile meeting lasted for eight hours and the ailing premier was not allowed to go to the restroom, which caused him severe pain.

Rubbing salt into the wound, Cheng Chu-Li, one of the premier's longtime aides, joined the inquisition, viciously attacking the premier by using the language peculiar to the Cultural Revolution, which might sound weird in another place and at another time. "He holds no regard for Comrade Su Ming, who is the Chairman's most faithful student," Cheng said as he pounded the lectern. "To show disrespect to Comrade Su Ming is an affront to our great Chairman. Comrade Su Ming is a beacon and a great standard bearer of the Cultural Revolution. To slight Comrade Su Ming is to attack the Great Proletarian Cultural Revolution!"

Friends against friends. Colleagues against colleagues. Si-Tu could not believe what he was hearing. Unbeknown to him, Cheng had made a deal with the ideological faction's members, who, betting on the Chairman's explicit support and their rise in the near future, had promised him the post of secretary of the Foreign Ministry if he attacked the premier at the closed-door meetings. The outrageous charges by one of his closest assistants saddened the defenseless Si-Tu. Cheng had only been a boy when they first met, and Si-Tu had treated him like an adopted son. How could he change sides so fast without any sense of guilt?

But the premier also painfully recalled that he had turned his back on his own longtime colleagues such as Tao Yin-Hu, Song Pei, Dong Zi-Tian, and Meng Bo-Xian. "When they were singled out to bear the brunt of Sheng's fury, what did I do? Didn't I join the attack to slander them, even when I knew the charges were not true? Worse, hadn't I carried out Sheng's order to murder Bao Feng-Nian?" Si-Tu recalled quietly.

"What have we become as a party?" he asked himself. A party of witch hunts? A party of hate? A party of vilification? A party of madness? A party of opportunists? A party of slanders? Or a party of one man and his fools?

A profound sadness overwhelmed Si-Tu, who was for the first time in his life beginning to fear that he might lose control over his body and mind, but for one name, one person…

13

"The chickens have come home to roost."

Relying on the ideological faction more than anyone else, Sheng launched the Cultural Revolution to condemn Song. After Sheng had gambled everything in this "Eternal Revolution," nothing seemed to be going the way he had planned. By deceptively stirring millions of brainwashed people and young students, the ouster of the head of the state tore the country apart, causing widespread clashes, unbelievable chaos, and devastating destruction, over which the "leadership group" had completely lost control. The fatal escape bid by Bao damaged the Chairman's aura of perpetual greatness, and underscored the folly of his wanton desire to establish himself as the next Marx.

A strong believer in all things Machiavellian, Sheng duplicated the game of checks and balances that he had arranged for the party leadership. He enlisted the military faction in his initial campaign to sack Song and bypassed the existing administrative bureaucracy. His expedient replacement turned into a national and international embarrassment when General Bao, the Chairman's handpicked successor, was killed while trying to flee the country. The disastrous split with Bao greatly shook Sheng, who now realized he had put too big a wager on the military. He then turned to Si-Tu for help, a man whose soft skills he had always feared and whose potential as a formidable challenger to his authority had always loomed large at the back of his mind.

As the influence of the resurgent Si-Tu grew at a time when the premier's administrative skills were badly needed by a nation in disarray, Sheng and his trusted ideological faction became increasingly uneasy. Jealous of the premier's popularity and envious of his broad powers in government, the ideological faction viewed him as the roadblock to their ascent. Backed by the Chairman, Su spearheaded the assault against the premier, who endured enormous pain while trying to defend himself against those horrendous insults and attacks.

The expediency of divide and rule had served Sheng's purpose. But his repeated use of the same stratagem had also left him with an ever-dwindling number of people he could rely on. Absolutism could breed nothing but absolutists. A captive of the tyrannical system he had created, the Chairman absolutely refused to trust anyone. He had never hesitated to exploit anyone, from his longtime associates to his wife, Su, or any faction whenever he needed their help. Nor would he ever hesitate to abandon them as soon as they were no longer needed. Just as he had plunged the nation into a civil war through brute class struggle, Sheng had turned the party into a bloody slaughterhouse—with colleagues fighting colleagues, and one faction killing the other—in order to preserve absolute authority in his own hands until the last day of his life.

To be an absolute ruler was one thing; to live in absolute isolation was another. He was at the pinnacle of his power, yet why was he feeling depressed? Was it because of his old age, deteriorating health, or something else? What went wrong in his life? What medicine could ease his tensions and maintain his vigor and determination? How could he find peace and counsel when he absolutely refused to trust anyone but himself? As Sheng had often done in the past, the lonely Chairman picked up the Chinese classics for solace. Through Su, he had asked the ideological faction to prepare a large print edition of one hundred ancient articles and biographies, which he perused eagerly despite his declining poor eyesight. The article that resonated with him the most was "An Old Tree," written by the accomplished sixth-century poet and essayist Yu Xin. It read:

A handsome, gifted, and stylish gentleman, Yin Zhong-Wen, was a well-known figure in the nation. When the Jin Dynasty was having trouble, he was sent away by the court to take up the post of a regional administrator in Dong Yang. Unhappy at being marginalized, the dispirited Yin strolled into the yard, stopped before an old tree, and noted, "Falling branches and scattering leaves, this old tree has lost the interest to live."

Unblemished white pines have been as pure as the snow of the North. The mystical catalpa tree, deeply rooted and sweepingly canopied, has grown into the rocks covering the mountains of the South. But the sweet tea olive tree is dying and the phoenix tree crumbling—the result of their transplantation from distant lands.

Acres of acres of solid and vigorous trees could live for several thousand years, even though they could have been cut down at some point. So venerated and worshiped, some of them had been granted the titles of high offices of the Qin Dynasty, and some bestowed honors as exalted as great generals. Yet none of them could escape from the invasion of bacteria and viruses, the menace of birds and pests, the abuse of severe elements, and the threats of blaze, fire, smoke, burns, and thunderstorms.

Uprooted from familiar hilltops and riverbanks, old trees wept while their wounded bodies bled. Dried up from inside out, the shrunken old trees caught fire, and their shattered stumps were covered with burning resin like streams of tears. Tumbling branches blocked caves, crushed stalks scattered throughout the valleys, destroyed trunks fell to the ground as fast as smashed ice, and splintered stems flew like demolished tiles. Eaten by cancers and tumors and plagued with bird nests and malicious bugs, the old trees lived with ghosts and demons of the wilderness.

How sad was I to have been born in this failing era, to have been sent to take a dead-end job, and to have lived alone in a yard covered with weeds. Watching the dying trees and grass, I pity their lives as much as I lament mine. Compilers of the *History of Huai-Nan* have stated, "What devastates the elderly the most is to watch the seasonal changes in autumn. When tree leaves fall each year, they know they are getting older and frailer than the year before." How precisely have his words spoken of my mind. When I planted the willows, they were so lovely and full of life. Now they are growing old in such a short period of time. How can mortal men stand such brutal reality?

"Am I really that old? Am I going to die like the old tree? Who will continue to propagate my ideas of the 'Eternal Revolution'? Who can I still trust and who can I even talk to in my current predicament?" the worried Chairman asked himself repeatedly.

14

The rapid deterioration of the premier's health, made worse by overwork and mounting political pressure, was good news for the Chairman, who was determined not to die before Si-Tu.

From the poor medical treatment at the hospital and the vicious attacks during the high-level party meetings that he was subjected to, Si-Tu knew what Sheng was doing. He called in Cheng.

"I want to apolo—" the assistant began as he walked into the office.

"No need to explain. I know you had to do what you had to do." The premier cut him short. "I have one last task for you. It does need some travel and I hope you will accept it."

"Yes, yes. I will do anything you say." Cheng was nodding furiously, as if to amplify his absolute obedience and complete loyalty.

"According to a report, a dozen of the best *Phoebe zhennan* trees have been found in the high mountains in Sichuan. Experts say those trees were at least three thousand years old and, after falling, could have been buried for another three thousand years. Only these fossilized *Phoebe zhennan* would produce the finest golden grains on the trunks, and, in the past, no one except the royal families could use them. You need to go to Sichuan immediately and take all the necessary measures to ship those magnificent trees to Peking. They will make the best coffins in this world, and we need to prepare one for the Chairman. Do you understand?" Si-Tu asked the assistant.

"Yes, yes. I do. I do." Cheng wanted to say more, but the premier stopped him. He left.

Si-Tu then called Fang Si-Liang into his office.

"Sadly, Cheng has turned against me and I can't rely on him anymore. I don't have much time left and just want to ask you one question—are you willing to carry out the last task that I am going to give you?"

"Yes. I swear. I promise I will do anything you say." Fang held back his tears, watching his shriveled boss wrestling with great pain and agony.

"Good," the premier said. "Here is a stack of papers. Please make at least a dozen copies of them, and make sure to send them to the twelve people I have named inside. Ask each person to make at least a dozen copies and send to twelve other people whom they trust the most for safekeeping. Do you understand?"

"Yes, I do," said Fang firmly.

"This may sound simple," Si-Tu said as he reached out for Fang's hand. Holding it, he continued, "but it is the most important thing that I have ever asked you to do. You must keep your promise and you must not fail. Moreover, when you see those twelve people, you must also ask them to promise that they will not fail."

"Yes, I promise I will not fail you," Fang answered.

"Good. I have made some terrible mistakes by hiding the truth in the past. I will not repeat that again." Totally exhausted and barely audible, Si-Tu was fast losing his voice.

When he was rushed to the hospital, the only word the doctors and nurses could hear was "wisteria."

"That's his childhood sweetheart, Teng," the devastated Hong Shi-Mei cried out hysterically—"wisteria" and "Teng" were homonymous in Chinese.

15

News of the premier's death threw the country into deep mourning. Thousands of citizens went to Tiananmen Square, the heart of Peking, to hold spontaneous memorials. Hundreds of thousands of black cloth banners and white paper flowers covered the capital, symbolizing a tragic death and profound mourning in the nation.

Inside the nearby but secluded Abundance, the euphoric Sheng was celebrating the demise. Noisy firecrackers were set off, a sign of joy and festivity.

A secretary came in and reported, "Chairman, this document was found on the premier's desk."

"Hmm, what is it?" Sheng asked, not in the least interested.

"I am not sure. It's marked as top secret and for your eyes only. Other copies have been sent to members of the 'leadership group.'"

"All right. Leave it on my desk." The Chairman had plenty of important matters to consider and was not about to let a dead person's last paperwork disturb his train of thought.

It was only several hours later that Sheng remembered the envelope when he was about to retire. As he opened it and started reading, his blood froze.

The document listed what the nation had been suffering during his Great Proletarian Cultural Revolution:

President Song Pei died like a dog in his cell and was cremated under an alias.

General Tao Yin-Hu was beaten to death.

Meng Bo-Xian died in prison.

Hundreds of political dissidents had been tortured and died in labor camps, including Yao Xi-Wa, Gan Zu-Xun, Mo Jia-Qi, Pan Jin, and Dai Tian.

Two hundred and thirty-seven thousand died in four thousand, three hundred armed fights. Seven hundred thousand were wounded and seventy thousand families destroyed.

Two and a half million public employees and officials were molested, assaulted, and brutalized. Four hundred and twenty thousand of them were arrested and incarcerated. One hundred and seventy-two thousand, eight hundred died.

Four million, eight hundred thousand people from all walks of life were charged and labeled as counterrevolutionaries, and six hundred and eighty-three thousand of them were tortured to death.

Five million, two hundred thousand rural residents were labeled as landlords and rich farmers, and one million, two hundred thousand of them were assaulted, beaten, and tortured to death.

One hundred and thirteen million people suffered assaults, beatings, molestation, and persecution. Five hundred and fifty-seven thousand are still missing or their deaths have not been accounted for.

Very likely, there are far more people than the above numbers who have suffered and even died, but whose names are not known or whose records are lost.

All told, nearly thirty million are dead and no fewer than one hundred million families have suffered much pain and losses during this "Eternal Revolution," which has destroyed hundreds of millions of the most precious artifacts, paintings, ceramics, sculptures, bronze, rare books, manuscripts, as well as ancient temples, tombs, buildings, and other treasures in our nation's history of three thousand years.

The prolonged fighting, chaos, violence, lawlessness, turmoil, and suffering have cost billions in losses, and the country's economy is on the brink of ruin.

"This is not a document. This is an indictment! How dare he? How could he do this me?" the enraged and frantic Chairman shouted. "Go! Go! Go out and stop the dissemination of this document! Confiscate and destroy all the copies! DESTROY ALL THE COPIES!"

Startled by the yelling, a guard rushed in and found that the Chairman had passed out behind his enormous desk.

Emergency doctors were summoned and they told Su that the Chairman had suffered a severe cerebral hemorrhage.

Sheng never regained consciousness and died within a month.

16

A week later the least conspicuous member of the party's Standing Committee, Xia-Ho Ding, rose to power by arresting Lin, Su, and Kang, a move that signaled both the end of the catastrophic Great Proletarian Cultural Revolution and the bankruptcy of the fanatical theory of "eternal revolution."

A search of their offices produced a document containing a brief list of appointments, which was presented to Xia-Ho.

In Sheng's handwriting, the document revealed his last wishes:

Su Ming—Chairperson of the Party
Lin Shi-Xiong—President of the Country
Kang Yi-Sheng—Premier of the Government

Signed: Sheng Bao

Although not filed in the official archives, the brief document was leaked to the media, and the term "The Gang of Four" entered the lexicon of Chinese history.

17

About a year later, Xi took Peter to visit Tania in a hospital near their home in Xisi. Much weakened and visibly frail, Tania was delighted to see the children; her face brightened up while looking at the recent pictures of her family and granddaughter. Fully relaxed, Tania reclined against the headboard and listened with complete satisfaction as Xi and Peter talked and talked, sharing and exchanging the endless stories of their divergent experiences over the years.

Tania passed away peacefully the next morning, with her patrician grace, or, as Peter and Xi would say, beauty intact.

Epilogue

MANY YEARS LATER CHINA ENTERED A NEW ERA OF rejuvenation.

"Honey, I wish *you* could give me a kiss like *that* sometimes." A delightful gray-haired woman was intimating the lovely passions displayed by a young couple next to where she and her husband were sitting in a transcontinental airplane over the Pacific Ocean from San Francisco to Shanghai.

The young couple was as animated as any honeymooners would be, especially the bride, whose vivacious face was radiant with joy and excitement.

"Look, David, it must be the East China Sea. We are close to our destination." Tossing back her beautiful long dark curly hair, she looked through a window over the unobstructed views below.

"That's a very nice piece of jewelry you have." The friendly and perceptive woman passenger commented on the bride's delicate necklace with a gleaming and cute tube-shaped pendant.

"Oh, thank you. This ceramic bottle used to be my grandma's." Responding to the compliment, the bride's sparkling green eyes and crisp voice spoke her pride.

"*How* exquisite her blue-and-white porcelain is. What a taste!" the senior lady lauded. "Your grandma must be from China."

"No, she was a Russian."

"Oh, a Russian? Really? What's her name?"

"Her name was Tania, who has loved China and the Chinese people all her life." Replied Tania the Younger, the granddaughter, beaming with the kind of beautiful tenderness, lovely affection, and self-assured understanding not commonly found in those of her age.